Ancient

By

R Kane

Ancient

By R Kane

Create Space Edition | Copyright 2016 R Kane

http://www.rkanepublications.com

This book is dedicated to my daughter who shows me every day there's beauty in this world that is yet to be seen or admired.

Thank you baby

Book One

'The belief in a supernatural source of evil is not necessary; men alone are quite capable of every wickedness'.
Joseph Conrad, *Under Western Eyes, 1911*

'Oh so hot no time to take a rest yeah
Act tough ain't room for second best
Real strong got me some security
Hey I'm a big smash I'm goin' for infinity yeah'

'If you think I'll sit around as the world goes by
You're thinking like a fool cause it's a case of do or die
Out there is a fortune waiting to be had
You think I'll let it go you're mad
You've got another thing comin'
You've got another thing comin', Judas Priest,
Screaming for Vengeance

Prologue

The cold fingers of winter gripped the coastal community of Savannah, Georgia tightly this night forcing many inside to burrow deep under blankets and covers letting the warmth there incite pleasant, peaceful dreams. A half-moon hung lazily in the cloudless night sky casting a pale light over the landscape creating ominous shadows to hide in for every corner it seemed. It was the kind of night where an active imagination might see something lurking behind the tree to your left, or that bush over there off to your right. The kind of night where grandpa's would tell the little ones' stories about an evil one handed man that would come for young boys and girls who dared to break mama's rules. It was also the kind of night where most people used the nominal amount of common sense granted to a man or woman and stayed in, it wasn't worth braving the cold, or maybe it was the off-chance there really was an evil one-handed man hiding out behind the bushes by the front of the house ready to kill you for not eating your Brussel Sprouts at dinner. Most people did not include Earl or Mooney unfortunately, depending on the way you looked at it. Neither man seemed to have much in the way of common sense which is why both were trying to slip quietly through one of the oldest cemeteries in Savanah at the moment.

It wasn't working for the pair though, being stealthy, not at all.

From somewhere, hidden by the night, a bird called out with a shrill shriek scaring no one except for the two men making their way through the old church graveyard. The large breaker bar that skinny six foot two Mooney carried over his left shoulder almost connected with his five foot ten partner Earl's large head as he spun around trying to see where the scream came from. Only a quick dodge by the stocky, and God help anyone who called his ample stomach 'fat', saved Earl from a nice set of stitches.

"Did you hear that Earl?" Mooney asked with his usual nasal whine in a whisper.

A ham-sized hand shot out and connected at the back of Mooney's long neck making a sharp crack and knocking the man's Atlanta Braves baseball cap clean off. Earl shook his head after hitting Mooney, watching the tall lanky man dance in a circle while trying to rub the stinging pain away. After a second of hissing, Mooney came to a stop looking at his fat friend with a hurt expression while still rubbing the spot on his neck.

"What the hell was that for Earl?" The man cried unbelievably loud.

"Keep it quiet you idiot." Earl hissed back through his considerably green teeth. "Unless you want someone to call the law and we both get hauled away."

"Well stop hitting me then!" Mooney demanded still whining.

He stepped back cautiously getting ready to run just in case Earl got the notion to chase him. Earl, though, just turned and walked away letting the light from the moon above show him the path between the headstones of the cemetery. Mooney watched him go for a second trying to decide if he really wanted to be here with Earl, and then thought about being alone in a graveyard at night got the better of him...and the scream from that damn bird didn't help but to make old Mooney run like the wind. He chased after Earl like a scolded dog catching up with him in just a few long strides of his legs. Better to stay with someone who could barely put up with you then hang around alone in a place of the dead on a night like this Moon thought.

"Are you sure about doing this Earl?" Mooney asked after a minute of following.

"No, I'm starting to doubt why I even brought your dumb ass along on this job tonight." Earl stated flatly.

"It's because no one else would come along with you Earl, hell you ain't got any friends but me." Mooney chirped happily as he smiled

Then another shriek came from the dark, loud and shrill, and Mooney ignored it as best as he could while walking next to Earl while absently rubbing the reddened part of his neck with his hand while remembering the pain from five minutes ago. Earl wasn't paying too much attention to Mooney at the particular moment, he never really gave the man a second thought most of the time anyway, and he might just ignore him for the rest of night if he didn't shut the hell up. No, Earl kept a close eye on the dates of the mausoleum plaques noting the fact that each one was from the Civil War or earlier. He stopped to get a quick bearing in the darkened surroundings when Mooney plowed into him, the tip of the breaker bar bouncing off the top of his bald head this time.

Mooney screeched like he had been shot jumping back away from Earl as the large breaker bar fell from his grasp to the ground with a muffled clang. His fist came up in a comic act to defend himself but the stocky Earl simply hit the exposed backs of the hands with his knuckles causing Mooney to jump into the air and hop around like a big old jackrabbit.

"Damn Earl that hurt!" Mooney spat just sticking his whole hand in his mouth.

"Well so did this!" Earl snapped back pointing angrily to his now bleeding scalp.

"I'm sorry Earl." Mooney said finally getting himself under control. "But the cemetery's scary at night son. Why the hell are we here again?"

"Because," Earl whispered looking around for the landmark again," there's an old Civil War General buried out here and I heard it on good authority that his family didn't send him on his way to the great beyond alone, but with a few of his favorite things."

"You don't think they buried him with his dog Earl? I'd want Buck buried with me if I had to die." Mooney stated with the legitimate honesty and the intelligence of a five-year-old.

"I'm going to bury you and that mutt alive if you don't shut the hell up! Now just follow me knucklehead." Earl spat angrily just before he saw something and a small evil smile started to creep across his face. The landmark the short fat man was so desperately looking for just appeared ahead in the moonlight.

The two walked briskly to a small angel statuette posed on a pedestal in bent prayer over the final resting place of someone, who didn't really matter to the pair. The angel looked pristine except for a large gouge to its childlike face, a mark that looked more man-made than by Mother Nature. They, meaning Earl leading and Mooney a step behind, turned left sharply between the headstones heading deeper into the graveyard. Now Earl could see what he had been searching for and his pace quickened to what some would consider a staunch run for him. Mooney's long legs kept up easily until his eyes caught sight of what Earl's had and instinctively he slowed his pace instead of quickening it like his friend. On the edge of the dark was the large structure of an old ominous mausoleum. The left side of the building was a solid mass of tangled ivy leaves, which grew and enveloped everything from the ground to the small spire on the roof. The exposed white marble of the right side glowed eerily from the pale moonlight it seemed, shimmered in wave's almost breathing life to some of the shadows that swirled here and there. Then he felt the cold hit him, not from the outside on his skin, but on the inside and right on his bones. Something wasn't right here, oh no, there was nothing right about this place. Mooney told himself over and over that it was only the wind blowing through tree limbs causing the shadows to move, but selling that to his imagination was a little harder. He had thoroughly decided he wouldn't visit this place in the daylight much less at night...and yet here he was.

"Earl, I'm not real sure about this bud." Mooney whined.

The fat man didn't pay any attention to his partner in crime, just like he hadn't paid him much attention to the last ten minutes or the last ten years, as they finally got close enough to touch the finely wrought iron gates of the mausoleum. Earl slowly reached out, ran a set of pudgy fingers over the metal, and looked up at the stylish raised letters that ran across the top of the doorway. The name was synonymous with the South and if your grandfather was an old rebel like Earl's then you heard it constantly at the dinner table when the stories of the past and what was right in the world at the time would begin to flow. Somewhere deep inside he almost felt sorry for what he was about to do, but then again an old trinket worth a few thousand bucks would sure help him get over the grief.

"Alright Moon, use that big beautiful breaker bar and get me in to see old General Whitfield here." Earl squealed excitedly.

"Oh, damn Earl, I don't have that bar anymore. I dropped it somewhere back there." Mooney exclaimed shrugging his shoulders and pointing a thumb back in the direction they just came.

Everything was quiet for a second, too damn quiet Mooney thought before Earl finally whispered with exasperation leaving his head slumped against his chest. "Why, in the name of the good lord, do I put up with you? How the hell could you lose that big bar you idiot?"

Moon began to answer but Earl obviously didn't want to hear anything because the fat man stepped away in disgust shaking his head. A second went by and then another as Mooney realized Earl was thinking of what to do now since they didn't have the bar. Earl would come up with something he thought.

Earl was smart. Hell he got as far as high school before dropping out to go work for his father at the lumber yard and Moon didn't even try for High School. Another minute went by and another without a response from the stocky man. Mooney began to wonder if they were going to leave, he'd sure like to leave, but then Earl suddenly spun and walked up to him.

"Ah, what we gonna do Earl?" Mooney asked quickly suddenly scared even more.

"We're gonna break down the mother of a gate Moon, run right smack damn through it!" Earl proclaimed.

Moon looked at him for a couple of seconds then turned and eyed the metal gates for only a second before pin wheeling back to his friend. "You're plum crazy Earl. That gate's metal and its real thick. We ain't gonna knock that down." Mooney proclaimed.

"You forgot the bar stupid so now we got no choice but to break it down." Earl said taking a couple of steps backwards.

"Why don't we just forget this whole dumb idea Earl and get the hell out of here, all right? Myrna at the diner might give us a cup of coffee for free if we do." Moon exclaimed walking up to Earl hoping the mention of busty waitress at the local eatery would change his friend's mind. Myrna didn't like Earl much, not at all really, but Earl liked to look at her none the less and if it got them out this damn cemetery then Moon was all for it.

"No way am I leaving Moon. I've waited a long time to meet the general there and I'm not gonna wait another damn minute. Now turn around and help me break down that gate or so help me God I'm gonna knock you out and use your skinny ass for a new breaker bar." Earl snarled clinching a fist so hard his knuckles turned white.

The look the man gave him said it all, there was no choice for Mooney since Earl meant what he said and always did what he meant. Therefore, the tall lanky man reluctantly turned and faced the metal gate with his fat friend and the two readied themselves to run smack through the middle of the barricade. They each leaned back together to get a little extra speed, took off at the target like a couple of crazy screaming hellions, and promptly met the enemy head on with less than spectacular results. The graveyard came alive with the sound of the impact, from both the men and the gate. The rusted hinges screaming from the sudden movement sent night birds screeching in fear. Mooney and Earl hit the metal gates with a meaty thud, rebounded off and across the grass in a ball, and came to a stop in a sprawling mass of arms and legs. A minute passed by before Earl stood back up rubbing his bruised shoulder and eyeing the gate with a hateful expression.

"That was real good idea Earl, too bad it didn't work huh. Well, I guess we can go now, huh?" Moon exclaimed sitting on the cold grass.

"Shut up Moon!" Earl hissed walking over to the gate.

He stood in front of the metal gate for a second or two seething in anger, and then Earl suddenly kicked it with his right boot. The blow shook the metal very little and in the end might have broken a bone in Earl's foot if not for the superior steel toe of his twenty-five dollar work shoes. The stocky man gave another kick, then another and another, and finally a fourth before stopping to catch his breath.

"Keep going Earl, hell you might just get in there son." Mooney joked with a single guffaw before realizing this was no time to be humorous.

A thought struck Earl suddenly, a real nasty one at that. He could see himself taking one of his twenty-five dollar work boots and stomping Mooney's ass flatter than the pancake it already was. A slight smile crossed Earl's psychotic face and he began to walk toward his friend Mooney with the express intent of trying to outdo that sudden nasty thought by using both boots in one hell of a stomp fest. Then he noticed something was wrong, well not really noticed as much as his gut now told him there was something really out of place. Moon had a look on his face of utter shock, or maybe he was just thinking real hard about something. The tall man always got that same stupid look whenever he tried to remember something, anything, like his own phone number Earl thought to himself. Finally, though he turned back to see what his dimwitted friend was staring at, and that's when Earl noticed the fingers slowly growing out of the mausoleum wall.

"Well...you did something son, but you know, I don't think we're gonna like it much." Mooney whispered still sitting on the grass eyes locked on the growing fingers.

The fingers continued growing out from the wall and according to the laws of nature and physics that should have just been about damn near impossible. At least that's what Earl's brain kept telling him as the fingers grew longer and longer till eventually they became a hand and then a wrist that protruded from the crypt wall just at eye level for his short stature. Then the wrist turned into an arm followed by a leg but then for a second the limbs stopped coming out from the mausoleum wall staying perfectly still. This was it. Earl and Mooney had plenty of time to start running for their old beat up truck parked at the entrance. Neither man moved though since both were just as fascinated by the strange limbs as the next set of grave robbers would have been.

"Earl, what is that?" Mooney asked

"How the hell am I supposed to know you twit." Earl hissed.

"Well you went to high school and I didn't." Moon explained.

Earl was going to remark about how he had never finished that damn school when the limbs began to move again. Both men yelped as the leg suddenly took a long step forward and the arm followed suit with both limbs suddenly pulling a vague shape from the marble, as if someone was stuck and needed the extra effort to yank free. There was a head and chest and lower abdomen, the complete right side of a man just everything split right down the middle. Earl and Mooney watched in dumb amazement at the spectacle that was happening right before their eyes. The man gave a second great pull to free his left side, and then there he was standing with his legs apart and his arms to his sides, like he walked through a door and not some marble wall. Moon began to whine as the reality of what was occurring started to sink into his thick brain and for a split second he was about to run, but his legs wouldn't respond to mental commands to get up and go. The man who had pulled himself from the mausoleum wall was young and stood tall with a long mane of brown hair in front of them. His clothes though were rotting rags and his shoes were all but gone from decay, yet other than that he looked perfectly normal with a chiseled chin, rather striking if you asked Moon.

"Oh, that was quite unpleasant." The man suddenly said with a proper English accent.

Earl blinked at the quick transformation wondering where the flash of light and fireball had gone. There should have been a big flash and a big old fireball. Even he knew all magicians use a flash of light and that big old fireball to distract you for the necessary split second needed to do the trick and this man was definitely some kind of magician, had to be. I mean how else do you explain what just happened, huh? From out of the side of a marbled wall steps a man with chiseled features dressed in some old rags in the middle of a cemetery in Savannah in the middle of the night. Only come to think of it now, Earl thought to himself, something was kind of wrong with this picture. Where's the beautiful assistant? What happened next all but convinced the fat man of the fact this new man was no magician, not in the least.

Those strong features of the strange man started to change, sinking inward as he clutched at his stomach in apparent agony. The skin on his face tightened over his cheekbones becoming gaunt and pale, his eye sockets became two large holes as the orbs shrank, and the long mane of hair on his head faded color to white almost instantly. Finally, everything struck both Earl and Mooney at the same time, but both had two completely different reactions from the sight of the man though.

Earl heard Mooney give one final screech but he never saw his friend's his eyes roll back as he collapsed to the ground in a dead faint. The fat man was far too busy at that exact moment backing away in an attempt to put some distance between him and the horrible figure. If he had seen Mooney then he might have avoided the tall man's large foot, which tripped Earl up and ended his chance at making an escape. He fell to the ground with an unceremonious thud practically bouncing off his plump rump back up to his feet. Earl looked over into Mooney's dead eyes then skyward as the sound of bare feet crunching cold grass reached his ears. Towering over him was the strange man who now looked more like the walking dead with his skin losing color to the point of becoming yellowish in the pale moonlight.

"I am sorry. I did not mean to frighten you." The corpse apologized in that polite English accent.

"That's okay, didn't mean to scare you either." Earl responded with a slight laugh full of fear.

"Do you happen to have the date?" The corpse asked politely

Earl couldn't believe he was having a coherent conversation with a corpse that appeared from the wall of a mausoleum in a Georgia graveyard. He must have hit his head on rock when he fell down, Yeah that's it! You hit your head when you fell over Mooney's passed out pathetic ass bud.

"2014...not really sure of the day though." Earl replied shakily.

The walking corpse turned back to the mausoleum and the floundering fat man caught sight of something poking out of the things curled lips, a long sharp canine. The tooth was way too long for a man or a woman and it was too sharp, like it was made for puncturing through...skin.

"Were you planning to rob the general's grave Earl? Is that why you tried to break in?" The corpse asked quizzically turning back to him with those hollow eye sockets. If you looked really hard you could almost see the thing smiling with its curled lips the fat man thought as a shiver rolled down his spine.

"Hell No! Moon and I were just curious about this place is all?" Earl replied with a fake smile and shrugging his shoulders still lying flat backed. Then what the thing had actually said finally hit home to the large individual on the ground and it scared him like nothing else had in his life sending another larger shudder though him. Earl whispered low as the fake smile slipped away, "How do you know my name?"

"Oh I know quite a lot about you Earl and old Mooney over there." The corpse replied.

"Why? Have we met or som-something?" The fat man asked with a stutter.

"No, we have never met Earl." The corpse said moving in close to Earl's prone body as the fat man's teeth began to chatter from fear. "Yet, I know your kind just the same little man. I know you beat your friend here when he makes you mad, that you are trying rather pathetically to gain the affections of a waitress named Myrna in a place called a 'Waffle House', and you cheat every chance you have at the Saturday night poker game with your other so called friends who in reality do not like you."

Again there was a small bit of silence before a stunned Earl whispered, suddenly mesmerized by the eye sockets. "Holy Shit, what the hell are you?"

"It would take too long to tell you Earl and frankly I am quite hungry at the moment." The walking corpse explained calmly bending over to stare into Earl's eyes.

"Wh-Wha-What?" Earl's stammered with his voice suddenly filled with fear.

"You see, I also know your blood is A-Positive, which curls my tongue ever so slightly, but as they say in Rome any port in a storm," the corpse hissed.

"Oh my lord in heaven," Earl whispered and then the corpse lunged at him.

There was a slight pop suddenly, like a needle or a long sharp tooth puncturing skin, and then quiet. Earl might have screamed but no one heard anything in the cemetery that night.

No sir, people were at home-snuggled deep in their blankets enjoying the warmth and savoring pleasant dreams.

Chapter One

The nightlife in the Buckhead district of Atlanta is as fast and as furious as it comes on a Friday night anywhere in the States. If you're someone, if you want to be someone, or just want to be near that someone who's been designated the 'cool person' for the week then Buckhead is where you go every Friday night in Atlanta. You can wander down the streets hitting a bar every ten feet guzzling expensive imported beer until you pass out in a drunken stupor in the cab driving you home, you know, if waking up face down in the backseat of a strange car is you're thing. What kind of music do you like? Well there's all kinds of tunes in the district, from Reggae to Rock to New Wave all play in certain themed clubs and along the way is an ample helping of the ruckus sports bar or grand eatery lining the saloon row. In Buckhead the cars cruise by slow and the women even slower, the guys dress in expensive suits or just pressed khaki's with matching button down shirts while the women sport short skirts or hip hugging jeans and boots. Hey, you have to look good to survive in the jungle of the single scene these days. Being in style isn't just imperative in Buckhead, it's a requirement that if not followed may get you thrown out a few establishments.

One particular bar, based on a street corner, boasted a special environment with music and ale of a distinct Irish flavor. People piled into the pub with the Gaelic sounds of the Emerald Isle playing through loud speakers that could barely be heard above the massing crowds. Men and women stood at a long bar, sat at small tables inside the pub, and even a few stout souls braved the cold of the spacious deck out back. Everyone was busy talking to the person they came with or trying to talk to a person they wanted to leave with, as in the case of any young man attempting to cozy up to a female. Laughs and merriment were all around, people meeting people and having a good time on a Friday night in the great South. Simon Barnes was just like everyone else this night standing at the bar with a drink in his left hand, the Armani suit he wore blending in easily with the elite of the crowd. He turned to say something to a woman who was sitting beside him, leaning seductively on him actually, and then suddenly turned back looking out past a set of double doors where people waited to enter the pub. Through the mass of people in the bar, and the ones walking by out on the sidewalk, Simon could easily see the individual standing silently across the street under the yellow glow of the old street lamp. The mysterious man wore blue jeans, a long sleeved white shirt with a simple short sleeved black T-shirt over that, and black Doc Martin boots. His long hair, flowing slightly in the small wind, covered the right side of his face. There was an image on the man's shirt but from such a distance Simon couldn't make anything out. The man was definitely out of place among the sharply dressed of Buckhead.

"Please excuse the effrontery sweetheart but I need to step outside and talk to a man for a minute." Simon said with a slight southern drawl as the lady pressed against him even more.

"Why certainly Sy, who is it anyway? Invite him over for a drink like the respectable southern gentlemen you are and introduce me." The woman remarked with a sexy smirk and wink.

"I don't think he's the sociable type Gwen honey." Simon remarked with a wink before stepping away from his companion and then out the double doors. He walked out past the bouncer of the pub, past the people wandering up and down the sidewalk, and across the street to meet the man. Simon walked with confidence, his fit forty four year old body striding as he approached the man with a large smile crossing his sharp facial features. The image on the front of the shirt finally came into focus and it shocked him for a second, the letters 'AC/DC' stood out in faded silver paint. Those long confident strides faltered for a second before Simon got his gait under control again. Father didn't mention the 'special' client was such a...causal dresser, especially someone who had so much money it took several spreadsheets to keep track of it all.

The man didn't smile in return. Only spoke flatly with little emotion for his greeting. "Good evening Simon Barnes."

"Good Evening Mr. Alexander. How are you this evening sir?" Simon responded holding out his hand for a polite shake. When Alexander didn't move to reply in kind with a gesture the lawyer simply put the appendage back in his pants pocket, Simon's broad smile slipping lower on his face as his exhaled breath crystallized in the cold air.

"I am sorry Simon, it is nothing with you. I do not like to shake hands, and please, do not address me as 'mister' or 'sir'. The salutation denotes a stature I no longer hold or wish to anymore." Alexander said abruptly. He had noticed the effect of not shaking hands with Simon and was now hoping to ease over any slight the lack of reciprocation might have caused.

"That's perfectly fine...sir." Simon replied with his smile before quickly realizing he just used 'sir' unconsciously. "I've been kind of spooked myself with your sudden call and all. My father always told me to be prepared for the time you might ring, but after twenty years I just sort put you at the back of my mind."

"Your father was an admirable man Simon, as was his father before him. I've trusted very few over the years but your family's stewardship has been a welcome boon to me."

Alexander said with a slight smile now creeping up at the corner of his mouth.

"Thank you sir, my father would appreciate knowing you said that." Simon nodded.

The 'sir' grated on Alexander but he didn't correct Simon this time. The man only wanted to show respect and in the end he had earned the right by virtue of his family's loyalty and patronage. "How is everyone? How are Kazahiro and Magda?" Alexander asked.

"All have been doing fine in your absence sir. The instructions you left about monetary allowances and such have been followed to the letter. If you would like me to contact anyone for you I would be happy to see to it." Simon remarked.

"No, please do not tell anyone about me." Alexander quickly shook his head cutting off any other talk of announcing his presence. "I do not want anyone to know about my return. I just want to be alone for a while in this strange new world."

Simon took a breath and spoke watching Alexander closely. "As you wish sir, but if I may add without you thinking I have overreached some confidence, Magda has ceased taking her allowance."

Alexander looked at his lawyer closely as his mind took in this revelation and processed it. "Thank you...the information is not a breach of our confidence Simon. What about the two men in Savannah, what is the news of them?" Alexander asked quickly choosing to move past the news of Magda and onto another topic, as if fleeing from any chance there might be more news of his consort.

"Nothing sir," Simon said as the vampire turned to look at a lovely passing female," the two have been charged with grave robbing and drunken disorderly."

"Have they talked at all?" Alexander asked turning back from the female.

"That's what brought about the drunken disorderly charge sir. The local constables felt the pairs' story lacked a certain...truthfulness you might say." Simon grinned with a nod.

"Good." Alexander replied absently.

"Are you okay sir?" Simon asked concerned.

The vampire turned looking all around the corner at the throng of people moving so quickly up and down the street. The world had certainly changed these last 130 years or so while he slept the dreamless slumber to escape his immortal existence, maybe changed too much for a vampire like himself to exist in it Alexander thought coldly and there, stuck deep in his soul like a poison thorn, the pain still lingered from the loss of her...his Christina. He couldn't be around anyone right now. The chance of being detected in a world he barely understood while still feeling the loss for her...it was too great a risk to take. All he wanted was to get his things and disappear again into the accepting silence of the night and being alone.

"Did you bring the requested items Simon?" Alexander asked already knowing the answer. His hand was out and ready before the lawyer could reach into the pocket in his coat.

"Yes sir," Simon remarked pulling a large envelope out from the inside of his Armani jacket. "Will you need anything else?"

"I will be getting my things and doing some business before being on my way in a day or two. We will talk longer at that time Simon...maybe we could come to an agreement about how to tell the others then?" Alexander whispered taking the envelope and tucking it away in the back pocket of the jeans.

"That sounds like an excellent plan sir. You know how to contact me. I'm at your service if you need anything else." Simon said with a large smile.

"Thank You Simon." Alexander nodded and then was gone faster than the southern lawyer could follow. Simon never saw the form of Alexander blend into the mass of people walking the street, but he knew his 'special' client was out there somewhere among them now. The lawyer shook his head clearing his pupils, but just as he did his mind told him that his eyes were perfectly fine. It was the mysterious nature of the 'special' client he would be taking on his father had explained to him when retiring, a client he had never seen his father winked to him over a glass of expensive bourbon. Alexander was and always had been a client of the Barnes Family and no other and the duty of seeing to him was passed down to Simon from his father and the duty was given to him by his father. The elder Barnes whispered with a twinkle in his eye, never think you're crazed or in the throes of some black magic when around Alexander. You see his father had continued, when it comes to Alexander certain 'peculiarities' were part and parcel of the client attorney privilege my father told me. Respect the rules I give you, follow them to the letter, and all will be fine his father whispered about the mysterious man just in time to take a sip of some very old and exquisite bourbon. Then the elder Barnes ended with one last bit. I have never seen this 'special' client Alexander myself, and your grandfather rarely had contact with him, but you must always be ready for his call my son, always be ready for his call. It is a duty of the Barnes family to see to him. Lord knows Simon missed his father and he respected the man so much he took on faith this 'special' client without so much as a blink for which there was no file except for a very old parchment with instructions written in a penmanship style no one had seen for a very long time and a ledger full of accounts and money. So lost in his thoughts was Simon that he jumped just a little when a female voice suddenly sounded from behind.

"Why didn't you ask him to come in for a drink Sy?" Gwen asked as he turned to look into her beautiful face.

"Gwen, my sweet southern angel, I told you he's not the sociable kind." Simon answered smiling at the women warmly.

The woman held up a small disc that flashed bright red quite annoyingly over and over in her hand as she smiled seductively with a raised eyebrow. "Our table is ready. He looked very interesting, a shame he couldn't come sit and have a bite to eat with us...maybe more?"

"My daddy once told me," Simon mumbled looking back into the mass on the street, "you never ask the grizzly bear how he caught the fish because he might want seconds."

"What?" the women asked giggling while looking extremely confused at the statement.

" Gwen honey, let's just go to the Cheese Cake factory, eat some overpriced food, and then go home and get naked on that big old bear skin rug by the fire place." Simon teased with a devilish grin of his own as his hand slipped down and pinched the women's firm bottom. She squealed with a laugh as the two moved off to the large restaurant across the street.

Alexander moved through the busy streets without attracting not so much as glance from anyone, not one pedestrian or car whizzing by looked in his direction. None knew of his passing and none would while he used his power to cloak his presence. Not a soul would see him unless the ancient vampire wanted them to know he was near. Alexander stopped at a corner, pulled out the large envelope from his pocket, and began looking it contents for something. He leafed past the stack of hundred dollar bills that easily amounted to a couple of thousand in his hand. A small piece of white paper caught his attention, and on it was scribbled a single address in fine pen with the sweeping curves of deliberate perfected penmanship. The name at the top of the address brought back memories and Alexander began to reminisce, but then a harsh voice brought him back to reality with a snap.

"Hey Bradley Cooper, I thought you were lost out in Vegas?" A voice yelled. The corner abruptly filled with laughter as Alexander looked up to notice he had been surrounded by a group of young men. He mentally chastised himself for letting the group get so close without noticing, dropping his concentration and power with a lapse thus letting someone see him. Time for memories later Alexander thought as he slid the envelope into his back pocket. The young men all stood behind a rather large man who had obviously made the humorous remark. The large man was dressed in a tight fitting shirt designed to show off his chest and arm muscles.

"Excuse me, but who is this 'Bradley Cooper?'" Alexander asked politely. The large man laughed even harder as the gaggle of boys also laughed harder, as if on cue.

"What the hell man, you been hiding under a rock somewhere?" The man sneered.

Alexander readied himself and smiled a crooked grin. "Not a rock, just a mausoleum in Savannah."

"What?" The large man asked quizzically more than just a little lost. The group of young followers fell silent as well as they pondered the statement.

"Never mind, it is obvious you have spent more time building your body than your brain." Alexander commented still smiling and still ready.

Tension began to fill the air as the large man suddenly realized he had been turned into the butt of the joke. His frame began to heave as he took in deep breaths and closed in on Alexander attempting to lord over the vampire, something the large man was accustomed to doing it seemed. The group of young males stood by anxiously waiting for their friend to pound the stranger into the sidewalk, as he had done to all the other poor bastards before this one.

"Mister, my name is Tony Brooks. I'm a 6'3, 235 pound monster who played half a season at middle linebacker for the New York Jets. Just wanted you to know who broke your tiny body into a thousand pieces when you wake up in the Intensive Care Unit at the hospital." The man growled cracking the knuckles on his right hand

"Well met Tony Brooks, though you may find breaking me slightly more than you are capable of doing." Alexander responded calmly letting his smile grow just a little bigger exposing just the hint of the large canines. Then suddenly Tony Brooks stumbled back from the corner holding his stomach before finally collapsing to the ground moaning loudly. The group of young followers looked at their idol, then back up to the empty corner, and then back down to the injured ex-football player at their feet. No one moved to help him because this had never happened before. No one had ever hurt Tony so no one in the group knew exactly what to do to help him. And everything had happened so fast anyway they weren't even sure how the strange man had hurt Tony. They just knew he was gone in the blink of an eye from the corner.

Two hours later Alexander stood across the street from a set of large broken iron gates, which at no time would have provided any sense of security and were obviously just some form of decoration...or had been. There was no fence to speak of, anywhere, around the gate. Two brick pillars supported a rusted iron horseshoe shaped sign for which the letters had long since vanished, been stolen, or just ripped from their supports by youthful vandals. Colored men dressed in clothes that obviously didn't fit their slim bodies paraded up and down the street screaming threats at each other every now and then. Alexander could see the handles of exotic guns protruding from the waistbands of their pants. Random cars would speed to an abrupt stop in front of these men, the person inside would talk for a second to one of the men, and a small packet would be exchanged for money with an entirely different man at which time the car would then drive away quickly into the night.

A second or two of thought and Alexander decided against trying to cross the street in the open, even though he could hide from their sight the encounter earlier made the vampire warier than usual. Maybe he couldn't hide in this new world as easily as he could the past one? Maybe these humans now had built up some kind of resistance to his kind? The questions rolled around in Alexander's head as he tied his long hair off into a pony tail, then from somewhere a succession of gunshots rang out and a man screamed about being shot in the back by a coward. None of the men out by the sign or the corner flinched, most just looked excitedly in the direction of the sound before going back to their own business. The others just shrugged the event off as if it were part of the nightly routine. Yes, Alexander thought, the less anyone saw of him the better. He stepped back into the dark shadows of an alley concentrating, willing his body to be lighter than the very air itself. Almost immediately his form took flight on winds that magically appeared and swirled causing him to rise from the dark shadows up into the night sky. Alexander turned his attention southwestward floating toward a certain building that drew him to it like a moth to a flame.

First, there was a crash of deadbolt after deadbolt as it was drawn back, and then at least a dozen chains being dropped from clasps. The whole effort sounded like an army moving its base camp, something Alexander was accustomed to. What he

The lights were out in the windows as he landed on the broken down porch where dead plants sat around in old pots. The poor things had lost their lives while also losing the fight to lighten the desolate area Alexander thought. The vampire took a quick look around then with a quick tap on the wood frame announced his arrival. He expected a sleepy eyed person to answer the door, and yet what he got was the exact opposite of that expectation and most curious.

First, there was a crash of deadbolt after deadbolt as it was drawn back, and then at least a dozen chains being dropped from clasps. The whole effort sounded like an army moving its base camp, something Alexander was accustomed to. What he didn't like was waiting and standing on the porch in the open, the soldier in him feeling exposed and vulnerable. Even after 2300 years it was a habit that was a part of him. Finally, the door opened and there stood an old wizened black woman in a dirty white robe with big fluffy slippers poking out from the bottom of the robe's hem. Her hair was as white as snow peppered here and there and it contradicted the dark glasses she wore that hid her eyes from the public.

"Just the man I've been waiting for," the woman remarked from behind the glasses.

If Alexander wasn't sure what to make of her then her last made him truly rethink the whole decision of coming here. He hadn't expected what he was looking at or that the elder lady would be waiting for him to arrive. She abruptly turned and walked into the dark house before her voice called to Alexander in a rough, hurry-up out-there tone.

"You might want to come in, looks rather strange for a white man to be standing out on my stoop this late in the evening. Wouldn't want the hoodlums round here taking a shot at you would we."

Chapter Two

"What do you mean by 'waiting for'?" Alexander asked the colored woman. She smiled showing a line of perfect white teeth to him before answering.

"It means my patience has finally been rewarded Mr. Alexander. Now, if you would stop being impolite and come inside. Davis was told by his father you were a polite man and he believed that something fierce. I'm sure you'd hate to disappoint the man if he were still alive, wouldn't you Mr. Alexander?" The woman stated walking away from the door.

The vampire stood perfectly still for a second before entering into the small abode. The first thing he noticed was how ram shackled the place looked to his eyes even in the dark, which was the second thing that caught his observant attention. There wasn't a light on anywhere in the room or house but he didn't need one to see the walls were in disrepair, the floor barely covered with a thin carpet, and a smell he wasn't sure of yet lingered in the air of the room. He knew what kind of place this was. He hadn't been gone from the world that long. This was a hovel, a place where those unfortunate enough not to be born into wealth or make it lived drudging out their days on what money they could secure or acquire.

"It's called a 'Project' these days Mr. Alexander." The woman called to him before dropping herself down into a recliner with a small plop of her heavyset body.

The remark struck Alexander numb. She had read his mind! But how could an old woman do that? He could tell if she was doing it, his senses were beyond super sharp, and had never betrayed him in over 2000 years. He could hear the heartbeat of a man miles away, could sense their blood pulsing through the veins of their bodies, and he knew things about people just by looking at them. A quick check over his shoulder reassured him the door was only a few short feet away if a sudden exit was called for.

"Oh don't Fret Mr. Alexander." The old woman said reaching up and removing the glasses. "You'll learn that Grammy doesn't need eyes to see the world for what it truly is."

Her eyes were covered with thick milky white cataracts covering all but the dark pupils that barely shone through. Fingers quickly went to work as Grammy cleaned the lens of her glasses with the fold of her gown that she had pulled out from under her leg. Alexander made a quick mental note, why clean your glasses when you can't see. The room was quiet for a second as

Alexander chided himself for being taken back by an old woman who was obviously crippled. Then he stepped forward and in front of Grammy. He stood perfectly still again looking deep into the old woman, staring at her, and trying to read her past in a mystical window only he could see. He stopped after a minute closing his own eyes tightly shut, what he needed to know now gained, her name and a bit of her past.

"I am sorry to hear about Jefferson Martha. His father's father was a dear friend to me." Alexander said offering his condolences. He had come to conclude a business proposition that had begun with Jefferson's grandfather but was now in other hands obviously.

"Davis was a good man and a better husband Mr. Alexander. His whole family was very special, so very special." Grammy said putting the glasses in the pocket of her night dress. "You've come for the locket haven't you?"

"Yes, I have." Alexander answered stilling feeling some shock at her knowledge of him. It was obvious that Jefferson Davis Wallace had imparted his knowledge of the vampire to his wife Martha here before departing the earth, that and the debt owed him and his family.

Grammy reached down in to the cushions of the recliner and as if out of the fabric itself, she pulled out a small bundle of white cloth. The material had long since yellowed from age, but the bundle was still perfectly wrapped fold for fold, just as it had been 130 years ago Alexander thought. He slowly reached out and took it from Grammy's hand noticing that she did not suffer from the shakes the way other senior citizens did. A small charge ran through him like electricity as his fingers closed on the bundle and the appendages tingled slightly as he unfolded each layer slower than the last. Finally, in the middle of the cloth in the middle of his hand sat a large silver ornate locket gleaming from something other than light. Alexander gently lifted the jewel from its cloth cradle and brought it to eye level starring at it for what seemed an eternity. Only the voice of Grammy brought him back to reality.

"Davis said that locket was mighty important to you Mr. Alexander. There were times when we could have eaten real good if he had taken to selling it, but he would just say 'we made a promise Martha and we have to keep it'. Davis was an honorable man, the strongest of any I have ever known while walking this world."

"I know...I could see it in his father's father." Alexander said bringing the locket back down and tucking it away in his jeans pocket. "I trust very wisely Martha"

"Davis said you were an honest man as well Mr. Alexander. He also said something about a payment when you came to get that Locket back?" Grammy remarked with a slight smile.

Alexander reached into the pocket of his coat producing the thick envelope filled with hundred dollar bills and handed it all to Martha, but she shook her head slowly. The move shocked the vampire again. It was a first for someone to reject a favor that he was bestowing. For 2000 years no one had said nay to one of his gifts, until now.

"Oh no sir, I don't want your money. It's your nobility I'll take in its place if you don't mind." Grammy said with the smile growing on her face.

"Pardon me, my nobility?" Alexander asked slowly trying to read Martha again but something blocked him and his sight this time. He could see nothing but a hazy fog that covered her mind and her intentions from the special window he used.

Martha rose from the old chair and crossed the room. She moved rather quickly Alexander noted for a woman of her age and disability, walked right to the open shades and looked outside as if her eyes still showed it to her. He watched closely trying to look through the special window again and something prevented it this time too, as if a wall had been erected to block his vision. The vampire cautiously crossed the room, but the movements were still too fast for the human eye to follow, and he suddenly appeared behind Grammy by the window looking out into the dark courtyard.

"What am I supposed to see?" He asked.

"You'll see in a second Mr. Alexander. Good Lord, two thousand years and your still impatient." Martha remarked without turning to look at him.

A minute passed by and Alexander was about to ask Martha to take the money for a second time with a little more force in his approach this time. There was nothing out there in the courtyard for the first thing and secondly he was wasting time standing here with a blind woman who was stubborn enough to refuse an ample amount of money. Then a shadow suddenly appeared walking fast across the courtyard from the northwest crossing with the small strides of a young one. Grammy smiled and Alexander watched as the shadow moved through the dark with swift steps easily dodging obstacles and objects that would make it tumble to the hard earth. Alexander could tell the shadow was going by memory, traveling the courtyard several times a day the young one knew where every danger was located. A step to the left here and a step to the right there kept it moving swiftly to the final objective, a window straight across from Martha's window. The young one opened the window, a small sheath of light popped out illuminating the surrounding area, and Alexander noticed that the shadow was a young girl of African descent. She only stayed for a second then climbed inside the window to the safety of her abode leaving Alexander suddenly and strangely feeling very alone.

"There's my payment Mr. Alexander." Grammy declared wandering back away from the window toward the back of her apartment. "You be her guardian angel and we're all settled."

"That is impossible." Alexander said suddenly appearing by Martha's side. The blind woman simply turned to him ignoring the vampire's rapid movements.

"And why's that?" She asked.

"Because that is not what the senior Davis and I settled on so long ago." Alexander stated flatly. If his anger was growing he was not showing one inch of it, but neither was Martha about to back down from her request.

"With all due respect Mr. Alexander my husband Davis, with his passing on and all, left the duty of the locket to me. So it's only fair to say that I now have the right to ask for my remittance in any fashion I so please." Grammy said looking right into the vampire's chest.

"Then take the money Martha. Use it to move away from here and live out your days in a place more suitable." Alexander spoke to Martha trying to use the tone of his voice to soothe the old woman into taking the money. Again, she only smiled and walked away from him turning down the long hall of the single level dwelling.

"No Mr. Alexander I don't need your money. I'll end my day's right here living the same way I have for these last forty or so years." Grammy stated.

"Why are you asking this of me Martha? What danger could this girl possibly be in?" Alexander asked her slowly.

Martha stopped, stood for a second, and then turned to the vampire slowly. She had not put her glasses on again, and with the moonlight pouring in through the slat of the blinds from the living room looked like a soothsayer Alexander had once visited. It was before Babylon, before his other life had crumbled to dust while he watched helplessly.

"Take a look around Mr. Alexander and tell me what you see. This place is the closest thing to hell on earth that there is. It eats the very souls from the living. My Davis and my son both died here in the Laurel Woods Projects from what those demons are doing outside with all those drugs. If they're not killing themselves then they're killing innocent bystanders with stray bullets and crack cocaine. You can't walk down the street because the addicts will kill you for your pocket change to get their fix for the night. That girl is a special gift Mr. Alexander and she'll go on to do great things one day if this place doesn't swallow her up first like it does all the rest. I've buried my share of special gifts Mr. Alexander and I'll be damned if I'm gonna have to bury her without using every weapon I got. If that means I call in all my debts, my markers, and IOU's including yours to my Davis then so be it because the ends more than justify the means in this particular instance."

"But I cannot do this Martha." Alexander said. "There are too many dangers involved right now for me to do what you ask and is this not something more suited for the local constabulary or even her mother."

"The Police are worthless!" Martha cackled loudly. " Those men don't care about us, and if they did then they would have done something to change this place long ago."

"I cannot change this place for you either Martha, it is not in my power." Alexander said trying hard to make a point.

"I don't want you to change this place Mr. Alexander, even if that were at all possible. Her mother's trying to do that all ready, which by the way is why she's in so much danger! All I want is for you to look after her. Why don't you meet her? See for yourself what she's like." Martha shot back.

"No," Alexander snapped emphatically," I do not mingle with people. I am more comfortable alone"

"You're talking to me and you talked with my Davis's father. What's so hard about just talking Mr. Alexander?" Grammy said.

"Those were different situations Martha, not to be confused with this one right now. I simply cannot do what you are asking me, it is not in me to be around people at this moment in time. There are something's I need to look into first before I leave you."

"I know it's got something to do with that locket and the reason you been gone for so long."

Alexander didn't say anything for a second, trying to come up with a tactic that might convince Martha to take the money and forget this crazy idea of him babysitting that young girl. He stepped forward and held out the envelope again.

"I am just not capable of this Martha and I do not care to explain why. All I ask is for you to take this money and forget this ludicrous idea of my protecting that young girl from the evils of this place."

"No sir I won't do that Mr. Alexander." Grammy stated with a huff. "Like I said I don't want your money! If you don't want to do what I ask respectfully for then you can go but my Davis once said you were the most honorable man he had ever met, that you couldn't stand to have a debt over your head, and for him to say that about someone was great thing. However, if you have an agenda to get to then don't let a closed door keep you. We can just call it evens and forget the rest."

The guilty tone of the last remark was enough to lower Alexander's hand holding the envelope full of money and give up the fight to change Martha's mind. He watched the old woman turn back around and slowly walk down the dark hall and then she stop just short of going left into a room that was obviously her bedroom. Martha simply called out to him not turning to look in the vampire's direction. A small smile ran across her mouth showing the white teeth again, the kind that proudly declares 'I win'.

"The door to your right is an empty bedroom that you can use Mr. Alexander. I know not to disturb you during the day so don't expect me to wake you up with a stack of pancakes now"

Then she was gone and Alexander was left standing alone in the dark apartment thinking silently to only his soul how he lost this battle. A 2300 year old vampire outsmarted by an elderly blind woman, where exactly did his plan begin to fall apart? The scene played through his mind second by second and each time everything hinged on one simple fact. Alexander was an honorable man, sometimes too much so now that he thought of it in this kind of perspective. He produced the locket from his pants pocket without really thinking of doing so and stared at the small jewel in his open palm for a minute, just feeling the metal against his flesh. A small latch on the locket's side gave a pop and the bauble opened slowly creaking as it did. There, protected from the harsh outside elements by the silver metal of the locket, were two oval hand painted pictures. A dark haired woman sitting with a small boy on one side and a fair-haired woman dressed in

Victorian era garb on the second. Alexander stood there fixed like a statuette just starring at his most prized possession, two small hand painted pictures.

Chapter Three

The Saturday night air was crisp as the bars in Buckhead filled to capacity yet again. Young people came and went with abandon all night not noticing the tall man standing in the dark corners of the dance clubs. Karen Spector rushed down the street stopping individuals, sometimes running into them, and asking frantically about her friend. Robin Caskey had disappeared from the bar just a few blocks down the street rather quickly leaving her shocked friend Karen and an unpaid bar bill behind. Karen had paid the bill but couldn't find her friend Robin anywhere. At first, she had just crossed off the incident as her friend seeing some buff guy and chasing after the beef, but then Karen had never ever seen Robin chase after any man, and she didn't need to. Panic set in then and after ten minutes with a no show from her friend Karen took off after Robin and now the search was in full swing. A few minutes later an ambulance flew by with the sirens blaring and the lights flashing brightly. Karen knew, no she felt just who that emergency vehicle was for and she began to chase after the revolving lights feeling her panic deepen with each step.

Alexander slipped by two female pedestrians moving along the sidewalk without so much as stirring their delicate hair. They never noticed him as the two halted to watch an ambulance whip by, but the vampire kept moving occupied in thought, he already knew where the vehicle was going anyway. This world is too big, too many strange things you don't know about his mind kept saying repeatedly. Yes, it was paradise for a vampire with so many unsuspecting victims that could be lured away down dark alleys and such, but it was uncomfortable to move around in, to 'be' in for a vampire as old as Alexander. The first thing, this 'Internet', what was so all consuming about it that kept people tied to it for days refusing to leave their homes or even eat? And these 'Cell Phones' that everyone carried around typing on, even the little ones, were true marvels to behold because they let one person speak to another through the very air itself. And the phones took pictures, both still and moving...MOVING PICTURES...what a wonder to see. For more than one hundred and thirty years had he slept in that mausoleum while everything around him changed beyond his wildest dreams and even his worst nightmares. Those phones, could one snap a picture of him? What if it could and it showed this world his kind?

Everywhere he turned there was some device, some new contraption that might be able to expose him to all these people. What if someone used this 'Internet' to show a picture of a vampire? Would there be anywhere in this world he could hide? Could he hide from the one who had chased him for so long, the one he was hiding from right now?

Yet, through all the doubt there was a fierce determination in the vampire's heart. Yes, this world had him confused and disoriented, but he would win out. He had no choice but to learn about it. All I have to do is teach myself Alexander thought, learn about the lost years and where better to do that then where he was going, something called the 'Mall'. He had seen the large complex called Lenox when he first came to Atlanta and it intrigued the vampire's curiosity. What would the need be of such a large building if not to house families and such. Then he found out it was used for commerce and it made perfect sense, it was the open markets but indoors now and in a vastly larger size, a place where people could wander from one provider to another parting with coin. With his interest piqued Alexander walked through the large glass doors and into the wonderland of a modern shopping mall.

The store clerk didn't remember the tall drink of water dressed in a black AC/DC Concert shirt entering her store and she sure as hell would have noticed him. Even though he looked plain on the outside she could easily envision rippling chest muscles, rock hard abs, and a set of biceps that could crush her very bones anytime he got the notion. The man looked at her, locked eyes with a smile, and instantly a scene from a romantic novel began to play in her mind. A strong wind was whipping her dress and long semi-blond locks as this mysterious man held her in a pair of rippling arms. She ran her hands across his bare chest which gleamed with sweat and bulged with more muscles than her skinny boyfriend Manx could get if he used steroids like Arnold himself. Then the mysterious man's face came into view and it was him, the man in the AC/DC t-shirt. The very one who was just a mere eight feet away from her right now at this very moment. Something began to build in her and it was spreading all over like molten lava, but was especially collecting right there in that spot where it felt best. Oh yes, right there you animal! She had to meet him. There was no chance she was letting this fine ass specimen of a man get away from her by God. She partly ran and partly walked straight up to him and announced her presence in her best, but sexiest, salesperson voice. "May I help you with a selection today sir?"

"Yes you may, what exactly is this?" Alexander asked holding up a compact disk case complete with artwork for a band called 'Skillet'.

The British accent almost floored her. *Oh my god,* her mind screamed, *it's as if Tom Hiddleston, and Benedict Cumberbatch and Henry Cavil all had a son, fused him into one hot body, and he was standing right here RIGHT NOW!* But even the sultry vision and lustful desire wasn't enough to keep her from realizing what her dream man had said. "Excuse me, but you don't know what a CD is? Where have you been for the last couple of years, huh?" She asked with a chuckle.

"Why does everyone keep asking me that? I was sleeping in a mausoleum in Savannah." Alexander expressed with exasperation without blinking. The manager though simply ignored the comment and began to explain the mysterious case to him in an excited voice.

"Well, this is a CD," the manager said taking it from the vampire, "and it holds music... sort of like a vinyl record from the 70's or a Cassette Tape from the 80's."

Alexander just nodded with wide eyes, when he went to sleep there had been rumors that a man named Edison had found a way of on putting music on a round tube that would play from a strange box when turned with a crank. Now though, music had been condensed down to a small round disc, truly amazing he thought as the woman next to him went on speaking. "But CD's are old school now. Everyone has an MP3 player or one their cell phones these days and they usually just download music off the Internet."

"An MP3 player, what is that?" Alexander asked quickly, his curiosity piqued even more.

The girl did a quick double take and smiled, yeah the question was really weird but that accent though. "It's a little device like a cell phone only it holds songs you upload off a PC or buy off of the Internet, or stole before the law got involved and cracked down on Napster."

The vampire grinned a little, "a cell phone can play music and take pictures and let you talk to someone through the air?"

"Yeah, with the right one you can do pretty much anything. So what kind of tunes are you into? Punk...Rap...No Wait! I know...you're a classic old rock and roll kind of guy right?" She said with a sly and very hopeful smile.

Alexander had no idea what she was referring to but he wasn't about to ask her just what made up each of those types of music. He was already drawing too much attention asking about cell phones so he only smiled and nodded to her hoping what he was about to experience was not going to make him want to go back to that mausoleum in Savannah.

"Who do you like?" She asked again. Her dream man stood for a second as if lost and she was beginning to wonder if he was an escapee from a mental ward somewhere when he was suddenly holding a CD in his right hand. Funny, she never saw him reach for it, but there it was in his hand as if he had been holding the thing all this time.

"These men, this AC/DC, I really like them." Alexander said holding out the CD.

"Oh yeah, should have known that from the t-shirt I guess. Not exactly classical rock, but a great band never the less. You don't look like an AC/DC man to me though, more like Phantom of the Opera." She stated smiling as wide and as inviting as she could. Oh God, please let him pick me up her grin screamed.

"I like all kinds of music. Maybe you could recommend something I could listen to...later?" Alexander replied to her with his own sly smile.

Oh yes, the girl thought, if that didn't sound like a pass and from her dream man no doubt. She smiled back at him, tilted her head, and batted the old eyelashes. There wasn't a man alive that could resist her now, she hoped and thought, and oh God please let this one be straight because if he's gay or just dead I might have to throw myself off the IBM Tower. "I could do that, but just for you."

"I would be more than gracious for your help." Alexander whispered immediately noticing the look in the woman's eyes. She was on the prowl, and so was he for that fact. "My name is Alexander, and you are?" He asked eyeing her deeply.

"I'm Shelly." She said licking her top lip. Oh she was most certainly on the prowl the vampire thought.

The two wondered around the store and she diligently pointed out a CD here and a CD there that she thought Alexander would just love to hear, and with each proffer she suggested he just download the album from the internet. A few simple albums grew into quite a handful but he remembered them all with expert precision and all the while keeping his eye turned to her. It made that special spot glow even warmer, brighter with every minute for Shelly, so much so she even offered to let him use her computer to download the albums onto and even stepped up suggesting she'd load the tunes on whatever MP3 player or cell phone he had. Alexander only nodded with his smile as they continued on. There were a couple of her favorite tunes and a couple she had never heard personally but came highly recommended. Finally, by happenstance, they stopped by the large wall racks where a number of rectangle boxes stood propped on one end, front covers displayed prominently.

"What are these?" He asked her while eyeing the rack.

"That's MegaBuster's colossal DVD movie selection. We have over a ten thousand titles in stock for your viewing pleasure...that is till Wednesday night." She said dully as if it had been said before, like a hundred thousand times before.

The vampire turned to her with a concerned look, "what happens Wednesday night?"

"The DVD rental business is going the way of all extinct animals like the CD and tapes, killed by Netflix and Amazon Prime." Shelly answered with a sigh.

"Is there any way I may see one?" Alexander asked eagerly.

"Yes you can," she said quickly stepping into the vampire's vision to get his attention back," You can rent one of our fine DVD's."

"Rent...like a room?" he responded.

"Yeah rent, as in take home for two days at $4.95 each. You just put the disc into your DVD player like so, push the play button, and sit back and vegetate for a couple of hours. You have a preference?" Shelly asked coyly while batting her eyes.

"Do you have anything on Vampires?" Alexander asked. He suddenly realized that he had asked for vampires without thinking, almost like a knee jerk reflex.

"Yes, a horror movie man. I just love horror movies, but everything with vampires really sucks these days. Let's see what I can find. Here we go all the horror movies we have. Just look for the ones you want." Shelly remarked happily with the same sexy voice while turning to wall of boxes.

Alexander's eyes were immediately drawn to a special box down to his left and paying close attention to move slowly he leaned down and picked up the carton. In bold letters and with a colorful background the box proclaimed 'the most suspenseful movie of our time' and 'a must see for all fanatics of Anne Rice'. The lettering spelled out 'Interview with a Vampire' in bold white and the face of some man with a crude smile displaying long incisors in a vicious manner. Who was Anne Rice? Moreover, when did she talk to one of us Alexander thought? He turned to ask Shelly about this woman but she was busy bringing him a number of boxes stacked under her right arm.

"Interview was okay but if you want a kick ass one then you have to go to the 'Fright Night' series and the 'Understudy'. I also got 'Bram Stoker's Dracula' because you can't be a vampire enthusiast without seeing it you know. It's kind of based on the book, or as close as Hollywood can get you know." Shelly said handing over the particular box bearing Bram Stoker's name in one motion.

"Bram Stoker?" Alexander whispered in surprise holding the box. "He actually wrote the book?"

"Yeah, it's like the quintessential vampire story. Based on Vlad the Impaler you know?" Shelly said nodding her head.

"Vlad...the story was never based on that maniac, Dracula was someone else entirely." Alexander remarked still eyeing the box cover.

"How do you know that? Don't tell me, you've met Bram Stoker!" Shelly said laughing. It was a joke right, had to be a joke?

"Very briefly, I answered a question or two for him before leaving for the United States on a ship." Alexander stated flatly. The statement was quick, to the point, and his eyes never left the box making Shelly suddenly feel like the poor bastard who let out a fart in the middle of the preacher's sermon at church. She stopped laughing and handed over the rest of the boxes, which numbered enough to overwhelm the vampire for a moment.

"Okay, it doesn't bother me your psycho as long as you keep talking and still look that good in the morning. The rest of the movies here are okay but kind of campy. The ones with Christopher Lee are good if you can get past a lot of really bad acting. I never understood why he did those movies; Lee was so damn good on his own."

"Who is Christopher Lee?" Alexander asked.

"I'm not going to even go there." Shelly said while walking away and giggling. "Let's just get to the register and check you out because the store is closing. Do you have a membership card? We can sign you up real quick if you don't."

"I was hoping to ask for some more assistance." Alexander inquired.

"Anything you want, and I do mean anything." Shelly said turning to him and smiling her sexiest smile once again. Oh God don't let him be gay!

"I do not have a DVD player as you say and I would be more than appreciative to borrow one if possible." Alexander proffered still grinning even though he knew the clerk was his now. The cat had most certainly caught the mouse and by far more than then tail.

"I have one at my place we can use." Shelly offered stepping close to Alexander. This was quite daring for her. She could feel her pulse race and her heartbeat against her chest bone. Shelly had never invited a man she had just met over to her place, until now.

"That would be very nice and maybe you could give me some more assistance in another area?" Alexander asked with his smile coaxing and drawing the young girl deeper into his will.

"And just what would that be?" Shelly asked batting her long lashes even more. At this point she looked like she was using semaphore to contact someone across the store.

"I wonder if it would be possible for you to show me where a man may acquire a few books of literature." Alexander said.

"I may, but what are you willing to give me in return for all this assistance?"

"I can assure you that tonight will be the most unbelievable experience of your short life." Alexander spoke low stepping in close enough to hover over the young girl.

"Okay...just let me get my keys." Shelly swallowed with a deep breath. Then she was running through the store barreling over one of her own poor workers like a middle linebacker for the Falcons. The girl never saw the blow coming and just ended up going feet over head through a display with a loud ka-bang as she practically bounced off the floor. Alexander shook his head and went back to starring at the cover of the display box for Dracula letting the memories come back to him. There he was with a young Bram at a small and very dark pub in Dublin answering several questions for the man in return for the procurement of a letter given to him by his Christina just weeks before...before he had to stop her from murdering other innocent lives.

"You ready to go lover?" A panting Shelly asked noticing her dream man slip back to the present as if he was occupied thinking aloud to no one.

"No one has called me that name in quite a while."
Alexander said offering his arm to the girl.

"Well I hope to call you that again later, and a lot louder
too." She whispered with a wicked grin. The remark totally went
over Alexander's head but he knew the grin, it was like an old
friend that had suddenly come to say hello after being away for
quite a long time. The two disappeared into the darkened mall
with a load of DVD's and one new cell phone in a bag the
vampire's carried. School was now in session.

The Sunday morning sun greeted the Laurel Projects in
Atlanta with a fiery burst as Stephanie rose from her bed
squinting from the bright light pouring between the broken blinds
on her bedroom window. A couple of second passed before she
forced her weary body from the warmth of the covers to the icy
cold of the outer world in a single move. You know it's going to
hurt so just do it in one shot her mother always said, funny how
the remark was of little comfort now. She threw on a robe
covering the large nightshirt she wore to ward off the cold and
began to move toward her door. Halfway there was an old chair
by her make up table, and being blind from just waking up,
Stephanie connected with it squarely right on her foot. Suddenly

she was blind, hobbling with broken toes, and spinning out of control toward the hallway. Only a great act of balance saved her from going through her own bedroom door like some kind of wild stunt out of a Wesley Snipes flick.

She moved down the hall of her two-room one-level apartment, just ahead was the door to her daughter Wilma's room. Stephanie walked past it not noticing the fact that it stood partially open this morning where normally it was always closed. The kitchen was bright as she put on a pan of water to heat for making the life sustaining coffee that would give her energy to face the day. A creak sounded through the house making Stephanie jump and begin to mutter how she had to stick it out in this damn neighborhood for the good of everyone. Right, for the good of one man was the real truth. Then the door to the kitchen flew open with a loud bang sending her leaping to the ceiling while screaming bloody murder at the top of her lungs. More bright light flooded through the open door causing Stephanie to squint, blurring the image in the door to doubles yet she recognized the small form standing there as plain as day.

"WHAT THE HELL IS WRONG WITH YOU GIRL?" Stephanie screamed at the two images.

"Nothing mom, just went out for a paper." Wilma said walking into the kitchen putting the morning paper on the table.

"Do you really think you need another cup of coffee this morning?"

"You'll need a doctor if you scare me like that again." Stephanie spat.

Wilma sat down at the kitchen table choosing to leave her mother alone. It was really for the best when she got like this anyway. The paper slid from the plastic protection bag with a pop as she opened it eager to read and learn. At 14, Wilma Livonia Jackson was not your normal pre-teen girl by any stretch of the imagination. She was considerably shorter than other girls at the middle school she attended and being named Wilma didn't help the situation one bit, but what was lacked in size was more than made up for in intelligence. Her I.Q. dwarfed her classmates and even surpassed the school teaching staff in all but the rare case. Once she developed and created a project for her science class that the teacher couldn't even comprehend. Wilma was given an A on the spot and she didn't even have to present anything. Of every class, though, the computer class was her favorite. She was proficient with the school's archaic computer system and showed it by surfing obscure parts of the Internet on her free time finding odd programs and patches to fix ailments the old desktops needed to keep running. Wilma wanted her own computer so bad she could spit, but reality was she had to wait until money was a little more abundant. Therefore, for now, she just looked through ads dreaming of the things she could do with those advertised high-end systems.

"What's happening in the world today baby?" Stephanie asked while blowing on a very large steaming mug of coffee.

"The usual, a couple of wars, a couple of political scandals, and some physicists say the upgrade for the Hadron Supercollider could bring about the creation of 'strange matter'." She said nonchalantly.

"Oh really," Stephanie remarked from behind the steaming cup of coffee," That's interesting, I guess"

"It is if you think about it. The Astronomer Royal says the upgrade could create particles called 'strangelets' and from there it's just a quick chain reaction to creating 'strange matter' which could potentially turn the Earth into a hyper-dense sphere...but it's just theory mostly." Wilma stated not looking up from the paper.

Stephanie blinked once in incomprehension as her daughter kept reading the morning newspaper. She took a drink from the coffee mug wondering if there was anything that Wilma couldn't understand or excel at. Then she remembered a little thing from the other night, the sound of a closing door.

"So where'd you go the other night?" Stephanie asked with a sly smile.

Wilma looked up from the paper finally and anyone could see the mixture of fear and the quick thinking going there behind her eyes. The kind of look a little kid will show when they know there caught breaking the rules and their mind is contemplating what the best option to take is, lying or acting dumb. Wilma had such a look for a second before regaining some composure and answering. Well, Stephanie found one thing Wilma wasn't good at, didn't she.

"What are you talking about?" Wilma commented turning back to the paper.

"Ah! Don't you try to blow this off girl? We can always see how you well remember things after a week inside the house." Stephanie remarked with a raised finger.

"Mom," Wilma shrieked looking up from the paper with a snap," I didn't do anything wrong"

"You went outside after your curfew is what you did wrong!" Stephanie stated.

Wilma was ready to dig in and fight for at least a modicum of rights when a small article on a back page of the paper caught her eye. Now suddenly the fight shifted from trying to gain some liberty to getting from the kitchen to the other article clippings she had down the hall in her room. Another victim, she thought, that brings the count to three including the two red necks from Savannah.

"Your right mom, totally, I just got bored is all... I'm sorry," Wilma said with a large smile.

"Excuse me," Stephanie retorted with a squint," you're giving up way to early here. What are you up to girlfriend?"

Wilma was slowly gathering her paper trying to just move on before her mother could build an effective retort. She needed to clip that article and it was gnawing at her like a trapped animal. Stephanie was about to jump on her daughter like nobody's business when a knock at the kitchen door acted like the bell signaling the end of the second round of a boxing match. Stephanie finally, after a minute, reached over and opened the portal slightly. A black man dressed in casual clothes stood on the small porch smiling broadly at Stephanie, a small gold cross-hung from his neck draping in front of the blue button down shirt he wore.

"Good Morning Stephanie and what a glorious morning it is!" He stated with enthusiasm.

"Good morning Lee," Stephanie said quickly primping her hair into place with a look of fright while letting the man enter the kitchen," So what's on the agenda for today."

Leland Hall stood just at six foot two even with a sturdy build from pumping weights most of his life. An ex-gang member, he turned his life to the works of God by street preaching in an effort to turn around the misguided youth and their wayward life.

He encountered resistance in the form of threats and physical violence but Leland was devoted to the lord and to his mission to save the Laurel projects. Leland was also devoted to his helper, more than she realized he secretly hoped for and feared at the same time. Stephanie worked tirelessly alongside him with the women gangs breaking the hold they had on the ladies of the Laurel. She was a wonder to watch counseling the women and giving them the attention and support they needed to get free the street preacher discovered. Leland felt that he could obtain real change for the Laurel with Stephanie's help. Maybe one day he could stop trying to save the projects and turn his full attention to the small wonder standing with him in the kitchen, who was at the moment trying to walk away quickly and quietly.

"We can talk about that in a minute Stephanie. Hello Wilma, how are you this glorious morning?" He asked cheerfully with a large smile.

"I am exuberant Mr. Hall." Wilma stated emphatically.

"Hey watch it with that mister stuff all right and try to use words I don't have to look up in the dictionary please." Leland joked setting both of the ladies in the room at ease.

"Is there a problem Lee?" Stephanie asked while watching her daughter run from the room, paper under her arm. She made a quick mental note to continue this conversation with her later.

"Well," Leland said with a deep breath," Do you remember Monster K?"

"The boy with the messed up hair you were trying to bring in? Yeah, I remember him. What's the problem?" she asked.

"It's complicated as usual," he replied walking over and taking Wilma's seat at the table, "his real name is Kenneth and I got him to finally come in and talk a couple of nights ago."

"That's great Leland" Stephanie remarked giving him a mug of hot coffee.

"I wish it were so but he's disappeared. He was supposed to come by my place last night but he never showed. No one's seen him since last night."

"I can get the word out, spread the net with the ladies and hopefully get something." She stated with genuine worry in her voice.

"That would be great. I think another gang member probably pulled him away. He was confused when he came to me, not sure what to do with all those mixed emotions and feelings. That's when they need me most, that's when the lord can help them out of that hole of despair they are in." He said shaking his head.

"I'm sorry Lee, what do you want to do now?" Stephanie asked.

"Pray to the lord. Come and talk to you." Leland said looking at her. The two sat in silence for a few seconds just starring deeply into the other's eyes. Down the hall, Wilma's hands worked feverishly with a pair of scissors cutting out the article out of the paper careful not to cut into the words of it by accident. Her mind was running at full power thinking of the three people mentioned in the articles and what might have caused their sudden anemia.

Chapter Four

Grammy sat in her favorite tattered old chair in the living room facing the large window that overlooked the worn out playground of the Project. She wasn't wearing her usual dark sunglasses. She never did when she sat alone in the dark of her own living room. Yet in the ghetto, you were never really alone were you, not with all that evil just outside the front door. The milky cataract that had covered her pupils and stolen the sight from her long ago couldn't hide the darkness of environment around her house, just feet from her front door. Like right now for instance, out there by that crumbling sign, a pack of young hooligans stood watch for another one across the street protecting him. That boy was the pusher; hiding in the shadows and selling the bags of that white devil dust to the fools who drove by with their stereos blaring loud enough to make you deaf, like no one else lived around here. The pusher's name was J-Rock, quite original Martha thought, using the same name as the filth you sold on the corners every night. *Nevertheless, I wonder if he knows what's going to happen* she thought and a little voice in her mind answered back quickly.

Not A Clue!

She turned her head slightly watching intently with her blind eyes just as a white Cadillac rolled past the pusher. On cue the rear window rolled down just as J-Rock withdrew a manila envelope, and with a simple snap of the wrist he tossed it into the window of the passing car as it never slowed. This was the mailman coming to pick up the money and run it back to the real dealers, the elusive men who ran everything here in the Laurel. The whole incident only took about three seconds and Grammy had known exactly each and every step in the sad act, it happened every night at this time. Payday on the docks you could say, but after tonight the bank would be closed for good. *Oh yes, that's all going to come to end, isn't it?* The voice said in her head with an evil giggle.

The Cadillac picked up speed and was out of sight while the pusher walked up the street a few feet to where another car had stopped and a hand waved from the driver's window. The hand was white wearing a gold watch, two gold rings, and a rather nice bracelet. More of the white folk coming down here to buy their drugs and here we are so eager to sell them that death they clamor for in a small clear baggie. Fools, both white and black, for letting this place and places like them exist, to drag us all down to hell she thought. Grammy then turned back to the window and across the courtyard she watched a small figure make her way through the playground, silently just as she had the night before and countless times before that. The figure slipped out and away to do whatever without stirring the attention or eye of any one of the men on the street corner. She knew where all the shadows were, the places to hide and move in. Poor girl, you shouldn't have to live like this Grammy thought one last before slipping her glasses on.

"You be careful child." Grammy stated rising from the chair with surprising ease heading back down the hall to the bedrooms. "As my late Jefferson would say, it's time to play my hand."

The empty room that Grammy let Alexander use could no longer lay claim to that particular adjective, one of being empty. Stacks and stacks of videos sat neatly around a small television and DVD combo in one while next to it a small laptop sat with an MP3 player and a pair of earphones, the small device in a red case still plugged in and downloading. Several stacks of CD jewel cases were neatly in place by the computer, not a single case was out of place but in perfect position to make each stack stable and able to obtain the lofty height of five to eight feet high. The center of the room was nothing but a semi-circle mountain of paperback books that came to a man's waist and in the middle of that architectural feat sat the vampire on a small uncomfortable chair, each hand holding an open volume. His eyes scanned just a few microseconds faster than his ambidextrous fingers which easily flipped the pages and those were a white whistling blur. The covers on both shut at exactly the same time as he looked up to the closed wooden door and called out to Grammy standing just beyond.

"You can come in Martha. It's only polite as you say." Alexander said calmly, both books coming to rest on the semicircular pile in perfect position.

The door swung open and she walked inside just past the jam, the dark sunglasses covering her eyes now lending a sharp effect to her white teeth which were exposed in a small smile.

"Well, well Mr. Alexander," she said with a small cackle," You sure have moved in. Now tell me, just how did you get all this in here without my knowledge, huh?"

"I have many talents Martha, it comes with my age. And it seems you have certain abilities as well, like how did you know I had these things?" Alexander asked not expecting an answer before crossing his legs.

"Oh Mr. Alexander, I just have a good pair of ears is all. I say, it must be a great thing knowing your gonna live forever. Sure does give one a reason to get up in the morning I'd say."

Grammy remarked shifting the conversation for a reason only she knew.

"Eternal life is not a blessing Martha." Alexander commented dryly, the friendly tone gone from his voice. "It is a loathsome parade at times."

"I'll have to take your word on it Mr. Alexander. I don't have any experience with everlasting life. Say, did you read all them books, listen to all them records, and watch all them movies?" Grammy asked.

Alexander rose from his chair and crossed the room in the usual blink of an eye coming to rest silently by Grammy's arm. She was still looking out at the chair as if he was sitting there in it but when he spoke she didn't jump or start from the sound of his voice.

"I have read every last sentence of every book. I have watched every last second of every movie and listened to every word on every CD." He said calmly.

"Why?"

Alexander smiled showing his sharp canine just a bit, "I need to learn about Society Martha, it is the only way to blend in effectively. Sleeping for more than 130 years left me out of touch with everything."

"Amazing what you can do when you put your mind to it. So you'll be moving on then I suppose?" Grammy asked turning to face him in his new position.

Yet, the vampire wasn't there anymore. He had already walked away from her and the spare room. Past Grammy and out into the musty living room, he looked out her large window to the rusted playground beyond. He heard her footsteps approach from behind and stand beside him at the window, looking out among the night as if her eyes could really see what was out in the courtyard.

"I'll be leaving tomorrow night Martha. I've arranged to have all my things picked up when I depart by some men. I wanted to ask if you will reconsider my offer once more." Alexander asked quietly.

"No sir I won't." Grammy said shaking her head. "Davis always said I was as stubborn as a mule. He told me once it was what he fell in love with the most about me but I can't really see that. I don't like stubborn people myself personally. Any way, it is not about the money Mr. Alexander, I don't need it or want it. I just want you to help out a little girl that can't help herself being in a bad predicament is all."

Alexander closed his eyes in frustration and finally responded after a minute. "I cannot fulfill that particular request Martha, anything else gladly but that."

"Well then, I guess our business is concluded Mr. Alexander. May all that reading, studying, and stuff help you 'blend in' as you call it? I'll wish you a Good night sir." Grammy said heading slowly back to her room.

"I will only bring her more trouble if I get involved, is that what you want for her Martha?" Alexander called to her, his voice tinged with anger and the building frustration.

"You want to know something Mr. Alexander. That little girl was born into this hell so somehow I don't think it could get any worse. The projects bring its own special kind of problems and to see it you have to look a little father than those books you read. I'm a little tired and not in the mood to show you as much so I'll say my good-bye's tomorrow night." Grammy explained then turned and proceeded down the hall to her bedroom. Alexander stood there for a few seconds more staring at where she had stood, and then like a whisper he left leaving the living room empty once more. The vampire had disappeared into the empty air itself it seemed yet if he had waited around a minute longer, if he could have looked into that dark bedroom next to the door jamb where Grammy stood, he would have seen a small smile creeping across her dark features.

Her small feet walked as fast as her equally short legs would carry her across the dirty cement sidewalk. Wilma looked around just once to make sure she wasn't being followed before taking her gaze back to the ground she pounded furiously with both feet. In the projects the first rule of survival was to keep your gaze low and don't make eye contact with anyone, unless you were looking for trouble and Wilma just wanted to get home as fast as humanly possible. Yeah, she had broken her mother's rule of not being out after dark again, and yeah it was a school night technically being Sunday, but the last showing of the original Star Wars was at the dollar movies this weekend and she couldn't miss out. Funny she thought, how a movie made before she was even born had caught her imagination, the lack of today's special effects didn't lessen the affect that story had on her. The movie, the story, it stirred something deep inside her imagination and she never wanted to lose that feeling, not for a single second. It was easy to see why she loved the old movie so because to live those adventures and fly through space and escape from dastardly villains meant she wasn't here in the projects anymore...to get away from its filth was enough to face the dark of the night and even Mr. Vader himself if need be. That's why she broke her mother's most sacred rule on a school night, but that didn't mean she wanted to be punished though, even Star Wars wasn't worth a taste of the belt. Wilma passed by a dark alley but she didn't look up, first rule of survival vigilantly observed. Back, in the depth of the dark alley, a movement flashed but it was so fast she wouldn't have seen it even if she was looking right at that spot at that very moment in time. She continued up the street not noticing the figure following from behind in the deep shadows cast by the arc sodium overhead streetlights.

Why don't you just do what you told her you would do and leave?

The voice had been running through his head for that last two hours berating and hammering his thoughts like a brutish whirlwind. The first hour he had wondered Buckhead looking for an ample victim to feed upon, but the voice kept up the assault, so much so he had given up on that course of action and tried to find some other way of distracting the voice. However, it was useless. In the end he simply chose an abandoned alley and crouched down behind the dumpster no longer seeking refuge or distraction. Oh, he had answered the voice. He had answered it so many times the response was like a recording from one of the many CD's neatly stacked in his room or the thousands of songs on that MP3 player he purchased. However, the voice didn't care for the answers he gave. No, it simply kept asking the same question over...and over...and over.

Why don't you just do what you told her you would do and leave?

"I am an honorable man and I cannot live with a debt over my head." Alexander mumbled to the dark.

Why don't you just do what you told her you would do and leave?

There was no way to stop it, you give the voice an answer and it just asked the same question again. You give the same answer and you get the same question in return. You give a different answer and you get the same question again for good measure. Try to run away and the voice just followed, try to hide and it found you even in the darkest of hiding places. Alexander was quickly tiring of the vicious cycle of this game, which brought him to the decision he was at now. Back to sleep his mind had proposed and Alexander agreed without hesitation, back to the sanctuary of deep unhindered slumber. There was no voice, no guilt, and no honor to drive him insane. There was no strange world to overwhelm him with so many new things and devices and rushing people that he felt like he was drowning. He would sleep and be alone again. Magda and the others would forget about him in time, no one would miss him at all. She had stopped taking his money so it had to be the same for his company. It would take little to make her forget his existence. Then he sensed something approaching the entrance to the alley. He didn't stand to see who because he knew it was a single being, a young girl walking fast trying to avoid attention. It was Martha's little girl. Then, the figure was past the opening of the alley, and not knowing why Alexander began to follow her at a safe distance using the shadows from the street lamps to hide from her. She was wearing a small purple jacket to keep out the cold of the night, but he could see from the shivers it wasn't really working that well.

Then the mystical window opened for him, and with each step he learned.

He knew her name was Wilma Livonia Jackson, born to Stephanie who was a single mother with a passion for discipline that drove Wilma crazy, even though deep down she knew it was for the best and it was out of love. He knew she would have to face a stern lashing with a leather belt if caught. If so, she would take the beating without a request for mercy because she knew she had broken the rules. He knew she was smart, so smart she was embarrassed by the fact sometimes, like when the teacher would ask her to correct one of the other students after they failed to answer correctly. Nevertheless, what came next simply blew the mind of the 2300-year-old vampire because after all that time this was a first for him, a first with the vision. Usually it was just the past that he saw, incidents and memories that occupied the vast spaces of the person's being, but with Wilma he was seeing her future unfold with each small, quick step she took. He saw a discovery in medicine that helped millions, organizations she founded to help so many others afflicted by other debilitating diseases, and somewhere was a family of her own in a large expensive house. Wilma Livonia Jackson was going to be a hero, a true hero, to everyone on the planet, even to him the once great Alexander of Macedonia. She embodied what he had sought for all these years, what he wanted that night in the Hanging Gardens of Babylon when the robed one had approached him from the folds of the dark. Compassion, from the tips of her toes to the top of her head, Wilma exuded it like a breath of fresh air for Alexander to inhale and revel in.

For a second he felt small, something he had never felt except one other time with one other person long ago. He felt below her, beneath what she was and would become in the future.

He was so taken with the new feelings that Alexander never heard the slow approach of the gold Honda Accord from behind. Like a snake, it had moved into position directly to his right and it might have slipped past him if not for the fearful glance from Wilma over her shoulder toward the creeping vehicle. He looked just in time to see the Honda rolling by slowly, stalking almost, and inside the dark vehicle he made out three young men dressed in black attire. Alexander looked back to Wilma and saw, with some relief, the girl had turned her eyes back to the ground obeying the first rule of survival while picking up the already fast pace of her walk. The Honda sped up accordingly though to keep up right behind her.

"Hey, isn't that the rug rat of that nosy bitch working with that street preacher?" J-Rock asked with a sneer.

"Oh yeah, I hate that bitch!" The man from the backseat snarled.

"Please, you ain't gonna do a damn thing except cry like that little girl when the mouth slaps you!" The side passenger remarked with a snarl and then a laugh. The nickname for Stephanie was well known by all in the Laurel.

"You two need to shut the hell up because I'm gonna tell you what we're gonna do! We're gonna send a message to that street preacher and the mouth for trying to take what's ours! You wanna hurt us. Well we'll hurt you right back! We own the Laurel and no one else! We run the Laurel!" J-Rock spat pointing at the little girl walking incredibly fast.

An evil grin crept across the face of the passenger exposing several gold teeth. "Yeah, we gonna make sure they understand who's the King in this project and who's the bitches!"

Alexander picked up his walk keeping the driver side window of the Honda right in align with his shoulder as it stalked Wilma. Even with the tinted windows he made out the driver, a tall black man with a blue bandanna wrapped around his head with the knot resting squarely over his eyes brows. The power of the vision took over and he knew the man's name was J-Rock, a name given to him because of the drugs he sold. He was a feared member of a gang here in the projects, and a cold-blooded killer through and through. Suddenly, the power window rolled down slowly exposing J-Rock to the world and just as Alexander saw him through the tinted glass.

"Hey there baby, you need a lift?" J-Rock yelled out at Wilma.

The passenger and rider in the back laughed loudly at J-Rock's request as the small form of Wilma lengthened her stride to try and get away from the men just that faster and to the safety of her home. The passenger leaned out and Alexander noticed the blue bandana with the large knot dangling just over the eyes of this man also. His fingers curled in some crude gesture, something called 'gang signs' he had found out over the last couple of nights.

"Yo baby! I know you young and all that but you got some JUNK in your' TRUNK!" The man yelled as J-Rock followed screaming out through his gold teeth.

"Give it up little sister!" The pusher yelled as all the men began to laugh louder.

The clairvoyant gift that Alexander used was the one true measuring stick he had for testing the people around him. He could see a person's past, see their actions, and see if they could be trusted with precious information or cargo. Until now, he had only come across two people where the gift worked differently. Grammy drew a total blankness, a wall of fog that hid her past from him like a veil. Then there was Wilma here, her future opening up in front of him like a play. Everything that this young woman would accomplish in her life rolled out for him in his mind's eye, only now there was a twist to what he saw just moments before. He saw the men accosting her, throwing her down in the trash, and stealing her virginity and purity like animals. Then he saw her lifeless body there in the street, no awards or praise given to a young girl who could have meant so much to this world. There was nothing for Wilma Livonia Jackson after this night, and that's what caused Alexander to react so violently.

―――――――――――――――――――――――――――

Wilma did her best to calm the frayed nerves and panic that was running through her body like a thousand volts of electricity. A huge chunk of her mind said run like hell and get to the house screaming for your momma all the way because no one messed with momma! However, she knew the men in the car were faster and in this neighborhood no one comes to the aid of someone else screaming for help. No way, that only gets you shot and there isn't a soul in the projects who likes to visit the Grady Hospital Emergency Room with a gunshot wound for not minding your business. Wilma voted for the other course of action that her mind gave her and that was to ignore the men for the next two blocks then duck into the dark apartment complex and hide out. She knew enough small holes where she could hide and get away. It was just a matter of making the next two blocks to the complex. The passenger screamed that he wanted to taste her, well he actually said something else but Wilma never really liked hearing the word that referred to her private area. The Honda revved its engine, a car door opened up with a pop, and the two blocks suddenly felt like ten long miles to Wilma.

She turned around to catch a quick glimpse and saw the passenger door opening with the man stepping out to obviously play catch-up with her on foot. Wilma instantly recognized him as one of the pushers out on the corner. She heard he had killed a boy before for trying to sell on his 'turf'. Wilma's panicked mind was close to snapping as she turned back to get just a few more feet in distance between her and the pusher, there was no more waiting to get two blocks her mind kept screaming. Up ahead a group of four or five mangy mutts were digging through some trash trying to find a good meal to fill their hungry bellies, maybe she could use them for a distraction or something. Then the pusher yelled something to her but he never finished the sentence, because the loud crash of metal giving away from a massive impact stopped him.

J-Rock fell out of the driver's side door to the asphalt with a small thud. The taste of blood filled his mouth causing him to spit out the red liquid. A quick check of his mouth and he found the bite mark on his tongue. He could hear Slim, his partner, screaming about his leg but J couldn't remember just what the hell had happened to his homie. He knew they were rolling up on some little honey planning to give her a good time and then here he was getting up from the street like some damn beggar.

"What the hell happened? " J-Rock gasped, which sounded a little funny with a tongue laceration, as his eyes came to rest on what was left of his prized Honda. It was now sitting totally sideways in the street blocking both lanes with the driver's side quarter panel smashed in to a small focal point just behind the headlights.

"Damn J! I think my leg's broke!" Slim screamed.

"Man, fuck your leg Slim! Look at my fucking car!" J-Rock yelled back.

"Fuck you and your car man! Get my black ass to the hospital Right Now," Slim yelled back at his main man and boyhood friend J-Rock.

"Hey you little bitch?" J-Rock suddenly screamed to the still form of Wilma standing on the sidewalk. "What the fuck did you do my car?"

"Man, fuck her up J! She broke my damn leg!" Slim screamed in anger from his prone position.

Wilma stood and stared in shock at what had just happened, and all of it right in front of her very own eyes none-the-less. Just a second ago she was trying to escape from the Honda and the men taking a small glance back to see just how close they were when the proverbial 'all heck' broke loose. She didn't see what had hit the car but she did catch Slim the pusher doing his impersonation of a trapeze act without the benefit of a net. It was somewhat cool watching him go end over end like that, but the landing is what caused his leg to have that peculiar bend it had right now, the kind a leg's not supposed to do. Wilma saw the other pusher with the bleeding mouth approaching her, she could see him screaming at the top of his lungs at her, but nothing registered in her brain. The ever present revolving replay of Slim spinning out of control had taken over Wilma's mind. Something else though was also in there as well, another voice, and it screamed for her to run but Wilma couldn't. She just stayed glued to the spot watching the pretty pictures of the past few seconds run by in her mind. She could see the pusher called J cross the street, his body going in and out of the shadows thrown by the arc-sodium of the only working street lamp overhead. Then the large ominous screaming man disappeared, well her mind said he really didn't disappear now did he. No ma'am, he looked like he was pulled, yanked even, right into the dark shadows by something. What 'it' was that ripped the pusher into the dark though Wilma didn't see and if you put her hand on a bible she would truthfully admit she really didn't care to know what 'it' was. The voice in her head suddenly turned commanding, growling and breaking her away from the trance she was in. It demanded she run like the wind for home now and

Wilma did just that with a quick turn bolting out of the area. As she ran past the pack of mangy mutts Wilma noticed they had formed a weird kind of scrimmage line blocking off the street. She could hear the sounds of a man screaming bloody murder. It kept sounding in her ears all the way home, as she climbed under the covers, and even in her troubled dreams.

"J-Rock? J MAN!" Slim kept screaming. He had pulled himself up to a semi standing position by clinging to the undamaged passenger door of the car.

It was crazy, one second J-Rock was ready to mess that girl up for crashing his favorite car and then he was...just gone. The street was quiet, way to quiet for Slim, and he began to panic before the screaming started echoing from the dark and he really lost it. Christ the screams were so loud Slim thought, almost hysterical shrieking. He had never heard J-Rock yell like that before, even when the man was shot. He wanted to get the hell out of there, his brain ordered it, but he wasn't going to leave his homeboy and any way the busted leg made any type of moving impossible. Suddenly, like someone just shut off the power to a radio, the screaming stopped coming from the shadows and the eerie quiet returned. The only sounds were the crickets chirping.

Slim really started to panic now. Fear began to sink deeper into the pit of his stomach like a huge bulbous lead weight.

"J, you there man?" Slim whined.

A sudden scraping sound caused Slim to gasp, his hand searched at the waistband of his jeans for the concealed gun he always carried there but it was long gone from the violent throw of the crash. He heard another sound, more like a footstep this time, followed by something spinning out of the dark at Slim tumbling end over end. He put his arms up just in time to block the flying object from hitting his face and it fell right at his feet with a meaty thud. It didn't take the pusher but a second to recognize the right hand of his homeboy J-Rock, or what there was left of it. Just above the wrist, maybe four or five inches, was where it ended in a tearing gash with just about half an inch of grey bone protruding out. The footstep sounded again and it was just inside the dark shadows this time, about three feet away from him.

"You would have brought harm to a sweet and innocent little girl. You would have disgraced her in the worst ways possible and then left her body for the dogs." A growling voice called out to him.

"Who the hell's there?" Slim yelled at the dark turning in small hops trying to find the owner of the voice.

"I despise men like you. I loathe men like you." The voice snarled with it sounding closer now.

"Nah man, you got it all wrong." Slim whined while slowly sliding his way down the car trying to get away from the voice. "It's not like that you know." He gasped with grinding teeth trying to ignore the pain in the broken leg, which felt like hot nails grinding slowly in the muscle, trying to poke their way out of his skin.

"You would have left her disgraced body for the dogs Anquan." The voice stated coldly.

"How'd you know my name man?" Slim asked quietly, the fear in his voice palpable. He made it to the trunk and began to turn to run down the street, or at least stumble, maybe even crawl if he had to. Whatever curiosity Slim had for knowing who the voice was or how it knew him was nowhere near the fear he felt. Running away from here was the first priority right now.

"I know your kind Anquan. I know you."

"Jesus Man Please! Just let me go please!" Slim whined while trying to limp away slowly with his back to the dark and the voice.

"Tonight Slim it is you who will be left to the dogs." The voice said coldly and as if on cue the pack of mangy mutts appeared out of the dark walking up silently. Their teeth showed through snarled lips yet not a one barked and not a single paw moved.

"No, no way man!" Slim screamed at the voice while going into a stumbling out of control trot because of his broken leg.

There wasn't a response from the voice this time, only the single snap of a finger, and the dogs bolted after their injured prey. Anquan, known as Slim on the streets, didn't get ten yards before the pack had caught and pulled him down. Teeth by the dozen ripped and tore at his flesh as Slim fought back with what ability he could but it wasn't enough. The hungry bellies of the dogs proved stronger then the pusher and after agonizing minutes it was over. From the shadows a lone figure stepped out and watched the dogs work. Alexander stood just inside the light of the street lamp, his chin covered in red blood, when his ears picked up the stirring moan of the third passenger in the back seat. He didn't move or hide when the boy stumbled from the car rubbing his head and back in obvious discomfort. He didn't say anything when the boy saw the hand and jumped or the dogs and whispered a prayer to the almighty Jesus. He only spoke when the boy finally saw him.

"Go home Kenneth, go home now lest my wrath take you like it did your two cohorts here." The vampire ordered.

Kenneth, Monster-K as he was known on the street, took off running for the safety of home as the vampire watched.

Alexander stood for a minute cursing his actions silently, for getting involved. He could sense eyes looking out of the dark at him, taking note of him, and it angered him even more. He simply disappeared leaving the hungry pack to fill its bellies.

Chapter Five

The area was lit up like the fourth of July with those damn
revolving lights on top of the patrol cars that Detective Otz
Renfroe hated so much. First red then blue then white, hell it
gave him one mother of a bad headache. The tires of his
unmarked Crown Victoria screeched as he came to a stop just
outside the gathering crowd. Homicide had gotten a call with
some sketchy details twenty minutes ago and just like magic,
Renfroe was now on the scene walking through the crowd of men
and women on-lookers. All he knew was there were two bodies
beside a wrecked car out in the Laurel Woods Projects and that
usually meant one of two things. The first, a couple rival gang
members landed on the wrong side of the street and got a few
holes put in them for trespassing. Or two, one pusher wanted this
corner and it already belonged to another drug dealer so the two
fought it out like the old west. Renfroe was opting for number
two since the Laurel was just a couple of blocks away and that
place was a breeding ground for pushers on these streets.

Renfroe stood 6'4 and weighed a good two hundred and sixty pounds. He got the name 'Bear' from his family and friends and it wasn't all because of his size. After being in homicide for the last six years Renfroe was burnt from the job, like a walking piece of toast his partner would say, that was if he had a partner these days. The city had dropped the budget conscious attitude and actually hired more detectives, just not in his precinct, the one that covered most of the projects and 'bad' side of town. No new partner or detectives in homicide for you Otz, maybe next year when we get more money so for now just get out there and catch the bad guys, but make it fast too cause we got another body somewhere else for you to go and see. Up ahead was the Sergeant in charge of the scene trying to keep some semblance of order to the chaotic display, too bad it wasn't working that well. Renfroe did the customary showing of his id while pulling out his notebook.

The Sergeant only nodded, "Evening Detective, guess no one else got the call huh?"

"There is no one else to get the call, so what do we have here Sergeant?"

"Well," the man said turning around and pointing the first sheet just south of the car," there's one body over there, young male looks like"

"Looks like?" Renfroe remarked with a sigh of exasperation already feeling this crime scene was going to turn very ugly.

"Yeah, the victim was eaten by dogs and Assistant Coroner Foster hasn't made the official call yet"

"Some dogs ate him after he di-Wait! Did you say Foster?" Renfroe asked carefully, slowly.

"Yes sir. He showed up about ten minutes ago."

"Are you kidding me, not Foster? Who the hell called Foster in?" Renfroe spat while throwing up his hands in obvious distress and turning a circle, as if he could call for a do-over and just get out this call.

"Sorry detective, he's the assistant coroner you know." The Sergeant said with a shrug of his shoulders and a look of 'I don't really care. I'm out of here in forty five minutes'.

"Yeah I know, one day maybe I'll get to do his murder. Where is he anyway?" Renfroe asked rubbing his eyes. The glare from all the bubble lights already had him wanting to grab the extra-large bottle of aspirin out of his unmarked unit's glove compartment and swallow about half.

"Up there, by the second body." The police officer said with an over the shoulder gesture of his thumb.

Renfroe sighed shaking his head and walked around the wrecked car and felt the headache jump up a few notches at the sight of the assistant coroner. First, the man was just your ordinary nothing special kind of guy. He weighed a few pounds more than 150 and nothing, stood all of 5 foot and nothing, and dressed in baggy cargo pants and a wrinkled polo shirt. He was just...nothing. Secondly, and this wasn't nothing, Foster at the moment was humming a tune while trying to dance or do something like a dance. The worst part was the assistant coroner was holding a piece of the victim, the right foot it looked like to Renfroe.

"Foster?"

"The thigh bone's connected to the knee bone..." Foster sang

"Foster?" Renfroe said louder.

"The knee bone's connected to the shin bone."

"Foster!" Renfroe finally yelled putting his hand to his eyes then squeezing the bridge of his nose hard.

The skinny man jumped from the loud yell and spun to see the Detective standing by the wrecked car. "Yes...Yes sir!" The coroner stammered saluting the Renfroe with hand that held the foot.

"Christ, please tell me you let them take pictures first before moving anything?" Renfroe asked massaging his eyes.

"Oh, yes sir! I followed procedures to the letter Detective!" The man said enthusiastically.

"Then what do we have here?" Renfroe asked.

"There are two males, mid-twenties, African-American. One dead from a dog attack and the other had vital body parts removed violently." Foster answered while walking up, his right hand still holding the victim's right foot.

"Run the last part by me again? And you can put the victim down any time you like." Renfroe asked, spat while preparing to write down what information he got.

"Victim number two here was ripped apart. I was reconstructing the body when you showed up detective." Foster said.

"Ripped apart?" Renfroe asked dumbfounded

"Yeah, both arms, both legs, and his head were removed violently." Foster answered.

"Someone ripped his arms and legs off? Who the hell would do that down here? And where is all the blood if he was torn apart?" Renfroe asked aloud to no one while looking around in a circle noting the pavement was as dry as a two year old steak bone buried in the dirt.

The assistant coroner shook his head giving his opinion, "it's because there wasn't a drop of blood in the body when the parts where torn away. All the wounds show little to no bleed out meaning the man had almost no blood in his body."

"No blood...in the body?" Renfroe asked with raised eyebrows in shock, a first being that most of the bodies he gets do the opposite.

"That's not the part you should be focusing on sir." Foster stated with a wink and a nod.

Oh God, this gets just worse and worse the detective thought. "What part?" Renfroe asked but the coroner had already walked over and kneelt down at the fender of the wrecked Honda motioning for him to follow. Renfroe shook his head frustrated while squatting down mumbling a certain expletive about enthusiastic coroners and their mothers under his breath.

"Do you see this?" Foster asked circling the dent with his index finger.

"It's a dent Foster! The guy probably got hit for Christ's sake!" Renfroe remarked.

The coroner took the severed foot he was still holding and neatly placed it against the dent and the entire picture struck home to Renfroe like a thunderbolt from the sky. The foot was damn near a perfect match to the shape of the dent. "Oh Christ," he whispered.

"Precisely, the shape of the dent matches the shape of a human foot!" Foster exclaimed happily, almost too happily.

"So you're saying someone - "Renfroe began to say before Foster cut him off.

"Yes sir, someone kicked this car hard enough to bend the frame, knock the engine of all four blocks, and break the axle and tear off the wheel rim. Whoever it was wears expensive boots, the kind you buy in a specialty shop for about a hundred dollars. I know this because the sole imprint pretty much matches one from another case I did two weeks ago. My guess, the boots are a pair of Doc Martins, size eleven." Foster said with a broad smile.

Renfroe snorted standing back up while shaking his head. "Uh-huh, your way off base here Foster. No human being is going to kick a car so hard its engine almost falls out!"

"You can't deny the evidence detective, its staring you in the face!" Foster whined.

"Look, "Renfroe said shaking his head and pointing to the dent, "I know you get a little carried away Foster but keep it reined in this time. I need a perfectly rational, explainable reason why the victim here is a puzzle instead of one piece, okay?"

"Aw come on detective? How can you deny this?" Foster said with a shrug of his shoulders and pointing to the dent.

Renfroe looked at the gleeful coroner, then to the severed foot in his hand being used as a pointer, and then back to the face of the man. "Easy, don't write it up in your report and I won't have to remember it, got that Foster? Don't...write...it...up." Renfroe ordered turning away from the coroner and walking back to the lead Police unit.

The assistant coroner didn't like the position he was just put in, the one where you make false reports. Yet, he wasn't about to let the good detective forget the footprint. So maybe a detail or two doesn't make it into the official report, there was always the special folder in his desk back at the office. The folder he kept for just such anomalies, disturbances, and downright weird occurrences. "If that's what you want detective Renfroe?" Foster called out while absently waving the right foot.

"You happen to have an ID of the victims yet?" Renfroe asked the Sergeant ignoring the coroner. There was only so much of the Foster experience he could take and tonight's limit had been reached and surpassed in world record time.

From the edge of the crowd, a voice called out to Renfroe. "Yeah I know them Otz."

The Detective turned to see an old friend standing by the yellow crime tape. He walked over and took Leland's hand in his feeling the tight grip, it was sure nice to shake a man's hand and not swallow it up with yours he thought. The two had met years earlier when Leland still ran with the gangs and Renfroe was just a beat cop walking the meanest street of Atlanta at the time. They respected each other, knew what the other would do, and just how far the other would go for a friend in need.

"How's the preaching life been to you Lee?" Renfroe asked

"I've saved a few souls here and there." Leland commented with a smile.

"That's good to hear," Renfroe turned back to the crime scene, "do you know the one in pieces?"

"Jamal Jennings, but everyone called him J-Rock in the neighborhood."

"That guy is our victim? Man I know him, local pusher and all around thug asshole." Renfroe said writing the name down in his notebook.

"Yeah that was J-Rock." Leland said then pointed to the other sheet down the street. "And that one over there is Slim."

"Never heard of him"

"You probably never would have. His name was Anquan Tucker, a follower who didn't get his hands dirty much, except to beat a pension check out of some senior citizen. J-Rock was the brains and guts of this outfit." Leland answered.

"Who'd do this kind of thing Lee? You think maybe the Deuces over on 14th street?" Renfroe asked.

"No way, the Deuces didn't do this. I don't know of any street gang that would tear a man apart like poor J-Rock there. It's all about the guns and AK's around here."

"I know, and Slim over there being eaten by the dogs, someone really lost their temper here tonight. You heard any noise of someone moving up around here? Maybe Eight Ball isn't holding down the fort all that well these days?"

"Nah, Eight Ball is still in control and running the corners around here. J-Rock there was one of his best workers, pushed a lot of stuff out here. This won't make Eight Ball happy one bit." Leland responded looking back and forth across the scene.

"So what we have are two dead pushers with no motive and no clue as to who did this and no suspects to match the MO that I see. This one's going to be bad, I can feel it a mile away right now." Renfroe sighed closing his notebook.

"Maybe, but I do know one thing." Leland said with a grin

"Yeah, what do you know Lee?" Renfroe asked hoping to hear some good news.

"I sure don't want your job." Leland quipped.

"I really don't want it either right now." Renfroe shot back.

The two men laughed at the last statement then Renfroe said bye to his longtime friend and the two parted. The detective walked over and asked a few more questions of Foster while Leland just disappeared into the crowd. The street preacher wanted to rush home and make a call to Kenneth's home, he didn't tell Renfroe everything. A couple of kids he used for information had seen Monster running like hell from the scene earlier, a straight bee line for home one had said with a toothy grin. That's what brought the street preacher around, to see what went down. What Leland didn't know was his phone was ringing off the hook at that very moment. When the answering machine picked up it recorded nothing but hysterical crying and sobbing on the other end.

"Good evening ma'am. I'm Officer Patterson and I need to ask a few questions if you don't mind"

"Oh, yes sir nice officer." Grammy said acting her best to be concerned while standing in her doorway. "Is there a problem officer? I saw all your lights and I just knew it was one of those terrible boys again."

"Yes ma'am, I need to know if you saw anything unusual tonight." The young officer asked.

"Well, I go to bed early cause I'm old you know, but just the other night I heard all this banging and smashing, good lord you would have thought the devil was coming for dinner." Grammy claimed clutching her chest in dramatic fashion.

"Yes ma'am," the officer said rubbing his head," but what I really need is to know if you saw something tonight?"

"Well I don't reckon so, wait! I did see a bunch of lights just about an hour ago." Grammy pointed out.

"Yes ma'am that would be us. We responded to a call two blocks from here and that's why I need to know if you saw anything else tonight." The officer explained scratching his head a little harder as he cocked it to one side. His patience was running out very quickly.

"No sir, I haven't seen anything but there was this loud noise last-"Grammy started to say as the young officer suddenly closed his notebook with a slap of the cover.

"No ma'am that's okay! I think you just need to go back to bed and rest."

"But the noise officer?"

"We'll look into ma'am and get back with you." Patterson said before moving on with a quick wave.

"You do that nice officer." Grammy called out before giving a gentle push to close the door. As soon as the portal closed her old self just showed up along with Alexander, who seemed to emerge from the dark shadows like a ghost. She went back to her old chair and plopped down in it with a small poof. "I don't think we'll be seeing much of Officer Patterson around here, don't you say so Mr. Alexander?" She asked with a cackle.

"This is not good Martha, not good at all!" The vampire retorted.

"Oh everything's going to be just peachy Mr. Alexander." Grammy sighed with a smile.

"No it is not Martha." Alexander said quickly walking over to the window. "I left someone alive from the car and there were others, street people that can provide a very good description of me or Wilma to certain individuals. Men like these have friends, brothers, and colleagues who just might decide that retribution is a perfectly acceptable response. These people could harm other people of this complex, or worse yet Wilma."

"Oh, stop fretting Mr. Alexander! As long as you are looking after our girl nothing's going to happen to no one." Grammy smiled, especially when she heard him mention Wilma by name.

Alexander turned to the window speaking as he watched the lights outside. "You know there are more people to be concerned with here than just Wilma."

"And just who should I be concerned about?" Grammy asked, but with the air of someone who really didn't care to hear the answer. Her plan was in motion and that was all that mattered to her.

"I am in hiding Martha, covering my presence in the world, and I cannot do that while trying to protect that girl! If certain individuals find out I am here then no one will be safe!" Alexander snapped.

"You hiding from other people or just yourself Mr. Alexander?" Grammy asked with a raised eyebrow.

The question struck the vampire square taking him off his usually fast feet. There was an awkward silence for a second, and then Grammy finished. "You once sat at the head of the table Mr. Alexander and that time is coming again no matter how hard you want to fight it. You just remember one thing Mr. Alexander, you keep our Wilma alive and everything else will fall into place." Grammy whispered with a smile.

The vampire was quiet while looking at her with a dark brooding eye, his mind a chaotic jumble as he stood trying to figure out what grand scheme the old woman had pulled him into. Obviously it involved Wilma, and he knew how special she was and was going to be, but he knew there had to be other young girls out there with the same endearing qualities as Wilma and yet Martha hadn't tried to help any of them like this. Yet, maybe she had tried. Maybe the loss of so many lives day in and day out finally took its toll on Martha and she decided to finally stop the loss right here and right now. And, what about his actions, he had suddenly almost against his will saved Wilma from a certain heinous and inhumane death. The great vampire Alexander, who had guarded himself against everyone for so long, who had watched men and women die before his eyes and never felt the need to intervene...until tonight where before he could think he was reacting to save a little girl. Maybe there was something 'special' about little Wilma. Maybe she did have some kind of power to sway a person to action.

"You almost got it Mr. Alexander. I have seen my share of the young die in these projects and they might have gone on to do miracles if they had grown older. But if you really want some answers then you got to do the one thing you're afraid of doing." Grammy suddenly said from her chair. The way Martha read his mind still sent a small shiver through Alexander. It was more than just a little disconcerting to have your thoughts picked out of the air like that.

"What is it that I need to do Martha?" Alexander finally asked.

"Just go talk to her. It's not as hard as you make it out to be Mr. Alexander and I think you'll be a little surprised with our Miss Wilma."

The room fell silent except for the sounds of the night and the people that had gathered outside on the sidewalks to watch the spectacle of the police. The vampire stood watching from the window, his mid toiling once more over the options that Grammy had given to him. After a short while his ears picked up the sound of the old woman snoring from the comfortable confines of the old chair. It looked like there was one more person he was going to have to watch over this night. He thought about Grammy's suggestion of going out and talking to the little girl but even the thought of such an encounter dredged up the past and painful feelings. Could he talk to her, could he be her friend, such a young one and his age? Before the vampire knew it he had produced the locket from his pocket, had it open, and was staring at the pictures again. Why couldn't he get close to someone again after all these years? Was her ghost still haunting his soul? A single whisper escaped from the vampire's lips and the words seemed to condense on the window in front of his eyes as they made contact with the glass.

"Christina."

Chapter Six

The Leopard Lounge, located off historic Peachtree Street, is just your usual nuevo-2014 hot spot that caters to the ultra-cool, and those who can afford to pay to be even though they're not. An old converted house with two bars where you simply come to sit in old lounge chairs, drink expensive martini's in a 60's motif and atmosphere, and then mingle with the highly scrutinized who just happen to be as cool as you are or who are just trying to be. Leopard print wallpaper hung on the walls, music blared from hidden loud speakers, and people stood in crowds around the bars. Brandie liked coming to the lounge because it was 'happening' and all her friends went there so she had to make a show, you know, to keep up appearances. Dressed in a black leather jacket, tight fitting mid drift shirt exposing her firmly tanned belly, and $400 dollar bell-bottoms she sat alone by the bar in what used to be the basement of the house perusing the male market roaming the Lounge and there was a lot of action moving on the floor tonight sweetie let me tell you she thought. Hunks of muscled flesh bound in tight T-shirts and expensive jeans sauntered by where she sat at the bar and with a discrete eye she followed each and every one. Brandie hadn't settled on anything yet but she certainly had some contenders in mind when a sudden figure appeared out of the corner of her eye from across the room.

Everything might have been perfectly fine if she had never seen the mysterious individual on the other side of the room. He was dressed quite plainly in a t-shirt, jeans, and black Doc Martin's. You know what that means don't you. It simply screams 'I still live in the 90's in my mom's basement and I dress just like a 90's High School grunge douche' and that was a definite turn off for Brandie. You had to have the 'juice' to make the show in her book baby. Yet, she couldn't fight or stop the sudden feeling that swept over her, compelling her to walk over and simply throw her body at him, to strip off her clothes and beg him to make furious love to her right there. The feeling of ecstasy became stronger and stronger with each breath, the lust in her threatening to drown her in a sea of maddening passion. The room wavered and Brandie grabbed the bar to keep from falling off the stool, sweat forming on her upper lip. She had to grip the cushioned edge with all her strength. She was close to screaming for this unbelievable ride to stop or she would go crazy when all of the sudden it did just that, it just went away.

Brandie crashed back to reality like a meteor hitting the ground and it took a moment to get it all back under control as she looked at the mass of people huddled around the oak bar in a semi-lost haze. No one was paying attention to her and no one else seemed to be bothered by the feeling. Oh where did you go you sweet, crazy ecstasy making me extremely excited in certain places Brandie thought? She absently reached down with her hand, rubbed the inside of her thigh with a slow long stroke through the thick bell-bottom jeans, and she shivered from the incredible sensitivity that was there. Brandie wanted more, this was a drug and damn it she wanted to overdose right now by God. She took a drink from the glass containing the Cape Cod she had ordered a minute ago with a shaky hand when the memory of the man standing across the room came back with the same suddenness the feeling had hit her with. He had the drug, he had the sweet feeling, and he was just over there. She spun on the stool looking for the mysterious stranger where he should have been standing but there was no one there now and you know what that meant, yeah...no drug. Panic hit Brandie, squeezed her hard as she rose from the stool looking for the man frantically, but she couldn't find him in the crowds of patrons at the bar. Then, just at the edge of that mass of people, she saw the black jeans and Doc Martins coat going up the stairs.

Heart racing she ran for the stairs pushing through, and occasionally over, any one in her attempt to reach that incredible man. Up the stairs, he went up the stairs her mind screamed as she bounded up the steps reaching the first floor and the main bar where even more people stood looking suave and ultra-cool. Where was he Brandie thought? I can't lose him! I have to find him! By the front door stood the typical massive muscled bouncer, Mike was his name she thought, monitoring the individuals and choosing who would enter and who didn't make the grade tonight. He was easily 6'3 weighing in excess of 300 pounds but Brandie didn't care as she charged right up to him with a desperate look on her face.

"Did a guy wearing an AC/DC T-shirt just leave Mike?" She asked frantically.

"Yeah, that guy just left." The bouncer said with a sly smile. "But he didn't look like your usual date material Brandie. He was re-." Mike, and his upcoming witty banter, was cut off in mid-sentence by a small hand gripping and then turning in his shirt pulling him down to the blonde-haired woman's eye level. Those small arms were a lot stronger than he expected as she spoke with an unusual guttural growl in her voice.

"Which way did he go brain dead?" Mike didn't have to decide whether to show Brandie where the strange man had gone, his arm shot out instinctively pointing toward the door. She let go and bolted out leaving a stunned giant guarding a swinging door.

The two-way street in front of the lounge was packed with cars, some parking by the club leaving just enough room for the occasional lone vehicle to pass going one way. Brandie ran right to the middle of the street looking in both directions for the man, but there wasn't a sign of him down either side of the road. The panic began to turn to despair at losing him, at losing the unbelievable feeling he gave out by the gram, and then a faintly audible voice slipped into the back of her mind like an old welcomed friend. Bandies knew it was the stranger and she began to smile as he whispered soothing words to calm her, making her bite her lower lip with anticipation. Someone walked past the zombie girl in the middle of the street staring but Brandie didn't care, the voice was talking and prompting her now. Directions it gave, the way to him it instructed and to that unfathomable passion. She would have killed for it if given the chance. Kill for lust, the old Brandie would have laughed at the idea, but that felt like a decade ago as she began to follow the words of the silent voice. Left then right she turned, up and down streets until finally, the chase was over and he stood just a few feet away in an abandoned alley. Brandie stepped over a fallen trashcan as her breathing quickened another step from the excitement that gripped her like a live wire, brought her senses to a level she never knew existed. Everything tingled from her feet to the tip of her hair as she stepped up to the stranger looking deep into his eyes.

"Do it again. Please lover, do it again!" Brandie whispered hoarsely.

Alexander opened his arms to allow her access and Brandie didn't hesitate for a second from stepping into the folds. She held tight to his body wanting, needing to be released from the spell he had cast on her. The sea of maddening passion began to rise again. Her stomach warmed with pleasure as Brandie stood trembling with eyes closed to the man who caressed her face with the back of one hand. She felt him push away a few strands of blonde hair on the nape of her neck as the warmth in her stomach flowed to that glorious spot between her legs heating her up until sweat beaded moist on her upper lip again. Alexander felt her crush him with arms filled with unrestrained sexual strength as he eyed the large artery on the side of her sweet tanned neck. He could see and smell the blood as it flowed faster keeping up with the heightened encounter between them he had conjured. The two long fangs glistened in the moonlight as he gently brushed the spot where he would put them.

Brandie moaned from the first touch trying to hold back the orgasm that was bursting her insides trying to get out. She was fighting a hopeless cause though as a second touch started the crumbling of her willpower and a third and final touch that felt like a small knife puncturing the hot skin of her neck sent her reeling and setting the orgasm loose. Brandie clutched her mysterious stranger like a vise with her arms and one leg, biting her lower lip to keep back a scream. Seconds later everything began to fade as the release of all the sexual energy left her weak and frail. Brandie welcomed the dark of deep sleep. Hell, she needed it after having sex like this!

Across town, Wilma was walking back from the small convenience store just up the street from the Laurel, the candy urge satiated after she consumed two 5th Avenue bars. After what had occurred last night Wilma at first wouldn't even consider going out in the dark again, but the sweet tooth was strong in her this night as her hero Luke Skywalker might have said. At least that's what she continually told herself as she was walking. The truth was she felt something, what she couldn't say, was watching her every move in the projects and on the streets now. Maybe it was the old lady across the courtyard? She knew about Grammy and the stories. She heard how the old woman could 'see' things as her mother had said but this was different. This was way out there past different landing somewhere in the left field of 'Spooky'. If Wilma had the chance talk to Grammy she could just imagine what the Voodoo woman, that's what all the little kids in the Laurel called her, would say with her old southern accent. *"Oh baby, God just sent an angel to look after his special little wonder is all"* is exactly what Grammy would say. However, Wilma didn't believe in God because if there was a Supreme Being then how could it ever let something like the Laurel exist. A place where death was as common as the air you breathed, where you went to bed at night with the sounds of gun fire while the noise of the pushers on the corners kept you up. There was no such thing as the 'Supreme Being' to her here in the projects and that left only one solution to her dilemma, there really was an 'angel' looking after her. That couldn't be the case though she thought. There had to a reasonable explanation for everything, and look she could even prove there was no 'angel' watching over her. All she had to do was devise a test, a good scientific experiment in a controlled environment. As ideas rushed through the young genius's head the sound of laughter caught her ears and just ahead were two young boys playing under the lights of the street lamps. Wilma knew the two instantly and she knew why they were out by themselves this late at night

"Reggie! Ronald! What are you two doing out this late at night?" Wilma yelled. The two young boys jumped from being startled, both had been occupied by playing with some old beat up hot wheels and never noticed the approaching teen.

"We playing!" Ronald yelled back.

"Yeah! We playing cars here!" Reggie chimed in.

"We 'are' playing cars is the correct way to say it boys. You two need to attend school more than just once a month! As a matter of fact, you two need to get inside, tomorrow is Monday you know." Wilma said shaking her head.

"We don't need no school!" Reggie stated turning back to his cars.

"Yeah! We don't need no school!" Ronald seconded.

"Yes, you definitely 'need no school'...where is your mother? Does she know you're out here?" Wilma asked with a raised eyebrow.

"Momma went in that house over there then came out walking all dazed and stuff." Ronald stated while rolling the car in the dirt.

"Yeah, we asked if we could stay and play and she said it was okay." Reggie declared defiantly.

"Did she now?" Wilma asked in her best stern tone, exactly what her mother would do even though she didn't mean to exhibit her mother's mannerisms.

Ronald and Reggie look to each other, shrugged their shoulders, and spoke in perfect unison. "Yeah, mama waved us bye and everything when she left."

Wilma looked in the direction the twins had pointed and felt a sudden twinge of anger deep down inside her small stomach. She knew what the two boys were talking about now. Their mom had paid a little visit to the 'candy man' for the Laurel. The run down shack of a house was actually the distribution center for the corners around here, the distribution hub for the drug pushers. A sudden thought entered Wilma's head, a good idea for that scientific test she was looking to conduct.

"Man what are we doing here?" Kenneth asked with a whine sitting in the passenger seat of the car that was hidden in the shadows on the street.

"Just tell me what you know about the house Ken and we'll leave." Leland explained pointing to a house that was uncommonly dark except for a single light on the broken porch. "That is the place where they sell the drugs from, right?"

Kenneth squirmed in the front seat for a second before finally trying to dodge the question from Leland. "Why don't you just call it crack instead of drugs man?"

"Whatever you call it the stuff is what's killing this neighborhood Ken! It's time for you to step up, be a man, and save this place!" Stephanie said from the backseat.

"And why did we bring the mouth along for the ride man?" Kenneth whined pointing to the lady in the backseat.

"Hey, stop that 'mouth' stuff Ken! You know what she's saying is right. I need her help to stop the drugs just like I need your help to put an end to what's killing the people around here. I need you to step up, grow up, and finally take some responsibility for what's going on here in your neighborhood man." Leland preached.

"You know she's starting to piss me off?" Ken warned with his best snarl that intimated no one in the car at the time.

"Then use that anger for good Ken and tell Lee what he wants to know!" Stephanie shot back.

"Man, you know they sell it from there! Everyone that lives here knows that they do! Hell, even the police know and they don't even try to stop what's going on. How am I supposed to stop it when the Police won't stop it?" The boy stated still squirming like a worm.

"Because a few can defeat the many, and even if it takes us bringing down one place at a time, we can win take back our neighborhood!" Leland answered.

"You know, whatever man, but why this place? I mean why start at the top? Can't we shoot for something small and not so, you know, important?" Kenneth asked.

"Simple my brother, I want the biggest and most important one on the block first. I want Eight Ball to see the hand of God smite him and his kind with a great blow and I want him to know who did it." Leland said producing a cell phone.

"You always go after the head of the snake Ken, never the tail, right?" Stephanie added trying to drive home the point.

"You know what I think...you both need help man. I mean you two are about to start a fight with Eight Ball and his crew and you're like all happy and shit! Do you know what's going to happen to you, your family, and any pet you may have living with you if you go and start something with Eight Ball?" Kenneth asked.

"I suppose something along the lines of what happened to J-Rock and Slim." Leland answered watching the reaction of the boy in the front seat of his car. Kenneth, at hearing the mention of last night's events, squirmed away from Leland and up against the car door getting as close to the metal as possible. Stephanie felt the hair on the back of her neck stand up at the sight of the boy. Another inch and he would have become part of the car door itself. Leland reached out to put a hand on the boy's shoulder but jerked it back when Kenneth jumped at his touch.

"Ken, what the hell happened to you last night?" Stephanie asked with a whisper.

"Lady, you don't ever want to know! Whoever you pray to in this life make a special request asking never to see what I saw last night." Kenneth whispered.

"Who was it son? Who killed Slim and J-Rock?" Leland asked with a whisper, calmly trying to reach the boy through his fear.

"I don't know man, and the crazy thing, somewhere deep inside I really don't want to know what that thing was. I can tell you this for sure though, it wasn't human!" Kenneth hissed with his eyes wide with fright.

"Well listen, I'm going to call a friend, he's going to bring the authorities and we're going to put a stop to this place you hear." Leland said turning back and pulling out his phone.

"You do that Lee! Let's bring this place down!" Stephanie chanted with fervor.

Leland's fingers were about to tap the buttons on the keypad with the proper numbers to place a direct call to Detective Renfroe when he felt Kenneth's hand touch his shoulder. The boy had spotted something out there in the street.

"You better dial fast man, that girl over there looks like she's gonna do something more stupid than what you two are planning. Isn't that mouth's kid?"

Leland looked up in time to see Wilma, he recognized her in a heartbeat, going straight for the house. The little girl was approaching the biggest and the most lethal crack house on the south side of Atlanta. The cell phone fell from his hand in slow motion. Leland felt his blood turn ice cold. His fingers slipped on the door handle in a frantic attempt to get out of the car and stop the little girl. He watched as Wilma strode right up to the door of the house and deliberately knocked three solid times with a balled up right fist. The rear passenger door popped open as Stephanie was already in motion moving faster than both the men in the car.

Why couldn't he have just walked away? Why did he have to kill those two men last night? Why couldn't Martha see what kind of danger he was to everyone? Even after the feeding, the sweet taste still lingering in his mouth, Alexander could not find solace or peace from the pestering voice in his mind. This was why he preferred to be alone in the world, not having to deal with the voice in his head or other people every waking minute of every day of this long drawn out life. When your alone you don't have to worry about hurting the one's you love because there isn't anyone for you to hurt. Yes, that was it, Alexander was tired of the pain he inflicted upon those who he let get too close. Moreover, here was Martha trying to make him get close to Wilma. If the old woman just knew of the torment, the suffering he had caused in his long infamous life then she would rescind her silly request. The death, destruction, and loss of humanity would be off the scale if there was an instrument capable of measuring it and this is what Martha couldn't understand.

The vampire had been so into his thoughts and the voice that he was upon the two boys playing by the streetlight before he knew it. He was deep in the shadows instinctively which is probably why the two little children never saw his approach, never even knew he was just a few feet away. Alexander marveled at their innocence, how they could sit there playing in the dirt while only five feet away a murderer stood watching. How many men had he trampled under the hooves of his horse? How many men died when he was chasing Darius across Persia? How many of his own soldiers, men who he knew by name and face, died at senseless battles he had never wanted? Hundreds upon thousands maybe, after a while you lose count and just see the faces as they pass by like ghost on the edge of your vision. You only hear their voices, loud and strong when they scream for your help, for your mercy, and later when they scream for the justice they were denied. And then there were the voices of the Generals, the very ones who wanted more land and gold, more subjects to control, and the unbelievable need for more power from it all. That's why he took the choice that night in Babylon. He had to escape the voices of the men, the Generals, and the pain of everything he had done. He was so engrossed in the revelation of his vision and memories again that he barely saw the kids jump from their sitting positions in the dirt to frantically standing and pointing. Alexander looked up to where the kids were gesturing and there was the little girl he had protected from the wolves of the Laurel Projects the night before. Wilma was defiantly standing up on the broken porch of an unnaturally dark house knocking on the front door hard enough to make the sound echo. Something stirred deep inside the vampire, his heightened senses screamed that Wilma was in trouble and it was substantially more than what the two men were going to do last night. Before Alexander could think about what he was doing he was stepping out of the shadows behind the two children, he wanted to scream out for Wilma to run but his voice was gone. He could only watch as the door to the house opened and the small girl disappeared inside so fast and vicious that both her small feet left the ground.

Wilma pounded on the door as hard as her small fist could stand from the numbing pain of each blow. She had stormed up to the front door of the house with only a single-minded purpose and that was getting to whoever ran the crack house...so he could test her theory of an angel watching over her. Boy, there had better be an angel because if there wasn't one she was going to be in a WHOLE lot of trouble. The shouting to her left is what took Wilma's attention away from the door of the crack house and out into the street just before someone yanked her inside. There, just at the edge of the semi darkness was someone screaming at her, pleading for her to turn back and get away from the house. At first Wilma couldn't make out the high-pitched voice or the figure but then the person ran into the arc sodium artificial light of the street lamps and she saw her mother waving both hands and screaming at the top of her lungs. Oh great, I'm really going to die for this one Wilma thought to herself, and my mother is the one who's going to commit the act. And then there was Leland the street preacher, just as adamant as her mother with waving arms it looked like, and abruptly Wilma had a change of heart. I mean maybe the idea of her confronting the dealers of this crack house wasn't the smartest idea to draw out her 'angel', or not draw him out as she had intended. A creak squealed behind her causing her to spin back to the door because it sounded like the knob was turning, and then she froze in mid turn. Out behind Reggie and Ronald and behind her mother and Leland now, just on the edge of the shadows was Grammy's angel. He stood just over 6 feet tall with long brown hair and a muscular build wrapped in a white long sleeve shirt with a another black one over it, but most important he looked human, just your average white man...really pale white man. No wings or halos or golden showers of light surrounded the being and the look on his face, it was as if he was afraid for someone. Wilma started to walk forward toward him without consciously thinking or ordering her legs to do such a thing when a grip that tore into her coat and flesh suddenly yanked backwards so hard her feet came completely off the wooden porch. It was pretty comical looking she assumed, and then the fear of what was about to happen set in.

"Oh Jesus Lord, they got her!" Stephanie screamed in panic. She immediately began to run for the house when a set of strong arms wrapped around her waist keeping her stuck in the street where she stood. Leland fought to hold Stephanie while looking around for help from Kenneth, but the boy's eyes were like saucers filled to the brim with fear as he walked up.

"Let me go! I got to get in there!" Stephanie demanded with a scream, but Leland held her firm. It took the entire sum of his strength to hold the woman but he wasn't about to let her go and do something crazy like break into the crack house and get herself killed.

"Stephanie calm down, you have to be calm! Ken, man, I need your help for God's sake!" Leland screamed trying to hold the thrashing woman.

"Listen mouth, you go in there and someone's gonna light you're' ass up too!" The boy yelled grabbing the woman with one hand, or trying to grab one of Stephanie's arms.

"WILMA! I HAVE TO HELP MY DAUGHTER" Stephanie screamed while struggling.

"I'LL GET HER BACK STEPHANIE! I PROMISE YOU I'LL GET HER BACK TO YOU!" Leland screamed back to her.

"And who's gonna help you two if you go and get shot trying to save her ass!" Kenneth yelled at the street preacher. Leland opened his mouth to warn the boy about Stephanie's right cross because she could throw one with the best of them and getting knocked out by a girl is sure fire not going to help your street cred here in the projects. Then something brushed past his side. He quickly turned from fighting the strong arms of Stephanie to looking for whatever it was that had turned his skin cold to the touch and that's when he saw a man quickly approaching the door to the crack house. He was dressed in a black T-shirt moving with a purpose and he simply walked right through the front door as if it wasn't there.

"Did you see that?" Leland asked in a stunned and somewhat scared voice. The sound acted like a soothing pill as Stephanie began to calm down a little.

"See what?" Kenneth asked still holding the somewhat calm Stephanie.

"What is it Lee? Do you see Wilma?" Stephanie demanded finally breaking free the street preachers suddenly sack grip.

"That guy just walked through the front door. I mean he just walked through it without opening the thing." Leland whispered.

"What...what guy?" Stephanie stammered

"He just walked through the door like he was a ghost or something." Leland gasped

"Oh man! Nah Man! Not again!" Kenneth whined looking at the house. The two men stood still watching as Stephanie spun to run for the house to get her daughter, and that's when the screams began to sound freezing her. People suddenly began pour forth through the windows like rats, running from the house in-groups as if they were fleeing the devil himself. Then a microsecond later the gunfire erupted like hundreds of firecrackers exploding from inside the house. Leland took a tentative step forward toward Stephanie then stopped not knowing what to do, part of him screamed to call the police while the other screamed just as loud to run in there and save Wilma.

Kenneth had given up trying to hold anyone back as well taking the more fearful approach of staying back and that's probably what saved his life that night. A minute or two or four later, if you asked just how long no one could give you an exact estimate of how much time, the house exploded like a bomb showering the neighborhood with debris, knocking out windows of other houses, and sweeping all three to the ground in a rush of wind and heat.

Wilma finally got her feet back on the ground when the short, but very strong man with a solid grip, stopped swinging her around like a doll. His breath stunk and he wore enough gold to buy out a house note if he wanted to, a typical pusher she thought just as the man snarled.

"What you want BITCH?"

Wilma was about to answer when two men rounded a corner, probably came out of the living room she thought, and walked up to the short man. Like picking up a baseball, the bigger of the two men snatched her away from the short stinky one and held her off the floor with just one hand.

"Is this the crazy mother that was beating on the front door?" The man asked with his own snarl.

"Sure thing Ice, I say we cold blast this Bitch!" The short stinky one chimed in fast.

"Wait-" Wilma began but the man called Ice shook her so bad her neck hurt and the room swam for a second after he stopped.

"No, wait a minute Tre', I know this fool. She's the kid for that one bitch with the mouth. You know the one always running with that street preacher! Oh yeah, we going to have some fun with this one, show her how we do things here in the hood. We're going to send your momma a message!" Ice said with a smile, every tooth except two gleamed with gold. Wilma couldn't imagine kissing that mouth.

"Oh man Ice! I want in on thi-" Tre' began to whine.

"NO WAIT!" Wilma screamed louder.

"Man, shut your ass up Tre' and guard the damn door before I put my foot in your ass!" Ice screamed back with enough intention to make Tre' forget about trying to get in on the 'fun' for the night. Wilma wanted to say something but Ice just yanked and pulled on her jacket dragging her protesting body as if it weighed just a few pounds more than a paperweight cutting off her protests. The pair rounded the corner and Wilma noticed she was right. This was the living room, or what was left of it anyway. The carpet was gone but the hardwood underneath was now covered with garbage and debris ranging from clothes to trash.

There were bodies lined up against the wall in coma like trances, from doing crack Wilma thought, and then the man called Ice stopped and spun her around until she faced him.

"Now little momma, you know what we gonna do with you?" Ice asked with a crooked, sinister smile.

"I don't care. The only thing I want from you is to watch you die you piece of trash!" Wilma hissed at Ice. Where this sudden bravado came from it Wilma wasn't sure, it even shocked her when it showed up. She wasn't normally this brave. The man's companion, who had remained quiet up to now, began to giggle at the little girl's defiance and that infuriated Ice to no end. Wilma looked into his eyes and knew she had just pushed the right button and that kind of scared her like nothing before.

In the foyer Tre' kept muttering under his breath after Ice had taken the girl out of the room, damn he hated being left out. One day, when he was in control, and by God he was going to be in control one day, he was going to have all the damn fun he wanted and he was going have it with anyone he damn well please and at any damn well time he wanted. Tre' was so involved in his dream of owning it all and damn well enjoying it that he never heard the creak of the loose boards on the porch, the usual early warning sign of someone approaching the house. He never saw the man who walked right through the closed door like a specter, his form shimmering for a second before becoming real again after he was past the wooden obstacle. Tre' simply turned back to stand watch by the door as ordered but the only thing he saw was the man standing there just outside of arm's reach, standing on the other side of the locked portal.

"What the fu-" Tre' started to say before the blow from the vampire cut him off, literally.

Alexander stepped forward and with a quick upper slash of his right hand cut Tre' in half from the third rib on his left side to the right shoulder with a single powerful move. Blood shot across the wall and stairs and dripped from the knife like nails on his hand, but not a drop hit Alexander. The short gangster never felt a thing. One second he was going back to work and the next he was shaking hands with the devil. His body fell to the floor in two pieces with a thud as the vampire strode by on his way to the living room where he stopped at the sight of it.

"Hey Ice, who the hell is that?" The companion shouted and pointed.

"Man, I don't know how you got in here past Tre' but first I'm going to blast you then I'm going to blast that no account fool for letting you're' ass in here." Ice shouted drawing a large chrome plated gun from the waistband of his jeans at his back. With a hard shove he sent Wilma spinning through a door way and into a separate room. She saw what might have been a kitchen with a stove and refrigerator that was missing the doors.

There was also a strange white man and woman by the stove and a whole load of boxes and barrels and stuff everywhere. What were they doing in here Wilma wanted to think, but then her head struck the corner of what was the kitchen table that held an untold number of 40-ounce beer bottles and Chinese to-go cartons with a loud whack. She fell into the darkness of unconsciousness never getting to wonder what was going on in the kitchen. Wilma did have the satisfaction of knowing her unplanned experiment had worked before she passed out though. She saw her 'angel' not once but twice this night and the second time she got close enough to see the disgust in the man's eyes.

Alexander watched Ice throw Wilma to the side and he heard the hollow thump as her head struck the table hard enough to knock her out. Damn it man, she's only a small girl he thought as Ice and his companion held their guns chest high and over to the side, just like in all those movies he had watched. All around the small room he smelled death, decay, and the rotting stench of human despair floating on the air. He had seen this before, experienced the same smells from the opium dens and merchants in the Far East and Europe during his travels. Every drug has its cost in both money and misery, and all have a deeper hold then any can imagine or prepare for. The drug pushers here extracted a dollar amount for their 'Crack' and then later the drug took its payment in the form of untold suffering. A human soul dragged through hell and back as it becomes a slave to the drug was only the beginning of the vicious cycle. Once you were hooked there was nothing vile enough that your addicted body wouldn't do to get the drug, and there were things so repulsive it made Alexander sick to think about them. And, just like the evil of slavery and its brood, there were the men who drew a profit from dealing the drugs and who considered themselves above the ones who they bound to the evil of the drugs for a penny or a shilling or a dollar as was the monetary trade these days. The anger welled up inside Alexander and just as Ice and his companion began to fire their weapons he marched toward them.

"Yeah You Punk Ass, take that and that and that!" Ice screamed with a sick glee as the gun began to smoke from the repeated firing.

At first the duo fired directly at Alexander hitting him square in the chest, ripping the t-shirt full of ragged holes, but the vampire just kept coming with a hard and purposeful step. Alexander's face began to change, his mouth stretched and pulled back in a snarl exposing large canines that gleamed with spit, his eyes sank deep into their sockets as the color changed from gray to jet black, and a guttural animal growl started to sound from somewhere deep inside his body. There was no blood, no explosion of bone, or any physical damage to the vampire from the hail of bullets. Then the guns began to kick and the bullets began to fly wide of their mark until the walls around the incoming Alexander started to splinter and crumble. This was all it took for the coma like users to gain some sense of being. Enough to flee the surrounding area and that meant the house. They jumped up to sprint through the kitchen, screaming like banshees while ducking out the backdoor into the night, running to flee the nightmarish image. Some of the men and women jumped out the windows falling the four feet to mother earth in non-graceful lumps. The vampire reached the two men just as their guns finally ran out of rounds leaving them with stunned expressions and the smoking barrels of their weapons.

"What the hell are you man?" Ice asked in a fearful whisper, the look on his face one of pure terror. He never received an answer as Alexander made a single swipe of his right hand that cut the barrels off both handguns like a hot knife through butter leaving the men holding nothing but the grips. Ice looked down at the useless weapon a second before Alexander sent him across the room and into the wall like a bag of bricks with a single punch to his chest. The other man screamed in a high pitched wail as the vampire turned to eye him for a second before continuing slowly into the kitchen to the still form of Wilma.

"Do not move one step!" The vampire hissed before turning away.

"Yeah, you got it my brother!" The man stuttered with fear.

Upstairs in the old house Alexander heard running, two more men were coming with more weapons ready to fight. He knelt slowly and picked up the body of Wilma gingerly and cautiously, cradling the young girl in his arms making sure to brace her head against his shoulder. The vampire looked up to see two individuals, a man and a woman, standing there staring back at him with wide eyes. Their skin was pock-marked, picked at by nails and fingers that were no longer under their control. The harsh smell of chemicals touched Alexander's nose as through the mystical window he saw them, this man and woman, as 'cooks'. They were making a drug called Meth in small batches to test, see if it could be sold to the poor souls around this area. Someone was looking to 'branch out' as they say, selling a new product to the populace to see if it would catch on.

"Holy Shit MAN, that WAS COOL!!!" The man laughed, his rotten teeth chittering and fingers dancing in sporadic tweaks.

The woman shook and jumped in place as she cackled. "Dude, you're like the Walking Dead! Your badder than Daryl MAN!"

Their minds are mush now, burned and scorched to the point they could barely function in this world Alexander thought as he turned to see Ice's companion hadn't moved and he could hear the other men running into the room now. He knew they had their guns drawn and were ready to fire. Ice's companion began to scream like a mad man and point at him as Alexander looked around and saw the stove sitting by the wall that was adjacent to the room where the men had their guns drawn. A plan formed quickly in his head for an escape as he stepped back from the stove. He was going to let the chemicals in this room do the work for him.

"Whoever you are you're not getting out here alive!" A voice yelled out.

"It's not working! He's got a vest on or something!" Ice's companion screamed still standing perfectly still on the same spot.

The 'cook' stepped up as he called out calmly and nonchalantly to the group in the living room. "Uh dudes, no shooting in here man, lots of stuff that goes boom, remember?"

"Yeah dudes, no shoo-"the woman started to say before she was cut off.

With a sharp stomp Alexander sent the stove through the wall and into the living room like a missile before spinning and cradling Wilma to his chest to protect her. Ice's companion let out a scream as debris struck him in the face and chest. The two men began fire with machine guns at the hunk of metal throwing sparks and small ricochets in every direction. Somewhere in all the chaos a stray bullet flew into the kitchen hitting a barrel of highly flammable chemicals. In an explosion of fire the room went up and the severed pipe that connected the stove to the natural gas line that ran under and through the house followed. For a split second there was a flash and then the world erupted in volcanic fury as fire and debris went in every direction. The resulting explosion leveled the house like a box of matches, shattered windows up to four blocks away, and killed the three men standing in the living room.

The man and woman never felt a bit of pain either as it all came to an end.

"WILMA!"

Leland rolled up to his knees to see the house gone, not a single board that used to be standing was there anymore. Stephanie sat on the street a foot from him screaming at the smoking pile of debris. He quickly stood up while reaching for Stephanie while his eyes never left the destruction of the former crack house. Leland put his arms around her to calm her, get the mother in Stephanie under control because he had to go searching for Wilma and he couldn't do that with her in hysterics. He was about to ask Monster if he had seen the man dressed in black go through the door or come running out when he heard the click of the hammer on a handgun being drawn back hand behind him. Leland, while still holding Stephanie, turned unsteadily around to see Kenneth holding a large .45 with a shaking hand, the barrel pointing at the man who walked through the door of the crack house standing just a few feet away. He saw Wilma in the man's arms and knew right away the girl was hurt, probably knocked unconscious during the explosion or something. The problem right now though was Monster here and what was going through his mind and where his hand was pointing the gun.

"Hey Ken man, can you put the gun down please?" Leland asked slowly.

Stephanie turned away from where the house had stood to see her daughter. Leland expected the mother to bolt for her most prized possession in the world, but Stephanie only moved slowly taking a careful step away from him and toward the man and Wilma.

"Ken, please don't point that gun at my daughter. If something happens and she gets shot-"Stephanie began to plead with the boy.

"I would not allow that to happen to her Stephanie." The man stated cold, like he was quoting a known fact, while never looking away from Kenneth.

"Come on Ken, man, just put the piece down now, okay?" Leland asked again.

"No way Lee, it's him! That's the dude from last night who killed Slim and J-Rock!" Kenneth stated with a voice as unsteady as the hand that held the gun.

"Listen Ken, Wilma is hurt and we need to get her to a doctor so put the gun down and we can talk this out all right?" Leland pleaded.

"Please Kenneth let me take care of Wilma. Please let me help her." Stephanie begged again.

"Is this what your mother wanted for you Kenneth?" Alexander suddenly asked. The question brought all three people eye to eye with the vampire.

"What do you know about my mom man?" Kenneth whined as the gun shook in his hand more.

"I know a lot of things about you Kenneth." Alexander stated making sure to look into and hold the boy's eyes with his. "I know how she worked two jobs to pay for your food, your clothes, and the roof over your head while you grew up. I know how when you were seven she purchased you all the presents you asked Santa for by only buying just enough food for the two of you to eat for two weeks, a sandwich meat called Bologna. I know she gave up saving for that new dress she had seen in the store window for church just so you could have money for a new pair of rather expensive tennis shoes. By the way Kenneth, where are those shoes?"

"They were ruined when I walked home in the rain one afternoon." The boy stammered shaking even more now. The .45 began to bounce back and forth and up and down as Alexander's words were taking a toll on Kenneth. Leland and Stephanie turned their attention from the boy to the man and back once more. Neither could believe what was happening right in front of them.

"I also know she used to sing to you in your crib at night, a song that you still remember to this day though you do not understand why. She only wanted the best for you Kenneth, sacrifice after sacrifice made to ensure you grew up a strong and responsible man. And this how you repay her Kenneth, being aligned with men like J-Rock? Is this how you honor what she has sacrificed for you, by befriending men who would rape and destroy a beautifully innocent 14 year old girl?"

The last piece was more than Kenneth could bear as the handgun dropped all the way down and hung from his loose fingers for a second before falling to the ground with a clang. The three men and Stephanie stood still for a second, and then Wilma began to move in Alexander's arms, slow at first before she finally opened her eyes. She looked out at Leland who gave her a big smile back, then she turned to her mother who whispered something to her, and finally to the crying Kenneth. Lastly she turned and looked up to Alexander himself. She looked into his eyes for a second and whispered gently to him.

"Did we escape from Hoth Han? Is Princess Leia safe?"

"Yes little one, we made it to safety." Alexander whispered just as Wilma slipped back into the darkness. He walked over slowly making sure he didn't move so fast as to disappear and placed her body in Stephanie's arms and as a mother's instinct took over she quickly cradled Wilma's head and hugged the little girl fiercely.

"I think she will be fine till you get her to a doctor." Alexander said turning to walk away and he got a few steps before Leland called out to him. The sound in the man's voice stopped the vampire from disappearing.

"Who are you?" Leland had asked with a noticeable desperation.

"He's Batman!" Reggie suddenly screamed.

"Yeah, it's Batman! " Ronald screamed just as loud. The two boys began to chant the theme to the TV show while dancing around and mock fighting just as they had seen Adam West and Burt Ward do on afternoon TV. Leland let go of a small laugh then turned back to find the man gone into the night, there wasn't a trace of him at all. Off in the distance the sounds of approaching sirens filled the night air and deep in the pit of Leland's stomach something turned over like a giant rock. Whether it was fear or elation he wasn't sure. All he knew was Wilma needed help, Stephanie was calm now cradling her daughter with a relieved smile, and Kenneth was about five seconds away from being totally hysterical.

Chapter Seven

"Do you think he's an angel Lee? I mean an honest to goodness-sent-from-God angel to keep an eye on Wilma?" Stephanie asked with a voice that sounded more like a person trying to solve a puzzle than one who was asking for help.

"I don't know Steph, I mean he might be, but why would an angel blow up a house? God has a hammer and he's not afraid to use it, but blowing up a house and risking innocent lives? I don't remember that one in the Bible." Leland answered with a whisper trying to keep his voice down in case someone was eavesdropping.

"What if he's some demon Lee and he has other plans for Wilma? I may have to go on the run Leland!" Stephanie whined taking her curiosity in the opposite direction and feeling fear for doing it.

"Listen Stephanie, I don't think it's time to go all Harrison Ford and make a break for it like 'The Fugitive', okay? You have a daughter, and a friend, who need you right here. The doctors are checking out Wilma and I'm pretty sure she's going to want you beside her when their done so be ready, and no jumping on her case for being outside, all right? Wilma's was just being a teenager and anyway I get first shot at her for scaring me half to death with that whole banging on the crack house door thing she pulled." Leland said with a chuckle.

Stephanie covered her mouth stopping a laugh from breaking free while slapping Leland's shoulder. "Okay, okay, I'll stop talking about Superman. Wilma's going to be okay Lee so if you need to go home and take care of things I understand."

"Do you want me to go?" Leland asked back trying not to sound hurt from the statement but feeling slighted nonetheless. His heart wanted to stay and it hurt just a little when the one he wanted didn't notice.

"No, if you want to stay then I'm glad to have you." Stephanie responded quickly before putting her hand over his.

The decisive moment my son Leland thought, you can either leave or stay. You have to make a good decision, the right decision, because let's face it the whole relationship is riding on this my brother. Yes, she has been talking non-stop about the guy who saved her daughter from a fiery death. Yet, she didn't ask him to stay and she didn't touch his hand. He could say yes and stick around, but what if she just wanted to talk about the guy saving Wilma again. Leland ran through the scenarios in his mind at lightning speed, which was pretty good considering he was totally lost in Stephanie's touch. Whichever one he went with he couldn't see the ending, couldn't make a decisive judgment. The street preacher sat staring at the woman he loved hand with an intensive look of someone trying to solve a philosophical problem. Stephanie stared back at Leland for a second with a raised eyebrow. Just what was wrong with the man she thought to herself? She finally got tired of waiting for an answer and decided to get one.

"I guess someone stepped out for a little bit."

The remark brought Leland out of his deep thought and back to reality. "What, oh yeah, should I stick around?" He asked with a slight smile.

"Oh no, that's already been decided." Stephanie stated confidently with a shake of her head.

"Oh really, wow, can you do me a quick favor then?" Leland asked with a shocked look.

"I don't know, I mean I only do favors for gentlemen." Stephanie remarked flirting with Leland playfully.

"Well it's a good thing I'm a gentleman then, huh?" Leland fired back with a sly smile.

"Then I guess I'll grant you a small favor?

"What did I choose? To stay or go?" Leland asked leaning in.

"Oh you definitely chose to stay sir, right by my side." Stephanie stated with a squeeze of her hand.

"You see there, my momma didn't raise a fool." Leland said matter of fact and both began to chuckle. A second later a doctor walked up to them. The mood changed instantly as both rose to greet the man dressed in the usual green uniform.

He gave them a quick rundown on Wilma's condition, which was good even though she complained of a headache. Wilma would have to spend the night for observation, but that was just procedure for anyone experiencing unconsciousness. The doctor didn't expect any problems tonight or the long term for his patient. Stephanie asked to see her and the doctor said it was okay so she headed off to the room, but Leland didn't move. He was unsure again of what to do so Stephanie took his hand and both walked down the hall and into the plain white room where Wilma was being looked at.

The crime scene was just as chaotic as the night before, only with more people, which meant the migraine would take that much longer to get rid of and Renfroe was sure there wasn't that much time in the entire world. He walked up to the Sergeant in charge already rubbing his eyes in anticipation of the pain that was beginning to bloom.

"What have we got here Sergeant?" Renfroe asked.

"A crack house that went boom mostly, don't know the body count yet." The Sergeant said looking up from his notebook.

"Were there were complete bodies or just parts and pieces?" Renfroe asked.

"Both, Foster found some pieces."

"Foster...again?" Renfroe moaned at the sound of the name.

The Sergeant only pointed over to a dancing Foster, the coroner was singing an old Stevie Wonder song called 'Superstition' while performing his duties. The man looked like a deranged Michael Jackson wearing two white gloves instead of the prerequisite one. Renfroe moaned again and turned back to the Sergeant.

"Do we have an idea what caused the explosion?"

"Foster says it was a gas explosion." The Sergeant said then looked up to Renfroe. "He also mentioned something about a footprint."

"What footprint?" Renfroe asked in frustration wondering what that lunatic was talking about.

"Well, he didn't actually mention it as much as I overheard him mumble about it sir. He said it matched one you saw on the front panel of that car last night, the case with the dismembered body." The Sergeant answered before watching the detective's expression turn from bewilderment to that look one gets when a puzzle finally clicks for the first time and you see the answer right in front of you. The next look the detective gave him after that scared the sergeant for a second, like someone had crossed a line they should have left well enough alone. He knew the look because it was the kind his mother gave him when he mentioned anything about his father. His father left them one night when he was young, the old 'I'm going out for some cigarettes and I'll be back in about, oh never' trick. If you ever said his father's name aloud around his mother then you had better be running for cover because something metal was coming at you, very fast and very hard. Renfroe turned, screamed at Foster to stop dancing and get his ass over here, and then the two huddled together for a few minutes. From the finger pointing the detective was doing and the cowering the assistant coroner had to do the conversation looked rather lopsided. Meanwhile the sergeant watched one of his men dealing with a particularly aggressive on-looker.

"Oh mister officer, mister officer," Grammy called out to one of the young police officers standing by the long stream of yellow crime tape.

"Yes ma'am." The officer responded with a broad smile walking over.

"I was wondering," she asked while chewing her gums loudly," is this in any way got something to do with them noises I've been hearing outside my window."

"Noise's outside where ma'am?" The young officer asked as he looked over to his partner and the man immediately remembered Grammy from last night. A quick motion of his finger in a circle around the temple was a not-so silent reply and the young officer knew what to do.

"Here Ma'am, if you have any more information just call the number on the card and the operator on the phone will gladly take down your information." The young police officer explained, even while Grammy was protesting the officer was able to shove a card into her hand and get away before the old woman could start up again about the strange noises around her apartment. With an inward cackle Grammy just smiled and headed off back toward home, it was enough to see the house destroyed she thought. It was enough to know Judgment Day had come for this hell called the Laurel. Just after she was out of sight of the scene and everyone, no prying eyes to watch, there was a slight gust of air and then there was Alexander at her elbow, as if he had been standing there these last ten minutes.

"That was quite amusing back at the crime tape Martha. You do take great joy in putting the local law enforcement through the screws as they say." He spoke.

"Oh Mr. Alexander, I'm just having me some fun at their expense is all. They never did nothing for me or anyone else when we called all those times needing them so I might as well get a few jabs in before I move on to the next life." Grammy smiled walking back to her apartment.

"And that is fine Martha, until you have need of their help before this is over, very soon maybe." Alexander remarked.

"And why in the world would we need the help of those fools?" Grammy asked with a shake of her head stopping by a dark corner next to her domicile.

"Others have seen me again Martha, it is harder to move in this world than I am accustomed to, and I am sure that the men who distributed the drugs out of that house there will know of Wilma and myself soon if they do not all ready." Alexander answered flatly.

Martha shook her head slightly while answering the vampire with a small smile. "No one in the Laurel sees anything Mr. Alexander. That's the second rule of survival in this jungle, you may see all but you never speak all, understand?"

"Do you remember last night when I said I was in hiding from others?" Alexander asked suddenly ignoring the humorous remark.

"I may be old Mr. Alexander but my mind is still as sharp as a tack!" Grammy answered with a bright smile.

"And that sharp mind has seen what I am hiding from, haven't you Martha?" Alexander asked slowly, almost whispering.

For a second Grammy stood still, then she took a deep breath and spoke carefully, choosing each word very carefully. "I've seen a man, but he's not a man in the sense we know a man to be. No sir, he hasn't been one of us for a very, very long time. He's black, and I don't mean in color like I am, but in spirit and soul. He has neither and he has known for some time you're out walking around in the world again."

The answer told Alexander she knew more about him then she was saying. Things he had tried to keep hidden and buried were surfacing with Grammy and her 'sight' so there was no longer a need to hide what he knew anymore. "The man's name is Akhenaton and at one time he ruled Egypt, but now he just wants to see me destroyed."

"The soulless man wants more than to destroy you Mr. Alexander. He wants to kill this world too, sink it into his very own nightmare." Martha whispered, adding what she knew and the vampire was beginning to think there was some invisible hand pushing him and Wilma along this path, pushing them together.

"What else do you know about my past Martha? What else have you seen?" The vampire asked looking to her.

"I know a little bit. I know about you taking over the world, I know about your supposed death from some mysterious sickness, and I even know about that knot you cut in half because you couldn't get it undone any other way. But all that stuff isn't what you're really looking for is it Mr. Alexander, no you're a smart man and you're looking for some specific things?" Grammy smiled beginning to shuffle along toward home.

"Do you know about Christina and Roxanna?" He finally asked knowing Martha would not be swayed with anything but the truth and Alexander already knew the answer before his friend responded.

"Yes sir I do." Grammy whispered low in a smug less tone, it was as if she was consoling the vampire for the loss of a lover. "And I know just how it's dug into you all these years."

"Then you know why I cannot stay around Wilma Martha. I will only put her in more danger, like Christina and Roxanna, and I cannot take the pain from hurting someone so innocent again. She will be hurt, Wilma, unless you stop whatever magic you are doing and free me from this duty you have asked." Alexander asked, almost pleaded with her.

Grammy shook her head and let out a small cackle of delight. She was still one-step ahead Alexander thought, still one long stride in front. He knew Martha had two different motives for what she was asking. He even suspected she knew what would happen these last two days. He was still a master tactician, Alexander thought, and the meetings with Wilma were perfect moves on a chess board or a battle field. To obtain that which you seek, be it victory in battle or the surrender of a city under siege, one had to have one's soldiers in place. He kept running into Wilma and she kept running into trouble, once an accident and twice a well-conceived plan the vampire thought. The only thing Alexander wanted to know was how, just how did Grammy get him and Wilma to all those spots together as she did, if she did?

"You give me too much credit Mr. Alexander." She hooted. "Yes I know about the two ladies and that is why I know you'll be seeing our little Wilma real soon."

"And just how do you know I will be meeting with her Martha?" He asked curiously.

"Now come, come Mr. Alexander, you know me better than that. I just figured that since she's already seen you and with this Akhenaton fella knowing you're awake now that the next step was really kind of simple. Go and sit down with the girl for a few minutes, talk and see what she's like."

"I cannot keep saving Wilma from this place Martha. It is beyond me to keep her safe from the Laurel every night and it is most certainly beyond my capabilities to keep the evil that infects the Laurel out as well. If you see an ending I do not then please, feel free to share it with me Martha. " He stated quickly, the fangs exposed for a second.

The old woman stopped just short of leaving the dark shadows and turned back to look at the vampire, her face set to a serious tone now and her milky eyes now aglow with her dark glasses removed. Martha had given way and turned into one of the Oracle's of old he would visit when he felt the want to, the one who sees all and knows all, and Alexander recognized the look because he had seen that face too many times for his liking. She breathed deep and spoke emotionless with a distant voice again choosing each word carefully. "You can see things too, can't you Mr. Alexander? When you look out on this place what does that window you look through show you? Go on, take a look now."

If the vampire was surprised that she knew of his ability he never showed it, Alexander was not one to be shocked by encounters with Oracle's. He did as she asked and looked out at the Laurel through that special window he used to view other people only now something took hold of the power in his head and the vampire felt a small surge. His eyes burned just a little as he saw nothing but the burnt debris and wreckage of what had been the Laurel Woods Projects. There was not a building left standing everywhere he turned and looked, not even a wall of bricks and as he looked back to Grammy, as she continued on, he saw something else that shook him.

"This place, all of it, was damned a long time ago Mr. Alexander. Evil can only grow so much, profit from human suffering just so long before the righteous fire comes and burns every trace of the dark, burns and cleanses it away. Whether it's by a lone avenging angel or a storm of holy conflagration, the Laurel will be destroyed Mr. Alexander and there's nothing anyone can do to stop it. The ones' who bring in that devil's powder to corrupt and kill will meet the same fate when it comes time for the Laurel to fall, join this place in the end of it all, but there is the unfortunate one who has been marked. There is one who will perish as well and she doesn't deserve to lose her young life because of fools."

"Little Wilma," the vampire whispered after a deep inhale. Grammy only nodded choosing to let her words sink in a little more, for the vampire to think on what she said before he spoke again. "Than what are you asking me to do Martha? If Wilma is not here when the Laurel is destroyed then she will be safe, right? Just ask her mother to leave." Alexander asked, almost pleaded with a low voice.

"If she was taken away from here, a hundred or even a thousand miles away, it wouldn't matter when the end comes. I've seen it with my dead eyes Mr. Alexander. Wilma's mother and that street preacher think they can save this place by staying here and fighting when the Laurel's end was decided long ago and by doing so they just brought the shadow of death down on them and our Wilma. They've done nothing but seen to the end of our little Wilma and themselves trying to save what can't be saved.

They won't leave if you begged them and even if they did the evil men who poison this place will just pursue and follow all of three to finish them. That's why I need you to make sure our little angel is safe Mr. Alexander, that her fate is changed and turned back because she has nothing to do with what Stephanie and Leland do. That she's not just taken away from here when the end comes but that she's safe for a good long time to come."

The vampire just shook his head before answering, "And how I am supposed to take Wilma away from here Martha, kidnap her and hide her for all time? How can I stop what has already been decided? If Stephanie will not leave with her and it does not matter if she does then what am I to do?"

"Oh Mr. Alexander, that's why I have need of your nobility like I said before. You won't leave our little Wilma to die here, not after these last two nights. I don't know how you're going to do it but you will Mr. Alexander, you'll save our little angel I just know it." Grammy whispered.

"Now I think you are the one giving me too much credit Martha." Alexander grinned weakly.

And now that she was done the look on her face changed, the old Martha returning as she smiled wide and slipped her glasses on. Even her old voice came back with ease as Grammy laughed, "let's just say I know what I'm doing Mr. Alexander, but you have to go and to talk to Wilma. You hiding in the shadows won't help her. Those nights are long gone sir, better you understand that now than later."

"I think I can 'see' that Martha, but I have my reasons as well for not talking with Wilma right now. I need to think about what has to be done a little more. I need to sit with someone else as well before moving on to Wilma. I need more information from him on the people involved...and permission." Alexander explained smiling just a little, accepting his fate now. The grand plan of going back to sleep in some graveyard lay shattered at his feet, and with it a new path laid out to walk.

"I understand getting the 'ok' and all, but who exactly are you worried for?" Grammy asked.

"Like you have seen in your visions Martha, there are others beside Akhenaton coming now looking for the one who destroyed the house, I am sure of it. I was a fool to think I would not be seen from the actions I have taken and now the men who are the most dangerous know about Wilma and me. These last two nights will be seen as an attack by an outsider, an incursion into their territory, and whoever controls this place will send in soldiers to crush anyone they think is associated with this attack. I need information to form a counter strategy because Wilma and her mother and Leland are targets now." Alexander said

"That is a lot to think about but I'm not worried as long as you stick around. I need to tell you one more thing Mr.

Alexander. I wasn't truthful a second ago with you. I know a little more than I was letting on." Grammy said with a sudden serious air.

"What is it Martha?" Alexander asked being drawn in by the older woman's tone.

"There's something else coming for you, it's not the dark man himself but something that's working with him reluctantly and he's trying to get rid of it for some reason. And there's more than one Mr. Alexander, it's like the four horseman of the Apocalypse riding out of the sky seeking you out of the crowd." She remarked flatly.

Alexander took the information in, ran it through his mind for a moment, and then stored it away to be looked at and analyzed more in depth later. "Thank you for telling me everything Martha." He said with a small nod of his head.

"Your welcomed Mr. Alexander but now you go and talk to Leland first to get your information, just don't wait too long. We're all working on schedules around here you' know." Grammy chuckled while turning into the horseshoe shaped entrance of the Laurel.

The last remark stuck with Alexander, it was like a fly that shows up while you're eating, and it just keeps buzzing in and out and all around. She knew about the part of his past no one else could know, knew how to make his path cross Wilma's, and what she knew of the future for this place called the Laurel scared Alexander just a bit. However, he let any worry go. Martha had an agenda and at the moment it seemed his part was to be a guard and hero. No, something else needed his attention right now more than Martha and her visions, even the one about 'riders' coming after him. What he needed now was to talk to Leland about the drugs and how they came into the Laurel, even though the thought of talking to the man bothered him. Alexander had an idea on how to protect Wilma now, a very rudimentary plan on how to have her 'removed' from danger before anything could happen. The only question to his strategy was how much risk would it bring to them all, how much attention would come?

This sudden plan would have him take on an impossible task to save Wilma, just like the one he had tried to save before so very long ago in a lost attempt to save his own former life. It would have him go against the people at the top of the drugs and its organization this crazed plan. Taking away a simple soldier or pawn only prolongs the conflict and has little effect, take away a General and you can watch armies move to try and bolster positions on the battle field and it would be in those moves that Wilma and her mother and Leland would be saved. He just needed know which 'General' to take away though and the tactful information on setups and deliveries; the kind of information that was vital and he needed now. He would never learn what was required from just watching the daily activities, not expeditiously anyway. The point of turning back was gone and no matter how hard he wished there were not, innocents had been dragged into this. If there was going to be a 'righteous fire' then every scrap of intelligence was going to be necessary to keep those he...cared for safe. And as usual he had more questions than answers after talking with Martha, like how did she know he wanted to talk with Leland?

Out of the corner of his eye Alexander spotted the white Cadillac rolling fast out of the congested neighborhood. Well, what better way to introduce himself to the men who ran the drugs around here than saying 'hello' in his own special way. It would take some of the light off of Wilma and her family too while focusing the attention more on him. Another idea ran through in his mind and it was simple if not prolonged, just had to pick out the right corner to deliver the message.

A sleek blue BMW driven by a large muscled man pulled silently into the parking garage next to the IBM tower in the Midtown area of Downtown, slowly rolled to the fourth level of an indistinguishable garage, and turned into a parking spot overlooking the streets below. In the back seat, a black man dressed in a white handmade three piece suit opened a certified package delivered to a lady at the cleaners on 12th and produced a single cell phone from its contents. He opened it with a practiced flip and hit the send button. Like the other times before the number was already programmed in and didn't show up on the screen like most other models of cell. The 'burner' phone rang once then after a click a voice answered with the polished air of a true salesman.

"What did we need to talk about Mr. Eight Ball?" The voice asked quickly.

"We lost the house on Ivy tonight." Eight Ball answered low.

"And how did we lose such an important piece of our distribution setup?" The voice asked.

"An explosion is the official word." Eight Ball responded low again, almost growling.

"What do you think? Is someone trying to move in on our operations?"

"No one's making a move against us, we still control most of the supply inside the city. " Eight Ball replied with confidence and some disdain. He hated talking with the Producer. The man acted like he was some kind of CEO running some big business. Hell, this wasn't Apple or Starbucks, it was just pushing drugs you

know Eight Ball thought. Get the shit in, sell it, and then get paid.
What else was there to it?

"Then what happened with our distribution point?" The
voice asked coolly.

"Police say it was a gas explosion. I tend to believe that."
Eight Ball said finally after hesitating. The flinch didn't go
unnoticed.

"Do I detect a slight disagreement with their conclusion
Mr. Eight Ball?"

"I've got some ears out on the street listening for me.
They say there was a man dressed in a black t-shirt on the scene
seconds before the house was taken out. He might have
something to do with what happened, but I'm not sure what to
make of it yet." Eight Ball said.

"Wild cards in the deck eh, well then, keep your ears out
and listening Mr. Eight Ball. Inform me if there needs to be
another meeting through the usual channels. We'll keep to the
schedule and use the house off Parker to ensure the product
inventory does not slow or stop." The voice commented.

"Will you pass the info up the chain?" Eight Ball asked
quickly.

"I think I'm required to Mr. Eight Ball, but you think we
should keep this to ourselves for now, why?" The voice asked
back with a hint of suspicion.

"I think I can handle this without any extra attention." Eight Ball responded.

"And what if the Boss feels extra attention is warranted?"

"The Boss isn't here and I don't want it to look like I'm not in control." Eight Ball stated through clenched teeth. The conversation was starting to make his anger rise ever so slightly.

"Frankly I don't care how you look Mr. Eight Ball. I care about the business and if it is running smoothly. I will pass the information along to the Boss and if he wants special attention given to this situation then that is what will happen, understand Mr. Eight Ball?" The voice commented and then the phone went dead with a slight pop before he could answer.

"I take it the phone call wasn't productive?" The driver asked from the front seat.

"I want Crazy D at the usual place in half-an-hour to talk about having extra protection on the corners. The green doesn't stop coming in, not for nothing. Then I want you to place a call to the rat and get me information on this 'man in black'. Believe me, if I find out someone messed in my business I will put a whole clip in their ass!" Eight Ball hissed slamming the lid closed on the cell phone. He handed it to the man in the front seat who set the cell back into the package it came in, but not before twisting it in two with his hands. The man then produced a can of lighter fluid, doused the contents of the box, and lit it on fire after placing it on the concrete of the parking deck. The blue BMW pulled away slowly as the small inferno destroyed the evidence of the cell phone.

"You still thinking about getting out from under the Producer?" The driver asked.

"Would I risk my balls skimming off the top if I wasn't going to go out on my own? Hell yes I'm going independent! I don't need to be treated like some punk on the corner! I got my cred the right way, put in my work!" Eight Ball spat, his mind still running through plans on beefing up security for his corners.

The cell phone closed with a pop, which echoed in the spacious study. A gentle breeze blew through a set of French doors just behind and left of a large ornate desk he sat quietly at. Lloyd Dunbar could hear the party, a gala he was hosting for some charity he didn't really care about, going on downstairs through the large oak door to his study. Maybe it was time to get out and move on to another venture he thought silently. Maybe someone was commencing a hostile takeover of the business? He flipped opened the cell phone again and dialed in a set of memorized numbers with an agile thumb. A rough voice answered, he gave the memorized password, and the phone went dead. The cell phone closed with a pop, just like a second ago. In a few minutes the cell would ring on cue with the Boss on the other end and Lloyd would pass on the information about the loss of the house on Ivy. He really hoped the meeting wouldn't take a long time, a rather large order of Beluga caviar was flown in special for this event and he hated to miss a single bite.

Across Town at the local Peachtree Dekalb Airfield, a Lear Jet made the usual approach and three-point landing on the runway. The plane rolled with engines humming over to a darkened hangar in an area of the airfield rarely used by the airport personnel or pilots. A large silver Town car sat gassed and ready next to a smaller Ford Mustang as the plane came to a stop and the door opened with a small pop and whoosh. The first out was a thin man dressed in an expensive Gucci suit followed by a medium and exotic looking female, a small leather jacket barely covered the thin shirt she wore and exposed midriff. Her mini skirt shook with every step she took, as did the long exotic white mane of hair that were pulled back by a large black cloth hair band, the length of white hair spilling down to just below her waist. Directly behind the woman three men stepped out, each having to turn sideways to exit the plane they were so big, all dressed the same in business suits and brown leather trench coats. The only difference between the triplets was each one had a different hair color, one was black, one was red, and the last blond. The black hair approached the female and spoke English with a heavy Russian accent.

"Where do we start looking for the vampire?"

"We will have to wait for him to make an appearance." The female said with the same thick accent. "He cannot be that smart leaving live bodies lying around. He will make a mistake and then we will corner him and end him."

"How do you know it's a 'he'?" The black hair asked.

"My Lord Akhenaton informed me before we left." The thin man in the Gucci responded before the lady could. "Remember, this Nosferatu has spurned our request for his loyalty. Lord Akhenaton wishes for him to be dispensed with and by doing so quickly your mother Svetlana will be returned to you by the ones who hold her captive."

The four Russians looked to each other with hopeful smiles before the lady turned back to the thin man. "This vampire and his kind, you are sure they will release our mother once he has been destroyed?"

"Yes, most assuredly so because those who defy our Lord Akhenaton, the ones who hold your mother captive, will not wish to have his vengeance visited upon them once they see what you four have done in his name."

The lady smiled a little more, "if it means our mother's freedom, then this vampire will never see his end coming."

"Good," the thin man responded with a sigh, "How long do you need to deal with him, a day maybe?"

The female's eyebrow rose just a bit as she answered his inquiry, "We have answered that question before Michaels. We will not attack this vampire without first knowing who he is and what he is capable of. I will not put my brothers in danger."

The thin man, Michaels, looked like he was going to let loose with a vicious diatribe that would literally smite the lady and all with his eyes tinged red with anger. Yet, just before doing so, he gave in with a wave of his hand and spitting his words. "All right, how long do you need for that?"

"We will have the answer once we know where to find the Nosferatu, as I have stated." The white haired female answered. Her eyebrow was still up and it was easy to see her suspicion and frustration was growing.

"I do not think this vampire will show for some time now though, maybe not till he needs to feed again." The red head suddenly remarked.

"And why do you say that?" The thin man asked in a tone one would expect from a person conversing with a three year old as he looked to the moon then down to the large man.

"I do not know why, it is just a feeling I have." The red hair remarked sniffing the air, tasting the night wind.

"Well, I'll have to remember your feelings are more perceptive than my lord's." The thin man stated with a flippant attitude and an exhale.

The woman was about to respond and come to the red hair's defense when the blond man called out, he was busy tuning in a small portable TV to the local station for the nightly news. He held it out to the woman with a childish smile as the newscaster talked about the explosion at the suspected crack house and how there were fatalities but none confirmed. The woman smiled at the screen while rubbing her hand down his cheek longingly like a devoted lover, she whispered something in Russian that made the man smile even more. The thin man shook his head and spoke up sarcastically. "How do you know the vampire is connected in any way to the exploding house?"

"We do not, but like my brother Gregor I have a feeling Michaels." The female remarked with a cold smile. For a second no one said a word, and then the thin man named Michaels produced a set of similar rail thin sunglasses from a breast pocket inside the suit coat. The others watched closely, waiting for the plan of action.

"I think Peter and you Yelena should follow any leads they can drum up from the females who were bitten. Gregor and Dimitri will see what is going on around these Laurel projects, see if this vampire has been good enough to leave us a trail to follow. We'll meet back at the hotel and go over what you find." Michaels said sliding the glasses on. "Is this acceptable?"

"What will you do Michaels?" Yelena asked suddenly somewhat confrontational. If there was something to the tone it didn't bother Michaels one bit as he just ignored it.

"I'm going to use my vast array of knowledge and powers to find out who we are dealing with, get his name and number you might say to push this along. We meet back at dawn so go out and do what it is you do." Michaels commanded with a wave of his hand.

"Da," the four all said at once. Gregor nodded his head again as the group got into the Town car and drove off in to the night leaving Michaels by himself. He watched the Town car's rear lights fade away before pulling a cell phone out of another breast pocket. He quickly dialed a number barely looking at the keypad and going off memory and feel. The other end rang only once before it was picked up by a man with short cropped blond hair and a smooth voice answered.

"Yes Michaels, what do you want?"

"I wanted to inform you we have landed my Lord Akhenaton and the Epova's have begun the search for the Ancient one." Michaels responded gleefully, a 180 turn from his mood just five seconds ago.

In a large living room in a 1950's Italian style villa tucked away in the hills overlooking Hollywood and Los Angeles the voice responded to the gleeful mood with a small grunt. "Well, I'll have to write this down as a day of grand celebration." Akhenaton said with a tone filled to the brim with mocking sarcasms.

"Yes sir we will, but I do have one question my lord?" Michaels asked quickly. The gleeful tone in his voice replaced with one of fear.

"Yes Michaels, what is it?" Akhenaton hissed.

"Sir, are you sure you want all of the Epova's killed by the Ancient One, Even Yelena? I mean yes she is very young and extremely brash but she's does show some promise for us, doesn't she?" Michaels asked hoping his lord would find some merit in his questioning of the plan.

There was a second of silence on the phone and Michaels knew his Lord Akhenaton was upset and the worst part was he was the one who made his lord that way. He clinched his teeth in fear for some unknown blast of punishment; Michaels just hoped it was quick. That was the best way, just get it over with. Yet the voice came back smooth over the phone, only dripping with anger. Anyone could have felt it coming through the small cell phone speaker.

"Okay, break out your notepad Michaels because I'm only going to say it once more. I'm trying to create a utopia here, the Garden of Eden, only in my own darkly horrific and nightmarish image and I can't do that with Alexander walking around threatening to make a mess of it." Akhenaton stated quickly.

"And it will be a splendid garden sir!" Michaels almost shouted, gleeful again.

"Shut up Michaels!"

"Yes sir,"

"I need Alexander to kill the Epovas, all of the Epovas, because that will make Svetlana very angry. When we let her out and she finds her pups dead at the hands of Alexander I'll get the Lycanthropes on my side meaning I won't have to worry about those nasty wolves getting in my way and my business. I also get a chance to disgrace, discredit, and otherwise alienate my greatest enemy. Two birds' one stone thing going on here, you follow?"

"Ah yes sir, the bad PR bit, now I understand!"

"So what's the problem then?"

"Well sir, how do I exactly do it? How do I get the Ancient One to kill the Epovas?"

The phone was silent for a minute before the voice replied. "What do you mean 'how'?

"Well sir, I ordered the pups to attack the Ancient One several times but Yelena has steadfastly refused to do it without first finding out who she will be attacking." Michaels pointed out.

"Whoa there, you can't let those pups find out who the vampire is Michaels because that will screw up all the work it took for me to get them out there, got it?" The voice said harshly.

The thin man nodded quickly trying to reassure his lord he was in control. "No sir, they will not find out I promise you. I was thinking I could lie and give them a false name. Maybe that would calm Yelena down a little."

"Ok, that could work. You can do that or you might have the pups deliver a dozen doughnuts with a good morning 'fuck you' to Alexander. That might get this thing to go down."

"Well yes, that might work sir-"Michaels stammer a bit before the voice cut him off. Is that a real thing he thought, a good morning 'fuck you'?

"Good Michaels, you're the man representing me out there so step up and deliver. But understand this, if for some reason Alexander doesn't kill the Epovas then I'm going to get really angry and we both know what happens when I get really angry, right?"? Akhenaton sneered into the phone.

"Yes sir" Michaels stammered from a sudden shudder of fear.

"Good, so don't screw this up!"

The phone went dead and Michaels stared at it for a long minute. His mind was racing, calculating, and forming a plan. There was no chance for a mistake here, no chance to 'screw it up' as his precious lord has stated. Michaels had to make sure the Ancient one, Alexander, killed the Epovas. There was just one problem; he still wasn't really sure how to do it.

***

The Blue BMW slipped into a different dark deserted parking lot pulling up next to a white Cadillac. The rear window of the BMW stopped in line with the driver's side window of the Cadillac and both dropped with the usual whir and precision of automation. In the driver's seat of the Cadillac sat a rather large man, one who engulfed the seat it seemed like. Eight Ball never really looked out at his enforcer and protector, but he still had a sneer when talking.

"You have the corners covered?"

"Yep, everyone's strapped with extra eyes and bodies standing watch." Crazy D said quickly.

"What are your ears hearing?"

"Some guy dressed in black stirring up shit, no name. There's also something else that's weird."

"What is it?" Eight Ball asked turning to look Crazy in the eyes.

"Both times this dude's stepped into our business he hasn't been alone."

"Who's with him?" Eight Ball asked quickly.

It took a second before Crazy answered. "A little girl, you know the kid of that loud mouth that runs with the street preacher."

Eight Ball took a second to take in the information, process it, and then form a plan. "Don't worry about that, I got it covered. You just make sure the green keeps flowing from the corners or I will put a bullet in your brain, you go that D?" Before Crazy could answer Eight Ball gave the signal and the BMW pulled out and away.

Crazy sat in his Cadillac for a second quietly seething with anger from being dismissed in such a manner. One day he thought, one day he'd be running the show and pissing all over Eight Ball's grave.

After the BMW rolled out Eight Ball's cell rang and he popped it open without so much as a glance. His mind was elsewhere, crunching facts and data like an overworked computer. Even his voice sounded distant as he answered the ringing device.

"Go" was all he said.

"You wanted to talk?" A voice questioned back.

With a snap of a finger Eight Ball's attention focused instantly on the conversation, the distant tone in his voice turning into intimidation. "I need info young blood, the 411 on our friend in black."

"I got nothing new, just a bunch of zombies on crack talking about a dude blowing up the house. No one whose brain ain't fried has seen the dude."

"That's not what I'm hearing young blood, nothing close to that. Another little G said the man in black's running with the loud mouth's rug rat. You know anything about that?" Eight Ball hissed.

On a silent corner under a single light thrown by a half busted street light a lone figure stood next to a pay phone arguing emphatically with one arm. "Listen man, that's all I'm hearing from the Laurel. Half the people say it's a ghost and the other half it's the devil come to end the world. All I know is I haven't seen the dude, not one hair."

"Okay young blood, I trust you not to leave me hanging. Keep up the good work and I'll reward you well, all right?" Eight Ball said suddenly becoming very affable.

"Yeah, we cool." The figure stated flatly.

"Good, call when you have something new." Eight Ball said and closed the cell with a quick pop. He slid back in the seat and put his brain back to crunching data again.

The lone figure under the street light stood still for a second, as if in deep thought, and then produced a quarter from a jean pocket and made a second call. The ringer on the other end sounded twice before being picked up and a very refined voice answered back. "Good evening my fine sir."

"Did my info check out? You believe me now about Eight Ball and the skimming?" The figure asked quickly looking over his shoulders feeling nervous.

"Yes, everything was the truth." The Producer stated, weirdly happily.

"So we're solid right?" The figure asked.

"Yes sir, everything we agreed upon will be yours at the conclusion of our business." The Producer remarked, again eerily happy.

"I'll be calling again to arrange it after everything settles down." The figure said.

"One thing my young friend, I need to ask something." Lloyd, the Producer, said quickly.

"Yeah, what?" the figure shot back with some agitation.

"I need to know about a man in black, I need to know if he'll become a problem." Lloyd asked.

The phone went silent for a second as the figure looked around again nervously eyeing the shadows for a sign of someone getting too close. There was nothing though so the figure turned back to the phone and spoke with a whisper. "I'm hearing he's a bad dude, some kind of a Rambo or something. Eight Ball's running scared to, he won't show it but everyone can see it plain as day."

It was Lloyd's turn to be quiet now for a second before responding the last statement. "Will we lose the Laurel if we keep the same course?"

"Hell yes! If Eight Ball don't get dropped by someone else then this dude in black is gonna do it." The figure said loudly into the phone.

"All right then that's what I needed to know. In the meantime you need to play along with everyone and make them think that you're still loyal to Eight Ball and if anything comes up about the man in black call me ASAP." Lloyd said with a sharp tone suggesting the call was over.

"I'm good." The figure said before putting the receiver down in the cradle. Kenneth turned away from the phone and checked over his shoulder one last time to make sure no one was looking. He didn't feel bad about turning in Eight Ball, only the fact that he had to fake loyalty until the inevitable took place. In the real world you waited for your company promotions like a good little boy or girl, but out here in the streets you took the promotions anyway you had to. If someone had to bleed or die for that happen Kenneth didn't care, he was moving up.

Lloyd closed the cell phone in his left hand and turned back to the one in his right. "I'm here Rico." He said coolly, as if he were speaking to a causal friend from college.

Rico Hierra wasn't even close to being anyone's casual friend. He was the biggest supplier of cocaine and marijuana for the South East and he was number one on the DEA's 'must apprehend RIGHT NOW' list. He also hated being asked to wait for anything, especially calls. "Who was that Lloyd?" Rico demanded, practically growling.

"It was our mutual friend, the one who brought the missing merchandise and money to our attention." Lloyd stated.

"What did he say?"

"Just checking in, making sure the information was accepted and all." Lloyd said jotting down a number on a pad on his expansive desk.

"Yeah, and what are we doing about our missing inventory Lloyd?" Rico asked, the anger gone from his voice. He actually sounded excited.

"The ball's already rolling on that Rico. I made a call to the Warehouse Manager and he's clearing out the rats on his end. I'll take care of this end."

"This la pija needs to be scared Lloyd, sweat a little you know before he's finished. And I want an example from this, something to remind everyone what happens when you bite the hand that feeds." Rico explained.

"I'm getting ready to do just that." Lloyd said with an evil smile.

"That's good Lloyd, very good. No one steals from me and lives." Rico explained.

"I'm sure everyone will be reminded who's in charge." Lloyd replied.

"What about this guy in black? Are we going to have a problem with him as well?" Rico asked sipping Patron over ice from a crystal glass, the yacht he was riding on rolling just enough to make him adjust his balance.

"I've got my spy gathering information on him, but for the moment we have a bigger issue with our man running the operation at street level. We have to take care of this or we will lose more than product and money in the end." Lloyd stated with the air of someone conducting everyday business.

"Okay, then do what needs to be done and call me with the details." Rico finished before hanging up the cell.

Lloyd's fingers though were already working the number pad of the second phone. Three minutes later it was done, the wheel set in motion.

Chapter Eight

Monday night was cold, which wasn't out of the norm with it being the middle of winter and all, but it was quiet, too silent even for a Monday night and that wasn't normal. After the main distribution house getting hit yesterday and all the other drama going round the last few days there should have been something happening tonight, especially with the man who controlled the dope putting down his foot, but there wasn't a thing going on. Eight Ball was leaving threats and bodies in his wake to protect his interest in the Laurel, all aimed at rivals. Four dudes beat so bad they might not walk again the other night for J-Rock and another shot dead last night in retaliation for losing Ice and it was early tonight. There was still a few hours to go until dawn so there was time to push the body count up to cover last night's mistakes, at least that's what X thought as he stood his corner. Casey 'X' Brown, the X stood for X-cellent or X-stasy Brown would state with a wide impish smile when the girls would ask what it meant. He never suspected that most of the girls thought it was just stupid and flat out ignorant. X was given his corner by Crazy D to work but not to hold or touch the product that was sold from there. All he did was take the money for the order and then send a message upstairs to a girl who brought the rock down to the customer. The perfect system X thought when Crazy D explained it to him a year ago. If the police hit him they caught him holding nothing and as long as X kept his mouth shut they wouldn't have a single thing to hold him on. X only had to worry about rival drug dealers moving in, and that wasn't going to happen with Eight Ball and Crazy D running the show, and anyway that's why he carried the 9mm Auto in his waistband. No one came to his corner and started any shit. No one started anything with Eight Ball backing him. Well, except for a few days ago when this dude dressed in black decided to show up to try take over the Laurel. Yeah, all that bullshit didn't worry X though, whoever this dude was who was trying move in he was sure as hell going to end up dead in the street from a dozen of Eight Ball's bullets. The extra protection for the night stood across the street in the form of two large dudes keeping an eye out just waiting for this punk in black to show up. Nothing to worry about X thought to himself while smiling, nothing to worry about at all.

Then X looked up from his phone that he was using to text a girl to see a set of headlights approaching, rolling up slow. This was a customer coming. X could tell by the way the car was moving toward him, inching up. He quickly picked out the two white kids in the front seat of the Dodge Charger, rich and sure as hell out of place in the hood. The guy was your usual blond hair blue eyed asshole X thought, but the girl was sweet looking...for a white girl. She had on one of those hoody's that squeezed a girl's breasts snug in just the right spots and from where he stood she had no problem filling out the material. The car came to a stop just in front of X, the window lowered, and the white boy rolled out a hand holding fresh folded twenty dollar bills while a gold bracelet and several rings draped off the appendages. X didn't move, only eyed the car and its driver. He didn't like white people.

No, check that, he didn't like rich white people.

"And what you want man?" X asked with a sneer. "The clubs in Buckhead are the other way homie."

"I need two bags for a private party." The driver remarked with his own sneer.

"Two bags of what man? If you looking for some groceries then you better try the Piggly Wiggly down the street!" X remarked, laughing at his own quickly thrown barb.

"Listen bruh, I need two bags for a private party. You can either make some money or watch the cash travel down the street to the next dealer. I hear it's a real bitch if you don't make your quota on the corner these days." The driver countered with an I-Know-I-got-you-by-the-balls look on his face. A set of perfect white teeth seemed to wink at X and his anger shot up right out of his skull.

He hated those perfect teeth. What he really wanted to do was stomp this rich white kid till he begged for mercy, turn and bang that rich white bitch till she screamed next to him, and then go back and finish killing this rich kid. But X knew better, he knew the kid was right. His momma didn't raise a fool. Eight Ball and Crazy D expected a certain amount of money from the corner, come up short with the cash then you better get ready to come up short with body parts, like fingers and hands. It only took a second for X to make a decision on keeping all ten fingers and toes.

"Drive down to the corner and wait for the mailman to come out the door." X spat taking the money from the ring laden hand.

The Charger rolled forward a few feet with the girl giggling and looking over her shoulder at X with contemptuous eyes. That hatred X felt for rich white kids deepened, he knew she was laughing at him. Yeah, laugh it up bitch he thought as he pulled out a cell phone. Let's see how much fun you have when I pop you and your boy for pissing me off he thought silently again while reaching around and touching the butt of his gun with his free hand. Out of the corner of his eye he noticed the extra protection wasn't there anymore, gone like a couple of ghosts he thought, and X started to think about calling Crazy but after a second he pushed the idea out of his mind. He didn't need any one protecting him, this was his corner damn it. X keyed the walkie-talkie function of his cell twice and on the third floor of the abandoned building on his corner, in a large room lit by some flood lights that caused shadows all along the outer edges, another cell chirped loudly. The only person in the large room of the condemned building was Shaniqua Williams, a sixteen-year old girl paid to be a delivery man for X on his corner. She made good money for basically sitting around all day and reading magazines, the life on easy street. The only real hassle was walking up and down the rickety old stairs, but at least it was exercise and her butt did look pretty damn good.

From the two chirps on the cell phone she knew two things. One, X made a sale of two bags of rock cocaine, and two she had to make another trip down the stairs. Shaniqua put down her National Star magazine, which proudly stated they knew where the love child of Elvis and a female space alien was living, and in an exclusive only they had, the girl would be auditioning for American Idol and was already a 20 to 1 favorite in Las Vegas. She walked across the room over to a large red tool box with a very large combination lock keeping it closed. Next to the box sat a can of gasoline and a box of matches, the insurance policy in case certain events ever took place, like a police raid or another pusher trying something. The numbered face of the lock spun easily from right to left and Shaniqua opened it pretty quickly. She pulled out two zippered bags, each one small containing even smaller bits of a white soapy looking rock. Shaniqua went to close the tool box when a hand suddenly appeared over hers and a voice sounded with a whisper from behind.

"I think it's time to close the shop my dear."

Shaniqua spun away from the voice to see a man standing in the room with her. She wasn't sure how he got up here and she really didn't care. The only fact she cared about was the one about someone besides her being up here. Shaniqua was sure X made a point about that, no one up in the room but him and her, no one! And look here, some strange white man dressed in a Metallica T-shirt. She drew in a deep breath ready to scream and go for the can of gasoline, or at least that was the plan. Yet she was suddenly sinking into the man's eyes, the black pools drawing her down and away. In a split second she changed her mind, she didn't want to go for the gasoline can. She didn't want to scream for X. The only thing Shaniqua wanted to do was to stand still and look at the beautiful man standing across from her. She was suddenly quite taken with him, maybe even more than just taken.

"I wonder what Xavier is going to do downstairs when you don't show up with the drugs."

She didn't care about X or the job anymore, everything she needed in this whole wide world was right here in the room. Shaniqua knew about love and lust, she was sixteen you know, but this was so far beyond those emotions. If the man had said run, jump out the window, and do it on fire then she would have gladly used the gasoline from the insurance policy to set herself on fire. All she wanted, the only thing she lived for it seemed, was to make this man who she just appeared a minute ago happy. A slow smile crept across her face, kind of like a three old who just noticed her daddy brought her a present home from the store.

"What do you say we find out, hmm?" The man said with a small grin. Shaniqua nodded her head slowly still smiling back at him.

Another minute ticked off the watch as X stood by watching the Charger which was waiting for the delivery. Shaniqua was really starting to piss him off, and in his present state it wasn't helping to keep him from going for his gun. And the two bitches in the car down the street, if one of them got out of that car, God help them all X thought to himself. He was so pissed he didn't even realize the fact he was grinding his teeth. There was a distinct possibility the pearly whites might disappear. Then the brakes lights on the Charger changed, shifted to the reverse lights, and that was the cue. Before it could even roll back an inch he was moving to a hidden door on the side of the run down building. X caught the look the rich fuck behind the wheel gave him and sneered, like it was his fault the delivery was all screwed up. Yeah, he was definitely going to pop a cap into that boy's ass tonight. X moved past some rotten walls, through a hole between the wall studs, and started up some rickety stairs. His mind was screaming, the first rule of Eight Ball and the corner broken. You never ever leave your corner, someone could roll by looking for stuff and if no one's there to sell it then there's no one there making money. And if you're not making money then you might not get to live, just the way it works in the hood. The old rickety stairs creaked and groaned under the weight, and stomping, from X as he crested the second floor on his way to the third floor before calling out the vault.

"Shaniqua, what the hell are you doing?" X screamed out expecting an answer.

There wasn't one.

"Listen you stupid bitch, I got customers waiting downstairs for their shit so you better move that fat ass of yours NOW!" He screamed out louder.

Again, there wasn't an answer.

When X did reach the third floor and the large open room he was ready to explode. Not only was the rich kid bitch downstairs going to catch a bullet, but this fat no account heifer was going to get one too. What he wasn't ready for was Shaniqua standing the middle of the room with a big goofy smile on her face. For a second he froze, numb from the shock, but then he saw the gas can at her feet. He looked over at the toolbox to see all the night's bags, each filled with crack, floating in fuel that was poured into the large metal container. This was a nightmare he thought, a total fucking nightmare, oh but the worst part was yet to come.

"What the fuck are you doing?" X spat at Shaniqua. She only smiled, pulled out the book of matches, and calmly pulled one from the book.

"Oh shit, don't you do it Shaniqua! Don't you dare do it bitch!" X yelled raising his gun in a single fluid motion toward the girl only it ended up pointing in the wrong direction all of the sudden.

X never saw the white dude until he was standing right in front of him, chest touching chest practically. X never saw the white dude grab the gun butt, along with his hand, and twist both sideways until the barrel of the 9mm was pointing at right at his own temple, like he was about to commit suicide or something. The white dude's grip was strong, almost crushing in fact, as X could testify to because he was quickly losing feeling in his hand and fingers. He couldn't move his arm an inch and he sure as hell wasn't about to try, no reason, he just didn't want to provoke the dude. All he did know was there was a new rule in the hood, the one where if you pulled the trigger you could get shot by your own gun.

"Hello Xavier, guess you're wondering what's going on here, eh?" The white dude said with an English accent, very prim and proper.

"Man, you got no clue who just fucked with. I'm working for Eight Ball you stupid-"X began to spit trying to sound as intimidating as he could, but something in the white dude's eyes said it wasn't working, not one word or letter.

"Does it look like Eight Ball scares me Xavier? Do I look in the least bit worried right now?" The white dude asked pushing the barrel of the gun into X's temple even more. "Maybe Eight Ball scares you? What will you tell him about all the drugs that were burned to ashes here tonight? A nice inventory from the looks of it and to know all of it will never bring a profit, oh my. Well I am sure that kind of a loss will hurt someone and their bottom line. I am also very sure Eight Ball will cut off more than a finger for all the money you lost him here tonight Xavier." The white dude remarked with a raised eyebrow and grin.

"You ain't gonna burn all that rock. You ain't that stupid!" X snapped back.

"Shaniqua sweetie," The white dude called out.

"We gonna have a cook out with hot dogs!" The girl screamed gleefully striking the match against the cover's course strike pad. It lit almost at once, the bright yellow flame bursting forth before down shifting to a deep blue.

For the second time tonight X knew the other guy was right. Even if an ounce of rock went missing it would drive Crazy D and Eight Ball into a bloodthirsty-shoot-you-twenty-times-in-the-face kind of pissed off rage. His mind began to race with fear and panic scattering thoughts and ideas until he finally pleaded. "Okay, okay. Don't burn the rock man! Anything you want, just don't burn the rock!"

"No hot dogs tonight Shaniqua, but maybe we can eat some tomorrow." The white dude said eyeing X the whole time. The girl blew the match out still smiling happily with blank eyes.

"Okay, what the hell do you want then man, my money?" X asked beaten.

The dude leaned in getting nose to nose with X. "What I want is for you to pull the trigger. Go ahead, I dare you."

"You're kidding right? No way man, no way in hell am I gonna kill myself!" X said on the verge of whining. He was truly beginning to feel terror. He always knew he could, and probably would, die pushing crack and his only hope was not to see it coming. Make the end nice, quick, and really painless. To see the gun, feel it scrape your head, was no way to die. It was too damn terrifying to X. A second rolled by and the quiet of the room heightened X's fear and panic to the point he began to hyperventilate. The gun barrel pressed even harder into his temple for emphasis as the dude spoke with a snarl, two long teeth gleaming in the low light.

"Then I want you to remember what you are feeling right now Xavier, never forget a second of it. From tonight forward this corner is mine and if I catch you setting foot on it again I will tear out your heart and put it in your mother's mailbox for her to find among her bills and shopping catalogs. There will not be a place to hide that I will not find you and there is not a person alive who can protect you from me Xavier, do you understand?"

"So, that means you're gonna let me go, right?" X asked with a forced smile answering the question with a question, which seemed the right thing to do at the time.

"Yes, I will let you go, but only after you do what I ask may you run all the way home Xavier." The white dude remarked coldly, which didn't help X feel any safer, not at all. He had no clue what he could do for a guy holding a gun to his head, but he was sure willing to try just about anything.

"Where are you going Bobby baby?"

Where the hell do you think I'm going Robert Cannon thought silently as he began to open the Charger driver side door?

The Cannon men, some of the richest in Atlanta, were known for courting only with the most beautiful women be it an actress or singer or even the occasional Pro Football Cheerleader. At this point Bobby would have sold them all for one who could just spell her name right.

"I'm getting my money back Kathy!" Bobby snapped stepping out of the car.

"It's Kasey baby." The girl said in a squeal hopping out with him.

"Kasey, Kathy, who cares really. I mean, it all starts with a K right?" Bobby said starting to walk over to the building.

Kasey trotted over, her ample bosom bouncing as she pulled at the hoody jacket, ignoring the remarks her beau just stated so nicely. "Baby, you can't be going in there, are you?"

"I have to go in there. It's where my money went." Bobby spat with frustration approaching the spot where X had disappeared into.

"Oh come on baby, it was what, maybe forty dollars. Is it worth, you know, risking our lives for forty dollars?" Kasey whined looking around fearfully.

Bobby spun around in a blur with his face was contorted into one of disgust and apparent loathing. Kasey took a step back from the look instantly recognizing the fact she had just crossed the line and hoping she wouldn't get hit. "Are you kidding me? No one and I mean no one takes Bobby Cannon's money and makes him look like a jackass. Now the plan is to go in here, kick the shit out of that street rat pusher, and get my money back. We're not in danger and we're not going to get hurt."

"I know you can beat that boy up baby, but this is the projects you know. What if someone sees us, me, down here?" Kasey whined trying to slip back into the good graces of her man.

"Then you can give them a blow job. That's what you do best, right? Just drop down and do that thing you do." Bobby said finding the secret makeshift plywood door that X went into.

"Oh stop it baby!" Kasey remarked blushing suddenly from the remark, as if it was meant to be a compliment.

"Listen Kasey, either stay her or go up with me I don't care." Bobby finally said heading into the building through the makeshift door.

It only took a microsecond for her to make a decision, and she was through the door before it could close, making sure not to touch the dirty wood with any of her perfectly tanned skin or $500 dollar jeans. Inside it took a minute for Bobby to reach the third floor scaling the steps two at a time with Kasey huffing and puffing behind clutching her purse with a death grip. At the top of the third floor they saw X standing in the middle of the room, his arms crossed on his chest, and a girl standing a few feet away.

"Hey asshole, where's my money or my rock?" Bobby demanded walking forward. Kasey instantly moved with him.

Before Bobby could make a second threat, or X could answer, Shaniqua suddenly produced the 9mm and pointed it at the pair. Kasey gave out a small scream as she saw it while Bobby froze instantly starring at the business end of the black gun.

"Now we got a party up in here, ah beep-beep, ah toot-toot!" Shaniqua screamed waving with her free hand around while holding the gun steady at the others.

"What the hell is wrong with her? What the hell is going on here?" Bobby asked X.

"She's not the one you need to worry about stupid!" X snarled.

Kasey, who was taking refuge behind her beau Bobby, never heard the man walk up behind her. She was too busy being scared at the girl waving around the large handgun at her and her lover. She did, however, feel his presence. Almost all at once she felt an overwhelming pressure on her neck, like something was about to slowly caress it with a long sensual bite. Kasey exhaled with a small gasp and slowly turned to see the man, or better yet his chest, and the Metallica T-shirt he wore. She couldn't see the muscles, but she knew they were there, and all of the sudden she wanted to touch them. There was an indescribable need to do whatever the man asked her to do, whatever he commanded.

Lost in the wave of lust was the room, the girl with the gun, and her very rich beau Bobby.

The poor man being held captive turned around when Shaniqua locked eyes with someone behind him. Bobby first saw his present girlfriend standing like a zombie by a strange man with a dull look in her eyes. He was about to ask just what the hell was going on when X answered the question for him. "That's who we have to worry about white boy!" he spat.

"Listen man, just give me my forty dollars and I'm out of here! And don't try to make trouble because I'm not into that shit, understand?" Bobby said watching with a shocked look as Kasey slowly reached out with a finger toward the stranger.

"Sorry Robert, but the money is gone." The man stated flatly, with a nice English accent.

"Fuck it, keep the money. We're out of here!" Bobby spat while watching Kasey's fingers creep slowly closer to the stranger's chest.

"Now Robert, wouldn't it be stupid to get shot over the sum of forty dollars." The man stated and there was something in his words, his tone that said getting shot was more than likely going to happen if he went for the door.

The guy was right Bobby thought. It wasn't worth getting shot over forty damn dollars, just give it up. But forcing him to stick around like some prisoner, now that's what really pissed him off so bad.

"What the hell do you want, huh?" Bobby yelled at the stranger pulling Kasey back away from the man before she could touch him. She actually looked like she was about to touch the man's chest with her finger for the love of God. Damn, he needed a new chick.

"In three minutes I need you to create a little diversion for me Robert, nothing much, just a quick run. I do require something special for this task though." The strange man said with a cold smile.

Then the click of the hammer of the 9mm being drawn back and cocked sounded through the room sending a shiver down spines. Bobby turned to see Shaniqua suddenly serious, the distant look gone from her eyes and replaced with a mean one, a stare of purposeful intent. She pointed the gun at his head with a rock steady hand and snarled.

"It's time to get naked boys and girls."

Bobby was about to tell the girl to just go ahead and shoot him because there was no way in hell he was going to strip, but then he felt a rustle next to him and turned to see Kasey standing naked as the day she was born all the while still starring at the strange man. Her hoody top, pants, and g-string pooled around her feet. Bobby turned back to see Shaniqua beginning to unbutton her jeans and from over his shoulder he heard X chuckle. "Better get to stripping white boy because I sure as hell ain't fighting that white man over there for my clothes." Bobby and X turned back to the man and whatever fight or anger there was in them simply disappeared...along with their clothes.

Approximately three minutes later the white Cadillac rolled up to a slow stop by the corner and a rather upset, and very large, Crazy D looked out the driver's side window for any sign of his 'employee' X. Nothing, not a sign of the little bitch D thought angrily as he turned looking for the extra protection he arranged for the corner, and again there was nothing there. That ember of anger began to blossom into a full fledge fire in Crazy's brain as he climbed out of the Caddy to stand on the sidewalk just a few feet from the street lamp. He could almost guess what happened to the extra protection. That good for nothing rat X that ran this corner probably thought he didn't need the extra protection, that he could handle anything on his own. Who cares if it was a direct order from Eight Ball? Crazy just wondered how X got the two guards to leave, but in the end it really didn't matter. Man, oh man, was Eight Ball going to kill that little trash talking wanna-be drug dealer bitch. X was a smalltime pusher with dreams of taking over the world, just like some small ass Tony Montana or something, but in the end all that dreaming was just going to get the fool killed. The large man looked at the building where the vault was and wondered if X wasn't up there trying to get him some with Shaniqua. Then he fumed more about X and his missing presence from the corner. In the hood Crazy D grew up learning the golden rule, you want to take over then you better be strong enough and man enough to do it. X wasn't either, and he didn't have the street rep to run a gang or even a Boy Scout troop with bad intentions. Eight Ball held his turf because he had no problem blowing your head off, and everyone in the hood knew it which gave him his street cred. The only thing X would control would be the way the bullet killed him, from the front like a man or the back like a little bitch. And the way he felt right now it was going to be from the back with a large caliber, the same one he was strapped with. Crazy D reached down with his meaty right hand to grab the handle of the large 45 caliber handgun in his waistband, but just as his fingers touched the grip of the gun the door to the abandoned building flew open and almost off its hinges. Crazy pulled his pistol on pure instinct, his finger on the trigger, but then he stopped as he couldn't believe his eyes at what was happening.

They stood huddled together in the cold, naked, by the plywood sheet acting as a door to the abandoned building. They didn't move, talk, or utter a single sound. They simply waited for the man behind them to give a signal, what that signal was to be no one had a clue, but they waited still. Bobby's eyes shifted back and forth looking for the right moment to make a break for it, once he noticed X doing the same thing. Bobby wasn't sure what he was going to do with no clothes and no money and no keys for the car, but he sure wasn't hanging around here. Kasey wasn't moving while standing next to him. She was still walking like a zombie and mumbling about the dude in the Metallica T-shirt for God's sake! Here they were butt naked with no money and no car keys and no way to make it home and this bimbo was crying about missing the asshole that put them in this unfolding disaster. That's it, game over. Bobby was done, through with the whole damn thing. He was going to make a break for it, I mean what's the worst that can happen he considered. The dude gets off a shot and hits him in the back, which was a lot better than standing next to some naked crying chick in the dark. He readied to blow through the make shift door with one blow, and then the desire for escape was replaced by something deeper and more pressing. Something he couldn't describe later to the police who found him, or even later to his father's lawyers.

All at once he felt afraid, so afraid it literally took his breath away. There was something behind them in the dark, something evil and vile. He could feel its hot breath on his neck burning the flesh there and his mind involuntarily conjured images of animals with long sharp teeth tearing flesh and breaking bone, his flesh and bone. It wanted to kill him, to rend him limb from limb. Bobby never felt this before, a stark terror so deep it made his legs quiver, and the weird part was he wasn't sure exactly what it was that was scaring him. Part of his mind wanted to look back, to steal a glance over his shoulder at the thing behind him in the dark. The other part just wanted to run away as fast as possible because the thing would chase him all the way home, even into his bedroom. A small cry caught Bobby's attention and he glanced over to see Kasey no longer sobbing about the man in the Metallica T-shirt. She was chanting over and over a prayer for the thing not to kill her. He looked over to X and the man was literally white, it was the first time Bobby had ever seen a black man turn white, but the man was scared just as bad as the rest of them. Bobby looked forward again while the terror grew, pressed harder on him, every passing second. He was close to screaming out for help, or just screaming to let the fear out, and then the thing lunged for him out of the dark. It came with claws barred, teeth gnashing air, and howling like a wild beast. Bobby didn't hesitate, he bolted for the door with X and Kasey and Shaniqua right behind. The plywood gave easy as the arc-sodium light from the street lamps suddenly flooded the small room.

The two white kids were first out of the door then followed closely by X and Shaniqua Crazy carefully noted mentally. All four were naked and not a one cared to try and cover up a single bouncing or flopping body part. Crazy thought the white girl had a nice rack, but it didn't compare to Shaniqua's naked fanny going up and down like two black muscular pistons. D might have to have a talk with that girl, show her what it meant to 'ride' the Crazy train, know what I mean. He was so taken with the display of naked flesh he never saw or even felt the approach of the strange man coming up from behind on the street, around the car. The man's arm reached out, flowing straight through the side panel of the Caddy for a moment before slipping out and becoming solid again as he closed in. When the man had reached just behind Crazy D his hand reached forward and out for the thick neck of the man, the hand clamping onto the stocky appendage like a solid steel trap. In one, unbelievably vicious, move the man lifted the large frame of Crazy right off the ground by the neck with one hand. Crazy got a second to take a breath before the pressure from the grip paralyzed him with mind numbing pain. He couldn't see who had yanked on him or where his gun went pin wheeling into the dark as all his limbs and hands spasm from the abrupt pain.

"Good evening Mr. Darrell Washington, also known as Crazy D. You are Crazy D I presume?" A voice with an English accent said right behind his ear.

"Let me go you asshole!" Crazy spat trying to limply reach back and grab the hand holding him.

"I can tell you with absolute assurance that is not going to happen for a few moments Darrell. You don't mind me calling you Darrell, do you? I hate to use nicknames when having a serious conversation." The accent remarked.

The pain from the hand grinding into the sides of his neck squirmed into Darrell's brain like fiery snakes causing his thoughts to scatter. He couldn't think, only react with a sudden growing anger at being attacked.

"Fuck you! Let me go!" Darrell screamed

"You know Darrell, for someone so big who has such a terrible reputation, you are truly nothing more than a mouse" The accent remarked flatly.

"Let me go and we'll see how long you last bitch!" Darrell screamed again.

Suddenly the accent took a large step forward propelling a powerless Darrell ahead of him in a rush. The street lamp post abruptly appeared in his haze filled vision and Darrell gasped as he was powerless to stop the impact of hitting it square right down the middle of his body. Pain exploded fresh in his mind from the crash of hitting the metal pole as the accent spoke low with a sudden menacing growl in his ear making sure to get his point across.

"There are two ways to do this Darrell, the hard way and the dead way, because contrary to popular belief Eight Ball is no longer the meanest animal in this neighborhood. There is a new monster walking the streets here in the Laurel and it is ME!"

"Yeah, just who the hell are you?" Darrell winced.

"Oh you know who I am Darrell, I'm Mr. Black."

"That name don't mean shit to me dude! Now le-" The large dangling man tried to sneer when he suddenly screamed from a sharp squeeze applied by the accent. The pain flooded his brain anew. Blackness began to circle his vision from the edges of his sight. The accent hissed into Darrell's ear and for the first time tonight the large man felt a twinge of fear. This could be it, the end of the whole damn match. At that exact moment the fear took over and Darrell was about to scream for the accent to stop, for the love of God to just let go!

"I'm not going to kill my messenger Darrell so stop thinking that nonsense. I need you to pass along something to Eight Ball, and I need you to remember what I say. Do you think you can do that Darrell?" Mr. Black asked.

"Yeah, whatever man!" Darrell screamed trying to hold onto the fear. His brain was on fire, his neck was about to break, and he was pretty sure he was about to pass out.

"Then give Eight Ball this message, word for word. The Laurel is no longer his to control. I'm here to take over his businesses; any and everything he does in the Laurel will become mine after this night. Anyone thinking otherwise will not see me coming, just like J-Rock and Ice from the drug house last night. Eight Ball's days are numbered as well as anyone else associated with him. Your friend X is going to tell everyone in the Laurel anyone dealing drugs better stop because the consequences will be deadly for them if they continue. Bobby and his girlfriend will tell everyone outside of the city to bypass this place if they come down here to buy their drugs, unless they want to end up like we did, naked and scared half to death. It is over Darrell. Eight Ball's time has come to an end and so has yours Crazy so pack up your things and leave with your lives because there is no stopping me from taking over!" The accent stated flatly.

"Eight Ball's gonna fuck you up man!" Darrell hissed just seconds away from passing out.

"That I highly doubt Darrell, but for now our little meeting here is done. Remember Crazy, leave and never come back!" The accent hissed one last time.

Crazy was about to say something, maybe a taunt or maybe not, when the hand holding him up just disappeared. The world spun as free of support he fell to the ground in lump, his arms and legs numb and not under his control at all as he flailed with all four like an overturned cockroach. A minute passed as Crazy let the pain from his neck subside before he gained his feet and stumbled for the Cadillac's open window. He held onto the open portal for support as he looked around for the accent. There was nothing though, nothing except the cold dark and the mist from his breath floating just in front of his face. Darrel cursed loudly once, something to effect of the accent performing of an act of self-gratification on him as he entered the Cadillac. Crazy reached over for the brown paper sack that should have been on the seat next to him, and felt nothing but cold air. That sack was his life, all six thousand dollars of it, the night's second take from all the corners in Eight Ball's territory. He looked over with a wince of pain from his bruised neck to see the brown sack full of money gone.

"Aw shit!" Crazy exclaimed knowing full well what Eight Ball was going to do about the missing money. It would be a tough choice to decide what was going to make Eight Ball more upset, the fact that X's corner wasn't making money or that all of the money was gone.

Yeah, this was going to be a real toss-up?

Mondays usually meant a lot of running around for Leland, what with getting ready for the week and all. He was out in the neighborhoods and projects making a show of force you could say instead of sitting on his ratty old couch. This was the day when he setup meetings with neighborhood civic leaders, set times to see the gang members he had pegged for conversion, and just generally getting his personal stuff together for the uphill battle of the week. Trying to pull a man out of the street gangs was a lot harder than it was to get in one and that was the Lord's truth. You only had to face the gang in a 'jump in', the ritual of beating the hell out of a prospective member to test their worthiness, but getting out you had to face the whole neighborhood and its wrath. Every day you had to deal with the people who called you a traitor, the ones who spit on you, and of course there were the death threats. Leland knew about the threats all too well, he had even survived a rather vicious attempt on his life one night while walking home from work. Some of his old 'friends' had tried to cut his throat and might have succeeded if not for a lone beat cop, one Otz Renfroe, who happened by. He was a good cop and one hell of a shot. Renfroe got a medal for shooting the knife hand of the guy who was trying to kill Leland. Now, seven years later, both had the goal of trying to save what they could from the projects, both were committed to stopping the drugs and both wanted to end the gangs in the Laurel. Three years ago he was joined in that fight by Stephanie Jackson and the trio made a formidable force. She took the girls, he took the boys, and Renfroe took the ones no one could save. Information flowed both ways between Stephanie and him and Renfroe, it always had, that was until last night when the man dressed in black showed up. He wanted to talk about the man in black some more with Stephanie, which is why Grammy Martha was watching Wilma tonight. As a matter of fact the old matriarch jumped at the offer cackling with joy.

Leland rose up from his spot on the couch next to Stephanie and walked into the kitchen while calling out to his guest "You want a drink Ken?"

"What I really want is to go home and catch some sleep man!" The boy shot back from the easy chair in the room.

"I'll take one Lee while you're up." Stephanie said with a smile.

"That's one coke on the rocks coming up for the beautiful lady!" Leland smiled walking into the kitchen with a quick step. "You sure you don't want anything Ken?"

There wasn't a response from the living room and with Leland's mind already preoccupied from previous events he didn't give the silence to his joke or question a second thought. All in all this wasn't the usual Monday routine for the street preacher, not after what had gone down the night before with Wilma getting hurt, the house exploding, and the man dressed in black disappearing from the destruction. Leland had seen the man walk right into the house, right through the front door like a ghost, and that shock was quickly followed by gunfire and finally the explosion. What kept blowing his mind was Wilma and how the little girl had been trapped inside the house when it was destroyed, which in reality meant there shouldn't be a lot of the little girl left, but that wasn't the case. Wilma was perfectly okay at home with Grammy, and it was all due to the mysterious man dressed in black. He had suddenly appeared behind Leland cradling the body of Wilma like a loving parent, not a scratch on either one. When Renfroe had called earlier Leland didn't say a thing about the man, just kept to the story that was already out there. The street preacher picked out a cola from his old fridge, opened it, and took a heavy pull filling his mouth. He started to drink while walking back into the darkened living room. A second later most of the coke was sprayed all over the room in a shower out of Leland's mouth from seeing the reason no one was talking.

Alexander had stood quietly hidden in the shadows of room for the last thirty minutes watching and listening to the two men and Stephanie talk about what had happened last night at what they called a crack house. What was about to take place did not sit well with the vampire, which is why it took thirty minutes for him to appear, but in the end Alexander knew it was necessary. This strategy he had to save Wilma, the plan which he had worked on all day and tonight, would need to remain a secret and as such he could not share it with the three here. He had to lie to them for their own protection Alexander told himself, for Wilma's protection. And yet he still needed information from all three to have this plan work, he had to draw them in with subterfuge and involve them with falseness so he could learn what was needed to see his scheme to fruition. Lying, oh how Alexander hated that most of his old human qualities. This had to be done he told himself and it had to begin tonight if he was to save Wilma. Therefore, when Leland rose to go and get a drink he had decided to make his presence known by stepping out of the shadows but he wasn't expecting the 'depth' of the response he'd receive when the man came back into the room a minute later. Kenneth though he knew would react just the way he did, completely shutting down and simply staring in fear while

Stephanie looked at him in amazement. Leland showering him with soda pop via his mouth in such a nice plume effect was not necessary, at all. Maybe I need to rethink how I meet people in this day and age he thought as he smiled at the street preacher.

"Is this how you usually greet your guest Leland?" The vampire asked.

"The ones who come right out of the wall, yeah I do. The whole thing's like a ritual." Leland shot back with an exclamation.

"What...what do you want man? You here to kill us or something man?" Kenneth stuttered finally while trying to crawl back through the recliner to get away.

"Stop it Kenneth!" Stephanie hissed at the boy while rising from her spot on the couch. Leland wanted to scream for her to stop as she approached the man in black but his voice was locked tight in his chest. "Please excuse Ken sir. He's not as mature as the rest of us. So you seem to know our names, maybe you can give us yours?"

"My name is Alexander" He answered still smiling.

Stephanie smiled a little wider and remarked oddly, like she was suddenly infatuated with the man. Leland caught the whole scene, took it in, and felt a sudden tinge of jealousy as she spoke. "I like that name, it sounds very regal."

Leland walked right up next to Stephanie to stand behind her, if it was an act of chivalry protecting his lady or showing a rival that this was his territory no one could be really sure. "Listen Alex, next time why don't you use the door like regular people, even though you're not really regular people and all. By the way, what are you?"

"Lee!" Stephanie squealed with embarrassment.

Yet Alexander simply brushed her off with a wave of his hand and a nod. "No Stephanie, it is quite all right. I came here tonight seeking information and counsel from Leland and Kenneth. I did not mean to frighten anyone and I am sorry for doing so."

"Yeah right big man. Your just here looking for information?" Kenneth mocked with a whimper.

"Yes I am, and I need the kind of intelligence only you can provide me." Alexander answered. "I need details on the men from last night and the night before, specifically their tasks and what they have to do with the drugs around here."

"And why do you want to know that?" Stephanie asked.

"I have been asked to end a certain danger for a friend and to complete said agreement I need information pertaining to the drug operations around the Laurel." Alexander responded.

"You got a 'what'?" Kenneth asked back with saucer sized eyes.

"He's going to take down Eight Ball." Leland answered with sudden realization.

"No way, he ain't really going to war with Eight Ball?" Kenneth asked Leland before turning to Alexander whining. "Why would you do that?"

"It's because of Wilma isn't it?" Stephanie asked rhetorically with a sudden gleam to her eyes, as if she saw everything for what is was now. "You've been watching over her, keeping her safe."

The room fell silent for a second as Stephanie's statement sank in, and with the lie he was about to tell stinging his tongue Alexander replied keeping eye contact with all in the room. "I have done a very poor job Stephanie. The world has changed so much, grown so much over these last years. It is much harder for one such as myself to stay hidden these days. The incidents last night and the night before will certainly signal to the men who flood the Laurel with drugs that someone is trying to take over, and I'm afraid they think that someone is me. I am also afraid they know about you and Wilma Stephanie. I never intended for this to happen, for everything to spiral so out of control, but I promise you I will not step away from keeping Wilma safe."

The room was quiet for a moment as Alexander's reply touched Stephanie, made her smile just a little more before replying. "Thank you,"

"So what's your plan?" Leland asked quietly.

"Plan, who cares about a plan, I still want to know what the hell he is!" Kenneth whined from the back of the room.

"KEN!" Stephanie practically screamed.

"Yeah his plan, Alex wouldn't have come here risking a meeting with plain old us without a plan, right?" Leland asked her quickly, puffing out his chest and acting like he had been disrespected, and all but ignoring what the vampire had just said almost. Stephanie shot him a mad glance, probably thinking this was some male showing of bravado, like two dogs peeing on the same fire hydrant but it wasn't. Leland wanted, needed, to show his surprise guest that he could hold his own and that he wasn't scared, well not a whole lot anyway.

Alexander smiled inwardly. He admired the street preacher for standing up to him, for protecting the woman he loved which is why he hated lying to him. "I have a plan yes, kind of simple but effective none the less. I do not intend to stop the flow of drugs in the city, that being a task too large for me to handle, but I can and will stop them from flowing into the Laurel."

The statement quieted the room again, just like before, for a minute but soon Stephanie stepped forward shaking her head. "And you think taking out Eight Ball is going to accomplish this? Dealers are a time a dozen in the projects Alex, as soon as Eight Ball goes down another three will take his place."

Before Alexander could respond though Leland turned to her, his eyes filled with excitement. He was slowly but surely catching on to this false idea Alexander was giving them with and thankfully the need to prove himself had passed...for now. "Not if you take out Eight Ball and the men supplying him! You bring down the whole thing and there's nothing left for someone, anyone to take over."

"What?" Stephanie and Kenneth remarked wildly with utter disbelief in unison.

"Do you know why Attila the Hun was able to take so many cities without so much as a sword stroke? The fear from his reputation was enough to drive the fight out of most leaving no one willing to stand in his way." Alexander explained.

"Oh, "Stephanie exclaimed suddenly catching on to what was being said," You're going to do an Eight Ball to the drug suppliers!"

The vampire blinked in bewilderment for a second before speaking again. "I do not have a clue what that means, but if it suggest taking down every dealer and pusher on the corners then it is somewhat appropriate I think. My plan is to make this ground, the Laurel, cost so much in blood and lost money that no one will want it. The reputation of the man in black will scare anyone and everyone into thinking twice before setting foot in the Laurel."

"And you're doing all this for her little girl? I don't know about them, but I sure as hell don't trust you!" Kenneth called out.

"KEN!" Stephanie and Leland screamed together this time at the boy. The screaming of the boy's name in unison was becoming quite amusing Alexander thought as he spoke.

"I have every intention of keeping Wilma safe, and due to my mistake of attracting attention to her that means I have to shut off the drugs flowing into the Laurel Kenneth. Trust is something we will all have to work out our own away from this room. It took trusting all of you a little for me to come here tonight. I need information on the men I disposed of last night, information only you have knowledge of. I trust you to give me that information Kenneth." Alexander said.

"You mean 'killed' right?" Kenneth shot back, his voice mixed with anger.

"Kenny!" Stephanie and Leland yelled once more at the boy, but Alexander was already answering.

"Yes Kenneth I killed those men, you're so called friends, and I understand your pain but that is not what you need to think about right now. You have a very important choice to make at the moment, two paths lay before you. Choose to either help me stop the men who poison these projects or you can burn with them. I'll only ask once and you must live with your choice for the rest of your life. "

The room fell silent as a certain revelation sunk in to Kenneth, Stephanie, and Leland. This man in black was for real. He had every intention on not only bringing down Eight Ball but anyone and everyone associated with him. The street preacher and Stephanie still were not sure what to make of this man but anyone who was against Eight Ball was on their team. Another one in the room was having a harder time with his decision though. Kenneth moaned slightly and stood up quickly.

"Come on man! Now I got three of you crazy mothers wanting me to talk." Kenneth spat.

"Why won't you tell us what we need to know Kenneth? You're acting like saving the Laurel isn't so high up on your list my man." Leland suddenly countered.

"Why did you have to kill Ice and J-Rock? He didn't have to kill my friends!" Kenneth cried quickly, his voice raising an octave. He felt outnumbered and began moving toward the door.

"Ice and J-Rock meant to harm Wilma, she was just lucky he was there to stop them from doing something, anything to my daughter you fool!" Stephanie shot back.

Just like the night before Alexander looked into the eyes of the young Kenneth and held him there by the door with his stare. "I cannot say I am sorry for what I did to either man Kenneth and I cannot say for sure they deserved to die the way the way did. All I know is they meant to harm Wilma and I was not going to allow that to happen." Alexander said with a firm resolution.

Leland quickly moved over to the door cutting off Kenneth's escape route. He didn't want to scare the boy any more than he was already, but then again Leland didn't want him leaving either. "Okay, come on guys, let's just calm down and get it under control all right. Think we can do that?"

"Aww hell no, I'm not talking while the mouth's in here defending the guy who killed my friends!" Kenneth shouted at Leland.

The mood in the room was quickly slipping away into uncontrolled anger, and Leland tried to think of a way to just get everyone to calm down. Then suddenly Alexander solved everything in his own special way, a way that Leland would become accustomed to seeing over the next week. To the point and direct wouldn't begin to describe how the man in black handled the situation in Leland's living room.

"You can give me the information I need two ways Kenneth, you can tell me freely or I can resort to other methods." Alexander growled quieting the room.

"What other methods?" Kenneth said trying to deepen his voice to hide the fear in it.

The vampire was suddenly across the room in a blink of an eye standing over Kenneth, staring down into his eyes. "Believe me when I say it is much more involved and thus extremely uncomfortable." Alexander whispered low and with an obscene amount of certainty.

The room was silent again, but just for a second or two, no more. Whatever emotion drove the people in the room seemed to drift away. The anger in Kenneth's body and voice disappeared as he whispered a quick question. "Were they really going to hurt Wilma?"

"If there were any other way to ensure little Wilma's safety Kenneth I would have taken that option. Now please, will you answer my questions?" Alexander answered, the tone of his voice softening now that Ken was calming.

"I just wished it had come down to something different is all. What do you want to know?" Kenneth offered quietly with a nod after a moment.

"First, let's have a seat, and then we discuss what I need to know." Alexander said motioning to the couch for everyone to sit. The two men and Stephanie moved slowly to the couch and sat while the vampire stood and talked.

"As you already know I have been protecting Wilma from the perils of the projects, and as last night showed, I have drawn more attention than I would like to have. I do not want to hurt anyone, but I am more than sure whoever is running the drugs through here will not stop if I ask nicely. That leaves me with only one choice and for that I will need information on the men who deal the drugs." Alexander explained.

"So what do you want to know?" Leland asked hoping to push the conversation along. In honesty, there was a small twinge of excitement inside his stomach. He wasn't going to trust Alexander fully yet, but something told him the weapon needed to bring down Eight Ball had just settled into his lap and that he could live with for the moment.

"I need to know the infrastructure of the group. How do the drugs get in and where do they come from?" Alexander asked.

"No one knows that stuff man, Ice and Eight Ball are the only ones who knew when and where the drugs came from, and now Ice's only speaking with God and Eight Ball never comes down here anymore." Kenneth remarked.

"Are you kidding Kenny?" Leland spoke up before Alexander could continue, his voice filled with disappointment.

"No way man," Kenneth said looking to both men," no one knows Eight Ball's supplier, not even Eight Ball himself probably. Only one soldier was allowed to pick up the product for sale on the corner and that was J-Rock. He went to the house that's in a bunch of pieces now by himself, always by himself, and came back later with the stuff the corners was supposed to sell. Ice would only deal with him!"

"That's crazy!" Stephanie spat but Alexander just let a small smile out and spoke up.

"No, it's actually quite brilliant. If you had a secret, the best way to keep it is not to tell anyone what that secret is right? Our man Eight Ball is just making sure there is no way to trace anything back to him, the less strings to cut the better if the time comes to protect that secret. I am sure there is a man between Eight Ball and the people who bring in the drugs, right Kenneth?"

"Yeah, I'm pretty sure but no one knows who that is, not even Eight Ball. Those guys are ghost man."

"So you're telling us no one knows how Eight Ball gets the drugs? The drugs just magically appear or something! That's not the way it worked when I ran with the Disciples." Leland asked with a measure of incredulity. Stephanie reached over and squeezed his hand trying to calm the street preacher.

"Yeah, well that's the way it works these days' man!" Kenneth shot back.

"Okay, so how are we going to stop the drugs from coming in if we don't know who brings them in?" Leland asked.

"Simple, we go after Eight Ball and the suppliers' reason for bringing the drugs in, the money." Alexander said with the same smile from a second before.

"What?" Leland and Kenneth said as one. Really, did they practice speaking in unison like that the vampire thought?

Stephanie though was onto the next step of the process, way ahead of the boys sitting next to her. She gave Leland's hand a quick squeeze while speaking. "We're going to rock the boat so much that Eight Ball's suppliers will lose a ton of money and pay us a visit."

"What?" Leland and Kenneth said in unison one more time, hopefully the last.

"In easier terms, I assume that a lot of money comes in due to the drug trade in the Laurel and surrounding areas. So, then I can assume further that if enough of a disturbance to this flow of money is made that Eight Ball himself will come down to see what is happening to his business. That is when and where I will take care of him." Alexander stated.

"And once he's gone we go after the supplier's, right?" Stephanie asked.

"Yes, I think the suppliers will show their heads then and that is all I will need to convince them to stay out of the Laurel." Alexander stated coldly.

"Wow, Armageddon, it sounds so easy." Leland whispered suddenly seeing how this whole 'plan' was going to work.

"What are you going to do about the guys in the middle?" Kenneth asked abruptly.

"What middle men?" Stephanie asked confused a little by the question.

"The guys like Crazy D mouth, the ones who run the corners. You know there's a lot more than just Eight Ball to take on here." Kenneth pointed out.

"That is the great thing about fear Kenneth, it fans with little force. I have watched many a city fall with no more than a vile reputation so I am sure keeping people away from here will not be that hard. I am convinced the middle men lack the metal to come here and deal on the corners after this week has passed." Alexander wagered.

"Okay, what about the addicts here? What are you going to about the junkies?"

"We have community shelters and churches that can help out with them Ken, but the first thing we have to do is drive the dealers and pushers out of the neighborhood. You can't get off the junk when it's right outside your door son." Leland answered.

"Man you're going to start a war with a bunch of mean-ass people you know, you ready for what that brings?" Kenneth pointed out again, his body language saying he was running out arguments and road blocks.

"I am no stranger to war Kenneth and if one has to be waged then that is what will be done. I would greatly appreciate any other way, any other choice than this, but we do not have another option at the moment." Alexander said.

"What about you? Are you ready?" Kenneth asked turning to Leland.

"I'm ready to do what has to be done," was the street preacher single answer.

"What's so special about Wilma?" Kenneth asked suddenly ignoring the death stare Stephanie was throwing at him with her eyes.

"That is something I am unable to explain to you Kenneth because I really can't explain it to myself at the moment. Something inside just tells me to do this and I have never been one to ignore the inner voices if you know what I mean." Alexander said hoping the boy understood what he was trying to say.

"Yeah, I catch what you saying man." Kenneth said with a nod. "I just had to hear it."

"Good," Alexander responded feeling a small bond form with the young man," because I am going to need your help in keeping her safe."

The room was quiet for a second or two then Leland spoke up asking a question. "What if there was another way, someone who might know a way around Eight Ball? That way you wouldn't have to go after the kids on the corners."

Suddenly Kenneth stood up as if a lightning bolt had just hit him and his face had the look of someone who had just realized an important secret was about to get let out of the bag. "No way man, don't you say it!" He snapped.

Alexander stood motionless watching everything closely, every word and body movement. No one knew about his sight, how he could see people and their past, and right now it was starting to show him some things about the people in the room. Confirming deductions and revealing truths as he simply watched and answered as needed

"Tell us what?" Stephanie yelled without realizing it.

"I wouldn't say a thing Kenny," Leland said slowly with purpose trying to calm the young man, "but this may help us and save so many people."

"Don't do it man, you gave me your word. Don't do it man, please!" Kenneth asked, pleaded with Leland.

The street preacher looked at the boy and one could easily see the internal struggle he faced. Cover for a friend or tell the truth. In the end Leland did the only thing his conscious and soul would allow him to do. "There's a boy named Chico that Kenny knows who makes special runs for Eight Ball."

"No way," Stephanie said with a shake of her head in disgust, "he's just a Puerto Rican hood rat who talks a lot of trash.

There is no way Eight Ball's ever had that boy make a run for him."

"He does too make runs for Eight Ball mouth." Kenneth remarked snarling. Everyone in the room could easily see his dilemma and after a second it seemed he chose Leland over his friend. "Chico makes runs that are off the books, special runs to make sure Eight Ball gets a little before the product rolls out to the corners."

"Eight Ball's been skimming off the top, getting ready to make a move to take over the Laurel for his own? That's gutsy, only I guess he didn't count on Alex here." Stephanie remarked flatly.

"How do you know this Kenneth?" Alexander asked giving his attention to the youth carefully, still looking for certain signs in his body language.

"I heard him once trying to impress some girls by saying he had made special runs for Eight Ball and his supplier a while back, made it sound like he was going to be important when Eight Ball became a major player." Kenneth explained sounding somewhat reluctant. No one took note that he may have tried a little too hard at selling his emotion.

"I know this is hard to do Kenneth, but in the end it will help the Laurel and its people like Leland said." Alexander stated trying to help the boy give up the necessary information, and maybe clear his conscience…maybe a little too much sympathy.

"Yeah, still don't make me feel any better." Kenneth whispered as the room grew quiet.

"You know Leland's right Kenneth. You know we need to go and visit this Chico tonight while it is still early and see what he knows or does not know. Will you help us find out where he is?" Alexander asked.

"It's time to step up and break free of the gangs Kenneth, become your own man." Leland said as the full attention and weight of the moment turned to Kenneth. He took a moment to reply, a long silent one.

"Let me go make some calls, I'll get the 411 and be right back." Kenneth told them and then bolted for the door before anyone could tell him different. Alexander starred at the boy intently as he left, his eyes never wavering or leaving Kenneth's back. The special window showing him things about Ken he had already assumed and was now confirmed.

"I'm going to check on Grammy and Wilma. Don't plan anything till I get back, not a thing!" Stephanie said running out the door behind Kenneth excited.

And now he was alone with him, the man who saved Wilma not once but twice. The man Stephanie, the woman he loved, couldn't stop talking about. Leland took a deep breath not really sure if he liked this. All he could see as he looked down and away was the carpet as he sat in awkward silence not really wanting to meet Alexander's gaze. The street preacher didn't look up to see the vampire starring out the door as if it wasn't there. If he did, he might have noticed how he was locked onto something or someone. He might have recognized the look on Alexander's face, the kind of look someone would show if they just had a hand turn into a full house in poker. Instead, Leland sat quietly not knowing what or how to talk to Alexander, and then the vampire spoke up. The suddenness of the silence being broken caused him to start for a second as he looked up to see Alexander staring at him.

"I'm sorry, what did you say?" Leland asked.

"I said I met him once." Alexander remarked pointing to the wall. Leland followed the pointing finger over to the far wall to where a solitary crucifix hung. The light from the lamps gave an eerie shadow effect to the face of Jesus. It took a second for the statement to register and when it did, Leland felt the pit of his stomach drop away as if he had just stepped off the side of a high-rise building. He turned back to the vampire with a stunned wide-eyed look.

"How old are you?" Leland asked in a voice filled with a dry cracking sound.

"If I told you the truth you wouldn't believe one word." Alexander said sitting down next to Leland on the couch.

"Why don't you try me?" Leland remarked.

Alexander looked deep into Leland's eyes without blinking. He wished he had met the street preacher in his past before the loss of his precious Roxanna. The pain of even remembering was like a weight strapped to his back, his soul felt torn and tattered from the inside out, and what strength he had was sucked away. Leland might have talked him out of the decision that took her life and the life of his son by the hand of his rival Cassander. Maybe the street preacher could have given him solace when the generals screamed for power and land and drove him to do such brutality? Nevertheless, that was so long ago and there was nothing he could do, or anyone else, to go back and change things.

"Why do you believe in him so?" Alexander asked still looking at Leland.

"Who, Jesus Christ?"

"Yes, the one from Nazareth."

"Because Jesus is the way to peace and love...because he can forgive us of all our crimes...even when we can't forgive ourselves for things we've done." Leland smiled somewhat sadly, as if the truth were painful.

"That's what some of the others said, those who followed him." Alexander responded.

"You were really there? You really met my Lord and Savior Jesus Christ?"

"Yes I did Leland, and I was very taken with him. I was passing through a small village outside of Jerusalem at night when there was this mass of people that came walking by, some running to keep up. He had stopped by the side of the road someone whispered and then I saw him waiting while people ran to his side. Some kissed his hands, some kissed his feet, and others only cried when they saw his form before them."

Leland smiled more and chuckled, "I would have done the same if I saw him."

"He looked rather calm as I watched from afar but I could tell he hated the attention, as if it were wasted energy. I hated men and women throwing themselves prostrate in front of me as well. To pass by people tossing flowers and such in my way was so...silly. I came to better a people and culture and all it seemed anyone wanted was to glorify me." Alexander sighed shaking his head.

"You were pretty important at one time huh Alex?" Leland asked now enthralled by the words the vampires spoke. The rabbit hole was large and the street preacher had jumped into it with both feet.

"Some might say that, but this man Jesus, he was more than I had been. When he spoke you could feel a calm come over the crowd of people, like a thirsty man who has just seen a crystal blue lake, and this mass of humanity sat and listened. His voice charmed the people's ears and his words put troubled souls to ease. There was no sense of danger with him. Later that night I approached close enough to just touch his hand and I couldn't. He was asleep only a few feet from me and I was in awe. I could see why people believed in him, faith came so easy and with no extra burden to your soul or heart with him."

"That's the gospel truth. What I wouldn't give to just hear him speak." Leland whispered.

"Careful what you wish for Leland, I asked for something once and now I sometimes regret ever mentioning a thing." Alexander said with a sour full tone suddenly.

Leland was too astounded to note the warning as he sat there in silence for a moment before Alexander asked one last question. "You think of Wilma as yours?"

"Yes," the street preacher whispered just letting his guard drop to speak from his soul, "she'll knock your socks off with how smart she is and she's just as beautiful as her mother. Any man would be so damn proud to call her his daughter...all except one."

The vampire sighed and nodded thinking of his son, "maybe all she needs is the one who thinks so much of her to say it to her."

The street preacher heard the words but barely registered a single one. He felt his heart lifted by Alexander's story, and he still was wishing for just the smallest chance to touch his lord and savior when a heavy paper bag landed in his lap. For a second he wasn't sure what it was, but then Leland opened the brown paper and his breath caught when he looked inside. "Is this what I think it is? I mean, did it come from where I think it came from?"

"I had a talk with Darrell, the one you know as Crazy D, before coming over and I explained the situation to him. I also took his gun and the money from the sale of the drugs tonight. It felt like the right to do at that moment." Alexander explained calmly.

"Oh my god, there's like three thousand dollars here!" Leland gasped.

"There's six thousand four hundred and twenty to be exact." Alexander smiled.

"I guess we were a little late with the 'not attacking the corners' plan. What am I supposed to do with this?" Leland asked still stunned from the number.

Alexander turned to Leland, the expression on his face one of seriousness. "I think using drug money to help a community rid itself of drugs would be the perfect case of irony."

The bag still felt heavy, but it was beginning to get lighter as Leland thought of all the good things six thousand dollars could buy. A broad smile appeared on his face as spoke. "I think you're right Alex. I really, really do. By the way, how do you plan on getting to where Chico will be?"

With a small smile Alexander looked to the street preacher, "I believe you have transportation, something called a Lincoln."

"Yeah," Leland stammered shaking his head, "I do but...how do you know I have a Lincoln?"

The vampire didn't answer the question, just smiled some more before turning back to look at the crucifix leaving Leland to ponder his own question. And no matter how much Leland thought about the question the answer that kept coming back was one that bothered him immensely, like just how much does Alex know about us.

The locked door to the spare bedroom was driving her crazy, or more like what was behind said secured portal, and she wasn't even sure why. Wilma just knew that ever since Grammy had asked her to stay away she had to see what was behind the barred bedroom door. "It's a simple lock, bet I could pop it with a knife." She whispered.

"Some doors are better left closed sweetie." Martha called out suddenly from her chair.

The noise scared Wilma, she was sure Grammy was asleep in the chair. "I wasn't going to do anything, honest."

"Uh-huh, just in case if you don't mind I'll go ahead and lock up my knives." Martha said with a small laugh. "Come on up here youngin' and talk to old Grammy for a little bit, keep her company."

Wilma took one long last look at the door with a frustrated sigh before moving up the hall and into the living room. She sat on the couch with a small plop making sure the positioning gave her a good view of the door. For a second no one said a word, but then Grammy broke the silence again with a question.

"So what's got you all flustered child?"

"Nothing, I'm good" was all Wilma mumbled still looking at the door.

"Uh-huh, and I suppose what happened last night isn't bothering you? I mean that was some miracle you walking out of that explosion and all, must have been some guardian angel looking after you." Grammy said rocking back in her chair.

The mention of the guardian angel immediately took hold of Wilma's attention. She turned so fast from looking at the door she almost fell off the couch fighting to stay on the cushions. Grammy held back a small smile while Wilma stammered with a remark. "What guardian angel? I never mentioned a word about a guardian angel. I never said a thing about a man on the edge of the shadows that night." Wilma responded so quickly that she instantly wanted all of the words back.

"Oh that's all right child," Grammy said getting out of the recliner and walking over the couch with her knees popping viciously from arthritis, "I'm gonna let you in on a little secret of mine."

"Yeah, what?" Wilma asked suspiciously.

"I've had me a guardian angel my whole life. No lie, he's been over my shoulder since I was knee high to my daddy, just like you. He even saved my life once." Grammy said with a toothy smile as she sat by Wilma.

"He did?" Wilma asked, less suspiciously.

"Oh yes, yes, he pulled me out of a stall of one of the meanest, most miserable horse on the farm my daddy worked back in Kentucky. My daddy had warned me to stay away from the horse around a hundred times before, but I was too stubborn for my own good much like you. My husband Davis said it was one of the things he loved most about me, but I think he was lying." Grammy said tilting her head.

The room grew silent for a second, which drove Wilma crazy, even more so than the locked door. I mean who stops right in the middle of telling a story she thought to herself. But if the stop was for dramatic effect or Grammy just going through her memories Wilma wasn't sure, and really didn't care. Martha on the other hand was following her script perfectly, like reeling in a big old catfish.

"So what happened with the horse?" Wilma asked after a second more of silence.

"Oh, excuse me child, lost my train of thought and all. Well, I chose one afternoon to go over to the barn and see about some chickens and the quickest way to go was through the stalls where the horses were kept and there was that mean old horse. Before you could put a stop to me I stepped into that stall and then I knew I had made a wrong decision because it took that mean old horse two seconds to come after me."

"What happened then?" Wilma asked leaning forward eagerly at the waist.

"Oh, that horse meant to stomp me to the very door of death, but it never got the chance. One second I'm screaming for my father and the next I'm on the other side of the fence, a man standing over me holding my hand as gentle as can be." Grammy said with a whisper. If Wilma had a sharper set of eyes, or even a mature inclination, she might have noticed the way Martha was hiding a smile. It was time to see if she really had seen Alexander.

"What did he look like?" Wilma asked eagerly oblivious to the eagerness in her own voice.

"Well, he wasn't black like me or white like the men in town who tried so hard to make me feel low. You know they always tried to make me into something I wasn't, like I wasn't as good as they were. But they were wrong because I never let myself believe I was second to anyone. No sir, no man no matter his color is better than the next in the eyes of God, you keep that in your heart child, understand?" Martha said with a pointed finger at Wilma.

How can she see me Wilma abruptly asked herself, but then she realized Grammy probably used some kind of sonic recognition. She could zero in on a voice with her hearing, like a bat, and that's what she was obviously doing here. "Yes ma'am, but can we back to the story. What did the angel look like?"

"Oh my, there I go again losing my train of thought, may the good Lord forgive me. Well, he was sort of tan with this long black hair tied back into a pony tail like some girl." Martha said looking at the roof feinting as if she was looking into her memory for a detailed recollection, but really she was just waiting to see what little Wilma would do.

Again, if Wilma were more mature she would have seen through the ruse. Martha was playing her and she hated lying to the little girl but she had to know if there was the connection. Even a small spark could start a fire; all you needed was the kindling to give it a little help. "Did he have a deep look in his eyes, like he could see though you?" Wilma asked with a whisper, almost afraid to utter the question aloud. Oh yes, there was the spark.

Martha turned back to Wilma with a quizzical look and a small smack of her lips, perfect acting. "Yes, eyes so pure they could see right to my very soul. He was quite, and I'm sorry to my beloved Davis for saying this, handsome and for a second I felt my little heart skip."

"So does mine." Wilma said with the same whisper.

"Does it now? Are you afraid of him sweetie?" Martha asked with that same whisper.

"No! I... nothing, don't worry about it." Wilma started to say before retreating from the question and the subject.

"I know baby, you only want to meet the angel, to get to know him, right?" Martha asked taking Wilma's hand in her own.

"How do you know that?" Wilma asked with a whisper. Martha could feel the goose bumps on Wilma's hands start pop-up.

"Aw sweet child, I'm Grammy...I know everything didn't ya hear!" Martha said with a broad reassuring smile. The goose bumps didn't go away but Wilma did give a smile and at least that made Martha feel a little better for lying and scaring the girl.

The parking lot of the Waffle House restaurant was dark and deserted, except for the sedan with the four individuals sitting inside parked in back of the building in the shadows. The cook and waitress had forgotten about the vehicle. Out of sight out of mind you know. Anyways, Mondays were always slow, a good time to get caught up on other stuff, like naps which the cook was doing at the moment.

In the sedan Yelena sat quietly with her four brothers, Gregor the red head, Dimitri the black hair, and the blonde Peter who was driving. They were just a mile or two away from the Laurel projects waiting for Michaels the Lesser Lich to show for their meeting. Yelena kept running over the information in her mind, trying to piece together what they found, but nothing worked. The vampire had destroyed the drug house last night and for some reason killed two dealers the night before. Of course the local law enforcement didn't know this or sense it. They had no clue to what was walking among them. The real problem, the stickler, was the why part. Why would a vampire risk detection these days for drugs? Did the vampire have some crazy idea of getting into the illegal drug business? If not, then why do something that would so blatantly expose him to the Great Lich Akhenaton? And to make it even more puzzling was the fact this vampire was alone, no others were seen with him. She and her brothers had been told their mother, the Grand Duchess Svetlana, had been taken by a group of nefarious Nosferatu and yet here they were watching only one who was acting alone. This vampire was making no effort to contact others and shouldn't he be if Akhenaton was trying to destroy him? There were more questions than answers and that picked at her, gnawed at her like a biting flea. Gregor suddenly called from the backseat breaking her train of thought.

"Michaels is here."

She looked up to see the Lesser Lich standing a few feet from the car. Yelena opened the door and stretched out her long legs while her brothers quickly exited to follow her lead.

"What have you found?" Michaels asked, his sunglasses hanging on the tip of his nose. Yelena was starting to find that a rude and a very unappealing look from the Lich.

"The vampire is male, six foot one with long black hair. He's dressed in a white long sleeve shirt with a black short shirt over it, black jeans, and doc Martin boots of matching color." Dimitri stated with a smile.

Michaels starred at the lycanthrope for a second before remarking, like a sniper lining up his shot. "Well, that's very detailed, but since I do not care what the vampire is wearing I care little for your description of his attire."

"Sorry sir." Dimitri whispered while hunching his shoulders. He looked remarkably like a five year old who just got caught reaching into the cookie jar moments before dinner.

"Well it's obvious you've seen the vampire but please tell me you have something more than this, tell me your mother and Ivan taught you better." Michaels said with a deep breath.

Yelena turned to him to speak, but for a second she hesitated. She wasn't sure what to speak of from what she knew from the information gathered. There was too much assumption being used to make connections. And there were questions with no answers, hell there were answers with no questions floating around in her head. Yet she had to report, give her analysis, so she just decided to tell it all in one flat burst.

"The vampire destroyed the drug house and killed two dealers the night before. Tonight he attacked a corner known for selling drugs sending four naked individuals running into the night and robbed a fifth man who came by to pick up the money for the sales."

"He's attacking drug dealers?" Michaels asked with a quizzical look, but the werewolves didn't answer. They weren't sure if the question was a real question or some rhetorical remark. "Is he trying to take over the drug trade in the city?"

"I do not know. The information is too small to see what the vampire's true intentions are." Yelena responded.

"We also do not know who the vampire is or where he is resting from the day light." Gregor added.

There was a second of silence before Yelena spit out the last thing they knew. "There is also a girl, a fourteen year old who has been at both incidents with the vampire. There is nothing connecting the two we have found except for this fact."

Michaels didn't respond to the last comment. He was too busy rolling the information Yelena had thrown out over in his head. Why would the Ancient One be attacking drug dealers? There was no reason for him to take over the drug trade, nothing in it. The Ancient One was already rich beyond belief, a walking God due to his age, and he had the Sisters and his brood to keep his interest bound to being awake. What is he up to Michaels kept thinking? Maybe there was a way to make this work for him. Yes, there had to be a way to use this, take advantage of it to help in the master's plan. Then Yelena finally grew tired of waiting and asked a question of him.

"Do you know the identity of the vampire Michaels?"

"Huh, oh no, not yet, he is hiding himself very well. Yet I will succeed in getting a name by the morning. I have to cast another spell and I'll have him." Michaels lied with a shake of his head.

"Okay, we wait, but for how long? We cannot risk the life of our mother much longer." Dimitri said with a nod. What a clod Michaels thought before speaking.

"It will not be long now, but in the meantime I want you to keep a close eye on him Yelena and Peter. Gregor and Dimitri I want you to find where he is sleeping from the daylight, do whatever it takes to find the location. Now go, and do what you've been told to do." Michaels said turning away from the group and heading back to the deep shadows of the corner parking lot to where he parked his car. He kept his head down deep in thought as he tried to make sense of this new change.

Yelena watched the Lich disappear into the dark. She took a quick sniff of the air to make sure he was gone before turning to her brothers. Gregor eyed her closely and spoke with a whisper first. "I do not like this sister, it does not feel right."

"I know, which is why we have to keep our eyes and ears open from this point on." Yelena whispered. No, it did not feel right at all. From the constant push to destroy the vampire to now waiting to end him, and all of this with her mother still in the hands of an evil group of Nosferatu. Yet, even the 'capture' of

Svetlana was starting to look very suspicious to the young werewolf, very suspicious indeed.

"I did good, no?" Dimitri asked quickly, his voice yearning for approval.

Yelena reached out a small hand and caressed the face of her brother with a loving touch while smiling warmly. "Yes my handsome brother, you always do well for us."

Gregor watched the show of affection and when it was done he looked to his sister, "I do not think this vampire took our mother my sister. There is something very...old to him I sense and the ones who took Svetlana were young ones."

"I know my brother, but if he does know who took our mother than he will pay for taking her." Yelena snarled before motioning to return to the car.

The four werewolves slid back into the sedan and it sped away from the parking lot with a small screech of rubber from the tires a minute later. The cook and waitress inside looked up just in time to see the brake lights turn out of lot and onto the street. The cook looked to the waitress and her at him. They shrugged, and then went back to their naps. Why stop a good thing, huh?

Chapter Nine

Otz pulled up a chair so he could sit instead of stand by the Assistant Coroner of the Night Shift's desk, one John Foster. It was good to be off his feet because the last 24 hours had turned into total chaos. Something was going down out on the streets, dead bodies were showing up everywhere and all of them dealers and pushers. All of the 'arranged' death pointed to a war among the runners, or God forbid the higher-ups, due to someone making a move for more territory and corners. Foster coughed catching Otz's attention and suddenly he wasn't so happy for the chance to get off his feet, especially if it meant sitting next to the AC. If you knew Otz then you knew just how much he hated the Coroner's choice for the night shift role and if you knew that then you knew about the special dreams Otz had each and every night concerning the assistant coroner and various torture implements. The obsession was about as healthy as going over Niagara Falls in a giant soup can, and Otz knew this, but there was not a thing he could to stop it because Foster just kept showing up at crime scenes. It was the Coroner's fault actually, Otz knew the man had it in for him and that's why he kept Foster around. You know, for the comedic potential of watching the police detective blow his brains out with his service revolver after he had to watch Foster do another dance while putting a body back together. Otz sat back in the chair with his mind still stuck on blaming the Coroner, put a large leg on the knee of the other, and looked at two photographs that Foster had pulled from a manila folder specially hidden in his desk drawer. The same drawer every other AC in the country keeps their 'special' folder in probably.

Oh yes, the sacred and 'secret' manila folder, the magic vessel that held the evidence Foster swore showed something or in his own words 'un-worldly'. So that's what he spent forty minutes coming across town in afternoon traffic for, Otz thought, some Star Trek obsessed nutcase with delusions that Superman just landed in Atlanta and decided to pick on the local drug dealers. The detective almost threw up when he saw the folder pop out of the desk drawer, and it wasn't from being sick. This wasn't the first time Foster went off swimming in the deep end of the pool. Hell the man should have enough hours logged from being there to be a scuba instructor. It still took Foster begging him for a solid minute before he finally gave in and said yes to look at some of the photos, not all of them mind you, just two or three. If you thought it was the skinny face with puppy dog eyes that broke Otz you'd be wrong, it was the hope that maybe he could keep his hand away from his service revolver for a few seconds and commit a murder.

To the untrained eye the photos didn't look the same, but to a detective with six years' experience in homicide and an Assistant Coroner with a PHD it was easy to find the where's and what's to look for. Otz looked up from the black and white glossies to Foster and spoke for the first time since sitting in the uncomfortable office chair.

"It's the same boot print as the car."

"What," Foster whined loudly, "of course it's the same boot print! Do you know what that means?"

"Yeah, it means we might have two guys running around the projects with the same size foot wearing the same kind of Doc Martin boots. Nothing the DA is going to wet herself over in uncontrolled excitement." Otz said with a shrug while throwing both photos on the assistant coroner's desk with a flop.

"No, No, No!" Foster said vehemently shaking his head grabbing the photos. "You're not looking hard enough at the pictures."

"Listen Foster, if I look any harder my freaking' head's going to implode! Now I told you I would look, and after you tricked me into coming here your damn lucky to get that much. I've looked and seen nothing extraordinary so unless you got something more substantial I'm rolling out of here to go and pick up another dead body." Otz demanded.

"Trust me this once Detective, I know you can't stand me and you probably have several torturous endings to my life dreamed up-'Foster was saying as Otz cut him off.

"You wouldn't believe the number."

"But will you just follow along with me on this one." Foster said ignoring the comment from Otz. The detective shook his head, switched legs, and motioned for Foster to continue his speech.

"I've been looking over the evidence and I can state emphatically who ever left this footprint in the front quarter panel of the car was at the house that exploded two nights ago." Foster said excitedly laying out the two photos side by side on his desk.

"We don't know if it's the same man Foster." Otz commented but Foster just smiled that toothy, lipless thing of his that made him quiver in disgust.

"Oh, but we can detective." Foster said pulling out a magnifying glass and two separate pieces of paper wrapped in laminate. Each one had the image of a footprint in black ink in center. "The man that killed Jamal Jennings and Anquan Tucker in the street three nights ago, he has the same extensive wear on the outside portion of his shoes, like he's walking bow legged.

The man at the explosion has the same exact wear on the shoe sole. The percentage that two people walk with the same exact pressure, step motion, and would have the same wear on a pair of shoes is unbelievably small. Here, check for yourself, I've made impressions from the crime scenes. See if you can find something, anything different."

The detective practically snatched the magnifying glass out of the Assistant Coroner's hand and then bent over the two ink images. Two whole minutes ticked by with Otz desperately searching for something different, but he couldn't find a thing. The Gods didn't answer his silent prayers to end this thing here and now, which wasn't the first time by any stretch of the imagination he had been ignored by the big people upstairs.

"Jesus." Otz whispered finally.

"Oh that's not all!" Foster shot back.

"What else is there? Something more than the matching shoe prints?" Otz asked with a tinge of fear in his voice, something Foster had never heard before from the large man. This wasn't going to end, this rabbit hole had no bottom, and worse...Foster may just be right.

"Oh yeah, a whole lot better. This same person must have been Houdini because this footprint from the crack house explosion wasn't made until after the explosion happened."

Foster suddenly whispered, painfully keeping his voice low as he pointed to the second photo.

"What?" Otz hissed loudly, then realizing the volume of his voice lowered it quickly. "No way, that's impossible. No one could have survived that explosion. A firefighter or some rookie flat foot stepping where he should have stayed the hell away from made that footprint. And how is there a footprint anyway? Didn't the water the fire fighters squirted all around wash everything away?"

The desperation in Otz's voice didn't register with Foster because he just kept pilling on the information threatening to break the detective's protective psyche. "The fire fighters didn't use a drop of water that night in this area, they didn't have to because there was no fire, remember? Now look at the footprint in the picture, the direction of the toes point north toward the street, away from the house and the explosion, and the print is a single too. There is not another shoe print in the vicinity. Our man started out right in the middle of the explosion, maybe three feet from ground zero where the blast originated. I know that because if the print was there before the explosion it would have been wiped clean from the concussion of the blast, not a millimeter of it left."

The last bit of information hit Otz like a brick as he gasped for a quick breath. That was it. He couldn't fight the beast any longer. Foster was right, damn it, he was right. Otz wasn't a fool and he could tell when someone upstairs had it in for him. After he caught his breath Otz looked hard at Foster with his best Clint Eastwood Squint. "Do you understand what you're saying to me?" he asked slowly.

"Yes I do! We have the scientific find of a lifetime here and it fell right into our laps. It's just too bad we can't call Jim Croce!" Foster remarked with a large smile.

"Why do you say that?" Otz asked confused and little scared. What did a dead folk singer have to do with this guy?

"Because, we have a person here that can break a car by kicking it and walks out of natural gas explosions with a skip and a how-do-you-do. I'm sure Jim would have wanted to meet Big Bad Leroy Brown here!"

Otz popped up out of his chair so fast it scared Foster a little. "You have a safe or somewhere to lock that folder away?"

"I'll just leave it in my desk drawer. No one knows about that place." Foster stammered feeling a twinge of fear and paranoia start to roll over him. Goosebumps began to rise on his semi-muscular arms mixing in with the light brown hair looking like ripples.

"There's not a chance in hell your leaving that folder in there, everyone knows about your desk drawer!" Otz spat looking around the lab.

"They do? How did they find out my hiding spot?" Foster whined feeling the fear grow exponentially with each second and the revelation his secret hiding spot wasn't so secret. A ghostly hand began to wrap around his stomach and squeeze ever so painfully.

"Okay here's the plan," Otz commanded pointing his finger at Foster chest," you take that folder out to your car and lock it away in the truck, not the glove compartment, but in the trunk understand? I'm going to talk with a friend, maybe try to think of some way to deal with this information."

"All right, but why do I need to lock away the file in my car?" Foster asked as the hand squeezed harder.

"If someone at headquarters finds that file and reads it then three things are going to happen, all very bad." Otz stated coldly turning to leave.

"What's that?" Foster cried out with the hand squeezing his insides doing it really hard now.

"If they believe it we'll end up in a ten by ten foot locked room at Area 51 talking to a bunch of guys dressed in black suits with big guns never to see the light of day again." Otz said opening the door to the room and turning back.

"And what if they don't believe it?" Foster called out quick to the detective.

"Well then, we just drive out to Area 51 and volunteer for the locked rooms. Those guys are going to be the only ones who will talk to us at that point." Otz said coldly.

"Oh dear God," Foster whispered as the fear gave his stomach a sudden severe squeeze.

Otz was about to open the door when he heard Foster yell from the desk. "What about number three? You said three things, what's number three?"

"Narcotics find's out about the folder and discovers we know who set off this turf war. Then we just end up in jail with the bad guys we put away. I'm sure they'll enjoy seeing us again." Otz answered ducking out the door and leaving the assistant coroner in shock.

Before disappearing out the door with a quick step though, just before it closed, Otz heard a very distinctive sound. The loud ripping, like a sheet of paper being torn in half inch by inch slowly, was Foster stomach finally giving in to the fear and paranoia. At least he held it in until I left Otz thought with a smile walking fast down the hall toward the exit.

Manuel 'Chico' Rodriguez drove the brightest, loudest, and with certainty the most obnoxious van that any human being could think about driving, or so some people told him with a shake of their head in disgust. The 78 Chevy was painted black and grey with bright green flames pouring out of the engine. A few people told him on several occasions that flames were orange and yellow but Chico just said it was his van and he wanted green flames because, you know, a flame can turn green under the right conditions. Nevertheless, what set the van apart was the large rendering of a seminude woman spread out on a couch, a 'looouuuunge' as Chico pronounced it rolling his tongue, barely covered by a sheet. Tonight he was riding with a homeboy, chilling in his ride while spotting some fine honey's walking around downtown.

"Hey there goes one man!" Memo yelled.

"Oh man, she's a blimp! Why you always point out the fat ones man!" Chico spat rolling his eyes while taking a quick shot at Memo.

"Man! Why you calling me messed up man when I'm not the one with green flames and some fat bitch painted on my van!" Memo retorted. He barely got the last out before busting out laughing.

"Man, shut the fuck up!" Chico shot back which just sent more wails of laughter through Memo. "Man, if you don't shut up you can walk your ass home."

The last threat seemed to work causing quiet finally as Memo knew Chico wouldn't hesitate to toss him out of the van. He had done it before to people more important. Suddenly Memo spotted a Hispanic store just up the street a bit and he pointed excitedly.

"Hey pull over man!" he said bouncing in the seat.

"Why man?" Chico asked whining again.

"Because I only shop at the finest establishments, and this happens to be a very exclusive place to shop." Memo said with a wave of his hand upward turn of his nose.

"Shit man, I've been in there before. It's just like every other store!" Chico yelled.

"Well, I want to keep the money in the Raza, know what I mean. I'm Mexican and I only spend my money in Mexican stores." Memo said with a mock air of dignity.

"Yeah whatever man! That little honey at the Cheetah last night wasn't Mexican and you sure put a lot of money in her neighborhood!" Chico laughed hard. Memo and Chico had been at the local Strip club the night before where Memo had filled the thong of one young woman with twenty's for most of the night.

"Come on man don't remind me." Memo wailed shaking his head. "And why didn't you stop me at some point man?"

"Because, I don't do charity work man! Now get out and get your' shit man, I need to be rolling tonight. I feel lucky holmes. I'm going to get me a little chica with some big-"Chico said holding out both hands in a cupping fashion at his chest.

"Yeah, whatever man!" Memo said exiting the van. He was just inside the door when his cell rang and he answered. A single word came over the speaker and then the line went dead. Memo closed the phone and turned back to the doors ready to go back to the van.

Just after Memo went inside the store, Chico heard his name being called by someone outside the van. When he looked in the rear view mirror and saw Leland he shook his head out of disgust. Out of all the people Chico couldn't stand Leland was at the top of the list as the man appeared in his window. I mean he had sole possession of first place locked up Chico thought with a hiss. The street preacher called out his name again and pointed to the front of the van but with the windows rolled up Chico couldn't make out what the man was saying about his 'Fly' ride.

"Man, what this fool want now?" Chico said rolling down the window. "What you want Leland?"

"Hey Chico, my main man, how things been?" Leland asked smiling from ear to ear.

"Hey man what you want? I don't have the time to be messing with you right now." Chico sneered.

"Hey, no problem bro, just wanted to know when you got that dent in the fender of this sweet ride?" Leland asked.

"Dent in my van!" Chico squealed looking dumfounded as he got out of the driver's side door. "I don't have a dent in the fender! Man if someone jacked up my ride I'll shoot me a fool with a whole clip!"

But as the small Hispanic man rounded the front and saw there was no dent in the chrome fender Chico felt his blood boil and for a second he was about to reach around for the .38 caliber pistol hidden in the waistband of his jeans. He shook his head and walked toward Leland "That's not right man, and you know it. Now get your ass out of here before I lose my patience!"

Leland raised both hands making sure to try and placate the angered young man because he sure didn't want any business with the concealed gun. Chico shook his head some more, muttered some Spanish, and reached for the door to the van. The door though swung open in a vicious arc just as his fingers touched the handle. The blow was hard and fast knocking the young man out before he even knew what hit him, one second he was upset and the next there was nothing but darkness. How long Chico was out he was never really sure, something wet splashing against his face brought him out of unconsciousness.

The water, or whatever it was, kept pouring causing the waking man to gag for a second and roll over to get away from a possible drowning. Chico got the gagging under control just in time to spit out a few words. "All right man! Stop with the damn water or I'm going to bust your ass!"

"Somehow, I am not really scared by the prospect of physical violence from you Chico." A refined voice told him. Chico rolled back over to see a guy dressed in black jeans, a black t-shirt over white long sleeve one, and a pair of Doc Martin boots. Another one of his homie's had a pair just like them, wore them all the time. Then the scene clicked for him, this was the guy in black, the dude trying to muscle in on Eight Ball's turf. Chico decided to play it cool, show some machismo when needed, and then run like hell when the opportunity presented itself.

"You know who you're fucking with man?" Chico spit moving to a sitting position.

"Manuel Rodriguez," the man said dropping an empty pitcher to the ground," a man of the street said you might give me some information on a little enterprise you've been 'running' with."

Chico looked around trying to figure where he was, it took about two seconds to see he was on some rooftop, but just where that rooftop was in the city only the guy dressed in black knew and he wasn't about to tell him Chico sensed. It was promptly confirmed a second later.

"Looking around isn't going to help Manuel, I took the liberty of getting us some privacy. I also took the gun you keep hidden in the back waistband of your pants. I want to be the only one with the surprises tonight." The man in black said with a small grin. A quick check with Chico's right hand confirmed the fact the pistol was missing from its usual spot.

"So I guess you expect me to just answer your damn questions." Chico spat giving the man in black a little attitude to chew on.

"That would be the best thing to do if you don't feel like flying." The man in black said cryptically.

"Wha-"Chico started to respond with a giggle and a smart-ass remark when his chest caved inward driving all the air from his lungs. He had the sensation of someone carrying him effortlessly across the rooftop but air and breathing was the first priority now so Chico pretty much forgot about everything else for the moment. When he got some precious oxygen back into his lungs his eyes looked down and focused on the spot where his feet now dangled. Moreover, when the picture finally registered in Chico's mind he began to scream like a little girl.

"Holy shit man, don't drop me!" He wailed. Chico's feet hung lazily out in space as he made out the alley some ten stories below. The only thing he saw holding him up was the arm of the man dressed in black so Chico clung to the cotton material of the long sleeve t-shirt like a newborn baby to its bottle.

"I think you better be quiet Manuel! All this noise might distract me. I might loosen my grip for a second and it's a long way down as you can see." The man in black stated.

"No! No!" Chico cried.

"Are you ready then to answer a question or two of mine Manuel?" The man in black asked calmly.

"Whatever you want man, just don't drop me!"

"Now that's what I wanted to hear. Let's start by your rank with Eight Ball's Organization?" The man in black asked.

"I ain't got any rank man!" Chico yelled.

"That's not what I have heard Manuel. I was told you have some personal connections, that you made some runs for Eight Ball. Special runs with special cargo." The man in black stated.

"They were lying to you man!" Chico screamed.

"And you are not right now?"

"Hell No! I just want to get back to the roof man!" Chico sobbed.

"Then tell me the truth Manuel or I get to see how high you bounce." The man in black demanded.

"Man, I can't tell you! If they know I'd talk they'd kill me! They'd kill my whole family!"

"At this point I would be more worried about my piloting skills. The old saying 'Any landing you can walk away from' really does not apply right I think." Alexander hissed, and for emphasis he loosened his grip letting Chico slip just an inch.

"Oh No, don't drop me man!" Chico wailed.

"Then start talking or start flapping your arms Manuel." Alexander spat.

"Okay, okay man! I make the deliveries for Eight Ball, the ones off the books. Just a kilo here or there, not enough to draw attention but enough to bring in a good piece of green, you know man. He was just skimming, getting ready to strike out on his own."

"Who's working with Eight Ball? Who brings in the drugs that go to the Laurel?" Alexander asked quickly, wanting to keep the pressure on Chico.

"I don't know man, but there's this place up off 285, it's the Shangri-La strip club. There's a bartender there, Shane, and I owed him a lot of green for a bunch of bad bets so one day I get this call. He says Eight Ball needs a special driver, none of his people will do, and if I make this pick-up and delivery everything will be square between us, clean slate you know man. I get some keys by Fed Ex the next morning along with driving instructions. I pick up the package and drop it off real fast like I was told." Chico explained.

"Who got the package?" The vampire demanded.

"Ice took it from me at the crack house, you know, the one that you blew up." Chico stammered.

"And where did you pick the drugs up?"

"A Gym in Duluth, stashed in a locker. I told them Shane sent me and they just let me right on by man. It's all true man, I swear to Jesus!" Chico said.

"Who runs the Shangri-La?" Alexander asked.

"A dude named Ray. Everyone says he connected, in deep with the Mexicans. That's where Shane got the whole kilos from! Aw come on man, let me back on the roof!" Chico whined.

"I believe you Manuel, but I think I'm still going to drop you off the building." The man in black remarked calmly.

"WHAT, NO WAIT, WHY?" Chico screamed so loud it turned to a shrill.

"I do not like having to work so hard for answers Manuel, and if the truth be known, I do not like you all that much either." And with that Alexander let go of Chico's shirt with a quick snap of his fingers.

Chico tried to scream for the man not to let go, but his voice was a second or two late with the plea, and the world began to float. He forgot about the words then and just screamed at the top of his lungs as the alley below began to rush up at him with blinding speed, the windows of the building whizzing by like some kind of crazy kaleidoscope. He flapped both arms, actually flapped them up and down like a bird, which caused his body to roll over instead of fly like he was hoping for, and then he was dropping headfirst. Impact was only seconds away. Chico stopped flapping his arms and brought them up to guard his face as he closed his eyes not wanting to see the end. Then, abruptly, he stopped falling. He was hanging by his left foot, or better yet, something had grabbed his foot right out of the air. Chico opened his eyes looking around and there he was, the man in black holding him by his foot just a few feet from the ground. The scene really hit home then and he noticed the fact that the man dressed in black was floating too. The two of them were hovering just off the ground like something out of Sci-Fi movie. Chico was just about to ask the man how he did that amazing scare-the-shit-out-me-by-letting-me-plummet-ten-stories trick when he felt his foot being let go. For a second time Chico wanted to say something only to be cut off by a loss of gravity, but hey at least he survived the second fall he thought. With a plop, Chico hit flat backed dead center in the middle of the alley. For a minute he didn't move and then the young Hispanic man rose from the ground wiping the crud of the street off his clothes while looking for the man in black, but there wasn't a sign of him anywhere. So with a certain bravado Chico began to walk toward the mouth of the alley to get back to his van, wherever it was.

"Man, if I catch that fool, his ass is mine next time!" Chico said walking faster toward the entrance.

He was just to the mouth of the alley when a shadow stepped out from behind him. Chico never saw the shadow raise the twenty-two handgun and thankfully he never felt the twin shots. His body dropped to the pavement in a lump, the legs simply giving out and letting the dead weight drop. The shadow stepped out into the light and Memo's face came into full view. He put the gun into the waistband of his pants then pulled out the burner flip phone and took a quick picture of Chico's body. Memo knew the Producer wanted proof of the hit because evidence was the only way to get paid in full. You have no proof then you get no cash. There was a slight twinge of regret for shooting his friend, but Chico was running on the side. In the hood stealing was second nature, but biting the hand that feeds you, well that was just stupid and the penalty for it was a bullet to the back of the head. Memo just wanted thank whoever it was that left him a voicemail telling him where to pick up Chico after he took off, or more to the point put an end to him.

But there was a bright spot, on top of the money for the hit the Producer would pay a nice bit of cash for the new information he had on the man in black, a pretty penny indeed. This was turning out to be a good night for Memo. Maybe he would drop by the Cheetah and see that little girl again. He turned away from the body and began to walk toward the street.

From the dark Yelena had seen everything, from the vampire dropping then catching the first boy to the second boy shooting the first. Now she was more confused than ever, nothing made sense. Why did the vampire drop the first boy off the roof? What did they say to each other? And why for the love of Ivan the Great Wolf did the second boy shoot the first boy after the colored man called him? It was all lunacy. Yelena needed answers, but did she dare take a chance on being seen? The second boy was rapidly approaching their hiding spot in the shadows and she had a second to make a decision. With a simple nod of her head Peter readied himself and when the second boy reached him the young wolf sprang into action. He raced out of the dark so fast Memo never saw Peter coming. The werewolf threw a perfect left cross punch to the boy's jaw dropping him on the spot with a small plop.

Yelena stepped out and ordered her brother in Russian to pick up the unconscious boy. She didn't want to interrogate him here, not out in the open. They would take the boy somewhere more private, like the vampire did with the first boy. Only the roof of a building wasn't her thing. She sniffed the air and instantly caught the scent of the vampire. He was still here, somewhere in the area. Yelena gave a quick wave of her hand and the two retreated quickly back into the shadows with Memo leaving only the rats and Chico's body to the night.

"What did Chico say?" Leland asked quickly, almost with too much excitement as Alexander approached.

"He said he made runs for a bartender named Shane. Kenneth was right about Eight Ball; the dealer was stealing from his suppliers at every turn. He said the bartender worked for a man named Ray who runs an exotic club called the Shangri-La where the drugs are distributed from, or so Chico swore to before he fell." The vampire answered.

"Ray? Not Ray Cummings? It can't be Ray Cummings, that guy's too small time to be that high up in this mess!" Leland said shaking his head.

"So you know of Ray?"

"The only Ray I know of is a fat bastard who sold crack and heroin out of an old Cadillac when I was running in the street gangs. Believe me, if you had ever met Ray you'd want to forget him as fast as possible, the guy's a disgusting human!" Leland exclaimed.

"He seems a bit out of place to be so prominent in the drug trade then." Alexander offered.

"Exactly, and to be in with the Mexicans, that's impossible. From what I know those guys only keep to themselves, no outsiders allowed!" Leland added but he noticed all of the sudden he was conversing with the night air itself. He turned to find Alexander but the man was gone. It took a second before the street preacher saw him standing by a tree they had just passed a minute before.

"What is it?" Leland asked Alexander. One second the man was walking next to him, and then just like snapping your finger, he turned back to where he had come from.

"Did you make the call to the boy, the passenger, to pick up Chico?" The vampire asked looking off into the dark.

The street preacher looked around nervous before answering, "yeah, but what's got you all spooked?"

"There's someone out in the dark over there, someone I have been expecting." Alexander whispered slowly, speaking low as if someone would hear. The scene just added to the whole atmosphere of creepiness that Leland was experiencing and fighting. Part of him said run but an equal and stronger part said stay, if this guy was capable of the things he had seen, and if he hated Eight Ball just as much as he did then he had to stick it out.

"What's out there?" Leland asked jumping at the sound of his own voice.

"Nothing," Alexander said with haste walking past Leland in a brisk gait," we need to get back and make sure everyone is okay"

"What's wrong? Damn it man stop!" Leland spat. Alexander turned around and looked at the street preacher who had taken an offensive stance instead of his usual defensive one.

"What do you need Leland?"

"What do I need? I need to know just what the hell is going on! You're going to tell me there's someone out there then just clam up like the X-files. No Way! I want to know just what's going down right now do you hear me." Leland ordered sternly. For a second Alexander stood quiet then Leland blinked and the man was face to face with him.

"If I told you there were other things out tonight like me, only not as nice, what would you do?"

"Like you...only not as nice?" Leland said swallowing hard. "I'd run like hell to the next county probably."

"There are some things that you are better off not knowing right now Leland. All you need to understand is stick close to my side, do as I request, and keep your eyes open at all times. Do you think you can do that?" Alexander asked.

"Yeah, anything you say boss." Leland stammered, and then he was off after Alexander trying to play keep-up with the brisk pace. His mind raced with the last statement by the man dressed in black as they made their way back to his car. There were others out there like Alexander, just not as nice. Leland wondered if they would be good guys, bad guys, or just true monsters but then somewhere down deep inside he hoped to never ever meet the bad guys like Alexander.

Chapter Ten

The cold night air felt good against Wilma's hot skin as she sat on the rusted remains of what used to be the playground slide. After being cooped up inside all day by an overly inquisitive Grammy she needed some fresh air, her mother didn't even let her go to school today. Wilma knew she had scared the devil out of her mother with the concussion and all, but was that any reason to lock her up like a prisoner. Heck, she was amazed that her mother let her out of the house tonight. Yeah, the dealers on the corner were missing which made it safer, maybe, but there were some still out there in the dark doing a nefarious business. Nevertheless, she needed some space to think and dear old Mom would have to take a back seat for a few minutes while Wilma got her head on straight. No matter how hard she tried to concentrate on what had happened at the crack house the face of her 'Angel' kept coming back. She could see his features so vividly; the shape of his chin, the flowing length of his hair, and the fearful look in his eyes. But why had he shown up so late last night, if he was an angel sent by some higher power to protect her then shouldn't he always be watching over her and stopping her from making seriously stupid choices. Because, if he was right next to her, just before the door opened he should have appeared and swept her away to safety right? No she thought, this wasn't an angel like off TV or the prayer network, this was something else entirely. The spark of scientific curiosity took over and Wilma was soon running theory after theory through her mind. She was so engrossed she didn't hear the approach of footsteps behind her. They stopped only when the dark gave way to moonlight.

Alexander had seen Wilma sitting alone looking up at the stars from the old beat up slide and breathed a sigh of relief. There wasn't a sign of anyone around, but his senses did detect a pair of wolves near, probably part of the same pack from the building where he left poor Chico. He knew there were two wolves intently watching the coming and goings of the Laurel, trying to find him or where he was staying obviously. The pack may or may not have known about Wilma, something to keep an eye on Alexander thought as a plan began to form in his brain, a way to use the pack to his advantage in this crazy scheme Martha had pushed him to start. He turned and looked at Leland wondering if there was any reason to tell him what he knew, what his senses knew for sure. *No*, he told himself, *the man is scared and barley trusts you right now so telling him anything else would just send him running for the hills.* Yet, he did owe something to Leland for just going along tonight and getting involved in what he thought was some noble endeavor to rid the Laurel of drugs when it was nothing more than a mission to save one small life. The truth, oh if Leland only knew what was going to happen to this place, what he Alexander had set in motion, would he still follow him into the dark? For that matter why was the vampire still here? Using the excuse he owed Grammy some kind of debt was beginning to wear thin with the vampire, and he had paid that duty in full at this point. So, the only reason he was still here was sitting out there on a rusted slide, a fourteen-year-old girl who had somehow gotten under the skin of this 2300-year old vampire to the point he couldn't walk away now if his undead existence depended on it. How she worked this magic was even more baffling since the two had not shared a single word of conversation. *It's about time to change that* he told himself.

"Let's go and see if Stephanie is all right Leland. I need to ask her a question." Alexander said taking a step forward before Leland's remark stopped him.

"Whoa! What do you need to ask Stephanie about?" He asked quickly.

"A question, like I said."

"Yeah, but I may know the answer so you won't have to ask her, cool?"

Alexander could see what was happening; it was kind of hard to miss. He decided to counter the situation, shift the conversation, to see how Leland would react. "Why don't you tell her about your feelings Leland?"

"Tell who what?" Leland asked back with shock.

"Why don't you tell Stephanie how much you care for her? How much you love her?"

"What do you mean? Aw man, it's not like that at all. I just respect her a lot. I mean what makes you think there's like something between me and her, huh?" Leland stammered.

"Well it just seems that every time I mention her name you get upset and short. And then there was the way she looked at me earlier tonight that seemed to have a negative effect on your mood. Are you jealous of me Leland?" Alexander asked with a slight smirk. The remark had its intended effect as Leland put up his hands and sped past.

"You know what, let's just go with what you said the first time and go talk to Stephanie. There's no reason to go digging into all this and that you know, I mean you're not Dr. Phil or nothing." The street preacher said with a huff moving off to go and see Stephanie.

Alexander waited a second, took in a deep breath to keep from laughing, and made a quick check again of the area. The pair of werewolves still occupied the same point watching, waiting for a sign of his arrival, but never once were they alerted of his return to the area. So maybe he was learning how to move around in this new world after all. Up the trail Leland was stopped looking around for him so Alexander moved to the street preacher in one move so fast the human eye failed to see it. Leland started a bit from the sudden appearance. The street preacher demanded, in a not so holy manner, for Alexander to stop doing that and the vampire acquiesced with a simple nod, and a hidden smile.

Stephanie was busy at the kitchen sink cleaning it for the tenth time, scrubbing the basin so hard it was practically shining like a mirror. She wasn't angry, oh no, she was way beyond the point of being angry. At the present moment Stephanie was hovering just around highly pissed. That's how it worked for her, get the hands involved in anything to work off the flood of emotions, or someone was going to get hurt. The boys left her behind to go off and talk to Chico, which really wasn't the issue, it was never that easy. No the problem was the fact she thought she was part of a team, a part of something, and then all of the sudden and just like that she wasn't. Why couldn't she go along? Leland said it was for her own good, her protection. What kind of bull was that? She was in just as deep with this as that chauvinistic, not picking up the obvious I-want-you-signal-that-I've-been-dropping street preacher!

"That's it, isn't it girlfriend? The man just can't see what you're putting out." Stephanie whispered out loud finally letting go of the worn out sponge in the sink.

A knock at the back door brought her back to reality and she turned around to open the door. Leland walked in and past straight to the living room looking a little miffed not even recognizing her while Alexander appeared in the doorway out of the blue.

"How did things go with Chico? Did he actually know something?" Stephanie asked Alexander purposefully ignoring Leland, who had chosen to show back up in the kitchen.

Alexander was about to answer the question when Leland spoke up from behind. "He knew a good bit, something for us to go on."

"Well, what's our next move?" Stephanie asked coolly turning around to eye Leland directly. "And I'm going this time, no matter what anyone says."

Leland was about to respond, maybe throw some gasoline on Stephanie's fire, but Alexander moved in quickly cutting off the street preacher. "We'll be acting on the information from tonight tomorrow evening. Leland is going to do some checking and then we can take it to task, but until then I want to keep it between us two, if that's permit able?"

"Good, I'm going, that's all I wanted to hear." Stephanie remarked eyeing Leland triumphantly with a raised eyebrow.

"I actually came here for something else Stephanie." Alexander stated quickly again to head off any words Leland might have, who by the way was beginning to look a little sullen leaning up against the counter with slumped shoulders.

"What do you need my permission for?" She asked back incredulously, shocked at the request.

Alexander paused for a second, which scared Stephanie a little, before speaking. "I want to talk with Wilma. I need to speak with her, explain things to her about what's happening."

"You've saved her twice Alex. You're more than welcome to talk to her if you want. I'd kind of like it actually. She's outside on the playground getting a breath of fresh air." Stephanie answered.

The response sent a small ripple of that jealousy Alexander had detected earlier through Leland. It was evident for only a second to the vampire, and he felt a twinge of empathy for the street preacher. "Thank you Stephanie." He said with a nod and began moving toward the backdoor again, but Stephanie stopped him before he could make good on his escape.

"Wait, please I need something too Alex."

Alexander stopped and turned back, a small spot of fear in his eyes. Leland snapped up from his leaning position against the counter, his body tense with anticipation.

"What are you? I mean are you an angel from God sent to protect Wilma? Or are you something worse? I need to know, I have to know." Stephanie asked earnestly, almost to the point of tears.

The small kitchen was deathly quiet for a minute as Alexander crafted his answer to the delicate question. "After I speak with Wilma Stephanie I will tell you everything about myself, but I have to talk with Wilma first. She is owed that much."

The kitchen was quiet again for a second time, and then before anyone expected it, even her; Stephanie moved in and gave Alexander a small kiss on his cheek. "Thank you for saving my daughter from this place Alex. I can never repay you for what you've done for us."

Leland nearly dropped to the floor in shock from the gesture, but Alexander figured some of it was due to that jealous streak also. So, taking some tact from Martha he decided to do something about Leland and his need to talk with Stephanie.

"You know something Leland. I think it's a perfect time to have that talk with Stephanie." The vampire said with a mischievous smile.

"What talk?" Stephanie asked turning to Leland, who by the way had turned a nice shade of white.

"Yeah, what-what talk?" Leland stammered trying to think of something, anything, to say to get his butt out of this one. "Um, yeah, talk...talk?"

"Now Leland, do not be shy. It's time to step up, as you say, and just confess all those emotions you have to Stephanie." Alexander smiled just before leaving the room in a blink.

Stephanie turned from where the vampire had stood to Leland with her full attention. She didn't even care that Alexander left the room without so much as opening the backdoor. "So what do you want to confess Lee?" She asked emphasizing the word 'confess' with a large hopeful smile.

Wow, the room was suddenly really hot and way too small for Leland. Add to that the obvious fact that Stephanie abruptly changed from being angry to being excited at the sound of him confessing and the distress level in the room cranked up past the safe zone right to DANGER! There was a very real chance the street preacher just might lose it and toss his Wheaties in the sink next to him. Leland took a couple of deep breaths trying to calm down, but with every intake Stephanie's mood changed. A lot of the excitement vanished being replaced with the old anger. He had to say something to keep her mood from slipping backwards and so Leland went with the first thing that popped into his panic filled brain.

"Aw man, that Alexander, you know he's joking right? That guy, he's a real kidder!"

Okay, that wasn't the right thing to say. Leland knew this because less than second after he said it he wanted every syllable back. Stephanie's lips drew into a tight line, and that was good because if they were open she might have said something hurtful. Instead all that came out was a muffled growl and a look of death that made Leland's stomach turn over three times, big looping somersaults. Stephanie shuffled over to the sink, grabbed the worn sponge, and started cleaning again. She did this to keep from strangling Leland with her bare hands.

All right, he was giving into Martha, giving into her premonitions about Wilma. The Lycanthropes were out in the shadows, only two of the four, watching him for some sinister purpose. He could wait he supposed, meet her later in safety, but now was as good a time as any. In the end he couldn't hide Wilma from them anyway so Alexander waited a second, took in a deep breath, and with no idea of how it would all unfold he walked up to Wilma Jackson. The little girl was so involved with her thoughts she wouldn't have heard his approach even if he wanted her too until he was standing just out of the light cast by the moon that made an almost angelical circle around her. He wanted so much just to stand and marvel at the sight, the same way he did with Jesus in that small village outside of Jerusalem, but time was growing short and he needed to talk with her.

"Hello Wilma." Alexander said in his most courteous manner.

The words startled the little girl so bad she almost fell off the slide as she whirled around in place. If not for her hand grabbing the railing of the rusted slide she might have taken a nasty fall. Alexander chided himself for scaring her. What a bit of irony, he saves her from two different life-threatening situations only to almost kill her with a couple of spoken words.

"Who's there?" She called out looking into the dark. Alexander stayed silent not knowing if opening his mouth would cause another near fatal accident. "Who's there?" Wilma asked again and this time she couldn't hide the fear in her voice. She was a strong girl for her age but after the last two days her strength was finally giving out.

"It's me Wilma, the one you called 'Han' last night." Alexander called out from the darkness.

"You're," Wilma said with a shocked expression at hearing his voice," the angel who came for me in the crack house and who stopped J-Rock and Slim from hurting me Saturday night."

"I am guilty of both, but I am no heavenly angel little one." Alexander admitted.

The little girl sat quietly eyeing the shadows of the dark with both eyes before finally speaking. "Can I see you, please?" Wilma whispered, almost as if she were afraid to ask for fear of shattering the moment.

In all the preparation to just speak with Wilma Alexander forgot he was still standing in the shadows of the street lamps and moonlight. He took a small breath, stepped out of the dark, and then slowly walked up to the little girl who sat with her mouth wide-open in amazement. He stood there for a second letting her take him in before saying anything to break the connection.

"And what seems to be so interesting about the stars tonight?" He asked looking skyward.

The question brought Wilma back to reality, back to the here and now as she looked upward along with Alexander. "I just come out here to think sometimes, get some air and clear my head of all the loose stuff bouncing around inside." She said as he looked back down to her and smiled a small smile.

"I get that way too on occasions myself." Alexander offered.

The two remained in an awkward silence; each not knowing what to say to the other even though they had prepared speeches in their minds. The silence may have gone on all night if not for Wilma finally speaking up with a squeaky voice.

"Can I ask you something?"

"By all means little one, ask me what you will?" Alexander nodded.

"What are you?" She asked quickly.

Second time tonight from the same lineage, good to see curiosity runs in the family the vampire thought to himself. Alexander bit his bottom lip trying to gather his thoughts and words to answer the question before finally speaking. "Well, I'm not sure how to put this so I'm just going to be as blunt as possible with you if that is permissible Wilma."

"Yes, finally an adult is going to tell me the worldly truth about something." Wilma mumbled with an air of victory and a small fist pump.

"And hearing the truth, is it that much of a victory these days?" Alexander asked.

"I have a small issue with authority, more to the point in being treated like a semi-adult, but please continue." Wilma offered quickly with a single breath covering up her remarks with a broad smile.

"A semi-adult, is that a new term these days?" Alexander asked again with a lost expression.

"If you were only asking me then yes it's a new term, someone else though would probably be lost like you." Wilma continued still smiling ear to ear.

"Oh, all right then, I'll make a mental note of that one." Alexander said with his own smile. "So I may continue then?"

"If you don't tell me something very soon I'm pretty sure I'm going to hurt myself and embarrass you in the process." Wilma stated rather flatly.

So with that Alexander took a deep breath in preparation to do something he hadn't done since 1895 with Grammy's future husband's father when the man was just about Wilma's age. With a steeled air he spoke and looked into Wilma's eye. "I was born in the year 356 B.C. to Phillip the Second, King of Macedonia and Olympias, his queen. I was given the rightful name of Alexandros but that soon became Alexander. I'm a vampire Wilma. I live off the blood of humans or other things if the situation requires. I have walked this earth for more than two thousand and three hundred years."

He hadn't spoken the words in so long and yet each one still had the same numbing effect on who ever heard them. Wilma sat perfectly still in shock for a second as her mouth fell open exposing pearly white teeth, the obvious sign of a studious brusher. Then the little girl suddenly stepped off the slide, hand up in the classic I-have-a-question pose before practically falling to the ground on numb legs. Without even a puff of air Alexander moved over to catch her gingerly by the arm, almost cradling her again. Without the aid of holding onto the vampire Wilma probably would have hit the ground unceremoniously hard.

"Did you just say you're Alexander the Great and a vampire to boot?" She asked regaining her balance and composure.

"Yes I am"

"You're a vampire!" she said with emphasis, almost daring Alexander to dispute what he just said.

"Yes I am"

"And at present," Wilma began counting on her fingers," your over two thousand three hundred years old."

"That would be correct, though I think I said that." Alexander smiled nodding his head after taking a second to recall his words to her.

"No wait, this can't be right. I did a history report on Alexander the Great for Mr. Robinson's class. You're saying you're the same Alexander that destroyed Thebes?"

"I wouldn't say I alone destroyed the city, but yes I was that man." Alexander remarked with a small huff.

"You're the same Alexander that chased the Persian King Darius across Asia? The same who said Asia would be won by the spear?" Wilma asked quickly.

"I see your report was quite detailed." Alexander commented. "Most people just remember the Gordian knot and my horse Bucephalus."

"I read everything about you I could find. It's kind of weird but I've always admired you, felt close to you after what I discovered."

Alexander blinked and whispered, "Why is that little one?"

"My father didn't want me either." Wilma whispered with a sad smile as the small confession rolled off her lips.

The act of breathing was just an illusion now, Alexander no longer needed air and his lungs no longer drew oxygen in. He mimicked breathing when he had to, when it was necessary to keep up an appearance, and yet with that one small statement he felt like someone had hit him hard enough to knock the air from him leaving him speechless. "Wilma...I'm...so sorry."

"I found him through the Internet and called him once without telling my mom." She moved on after a moment looking at him with that sad smile still. "He told me he didn't have a kid and even if he did he wouldn't have some silly girl hanging around. You did all these great things without a father so I thought if you could do without yours I could do without mine."

"Your father was wrong Wilma, as was mine." Alexander stated with warm compassion,

"I know," she sighed and shrugged her shoulders moving the conversation on and the vampire found himself thanking her silently for it, "I read a piece once in history class and it's always stuck with me. In it you never used war to destroy or suppress a society, but as a last option to obtain unity for it. You tried to make us all one tribe and that's a great thing I think."

The remark embarrassed Alexander for a second, almost to the point of blushing, responding with the same far-away smile. "Thank you little one, I'm honored by your words."

"No, wait, this can't be true. This goes against reality and science and plain common sense." Wilma suddenly said shaking her head, denying the explanation Alexander had just spoke.

"Please Wilma. Do you really need proof after the house and the car? I know it's hard to accept but you need to understand what I am and why I am here." Alexander asked with a raised eyebrow.

"Oh yeah, you have a point there. Okay, let's say for science's sake that you are a vampire and you do drink blood, how did you become a vampire? Was it something like out of Anne Rice or Bram Stoker?" Wilma asked in an excited state that seemed to be growing exponentially. Alexander also noticed that she hadn't moved an inch since his opening statement, not a centimeter away from him. Wilma was either strong willed and curious or still in shock and he was choosing the first two from the way she was asking questions.

"The transformation is difficult to explain little one, it is something one must experience to be described." Alexander answered as best as he could.

"What was yours like?" She asked quickly following his answer with another question.

"Mine is a long story little one, you may need to sit down before it's over." He said. The question was bound to come up and Alexander knew there was no use in trying to hide his past from her. With a sweep of his hand, the vampire motioned Wilma over to a bench where the two could sit and talk like friends and not like adversaries on the street. Wilma didn't move at first, but slowly she went over and sat down, when she turned back to look for Alexander he was already sitting. The quick movement threw her off for a second. A double take was needed to insure nothing was done with smoke and mirrors to fool her.

"My transformation little one came about because I wanted it to, because deep inside I needed to be released from a great burden." Alexander began.

"Released from what burden?" Wilma asked

"I no longer wanted to be Alexander the Great, military genius and boy king."

"Why?" Wilma asked with a whisper.

"I was so tired little one, near the end I realized what I was doing was not what I wanted. I wanted to bring this world together so the cultures could combine, help each other to grow and enrich everyone. I simply wanted peace and prosperity among us all, but instead I brought war and misery because the men under me wanted nothing but power." Alexander answered.

"How could you say it was all bad? You gave the world the Library at Alexandria, a wealth of knowledge for everyone. I would give anything to walk into its halls just once, to see the philosophers and thinkers going over papyrus after papyrus and the words written on them." Wilma whispered low.

"Yes little one, the Library was spectacular to behold, but one good deed does not cleanse a soul." Alexander responded.

"I think you did the best with what you had to work with, at least that's what my mom tells me when we're short on money. You've come the closest to uniting us, we'll never be that close again." Wilma offered. The vampire smiled slightly at the touch of compassion from his new friend.

"Your mother is quite the philosopher Wilma. Maybe if I had her to counsel with things all would have turned out differently." Alexander said looking up to the stars.

"So what really happened the day you died? Every culture it seems has a different version of just how and why you died, but it's obvious they all missed it by a longshot." Wilma asked quietly, almost in reverence.

Alexander looked back down, took another breath, and started to talk. When the words first started he found them hard to say, but as each one rolled off his tongue the letters became easier and easier until finally Alexander was telling the story of his birth as a vampire to Wilma.

"Do you know of my journey through Egypt?" He asked

"A little, like you were made a Pharaoh, created the city of Alexandria, and conquered most of the lands between the Tigris and the Euphrates River." Wilma answered confidently and quickly with a smile.

Alexander eyed Wilma with amazement as he spoke, "that is the short version I guess you might say. Just how much do you know about me?"

"Oh, I know a good bit." She said smiling even more.

"So you know about my journey to the Oracle of Zeus Ammon then?"

"I read about it, but the historians can't seem to agree on what the Oracle told you. Most say you told by the Oracle you were a God." Wilma remarked.

The vampire leaned in close and whispered. "I never put much stock in seer's and such, but maybe that time I should have."

Wilma leaned in too almost touching Alexander's nose with her own. "What did she say?"

"She told me I was the true son of Zeus Ammon. " Alexander said while perfectly still looking Wilma dead in her eyes. " Yet, even the son of Zeus isn't immortal. She told me not to enter the Hanging Gardens of Babylon. There was a great danger there waiting for me, to change me and take me away."

"So that's where you were changed, the Hanging Gardens?" Wilma asked excitedly suddenly sitting back again.

"Slow Wilma, slow. Let me tell you some more first." Alexander laughed and raised his hand. "My army had secured the surrender of the city of Babylon without a fight, the way most cities fell when confronted with the prospect of waging war with Alexander the Great. While my soldiers and staff ran through the city acquiring its riches, I went against the words of the Oracle and visited the Hanging Gardens built by Nebuchadnezzar. My word but were the gardens beautiful Wilma, with plants and trees growing everywhere you turned, and the wild birds and animals running about. It astounded me someone could build something of such beauty. I wandered its halls and paths for hours until I came across a man dressed in Greek clothing standing off in the shadows created by the dense branches of the trees. As I approached he asked if I was Alexandros the great conqueror. I told him I was and asked if he could give me his name. He told me his name was not important, not yet at least. There were other things at the moment that were more serious, like the prophecy the Oracle had told me."

"He knew about prophecy?" Wilma asked with a gasp and clutch of her hand to his arm.

"Oh yes, he knew a lot of things about me, just like you little one." Alexander said with a raised eyebrow before continuing on. "I asked how he knew of the prophecy but he responded asking how I could have conquered so many lands and subjugated so many people when my heart wasn't that of a tyrant like my father. He asked how much longer I would let the generals and other smaller men kill in my name before I put an end to it. He said I was the feeble lion who ruled a pride filled with avarice and lechery, not one ounce of nobility among any of us. His words infuriated me, drove me to taste anger on my tongue. The words stabbed at my manhood and ego. I stepped forward saying I was intent on showing him his heart on the point of my sword when he was suddenly gone in the blink of an eye. Rather his form was gone but his voice was still there sounding in my mind like he was only inches away from my ear."

"Whoa!" Wilma whispered losing herself in the vampire's words as he continued on.

"I know, so I called out to the voice demanding to know who or what manner of demon it was, but laughter was the only answer I was given. The voice said it knew what my true intentions were and how I had let the generals twist everything I wanted to evil. After this night though it would all change. From this night on I would start to see the true pain I had let happen, the misery I brought to the world."

"Wait a minute! Didn't the man know what you were trying to do? And what did he mean by 'misery'?" Wilma asked sarcastically.

"I thank you for the support little one." Alexander said with a tip of his head.

Wilma blushed for a second and looked at the ground. "You know...I'm just saying...you're welcome."

"Are we ready to continue?" The vampire asked.

"Oh yeah, sorry, please continue." Wilma said with a nod of her head.

"I asked what misery he was exactly talking of, just like you have, and all the voice said was my time was at an end. All men must be judged for their crimes, answer not only to the Gods but their own souls as well. My judgment would come after my awakening. I yelled back saying no man or demon would judge me. I would never allow it, yet the voice said there was nothing to stop it now. It said I would know when Darius the Persian King was dead that my end would almost be at hand."

"Hearing something like that would make me pass right out." Wilma whispered with a shocked expression.

"Yes Wilma, I was more than a little upset as I called out to the voice again saying I would not be judged by anything in this world. All I heard though was the hollow laughter in my head. I ran from the gardens with it ringing in my ears, calling out that I would return to Babylon no longer a conqueror but conquered. As soon as I reached the outside streets I saw something I had never seen before." Alexander stated with a drop in the volume of his voice at the end, like the memory was still too fresh for him to accept.

"What did you see?"

"The misery little one, it was everywhere. Every eye I looked into, at every turn, seemed to throw it back at me. The voice was right I realized. I was starting to see what I had done to the people of the city, to even my own loyal soldiers. Between the eyes and that hideous laughing tormenting my mind I did not sleep all night, but I did come up with a plan." Alexander said with a halfhearted smile.

"What? What did you come up with?"

"Now you have to remember at the time it was a brilliant plan Wilma, and it was so easy." Alexander said raising a finger. "The voice said that my end would come when Darius was dead, so the way to defeat the demon was to make sure the Persian King did not die."

"Oh yeah, that would have been a great plan, you know, if he hadn't died and all." Wilma said agreeing whole heartedly with Alexander while smiling weakly.

"Yes, that did dampen the outcome didn't it? So the next morning, after I moved my soldiers out of the city, I rode to Susa and took it. I took my army to the capital of the Persian Empire Persepolis itself and captured it, but to my dismay Darius had escaped. To most I must have looked possessed, but they never knew why I was chasing Darius so doggedly, how much I needed the man to remain alive. If he was breathing then I could, would, get answers to the questions in my mind. I still saw the pain and misery in people's eyes and of course the demon's voice never wavered during this time. It still taunted me, keeping me awake at night. It would tell me of the approaching end, how I would finally be judged."

"Judged?" Wilma said shaking her head.

"Yes little one, judged. I was to see all the pain and suffering that I had caused to everyone over the years. I would feel their pain and drink their suffering the voice said like a potion. Darius would die and my punishment would begin." Alexander explained with a low voice.

"So you chased Darius to keep him alive?"

"Yes, only it was not to be as you know." The vampire chuckled with a sigh that was filled with irony.

"But his own men killed him. You didn't do anything, that's so unfair." Wilma whined with the same low whisper.

"Your right little one, but in the end it was a fool's folly to think I could stop what was happening. The fates ensured the end by blocking my every attempt to keep Darius from his fate. He fled in a coach to escape me but the fool ran from the one person who tried to protect him. When I flung open the coach door and saw his dead form lying there, something inside my mind broke and I screamed, more in anger then fear. I had fought for so long to stop the prophecy from coming to fruition, for days upon days, and then it came true anyway and my hope was gone. I could hear the demon laughing at its victory in my head." Alexander said with a shake of his head.

"So that's why you started acting deranged, out of control." Wilma gasped, as if the light bulb finally went off in her head.

Alexander let out a small laugh, she really did know a lot about him. "From that point everything was all surreal, pointless. I dressed in Persian clothing and burned the wagons of the riches we had obtained through our many battles and conquest. The Generals pleaded with me to stop the insanity, my friends begged me to stop my actions, but I was waiting for the end to come. I could not sleep at night because I only heard the voice, I could not eat because nothing would stay in my stomach, and all around me all I could see was pain and misery. I could not stand it any longer so I decided to end it."

"But you took India during that time." Wilma remarked.

"The Generals took India little one. My soldiers who were loyal to me took India little one, not me." Alexander countered still smiling.

"What were you doing?" Wilma asked

"Seeing the world for what it was, just like the demon in the gardens had spoken of, seeing what I had created through my own eyes Wilma. In all my conquest, I never really looked into my enemy's eyes or heard the sounds of battle for what they really were. Now I was seeing everything and it sickened me so much I simply refused to be...me. I dressed differently and married a Persian Princess to ease tensions, to escape being Alexander." He choked on the last part making Wilma wince for a brief second.

"And the worst was yet to come." Wilma whispered feeling just like she said.

"Yes little one, the bottom of my despair was still to come. I lost my horse Bucephalus, my old friend who had taken me into every battle without so much as a threatening cut to him, and then he was wounded and died in one fight. I was so distraught, so torn inside. I sought to battle any warrior on any ground at any time without any sort of plan. I did not care about a thing including my life."

"Trying to commit suicide in battle, they call it 'suicide by Police' these days."

"Really, I'll have to keep that one in mind too." Alexander said with a quip.

"My friend Sasha's father did it a year ago. He beat her mother into a coma on the front porch step with the butt of a gun and when the Police showed up he shot two of them before they shot and killed him. Sasha lives with her Grandmother in Chicago now." Wilma said quietly turning away from the vampire, to hide a tear or not he wasn't sure.

"I'm sorry for you once again, and for her Wilma." Alexander offered wanting to touch her small shoulder, but something held his hand in check.

"I'm okay. I got over it after a while. You were telling me about India and how you were trying to end it all or something like that." Wilma said quickly trying to shift the conversation away from her pain.

"You could say that, and in India it almost happened. I stopped the army to fight a village of warriors called the Malhi. The battle was long and fierce. I personally charged them several times not caring for my wounds or my men, the battle lust only stopped when an arrow pierced my breastplate. I thought for a second my life was done and all the pain and torture of the last months was gone for good. I could finally have peace. I was actually relieved lying there on the ground."

"But you survived," Wilma said suddenly turning her body back toward him so she could take in the experience and the story better," Only to try and cross the Gedrosian dessert."

A small smile played across Alexander's face as he talked, but Wilma could tell it was one of pain not joy. "The Generals thought we could make it, but I knew it was a death march, and yet I sat quiet and let them lead us into Hell. I watched a third of my men and friends die out there in that dessert. They died because I could not lead them Wilma, I failed them all so miserably."

"You can't blame yourself, what happened was out of your control." Wilma offered with a sympathetic tone, trying to ease his pain even though she wasn't sure how to.

"Maybe little one, maybe." Alexander responded back with a raised eyebrow.

"What caused you to return to Babylon?" Wilma asked quietly.

He looked to her with a newfound admiration. The girl had obviously done an excellent job on her report for Mrs. Robinson. She looked right through him to the pain stored in his soul.

"It was the death of my dear friend Hephaeston that finally made me decide to return to Babylon, the physicians said it was a fever but I knew deep in my heart it was something else. It was him, the one from the gardens. I knew it the way I knew the sun would come from the east and fall to the west every day in the world. He had followed me so long tormenting me and now he committed the foulest act to drive me back to the Garden. That was the last thing I could endure, there was nothing left for me to give or to fight for so I decided to go back to Babylon and confront the demon at the gardens."

"What happened when you got there?" Wilma asked enthralled.

"I found him standing by the same tree he was by the first time I was in the hanging gardens. Even through the dark of the shadows I could see the smile on his face. He asked me if I had returned as a conqueror or one who was conquered. All of the sudden, and I'm not sure why, but sheer fury just over took me. I pulled my sword from its scabbard, pointed it at the demon's chest, and screamed I would be free of this curse tonight. By either his death or mine the curse would be done. I was ready to kill or die; there was no hesitation in my mind."

"The demon just laughed and smiled saying it would be ironic if I killed the one being that could end the pain. It actually asked me if I was ready, prepared to face my next battle and be truly free, not just from the last months but from the generals and this life of being Alexander the Great. The question drove the very air from my lungs it shocked me so, the prospect of having this hellish existence end was the farthest thought from my mind. Yet now here it hung in front of my eyes like a carrot on a string, just out past my fingertips every time I reached for it." Alexander whispered.

"So you chose the transformation?"

The memory of that night was still fresh. Alexander could almost smell the flowers of the garden on the night's wind as he spoke low. "I lowered my sword and asked him to release me and he asked if I knew what pain was, the true pain of the tormented soul, and the pain at the loss of someone closer than a brother. I could only whisper yes. He asked if I knew of suffering, the bitter taste of it, the agonizing feeling of watching so many die for nothing but greed. Again, I could only whisper yes. He laughed once more and I asked why he tortured me so. He replied with a calm voice that it was necessary for the next step, that the great Alexander had to be shown that he was simply a man at the end and all men must pay for their crimes."

"And that's why you chose the transformation, to become a vampire? Because you had to pay for something you didn't even do?" Wilma gasped from shock.

"Yes and no little one. I know now that I didn't bring misery to the world, but I did nothing to stop the generals from doing so. Truthfully, the only price was my life as a conqueror and in the end I realized I was more than willing to pay it." Alexander said letting the smile on his face slip away.

"Why though? Why walk away?" Wilma asked not following the vampire's last statement.

"The transformation doesn't come without a cost Wilma. It takes something different from everyone it touches. My price was my life as Alexander the Great...and my Roxanna. I no longer ruled the world or any of the people that walked on it. In less than a day I had gone from a conqueror to what you see before you. I was no longer married to my love." Alexander explained holding out his hands.

"In less than a day you became a vampire! Was it anything like in "Interview with a Vampire" where Tom Cruise bit Brad Pitt's neck then opened his own veins to let him drink?" Wilma asked suddenly excited, the pains of Alexander's story quickly forgotten in the name of scientific curiosity...or something like that.

"Well, I don't remember much from my experience, but I can tell you this" Alexander started.

"Yeah," Wilma leaned in with her voice dripping from excitement.

"It's a secret." Alexander whispered leaning in as well.

"What," Wilma whined shrinking away with a look of disgust," Are you kidding me? What do you mean a 'secret'?"

"It's just that little one, a very well-guarded secret among our kind." Alexander sighed with a small sigh.

"Come on, really? I can't wait till I'm old enough to know something important so I won't tell you or any other adult!" Wilma spat sitting back and pouting.

"Well, I'm sure you'll do just that little one!" Alexander replied with a smirk.

A second or two of silence went by before Wilma finally broke and spoke up, the disgust from earlier still sounding in her voice. "Well, can you answer a different question then?"

"What's it like being a vampire?" Alexander asked for her.

"Oh, you READ minds now?" Wilma asked with exasperation.

"No," Alexander said shaking his head," the question just comes up about this time in every conversation like this one."

"Oh, well what's it like?" Wilma asked, the anger slipping from her voice finally.

"Just like you little one, only with certain restrictions."

"No," Wilma said this time shaking her head," I mean is it like Anne Rice and Bram Stoker or is it like the movies? Do you know Kung-Fu like Blade and ride a black motorbike? Or do you sit around the living room dressed in period clothes biting on a pretty girl's necks?"

"What exactly are you trying to find out Wilma?" Alexander asked back shaking his head and feeling suddenly lost in the conversation.

"I mean you have to have some kind of superhuman powers to walk out of that building explosion last night, right?" She asked with a little attitude.

"I guess you can say my advanced age has brought me some added extras." Alexander agreed seeming more than a little evasive.

"What kind of 'extras'? Do you turn gaseous like in the movies and books?" Wilma asked, her voice sounding excited yet again.

"No, and I know of no vampire that can." Alexander said searching his memory to make sure.

"So if you didn't turn gaseous and go under the door last night how did you get in?" Wilma asked, the excitement in her voice being traded out for some good old fashioned curiosity.

"I just used the front door." Alexander replied.

"But," Wilma responded as her balloon began deflating," I didn't hear a crash of the door being ripped from the hinges."

"I left the hinges intact. I simply passed through the door."

"You did what?"

"I can pass through solid material Wilma, but it drains me and it can hurt something fierce if I do not watch what I'm doing."

"Like a ghost, you can just walk through walls and stuff." Wilma uttered in sudden shock.

"Yes little one, like Casper I can just walk through a wall or anything solid when the feeling strikes my fancy." Alexander said with a grin.

"And all the gunfire, I assume there was gunfire because those guys always shoot first and ask questions later, did you just 'pass' through the bullets too?" Wilma asked painstakingly wording the question according to her scientific nature.

Alexander took a second to structure his answer for Wilma. "Not really, I just sort of let the bullets bounce off me. I have really tough skin. The only problem was I lost my AC/DC T-shirt in the process. I really liked that shirt."

"So you're bullet proof?"

"Yes."

"And you're impervious to explosions?"

"I think it depends on the level of the explosion, which would have to be very big to hurt me." Alexander answered with a nod.

"Good Lord! Then there really isn't anything that can hurt you, is there? Not the hail of bullets or the explosion from last night." Wilma said in astonishment.

"You remember the T-Rex from Jurassic Park?" Alexander leaned in close and asked with a whisper.

"No Way!" Wilma whispered already guessing the answer from the vampire.

"The beast wouldn't even leave a scratch on me." Alexander continued with a small wink of his right eye and a playful smile. Wilma could only stare in amazement at the new friend she had made, or on second thought, had found her.

———————————

The kitchen was still quiet, after fifteen minutes of scrubbing the same spot in the sink and Stephanie was still mad enough not to want to talk to Leland. He shifted from one foot to the other nervously trying to figure out what to do. On the one hand he could venture a quick question, a recon into the battle field to see what would happen. Minimal loss of life and he could detect any land mines that were waiting for an unlucky step. Yet, that wasn't Leland's way with Stephanie. He always took the second choice, to be upfront and truthful about anything and everything with her. Did it come from his feelings for her? Yeah, maybe...no, it most certainly did. He felt a longing so deep and strong for her that there was no way he could lie to her, not in her face or behind her back from the corner. So, the only choice left was to do this thing, do it right from the heart.

"Stephanie, we need to talk." Leland called to her.

"Nope, you don't need to talk about anything remember? That Alexander, he's a real funny guy, don't you remember?" She answered back full of spite while scrubbing harder on the sink.

"Stephanie, stop scrubbing that damn sink and look at me." Leland said forcefully.

The tone was new to Stephanie, something that took her by such surprise it scared her for a second. She dropped the scrub brush in the bottom of the sink while turning around. Leland locked eyes with her for another second not saying a word. Stephanie felt a tinge of anger at being frightened by the Leland's tone, so much so she was about to make it known when the street preacher reached up and pulled off his T-shirt and his undershirt. The move shocked Stephanie again, but not enough to keep her eyes from wondering over Leland's muscled torso. The street preacher began to walk over and Stephanie felt her breath quicken with an old but familiar anticipation. This was a different Leland, a more assertive man than the gentle street preacher. He looked meaner, like a gang banger right off the corner.

"Lee, what are you doing?" she said with a forced giggle that masked her concern.

He stopped right in front of her and pointed to a set of tattoos on his right pectoral. Two rows of two perfect representations of the Club from a deck of cards. "Do you know what these mean?"

Something wasn't right. The mood was all wrong, too serious she thought before speaking. "Those are gang tattoos from your old days, right?"

"Yes and no, there's more to them than just that." Leland said pointing to the top one. "These were given out to the Tenth Street Disciples as badges of honor for certain completed tasks. This one was for beating up a Latin King by the name of Jesus Calderon. I used a brick and put him in the hospital for three weeks with internal and bodily injuries so bad he still has problems walking today."

Leland moved to the one below. "And this one was for shooting a member of the Black Gangsters who disrespected our turf by selling his drugs on it. I didn't kill him, but someone else did six months later with two bullets to the back of his head in some trashed out alley. They didn't find him till the rats and dogs had their fill."

"Why are you telling me this Leland?" Stephanie remarked tentatively almost afraid to hear the answer.

The street preacher ignored her question though moving onto the second row, top one. "This one was for enforcing the collection of dues owed the Tenth Street Disciples by various individuals such as store managers and prostitutes. You don't want to know how I did the collecting; it involved a baseball bat, heads, and some very unpleasant work."

"Okay Leland, I get it." Stephanie said trying to stop the confession.

"And this last one," Leland said intent on finishing what he started, "was for dealing. I made the most money because I hustled the fastest. No one out sold me on the corners."

"Why the hell are you telling me this?" Stephanie found herself screaming. She was so upset at hearing the confession that she was through with hearing another word. "What, are you trying to prove how much of a bad ass you are compared the Alexander? Well, you win Leland. You're the meanest mother on the block!"

"I was, but not anymore. Here I am trying to save this place and the people in it and I can't even do that without the help of some strange white man and on top if it all, the woman I care for is falling in love with him!" Leland growled closing his eyes and grinding his teeth holding in the anger. It was just like the old days he thought as the red haze clouded his mind, back to when I would get so mad at the smallest damn things.

The kitchen was quiet again thankfully Stephanie thought, maybe too quiet she was thinking when Leland took a step back from her suddenly. He looked like the old street preacher now, gone was the gang banger from the corner replaced by the man she loved as he whispered. "Do you remember the first day I saw you?"

"Yes, it was after Wilma and I moved in. We had just returned from the grocery store and you helped me carry in the sacks. You were the only gentlemen in this whole damn place." Stephanie answered feeling a little safer. She wanted so badly to ask him what he meant by what he said just a moment before, did he really say he cared for her?

"I fell in love with you that day, hopelessly over the moon out of breath in love. I haven't stopped thinking about you for the last year." Leland said looking straight in her beautiful eyes while stepping back again to lean up against the counter.

The last literally knocked Stephanie for the proverbial loop. She had hoped for so long to hear the words 'love' and 'you' from Leland and any combination of the two would have sufficed, even in such an awkward confession as this one. "Lee...why didn't you say something before now?"

"I'm not good enough for you Stephanie." He answered back shaking his head.

"What do you mean you're not good enough for me?" Stephanie shot back stepping across the room to confront the street preacher.

Leland shoved his shirt back over his head, pulled up his sleeves, and then held out both hands palms up to Stephanie. "What do you see? Nothing I bet but normal skin and hands. Me, I see every damnable deed I have ever done. How could someone as sweet as you and as pure as Wilma love a man who has beaten, maimed, and destroyed innocence in this world?"

"By forgiving you of your past," Stephanie whispered quickly without a moment's hesitation while taking Leland's right hand and placing it over her heart. "I accept what you were, what you are now, and what you will be in the future Leland Hall because I love you. I have since the day you carried in my eggs and bread for me."

The moment was too much for Leland as he looked away from Stephanie's eyes. "No, I can't do this. I can't do this."

She took her left hand and gently, but firmly, pulled Leland's face back to look into her eyes. Stephanie saw a small set of tears running down Leland's face and she felt his heart racing as she spoke. "Why can't you be with me now? Are you afraid of something or someone?"

"Of me, I'm afraid of hurting you or God forbid Wilma. I couldn't live with myself if either of you were hurt because of me!" Leland spat wanting to turn his head away.

Stephanie didn't lose contact this time. She held Leland with her eyes, her hand, and the strength of her heart. "I know you won't hurt us, and you know how I know this? Because I know you're a good man Leland Hall. Out of all the men I have known in this life you are the noblest of them all."

"Even next to Alexander?"

"Yes, even next to him," Stephanie smiled warmly.

Leland stood still for a second as he came to a sudden gut reeling realization. He had confessed his love for Stephanie and she was still standing in the same room. She hadn't taken off running into the dark screaming with fear or disgust. Maybe, just maybe he was good enough to love her.

"Okay." Leland muttered finally.

"Okay." Stephanie said back feeling his heart begin to slow down finally.

"I'm good with this...I'm good with this," Leland said with a small smile.

"Yeah, so am I." Stephanie giggled sounding like a school girl with her boyfriend by the lockers in the hall.

"There is one other thing, though." Leland said cupping her cheek in his left hand.

"Yeah, and what's that?" Stephanie said enjoying the warm touch of Leland's hand on her face.

He leaned forward and kissed Stephanie affectionately, slowly caressing her lips. It lasted only a few seconds, but for the two it felt like a yearlong embrace that had been waiting to come to fruition. Leland broke the embrace and looked deep into her eyes not speaking for a second.

"So what is it?" Stephanie asked feeling a little nervous all of the sudden. What if he didn't like her kiss? Did he taste something weird? Did she have bad breath?

"Nothing, it's just after waiting a year to do that it was everything and more, kind of knocked my socks off." Leland grinned.

"Want to do it again?" Stephanie asked with a mischievous eye.

"I get to do it again!"

"As many times as you want,"

The two stood holding each other, kissing like young sweethearts and enjoying love again. When Wilma came in later she found the two drying some dishes and talking over the sink. She couldn't be sure but she felt some of the conversation had to do with how the two were going to tell her about their relationship. Funny, but Wilma always knew her mother and Leland were in love with each other. Everyone in the Laurel knew the two were in love so why did it take them so long to realize it.

"You spent the last hundred years or so in the grave of a Southern general from the Civil War waking up just a few days ago because a couple of inept grave robbers just happened to be too loud." Wilma said running back the story Alexander had told her just few minutes prior.

"Um yes, that is a fair telling of events." Alexander said with a nod of his head.

"Wow," Wilma remarked with open eyes then just like a typical teenager fired off a question," Why did you go into hiding?"

"It's complicated little one, a story for another night perhaps." Alexander stated

"Okay, but you shouldn't worry about hiding so much. Go out and buy a custom car, live and see the world. Go places, any place, and just see everything. Staying hidden in the dark never solves anything, or so my mother says." Wilma demanded.

"All right, I just may do that little one."

"So what do you think about the Twentieth Century?"

"From what I have seen and heard, it's quite exciting I will admit." Alexander replied.

"And why's that?"

"There's so much energy out there little one, it's like there's always something happening somewhere at any time during the day or night. The Internet has given the world a portal to communicate, the music is fast and furious, and the city here never seems to sleep."

"That's what they say about New York City." Wilma said with a smile.

"What?"

"They say New York City is the town that never sleeps, or at least that's what Frank Sinatra use to sing about." Wilma answered.

"Ah! Frank, he was a really good singer, the golden voice that made the ladies swoon." Alexander pointed out.

"You like Frank Sinatra?" Wilma giggled uncontrollably.

"Are you laughing at me?" Alexander asked with a chuckle being overcome with his own mirth at the Wilma's laughter.

"No! It's just a man dressed in a concert T-shirt with boots and jeans seem more like the rock-n-roll type then the oldie but goodie crooner." Wilma said between gasps as she tried to get a hold of her laughter.

"I like all types of music. I like Metallica and Hard Rock, Classic Rock like Heart, Rap has some good music and lyrics, and Country is good to sit down and listen too while having an ice cold beer." Alexander stated with a broad smile but still hiding the large incisors from the view of the little girl.

"Oh my God, you sound like you walked into Best Buy and said 'I'll take it all, box it up right away!'" Wilma practically yelled.

"I did kind of do that you know." Alexander chuckled trying unsuccessfully to hold back his own laughter now.

"Is there anything you don't like?" Wilma asked

"Not really."

"So does the open minded streak extend to Books?"

"I've read everything from King, Koontz, Rice, and other horror counterparts. I read all the works of Clancy, Turrow, Grisham, Andrews, Rowling and others. I haven't read that much in the last two days though because I have been rather busy." Alexander said.

"Whoa," Wilma said with an open mouth at hearing the list," How many words do you read a minute?"

"Which hand, right or left?"

"Oh Wow! Do you watch movies that fast?"

"Well," Alexander said with a shrug," it's easier to get a good number in when you fast forward through them"

"Are you kidding me? You fast-forward through Star Wars...and the first Batman or Batman Begins...and whatever else?" Wilma asked in disbelief.

"Yes," Alexander answered cautiously, his senses picking up Wilma's growing distress.

"Why did you do that? I mean you miss all the nuances that way!" Wilma said with a high-pitched voice, the pain in it evident. It was as if Alexander had broken the highest law in the land according to Wilma and she was giving the closing argument at his trial.

"Nuances little one?"

"Yes! I mean you don't see the way Luke Skywalker look's at Leia with that puppy dog kind of love in his eyes or the playful grin from Han when he gets under her skin." Wilma pointed out with animated hands going up and down to add to her point.

"But Luke and Leia are brother and sister." Alexander countered with a single raised eyebrow.

"Of course I know that! But you don't know that in the first movie!" Wilma wailed

"Oh, I'm sorry." Alexander said with a slight smile

"And you don't see the way Michael Keaton played Batman with the precision that should have won him an Oscar! Or the great direction and devotion to the story and plot that Tim Burton displayed!" Wilma demanded.

"Oh yes! I do remember that now." Alexander added slowly trying to calm Wilma with just a slight placation. He hadn't really noticed what she had seen. He probably wouldn't have even if he slowed the movies down.

"Yeah and just how did you notice it when the movie's going by at a 100 miles per hour?" Wilma asked with dripping sarcasm.

"If I promise to watch all those movies again Wilma, but in their true artistic form, would you please grant me a second chance? I throw myself on your gracious mercy" Alexander asked with a sweet smile.

"Okay mister, but just this once and don't ask for it a second time all right." Wilma smiled playing along him.

"I never will little one." Alexander laughed happily. The two sat for a second or two just looking at each other warmly when Wilma glanced at her watch and saw the time. She jumped to her feet grabbing her left wrist as if the thing might fall off if she let it go for even a second but she was just making sure Mickey mouse's hands were pointing correctly. The two had been talking for almost two hours, which was two hours longer than she was supposed to be out.

"OH MY GOD, look at the time! I got to go, it's late!" Wilma said tearing off then suddenly turning back and running back to Alexander. Before he was even prepared, she had bent down and placed a kiss on his cheek, the small lips gently but firmly placing the gift right in the middle of the bone.

"Will you come and talk to me again, please?" She asked with eyes that implored to hear a positive answer.

"Yes little one, I will come and talk with you again very soon." Alexander answered before the voice in his head could object. He didn't need to have a relationship with a human right now he thought as he watched Wilma run away happily. He didn't need to care for someone right now, yet it never stopped him from saying yes to Wilma. Did his heart want this? Did his soul? Alexander wasn't sure. All he could do was hold on tight to the handrails of the cart on this crazy ride Martha had set in motion. Then he pulled his left hand from the pocket of his jeans and there tightly in his fingers grasp was his silver locket, the latch opening as if of its own accord. The picture's starred back at him, the woman and boy on one side and the blonde woman on the other. A small whisper escaped his lips. Maybe he did know where the yes came from after all.

"Thank you my loves,"

Then he looked up and away in the other direction from Wilma's house. His senses picked it up, a certain someone on the move, so Alexander decided to follow. He was gone in a flash, the wind and the night the only companions for the bench now.

The vampire was gone so fast that Dimitri had to make a quick double take. He and his brother watched the vampire from their vantage point, doing as instructed by Michaels. When his eyes finally proved to his brain that their prey wasn't on the bench he turned to Gregor. He was about the shake his red haired brother when he noticed his lycanthrope kin staring fixated on a window. Dimitri waited a second not sure what to do, he see-sawed between waking his brother and not wanting to get slapped. Finally though he gripped Gregor's shoulder and gave a quick hard shove causing the lycanthrope's head to snap.

Before the push something had been exploring at the back of Gregor's mind, touching and feeling like a blind person but with clear intentions. Whatever it was it wanted inside his memories. At first he just pushed away the ghostly fingers, but they kept coming back. Finally enough was enough and he turned around fully expecting someone to be standing behind him, but there was nothing there and no one to engage. He looked around carefully to make sure he and Dimitri were alone, and of course they were. He was beginning to turn back to watching the vampire when his gaze came across a set of windows and something behind the glass stopped him dead in his tracks.

There, sitting in an old recliner was an old woman clutching a photo in frame. How Gregor knew this was a mystery since he couldn't see past the drapes, but he knew she was there. He knew she was the one groping at his mind trying to get in. At first he thought she was sleeping, her chest moving up and down slowly in the old robe and worn nightgown, but then he saw it for the ruse it was. She was wide awake and she was looking right at him. What was she doing he thought to himself silently, what was she doing?

Oh don't worry about dear old Grammy. I just wanted to know about my new neighbors is all?

The voice was strong and loud, but the old woman didn't move her lips. She was speaking to him through some kind of telepathic connection, right into his mind.

I know all about you and your family Mr. Wolf. I know what you're here for and I know you came with a man who you don't fully trust. That's a good thing Mr. Wolf, you shouldn't trust him. There's other things' going on here, things you're not supposed know about. I'd watch my step if I was you.

Gregor was shocked, no stunned. He was about to ask the old woman what she knew and how she knew her information when Dimitri suddenly shoved him from behind.

"What the hell are you doing?" Gregor spat looking from Dimitri back the window.

"The vampire is gone. He disappeared a few seconds ago, I blinked and he was gone." Dimitri answered cowering slightly.

A wave of guilt washed over Gregor, he didn't want his brother to fear him. Family was the most important thing to him. It came before anything and everything else. He reached out and lovingly grasped his twin brother by the neck. "I am sorry, I did not mean to frighten."

"What happened? What was going on with the window, did you see something?" Dimitri asked quickly trying to look past his brother's ample frame to the window.

"It was nothing. We will discuss it with Yelena later. Now we have to find the vampire or else Michaels will skin us alive." Gregor said moving out.

Dimitri didn't hesitate a second to look at the window but he saw nothing but dirty drapes. He followed Gregor as the pair moved through the dark shadows of the Laurel Project without garnering so much as a glance. They moved effortlessly and silently until Gregor came to a sudden stop behind some bushes. He quickly turned to his brother, gave the sign for silence, and then pointed out to an open area on a corner. There, under a bright light of a street lamp stood a single figure by a single solitary phone booth. Gregor took a sniff of the air cataloging the scent in his brain for future reference. The pair stood still and observed their new interest forgetting momentarily about the vampire they were supposed to be following.

The street light was bright, too damn bright if you asked Kenneth. He walked over to the payphone under the harsh light briskly while pulling out a couple of quarter's intent on making a phone call. Then something popped, more like a branch cracking, just to his right out in the shadows. Kenneth froze instantly with fear staring at the dark where the sound came from. He knew he was playing a dangerous game, if anyone of the side he was turning on found out what he was doing then it was good bye Monster K. A second passed, then another, and the whole time he refused to breath or move. What if it was someone from Eight Balls posse? What if it was Leland? Hell, what if it was the man in black? Suddenly Kenneth wasn't feeling all that good about his plan or his immediate future. Maybe being King of the Hood wasn't such a great job now that he thought about it.

Then, almost on cue, a small flea bitten mutt with the mange hobbled out of the bushes. It stopped at the sight of Kenneth and then began to try to growl its displeasure at him. The pathetic snarl, the mutt was missing a few teeth, was matched only by the whiny growl. It didn't scare or intimidate anything, especially Kenneth. It just seemed to really piss him off. "Man, you better take your raggedy ass back on into the bushes!" He screamed while throwing a punch in the air in the direction of the dog.

The mutt at first didn't do a thing but stare with indifference at the strange human, but then gave out a small yelp and dashed back into the bushes where it came. At the victory Kenneth felt a sudden surge of empowerment from the top to bottom of his body. He sucked hard on his bottom lip while beginning to bounce his head up and down to an imaginary beat. The King of the Hood was back baby and you all better recognize or someone was going to get hurt. Kenneth was so engrossed at seeing his new future as the King that he never saw the slow approach of the car behind him. The sedan crept up until it was just a few feet away before suddenly turning on its bright lights and flooding the area.

The King of the Hood disappeared in the blink of an eye replaced by the scared teenager Kenneth. He stopped head-bobbing and sucking on his lip because the fear told him to. The front of the sedan moved past him at the same creep, but to him it felt as slow as a Hertz going to a funeral. It was hard to breath, pulling in air and then pushing it out was so hard it was making him sweat. And then finally, mercifully, the back window of the sedan appeared and it stopped with perfect precision right beside him. The tinted window was dark enough to keep prying eyes from seeing inside, and Kenneth was happy for that right now until it started to lower and when the face inside popped into view he screamed, yelped might be the actual adjective, like a little school child who just saw Santa at the mall. The right lifeless eye of Crazy D stared back from inside the hood of protective plastic. The left one was gone from what Kenneth could see, along with most of that side of Crazy's head.

"What's a matter young blood? Act like you ain't ever seen a dead body before?"

The sound of Eight Ball's voice snapped Kenneth away from Crazy's one-eye pirate look to the dealer exiting the sedan from the other side.

"Holy shit, you killed D?" was all Kenneth could muster through stuttering teeth.

Eight Ball marched around the end of the car and Kenneth noticed the smoking gun in the man's right hand. All the nasty images of what would happen if he got caught came screaming back and Kenneth felt his knees go weak causing him to take three involuntary steps back. Missing fingers and getting shot in the face was just the tip of Eight Ball's pain plan. The dealer stopped right in front of Kenneth pointing a long index finger into his face.

"My empire, my life young blood, has turned into a crumbling pile of shit. My patience, along with my cool, is gone. Yeah, I shot that fat mo-fo and I'm going to shoot you in the face too young blood unless I get some answers."

When all the 'I'm-taking-over-the-world' stuff started Kenneth had backup plans, what to do in case he was caught or someone was getting too close. They were damn good plans too, some of Kenneth's best work to date. And right now every one of those plans was gone, every step and order, lost due to the sight of the meanest drug dealer around pointing a finger at him and his friend shot in the head. Okay, so he didn't plan on this happening. All he needed was a minute to think of a way out, Monster K wasn't done for yet.

"You ain't thinking of lying to me, are you young blood?" Eight Ball suddenly said raising the smoking gun to about an inch in front of Kenneth's eye.

All right, that was it, Kenneth shut down with a vapor lock of the brain so bad it was pathetic. He couldn't remember his own name, hell he was lucky to remember to hold his bladder in check. And then, out of the air of the night, it felt like a little voice just started speaking in his mind. It told Kenneth to calm and what to say...and he did both without a second of hesitation.

"You can't find Chico or Shane can you?"

The question startled Eight Ball, shook him for the briefest of seconds. Then he cocked the hammer back on his nickel plated .45 which was pointed in Kenneth's face. "What'd you say? You better start talking young blood or so help me I'll make sure your momma has to have a closed casket for you!"

Kenneth wasn't sure where the words came from but they gave him courage, that and the fact he could see the effect on Eight Balls face. A surge of energy took control as he spun away from the dealer and out into the open street. "Aw damn man! I backed your ass with everyone. And now I find out its true!"

"Bitch, I'll shoot your ass right here and now if you don't' start making sense!"

"You're skimming man, taking a cut off the top!" Kenneth wailed.

The last stopped Eight Ball in his tracks. The gun lowered pointing to the ground as he stared at Kenneth with a look of bewilderment. "How did you know?"

"Chico told me this afternoon man, told me he was about to go big time with you and if I stayed loyal we'd all own this hood. He said you were taking a cut under the table, getting ready to make a run at being an independent. I said bullshit, no way Eight Ball's that stupid to try and take on the big boys without having an army ready."

"He talked?" Eight ball sputtered.

"Oh yeah, Chico talked so damn much he's got your ass in hot water now!" Kenneth yelled pouring it on thicker with every syllable. "Is that why you shot D? Damn man, you shot Crazy over this?"

"Damn, the boy talked." Eight Ball stammered almost ignoring Kenneth talking.

"Yeah, well you don't have to worry about that now. Chico's probably not talking to anyone either." Kenneth said rubbing his mouth. This was too easy. He had Eight Ball running like a white girl playing one of the Williams sisters on the tennis court.

"Why? What happened to Chico?" Eight Ball asked quickly locking his eyes with Kenneth's.

"You have to ask? Its obvious man, what you've been doing made its way back to the supplier's man, the big boys. They probably took care of Chico man, the ones you undercut and betrayed!" Kenneth shot back while holding his own evil smile in. "The man in black, he probably did it! I'll bet you a million dollars he's working with them!""

The mention of the name made Eight Ball take a step back in fear. "The man in black...you think he's working with the Producer?"

"Hell yes! He's the perfect assassin, like something out of the movies man. This dude is going to scare the hell out of you before finally moving in and finishing the deed!" Kenneth pointed out so helpfully.

"Yeah, that's what they always want. Turn you into a bitch and then shoot you in the back!" Eight Ball said tapping the barrel of the .45 to his heart. "But not this Negro, I ain't turning into a bitch."

"Oh man, that's the wrong thing Eight Ball. You got to go man, get out of the city tonight! It's the only way you're going to stay alive!" Kenneth gasped, prodding the dealer like the expert he had never been to leave town.

"I already said I ain't running! If they want a war then they got one!" Eight Ball yelled, demanded, while storming around the sedan to the passenger's side backdoor. He pointed to the massive driver, who no one had noticed exit the car, and barked an order. "Get me all the shooters still loyal to me and have them ready to go by tomorrow night."

"Where they going?" The driver asked with a shrug of his meaty shoulders.

"The Shangri-La, Ray's joint. I'm going to cold blast that fat ass and any ho working the place." Eight Ball said shooting a look over to Kenneth.

"You sure about this man, I think getting out of town is a whole lot better idea?" The boy shot back.

Eight Ball didn't hear it though. He was already piling into the car. His mind was on Ray and the others who were taking him down. They were going to learn real quickly what fucking with a real hood rat would get you, a very big bite and a foot in the ass.

The window closed slowly and Kenneth silently said a goodbye to his friend Crazy D. He wasn't sad about the death, this was the hood and sometimes friends die here. Nope, Kenneth was quite happy with himself as he watched the brake lights of Eight Ball's sedan disappear. He had manipulated the meanest dealer around, turned the man into his bitch. Yeah it started out a little slow but then his super brain kicked in and boo-yah, it was over just like that. Eight ball was nothing more than a pinball getting shoved where ever he wanted him to go. And the bit at the end about not going after Ray at the Shangri-La, hell he knew Eight Ball was going there first and nothing was going to stop him. Well, might as well give the heads up to the people he's coming after. Kenneth went back to sucking his lower lip as he popped in two quarters and dialed a number only he knew. After the two usual rings the usual voice answered.

"What do you have for me?"

"Oh Mr. Producer, I have some very nice stuff for you tonight. Let's start with a certain dealer paying a visit to a certain strip club." Kenneth said finally letting his evil smile out.

After ten minutes the youth hung up the phone, checked his surroundings for anyone watching, and then walked away from the phone. Dimitri knew clandestine work and this wasn't even close. The boy never once checked the phone for a tap and his observation skills were atrocious. He didn't look for any one trailing him, the most basic necessity when it came to espionage skills. And what was the man in the sedan doing driving around with a dead body in the back seat. It was an obvious assassination here in this place, but why does one bring a dead body with them? The whole point is to kill the target and then dispose of the body, per the rules of assassination and espionage. The whole thing was confusing and he was starting to get a serious headache.

"We need to get back to Yelena and tell her what we have seen tonight." Gregor suddenly said exiting from the shadows to Dimitri's left.

"And tell her what? I don't understand one thing of what we have just seen." Dimitri exclaimed following his brother out of the safety of the darkness.

The pair stopped just outside of the ring of white light thrown by the street lamp. Gregor turned and took a sniff of the air noting mentally the boy was out of range, and so was the vampire still. He looked back to Dimitri and hoped to soothe his brother. "I'll explain everything when we see Yelena, but now we have to leave."

"What is wrong? Do you sense something?" Dimitri asked suddenly weary of everything around him. He scanned from left to right so quickly he couldn't have seen a purple elephant if it was right in front of him.

He didn't mean to scare his brother so bad, but Gregor didn't feel safe anymore. The old woman talking in his head, the vampire disappearing, and now this boy with his plans to overthrow this Eight Ball, it was just too coincidental. And how did this boy, who was floundering at the start of the confrontation, suddenly became a master manipulator in the middle. No, something was very wrong. It was like someone was using them, pushing them like chess pieces around the board. Gregor just wanted out and back to the pack.

"No Dimitri, there is nothing wrong. It's late and we need to report in so let's go, okay?"

"Okay, we go." Dimitri responded. A second later they were gone and the street was empty again, until a familiar shadow fell across the phone.

Alexander waited until the lycanthropes moved off before exiting from the shadows himself. There wasn't a soul around except for the poor dog who had scared Kenneth so bad just fifteen minutes ago. The small mutt laid cradled in his arms content to let the long nails continue to scratch his head. Yeah his belly was empty but that didn't matter, this was pure joy and happiness crammed into a milk bone baby!

The vampire was taking stock of what just occurred between Eight Ball and Kenneth. His mind whirled and spun with a pointed sharpness making use of an intellect more than twenty-three thousand years old. His plan to have Wilma saved was moving along quite well he thought, and the werewolves would only help now with it, unknowingly add the last piece to his puzzle. Some things stood out though, the help he gave to Kenneth in standing up to Eight Ball just a minute ago. He really hoped that didn't come back to haunt him, and it probably wouldn't, but it was always better to be prepared just in case. And now he knew who the lycanthropes were, three men and one woman. They were young though, much too young to be chasing and confronting him. He could only wonder what Akhenaton was up to? He did know one thing for certain; a trip to Shangri-La was most assuredly on now. Everyone was going to be at that party and we wouldn't want to miss that would we?

The dog gave a small yawn and turned its head ever so slightly so the nails could get just the right spot. Alexander scratched the head carefully, took one last look down the street, and then stepped back into the shadows again. Now, the street was definitely deserted for the night. Well, there was the bum that wandered down it an hour later, but that's not important.

Chapter Eleven

Even before Renfroe pulled up to the crime scene he could feel in his bones there was something wrong with this call. He was a burnout and he knew it, hell no way to hide it, so when calls came in he just answered them with about as much enthusiasm as a man going to his dentist. Yet, when the phone rang ten minutes ago, he felt his heart jump a bit, as if he was back on the first day of homicide again. Maybe it was the name that landed on the board just five minutes before, Chico Rodriguez. He knew the name and knew it was connected to Eight Ball which these days which meant he was at the top of the suspect list, one more time. Well, at least to Renfroe anyways. He let the phone ring out for four long blasts scrambling to pick up the receiver before the automated answering system picked up. The voice on the other end was talking but Renfroe wasn't listening, he looked down to see his free hand going for the notebook he kept in the pocket on his sport coat. Christ this was different, he as actually going to take some notes, that was a first in how many months? Hell, how many years? He told the dispatcher on the other end to repeat everything from the start and with a long deep breath he got control of his shaking hands and took notes. Now he was here and his heart was still jumping, skipping a beat every few seconds. There, just beyond the tape, stood the Assistant Coroner Foster. As Renfroe walked over to the Sergeant in charge he noticed the man wasn't dancing or singing, straying from his usual antics for a crime scene.

"What have we got here Sergeant?" Renfroe asked with a huff.

"A young male, Hispanic 22 years of age, goes by the name Memo. I think he runs with your other body from tonight, Chico Rodriguez. "The Sergeant answered looking up from his notebook.

"This guy runs for Eight Ball's crew too?" Renfroe whispered feeling his heart skip another beat. "Do we have a cause of death yet?"

"You'll have to ask Foster that one. He's keeping it all close to the vest tonight for some reason, which doesn't bother me in the least." The Sergeant remarked just in time to see Renfroe almost collapse. "Whoa, you okay detective?"

If his heart was skipping beats then it just missed a whole bunch of them. Renfroe felt the world spin for a second at the mention of Foster keeping secrets from the sergeant in charge. This was bad, the image of a certain manila folder containing certain secrets popped up in his brain and a wave of nausea struck. Renfroe fought it all off though, he had to. He couldn't let anyone even think for a second there was something going on. He forced his legs to keep him upright and then turned back to the sergeant. "Yeah, I'm good. Keep everyone back while I go talk to Foster, okay?"

"Yeah, will do," The Sergeant said watching Renfroe walk toward the coroner before going back to his assigned duties of crowd control.

When Renfroe got close he could tell something was wrong with Foster. The man was standing over the body mumbling to no one in particular while rubbing his non-existent chin repeatedly. "What you got Foster?"

The coroner turned to him and the look he got from the short skinny man didn't help the irregular heart beat in his chest. "What do I have, oh yeah, I have a male 22 years in age from what his driver's licenses says-"

"How was he killed?" Renfroe said cutting the coroner off quickly.

"Killed? Oh yeah! Uh...his heart, yeah that's it, his heart was cut out. Well cut really isn't the right word –"Foster was saying before Renfroe turned and pulled him off to the side. The detective obviously wanted a private conversation since he chose a spot away from the crowd and the police.

"Was it our boy?" He asked quickly.

"Our boy?" Foster asked back not following Renfroe's lead at all.

"Yeah, the guy from the crack house that exploded last night and the Honda the night before. Remember that guy?" Renfroe pointed out sarcastically.

"Oh yeah, that boy, our boy!" Foster said nodding his head emphatically

"Yeah that one," Renfroe exclaimed mocking Foster last statement," What's wrong with you? Why the hell are you acting so goofy?"

"I've never seen anything like this before Detective. The whole thing's thrown me a little." Foster explained wiping his mouth.

"What is it?" Renfroe asked suddenly feeling his heart start to skip a second beat along with first one now.

"The victim's heart, it wasn't cut out like I said, it was more like torn out by brute force with a lot of trauma to the outer chest area." Foster whispered.

"What do you mean trauma to the outer chest area?" Renfroe asked back, the usual sarcastic tone gone from his voice. Oh yeah, this had 'really, really evil' written all over it.

"I mean it looks like the heart was ripped out by an animal with a large maw, like a Grizzly bear or something akin to it.

There is a lot of posterior damage, jagged flesh with some obviously missing... "

"Jesus! But there aren't any bears in Atlanta except in the damn Zoo!" Wills exclaimed with a gasp.

"Now you know why I'm in a little bit of shock. It isn't every day in the city you get to see a Grizzly attack first hand!"

"So it wasn't our boy?" Renfroe asked already knowing the answer to his question, but he wanted and needed to hear it from Foster just to be sure.

"Nope, we got nothing in the way of physical evidence in the area so it's just a gut feeling about this one. This was done by someone or something with a very large mean streak in them."

"Why do you say that?"

Foster swallowed hard and then uttered each word like it was a cold piece of ice on his tongue, "because he was alive when his heart was torn out. The guy he ripped apart Saturday night, he was dead before being shredded but this poor bastard...he was kicking and screaming."

Renfroe didn't ask another question, he didn't need to as he walked over to the white sheet seeing the large red stain in what was the chest region of a young body. A small part of him wanted to lift the sheet and look, confirm to his reeling brain that this was real and it was happening. However, the larger part of Renfroe that wanted nothing what-so-ever of that scenario won the vote by a landslide so the sheet never moved from its position. Renfroe opened up his notebook and scribbled a few notes in it. He wasn't sure why he was taking notes anymore. He really didn't want to solve this one. He really didn't want to know who did this because that meant he'd have to meet said person and that prospect sent shivers down the big man's spine. With a slap of the leather cover Renfroe walked away from the scene leaving Foster to finish the job of loading the young man's body into the meat wagon.

Even from this great distance and in the deep dark of the abandoned building Yelena could make out the scared look on the big plain-clothes officer, he was probably with homicide she thought. She could see the blood run out of his face as the short skinny one told him about the boy, how he died specifically she thought as she watched the big man get into his car and drive off. This wasn't good, not at all. She didn't mind killing and yet neither did she love committing the act, it was just that...an act that had to be done some times. She was asked if she could kill for the Great Lich Akhenaton before they had flown out here and she told Michaels it would never become an issue if it meant saving their mother. Killing was part of the job you might say, a dirty necessity some might have trouble with but was just second nature to Yelena. She tasted blood on a regular basis while fighting at her mother's side from an early age and every drop she drank without pleasure or disdain. When the boy was screaming for Peter not to kill him and then praying to Jesus Christ to save his soul right before the end she didn't flinch or move to stop her brother. It was just the act and it had to be done.

And just what are we doing here she thought? The choice to join the Lich to complete his task was never the question, to save her mother she would do anything, but she never had imagined 100 years ago she'd be standing in an abandoned building feeling paranoid about the Great Lich and what his 'plans' were? This boy, his death, it weighed on Yelena more than anyone else's had in her past and not for the reason of guilt. The problem with the killing was the 'why', as in why was this all happening around them? Nothing made sense, not this vampire or his actions again this night and now her brothers and she had been dragged into an unplanned death because of it. You see, that was the other problem, it was now driving away in an unmarked Police cruiser. Technology made it so much harder to mask and hide things these days that you had to plan before taking a life. Damn, where was all of this going Yelena thought silently.

"Do you think they can trace this to us?" A voice from the dark behind her called. She could tell it was Gregor, he sounded worried. That was Gregor's job, to be the devil's advocate. Yelena knew her brothers well, and she was easily the strongest among the pack, but she also needed each and every one of them. They each played an integral part, a spoke on the wheel that kept the Epova Family alive.

"I do not know? If the detective is as incompetent as the others we have come across then we are safe. If he is exceptional then we will have a problem." She responded to Gregor.

The red headed wolf turned to his brother and gave the wolf a scolding look. The second Peter lowered his head Gregor felt a sudden pang of regret for admonishing his brother. Yes he knew he had to do it because Peter had endangered them all now, but he still loved his brother with all his heart. Peter mumbled an apology in Russian. He still refused to speak anything else.

"It is fine brother. We will endure as we have always done. The family is strong and Yelena will lead us safely through as she has always done." Gregor responded to his brother patting the big man on the face before walking over to his sister.

"It was my fault," Yelena remarked with half-a-smile while taking Gregor's hand," we had our information and Peter reacted before I could stop him to ensure the boy would be silent."

"It is done, no more need to worry. Did you learn anything?" Gregor asked

"He killed his friend as ordered, cleaning up a mess with some drug dealer who was taking money. He was to go to an exotic club called the Shangri-La later to retrieve his money for the assassination." Yelena stated but she drew in quick breath at the look on her brother's face. "What is it Gregor?"

At the mention of the Shangri-La club Gregor felt his blood go cold. This was too coincidental he thought again. He quickly told all in the room about his eventful night, from the vampire disappearing into thin air after conversing with a little black girl to the boy on the phone mentioning the Shangri-La club. And when he came to the old lady talking to him in his head though, telling him not to trust Michaels, well that was like setting off a bomb. Everyone gasped in shock.

"What do you make of what she said?" Dimitri asked quickly looking at his sister.

"I do not know brother. It worries me greatly though that we have another individual in this mess." Yelena pointed out quickly while chewing her bottom lip in deep thought.

Peter broke in speaking very fast and pointing excitedly to Gregor.

"Yes Peter, maybe the old woman and the little girl are connected, but there is nothing pointing to this. The vampire could be protecting both, but why? All we know is the vampire has risked drawing attention to him by attacking drug dealers. What we are guessing at is the little girl and now the old woman.

And we still do not know who this vampire is but he is not a fledgling and that I am sure of." Gregor stated shaking his head.

Dimitri was about to speak up, bringing another point to the table, when his sensitive nose picked up a familiar scent close. Almost at once the pack smelt it, Yelena's eyes squinting in displeasure as she turned to see Michaels walk out of the dark of the open doorway. She hated being spied on, it was a pet peeve let's say. Just another reason to distrust this man she thought.

"Good evening ladies and gentlemen, are we having a meeting that I wasn't invited to?" Michaels asked sarcastically while walking to the center of the group.

"We are validating our speculations, going over facts to ensure they are correct. We would hate to make a mistake and embarrass you." Yelena suggested adding her own bit of sarcasm to the statement.

"The only mistake my dear is not bringing what you discover to me immediately. Make sure it doesn't happen in the future, now what do you know." Michaels stated looking to Yelena.

She didn't move to answer the Lesser Lich though, only giving her brother a secret signal to speak for her. Gregor took in a deep breath and then laid out what he knew in a manner that Michaels might understand. "We can only surmise at this point but we think the vampire will be at an exotic dance club called the

Shangri-La tomorrow night. We observed a boy with the local drug dealer tonight arguing and before the dealer departed he mentioned paying back another associate for a betrayal with a small force of armed men and we think that is where this Nosferatu will be. The local dealer, I assume, is making a move to better his position in the drug trade around here."

Michaels stood quiet for a second digesting Gregor's last before responding. "And what makes you so sure the vampire will be at this club? Why wouldn't he go after the local dealer and just end him?"

"The vampire has already hurt the local dealer. The corners around the apartments have already been deserted so the next logical step is going after the ones who supply the drugs and this club must be where the drugs are kept. Why he doesn't finish him we are not sure of yet." Dimitri said speaking up before Gregor.

Michaels though seemed less than impressed with the man's statement and turned back to the pack's leader, Yelena for assurance. "Do you agree with this? Do you think the vampire will be at this club?"

"Da, I agree with what my brothers say." She agreed holding back a snarl of contempt.

The room went silent as Michaels seemed to enter a trance watching the police lights through the broken windows of the room. A minute went by and Yelena was about to ask just what the Lich was up to when he turned back around with a snap. For a moment the look Michaels wore scared her, like he was suddenly struck with a dark epiphany, while he spoke with a whisper. "I have an idea."

"What?" Yelena asked suspiciously.

"I trust what you have found, but I also want to be cautious and not lose a chance to strike. You'll split into two groups, Gregor and Dimitri will go to the club while Yelena and Peter will follow the local drug dealer. This will cover both ends and whichever one the vampire shows up at you can strike and destroy him." Michaels smiled wickedly before walking away from the group.

"I thought we were waiting till we knew more about the vampire, at least learn his name?" Gregor asked quickly pointing out a flaw in the plan.

"Bah, I've already discovered the vampire's name and it is one we are not familiar with which means he is too young to worry over. Lord Akhenaton has given the order to destroy the vampire immediately. Now go rest for tomorrow night's activities." Michaels said waving off the question like so much banter.

"I do not like this idea. If we are to attack this Nosferatu it should be in force to ensure its demise and our safety." Yelena spoke up eyeing the lich with a cold brutal stare.

Michaels bristled at the objection to his plan, especially from Yelena. Why was it so hard to get one vampire to kill four young werewolves? "And I said I did not want to miss a chance. This is the plan Yelena, follow it or face the displeasure of Lord Akhenaton. Do you want your mother back in one piece?"

The room was silent again, but Yelena wanted to fill it with one long scream. This Lesser Lich was going to get one of them killed and may Akhenaton have mercy if it was one of her brothers. She might have actually screamed if not for Gregor's hand appearing on her shoulder calming her down. If this is what is asked of her to facilitate her mother's return then that is what she would do gladly. Yelena nodded to Gregor signaling she was okay and then to Michaels signaling obedience before leaving the room through the open door. The pack followed suit and when they were out of ear shot Gregor spoke.

"I do not trust that man sister. There is something very wrong with him and his plan. This vampire is not young as he said."

The two walked on for a second before Yelena answered him. "I do not trust anyone but my brothers at the moment and for the foreseeable future."

After he could no longer hear the werewolves walking away Michaels quickly flipped open his cell and dialed a memorized number. The phone on the other end rang once before being picked up. The same smooth but agitated voice from before spoke quickly.

"You have a plan now Michaels, please tell me you have a plan."

"Oh yes Lord Akhenaton, I have a dastardly good one. It just kind of hit me out of the blue you might say." Michaels answered giddily.

"Dastardly? Who says that these days Michaels?" Akhenaton commented.

"I'm sorry sir!" Michaels apologized as the phone line went to dead silence.

"Plan Michaels, what is it? Focus for me man!" Akhenaton snapped with a demand.

"Oh yes, the plan, well it's very simple and very direct." Michaels said with an evil smile.

"Good because this conversation sure as hell isn't!"

"Yes sir, I've split the pack into two groups to follow two possible leads. I've also ordered either group to attack Alexander, which ever lead the Ancient One appears at. Whichever pair he kills the others will feel the need for vengeance and they will gladly go to their deaths. The Epova's will be no more." Michaels said clinching his fist for emphasis.

The phone was silent again for a second before Akhenaton answered. "I like it Michaels, just one minor thing."

"What my Lord?"

"You better hope Alexander does what you want because if he doesn't then I'm going to hurt you so bad Michaels words won't describe it, understand?"

"Yes my Lord, I ensure you this plan will work." Michaels said feeling a sudden twinge of fear. What if Lord Akhenaton was right? What if the ancient one didn't kill the pair like he was supposed to? Oh, that would be bad, a definite fly in the ointment.

"Well then, good job Michaels, keep up the great work and call me when those four puppies are dead as door nails." Akhenaton said before hanging up.

"Yes my Lord." Michaels said to the silent cell phone. All the confidence he was feeling a moment ago suddenly wasn't there anymore. It was replaced by a bout of uncertainty and about twenty million questions.

Across the way the lights from the police and such light up the area for another two hours as CSU and others collected evidence. They didn't get a lot, maybe enough to fill two separate large plastic bags. The body held most the evidence, maybe there was some DNA or a fingerprint on an eyeball. Right, that only happens on TV one of the techs laughed. One of the other techs said the lack of any physical evidence would hamper the investigation and a police officer could only agree.

This case was probably going cold after a week, if it took that long.

Chapter Twelve

The last twenty-four hours went by slow for Alexander, the ancient vampire stayed silent and deep in thought most of the time with the exception of going out and feeding. There were second thoughts about talking with Wilma after sensing the approach of the Werewolf pack. There was too much of a risk he knew, yet he was willing to face the danger because he found himself wanting to talk with her. There was a lift in his soul when she was near. How had he allowed this to happen was still a conundrum, he had never felt the need to converse with someone like this before with the exception of one, a playwright with a very dry wit who could make him laugh wildly. So tonight, like the one before, he had left Martha's earlier than usual and taken a seat on the bench in the shadows of the old playground. The darkness was still a welcoming comfort to him. Wilma would know instantly who was sitting on the bench and join him for nothing more than some simple pleasant conversation. In fact, his senses picked up the sound of her shoes scraping the stoop outside of the house. Wilma was trying to sneak up on him, probably trying to scare him. Good luck with that he thought before turning his thoughts to more serious matters. Alexander sat perfectly still, his mind wrapping itself around the plan he had crafted to save little Wilma.

Everything had gone as he expected with the first piece, even the betrayal by Kenneth. Everyone had played their part moving the plan along to the next phase, going after the suppliers. Yet, he didn't feel safe about the next phase. No, safe wasn't the right word, good was the word. Yes Eight Ball was still hanging around but from what occurred last night with Kenneth he could deduce that the dealer's time on this earth would be short. No, what he was worried about were the wildcards.

What were the lycanthropes doing stalking him? They didn't come to Atlanta to see the Laurel, which left the only reason they would be here being his presence here. It was apparent Akhenaton had sent them and if he had then it wasn't to say hello. The Grand Lich was obviously falling back on the old blood feud, but the confusing piece was why he sent such young pups in the first place. They had no chance against him, unless he somehow fell asleep and they stuffed a very large bomb inside his clothes. So why did the Lich send them, an able group but lacking experience, against him knowing the impossible odds? He also worried about desperation and the pack, the crazy things that happen when panic sets in. They knew about Wilma, they might move against her in some way?

Wilma was still slowly creeping up on him, each step painfully placed. Alexander made a slight mental note to remind her about the squeaky shoes.

There was also the war he was waging against Eight Ball's suppliers, a fruitless endeavor if you took into account his vision and Martha's from the other night. Why do all this when in the end the Laurel was just going to burn? Because, when it would burn it would take a small sacred life and the vampire couldn't let that happen which is why he had set this plan of getting Wilma away into motion, or better yet have someone take her away for him. So, he had little choice but to keep going the vampire thought, knocking away one stone after another until that someone higher up came for him...and Wilma. Alexander succeeded in bringing down Eight Ball and he knew it was all for nothing if the suppliers were still in business. They would just find another Eight Ball, start up selling again, and the vicious circle was back in place and Wilma would still be here and still in danger. The only way to save Wilma was to make the Laurel untouchable, not worth trying to sell drugs, even if the temptation was strong. He intended to make it so expensive to deal drugs here that the price was too high. Of course this meant causing a significant amount of trouble, which in turn meant exposure.

He was a vampire, taught to hide in the shadows and never run the risk of letting 'them' see you. Occasionally you had to have some help like that of Simon and Davis's father, but you never befriended a human as he was with Wilma. The risk was too high for both parties. He wouldn't let Wilma get hurt because of him, the thoughts of Christina floated back and he pushed them away just as fast. He absently wondered if the werewolves had already found Eight Ball. He knew they had overheard Kenneth talking to Eight Ball last night and by now they were planning on going to the Shangri-La. They probably knew as much about the drug world around the Laurel as he did. Lycanthropes were masters at the game of espionage; they probably taught the KGB everything they knew.

Therefore, the final question was really simple. How far do you take this 'war' with the others? Alexander was prepared for a conflict with any force, but how prepared was Leland or Stephanie? And then there was the final piece of his plan, the dark gamble that would get Wilma to safety just before it all burned. If it worked then he was a hero who vanquished the evil dragon, but if it failed then the mausoleum in Savannah would be his final resting place for all time.

The little girl had slowly closed the gap while he was thinking and she was only inches from scaring the wits out of him when the vampire spoke up. "I see your mother made spaghetti tonight."

"What? How did you know who it was? How did you know I had spaghetti for dinner?" Wilma asked while getting into her usual cross legged sitting position on the bench.

"I could smell the garlic and you're the only one I know who would try to sneak up on a twenty three hundred year old vampire." Alexander remarked with raised eyebrows.

"Okay, so you're Superman, I'll remember that for next time. Hey wait a minute, you can smell the garlic?" Wilma said with a mocking raise of her own eyebrows.

"It's a little strong, but not as bad one would think." Alexander winked with a slight smile.

"And it doesn't bother you?" Wilma asked.

"If used in moderation I have no complaints." Alexander responded.

"So vampire folk lore doesn't pertain to you?" Wilma asked with a small smile.

"Some parts more than others."

"Garlic does nothing, how about holy water?" She asked quickly

"To drink or bathe in?"

"What about a wooden stake driven through your heart with a mallet?" She asked in checklist style.

"That would kill anyone, dead or undead." Alexander stated with an appalled look.

"Can you enter a church?"

"Yes"

"Does sunlight burn you?"

"Not anymore"

"Not anymore?" Wilma asked.

"I can walk in broad daylight if I wish, just another benefit of being so old I guess." Alexander answered with a grin.

"You not hurt by bullets so I doubt there's anything that can cut you except for maybe a high powered industrial laser. So, I can summarize that you are the closest thing to a walking God that there is on the earth." Wilma stated.

"Why are you asking so many questions little one?" Alexander inquired with a small grin.

"Oh no particular reason, just want to get my facts straight is all." Wilma said with a broad smile.

"I see your keeping up your journal." Alexander remarked.

"How did you know about the journal?" Wilma cried out.

"Just remember the age and that should answer all your questions."

"Is it difficult being that old?" Wilma asked after a second with a low whisper

"Sometimes little one, but I have met some interesting people over those long years." Alexander stated.

Wilma fell silent for a second before slowly reaching into her coat and pulling out a large book. She treated it with an irreverent touch making sure not to crinkle the dust cover or damage the precious volume in anyway. The large gold stamped letters caught just enough of the streetlight to tell an observant Alexander what the book was about. 'The complete works of Shakespeare' flashed once as Wilma slowly ran her fingers across the raised letters.

"I love his works," Wilma said never looking up from the tome," the way he weaves words into the simple magic that inspires a magnitude of dreams. I saved my allowance for a month to buy this book while stopping every day at the store to make sure it was still there. I've never read a page because I didn't want to ruin the magic on the pages."

"The book is quite a treasure Wilma." Alexander said looking at her.

"Do you think I'm pretty, like the way he describes Juliet?" Wilma asked looking up at the vampire with quickly moistening eyes.

"Of course little one, you're very pretty." Alexander answered back with honest emotion.

"I think Gabrielle Union is beautiful, Halle Berry and Cate Blanchett are gorgeous. I so want to be as beautiful as Carrie Fisher in Return of the Jedi as funny as that sound's. I'm just plain compared to most of the actresses I've seen in the movies or the other girls in my school. I'll never be like them, never ever."

"That's not true Wilma."

"How do you know?"

"The rose does not bloom until it is ready Wilma. Give yourself sometime to grow little one and you'll blossom into a beautiful woman just like your mother."

She looks like she's blushing Alexander thought as Wilma smiled looking to the book before turning to look at the night sky. In that smallest moment of an instance he could see who she would become and Alexander wished he could tell her just how beautiful a woman she would be, but he kept quiet as Wilma spoke. "Do you know why I love Star Wars so much?"

"No, why do you?"

It took a minute for her to start, just a moment to start the ball rolling before Wilma was peaking again. "Because it's not here, it's not the hood or the Laurel. Up there in some galaxy far away you don't have to worry about getting shot with a stray bullet or getting mugged by some drug addled maniac looking for money to buy a fix. Up there...it's so far from being here I sometimes cry...I don't want to be here anymore."

And how does one respond to that Alexander thought in bewilderment? He tried to think of something to say, anything to say, but the vampire was lost to the attempt. The two sat silent for another second, and then Wilma suddenly held the book out for Alexander to take. The gesture drove a knife in to his heart a second time. He still couldn't think of anything to say or do. He just looked from the book to Wilma.

"I want you to have it for saving my life." Wilma said quickly, warmly.

"Wilma, I can't take this." Alexander struggled with the words.

"You risked so much to help me Alexander, more than I could probably imagine. You deserve a reward for taking that chance." She said laying the book in the vampire's lap gingerly.

Alexander slowly reached down and took the book in one hand using the same gentle care as he had seen Wilma use not to damage it. He felt a twinge of pain deep in his soul. When he ruled the world dignitaries brought gifts, treasures, and prizes as offerings of good will, but Alexander never remembered one such as precious as this book. The vampire looked to his friend then reached down and slowly rubbed the imaginary dust off the front cover.

"William would have been so taken with you Wilma." Alexander said turning back to the little girl shaking his head in sudden awe.

"What? Why?" Wilma asked with deep reverence. Oh if he only knew how much she loved William Shakespeare.

"You're a visionary. You are unafraid of the future and the change it brings. And you would have laughed so much at his jokes." Alexander said with a smile.

"William Shakespeare told jokes?" Wilma remarked with surprise.

"Oh he had the most diabolical wit little one. The man could make you cry one second and laugh yourself silly the next." Alexander smiled, his face now filled with reverence.

"I would have fallen at his feet. Listen, I'm spending the night with Grammy because Leland and my mom are going out to save someone's soul or something so I have to go." Wilma sighed touching the book one last time. She looked up at the vampire, her eyes beginning to mist, and then she turned and ran from the park bench. She stopped on Martha's stoop and waited for the old woman to open the door. Wilma ducked in without looking back as Martha patted her on the back.

Alexander sat perfectly still on the bench watching the pair. Martha looked up and around and then right to him giving a small wave before stepping inside and locking her door. He wasn't even sure how long he sat motionless in shock from the gift and Wilma's words before a voice called out to him. He knew Leland and Stephanie had walked right up to him and he had never sensed their approach. Oh what an effect this little girl had on him. The vampire reached down and rubbed the book cover gently as Leland spoke.

"So what's the plan?" he asked.

"We need to walk to the Fox Theater, I'm meeting someone there." Alexander said rising from the park bench so fast Leland and Stephanie didn't see it. The pair also did not see the large book disappear. No one would have and no one would have known where the vampire had hidden it.

"Who are we meeting?" Stephanie asked as she fell in step with Alexander and Leland.

"A friend of mine, he has some information and transportation waiting for us." The vampire answered.

The trio walked in silence for much of the distance, they slipped along the sidewalks and storefronts unnoticed. Alexander always stayed to the inside next to the store windows, making sure to keep in the shadows produced by the lights of the street lamps. When the FOX was in eyeshot Stephanie spoke up breaking the silence of the group.

"Alex, do you mind if I get personal for a second?"

"That depends; I'll answer what I can." Alexander remarked.

"Last night, you never came back to tell us what you are. Can you tell me now? If it's too personal then I won't worry about it." Stephanie said hoping she just hadn't crossed the invisible line of impropriety.

The question caused the vampire to stop, the unstated intention of not trying to disrespect obviously catching him off guard. Leland actually stutter-stepped for a second, but he pulled himself together though with the practiced ease of the street.

"Are you afraid of offending me Stephanie?" Alexander asked with a small grin.

"Yeah, it's not polite to ask a person what they are, right?" She responded.

"Of course it's not." Leland said emphatically

"Thank you babe," Stephanie shot back with a wink and a smile.

"Hey, I got you're back my lady!" Leland said holding out a fist which Stephanie hit showing her solidarity to her man.

The pair turned back to Alexander who was watching the whole exchange between the two with a raised eyebrow. Well, it was good to see Leland had finally said what needed to be said which meant the vampire no longer had to worry about that jealous streak in the man. "Well, I'm glad to see with my help Leland finally took the step to telling you how he really feels. I'll tell you what Stephanie, after I finish with my business and we're on the road I will tell you everything you need to know."

"Yeah, that'd be great!" Stephanie said with a shrug of her shoulders.

"Good, let's carry on then. I do not want to be late and keep my friend waiting." Alexander remarked starting forward again.

"Need to know? What's he talking about?" Stephanie whispered to Leland.

"Don't ask baby just understand there's things out tonight that are like him only not as nice." Leland whispered back pulling Stephanie along as he followed the vampire.

"That's exactly right Leland." Alexander yelled back just before walking past the busy front entrance of the FOX theatre. Patrons moving through the ticket lines hoping to get a seat for the play "RENT" never noticed the dark figure as he passed by, only the small breeze of his movement. Leland and Stephanie lost the vampire in the crowd for a second before spotting him over by some lawyer. The street preacher knew the man was lawyer by the Armani suit, the gold watch and rings, and the fact he had the balls to flash them around without a care in the world. All it would take would be some young punk with enough attitude to gang rush him and take all that gold. Leland kept his opinion to himself though as he walked up the left of Alexander. He and Stephanie watched as the lawyer and the vampire interacted.

"Is this the information I asked for?" Alexander asked.

"Yes sir." The lawyer stated handing over a folder. He waited patiently for Alexander to read the papers before moving on in the conversation.

"Simon, I would like you to meet Leland and Stephanie, friends of mine." Alexander said while closing the file.

The lawyer quickly held out his hand, which Leland and Stephanie shook, the lawyer's grip was tight and sure. This told Leland that Simon wasn't afraid of black people, must have defended a lot of them in court the street preacher thought to himself. Simon turned slightly then showed Alexander to the side parking lot beside the theatre, over to a parked car. It was painted jet black with a glossy finish that reflected the lights of the city like diamonds.

"And here's the car you requested sir." Simon said handing over a set of car keys to the vampire. The group turned together when a squeak from Leland brought him sudden attention.

"This isn't what I think it is." He asked in whisper, the reverent tone the same Wilma made when she spoke of Shakespeare.

"It's just a car Lee." Stephanie remarked and the look she got back from the men actually worried her for a second or two.

"No ma'am, it's a 1973 Chevy Chevelle 454 with speed shift, extra fat racing tires on the back, and tinted windows."

Simon remarked in shock, like it was sacrilege to have to explain this work of art to someone.

"With the sound system I requested." Alexander asked eagerly.

"To the letter sir, I had the technicians install the All-in-one head unit, amplifiers, and speakers this afternoon. I had to pay a little more for the car and the stereo installation because of the short notice and all." Simon explained.

"An all-in-one built in head unit, like navigation system and DVD and CD and all in one!" Leland gasped trying to peer through the tinted windows.

"A top of the line unit custom installed!" Simon said with a broad smile

"You boys and your toys," Stephanie giggled shaking her head while watching Leland drool on himself.

"I would say it's all satisfactory Simon, you have once again more than met my request." Alexander stated with a smile.

"More than happy to be of service sir, now if you will excuse me, I have a certain lady friend waiting for me." Simon said. He waved once to Leland and Stephanie then turned and disappeared into the mass of people gathered by the front of the FOX. Alexander opened the door to his new car then unlocked the passenger door for Stephanie, who slipped into the back seat. Leland though took a few extra seconds to slip slowly into the car.

"I thought you wanted to keep a low profile." Leland asked Alexander.

"I do Leland." The vampire said.

"Then why did you buy a tripped out car like this? I mean this thing is a classic, done up sweet, and it screams look at me to everyone."

"I'm just following some advice from a friend. You know, living a little." Alexander answered slipping on a pair of Ray-Ban sunglasses.

"You're not going drive wearing those glasses on are you?" Stephanie asked with a quivering voice while slowly reaching for the five-point harness that served as her seatbelt.

"I think you should be more worried by the fact that I have never driven before this moment. Now, the brake is the skinny pedal on my right foot and the gas is the fat one on my left, isn't it?" Alexander said concealing a wicked grin.

"Oh dear God in heaven," Leland whispered quickly securing his harness.

"So where are we going?" Stephanie asked scrambling to fasten the harness around her as well.

"Are you sure you want to do this Stephanie? Once in there is no way out but through." Alexander asked looking at her through the rear view mirror.

"I want to go Alex, to see this through with Lee." She said popping the harness clip closed with an audible snap.

"Then we're off to see Ray. I need to ask him a few questions concerning the Laurel."

Stephanie didn't get a chance to ask who Ray was or where he was. The 1973 Chevelle kicked to life with a roar of the massive engine, the speakers began to wail George Thorogood's "Who do you love?" at an earsplitting decibel level. All eyes on the block turned to watch the jet-black car as it pulled out of the lot, the tinted windows reflecting back the bright lights of the FOX theatre. Suddenly the tires squealed and smoked as the engine bellowed from a surge of the gas pedal, the torque too much for the extra fat radials to sustain traction with the asphalt. The Chevelle rocketed through the night dodging cars left and right as it sped toward its destination. One of the many people waiting in line could have sworn he heard screaming coming from the car as it sped past.

The blue BMW pulled into and parked in the garage parking lot again tonight, but this time Eight Ball didn't have his usual package from the usual courier service. He stepped from the car, after his bodyguard had opened the door for him, unfolding the six foot frame dressed in another white Gucci suit. Eight Ball looked around slowly surveying the area of the parking deck scanning for any sign of something, or someone. Once he was satisfied he was alone in the area he turned to his body guard.

"You got everyone? They know what's going down tonight?" He asked pointing a finger.

"Oh yeah," Nelson said stepping around the car to present himself, "I got a ten men crew up. They'll go in slowly in pairs so as to keep attention low. When the sign is given they start cold blasting the joint."

"Good, cause tonight I'm setting myself up like a King baby. I'm cutting out my slice of the pie, getting my business taken care of!" Eight Ball spat.

"Yeah, that's good an all dawg, but what you gonna do about the product?" The bodyguard asked.

"What do you mean?" Eight Ball asked.

"I mean if you go and shoot Ray and his place all up the Producer probably won't deal with you man so who you going to get the product from?" The bodyguard said shrugging his shoulder.

"Man, do you think I'd be doing this if I didn't have other shippers lined up? I got a whole list of people, and why the hell are you asking anyway? I mean who's running this damn show anyway." Eight Ball answered screaming and locking eyes with his bodyguard.

"Okay brother, okay." The Bodyguard said holding up his hands in a move to calm his employer down. The two stood in silence for a minute or two before he asked Eight Ball another question.

"You ain't gonna deal with the Jamaicans are you?"

"If they got a decent price and good product then hell yeah I might deal with them." Eight Ball said pacing behind the car.

"Aww dawg, you can't deal with them?" The bodyguard whined.

"Why, you prejudiced against Jamaicans or something?" Eight Ball asked.

"Everybody knows they do voodoo man, and before you see it coming, BAM you're a zombie. Now I know this guy on 16th who moves large, I mean kilos and kilos of product man. You get in with him and its party time dawg." The bodyguard said pointing a finger for emphasis.

"You mean the crazy ass Columbians? Damn man, what do you think I have to deal with now? " Eight Ball yelled.

"Aww dawg, that's just one group. This guy, he's legit and he's not like those other crazy Columbians man! You can trust him." The bodyguard responded.

"Yeah, okay, what the hell time is it man?" Eight Ball asked nervously still pacing back and forth.

"It's 10:50." The Bodyguard said.

"Damn, this waiting shit is going to kill me!" Eight Ball said turning away from the bodyguard and starting on another lap.

Out in the dark of the parking deck Yelena and Peter walked up as close as the shadows would permit. They each picked a pillar to hide behind and watch the antics of the local drug dealer from afar. They could easily see him pacing back and forth nervously while his bodyguard kept up about people to buy more drugs from. Yelena sniffed the air quietly noting all the scents. Something bothered her, a smell that wasn't right. The car exhaust and garbage and other smells of the city masked the scent but she knew it was human, male. They weren't alone in the parking deck like they thought and it wasn't the drug dealer she smelled either.

Yelena looked around and sniffed more trying to zero in on the scent, but it was too buried by everything else around. She couldn't lock in on it and decided not to pursue it any farther. They weren't here for that anyway. They were here for the vampire, if he decided to show up. There was a chance this was all for naught and that also nagged her. Finally, mercifully, she pushed all the rambling thoughts out of her head with one big shove. She settled in to watching the drug dealer pace behind his car while the noises from the city echoed in the deck.

Chapter
Thirteen

The Chevelle sat in the parking lot of the Shangri-La Nude Review Emporium, the three occupants sitting perfectly still in their seats. They had been sitting there for thirty minutes, not moving from their spot, just watching the occasional drunk stumble from the building. A group of men entered earlier hollering and chanting 'party' as they walked in the front door while another man cautiously walked up and looked around twice suspiciously before entering. Alexander wondered if the man was embarrassed, maybe he was ashamed of having to visit an exotic dance club. The man was somewhat mousy with thick glasses and a suit that looked cheap and old at the same time, a dated fashion statement in any period he had lived in. The vampire didn't think long on this long though, he went back to the original reason for the trio sitting in the car in the parking lot.

They were here, waiting on the inside for him. He had sensed the wolves the second they had driven up. The two Russians were trying to conceal themselves but it wasn't working. Alexander began to wonder again, why Akhenaton would send such an inexperienced group like these pups after him. There were ulterior motives written all over the decision. Then he saw a pair of Eight Ball's men, dressed in a trench coat and a parka slip into the building. He knew who they were; it didn't take seeing their past in that special window to identify them. This was the fifth pair he had counted, all ten were men...the gang was all here now. A minute rolled by as he checked his watch one last time. Time to put the plan he had been working on for the last few days into effect and rely on his knowledge of warfare. If everything went as it should then Wilma would be saved from her fate by the very men who had brought it about with their drugs and it would happen soon.

"Are we going in soon? I have to go to the bathroom." Stephanie asked from the backseat.

"Excuse me?" Alexander asked back coming out of his trance.

"Are we going in soon? She really has to pee." Leland stated for Stephanie who sighed. It didn't seem proper to announce loudly how her bladder was about to burst.

"Are you sure you two want to go in?" Alexander asked one last time.

"Why do you keep asking us that?" Leland shot back with a twinge of fear.

"Do you remember when I told you about things like myself?" Alexander countered staring Leland in the eye. The unveiling of his past to the pair, and thus the fact he was a vampire, wasn't as thrilling as it had been the night before with Wilma. Both had sat there with mouth agape just staring back speechless, which was just how he had expected the street preacher and mother to react to the information. It's why he waited so long to tell them.

"All right, just 'what' things are out there?" Stephanie asked suddenly turning and looking out her window.

"It would take too long to explain, just be prepared for the unexpected and if need be run like the wind for the exits." Alexander said seriously.

"Oh, wait a minute. What exactly are you planning to do in there?" Leland asked in shock.

"It's not what I have planned that you must worry about Leland." Alexander replied one last time opening the door. He was out of the car and walking away before Leland could get out. The five point harness was giving him just a smidgen of trouble.

The street preacher struggled to get out of the Chevelle as fast as he could with Stephanie on his hip all the way out. "Okay, did he just tell us he's a vampire?"

"Yep, he did," was all Stephanie said as an answer.

"And he's Alexander the Great, THE Alexander the great!"

"That he did sweetie!" Stephanie stated trying to spot Alexander in the semi-dark parking lot with long sweeps of her head.

"Okay, now for the real question, do you believe him?" Leland asked turning to her.

"All I know Lee is he saved my daughter from a crack house that exploded and she was in one beautiful brown piece. From what I've seen over the last couple of days I'll believe anything he says." Stephanie remarked.

"All right, that's good. I feel the same way, just wanted to check with you first." Leland added with a quick smile.

"Aw, that's sweet baby, but I think we need to catch up to Alex before our friend the vampire does something." Stephanie said taking Leland's hand.

"Oh yeah, you're right!" the street preacher gasped gripping Stephanie's hand and heading for the entrance of the Shangri-La strip club.

They trotted up to the entrance trying to catch Alexander but the vampire was through the door without looking back. The street preacher opened the door as Stephanie ran in and then he leaped into the dark entrance of the strip club.

"Foster!"

The assistant to the Coroner nearly fell off the bar stool he had planted himself on when he and the detective had arrived. After getting his seat, Foster spotted Toni, a nicely shaped dancer who was busy walking around trying to drum up business in the darkened club. The minute his eyes connected with the auburn haired beauty the smoke from the room didn't bother him anymore, the loud music didn't grate his ears, and the feeling of being infested by a thousand germs running along his body from touching things suddenly went away. Two hours later and about two hundred dollars in Toni's garter, Foster was steadying himself after Renfroe broke the hypnotic trance of the dancer.

"What, did I miss something?"

"Yeah," Renfroe said pulling him away from the young dancer, "your measly paycheck from the city. What are you doing with her?"

"Oh, Toni, she's a great girl. Did you know she's putting herself through school by working here? She wants to be a Radiology Technician." Foster smiled with a quick nod.

"They're all working here to pay for school. Even the ones' who didn't graduate from high school work here to pay for college." Renfroe spat.

"Are you saying she's lying to me?" Foster asked in shock.

"She's treating you like an ATM machine. She's getting every last dollar out of you before moving on to the next victim okay. And getting friendly isn't why we're here in the first place."

"She is not hustling me! Toni is a very smart, generous, and a tender hearted human being. And since you brought up the fact, why the hell are we here in the first place?" Foster retorted.

"I got a tip from a buddy in narcotics. The boy who was found in the alley shot in the head was allegedly running for a bartender out of here, someone who had been skimming and running on their own. The higher-ups didn't like this I guess because the boy got a bullet and the local authorities only found about twenty pieces of the bartender washed up across Lake Oconee. The owner of the Shangri-La here, good old Ray, has a few connections including a link to certain organizations in Mexico and a shady relationship with a mid-level pusher named Eight Ball. None of this can be proven of course, which is why Ray is just beyond those doors going to the back." Renfroe stated.

"Why doesn't Narcotics just bust him? Better yet, the Feds come down on him with some RICO charges. And why have we been here for the last two hours?" Foster asked leaning up against the bar again.

"All hear say," Renfroe said looking around, "can't get an indictment on what a couple of street punks say. And with some high up power connections no one can touch Ray there, except maybe someone moving in on the turf."

"And you think whoever killed the boy is trying to take over?" Foster asked.

"That person, and our super-secret suspect, could be one in the same. Whoever it is, they've worked their way up the chain right to Ray here and I got a gut feeling tonight's his turn in the barrel. Now, if you don't mind, can you help me keep a look out?" Renfroe pointed out with a nod of his head at the end for emphasis.

"Yeah, okay, but exactly what am I looking for though?" Foster asked perplexed.

"Anything you think is out of the ordinary, like some guy walking through the front door trying to hide a howitzer under his coat." Renfroe remarked spotting someone just coming in the front door.

"Oh, that'll be easy in here." Foster said sarcastically, but Renfroe was already on the move.

The inside of the club was dark, smoky, and loud to the point of being unhealthy. Large speakers suspended from the ceiling propelled the loud techno and heavy metal music that caused the very floor to reverberate with each bass shot. The building felt like it had a pulse and it was a fast one. Along the north section was a large bar that stretched the length of the wall then turned the corner going east with that wall until it came to a raised stage. This was the main dancing stage complete with a brass pole and lighted floor. The south wall held a small stage and so did the West wall, all occupied by a scantily clad woman dancing seductively. Alexander could move around here without worry, everyone was looking right at the stages and not at each other. The dancers were staring at the men who were staring back intensely, but not at the woman's face. He easily moved between the crowds, no one looked at the large figure with dark sunglasses moving among them like a ghost. He walked toward the double doors that he knew led back to the kitchen area and beyond that to an office where Ray Cummings sat waiting for the whirlwind. The man knew Eight Ball was coming and Alexander knew he had men waiting to counter them...all except him. Poor Ray would never see the vampire coming.

The doors he was so intent on walking through abruptly swung open and a man dressed in a black suit with a dark red shirt stepped out. The man's shaved head gleamed from the flashing lights as he passed by the vampire within inches yet never noticing Alexander was close enough to bump him if he wanted. Alexander stopped and watched the man, the special window he looked through opening again as he saw the man's past. He instantly knew where the man had been and why. Ray had another uninvited visitor this night. Someone else had noticed the opening that the Laurel was now in the ever shifting drug trade. Everything was going better than planned he thought, better than he hoped.

The vampire moved to the doors, stopped to look over his shoulder, and smiled slightly to no one. He knew the two werewolves were out there somewhere in the dark room. The lycanthropes were hiding, but he knew they were out there. The whole place was a trap, they had hoped to catch him unaware but the only ones caught would be the ones who had laid the snare. Tonight, the field of battle would change and the odds would be in his favor from here on out. Then, with a simple small push, the vampire moved through the swinging doors and into the back. Behind the metal doors was the kitchen area where a steel prep station was opposite a large grill and frying stations. Alexander walked down the make shift hall the station made from its position, a single man working the grill never noticed the vampire as he went by. The large kitchen closed in to continue making a single hall going to the back to an ordinary door where a large man stood watch. The vampire smiled as he walked up without so much as a blink from the man, he waited a second, and then he spoke scaring the bodyguard half to death.

"Is this Ray Cummings office?"

"Holy shit on a stick!" The man screamed pulling out his gun with a single move. Alexander simply grinned at the sight. He showed no fear of the large barreled gun that was pointed at his head and face.

"What are you doing here Lee?" Renfroe called out.

Leland could barely hear the detective for the loud music coming from the sound system, but he knew Renfroe's voice and suddenly his stomach knotted. What was his old friend doing here? Did he have a lead or something? And what about Stephanie, what would she think? The questions continued to fly in his head as he took the large man's hand in a firm shake.

"Hey, what are you doing Otz?"

"I asked you first. Good evening Miss Jackson." Renfroe said greeting Stephanie.

"Good evening detective, how are you?" Stephanie asked back trying to be polite while her eyes kept scanning for Alexander.

"I'm fine Miss Jackson, are you two looking for someone?" Renfroe inquired noticing the way she was looking around the smoky room. He also took note of the fact she wasn't the type to frequent strip joints, at least it seemed that way.

"Yeah we are," Leland said speaking up quickly trying to make the lie up as he went, "I have a boy wanting out but he doesn't want to be seen with me. We both agreed to come here, talk it out you know."

"You came to a strip joint to talk a boy out of the gangs? This boy is of the legal age to enter this establishment, isn't he Lee?" Renfroe asked eyeing the street preacher suspiciously.

"Yeah man," Leland said with a nervous chuckle, "no one knows me or Stephanie or Joe, perfect place to meet."

A dancer walking past suddenly, stopped and squeezed Leland's left buttock causing him to jump and squeal just a little. "Hey baby, long time no see. You still got that incredible tongue?" she said with a sly smile. The street preacher looked from her back to Renfroe back to Stephanie to the dancer and finally back to the detective. For a second his brain locked and the lie went off the track along like a large locomotive, but then again this was the street preacher and like a true trooper for the righteous he righted the ship.

"I helped her find the Lord." Leland remarked with another nervous laugh.

"The Lord, excuse me?" Stephanie asked with a raised eyebrow.

"Yeah, you know, we met at her place and talked about how Jesus could help save her life." Leland said shrugging his shoulders.

Stephanie was about to call Leland on his obvious bullshit when the doorman, who had been staring at her, suddenly made the connection. "Foxy brown, is that you? Hell yeah that's you! I'd know that ass anywhere."

The remark froze Stephanie with fear while Leland and Renfroe were shocked to silence. She turned to see an old friend from a life she had said a happy goodbye to so many years ago. "Hey Luther, how's your daughter doing?"

"Oh, she's doing great, going to college at UGA." Luther the large sized doorman said with an equally large sized grin.

"Wait, wait, you use to strip?" Leland exclaimed with a yelp.

"Oh man, she was great! She used to do this thing on her last stage dance with her G-string where she would cut off one side then rip the other while bending over. The place would go nuts, well the ones who were there anyway." Luther offered up for general consumption. He obviously didn't see Stephanie giving him the universal sign to shut the hell up.

"Well, did you dance here Miss Jackson?" Renfroe asked trying to hold back a laugh. It wasn't from her past creeping up but more from Leland going nuts just to his left.

"Yeah, did you used to shake it here or what?" The street preacher asked with a small whine.

"No I did not," She hissed through pressed lips while eyeing Luther with a death stare, "it was a dive over by the airport. I made sure no one would recognize me, ever! I only did it for a while to pay off some bills that Wilma's father ran up before abandoning us in the night. I had no choice. It was degrading, embarrassing, and just a little desperate."

Leland felt a pang of guilt at Stephanie's admission, the talk in the kitchen from last night replayed in his head. He had to be good enough for her, a man to her when she needed it. She was obviously upset and ashamed about having to strip to get by. Leland reached out and took Stephanie's hand gently. "I'm sorry, I shouldn't have judged you."

"It's okay, in the past, or so I thought." Stephanie said giving Luther at the door one last death stare.

"Can I see you dance?" Leland asked with his best boyish grin tinged with a little mischief.

"Maybe, if you ask nicely later. I think I may have a thong or two lying around." Stephanie responded with a tone of heavy arousal and batting of her eyelashes.

"Oh yeah, you do, huh girl?" Leland said responding just as hard with his own arousal.

"Oh man, you gonna have some fun tonight!" Luther screamed holding a thumb up.

"Yeah, thanks Luther." Leland whispered trying to ignore the man mountain by the door.

"Excuse me, I hate to break into the obvious sexual play going on here, but can we get back to the present for a second." Renfroe asked patiently.

"We're sorry, got kind of side tracked there." Stephanie giggled.

"Sure you did," Renfroe said with a cocked eye, "now why don't you tell me why you two are really here?" The knot in Leland's stomach tightened, just like the noose around his neck.

The inside of the main office was junky, papers were scattered everywhere instead of being inside the large metal file cabinets that occupied the back corner. An old, scratched desk sat almost to the back wall, there was just enough room for the fat body of Ray Cummings to sit behind it. The man was short and balding, not the type Alexander thought would be running an exotic dance parlor. It was all kind of stereotypical if you asked him. The room was filled with large men, three to be exact, that looked like ex prison convicts or escaped ones for that matter. All the steely eyes in the room looked Alexander up, then down, and finally back to his face. Ray looked at him for a long second then busted out laughing before the others joined in as the room filled with loud guffaws. Outside, in the club itself, the song 'You've got another thing coming' by Judas Priest was playing as the DJ proclaimed to get out your money and pay the honeys on the stages. He stated with pure salesmanship that the girls won't get naked unless you put a dollar in the garter men so do the right thing, let's get the ladies paid!

"You have to be this guy in black, right? Is the part where I get scared of Ray Charles here?" Ray asked his thugs obviously digging at Alexander's sunglasses while getting his amusement under control.

"I'm no one special. Though I can see someone you talked to earlier today must have a very different impression of me. All these guns Ray, are the weapons for me?" Alexander stated letting his eyes scan the room before coming back to Ray.

"Depends, you see I got eyes and ears everywhere mister man in black. You don't get to where I am without some inside information, know what I mean? I even got this special one, really inside you know, which gives me a call and says there's a man causing us all kinds of trouble, a dude dressed in black. My inside man says he's a real mean son-of-a-bitch, tear my damn head right off and I'll even end up worse than Chico or that bartender who was stealing from me if I don't keep an eye out for him. Yet, now that I see who the man in black is, I'm just not that scared. I mean a Foreigner t-shirt and jeans, what kind of a killer are you?" Ray gasped from laughing while wiping away a tear with a fat finger.

"Looks like a real Johnny Bad Ass to me." One of the bodyguards remarked sending more laughter through the room.

"Hey man, did you wear those stupid sun glasses thinking we wouldn't hit you or something?" Another man said between guffaws.

"Yeah bad ass, you gonna hurt me now?" Ray asked wiping away another tear.

"I may not have too Ray. The ten armed men who walked in the club before me seem intent on shooting you or I could just wait for three days and let the bald man who just left you have two men shoot you in the chest outside your club here." Alexander said coolly letting his reputation and the lie about the three days sink in ever so slowly.

The room went deathly quiet. The music out in the club had changed to Metallica's 'Enter Sandman' as a second passed in the office.

"What did you say Bad Ass?" Ray asked with low and serious tone bordering on confusion.

"My name is not Bad Ass Ray, and your time on this Earth is coming to a very messy end if you stay here in Atlanta. If I were you I would leave tonight and never look back." Alexander explained with a flat calm tone.

"What the hell are you're talking about? We got this place covered just waiting for Eight Ball's boys to try and roll in." Ray chuckled nervously as his hand slid slowly under the desk, an obvious move to grab for a hidden weapon, if there was one down there between the table top and Ray's ample belly.

"If you need more of an explanation Ray then by all means let me make this simple. Your people were supposed to keep Eight Ball's men out, yes I know about his scheme to kill you as well, but your plan did not work Ray. Now you have a real issue out there in the club because there are ten armed men ready to start shooting any second. Do you think you're people are prepared for that kind of frontal assault? I think for your sake you better hope they can defend their positions or your club here is going to need a lot of repairs come tomorrow morning as well as a doctor for yourself. And if those men fail to kill you then the messenger who just left, the one who gave you a message from a nefarious but prominent 'Family' from New York most certainly will. What did the messenger say exactly Ray? Was it something along the lines that said prominent family is planning to move in on the Laurel as well, taking it over in Eight Ball's absence, and if you don't work for them you might meet with a serious life threatening event?"

"Bullshit, how did you..." Ray spat.

"I would not lie to you Ray." Alexander said with a smile, seeing the fear in the fat man's eyes as he locked onto them. "When you tell the messenger you have no intention of working with them tomorrow morning upon his return to what is left of your club he will relay that answer to the man who gives him his orders. Three days later you will be shot in the chest by two men carrying what you call 'shotguns' for saying no to their request. You will die out in the parking lot of your club here Ray or you might be shot by the armed men Eight Ball sent in here to kill you. So you see there's no need for me to do much Ray...except wait ten minutes or three days, either way your fate is sealed and I am free to move onto the men who give you the drugs."

"Bull..." Ray exhaled so low his words were barely audible. The fear in Ray's eyes making the pupils there look like the size of pool balls now. It was so easy Alexander thought, like taking Thebes almost as he growled low.

"You see Ray I just stopped by to ascertain the two names of the men who supply you with the drugs for the Laurel. And what do you know, I just found them."

Renfroe looked away from Leland, he knew the man was lying and according to standard police procedure he was just letting the street preacher squirm a bit. That's when he spotted the first hit man. He was wearing a leather coat and a ball cap embossed with a marijuana leaf, the symbol of Eight Ball's runners. Renfroe noticed Leland's babbling had stopped as the detective scanned the darkened club quickly, but not fast enough to draw attention. He knew the street preacher and ex-gang banger saw what he saw. The detective counted at least seven men among the crowd and he knew there was more out there just waiting for the sign to start shooting.

"You got them picked out Lee?" Renfroe asked slowly.

"I see ten mixed in around the club, probably got sub-machine guns under their coats." Leland stated just loud enough to be heard.

"What's going on? What's wrong Lee?" Stephanie asked gripping the street preacher's arm.

"It's nothing baby, I just need you to stay at my side and follow me, okay?"

"I'm like glue sweetie."

"Do me a favor Lee, you see that skinny guy at the bar being taken for every dime in his bank account?" Renfroe asked keeping track of the gun men.

"You mean the skinny guy with the fine looking red head?" Lee asked back.

"Yeah, he's the one. I want you to walk over there, stand by him, and when all hell breaks loose both of you get your ass over the bar and take him with you, understand?" Renfroe stated keeping eye contact with all the hit men.

"No problem, I was thinking of heading that way right now." Leland remarked turning his body in the bar's direction.

"What?" Stephanie inquired with a shiver.

"I think someone's about to make a move in the neighborhood drug business ma'am." Renfroe stated.

"Oh Damn!" Stephanie whispered.

"How do you know about that guy who just left?" Ray asked with the fear in his voice now a pure panic.

"Oh I have no personal knowledge of him Ray, just who he is and who he works for." Alexander answered with a smile.

"You don't know shit!" Ray exclaimed with that twinge of panic in his voice.

"Well, I do know you distribute drugs for Mr. Dunbar out of this club. I know you got this job in his enterprise as he calls it because your friends with Mr. Hierra. Let's see if I have how it all works, Mr. Dunbar smuggles Mr. Hierra's Cartel drugs into the country and then gives the loads to various people, like you, to sell out of places like this. I will say this, it's very good to have friends in high places, this is quite the step up from dealing drugs out your trunk, is it not Ray?" Alexander chuckled, reveling in the look of shock from Ray.

"How do you know all that about me?"

"Oh it's a gift really, but all I came for was Mr. Hierra and Mr. Dunbar's names. They're the ones I want to meet with so I do not need to talk with you further Ray. Quick check though, I did get the names right did I not Ray?" Alexander asked as his voice dropped to a deep growl.

The room was silent again. Alexander could tell Ray was going over his options right now in that small brain of his. The man was trapped, confront the army in the club or attack the man who knew the names of your employers, names who you were supposed to take to the grave if needed. This is why he waited in the parking lot Alexander thought, waited for the timing to be just right. He wasn't scared of Ray's thugs, not in the least, but this here was what he wanted, psychological warfare. The fat man behind the desk was overwhelmed, outsmarted, and obviously stupefied as to what to do next. He could see Ray felt helpless and that's what Alexander wanted, was his very intent on obtaining that paralysis by waiting. In the end Ray made a choice, it was the only one the fat man could take in his position. Alexander was moving before the order was given.

"Kill him boys!" The fat man screamed trying unsuccessfully to slide under the desk.

Almost at once everyone in the room started to move, the bodyguards reaching under jackets to draw their guns and Alexander stepping forward toward Ray. The men barely had their hands on the grips of their weapons when the vampire stomped the front desk sending the piece of furniture backwards into Ray, and both the desk and the fat man into the wall with a loud crunching thud. Alexander let the anger in his blood loose, his fangs grew instantly and his face changed features morphing and melting into a mask of death as he let his darker side free. Eye sockets deep and black stared from behind misshapen cheeks over a mouth that stretched from ear to ear with rows of long teeth. Ray looked up and screamed at the visage of the thing that had his arm and body trapped against the wall with his own office desk.

"I have a message for your boss Ray, one you need to deliver!" The thing said with a guttural hiss.

The bodyguards stood holding their weapons in a shocked trance as the thing that was once human turned on them suddenly. They stood watching, not comprehending what was happening, as if reality had taken a rain check. There was a man there a second ago, wasn't there they thought. Yet, this wasn't a man in here with them now. This was some kind of a beast with long claws and teeth, and it was ready to kill. Then, because the fear finally overtook the shock, they all opened up on the thing firing every round in their arsenal at the body directly. Ray barely got down and out of the way of the barrage of bullets. He lost a few inches of skin on his arm just trying to slide down to the floor as the wall behind him blew apart from all the rounds that struck it. The booming from all the guns being fired lasted for a minute or more but there wasn't a scratch on the beast, not a single cut. Ray could hear more firing, but it was faint and he realized those guns were going off in the club itself. The man in black had been right; Eight Ball's hit teams got inside the club and were after him. Damn, this was bad the fat man thought. Then the bodyguards began to scream and Ray closed his eyes in an attempt to wish the evil thing out of his office.

Leland and Stephanie were halfway to the bar when the 'hell' Renfroe had described happened. The skinny guy Renfroe had pointed out was too busy feeding the auburn hair dancer olives to notice anything going on in the club. If you asked Leland, this guy didn't look like he could notice a drug deal was happening even if you gave him a script and a set of cue cards. Suddenly, from behind the metal doors Leland thought led to the kitchen, gunshots resounded through the club. The booming wasn't loud enough to overpower the sound system so at first no one moved. They just looked around stupidly wondering where the fireworks were coming from. Leland's experience from the street though told him different and he was running at the skinny guy screaming for him to get over the bar. From somewhere behind one of Eight Ball's shooters stood up and produced a Tec-9 from under the leather coat.

"Get over the bar!" Leland screamed at the man who was looking up lost with an olive in one hand.

"Light this mother up!" The shooter screamed as the Tec-9 began to rapid fire. Renfroe was moving already though and he struck the machine gun wielding thug with a running block that sent the man over a table and into another one.

Leland watched as the skinny man suddenly realized what was happening and with a quickness leapt over the bar dragging the dancer with him. The street preacher and Stephanie followed suit, both jumping in unison over the wooden structure just as the others in Eight Ball's hit squad began to fire into the club. Rounds from one of the Tec-9's slammed into the bar splintering the wood. The bottles on the racks above the bar shattered causing liquor to flow from broken containers like a river on the mat that Stephanie, Leland, Foster, and Toni sat on.

The others in the squad unloaded in short sweeping burst shooting into the DJ booth, the bar, and anything else that was part of the club. Renfroe watched the club erupt in pandemonium as Luther the doorman, both bartenders, and some of the waitresses pulled out there guns and began to fire back. Even a couple of guys sitting in a corner pulled out semi-automatic pistols, Glocks it looked like, and got into the act by trading bullets with both sides. In a couple of seconds it was worse than the O.K. Corral in the strip club. Renfroe pulled his forty-five caliber long slide from its hide away holster just as some of the patrons screamed and fell to the floor shot. Damn, he was intent on arresting a few of the squad but that was quickly becoming secondary to just stopping the hail of gunfire. Then he saw the Tec-9 of the man he had knocked down suddenly turn toward him. Being a veteran of the Atlanta Police Department Renfroe didn't freeze or hesitate. He was gone in a single step as bullets from the sub-machine pistol chewed a crooked trail along the wall behind him. A dancer who was working the third stage dove to safety just as the detective passed by, the bullets following closely behind. Renfroe fired back blindly, which was still damn good as it kept the man pinned down and unable to draw a decent bead on him. He dove behind some tables getting a momentary breather from the action. When he looked up he saw the doorman and bartenders firing back with their guns as the battle shifted to a classic standoff with the hit squad. Each side was dug in now behind whatever cover they could find exchanging gun fire with practiced precision.

Renfroe checked his side arm and found the slide locked back, it was empty. He hit the button to release the depleted magazine and popped in a new full one he got from the holder on his belt. The slide on the forty-five closed with a pop as Renfroe caught two men from the hit squad moving to the back through the metal doors. He rose and moved after them but between dodging bullets and strippers hunkering down for cover it was slow going through the club.

From behind the bar Leland took a quick look, a peek to see if they could get out of this crazy shooting gallery. He watched a customer trying to run for the front door take two in the stomach and quickly decided it was safer to stay put. Leland looked around for another exit when he saw Renfroe moving toward the metal doors to the back. The street preacher knew the detective was moving that way for a reason and hopefully it was because there was a way out back there.

"Okay, we're going to get out of here. Stephanie follow me, you two stay behind her." Leland ordered Foster and Toni.

They huddled up behind the front of the bar, four heads slowly peeking over ready to run like mice for the metal doors. Leland took a quick breath ready to drag Stephanie with him to the back but before he could he saw something that froze him with utter astonishment. Some red headed dude was walking right through the club, right down the middle of the fire fight, without a care in the world. Several bullets from a hit squad member slammed into his chest at point blank which staggered the large man but didn't stop him. The hit squad shooter was out of ammo so he decided to just run at the large man intent on bashing his head in with the smoking Tec-9. The shooter didn't get close because the large man simply reached out and grabbed the shooter by the throat. He picked the smaller man up deftly off the floor and then shoved his hand right through the shooters chest. Stephanie and Toni both screamed but Leland and Foster didn't make a sound. They only watched as another shooter with an empty gun jumped on the large man's back followed by another. There was a small lull in the shooting as people began to move. The hit squad was busy with the large dude and also trying to keep the club personnel from picking them off. The tide of the fight had shifted and with it Leland decided it was time to go.

"Come on!" He screamed pulling Stephanie with him over the bar. Foster and Toni followed closely as suddenly the bullets began to fly again. It seems Eight Ball's shooters still had plenty of fight to give it seemed.

Two members of the squad ran through the metal doors heading to the back for the office as their plan called for. They were here to kill Cummings and bring his head back to Eight Ball in a bag, a little out of the ordinary but the drug dealer was paying extra for a souvenir. Only the plan hadn't called for what they heard, because there was screaming coming from the back office as soon as they broached the kitchen. The two men froze at the sound, neither sure what to do now. All of the sudden the door to the office exploded outward as a body crunched against the wall, the man's limbs bent in all sorts of wrong directions. That was all the time Dimitri needed, he came at the two hit men from his hiding place from the corner of the kitchen like a bolt of lightning. One of them got a chance to scream for help and the lycanthrope made a mental note to work on his stalking technique.

The office was a blood bath. Ray could see it running on the floor from his vantage point under the desk. The screaming finally stopped but the shooting could still be heard, actually with all the sounds of gunfire it must have been like world war three out in the club. An arm plopped down on the floor followed by what looked like a foot dressed in a Doc Martin boot, something a teenager might wear. Ray didn't remember any of his guys wearing those kinds of boots. I mean I would have noticed one of my boys wearing a cheap pair of Doc Martin boots he said to himself. Nevertheless, he really didn't pay attention to the little things like that. Maybe he would start if he got out of this alive. Maybe he would go to the park and smell the roses, dance barefoot in the dew-covered grass if he was still able to walk. Suddenly the desk shot away from the wall exposing Ray and his hiding place, and he knew the man in black was standing over him. Ray rose up slowly onto his knees chest against the wall looking over his shoulder, and there he stood dressed in his now bullet chewed t-shirt. Gone was the frightening face, replaced by the normal one he had walked into the office with just a few minutes ago.

"Hello Ray, nice to see you were not hurt in all that mess." The man said.

"What are you?" Ray stuttered with fear.

"Would you believe the tooth fairy?" The man asked. Ray simply shook his head 'no', and then he was being picked up off the ground like a sack of potatoes and pressed into the wall, so very hard. Ray's face was slammed into the sheetrock and he felt the steel grip of the man's hand on the back of his neck. His feet didn't reach the ground and the wall cracked under the pressure of the man's enormous strength.

"I need to leave a message for Mr. Hierra and Mr. Dunbar Ray. I need you to take this message to them as soon as possible. Do you think you could do that for me?" The man asked.

"Yeah, yeah, I'll even do it in person if you don't kill me, okay?" Ray whimpered.

"I own the Laurel and the surrounding neighborhood now Ray. Two days ago I began my takeover and tonight it is complete. Your drugs will no longer be sold there, understand? There will be retribution upon both Mr. Dunbar and Mr. Hierra should they disobey this order, understand?" Alexander snarled.

"Yeah, Laurel Woods is out!" Ray gasped.

"After you deliver the message I would give serious thought of leaving the state Ray, maybe even the country, understand? Remember what I said Ray, the messenger will have you killed in three days if you see him in the morning." Alexander hinted.

"Oh man, I am so out of here! You don't have to say anything twice. I understand, bit the road before it hits me...got it!" Ray pleaded.

"Good" was all Alexander said, then Ray felt the hand let go of his neck and his heavy body fell to the floor with a crash. He rolled over expecting to see the Doc Martin boots walking out the entrance to the office but there wasn't anything there, only the missing door and what was left of his bodyguards lying around in pieces.

Renfroe dodged people, bullets, and flying glass as he ran from overturned table to overturned table for cover. He was trading shot for shot at any man with a Tec-9 hoping to keep them pinned down so he could cross the floor. Renfroe instinctively ran the last few feet for the metal doors to the back exploding through them just as the last rounds from a Tec-9 slammed through the thin sheets. He leaned up against the wall by the doors, popped out the empty clip letting the metal holder fall to the floor, and then reached under his jacket and grabbed a replacement. The new clip went in with a click and Renfroe closed the breach with a loud pop readying his body for the two men from the hit squad he chased into the back. That's when his eyes caught the scene just to the left of him, Renfroe was so busy reloading his service pistol he didn't see the dead bodies. The two men, or what was left of them, were the same ones that had come in here only minutes ago. The baseball cap sitting in the growing pool of blood was the same that all the Tec-9 toting men were wearing.

"Sweet mother of the Goddess." Renfroe exclaimed with a whisper. The click of a boot brought his gun up with a snap, leveled and ready to fire. There, in the hall that led back to what might have been an office stood a man dressed in black jeans and what was left of a t-shirt. He saw a body lying face down in a painfully crumpled position in the debris of what might have been a door at one time. In a split second Renfroe knew this was his man. This guy blew up the crack house and killed the two dealers out in the street by kicking their car out from under them.

"Don't move! I'll shoot you dead where you stand!" Renfroe yelled out in commanding police fashion before realizing the gun was probably useless. All the man did though was simply smile and point to his right, Renfroe's left.

"I'd watch out for the boogey man if I were you." He said in a perfect English accent.

The warning was too late though as Renfroe never saw the body coming at him, he only felt it strike him like a ton of bricks. Somewhere out in the club a stray bullet struck an overhead sprinkler setting off the fire protection system. Renfroe heard the pop and whoosh as it suddenly started to rain in the kitchen of the Shangri-La exotic dance club. The detective went into full battle mode with the flick of a switch in his brain. He didn't think any more about his actions, everything happened naturally. Renfroe hit the large man with an elbow driving him up and away from his gun hand, the police hand-to-hand combat training coming back as if second nature. He spun and kicked the man square between the legs, and for a second it looked like the blow might drop him as he stepped back and away. Renfroe though watched in disbelief as the man stood back up, a loud growl emitting from somewhere deep inside him like a large wolf. Again, just as training had taught him, the detective gripped his gun as tight as he possibly could.

"You will die very badly for that." The man snarled with a heavy Russian accent between growls.

"Yeah, I figured as much." Renfroe replied just as Dimitri grabbed him by the coat.

The Russian picked Renfroe off the floor as if he weighed nothing, then the world spun for the detective as he cleared the steel prep station like a thrown baseball. All of Renfroe's weight struck the overhead canopy above the grill then he landed on his back with a sick plop half on half off the large appliance. His jacket began to sizzle from the heat and Renfroe rolled off and away feeling the skin on his neck and head begin to burn. The wet floor cooled him instantly and Renfroe gave serious thought to just lying there when he saw shoes walking his way, it was the

Russian who just used him like a basketball. He tried to raise the gun, which he was still holding onto just as training had taught him, but the blow had scrambled his brains internal circuits. Renfroe commanded his finger to squeeze the trigger and nothing happened, the gun simply laid flat on the floor in the grip of his right hand in a growing puddle of water.

After running past several injured people, having bullets whiz by within an inch, and beating the odds of getting shot Leland and the others arrived at the metal doors. Only now the street preacher froze, stopped at the very entrance he almost died trying to get to.

"What is it?" Foster yelled clutching Toni behind him to protect her.

"There's another big guy beating up Renfroe in the kitchen, dark hair this time." Leland yelled back to Foster.

"You sure?"

"I can see the guy through the crack in the doors!"

Foster turned from the street preacher for a second and reached down to pick up a stray pool cue. He snapped it across his knee and handed the fat end to Leland. "We have to go in and help him."

"Are you sure?" Stephanie yelled.

"We got to go. Stay here with her and keep your head down!" Leland ordered.

Foster moved around Stephanie and Toni instinctively hunkered down by her. Leland and the coroner looked each other in the eye, gave a quick nod, and then flung open the metal doors with a loud warrior scream.

Dimitri might have killed Renfroe. The detective was in no position to fight back after the throw. The man was just lying in a pool of water, his feeble attempts to raise his weapon looking comical. Then the metal doors flew open and two men charged the lycanthrope wielding broken pool cues like swords and screaming like mad men. The first one, a black man, broke his stick across the head of Dimitri but the werewolf just shrugged off the attack and slapped him away. The second, a very thin man, stopped and dropped his stick to the floor. He smiled broadly, gave a small finger wave, then turned and tried to run. The werewolf reached out and grabbed the shirt of Foster reeling him in like a prized tuna. Dimitri was going to snap his neck when he felt the cold steel of a pistol pressed against his stomach. The werewolf looked down surprised to see the fat man had drawn a weapon.

"See you in hell!" Foster screamed before firing the gun twice.

The bullets struck Dimitri just above the navel pushing him backwards and away from Foster. The power of the gun though was not enough to kill him. The bullets barely broke the skin. It was just powerful enough to make the werewolf really mad. Dimitri growled again, only deeper this time, as he walked toward the shocked skinny man. A sudden second shot rang out from the werewolf's left and he turned to see Renfroe, his pistol now raised and drawing a perfect bead. The gun fired rapidly, one shot after another, and all struck Dimitri in his chest. Renfroe stitched him from the center of his chest straight up and to the left, the last shot striking Dimitri right in his collarbone.

These rounds were different. They were bigger and more powerful than the one the other man had shot him with. Dimitri stumbled back against the wall, his chest, and neck screaming with fiery pain from the attack. He howled loudly, the eerie yell sent shivers through Renfroe, Leland, and Foster, but Dimitri refused to go down. He pushed away from the wall eyeing Renfroe. The breach on his gun was open, no more bullets! Dimitri charged with a roar intent on pulling the man apart limb from limb, he wanted him alive long enough to see his own heart before dying. Renfroe could only close his eyes, there were no rounds left for his gun, and even if he had some the last seven didn't do a damn thing. He hoped there was enough for Foster to identify later, and then he grimaced at the thought of the assistant coroner touching his dead body.

A second went by, then two, and finally a long third one. Where was the attack, the screaming painful attack? Renfroe, just as curious as anyone else, opened his eyes to see where the large man had gone. He looked up through the pouring rain to see the man with the torn up t-shirt holding the charging larger man by the throat with one hand and one of the Russians hand with the other. From the look on the large dark haired man's face he was taking great pains to keep breathing.

"I was wondering when you would come out of hiding little pup. Now, let's see who you are." Alexander asked with a grin while locking eyes with the struggling lycanthrope.

Dimitri couldn't retort or answer. He was busy trying to force open the hand of the oldest vampire in existence with one hand in order to breathe. Alexander's grip was like steel, his fingers squeezed until the sound of crunching bone could just barely be heard above the falling water. The lycanthrope growled in anger but Alexander ignored him, the fight was his and Dimitri knew that well enough. The vampire pulled lycanthrope closer, right next to his ear, as if giving it a secret message only he was allowed to hear.

"I know who you are Dimitri Epova," Alexander whispered into the werewolf's ear, "and I know about Yelena and Peter and Gregor too, so hiding in the dark will not help you anymore. My name is Alexander, yes that Alexander. I do not know why Akhenaton sent you on this suicide mission but believe me when I say it is one if you're family challenges me Dimitri. Leave me be pup, I am ancient, older than you can imagine. Think well before crossing my path or my friends after this night."

Then, with a giant shove that looked more like Alexander was casually flexing his bicep, Dimitri flew out of the kitchen and through the devastated club. He crashed through tables and glass landing between what was left of the hit squad and the club personnel. For a second the shooting stopped as the dark haired missile came to rest at the base of the second stage among a pile of debris. A second later the shooting started up again as if nothing had stopped it in the first place.

***

"Holy-"Stephanie screamed above the sound of the sprinklers and gunfire.

"Shit!" Toni screamed as well finishing the sentence.

Both women stared in shock as the man who had crossed the room like a MX missile and slammed into the stage with enough force to kill a person only rolled over and coughed up small spot of blood. A voice boomed loudly over the den of the fighting from the corner by the DJ booth. Stephanie and Toni looked over to see the red headed man from earlier by the stage screaming.

"BROTHER!"

Around the red head's feet were the bodies of the hit squad that had jumped him. He stepped forward to go to the other man's aid when the DJ popped up from behind the protective walls of his booth and fired a sawed off shotgun at the red headed man. Toni screamed again and grabbed Stephanie who clutched the young dancer back. Almost at once both of the women noticed the blast from the shotgun didn't do anything to the man. Nope, all the attack seemed to do was really upset the man Stephanie realized. The DJ noticed also because he gave a small scream before ducking back behind the booth walls. The large man stood for a second in front of the wall the DJ ducked behind, ignored a bullet that struck his back, and then with a quick rabbit punch drove his fist through the wall like it was papier-mâché'. There was a scream by the DJ before his body came through the hole unceremoniously, folded in places that the human body doesn't and shouldn't bend Toni noted.

The large man with red hair turned from the booth and the dead DJ running back through the melee to his brother. Two bullets struck his side and chest but the man ignored them as if they were flies. He bent down and picked the dark haired man by the arm and the pair started for the door, one leaning on the other for support. Luther the bouncer stepped out from behind his table and pointed a shotgun at the pair but it didn't stop the men one step. The red hair slapped the barrel of the shotgun away just before it went off. And before Luther could regain his balance or raise his weapon he was out of the fight. The red hair reached out and grabbed a handful of the doorman's coat and skin in a death grip and began to push. He lifted Luther an inch off the ground and started going backward intent on using the doorman as a battering ram. The front doors exploded as Luther and the pair went through them and out into the parking lot with one big rush.

"Well, there's another exit!" Stephanie said to Toni with a shoulder shrug. A round struck the wall just over their heads and they both screamed.

A second later a hand grabbed Stephanie's arm and for a second she was about to knock who ever owned that arm out, but Leland's face suddenly appeared.

"Come on, we're going out the back!"

The two women ran through the metal doors to the back leaving the occupants in the club to finally finish the gun battle. A minute later the last of the hit squad dropped to the bloody carpet with two large holes in his chest from someone's weapon. An eerie quiet took over as the guns finally quieted.

Renfroe looked up to see the man in the torn up t-shirt and blinked coming to a certain realization he couldn't prove if he tried. Yes, this was the man who had killed the two dealers and blew up the crack house, yet somehow he wasn't the bad guy in this whole mess. Don't ask him how he knew this, I mean chalk it up to good old-fashioned police intuition if you want. The man in the t-shirt turned to him, smiled showing perfect white teeth, and then disappeared in the time it took Renfroe to blink again. And then out the rain Foster was next to him, helping as much as possible to get his weight up off the slippery wet floor. Renfroe looked around and saw Leland and Stephanie pulling Toni toward the back, but the man who he really wanted to see was long gone. Renfroe turned back to Foster as they walked toward the back and an exit.

"Where'd he go?" Renfroe asked.

"Leland and the girls are heading for the exit, don't worry." Foster answered.

"Not Leland, the guy back here. Did you see him? Tell me you saw him too Foster!" Renfroe demanded.

"Yeah I saw him, dressed all in black and kicking everyone's butt." Foster said pulling Renfroe's arm around his shoulders

"That's the one." Renfroe remarked as the two left the kitchen.

Fingers danced across the number screen of his smartphone as the messenger dialed his boss. Basilio Costa, C-Note to his friends because he never carried anything less than a hundred-dollar bill, smiled broadly as he listened to the cell phone connected on the wireless network. This was perfect; just what his boss Don Russo needed to get the family's foot in the door. He could almost kiss that allocco Eight Ball for shooting up Ray's place. That fat bastard would come running to Don Russo after tonight looking for protection from Hierra. Perfect he thought, just perfect. Basilio never saw the man approach from behind. No one else would have either for that fact.

"So how did the meeting go with Ray?" a voice thick with Brooklyn called out from the cell's speakerphone

"It went, Ray got your message, but what happened afterward would interest you far more." Basilio said with a grin.

"Yeah, what happened?"

Basilio didn't answer the question. The voice waited a second before yelling into silence. "Hey Basilio, where the hell did you go?"

"Good evening Don Russo." A strange voice with an English accent answered back.

"Who the hell is this? Where'd Basilio go?" the voice asked quickly.

"My name is not important, but the message your man is going to bring you will be." Alexander said while looking down at the ground at Basilio. The messenger was trying to remove the vampire's foot, unsuccessfully, from the center of his chest.

"Yeah, and what message is that?"

"The Laurel Projects are mine, step into any part and I'll destroy you and your family."

"Excuse me? Just who the fuck are you?" The voice hissed in obvious anger.

Well, it seems Don Russo doesn't like taking orders Alexander thought. "Heed my warning Don Russo or suffer the consequences, like your messenger here."

Russo's voice bellowed from the speaker but Alexander paid it no attention as the conversation, what he wanted to say, was done. He gave the small metal box a sudden hard squeeze and it imploded in his hand with a pop raining down broken electronic pieces on Basilio's head. The young man was beyond agitated, so much so he didn't fully appreciate his position at the moment.

"Man, I am going to fuck you up for breaking my phone you bitch!"

Alexander leaned into his foot increasing the pressure on Basilio's chest exponentially with each passing second. The messenger began to gasp for air like a fish out of water trying to force oxygen into his lungs which were crushing beneath the vampire's foot. The scene looked quite comical to Alexander, the messenger gasping and trying to be intimidating at the same time wasn't working, so much so he was fighting back a fit of laughter. Yet this wasn't the time for a laugh so Alexander ignored the humor and turned to the task at hand, delivering his message. He backed off of his foot giving the boy under it a break for a second, enough to breathe again. The fresh air didn't have the desired effect on the messenger though. He still didn't appreciate his position at the moment.

"You think I'm scarred of you?" Basilio sneered between deep breaths.

"Oh, I know you're not scarred of me, but I do know what you've been frightened of since that day at your Grandparents little Basilio." Alexander said coldly.

"Yeah, whatever, you don't know shit asshole?"

Alexander leaned in again and smiled broadly. "Then let's see how loud you can scream."

Basilio began to laugh, who does this fuck think he is, huh? Then the man's face changed, it was so quick it caught Basilio by surprise. The features went from human to something hideous, nightmarish. The closest thing he could assign to the visage was a picture his brother showed him once when they were young and staying at their Grandparents house in Queens. That picture scared Basilio to his soul, he never told anyone about how bad it affected him. The image was out of the old the bible on his Grandmother's nightstand and it showed Satan standing over a prone man cringing in fear, sort of like he was now. The face was pure evil, the eyes struck fear straight into his young heart, and the teeth looked like they could bite right through his bones. Those same teeth gnashed now right above him while those evil eyes glared down on him. Something in Basilio's psyche snapped at the sight of the picture that day. He could feel the devil looking at him right then and there in his Grandparents bedroom and it was the scariest feeling Basilio had ever felt in his short life. He ran from the room screaming, he didn't sleep for a week, and up to this very day he still had that feeling of being watched when he happened upon a depiction of Lucifer. Basilio screamed until the Police arrived 10 minutes later, during the examination from the Paramedic, and even for a few seconds after a powerful sedative was administered.

***

Leland and Stephanie broke away from the dancer and made a bee line back to the Chevelle. The street preacher looked around quickly, scanning the area for any sign of Alexander. He turned back to Stephanie and immediately noticed her shivering from the dousing by the sprinklers. Leland pulled off his jacket and wrapped it around Stephanie slinging water from it in the process. She didn't stop him; even wet the jacket might provide some warmth.

"Are you both well?" a familiar voice asked from the driver's side of the car.

"Damn man, where have you been?" Leland spat back at the vampire.

Alexander unlocked the Chevelle and then looked back to Leland. "I had to stop and talk with someone, give them a message to pass on."

"You do that a lot, maybe too much." Leland said opening the passenger door to let Stephanie jump in, and a soon as she hit the seat she promptly turned to Alexander.

"What the hell was that in there?"

"That was a Lycanthrope." Alexander answered. He pulled out the parking lot just as Leland slammed his door shut and seconds ahead of the first sirens approaching on the horizon. The vampire hit the switch to start the heater up in the car which was so welcomed.

"A what?" Leland yelped.

"That was a werewolf." Alexander answered again while guiding the car into the stream of traffic on Peachtree-Boulevard.

"A werewolf! Is that what you meant by 'things like you'?" Leland demanded.

"Yes," was all Alexander offered.

"What's a werewolf doing here? I think someone in this car forgot to pass along some vital information, know what I mean." Stephanie stammered through chattering lips and teeth.

"The werewolf was Russian, from a long lineage of lycanthropes. His name is Dimitri Epova. He has two brothers who are all equally as powerful and as formidable as he is. Their older sister, Yelena, leads them. Lycanthropes still exhibit the pack mentality of their ancestors and never stray far from their family units." Alexander explained.

"Why are you telling us this?" Leland asked suspiciously.

"Simple," Alexander said turning to look at him and Stephanie, "the Epova's have raised the stakes in our work."

"Why is that?" Stephanie asked.

"The last few days the Epova's have been doing reconnaissance around the Laurel, following me when they could. They were sent here to destroy me, but the person handling them is playing at something else entirely. The Epova's are too young to take me, too immature to make even a decent fight of it. And by now I am sure they know about all of us, even little Wilma." Alexander answered slowly letting the car drop into a silent lull as it sped up the road.

"So their like a wildcard, you never when they'll come around or what they'll do." Leland said finally keying in on the situation.

"That they are," Alexander said keeping the gas pedal on the Chevelle down, "I'm still trying to ascertain why only two came tonight. It's a mad dash to destruction to attack me with just two. The Epova's may be young but they're smarter than that."

"How do you know they're that smart?" Leland asked.

"You have to think like a werewolf Leland." Alexander said.

"How does a werewolf think?" Leland asked exasperated.

"They are cunning and ruthless, not above killing someone to achieve a goal. The Epova's probably trained the KGB on everything they know which is how they found the Shangri-La." Alexander answered.

"Do you think they'll cause a problem?" Stephanie asked from the back.

Alexander took a second to respond. It was the moment of truth, or deception depending on how you looked at it. If he told them what was coming then his plan wouldn't work. A sour taste took hold in his mouth as he spoke. "You need to be aware of what we're up against now, to be ready for anything."

"You think they might come after us?" Leland asked Alexander, but he didn't get a chance to answer.

"I don't care." Stephanie said from the back with a firm voice and a tone which said her mind was made on this. The chattering of her teeth had passed as the inside of the Chevelle began to warm nicely. "I trust you Alex, I trust you with my life and with Wilma's."

The statement made Alexander fill with shame, would Stephanie be so willing to trust him if she knew what he was hoping for? Maybe she would, but then again maybe she wouldn't. "Thank you Stephanie for your trust."

"Wait! How do the werewolves add up in our plan? How does this help us in stopping the drugs from coming into the Laurel?" Leland asked quickly.

"I know who supplies the drugs to the Laurel and who supplies that person. The Epova's do not, and that is where I will change the rules to our game." Alexander stated.

"What rules? I still don't follow." Leland asked shaking his head.

"Faith Leland, everything will become clear soon." Alexander said with a smile as the Chevelle sped through the night. The street preacher didn't like that smile, it was the kind his mother always gave him when he would ask why she didn't want to give an answer too. And he knew it was useless to keep asking, just like with his mother, and his head hurt anyway so Leland just sat back and watched the lights sweep by one by one.

"They got them all!" Eight Ball screamed out in disbelief, his voice echoing.

Eight Ball's bodyguard shook his head in disbelief also before recounting what his contact had told him just seconds before on his cell. "They were waiting on us man, everyone in the place had a gun. Only one of our guys got out without a scratch and he's making for the state line to Alabama as we speak."

"Waiting on us how?" Eight Ball spat.

"Someone told them man, someone who knew we were going to Ray's! We got a rat in the house brother, a big fat ass rat!" The bodyguard pointed out.

A split second was all it took for Eight Ball to realize who sold him out, the time for a synapse in his brain to fire and close. He slammed both hands on the trunk of the car staring so hard through the metal he was seeing the interior carpet. "That fuck, he was playing me this whole time! That motherfu-"

A single plink, the same sound a bullet fired from a silenced sub-machine gun makes when striking a glass windshield, cut him off. Eight Ball looked up to see the hole in the back window just as the weirdest thing happened. Time slowed down, I mean dropped down to a crawl, and everything seemed to happen in some weird ESPN slow-motion type thing. He turned to his bodyguard and watched the man trying to pull his pistol from its hiding spot on his waist just as a bullet sliced through his ample sized throat with a bloody splash. Eight Ball could actually see the skin quiver and shake from the bullet's impact; it was kind of cool he thought. Another round hit the bodyguard's stomach causing the large man to fall back and inward, like he was a folding chair.

A final third bullet hit his chin exploding his face in a slow unfolding blossom of bone and blood.

Eight Ball spun away from the spray of human debris that was his bodyguard's head and stopped just in time to see the two hit men coming for him. In that same weird slow-motion he saw the yellow flashes and puffs of smoke from the gun barrels. His body wanted to run, instinct honed by years of hard street life screamed to flee, and yet deep inside Eight Ball knew this was it. All rides come to an end, don't they? The roller coasters at Six Flags always stop in their little houses when the fun's over, nothing different about life.

Something exploded in Eight Ball's stomach and again in his groin. Pain began to yell in his brain as another bullet and another slammed into his body, both rounds dead center in the middle of his chest. Another round hit his chest above the right nipple as the force lifted him free from mother earth. The energy dissipated quickly though and Eight Ball fell back on to the trunk of his prized BMW. The dealer with aspirations to rule it all was dead, his ride on life's roller coaster at an end.

The two men moved with purpose after Eight Ball was finished. They stopped firing and briskly walked over to the dealer, giving a final coup de grace with a bullet to his head before turning and heading away in the same purposeful walk. They stowed their guns under their coats swiftly intent on getting out of the area fast but under control. The one on the left made it just to the shadows when a paw slightly larger than a Grizzly Bear and claws like rail road spikes shot out of the dark with a swipe. The blow instantly disemboweled the man and before he could scream a second claw went for his head. In a second the skin on his face was gone, stripped to the bone, and his neck broken like a twig.

The other hit men swung to his left bringing the machine gun barrel up in the direction of the shadows where the paw came from. He never got a chance to fire his weapon, not even to line up a shot. Out of the dark from behind him Yelena stepped cool and quiet, without an audible sound, and moved to the man's side. She grabbed the back of his head with her left hand, the gun with her right, and with a single squeeze brought both hands together. The crunch of metal meeting bone was loud and it echoed in the parking deck as the man flopped to the concrete in a heap. Yelena looked up from the prone figure to see her brother step out of the dark with torn clothes from the transformation. His body was lupine now, legs and arms and face morphed to a semi-wolf visage. The suit and shirt were covered in blood and both shivered along with his body from the thrill of his recent kill. Yelena looked down again and contemplated silently, should she wake the man and interrogate him to get some information before killing him? That's what Michaels would want, expect from her and the pack. Yet, she thought, why should Peter have all the fun? Her brother watched on in silent excitement as his older sister transformed into the formidable White Wolf.

She wasn't sure what raised the hair on the back her neck, but it snapped Wilma away from her book with a flash. Grammy's living room was dark except for a single lamp she sat under with one her favorite tomes, Tolkien's 'The Return of The King' spread out on her lap. Wilma scanned around the corners of the room knowing full well there was no there with her, except for Grammy snoring in her chair, yet she could feel there was something out there in the dark raising her flight response. Her eyes didn't pick up a single person or object except for Grammy and the living room furniture. Then, just on the edge of her thoughts, something touched her ever so slightly. Like a butterfly, it was there just floating on the very edge of her consciousness beckoning her to come and follow it. Wilma rose from the couch slowly to keep her movements quiet while setting her book down on the cushion gently. She gingerly stepped over to the window and looked out past the old worn out playground to one particular street light that cast shadows in a long arc. Not a thing or a person was out tonight, unusual for the Laurel. Wilma felt something else was out of place though and decided to look closer. She began to probe with her eyes again examining the shadows closer to the buildings. A second later she saw him.

There, just on the edge of the shadows by the bench she sat on with Alexander she spotted a man in a black suit with a red tie and rail thin sunglasses. Instinctively she reacted, he wasn't Alexander, and without thinking she reached for the latch to make sure the lock on the front door was set. Yet, just as her hand touched the cold metal of the deadbolt, she heard Grammy speak from her chair.

"You don't have to worry about the bad man trying to get in here girl. He can't come in where he's not wanted."

"What is it? Who is he?" Wilma whispered in a frightened voice.

Martha rose from her chair and shuffled over to the window standing behind her small friend. "He's here because of your angel my dear. Sometimes good men have demons too."

"A demon's after Alexander?" Wilma asked with a frightened squeal.

"Oh yes girl, evil walks the earth in many forms. It comes as the men from the gangs who tried to hurt you the other night. Other times it's the men in the police uniforms who choose to ignore what's happening around here, and then there's the powder that's shoveled in here on a daily basis. "

Wilma listened intently to Grammy, but her eyes were locked on the man outside the window. He wasn't Alexander; this wasn't something nice. This was something best left outside in the dark shadows. Wilma stepped away from the window with a small shutter step because the sudden fear gripped her legs so hard she almost fell. The only thing that stopped her from bouncing off the floor was Grammy.

The stranger outside the window stepped closer, threatened to approach the front door the little girl knew. Wilma leaned back into Grammy for strength, she needed it. Her legs shook from the fear. This wasn't Alexander; this wasn't nice her mind repeated over and over again. She never stopped listening though as Grammy began to speak again from behind to soothe her fears.

"But you can never shy away from evil girl, never back down to it. Once the demon has you it won't let go no ma'am, it will hold hard to your soul. But if you're strong and show no fear then evil can't win you over. You remember that to your grave girl. Evil can do no harm to the ones of pure heart."

Almost at the same time that Grammy ended her last syllable the stranger stopped. He winced and grabbed at his head, like a sudden spike of pain had been driven into this frontal lobe. "Away with you demon, get away! You can't hurt anyone in here

tonight! Good lives here! Pure Heart hardens theses walls!"
Grammy hissed.

Wilma's breath crystallized just in front of her face and it
seemed for a second that the room fell deeper into the cold of the
night. Wilma shivered and she crossed her arms in front of her
chest without thinking to fight off the cold. However, her eyes
never left the window or the thing just on the edge of the
darkness in front of the building. The man stepped back grasping
harder at his head, and then he snapped straight up and stared at
the window, at Grammy.

The old woman giggled and placed a protective hand over
Wilma while she looked back with her milky white eyes out the
dark. "You can't defeat me demon, and you can't defeat my angel
of light. Back to your dark pit, back to damnation demon!

A minute went by with the staring act uninterrupted
before the stranger in the shadows finally moved. He stepped out
into the light of the street lamp causing Wilma to flinch and creep
back deeper into Grammy's body. The man was normal height
and skinny with a small black goatee, a man who might catch your
attention on the street. Wilma sensed without thinking that his
good looks were deceiving. This man was evil to the bone. He
smiled and she winced at the sight, it was ugly and scary all at
once.

Grammy gave a hackle and moved to the door but Wilma grabbed her hand before it could touch the metal knob. "What are you doing? We can't go out there!" The little girl wailed.

"Wilma, baby, ain't nothing out there going to hurt you! I wouldn't let nothing happen to you my angel." Grammy said with a broad smile.

'What!' Wilma's mind screamed. There's a guy out there in the dark that's pretty dang scary she wanted to yell, and look out the window if you don't believe me. Yet, when Wilma checked out in the dark shadows again the man was no longer there. Gone like a bad dream. Not a sign of the man. Wilma's legs tried to give out for a second time, not because of fear but astonishment. What was going on here? That guy, the evil dude in the nice suit, he was right there...wasn't he? Wasn't he a demon from Hell sent to collect her soul or something like that? The room spun for a second and Wilma turned back to Grammy for some kind of an answer to what was happening.

What the little girl got though was another thing indeed. Grammy had the door open and was waiting in the doorway patiently, like this was all part of some bizarre plan. "Come on girl, it's time for you to hear some answers."

"Are you kidding me? You're going to tell me something?" Wilma remarked walking over slowly, cautiously to the door.

"You, angel, deserve them because this is all about you in the end. You hear that?"

"What?" Wilma yipped looking around scared, trying to catch sight of the boogeyman again.

Grammy scanned the night and smiled before speaking. "It's a first in a long time child, the sound of peace. No dealing on the corners, no one shooting in a drive-by, just a quiet night."

The night was quiet Wilma finally noticed, a little too quiet maybe. Yet, even after seeing the stranger outside the window, she felt the peace Grammy was alluding to. It was quite the different feeling, weird not having to treat your front stoop like the jungles of Vietnam. Wilma took a tentative step just past the door and Grammy placed a hand on her shoulder.

"Come child, you're safe with Grammy."

The pair walked out into the dark then, right past the spot where the stranger had stood, hand in hand to some secret place. Wilma wasn't sure where she was going, all she knew was she would finally get an answer from an adult. It may be to a question she could care less about, but it was an answer. You choose your battles carefully; win what you can when you can Alexander would say. So, with a deep breath to hold back the fear she walked along side Grammy.

Chapter
Fourteen

The rotating flash from all the bubble lights gave the parking lot of the Shangri-La an eerie carnival like atmosphere. The whole place went from a harsh white to a serene blue to a hot red, and all at different intervals and lengths of time. Police cars, ambulances, news vans, and just about every other curious bastard had found their way to the strip club in the last hour. Funny how a full blown shoot out brings out the best in people, isn't it Otz thought. Renfroe sat hunched on the bumper of one ambulance while the medic cleaned the wounds on the back of his neck and head. The antiseptic stung a bit but Renfroe was too busy trying to answer inquiries from a friend and fellow officer about what he was doing here at the club to care about his own pain. The lead detective over this whole damn mess was asking a lot of questions and Otz was lying for each and every one.

"So you ended up down here because of the two dead pushers from last week right?" Fred Thompson asked.

"Yeah Fred," Renfroe said standing up from the bumper slowly with a grunt, "I was meeting with Ray to ask him a few questions when the party crashers showed up. I don't know why I was chasing Ray, that fat bastard wouldn't answer a question if he had too, know what I mean."

"That's for sure. Now, why is Foster here?" Fred asked looking over his shoulder to the coroner. The man was standing next to Toni, who was wrapped in a blanket, and it looked like they were exchanging phone numbers.

"Getting lucky from what I see. Since when is it a crime to go to a strip club Fred?" Renfroe said stretching.

"No law I know of. Okay, go home and get some rest. I might have a few more questions later all right?" Fred said walking away from Renfroe.

"You know which desk I work at Fred, just stop by anytime." Renfroe answered then turned and walked over to his unmarked car. He massaged a sore muscle or two while waiting for Foster to finish with his new friend. A plan was unfolding in his head, straight and organized like always, and it included the assistant coroner. Renfroe wasn't sure what the Russian was but he had a good idea and that meant he had do something he didn't want to do. It also brought up an interesting issue about Foster, did he really want the assistant coroner in on this part of his personal history, his personal circle. The detective had always been a private man and that's just the way he wanted to keep it, but Foster did risk his life for him. And this thing with the Russian, maybe he needed to team up finally. Renfroe stopped thinking and smiled briefly when Foster walked up after finishing his exchange with Toni.

"So you got her number huh?" He asked awkwardly.

"Yeah, kind of amazing I guess." Foster said with a small smile.

"What sealed the deal?" Renfroe asked quickly with more confidence.

"I think it was my enormously large penis." Foster responded with a serious air and tone. The remark hung out there for a second before both men started to laugh at the hilarious retort. Renfroe held up both hands in mock terror.

"Too much information," He guffawed.

The two finally got a hold of their laughter and then giggled for a few more seconds before finally subduing the funnies. Renfroe had never laughed with Foster and for the first time he gave the skinny coroner the smallest amount of respect for the funny remark. He wiped away a tear while shaking his head, and then set himself for what he knew had to be done.

"Thanks Foster, for what you did in there." Renfroe said sincerely.

The remark wasn't lost on the coroner, Foster stood perfectly still for a minute just taking in the compliment. His facial expression was one of amazement mixed liberally with joy, the man was actually stunned. However, Foster finally sighed and spoke in an appreciative tone.

"Thanks Otz" was all he said.

"No problem," the detective responded while looking around, "what did Thompson ask you?"

"The usual you know, why were you here? What happened?" Foster said with a wave of a hand.

"What did you tell him about the kitchen?" Renfroe asked.

"I didn't," Foster answered looking the detective in the eye, "I can't say for sure what that thing was in there so I didn't mention it to Thompson."

The two stood in silence for a second before Renfroe asked the question he really wanted the answer to. "Did you see the guy in the black, white long sleeve shirt under a T-shirt?"

"Yeah, the guy with a pony tail, I saw him plain as day." Foster answered.

Renfroe felt a surge of relief spread through his entire body as he turned and walked to get into his car. Yeah, it was the second time he had asked but having the confirmation twice that their man existed and someone else had seen him proved that he wasn't crazy. He wasn't a total burn out yet, there was still some life in his tired mind. The seat of the unmarked car felt good to him as he got in and closed the door with a quick snap. The decision if it was okay to allow Foster in his personal circle was made in a split second.

"You go home, get a shower, and few hours of sleep. I'll be by to pick you up this afternoon." Renfroe said looking out the window of the car.

"What are we going to do?" Foster asked.

"We're going to try and find out just what that Russian was." Renfroe remarked backing the car up.

Foster stood in the parking lot for a second looking stupid, but if you could see inside his head you would know the reason for the sudden mannequin imitation. The assistant coroner was scared. He had survived this night of terror only to find himself going after the thing that had tried to kill him. He didn't want to know what the Russian was because all he really wanted was to go back to being an assistant coroner working the night shift at the morgue. Dead bodies can't disembowel you or twist your head off your neck like taking the cap off a Coke bottle. Then, out of the blue, a soft touch of fingers brushed his back and Foster jumped from the feeling, his heart skipping a beat.

"Holy hairy mother of Christ," Foster yelped.

"I'm sorry," Toni said holding up her hands that were wrapped in a firefighter's blanket, "I didn't mean to scare you."

"It's okay, just after tonight sneaking up on me isn't a good idea." Foster said catching his breath and heart.

"I'm sorry," Toni said again with a grimace.

"No really, it's okay." Foster said with a broad smile.

"Listen, I know this is a weird request and all, but after what happened I really don't want to be alone for the rest of the night." Toni said blushing.

"Yeah, it'll be hard getting to sleep." Foster remarked oblivious to the signs Toni was giving. Yet, she just giggled and shook her head.

"I was sort of hoping to go home with you if that's all right." Toni said biting her lower lip in a way that made most men melt like ice cream run through the microwave.

The request left Foster in a vapor stupor. It may be hard to believe but a woman had never asked to go home with him, ever. He tried to answer yes but the only sound he could make was a high squeal pitch, like a truck that had hit its air brakes. Finally, after a few tries, he got a discernible answer to Toni.

"Yeah, sure, I thought, though, you might want to go home with your boyfriend you know." Foster remarked.

"My only boyfriend of late takes D batteries." Toni joked taking Foster hand in hers.

"Oh!" was all the coroner could say. The two turned and walked away from the crime scene, they're hands entwined as the lights from the bubbles cascaded over them. A police officer watched as the two walked away and the scene struck him weird.

He made a quick mental recognition of the pair. They rather looked like Fred Astaire and Ginger Rogers.

Renfroe was pulling onto Peachtree Industrial Blvd on his way home when his scanner screamed and the dispatcher sent over a message. In a nasal voice she told the field units of a request for a homicide detective to show up at a scene on the south side of town. Two black males were found in a parking deck by a blue BMW, their bodies shot multiple times, and also on scene were two more bodies severely injured and mutilated. Renfroe felt his hands go weak, the car swerved for a second as he momentarily lost control. It was weird but somehow he knew who one of the black males was and if his hunch was right he knew what happened to the other two. That meant the Russian wasn't alone, not by a long shot.

Chapter
Fifteen

"What is she doing?" Stephanie gasped.

There standing under the ruined gate of the Laurel and a street light were Martha and Wilma. The little girl spotted her mother and instantly jogged over taking Stephanie's hand with an excited jolt. That's when Wilma noticed how wet her mother still was.

"Why are you so wet mom?"

"Long story baby, why are you outside?" Stephanie said with a wide mocking smile.

"I think Martha's up to her old tricks." Alexander said from the side, almost appearing out of thin air.

Wilma and Stephanie both looked ill suddenly, the color draining from their faces, but Grammy was the only one speaking. "Oh Mr. Alexander, I'm just bringing it to the light you could say."

"Listen sweetie, "Stephanie began giving her daughter's hand a gentle squeeze, "I have a lot to tell you, about what's been going on the last couple of nights in the neighborhood."

Wilma raised her hand and squeezed her mom's hand back. "No need mom, I kind of figured it out before the crack house went boom. You know, I'm kind of smart and putting one plus two together was really easy in this case."

"Oh, okay. I thought I had that secret under wraps." Stephanie said eyeing her daughter with shock.

The little girl looked over and smiled brightly at Alexander. "Hi!"

"Good evening little one." Alexander said with a small grin back and a nod.

"That must have been some party?" Wilma remarked pointing at the many holes in Alexander's shirt.

"I ruined another shirt, a good one at that too. I might look into changing my greeting, may be a different way of saying 'Hello'" Alexander stated avoiding the question with perfect flair.

"Wait a minute, Grammy...you know Alexander here?" Leland asked.

"Do I know him? Why yes lord I know him. And better yet, I know why he's here with you!"

"Well then, I guess Grammy got us all. We all know about the other, and now we know what the other was doing." Leland said shaking his head.

Martha let out a cackle along with a loud slap of her own thigh as her right hand struck it. Everyone looked shocked as the old woman spoke loud and clear. "You can bet on that Lee, I even got to eat my cake too when that house of the devil went boom."

Everyone eyed Martha with a suspicious eye, and Wilma was about to ask what she meant when a cell phone ringer suddenly blurted out causing Leland to break his trance. He pulled the small compact phone from his pocket and answered it thankfully stopping the shrill sound it was making. The group stood in silence while he took the call and it wasn't good they could tell from the way the street preacher acted. Leland spoke softly, carefully, acknowledging the person on the other end every few seconds. Stephanie thought it sounded like Kenny but she wasn't totally sure.

"He's dead," Leland said slowly after hanging up the phone, "Eight Ball and his bodyguard were found in a parking deck full of holes by that blue Beamer he used to parade around in."

Stephanie looked to the ground in shock, the news settling in slowly. "I'm glad we stopped him, but it feels hollow. I mean I knew what was going to happen, but now that it has it seems weird. Did we do the right thing you think? We didn't we get him killed, did we?"

Wilma squeezed her mom's hand feeling a twinge of guilt at hearing about Eight Ball. In the end she wasn't sorry to hear about his death, and maybe that was wrong, but it was what it was.

Leland reached out and rubbed Stephanie's shoulder and back with reassurance while speaking. "Eight Ball chose his path, chose to ignore anyone reaching out to him, so in the end he was his own enemy. No one can live in the drug world and expect to be there long, not a soul."

"Oh please, what's all this sadness over that no account boy for!" Martha called out in disgust.

"Come on Grammy, we're all children of the Lord at the end of the day." Leland said with earnest.

"You think the Lord is going to come down and save anyone in this Project Lee? You're crazier than I thought if that's the case. Eight Ball dealt that junk and the wheel of vengeance turned on him and if he got it earlier than it should have been, well that's just a cookie in my jar." Martha shot back.

"This place is going to be a battlefield by tomorrow night Grammy. Someone is going to make a move at taking over this piece of turf no matter what. People are going to die Grammy, innocent people who had nothing to do with this plan, our plan. I'm sorry if we feel a little remorse at that!" Leland retorted.

"Innocent people been dying in this hell hole for years Lee, of all the people here you should know that best. Fate dropped a chance in my lap to save that angel right there, and may be even free this place from the grip of the devil's white powder. I took a bull by the horns and made a decision, one I thought you might understand but I see I was wrong!" Martha alleged.

"Grammy, it's not that simple." Leland began, trying to explain his feelings.

"BAH, simple ain't got anything to do with it! You want to end this thing?" Grammy demanded.

"Yeah" Leland exclaimed.

"You want this thing over with Stephanie so your precious daughter can be safe?" Grammy demanded of the woman.

"Yes Ma'am!" Stephanie exclaimed as well, her posture straightening with sudden steel will.

"Then you stand back and let Mr. Alexander do what he knows how to do. I've watched too many babies die in this place to watch another angel follow them into the grave. If Lucifer wants my soul as the cost for saving Wilma Jackson then I'll gladly pay that bill. I won't sit by and watch her die by some thug's hand Lee. I refuse to do that anymore!" Grammy said emphatically shaking a finger. The tension in the air was thick and hot threatening to boil over for a moment as everyone became silent.

"Do you really think you can stop the drugs from coming in?" Wilma asked quietly taking the mood of the group down a notch or two.

"I have a plan little one." Alexander stated tasting the foulness on his tongue again. He held back the look of pain on his face, the hurt of having to lie to Wilma. There was no way to stop the drugs from coming in and in the end there was no possible grace which would save the Laurel from being burnt to the ground.

"Is it a good plan?"

"Oh yes, I rarely think of any other kind." The vampire said with a wink.

"And you want to know what the next step is?" Stephanie asked Wilma, but it was Leland who answered.

"We go after the men who supply the corners. We go after the head of the snake. I'm sure Alex got the names of the suppliers from Ray, right?

"That I did," the vampire stated with a nod.

Stephanie finished the street preacher's explanation with a wink. "And we convince them that the Laurel is way too expensive to deal in, just like Alex said before, too high a price to pay for them to keep coming down here."

"Wow, a simple but effective plan. It is pretty good." Wilma said looking over to Alexander with a smile.

"How would you know?" Stephanie asked giving her daughter a playful poke in her stomach causing Wilma to giggle.

"Thank you." Alexander said politely, fully acknowledging the compliment from Wilma.

"Wait a minute though, what about the werewolves from the club?" Leland asked quickly.

"What werewolves?" Wilma cried out.

Stephanie pulled her daughter into a quick bear hug while trying to calm her with humor. "Lee just meant a bunch of mean old dogs, better watch it or they'll get you! Quick, we better get home!"

Wilma let out a scream as Stephanie's fingers danced in a devilish tickle across her ribs once more. Leland followed the pair as the trio made their way to the backdoor of Stephanie's apartment. They all disappeared inside under the watchful eye of Alexander as Martha asked a question from behind.

"What's this about werewolves?"

"The four horsemen you warned me about three days ago. The horsemen are actually Werewolves who have come to kill me." Alexander responded calmly, as if it were normal to be hunted by werewolves these days.

"Oh, that vision. I have so many these days it's hard to keep them all straight." Martha chuckled.

The vampire turned to Grammy with a raised eyebrow and a question. "Did you mean what you said about finishing this Martha, are you still hardened to this path?"

"As long as Wilma is safe, you can kill the whole damn lot of gangsters round here." Grammy stated flatly. The remark brought a long look from Alexander and that burled Grammy just that much more. "Are you worried or something?"

"No, I told you other people would get hurt in this if I preceded Martha. I only wanted to insure you were still willing to carry on with everything." Alexander stated flatly, steely, still watching her.

"As long as you stay the course Mr. Alexander, I got nothing in this world to worry about." Grammy replied with a smile.

"What makes you think I won't Martha?" Alexander asked, his stiff demeanor turning soft.

"I know you love that little girl now but if for some reason I'm not here on this earth before she's safe, I need you to make me a promise Mr. Alexander. I need you to promise you'll finish this no matter what." Grammy said leaning heavily on her cane.

"Why do you think you're not going to be here Martha?" Alexander asked truly perplexed.

"I'm not saying I won't be here, just in the case that I am not." Grammy said with a bigger grin. She slowly walked away leaving Alexander alone on the small pathway.

His mind turned to the plan, what would come in the next few days. He felt instant guilt and regret, what he had started in motion was coming for his friends. Alexander told himself he would protect them, keep them safe no matter the cost, but it didn't stop the wave of emotions. After being gone for so long, to have friends again, it was hurting him so much to know that he was using them. Yes, this was all for the good of protecting Wilma, but even that rationalization wasn't enough to stop the guilt. Alexander reached into his jeans pocket and clutched the locket drawing strength from it, drawing the courage to see through what he had started just a few days ago.

Book Two

'Stare in wonder, who's here to bring you down?
Find your martyr; I'm sure you've made the crown
So light a fire under my bones, so when
I die for you; at least I'll die alone'

'Ain't nothing for me to end up like this
There's no comparing me this time'

'All my heroes have now become ghosts
Sold their sorrow to the ones who paid the most
All my heroes are dead and gone
But they're inside of me, they still live on'
Heroes, Shinedown**, *Us and Them*

Chapter One

Yelena's distrust and animosity for Michaels was absolute, to the very point of hate with a swift and passionate undercurrent of loathing, and the way the Lesser Lich was acting only fueled her suspicion. The evidence pointing to a secondary secret outcome for the pack in this partnership was nothing short of overwhelming. There was another plan in play, one that had a very unhealthy ending for Yelena and her brothers. The only real question at the moment, the one rolling around in her head, was where her mother Svetlana was being kept. It was the only thing keeping her from killing Michaels with her bare hands at this time. Was her mother in danger by some rogue clan of vampires or by Akhenaton himself, was she even alive? Michaels here was just an errand boy for Grand Lich, he wasn't even a full Lich like his precious lord. She wasn't sure of the exact steps or components needed to perform the arcane ritual to become one of the most powerful undead in existence, but she knew of only one person who could do the complicated incantations, the same person who had worked the necessary dark magic to its nefarious end with perfection once already and was now invincible. Akhenaton, the onetime Pharaoh of Egypt who had been called mad and insane by some, was also a powerful sorcerer who had taken his own life essence and during said ancient ceremony transferred all of the energy into a large magnificent blue Sapphire gem through the powerful conjuration. In effect, after one night, Akhenaton was immortal. He was no longer bound to the flesh or laws of this world, and nothing on this earth could stop him because if you destroy the body he lives in then he simply takes another, shifting with ease. The Grand Lich feared nothing save for one, his only weakness being the gem. If it should fall into the wrong hands and be destroyed, he would also cease to exist.

Only Akhenaton knew of the necessary steps to become a Lich. The only one who possessed the knowledge of the incantations so when he converted a disciple he would always perform the ritual, but while casting the spells he would change something Yelena was told by her mother Svetlana. The Grand Lich would alter some part of the ceremony and thus bind the new disciple to him through the dark magic and hate he used to transform him or her. This made the new follower nothing more than a slave to its new master for all eternity. The Grand Lich controlled all the undead he created, most of the magical beings bowed down to him, and a few of the magic bearing ones on the west coast called him an ally but now he was starting on the east it seemed. And here stood one of those slaves bound to him in their hotel suite holding court over them like some kind of a judge administering punishment to a youth who had been caught committing a crime, and it was this fool Michaels who was the one who had them confronting the oldest and most powerful vampire in pairs. The dead man was either insane, stupid, or running a devious plan and Yelena was sure he was too cowardly to do something like the last on his own. Michaels also wasn't insane nor stupid either, though history might tell her different on both. So that left only one answer, the one she was struggling with right now.

If her intuitions turned out to be true then everything she had assumed and trusted would be waiting for her and her brothers at the end of this accord was a lie. Her mother had warned her once to never trust any Lich and yet Yelena had done just that to find Svetlana and look where her and her brothers were now. No mother and now there might be little chance at living past this week. She had pledged to her father, her mother, and her Lord Ivan to protect her pack and house with her life, to protect her family's' long history of honor with nothing less than her very being and yet here she stood trying to make sense of why Akhenaton would put the Epova family under the knife, treating them like so much grist for the mill. How could she have let this happen?

Was it for some power play she asked herself, is that why the Grand Lich would send them against the Ancient One? For the last thousand years the magical beings of the world, from lycanthrope to vampire to wizard were just rambling solitary groups scattered across the lands of the world calling no country a true home. There was no alliance but to family, no loyalty but to one's own patronage unless you needed protection. The Epova's lived by the rule and order of the pack's mother, Svetlana, and she had lived by no one's rule save one and that was the protection of her family after her mate had gone missing. She was an Elder who was not afraid to fight anything for her territory and to protect her own, until an enemy came along that the Duchess could not fight. A Nosferatu by the name of Gaul had for a reason young Yelena did not know marked the Epova family for death, all of the pack, and Gaul had many a follower and brood. Yelena and her brothers were still too young to run with their mother, unable to fight and defend themselves, so Svetlana had called for the Great Wolf Ivan to ask his help, and one night later he appeared. The strongest of all the lycanthropes Ivan came to the pack mother and gave her two choices, she and her family could join under his house and have the safety of numbers or they all would die by nightfall at the hands of the Nosferatu Gaul and his kind. There was no choice. To face the Nosferatu and his followers in a fight with such a young pack was suicide, so Svetlana chose to move her family under the rule of Ivan and life as one with his other packs. There was no longer a single house of Epova, no sense of distinction, and it was then Yelena started to hate vampires, loathe them for what they had done and taken from her family. And that is what Akhenaton had used to pull her in so deep and so fast, that anger buried deep inside, Yelena thought before the epiphany came.

It clicked, like a lock being opened with a loud pop. The Grand Lich had Svetlana, he was the one who took her and he did so because of other packs. There were other packs of werewolves who refused his rule, other lycanthropes like the Great Wolf Ivan that hid during the day and hunted at night. They chose freedom over Akhenaton's 'fealty' and had for years as he sought to catch them, break them, and subjugate them like he does everything else. There was only one reason, one act that would bring them out of hiding to stand with Akhenaton. If the vampires began to massacre packs of werewolves, killed all those living in peace and left none alive, then the elders of all the Houses might think of taking an offer from the Grand Lich if it was a certain Ancient One committing the acts of murder. The werewolf packs might even unleash all of their fury on him. Yelena closed her eyes as it all made sense now, how Akhenaton had used them and would continue to. He had and would continue to play on the natural disdain the werewolves had of the vampires, the scorn the Nosferatu had for them, and in the end he would make a war that no one would survive. She felt the chill of the betrayal, felt it run down her spine and into her soul like a dagger of ice. This couldn't be happening, sentencing them to death, every wolf and vampire, it would be carnage. The Great Wolf, her sworn lord and ruler, might sense what would be coming if he were here...but he wasn't and even if he was then Akhenaton would just have him destroyed as well.

And there were others who would suffer the Grand Lich's wrath as well, other wolves and wizards, even the Sisters and their small band of Nosferatu. Magda and her brood were the children of Alexander living just miles from Akhenaton, hunting right under his nose out in Los Angeles. The Grand Lich hated, no despised, the ancient vampire Alexander to the point of an obsession. She wasn't sure what transpired to cause the hatred between the two, and right now she didn't care. Yelena was just trying to think of a way to get her brothers and her mother to safety and she knew a single handed effort would get her nowhere. The Sisters, they could find Svetlana while she could ask the one being who could save her and her brothers for his assistance. Would he help them though after they had stalked him, tried to confront him? Would Alexander even listen to her after what had happened between them?

"Am I boring you Miss Epova?" Michaels called out.

The question snapped Yelena out of the trance she was in and she stared at the man who was dressed in an Armani suit with matching black Italian leather shoes. That animosity in her for Michaels suddenly spiked turning to a mean case despising. The urge to run across the room at Michaels and tear his body cowardly limb from cowardly limb flashed like a flame catching dry wood. You never, ever, betrayed an Epova.

But she didn't do it. Yelena put her murderous thoughts to the back of her mind and focused on Michaels while speaking clearly, concisely. "No sir, you are not boring me. I was thinking of why no one was able to discern this vampire was the Ancient One."

"The vampire is not Alexander, I have told you this! I would have known if this imposter was the Ancient One from my spells and observations." Michaels answered back with a snap. Yelena only nodded then looked over to her brother Gregor whose face was a mask. Michaels wouldn't have noticed but she knew exactly what her brother was thinking. He had put two and two together also and now he was dealing with the implications. Yelena felt a pang of guilt and the only thing she wanted to do was hug him, take away the cold stunned feeling she had just dealt with.

"He told me his name, twice, while ripping my throat out almost!" Dimitri whined from his spot on the couch.

"You must have heard wrong!" Michaels spat. He was quickly losing patience with the wolves and the conversation as anyone could see.

"I know I was a bit occupied at the time trying to breathe and all, but I am sure of what I heard." Dimitri shot looking around the room for help, but there was none coming. Gregor and Yelena stayed quiet while eyeing Michaels carefully.

"Do you want to challenge me on this pup? Maybe we should call Lord Akhenaton and ask him, hmm? What do you say pup?" Michaels hissed, his eyes narrowing to slits.

The room dropped to dead silence for a second as Dimitri pondered the question. He looked more than willing to take the challenge, and then he turned to his sister. She gave him a sign to cease, something no one would notice, before turning back to Michaels. "No sir, there is no challenge."

"So you're saying you do not want to call Lord Akhenaton?" Michaels said quickly, pressing his will over Dimitri.

"No sir, there is no need to call the Grand one." Dimitri said lowering his eyes, giving in to Michaels.

"Then you're not challenging me?"

"No sir."

"Are you sure?"

"Yes sir." Dimitri growled, his patience waning under the ego of Michaels.

"Good," Michaels said turning to the others nervously pacing, "don't presume to step out of line with me again. Instead of chasing after foolish notions and conjecture what we need now children is a plan. What we need is to anticipate what this vampire is going to do so we can destroy him once and for all."

"That is not a good plan Michaels, it will not work. We have no information that will tell us what we need to know, as in where this vampire is hiding." Gregor said watching Michaels closely. He noticed the man's eyes come alive with fire at the mention of the plan being ineffective. Someone might take the look at its face value, a man's ego being stepped on. Gregor knew better though, he knew now what it and this meeting was really about. Michaels response to his question was the final piece that closed the deal.

"Are you trying to upset me?" Michaels snarled with a disgusted air.

"We are not trying to upset you. What my brother is saying is we have nothing to give us any indication what the vampire is going to do next. We have run out of options to locate and end him." Yelena spoke carefully with painstakingly chosen words. She made sure to not say 'Ancient One' as the vampire even though she knew this Nosferatu was Alexander.

Michaels turned to her and locked eyes. "You are trying to undermine me with my lord that is what you are trying to do pup."

"We are doing no such thing!" Yelena spat back.

"You're evading your promise to Lord Akhenaton by not fulfilling the request of his to exterminate this vampire! Your mother's life is for naught and you have no one to blame but yourselves!" Michaels hissed vehemently.

Gregor rose from his sitting position on the arm of the couch and crossed his arms across his chest making his posture one that he hoped would be seen as non-antagonistic but also defiant as well. "Do not threaten our mother Michaels, ever! We will willingly destroy this vampire as you want but only when the obstacle hindering us is removed. We have no clue to where he has gone."

"You know where he is. You know he stays somewhere in that slum." Michaels countered quickly.

"We have no address or building number. We cannot break into every room of every house searching for the vampire." Gregor explained keeping his voice level and calm.

"You know he's attacking the drug dealers! Spy on them and wait for the vampire to appear."

"The dealers are not stupid. They have left the area to save their own lives and we cannot watch every corner around the large complex Michaels. It is impossible to know where the vampire will appear or attack."

"Then what do you plan on doing?" Michaels practically screamed.

"That is the obstacle sir. There is nothing we can do." Dimitri finished shaking his head.

It wasn't the dim reality of the situation that burned Michaels as much as the fact that these menial wolves were still alive. He had set them in motion, pushed them in the right direction to confront Alexander, and then they refused to die! It was just like Svetlana's worthless lineage to fail, they were all good for nothing flea-bags. And now they were pointing fingers at him, blaming him under muffled breaths and accusing stares. He still had one card though, and when he played this one it was a full out attack. No more trying to play it smart, just get the damn job done and go home he thought. Michaels stopped his pacing and stood still in the center of the suite to get everyone's full attention.

"We still have one thing left, the old woman."

"The old woman who spoke to Gregor in his mind," Dimitri asked quickly, struck dumb with shock

"That is an even worse idea Michaels. We have no information on her and there is no guarantee she will talk or tell us anything." Yelena pointed out.

"We're not going to talk with her Miss Epova. She will be our bait for the vampire!"

Gregor stepped back and watched with wide-eyed amazement at his handler and his last statement. If he hadn't already guessed what Michaels was doing then this would most certainly have been the final straw, the last clue he needed to bring everything into focus. It was more than evident the pack was in danger, being turned over to the Ancient One by Michaels. Yes, Gregor knew the vampire they had been following and attacking was Alexander. He didn't have any solid proof for his over-analytical mind to bolster the claim and he didn't need any. He had Dimitri's word on what he heard and that was all he needed. At the end of the day all he needed was the word of his family. Gregor looked to his sister, gave her the same sign, and went back to listening to Michael's madness. In a couple of hours he would talk with Yelena and then only the Great Wolf knew what they would do next.

At the same time across town on Roswell Road Renfroe pulled his Crown Victoria into the small parking lot of the Phoenix New Age store with Foster sitting next to him, a dreamy look on his face. Renfroe was still having a hard time believing what he saw when he went by to pick the man up from his apartment. There, standing in a terry cloth bathrobe, was Toni the exotic dancer from the night before. She was wrapped in Foster arms giving him quite the sendoff kiss. Toni was naked under the robe too, he could tell. Then the image of her and him in bed popped into Renfroe's brain and for some reason it just didn't make a bit of rational, deductive sense. How did he end up with her? Renfroe shook his head to clear the image out as Foster trotted up and hopped in the car. Toni waved Foster goodbye and blew him a small kiss as they pulled out of the apartment parking lot with screeching tires on their way to the store.

Renfroe put the car in park then turned to Foster and spoke in his best commanding tone. "When we get inside, just let me do the talking." Renfroe stated.

"Yeah, no problem, I'll keep it mum." Foster said with a shrug of his shoulders.

The two got out and walked into the store through a small front door that hardly admitted Renfroe. They were barely on the inside when Foster eyes had adjusted to the low lighting of the room. Soft tantric music played as incense floated on the air, serenity seemed to flow from every corner and turn. Foster could tell the store had once been a house as the front room had separate openings to other rooms, like the living room of his parents only without the plastic covered couch and chair. One room was dedicated to the Wicca and Celtic religion, one to Native American studies while another to Eastern philosophies like Buddhism, and in the back was a large room with rows of bookshelves and other assorted metaphysical items and studies.

"What is this place?" Foster asked in a whisper.

"Home," Renfroe said as he walked over to the counter by the front door they had walked in.

"Bear," a young man said to Renfroe as soon as he spotted the large man, "blessed be. It's been a while since you came in here."

"Where's Adria?" The detective asked ignoring the man's comments. Foster was about to say something when a gentle voice called out to Renfroe from behind.

"I'm here Bear."

Foster turned to see a beautiful raven-haired women standing in the doorway to the Wicca room, a shawl wrapped around her slender body. She stood maybe an inch short of five feet tall, the gray dress she wore flowing out from her in a pool on the floor. The material of the dress ebbed with a shimmering movement of light adding to the mesmerizing effect and the scene took Foster's breath away. She looked like an angel or as close as there could be to one.

"Hello mother." Renfroe answered back.

"Would you like to talk to me about something?" She asked smiling warmly.

"I need your help mother. I need your 'special' help." Renfroe answered then added.

"Well then, I am more than pleased to help. Come back to my sanctuary." Adria said offering her hand to her son. Renfroe walked forward slowly, almost reverently, before taking Adria's smaller hand in his and the two disappeared.

"Where are they going?" Foster asked the man at the counter.

"They're going back to Adria's sanctuary, it's a room in the back that she does her readings and work from." The man answered.

"Oh, okay. Listen did I hear him right? Did he say 'mother' to Adria?" Foster asked with a quizzical look.

"Yes he did," the man answered with a slight smile, "Bear is the oldest son of Adria."

"Wow, I figured Renfroe's mother abandoned him because he was so damn mean!" Foster laughed. He stopped a second later as the man didn't respond in kind making the moment slightly awkward.

"My older brother has his quirks, but once you get to know him he's really kind of cool." The man stated with a small smile.

"You're his little brother?" Foster asked with a blink of his eyes.

"All my life," The man said with a broad grin.

"Oh wow, that's great!" Foster said trying to respond in kind but finding it a little hard. Renfroe had a mother and a little brother, who'd have thought?

The room was wasn't large but it felt deceptively spacious and warm. There wasn't much furniture save for two wicker chairs around a small table draped in fine cloth and a matching smaller version of the chair in the corner. Forest green adorned everything from the color of the walls to a set of throw pillows that sat on the floor around the small table. Incense burned on the table, lavender and vanilla hung in the air and seemed to induce graciousness. Renfroe followed Adria in and watched as she closed the door then moved over to the wicker chairs. She extended her hand signaling for him to take the other chair but he waved her off with a slight shake of his head.

"I'd prefer to stand, makes it easier for me to pace." Otz stated.

"You were always filled with energy weren't you my little Bear." Adria said with a smile that enhanced her already remarkable beauty.

The two stood in silence then. Adria holding the deck of her tarot cards while Renfroe stood soaking up the atmosphere of the room. He had forgotten the smell of his mother's private abode, the way it instantly relaxed you and freed your mind from the stress and anxiety of the outside world. Childhood memories flowed back to him of the large open woods he played in with his brother at their house in the country. They would lie down in the thick grass and look up to the tall canopy the trees formed and feel nature flow over and through him like a giant running river. How long ago were those days? It felt like eons instead of years. How could some things change so much in so short a time?

"I ask myself that question all the time." Adria called out.

"What?" Otz replied coming out of his trance.

"Do you still honor the sabots Bear?" Adria asked.

"I still honor the pagan holidays, though I might have missed one here and there."

"Do you still cast spells?"

"On occasion, but I didn't come here to answer questions mother. I came here to find answers to a few." Renfroe remarked in an attempt to bring the conversation back to center. It may have sounded harsh but it was his way, straight to the point.

"You need to know about the man in black don't you?" Adria asked. The question would have thrown the average person, Adria forging ahead in the conversation with a bit of information the person had never mentioned. It was her way, and she meant no harm with just asking her son about the one thing he needed to know without saying a word yet. Renfroe was more than comfortable with his mother's precognitive abilities though. He wasn't scared or apprehensive in the least little bit when she displayed her powers to him.

"Yes, I need to know about him and a Russian. I need to confirm a suspicion or two with your help mother." Renfroe answered.

"Well," Adria said beginning to turn over the tarot cards, "let us see what I can find out for you shall we."

"And why do you call him 'Bear'? I thought his name was Otz?"
Foster asked politely.

"His name is Otz Renfroe," the man behind the counter said,
"but we've been calling him Bear since his early childhood."

"Why, because of his size?"

"No sir, it's because his totem animal is a bear." The man
answered.

"Oh, that would make sense. By the way, my name is Foster."
The assistant coroner offered holding out a hand to the man. He
wasn't sure what a 'totem' animal was but Foster wasn't going to
ask about it anyway. The chance to find out about Renfroe was
just too good to let go.

"My name is Joel."

"So Joel, Renfroe is a witch or something like that?" Foster
asked.

"You would have to ask him that question. We all call ourselves
something and Bear is a private man who likes to keep everything
close, there's no surprise that way." Joel stated apprehensively.

"Oh, I see." Foster remarked again. He slowly walked away
from Joel to explore the marvels of the bookstore and to digest

his new found information. He would have never thought of the big man being a witch.

"I see the man your here to ask about. He is old and wise, moving with the shadows through time. Yet, he's engaged in a bargain of some kind now, a deal or repayment of debt. He's your ally in this battle Bear so do not anger him or give him reason to alienate you." Adria stated staring at the fan-type arrangement of the Tarot cards on the table.

"He saved my life last night." Renfroe remarked back low.

"I see," Adria said with a raised eyebrow while keeping her eyes and concentration on the cards, "I will have to thank this man someday for doing such a noble act."

"What about the Russian?" Renfroe asked quickly, feigning ignorance at his mother's remark.

"He is a strong advisory," Adria remarked turning over a card from the deck, "he is not to be taken lightly in strength or perseverance...or number."

Renfroe eyed the cards hard as he whispered, "Number, you mean there's more than one?"

Adria ignored his question and turned over two more cards, at the placement of the second card she paused. Renfroe knew she had found something, he had watched his mother enough to know her mannerisms. When she did this the cards had revealed something dark and she was trying to decipher the message exactly.

"This man belongs to a family with a long lineage, a past that weaves to and fro but points to a single star. He has brothers and a sister and all three ride with him. They are a pack hunting together, killing as one, like wolves." Adria remarked.

"He has a family...a pack? Can you see what they're here for?"

"They've come for the man in black. It seems my dearest son you have become entangled in a personal war, a very old conflict." Adria answered finally looking up from the cards.

Renfroe stood still for a second ingesting, rolling over, and examining the information as precisely as he could. His mother's readings were like this, confusing at the beginning yet if unraveled the right way could lead one to the answers you needed. He just had to figure out the puzzle, had to find the right key to open the encryption matrix.

"There is something else here Bear." Adria abruptly said cutting off Renfroe and his thoughts.

"What is it?"

"You must be wary of your allies Bear, or you will be betrayed." Adria spoke softly.

The man in black instantly came to his thoughts, but then he pushed it away. Renfroe wasn't sure who the last part his mother was speaking of and he could spend the next week trying to figure it out and never come close so he stored it along with the other information from the reading. He walked over to his mother and slowly reached out to touch her cheek, his fingers gingerly rubbing along the smooth skin of Adria's face. If he could cry a tear one might have slowly rolled down his cheek through rough stubble.

"I'll be careful, I promise mother." Renfroe said.

"I know you will Bear," was all Adria said as she watched her son leave the room. There was no need for more words. The simple gesture of touching her cheek conveyed the love the two felt for each other.

Foster saw Renfroe marching toward the front door and he scrambled to catch the big man as fast as he could. Even with the effort he barely caught up with Renfroe as the man opened the front glass door to walk through when Joel's voice stopped them both.

"Can you do something for me Bear?"

"Yeah, what's that?" Renfroe asked back.

"Come back in one piece big brother." Joel remarked before giving a small salute.

"I plan on it." Renfroe offered. Then he was out the door in a flash, squinting against the harsh sunlight, and Foster following up quickly.

"We need to go to the Laurel Projects. I have to speak with a friend there but first we need to follow up on some other information." Renfroe stated getting into the car. After climbing in he turned to find Foster staring at him intently, almost studiously. "What?" He asked quickly.

"Nothing, I just never would have thought of you as a witch is all." Foster commented.

"Joel," Renfroe said shaking his head as the car squealed out of the parking lot, "Of all the people you had to talk to in there, you had to get my little brother."

"Do you cast spells and stuff?" Foster asked with genuine interest.

"Don't make me shoot you Foster." Renfroe stated with a growl. The coroner sat in silence as they started to travel to the Laurel. His piqued curiosity was not even close to being satiated but messing with Renfroe who carried a loaded gun quelled any thought of probing farther.

The detective's cell suddenly blurted out its ring tone which echoed in the car. He answered the cell with one hand with a gruff 'Renfroe'.

The conversation didn't start good and it went downhill fast. Foster could tell from the look on the detective's face and the fact the car's speed went up twenty MPH in five seconds.

"Now, you want it right now?" Renfroe screamed into his cell.

Someone on the other end said something that just added to the detective's anger. Foster peeked over to look at the speedometer and it was somewhere above 90, not real safe. Renfroe growled some obscenity abruptly ending the call and chucking the phone into the backset for good measure.

"What is it? And please slow down, it's getting a little scary here" Foster requested.

"We have to go to headquarters. IAD wants to talk with both of us."

"IAD wants to talk with both of us?" Foster whined

"Yep, we're in their sights now."

The car was really hot, and it was moving a lot Foster realized. It was too hot maybe, and maybe there was just a little too much swaying in the car. That's what had to be making him nauseous, or maybe it was the fact Internal Affairs suddenly wanted to talk now.

The wolves were gone, gathered in their room obviously devising some plan to make him look even worse to Lord Akhenaton. Michaels paced in the large living room area looking down to his cell a fourth time and could no more bring himself to dial the number for his lord than the last three times he had tried. He put his hand that held the cell phone behind his back and continued to stare out the window at the Atlanta sky line. Out of sight out of memory he told himself hoping it all would just go away. All the pressure with checking in, trying to get the Ancient One to kill the Epovas, and the possible chance of bodily injury upon failure was too much for him. He needed a break.

Suddenly his cell went off in his hand causing Michaels to jump and drop the small metal box to the floor with a thump. He cringed at the ring tone blaring from the cell as it lay in the thick carpet of the suite. Michaels knew who was calling and he knew nothing good would come from answering right now. Yes, just let it ring until it stops he thought, let the other end think your unavailable. Yes, that was a good idea, you were taking a nap in the bedroom and you just missed the call his mind yelled out.

Yet he just could not answer it so somewhere around the twentieth ring Michaels picked up the cell and stared at the screen for a moment before answering.

"Why are the Epova's still breathing?" Akhenaton asked in a voice that dripped with anger.

"Sir, please, I'm trying my best and the Epova's will not-." Michaels stammered somewhere between explaining and whining.

"And what did I say the last time Michaels, what did I say?"

"That my plan had better work or there would be dire consequences." Michaels cried.

"YOU'RE DAMN RIGHT," Akhenaton yelled into the phone making Michaels jump, "I'M GOING TO REACH THROUGH THIS PHONE AND TEAR YOU'RE SKELETON OUT OF YOUR SKIN! FAILURE IS DEATH!"

"AHHHH, NO!" Michaels wailed collapsing onto the couch as if he fainted. Here it comes he thought, unimaginable pain (if he could still feel pain it would be ghastly for sure) followed by the dark nothingness of death! If his heart was still alive and beating it would surely leap from his chest and explode Michaels thought. Here it comes! Yet, a second passed and nothing happened. Then a second and a third second went by before Akhenaton's voice sounded from the cell being crushed in Michaels's right hand.

"Come on, I'm just messing with you Michaels, having some fun. No gloom and doom here for you buddy."

"Sir?" Michaels asked weakly and totally confused.

"You're safe, but did I not tell you how much trouble Alexander would be in your plan. Did I not call that or what?" Akhenaton said jovially.

"Um, yes you did sir," was all Michaels could bring himself to say for the moment.

"That vampire didn't get to be the biggest pain in my ass by doing what we thought or wanted him to do Michaels. But his day's coming, and sooner than he could ever imagine."

"Sir, what exactly is happening here?" Michaels asked genuinely confused.

"A change of plans Michaels, I need you to keep an eye on someone for me. There's a woman with a lot magical power and precognitive abilities I need." Akhenaton explained coldly.

"Keep an eye on sir, or do you mean kidnap? And if she can see the future want she see us coming to get her?"

"Wow, that's a lot of questions about my carefully thought out plans, maybe I should have ripped your bones out of your skin just for fun, eh?" Akhenaton hissed.

"I'm you're willing servant sir, direct me at you're will!" Michaels begged trying to climb out of the sudden hole he dug and then fell in.

"Well, what I'm thinking is you might need some help, which is why I've sent Ick and Phlegm to give you some assistance."

At the sound of the names Michaels sat bolt upright on the couch, a look of fear gripping his face. "The ghouls sir, are you sure you need to send the ghouls?"

"Yes Michaels, I'm sure I need to send them because they can help you on two fronts. Tell me, what happens if someone gets bit or gets a deep cut from one of my ghouls?"

The Lesser Lich looked around nervously still not totally convinced he was out of danger as he answered. "The bite is poisonous sir causing a deep form of paralysis yet the victim still has all their mental faculties. The victim can feel and think just not move. "

"Right, dead to the world for all rhyme and reason and what does that paralysis help us to do Michaels?" Akhenaton carried on.

"We can control the victim sir...take control of their bodies and have the victim do our bidding."

"That's right, a little dark magic and we get a worker bee that doesn't rot. This is why I gave up making regular zombies Michaels, the ghouls are such better weapons and one can make a room full of trapped followers in a matter of seconds."

"Yes, sir, perfect weapons...I just wish Ick and Phlegm were more like the harmless things off Harry Potter than what they truly are." Michaels said disdainfully.

"I more than agree Michaels, their breath alone is horrendous and that's before you add in the way they look, but don't distract me. Here's the plan Michaels, no deviation. First, I've already given Ick his orders to shadow the woman for a couple of days before snatching her, just keep an eye on him and make sure when he gets her she stays in one piece. No missing fingers this time!"

"Yes sir, all fingers intact and working." Michaels agreed. The last time the ghoul had 'retrieved' a person for Akhenaton the poor man only had seven digits left. That was another problem with the ghouls, they liked the taste of flesh just a little too much and if you didn't watch them closely you might come up short a finger or toe...or both.

"Second, take Phlegm and finish the Epova's, don't wait for Alexander to do the job. Once the ghoul claws and bites the pups you'll have full control of them, no more stalling from Yelena. You can plant whatever evidence you need later. I'll convince Svetlana that Alexander killed her family and those ignorant renegade wolf packs will come crawling to me looking for revenge. Got it?"

Michaels swallowed hard submitting everything to memory, missing the sounds coming from behind his bedroom door. "Yes sir, I have everything. When will the ghouls arrive?"

"Oh, I sent them via express mail before I called you on the cell. Both are waiting for you in your bedroom." Akhenaton stated. One could almost picture the smile growing on the Grand Lich's face as he sat behind his big desk back in the mansion in LA.

Michaels turned slightly toward the door to his bedroom and saw it suddenly pop ajar. The hinges squeaked loud as the portal swung just an inch or two inward exposing a strip of the dark inside. A set of yellow slits appeared and deep labored breathing floated out of the dark room. The eyes locked onto Michaels as he spoke into the cell with a dry mouth in a fear filled whisper.

"Oh, that's a wonderful plan sir!"

All at once the Epova's looked skyward and sniffed the air. There, just on the fringe of the ventilation, was a scent they all knew and loathed. Only one thing made that scent, the one thing that signaled their end. They all looked back down, a mask of disgust on their faces. All at once they whispered the same word.

"Ghoul"

Dimitri turned to Gregor and spat. "Then we are truly dead to Akhenaton. He will have Michaels hunt us down if we flee."

"That we are brother and that he will. Michaels will no longer wait for the Ancient One to kill us." Gregor said crossing his arms over his chest.

"I am sorry my brothers," Yelena said with a bowed head," so sorry for getting us into this. I should have seen what was being set against us-."

"No dear sister, this is not your fault" Gregor said cutting her off, lifting her head with his hand on her chin so she was looking at them all. "We have been betrayed by the master betrayer, but we will not be broken or defeated. We may have no one to turn to or anywhere to hide from the Grand Lich but we will not cower in a corner."

"Da, we will not die without a fight!" Dimitri said with clenched teeth and a tight squeeze of his fist.

Peter reached out and grabbed Dimitri's fist in a show of solidarity. He said something in Russian that brought a laugh from the dark haired werewolf who in turn grabbed his brother Peter around the neck in loving hug. Gregor stood back and smiled watching his two brothers laughing when his sister spoke up breaking the moment.

"There will be no need to die."

The brothers stopped and all as one turned to Yelena starring at her. Gregor eyed his sister with a close eye. "What are you suggesting Yelena?"

"I am going to find the Ancient One. I will tell him of our situation and garner his protection." Yelena said with one breath getting her words out before anyone could object to them.

The expression on Dimitri and Peter's face wasn't supportive in the least; it was more like shock mixed with a little 'are you crazy?' And Gregor's look just scared her, but Yelena didn't budge or back down. Yes, Ivan had ordered no alliance with any Nosferatu under any circumstance. Yes, all four hated the vampires with all their beings could muster but this was the only choice, the only option they could take to stay alive.

"Are you serious sister? The Ancient One will kill you. He will rip you from limb from limb! All Nosferatu are evil, like Ivan has told us." Dimitri exclaimed with a wail.

Gregor turned to his brother with a scowl for over-reacting and the look brought Dimitri back to his senses before going back to Yelena. He took a deep breath and then spoke carefully. "Do you think you can convince Alexander to take protect us?"

"Maybe, I have to try or we will certainly never see mother again."

"What if he demands servitude for our lives?" Gregor asked quickly, to the heart of what concerned them all. Peter grabbed Dimitri and spoke something to him in Russian, but the black haired wolf responded with a finger to his lips demanding silence as Yelena growled.

"No, I won't agree to that. We have seen how others treat us, especially the Nosferatu. We will be no one's slave after this night! I will not trust the Ancient One. I will only use him to assure our freedom and survival from the Grand Lich."

The answer had a calming effect on her brothers Yelena noted. Her ruse had worked. She had every intention of giving the Ancient One something in exchange for her brother's life, and if they knew what that was then there was no possible reason they would let her leave.

"How will you find him?" Dimitri asked.

"The old black woman from the housing project, she will know where to find him." Gregor answered.

Yelena gave a nod of her head choosing not to speak. The pack stood in silence for a minute. They knew what their sister was about to do, what the ominous implications of going against the Grand Lich Akhenaton were, especially now with no Ivan or protection from his House. They each took the other's hand embracing one more time, sending out impulses with their touch, absorbing the love for each other in case something dreadful were to happen. And when they broke the connection the three brothers watched their sister and leader leave the room. Each made a silent prayer to the Great Wolf asking for Yelena to return safe and with the aid of the Ancient One.

Chapter Two

Even hiding from in the shadows thrown by the street lamps Alexander could tell something was wrong with Wilma. She looked around nervously at the smallest night sound, flinching at the chirp of a cricket once. Something had frightened her, and he had a good idea what the something was. He had felt their presence over the last couple of nights, but not today or tonight. The Epova's had taken up residence, watching and waiting for him to appear so they could lock down the position of his sanctum. Alexander knew they had seen him with Wilma and Martha by now. The Epova's, all lycanthropes for that matter, were methodical when it came to unearthing information, they had a reputation and it was well earned. Yet the reality of the situation had risen to a new level, before it was just his life on the line but now it was this little girl's welfare as well. Alexander reached into the pocket of his jeans letting the locket that was stashed there fall gently into the palm of his open hand. The silver felt cool, reassuring to his touch. In only a short time Wilma Jackson had reached a certain status in his heart that only few could claim to have reached. The little girl had thrown his comfortable and laggard solitude into complete disarray, just as Christine had done so long ago in London. Could he live through that again? Could he stand to lose her as he did Christine?

"Alexander? Are you there?" Wilma whispered suddenly. Her voice was filled with fear, which snapped the vampire out of his trance immediately.

"Yes little one, I'm here." He replied warmly stepping from the shadows.

Wilma breathed a sigh of relief, then walked over and hugged Alexander's waist. She squeezed as hard as her small arms would permit as he slowly ran his hand over the top of her head feeling each strand of her hair. The two didn't move or speak for a second, only enjoyed the embrace.

"What is wrong little one?" Alexander finally asked.

"There are other things out in the world, vampires like you, aren't there?" Wilma asked from her bear hug.

"Yes little one, there are others like me in the world." Alexander answered.

"I guess they're not as nice as you are, huh?" Wilma asked.

"No little one," Alexander answered feeling the fatherly instinct take over, "they are quite evil you might say. Yet, there are those who are as nice as I am, some even nicer."

Wilma finally let go and brushed away an obvious tear on her cheek. Alexander didn't say anything. He protected her dignity with the same ferocity that he used to protect her life. There was nothing to gain by embarrassing her and everything to win by allowing Wilma the second or two needed to gain some composure. She turned and walked over to the park bench taking a seat just as Alexander appeared beside her.

"The werewolves, the ones you mentioned from last night, are they nice too?" Wilma asked slowly.

"I do not know little one, I haven't yet had the chance to talk with them. Why are you asking about them anyway?" Alexander responded fully intent on listening to Wilma, but then his senses picked up a familiar presence. She was just in the dark behind them, watching and listening. He quickly adjusted in the seat, a subtle shift that Wilma didn't notice but allowed him to focus on both her and the new arrival.

"I think one of them made a visit here the other night." Wilma whispered.

"Oh," Alexander said realizing the reason why she was frightened and why the conversation was going in its direction, "what happened?"

"I was reading by Grammy's big window, she actually lets me do it which is cool. My mom won't let me near the windows in the living room, you know, a stray bullet might come through." Wilma confessed.

"Oh, I didn't know." Alexander lied. He already knew what a harsh reality this world was to her.

Wilma took in a breath, waited a second, and then carried on. Alexander didn't prod or push, only let her go at her own pace. "It was a man, a white man, standing out by the trees in the dark. He was wearing a black suit with a blood red tie and I could feel him in my mind, like you sometimes, only he was different. I knew he was evil and he was here to hurt me. I was so scared I couldn't move and if it wasn't for Grammy driving him away there's no telling what would have happened to me. But that's not the weird part?"

"It wasn't. What was the weird part Wilma?"

"I don't know how to say this so I'm just going to say it. He wasn't one of the werewolves, but I think he's hurting them in some way. I don't know how I know; it just feels that way, understand?"

Alexander felt his anger grow exponentially for the boldness of the werewolves as well as his guilt for not being with Wilma when she needed him. He hid his emotions as best as he could when he spoke, but it was impossible to keep the guilt under thumb. "Yes little one, I understand. I'm sorry for not being there to help you Wilma. I should have been being your sworn protector and all."

"It's all right now. The whole encounter sort of brought back something I had forgotten about." Wilma said shrugging her small shoulders.

"What was that?"

"I have this dream, it's kind of corny, but it's my dream and I like it." Wilma said with a quick smile.

"You mean the one where you help all the people in need around the world? I like that one too." Alexander responded with a smile before realizing he just let the cat out of the bag about invading her privacy.

"How did you know about that?" Wilma asked quickly in panic.

"Dreams are the easiest thing to read in the mind sometimes. There expressions of your heart and soul, only visible at those times when you let them grow gossamer wings and escape." Alexander stated hoping Wilma missed the whole implications of reading her mind when she wasn't looking.

"So you don't think it's corny to try and solve all the world's problems?" Wilma asked shyly.

"I think it is one of the most admirable qualities about you and I know you will go farther in your attempt that I ever could Wilma." Alexander answered so honestly it had an immediate effect on the little girl. Wilma blushed, shaking her head hoping to hide the glow in her cheeks from Alexander. She was so embarrassed by the remarks until a scarier idea suddenly popped into her head. Wilma turned to Alexander, actually spinning on her butt.

"You can read my dreams?" She asked with fear in her voice.

"Yes?" Alexander asked back suspiciously, thinking he almost got away.

"You didn't happen to see the one with Taye Diggs?" She asked cringing.

"Oh," Alexander responded holding up a hand, "I turned away from that one right away."

"Thank God!" She gasped while wiping her brow.

The two looked at each other and smiled, an instant moment of understanding between them. She knew she could trust Alexander with anything. He was the only adult who understood her for who she truly was. He knew he could trust Wilma now as well. She would never give him away and always prove to be his greatest ally. They sat in a stoic silence until Wilma asked an awkward question.

"I know this might be a little weird too, but do you own a locket?" She asked quickly with a whisper.

Alexander starred at her for a second, the question raising a small warning flag in his mind. How did she know about the locket? Martha was the only one who knew so she must have mentioned something to her.

"Yes I do, but why do you ask little one?" Alexander asked back

"I keep having this other dream, it's brand new and it's happened every night for the last three nights. You're in it, we've just finished talking, and you're walking away from the bench because we're done for the night. That's when I find this silver ornate locket on the ground at where your feet had been and I'm not sure how but I know it's yours, but before I can say something you're gone. I pick it up and I know you left it for someone when you went away, to keep safe and hidden until you returned because it's so special to you. I feel like I have to open it up, like some force is telling me too, and after I do I see on the inside there are two images. The pictures are the hand painted kind, from the Victorian era by an old man in a shop in small village in the Alps. I don't know how I know the last part, I just do. On the left is a picture of a woman and a boy, your wife and son from before your were changed. And on the right is a beautiful blond woman dressed in Victorian clothes. I don't know her name though." Wilma explained looking to him. There was a moment of silence, of sadness, as she watched her angel take in a deep breath getting ready to talk.

"Her name was Christina,"

"Who was she?" Wilma asked with a reverent whisper.

"A lovely creature," Alexander suddenly found himself revealing his darkest story, "much like you little one. She was a woman of unrenowned beauty, both on the inside and out.

Christina was born into a wealthy family but she preferred to spend her nights and days helping the children of the street. One night she left a brilliant ball clothed in the most expensive dress in London at the time to visit a hovel in the city slum. She spent the night with a sickly child, sitting with a boy who had developed a severe and strong fever."

"Christina was the first woman I fell in love with after the death of Roxanne, the woman in the picture with my son. I have come across other woman who intrigued me, who showed me beauty, but Christina actually breathed life into the hole in my soul. We spent hours discussing anything and everything. There wasn't a subject she did not take too or could speak about. She would discuss philosophy one minute and then switch to literature the next and end up talking of the gossip of the day about influential society members. One night, without so much as a word planned or thought of, I told her about myself. I told her about my life, my transformation, and my darkness. She never flinched Wilma, my dear Christina, and only smiled taking my hand in hers confessing that she had already known something was different with me."

"We were in love, little one, and for the first time I wanted to make the transformation happen. For the first time in such a long time I wanted another companion at my side. I wanted Christina to ride the night winds with me."

"Another companion, you mean you made her a vampire like yourself?" Wilma asked.

"I'm a selfish person little one, a single companion is never be enough. I've transformed others over the years, but there's always a feeling you must have before doing so. I never felt that with her and I should have turned away because of that." Alexander explained.

"What feeling?" Wilma asked again.

"A primer you might say," Alexander answered looking Wilma deeply in the eyes, "an instinct that says this transformation will succeed. This feeling always precedes a transformation. It's a way to know if it will happen correctly."

"And if you don't have this feeling then the transformation won't happen right?" Wilma asked intently.

"Nothing can stop a transformation little one, all the feeling does is signal when a possible companion can be brought into the fold." Alexander explained.

"Do you get that feeling with me?" Wilma asked, her eyes glowing with anticipation. Alexander couldn't miss the intention in the look and it saddened him just a touch.

"No little one," Alexander said watching the disappointment in Wilma's eye as he felt a small touch of relief, "and I will never try to transform another without that feeling."

"You tried to transform Christina without the primer?" Wilma asked.

"Like a fool in love I ignored everything including common sense. I wanted her with me so badly I went ahead with it and in the end I killed her Wilma, twice over. The transformation changed her, she was no longer the beautiful woman that had taken my soul and healed it. Now, there was only an animal that killed for pleasure and not necessity. She left bodies lying in the gutters of alleys and they were mostly children not much older than you are now. Weeks passed as she hid among the rats in the abandoned buildings along the wharf." Alexander exhaled letting the pain flow out as he stared at the ground. He had never intended on telling her this much, but as the wound opened the sorrow in his soul seemed to spill out.

"Oh my God, what did you do?" Wilma hissed in shock.

Alexander didn't hear the question from her. His vision had turned inward in a weird trance as that faithful night played across his mind like one of the horror movies he had watched on his small TV. He had tracked her to an alley and found her feeding on a young girl, maybe twelve at the most. When Christina was finished she stumbled away from the body toward the entrance of the alley trying to find her balance like a common drunk. He dropped down quickly from the roof where he was hiding, through the dark, landing lightly in front of her before she could react. The fresh blood had dulled Christina's senses to his approach, his left hand was around her neck and closing as her sluggish eyes went wide with the realization of what was happening. She thrashed and tore at his hand but a scratch never appeared and he didn't feel a thing. As her neck began to crack and break he whispered 'I love you' while looking into her frightened eyes. For a second she stopped fighting and he could see his Christina again. She gingerly reached out to try to touch his face one last time and a small tear slowly rolled down her beautiful cheek. When the energy of life finally left her and he knew she was gone, he took both bodies away and burned them. Alexander stood and watched as the ashes drifted away on the nightly breeze and he swore never to make another companion again.

"Alexander?" Wilma said shaking his hand lightly.

"Yes, my dear." He said coming out of the trance. Off in the distance gunfire erupted and someone screamed.

"That sounds close, I'm going inside." Wilma said rising from the bench.

"I think that's a wonderful idea, I'll see you tomorrow little one." Alexander said smiling.

"Will you promise me something?" She asked suddenly.

"How may I serve you?" Alexander said rising from the bench with a bow.

"I know you won't let anything happen to me and that really helps in the sleeping department, but promise me that you won't hurt the werewolves, especially if there's a girl werewolf with them." Wilma stated with a wide eye, pleading look.

"Why do you want me to spare the werewolves little one?" Alexander asked surprised.

"I don't know it's just a feeling. This man, the one that came by last night, he's hurting them somehow or going too soon. They need help is all, and you can give it to them."

"I don't feel safe with this request Wilma," Alexander began before Wilma broke in.

"Please Alexander, their scared and they need you to help them. I can feel it." Wilma whined.

"How do you know there's a girl werewolf among them Wilma?" The vampire asked still perplexed but willing to acquiesce to her want.

"Just part of the feeling, I can't explain it. So do you promise or what?"

Alexander took a second to kneel taking Wilma's hand in his. He looked the girl deep in her eyes and spoke seriously. "I will abide by your rules my lady. I pledge my existence and my strength to protect you Wilma."

"Thank you my Knight." Wilma replied with a small smile and curtsy. She reached down and ran her fingers along his cheek and for a second it looked like she might ask him for something else, but then she turned and walked to her bedroom. In a split second, she was inside and the window shut.

Alexander rose from the kneeling position and watched Wilma's window for a minute or two. He had pledge to keep her safe, yet part of his brilliant plan made that pledge a simple lie. There was no turning back and the only way through was forward now. He gripped the locket tightly in his hand and felt a small ghost like handgrip back for a second. Christina had approved he thought. Then he spotted a Lincoln rolling slowly down the street, two men inside dressed in expensive trench coats in the front and a third in the back. The man in the back wore a goatee and slicked hair, Alexander knew instantly who it was. A second Lincoln that followed closely behind slowed to a stop by the corner and a figure ran from the dark and jumped in the back quickly. Just as planned Alexander thought. Everything was rolling to a conclusion like the fine gears of an ornate clock. The two cars sped off into the night leaving the vapor trails of brake lights that faded in the distance. Alexander knew where the cars were going. He had the address written down on a slip of paper he had gotten from Simon earlier that very afternoon. He and Leland and Stephanie would pay a visit to the occupants later, but there was some business that needed attention before that.

Out in the shadows Yelena was struggling with the shock of the last few minutes. Never, and she was searching every memory cell in her brain trying to remember, had any pure human said something like what the little girl had just requested of the Ancient One. All through Yelena's life the need to be wary had been repeated over and over to her like a mantra, humans will kill you her elders had all told her. You, the werewolf and the vampire, are the makings of their nightmares and you are reviled. You are detested and shunned. They, these humans, will never accept you into their world or their daily lives. And yet here was this young girl ready to do just that very thing, even more than that it appeared. She was asking for mercy...for her, for Yelena, and the girl had never even met her. This little one had begged for the oldest vampire there is to save her, a young werewolf.

"Her name is Wilma."

The voice, it was one Yelena had never heard before and yet she knew it was Alexander's and she knew though never being told that it was never good to have the Ancient One behind you hiding in the dark. By the time it took her to spin and face him the vampire was on her moving so fast he was a blur. His hands wrapped around her shirt and jacket forcefully pulling her into him lifting her feet free from the ground while his mouth went right to her neck, his fangs an inch from her jugular. There was nothing Yelena could do except clamp her eyes shut as the vampire's hot breath washed across her neck and face. Alexander was too powerful and strong, too quick, and he had her trapped unable to pull away as her hands latched onto his with a death grip. The only thing she did was blurt out the first thing that popped into her panic stricken mind.

"You promised her you would spare me!"

There was a long, what felt like an eternity to Yelena, pause before Alexander loosened his grip just a little and her feet were back on the ground. His fangs were still out and his voice was a growl as he addressed her still holding her close enough to touch his nose to hers and look into her eyes and strike. "You have twenty seconds to explain why you failed to heed my warning or I will break my promise to Wilma and rip out your throat."

It was the eyes that told Yelena the Ancient One was speaking true. Even in the dark, and with the orbs of his eyes as black as coal, she could sense he meant every letter of every word he spoke. Alexander would tear out her throat and then live with the consequences she thought as she swallowed and whispered. "I have come to seek your protection, for my brothers and my mother."

"Fifteen seconds," Alexander replied ignoring Yelena's request.

"Akhenaton and Michaels sent my brothers and me against you so you would kill us! They want you to kill us so they can control the other packs." Yelena cried feeling trapped again.

"Ten seconds."

"We need your protection from Akhenaton! He has brought in Ghouls to finish us!"

"Five seconds." Alexander said closing the distance again on Yelena his fangs inching closer to her throat.

Being in her present position was something new to Yelena, the icy feel of desperation closing its grip on her heart. The Ancient One wasn't listening and the clock had run out on her pleas so fast. Before thinking about anything she made her last offer turning her head exposing her neck for the vampire willingly, hoping the bite would be quick. "Take me Ancient One as you want, but spare my brothers please. Spare my brothers and my mother."

Alexander stopped an inch from Yelena's jugular again as the reality of everything set in for the werewolf. She began to cry, a small tear at first that turned to a small sob. "Please Ancient one, I give myself to you, but spare my brothers from Akhenaton." Yelena said pulling herself together and reigning in her emotions.

"You would give yourself to me?" The vampire growled menacingly.

"Da...I'll do whatever you want, but please save my brothers and my mother from Akhenaton."

Alexander looked down to see her exposed breast in a lacy bra, the taught muscles in her stomach rippled in light of the street lamps as she gasped. He rolled his head around to look at her tear stained face. "Anything I ask pup?"

"Take my blood Ancient One, I will not fight you." Yelena stammered trying to avoid what she knew was coming, force the vampire to drink her blood instead of the one thing she hated above all. In her stomach the fire of anger began to smolder as the feelings of loathing and the repulsion for the vampire began to show finally. Oh how she hated the Nosferatu for what they had done to her family, how she detested them like the filth they were, but then the memories of her sweet mother and her brothers appeared and the fire in her belly cooled just a little. They needed her to do this or the Grand Lich would have them killed or worse...made into mindless zombies to do his bidding for all time. She had to do this.

"Oh, it's not your blood I want little Yelena."

"What," she asked shakily hoping against hope he would not want that, "what else could you want from me?"

"I think you have an idea. I also think the very idea of it detest you."

The fire that was cooling in her stomach suddenly stoked to a raging burn through Yelena. The images in her mind of her loved ones disappearing as the anger in her caused her to breathe shallow as she glared into his eyes. "Is that what you wish Nosferatu, to make me your slave of lust? Is my blood not worth the same as what you would do with my body?"

Her answer was a simple smile from Alexander, his fangs gleaming in the low light, and then something swept over her so powerful it drove the anger and loathing from her in single sweep. An emotion, a deep desire, she had kept so secret Yelena had never spoken word to anyone of it flared and broke loose from her control. All at once the werewolf was swimming in the heat of her own desire as she gasped and the world around her changed from the grungy outside of the Laurel to a large bedroom in a house she had never been to. A large four post bed was just behind her, how she knew this without looking was a secondary thought to how she ended up by it in the first place. Where were the Projects they were just in? She looked down to see her clothes had changed too and now she wore a lacy corset and panties, both holding everything tightly in just the right places as well as long white gloves. Then she heard a growl, deep and hungry and coming for her out of the dark in the room.

"What I want little Yelena is a hunger you have closed off for far too long because you fear giving up control...you fear you would like it too much." Alexander whispered here in the real world while slowly reaching down and running his hand across her stomach muscles.

She heard his words in this strange world, felt each syllable send a ripple through her driving the lust higher in her body. How did he know? How did he know about this? Then he stepped out of the dark shirtless and the look in the Ancient One's eyes melted Yelena as the desire she swam in pulled her under with one quick yank of both her legs. She inhaled so deep her sides hurt in the corset as Alexander stepped forward with so much intent in his eyes that she felt pushed by the force of it just a little. Then he was on her a second time grabbing her forcefully in his arms and lifting her free of the floor once more before taking two long steps carrying her to the bed and dropping her down roughly. Her hands went up to his shoulders pushing on the muscled joints weakly in some silly token attempt to keep him away as she let out a small whimper of urgency. How did he know my true desire was to be taken, claimed like this?

"This is what I want Yelena, what I will take for sanctuary." The vampire growled running his hands up her side under her opened shirt in the real world before embracing her in a strong hug, squeezing her. In the dream world he reached up and grabbed her wrists and with a hard move gripping both in one hand and pushing the appendage into the bed above her head holding her hands there as he pressed down into her with his body. "Only now will you give in to what I know you want?"

"Yes, yes I will, I will go to you anyway you wish." Yelena gasped quickly and snarled here in the reality as her hands reached up wrapping around Alexander's head pulling him to her neck so he could devour her. She even wrapped a lone leg around his rubbing up against him she wanted him so much now. By the Great Wolf did her blood boil? In that dream world pinned to the bed beneath him Yelena felt his free hand slide down her body just a moment before the sound of ripping cloth made her gasp again. In the corner of her eyes she saw the Ancient One toss the torn panties away and then felt him push into her lower body more, pressing into her bare flesh with his waist just a moment before she felt him enter her.

"Would you little Yelena? Would you come to me dressed as I wished? Come to me letting me do as I wish?" Alexander's husky voice asked while his hands caressed her smoldering skin in the real world.

"YES," Yelena yelped with abandon and free of restraint with a loud gasp. In the dream world she let out a scream of ecstasy, a howl as the wolf in her gave over to Alexander letting him do as he willed with her. Whatever he wanted...whatever he wanted.

And then he was gone, his hands no longer roaming and caressing her body here in the real world. It was so sudden it startled Yelena, the dream world gone as well in a blink. The disappearance was so fast she stood exposed for a moment in the cool winter night air before realizing what she looked like. Yelena pulled her shirt close looking around carefully, her soul now feeling so empty that it bordered on being abandoned. "Ancient one?" she called out low in a voice filled with fear and from her right he answered.

"Yes Yelena."

She turned to see him standing there eyeing her normally, the fangs were gone as well as the dark eyes. He looked so unbelievably attractive there in the light, nothing like she had heard about him from others she had crossed paths with, and it was the look that added to the feeling of loss she felt. Why did he stop she asked herself? Why did he not take me? "What is wrong? Did I displease you Ancient One?" she asked cautiously but with earnest.

"No, on the contrary you've done quite well and even impressed this hardened heart. If you pass my last test then I will give you, your brothers, and Svetlana sanctuary from Akhenaton as you have requested. Is this acceptable?"

"What test? I thought you wanted thongs and lingerie...and me? "Yelena questioned in utter confusion after swallowing hard.

Alexander crossed over to her in a blink and locked eyes with her. She stood perfectly still clutching her shirt around her, feeling the imposing weight of Alexander's ageless presence for the first time as he spoke. "I need to see three things from you before I will help you Yelena. The first is courage which you have shown by coming here looking for me. The second is loyalty, because you were willing to give yourself to me physically to save your family, which is the most detestable thing you could think of doing, but which you would have done without being forced if it meant the safety for your loved ones was assured showed me this."

As hard as she tried she couldn't look away from the Ancient One's eyes. Finally, and mercifully, she was able to speak and it took a small modicum of effort to make sure the words didn't come out jumbled." Do you treat all females asking for help like this, or did I do something special to grant such an honor?"

"Every woman I have 'touched' like this has reacted differently. Some have seen me as a gentle lover kissing them sweetly to wake them from a long deep slumber while others such as you have a need to be taken and claimed, to hold nothing back from the one they want. I must admit, you are the first in a very long time that I wish to 'touch' again and again, over and over." Alexander replied tongue-in-cheek with a wicked smile.

The remark and the look sent Yelena blushing as she looked away quickly trying to hide her red cheeks. "So what is the last test Ancient One?"

"The simplest of all, can we trust each other? Will you follow me if I ask you too? If I have a need will you help me without condition or question? Can you walk with me and give me the loyalty of a friend? Can you trust my word?" Alexander explained.

"So all you want is my friendship and in return you will keep my brothers safe, and my mother too?" Yelena asked incredulous, not believing the terms. Deep down she kind of wanted to go back to the bed, to be his letting him take her.

"I won't promise a pain free escape, but I will get her and your brothers to safety." Alexander said offering out his hand.

Yelena starred at the vampire's hand for a second, as if sad for having to choose this path, before slowly reaching out and taking it. The grip was strong and tight, telling her he considered her an equal in his eyes. The shake lasted but a second before he turned and began to walk away while talking over his shoulder. "Come along Yelena, you still have that last test."

It took a second for the female lycanthrope to get past the shock of what just happened before she started moving forward. She quickly fixed her shirt while catching up, practically running. The two moved into the shadows of the dark toward the front of the projects and the streets beyond.

They had been waiting by the bench maybe ten minutes after dropping off Wilma at Grammy's, but it felt like an hour. Leland was jacked up, ready to carry out the plan for the night while Stephanie stood patiently and watched her man pace. She was getting a good little giggle going watching Leland walk briskly from point A to point B over and over.

"Where do you think he is?" Leland asked nervously scanning the dark with his eyes.

"He'll be here Lee, give him time." Stephanie answered shaking her head.

"I just hate waiting is all, you know, it gets me all jumpy." Leland offered making another turn back to walk in front of the bench.

"Uh-huh, and this is what you're like when you' impatient?" Stephanie asked.

Leland was about to answer when he was suddenly interrupted by Alexander appearing to his side right out of the thin air smiling. "Good evening Leland."

"Ah!" The street preacher screamed stepping back," Man, you have to stop doing that!"

"How am I supposed to have fun then?" Alexander asked with a gleeful smile.

"Yeah, scaring the black man to death is a whole-lot-of-fun." Leland shot back.

Stephanie was trying unsuccessfully to hold back her giggles at Leland's expense as she shook her head. "So what's the plan Alex?"

"We are going to this place," Alexander said pulling a folded slip of paper from his pocket and handing it to the street preacher, "Do you know the way to this address?"

Leland took the paper from Alexander and glanced at it, whistled, and looked up at him. "This is a swanky hotel downtown, just a few blocks from here. I hear the room rates run the same as a new Mercedes for a night."

"Well, we might feel a little out of place then." Alexander stated.

"Why's that?" Stephanie asked.

"We have to make a call on someone and I think we might even crash a party they are having tonight." The vampire answered with a wicked smile.

"As long as there are no guns, the Shangri-La last night was enough excitement for one man's life." Leland said shaking his head, a second later he noticed Yelena just behind the vampire. How did he miss her he thought as he spoke up? "Who's your friend, and what exactly is she doing here?"

All eyes shifted to the Russian as Alexander made the introductions. "Oh yes, Yelena this is Leland and Stephanie. Leland and Stephanie this is Yelena."

"Hi," Leland and Stephanie said meekly, together, with a half-hearted wave.

"Good evening." Yelena replied with her Russian accent thick and strong.

"Oh, you're Russian, that's nice." Stephanie stammered with shock stating the obvious.

"Da, I am Russian."

"Well that's great. We don't get to meet many people from Russia around here as you can see. I hear it gets really cold over there in the winter." Leland remarked nervously, almost to the point of being forced to say anything at gun point.

Alexander noticed the stiff posture of the three and the fact they were not really hitting it off. They didn't have the time to endure long pleasantries so Alexander decided to move things along a little faster, just a small nudge with the right amount of pressure.

"Yes, she's one of the werewolves I told you about last night Leland and Stephanie. Yes, it was her brothers Dimitri and Gregor who tried to kill me, but it was all a big misunderstanding and we're past it now. There, it's all out in the open, so let's get on the road and pay a visit to the men who supply the drugs to the Laurel, shall we?" Alexander turned and walked off toward the parking place of the Chevelle while the others stood in shocked silence.

"You're a werewolf?" Stephanie asked after a minute with a surprised look.

"Da," Yelena answered low with a small nod.

"And the big guy with black hair last night at the strip club, he was your brother?" Leland asked with the same surprised look.

"Da," Yelena said with a nod of her head again before turning and running to catch up to Alexander. At the moment he was the only one she felt very comfortable with, which was so surreal and a definite departure from what she had been taught about vampires.

Leland and Stephanie turned to each other to speak but it was Stephanie making the first statement. "Trust in the vampire baby, just trust in Alex!"

"What! Did you just hear what you said?" Leland whined as Stephanie took his hand and began to pull him toward car. "The woman I love shouldn't be saying 'trust the vampire', it's not natural! And don't get me started about the werewolf!"

Chapter Three

    Lloyd Dunbar had more money than the King of Siam, and that was the God's honest truth because Forbes said so in its yearly rakings of the top Billionaires in the US. He ran one of the largest corporations in the Unites States, a conglomeration of businesses ranging from department stores to real estate ventures to a television station to a software development studio and even a small book publishing company. Hell, he even owned two or three recording studios in the Atlanta area that recorded and produced Rap records. He couldn't stand the music, just the money it brought in. However, a few years ago, Lloyd became truly bored with all of his business achievements and pursuits. Someone told him at a party a while ago that once you've made your first million the success just drove you to make the next million. Well the same couldn't be said for a billion. Once you got to that amount of money getting the next billion was incredibly boring. He had money and women and power so what was left to conquer in the world? He didn't want to climb Mount Everest or anything stupid like that, it wasn't his thing risking life and limb to stand on top of some really large rock for ten minutes. Then he ran into Rico Hierra while vacationing in Mexico and when he discovered what the man did for a business, a high ranking man in the Cartels, well the rush of the old days just came flowing back breathing fire into his tired soul again. When Rico had come offering a business proposition, for Lloyd to use a shipping company in his conglomerate to bring drugs into the country and in return he would see a profit from this illegal operation, oh it was like tossing a lifesaver to a drowning man.

Why, you ask, did a man of Lloyd's position say yes to this proposition? Simple really, and it had nothing to do with the money. As crazy as it sounds, the personal company of the business acquaintance thrilled Lloyd to no end. He had, over the years, literally cut the throat of many an executive in building his empire and he loved the feeling of watching another man's future die and the look on said man's face as he realized it. That was power. To crush a man under your boot, there wasn't a feeling like it anywhere or any drug to duplicate. Yet it was very...lonely if he had to describe it. How do you explain to someone, like his wife who enjoyed pedicures and dirty martinis too much, how that ruthless streak that resides in your very DNA leads you to destroying someone? Now he had a double life where he could watch a man die, really die, and then go to the Governor's ball and mingle with the elite. Lloyd Dunbar was an inventor you might say, he had found the perfect way to have his cake and eat it too. Soon Lloyd was not only bringing the drugs in, he was helping to run the business here in the Atlanta area and like all good businessmen he was looking to move up the corporate ladder. In addition, with the way Rico was going on right now, ranting in the middle of the sitting area of the master bedroom of the expensive suite he was renting, someone was going to die in a very bad way. That might be a death worth taping for viewing later.

"So Eight Ball didn't say a thing to you about what was going down there in that shit-hole the Laurel?" Hierra asked tight-lipped, a horn could be heard blowing down on the street through the closed French doors that led to the outside patio.

Lloyd released a puff from a rather expensive cigar watching the smoke ring rise slowly to the ceiling of the bedroom before answering. "I've already told you what he told me Rico. Eight Ball never knew who was moving in on the territory, and apparently he never will either."

"That suits me just fine!" Ray yelped from his chair beside Rico, the large drink slightly spilling from his shaking hands. The fat man was still having a time trying to steady his nerves twenty-four hours later.

"And what about this pinche pendejo dressed in black, you don't know anything about him do you Ray?" Rico asked quickly.

The large man took a big swig of the drink before answering. "All I know is he shows up and gets shot about sixty times and doesn't even flinch. Meanwhile, some crew Eight Ball hired is shooting holes all in my club and my customers!"

"And you see that's where I don't get it. You said this guy just walked right in and let you're men shoot him. I'm just a little confused by this? Who does that?" Rico said eyeing Ray suspiciously.

"I told you the truth man! Why the hell would I go back on you when you took me off the streets, huh?" Ray shot back.

"Maybe your men missed?" Lloyd chuckled rather off the cuff, more to solicit a response than an answer. Oh he got one too from the fat man in the blink of an eye.

"Listen," Ray said with a snarl, "I don't hire humps! I only hire the best protection and these boys don't miss. They fired enough rounds into that guy in my office to be confused for a SWAT Team and he still walked away."

"I don't doubt you Ray, it just seems kind of coincidental is all. First you have a man stealing from the till and then this man in black shows up on your door step trying to take over, very good timing if you ask me." Lloyd remarked.

"What? Are you calling me out or something? Listen man, I don't steal from the company supply store, EVER. Eight Ball decided to bite the hand that fed him and got his ass killed for doing it. That's it, end of story, and close the books." Ray challenged with a shake of the whiskey glass spilling more of the golden liquid.

The CEO shook his head smiling, "How long was Eight Ball stealing Ray? How much did we lose while he was running the Laurel?"

"I don't know. I don't have fifty assistants running around me all day look doing my bidding like you do. And why the hell are you here Mr. Billionaire? Isn't playing drug runner beneath a man like you Lloyd?" Ray snipped taking a drink from his glass.

"Well," Lloyd stated taking a second puff of the cigar, "I liked to keep a watchful eye on my business dealings Ray, unlike you it seems. I mean you did get most of the product back, but where's the money big man? Don't tell me you killed that bartender before finding out where the money is?"

Ray spun away from Lloyd and pointed a fat finger at Rico, the drink spilling some more. "I got the stuff back, but it was the CEO asshole here who was supposed to get the money. Only his two men shoot Eight Ball full of holes instead of asking him what bank he goes to, and then those guys go missing. Now who are you going to blame for that?"

"I blame all of us Ray. None of us had a clue what the hell that idiot Eight Ball was doing down there in the Laurel, but I can tell you this, we better figure it out real fast. We better know what the hell we are going to do to keep this under control because Russo and his people are not going away. I'm just not losing money here. The people I work for are losing money my socio comanditarios. The Cartel never loses money and forgives, understand?" Rico stated in a demanding tone.

"Listen, all I know is my club is full of holes and I got one bad mother on my back. I'm on a plane back to Brooklyn tonight!" Ray said with another hit of the whiskey ignoring Rico's comments. He didn't know what the Spanish part meant anyway.

"So, what are we going to do about keeping the Laurel Lloyd?" Rico asked turning away from Ray while sipping tequila instead of whiskey from his glass.

"Oh that's not my department," Lloyd said turning his attention back to Rico instead of Ray as well, "I just bring the drugs in and Ray here distributes them. I have nothing to do with the sales infrastructure at all."

"Yeah, whatever," Rico grinned at Lloyd with the beginnings of a wicked smile.

The Windermere Bay hotel was opulent, extravagant, and unique. It was built for the rich by the rich, which is why you probably needed a qualifying financial statement and credit check to get a room. Everyone inside watched as the loud black Chevelle rolled by slow, as if taking note of the front entrance to the hotel, but no one paid attention to the four people who walked through the spinning doors ten minutes later. They were not worth the effort to watch, the employees and people in the lobby wearily surmised. The group didn't look famous or rich and as such there was no need to bother with gawking. Someone else, like Security, could tend to the issue of escorting all four off the property. Two men took a second to notice the chick with the hard body and pure white hair, but then they went back to what they were doing before she walked in, which was typing on their respective blackberries.

"I need to make a phone call, everyone head up in the elevators and wait for me on the tenth floor." Alexander ordered. Leland and Stephanie and Yelena only nodded before moving over to the large entrances for the moving metal boxes and waited. The street preacher had just hit the up button for the elevator when a ham sized hand landed, or more like plummeted from the sky to crash unceremoniously, onto Leland's shoulder with a loud plop. All three of the group turned at once looking over their shoulders at two very large men wearing suits that barely contained their muscles. This can't be good Leland thought.

"This is a private establishment sir. If you don't have a room I'm going to have to ask you to leave, immediately." The ogre with his hand on Leland said eyeing him menacingly.

A second passed, the air growing tense enough to taste it. This was bad; if a fight suddenly broke out in the lobby then it was over, their secret infiltration mission blown. And if that happened then the dominoes would cease to fall. Yelena knew the consequences of her siding with the Ancient One, if the Grand Lich found out then it was the immediate death of her brothers, and he would most certainly find out if every news source from here to California ran the story of two men being eviscerated in the lobby of the hotel. She was risking more than just her life so there could be no failure, no chance of anyone finding out, especially Akhenaton. Yelena knew she needed to strike quickly, take out the two large men before they had a chance to call for help or backup. She just needed a second to do it, a little distraction, but instead Yelena did something totally unexpected even to her. She maneuvered her body to the left, just enough to get between the men and Stephanie, like she was ready to protect the human. This was a first and for a second Yelena could actually see herself, like some out of body experience, blocking Stephanie from the two security guards.

"Yo man," Leland suddenly said harshly eyeing the man back coldly, "unless you want to visit the ER at Grady tonight you better remove your hand right now."

The second guard only hissed moving in quickly, seeming to favor confrontation over talk. "All right little man, you want to get physical then we'll dance with you!"

This was it. She was going to have to kill the two guards Yelena realized calmly. She made a claw of her right hand, which was hidden at her side, and made ready to slash the second guard when Leland broke in carrying on in his ruse. Yelena wasn't sure what the man was doing but if it got them out of the middle of this dilemma without bloodshed then she would play along cautiously.

"I don't think you understand what I'm delivering to a certain 'individual' on the 8th floor!" Leland said pointing to Stephanie and Yelena with his thumb.

The two men stopped abruptly at the sound of the 8th floor. They both turned to stare at Stephanie and Yelena suspiciously. The first guard never let go of Leland though, just gave the street preacher's shoulder a hard squeeze. "These are the professionals for Double J? They don't look that high end to me?"

Yelena was about to ask just what this 'professional' was that the guard was referring to when Stephanie's left hand gingerly slid around her neck with a seductive touch. The finger tips slowly dancing across her flesh made goose bumps pop up on the skin of Yelena's abdomen, which Stephanie's right hand began to caress seductively also, the fingers just sliding along the waistline of Yelena's skirt. At any other moment the lycanthrope would have reacted with a mixture of terror and a quick Karate strike to the neck, but not this time and certainly not now. She instantly put two and two together. The 'professional' the guard had so eloquently called them was nothing more than a woman of pleasure. Well, if that's what they wanted to see then she could go along. She reached back with her own hands running them along Stephanie's curves stopping to rub every few inches.

The scene froze the men, including Leland, for a few seconds before the first guard regained his senses and turned back to the street preacher. "All right, but next time they go through the loading dock in back. We need to keep a low profile in the lobby, dig?"

"Some photog's were back there man, maybe you and Godzilla here should check it out after you let go of my shoulder!" Leland hissed jerking his arm away from the security guard.

"Hey, think we can get our pictures taken with the hookers?" The second guard asked pointing at Stephanie and Yelena with a broad smile. The girls broke for a second, Yelena circling to her left and entwining her arm with Stephanie's going back to the seductive embrace.

The other guard called his partner stupid mumbling hookers like to be called professionals these days while actively pushing him away. The doors to the elevator popped open, not with the metallic ding which accompanies most elevators at other normal buildings, but with a musical flare. Leland and Stephanie and Yelena walked in and as soon as the doors closed all three collapsed against the walls with a thud, the shock of actually getting past the guards overwhelming them.

"Who is this Double J?" Yelena asked leaning against Stephanie.

"Jimmy Jonas, he's an actor shooting a TV series outside of town, white guy who likes multiple girls at one time, you know, for...fun." Leland said turning to look at the pair to his right.

Stephanie was still entwined with Yelena sort of, but not as enthusiastic as before. She looked up at him and spoke. "What I would love to know is how you knew he was here?"

"My running mate Dawes knows his manager, he called me and wanted to know if I would like for the kids to meet the man, you know 'look at the big Hollywood actor helping out the underprivileged kids' stuff. I had to respectfully decline though, what with J recovering from drugs and all the sexual promiscuity rumors I just didn't feel good about it. Now I know I made the right decision." Leland explained.

"I knew you were a good man," Stephanie said pulling away from Yelena then turning back to her quickly, "You're skin is really soft and your hair smells great, what do you do?"

Before Yelena could answer the elevator gave a musical flare again and the doors opened on their floor. In the entrance stood Alexander who looked to Stephanie and Yelena with a mixture of humor and enlightenment. "One day you both will have to tell me exactly what that little dance was about downstairs."

"Oh, just going with the flow. Yelena's a good friend!" Stephanie said taking the lycanthrope's hand and giving it a squeeze.

"Da, good friend!" Yelena added with a smile.

"Right, if going with the flow is giving all the guys in the lobby stiff pants and wet dreams for the rest of the week you two did great." Leland said exiting the elevator.

"I didn't hear you complaining!" Stephanie said with a quick snap.

"And you never will." Leland shot back with a wink as the group walked off down a corridor.

"I know you Dunbar. You're not satisfied with just running the drugs. I bet you got some kind of a plan already setup to take over just in case Eight Ball ended up dead, am I right?" Rico asked with a crooked grin.

"Well I do have a few ideas that may help, you know, for just such an emergency." Lloyd replied with his own devilish smile.

"Are you two crazy? This guy is coming back I tell you and he's not going to let you deal in the Laurel or anywhere else! He told me so and I for one believe him! Especially since he's bulletproof and picked my fat ass up by my ever-loving neck!" Ray demanded with a shake of his head.

"So what's the plan?" Rico asked Lloyd while running a lone finger through his goatee and ignoring Ray's whining protest. The fat man was quickly working Rico's last nerve.

The hallway leading up to the door to the suite was long and dark giving Alexander and his group enough shadow to cover their approach. A single guard stood watch by the door meaning someone important was home, but the vampire already knew who was staying in the room. He turned back to the others to give one last instruction on his plan.

"Remember, give me three minutes and then create a diversion, understood?"

"Da," Yelena whispered back.

"Stephanie and Leland, make sure there's no one coming from behind. If there is get Yelena's attention and then escape to the Chevelle."

"Got it," Leland nodded.

Stephanie had other ideas though and wanted to know just a little more. "What are you going to do?"

"In the immortal words of Mel Gibson, 'I'm going to go pick a fight'" Alexander said with a small smile.

"Oh, okay." Leland whispered accepting the remark. Then he remembered what happened in the movie and his eyes went wide.

Alexander gave the group a quick nod and then he was gone in the shadows, moving up the hallway along the wall. He made it to the guard's position without the man so much as guessing he wasn't alone in the passageway. The vampire moved past the guard without ruffling a hair and slipped through the door and into the suite without opening the portal.

The inside was dark except for the dim light from a TV, which gave Alexander an advantage. He quickly took note of the two men sitting on a couch in front of the large screen watching a football game from New York. The fact the back of the couch was to the front door was perfect, Alexander couldn't have laid out the suite any better for an assault if he had done it himself. On his right was a door that led to a bedroom and a familiar presence. To his left was a set of doors and he knew beyond those was the main bedroom with a small sitting area and that's where he wanted to go because the ones he wanted to see were right in there.

"Simple really, I'll keep supplying the drugs like I have been. We find someone to replace Ray here, and I take over the operation in the Laurel and surrounding areas." Lloyd remarked with an air of confidence.

"I knew it," Rico shook his head with a deep laugh, "and you get a bigger percentage of everything of course?"

"Only a small percentage Rico, you and your Cartel associates still get their usual payout. My end just increases due to a management promotion and increased risk." Lloyd explained with a smile.

"Did you just say 'management promotion'? Lloyd, this isn't one of your corporations where you just sit on some board and make useless decisions that don't affect you personally or professionally." Rico stated.

Lloyd just smiled on and spoke casually like he usually did when he was negotiating. "I know what I'm doing Rico, drug dealing is still a business with the same principles of supply and demand. I have some ideas about how to control the product and promoting inventory while increasing profit."

"Oh I get it, you're going to have your own version of a white sale huh? Only, there won't be any towels or sheets, just coke and crack lining the shelves." Ray said with a quick laugh.

"Advertisement is an integral part of any business model Ray." Lloyd chuckled too while taking a deep inhale of his cigar.

Rico leaned forward in his chair and stared hard into Lloyd's eyes, snarling as he spoke. "This is not a business model, this is drug dealing Lloyd. The very nature of it is one of death. You kill to keep your territory, you kill to keep your pushers in line, and you watch the users slowly die from taking the shit you peddle to them on a daily basis. There is no room for fucking advertisement, do you understand? You got the balls to defend your turf against Russo and his people when they come for it?"

Lloyd didn't respond immediately, he simply stared in disbelief at something just past Rico's shoulder. When the Cartel figure turned to look there, standing about two feet away was a tall man wearing a Def Leppard T-shirt, black jeans, and a pair of black Doc Martin boots. The kind the kids in high school wear because everyone seemed to have a pair.

"Oh Sweet Mother Mary of a hairy Christ," Ray cried sulking down in the chair, as if the thing would hide his large girth.

"And who the hell are you?" Rico hissed.

"You're the man in black, I presume?" Lloyd guessed, which really wasn't a guess at all since the man was wearing all black except for the long sleeve shirt.

Alexander replied. "You would most certainly be correct Mr. Dunbar."

"Well, do you have a real name Mr. Black or do I keep using your Crayola alias?" Rico asked with a snap.

The vampire chose to remain quiet as he circled the room just fast enough to seem slow, right the front of the men, while watching Ray squirm and cringe at his approach. He looked form Rico to Dunbar and back noting the looks on the man's faces before answering.

"Mr. Black can do for now." Alexander finally responded.

"Well that's very 'Reservoir Dogs', I love it!" Lloyd shot back with a smile.

The group sat in silence for a second, except for Ray's crying, until Rico finally spoke up.

"So what do you want Mr. Black? You want a piece of the Laurel for yourself, is that why you're messing in my business?" He asked in a thick Spanish accent.

"I came by to see if you were going to pay some heed to my warning that Ray gave you, and I know he gave you my warning. By the way, did I not tell you to get out of town Ray?" Alexander stated.

"I was just about to leave to catch my flight right now." Ray cried falling to the floor because his legs wouldn't work. He began to crawl slowly to the door.

"You think you're just going to walk in here and take the best piece of territory in this city away from me!" Rico hissed.

"I already have the Laurel Rico and if you try to take it back I will kill you, do not doubt that." Alexander stated flatly, calmly.

"Now gentlemen, threatening each other won't solve any of our problems. If we just sit and talk I'm sure we can reach an agreement." Lloyd said rising from his seat and trying to mediate.

"You don't have shit pendejo, and Rico takes anything Rico wants, understand? If I want the Laurel I'll have the Laurel on a fucking platter!" Rico spat, not backing down from Alexander.

"There is only one way to save any of your lives and that is to stay away from the Laurel starting tonight." Alexander stated flatly again never taking his eyes off Rico.

"I'm Rico Hierra pendejo! You think I'm scarred of you Mr. Man in Black! I can deal with you. You just bought yourself a whole world of hurt!" The Cartel man threatened with a shake of his head.

"In the grand scheme of things Mr. Hierra you are nothing but a small, insignificant part to me. The threats you throw around are hollow and meaningless, much like the man you are and always have been."

Rico rose from the chair in a bolt at the man in black's accusation about his importance and stormed forward, his hand reaching into the folds of his expensive suit jacket. Ray screamed with a wail tossing what was left of the whiskey out of the glass when he covered his face. Lloyd jumped up over the back of his chair trying to find cover while hoping to keep Rico from splattering blood all over him. His shirt was silk for God's sake, priceless. Not one of the men was prepared for what happened next though. The whole scene was over before it almost began.

Alexander actually let Rico pull the small gun from his jacket and get to within a step before reacting. The vampire reached out slapping Rico's wrist away like he was swatting a gnat, the gun flying through the glass of a set of glass French doors and onto a patio. The blow made the drug smuggler stumble for a moment and Alexander continued the man's off balance dance with a push of his other hand sending the man sprawling over Dunbar's chair. Lloyd barely got his hands up as Rico slammed into him like a rolling boulder sending them both backwards onto the floor in a heap. As Rico crossed the neo-European style chair he took out the equally neo-European looking lamp providing most of the lighting for the room, except for the spill from the outside lights through the French Doors, which wasn't much. In a split second almost the entire bedroom was bathed in dark shadows except for a small corner by the doors leading into the living room, exactly where Ray was crawling for right now. He was just a few feet away when the portals burst open and the two guards from the other room spilled in with guns drawn and trigger fingers ready. Light from the TV made the shadows waver in the room as the men swung their guns from side to side looking for something to fire on.

"Wait! Don't Shoot!" Ray screamed just as the front door to the suite exploded sending shards everywhere in main room. The started to drop into crouches while spinning round to engage what was coming for them. Neither knew the real threat was right beside them in the dark by the door; not even a warning from Rico helped the pair as the diversion worked perfectly.

The lone guard out in the hall by the entry door to the suite reacted instinctively to the sounds from inside the room behind him. He dropped his center mass for better stability in the coming fight while presenting a smaller target to strike at. He also started for the forty-five under his coat, but his fingers never touched the special Pac-Mar handgrips on the weapon. A sound caught his heightened attention, someone running right at him full out. Then out of the shadows the guard saw Yelena for a brief second before she was on him; the flash of her white hair was stunning and deadly.

Yelena leapt at the guard's lead leg placing her left foot deftly on the limb and then using the leg as leverage sprung upwards like she was shot from a gun. She brought her right knee up at the same time delivering the hard bone of the joint right into the guard's chin with battering ram force. As his body began to rise she stomped with her right foot into the man's chest with all her force sending the dead weight of the guard backwards now. He slammed through the door to the suite shredding it into splinters, Yelena standing on him all the way to the floor.

"Look Out!" Rico yelled from the corner, rising up to a semi-prone position, just enough to see over the edge of the chairs. Dunbar rose up beside Rico just in time to see what was going to happen to the two guards who had rushed in.

Alexander came out of the dark like a tiger, his attack swift and vicious. He grabbed the first guard in a solid grip and heel stomped the large man like he was a small bag of wheat through the doors and into the living room with a loud crash. The sound of the landing was barely over before Alexander turned to the second guard. The man didn't have a chance to even level his gun on the vampire. Rico and Dunbar heard the guard in the living room scream for God to help him and then a wet crunch, but they never took their eyes off the man in black. They watched as he reached out with a snap of his hand and wrapped his long fingers around the guard's throat squeezing so hard, so fast, that the man's neck snapped with one great wet pop. The second guard gave out a small gurgle as his eyes rolled back in their sockets and Alexander dropped his listless body to the floor.

"Sweet Mother of a hairy Christ," Dunbar whispered again as Rico rose from the floor. The Mexican Cartel man expected Alexander to come for him, and so what if he did, by God Rico Hierra was going to die like a man and not a woman. What he got was though was unexpected.

"Leave the Laurel alone Mr. Hierra," was all Alexander said standing calmly now.

"Or what pendejo, you think any of this scared me tonight?" Rico asked with defiance.

Yelena entered the room, blood dripping from her right hand onto the carpet as Alexander answered Rico. "I'm not someone you want to make angry Rico. I can kill you without blinking, just ask her." Alexander insinuated nodding to the female lycanthrope.

"I think you and the bitch better find a hole to hide in pal because this discussion isn't over." Rico hissed back.

Suddenly Alexander wasn't there in the bedroom, he had moved across space and time so fast he disappeared and reappeared a second later past the large French doors, which were open now or had been opened so fast no one noticed, to the small patio. Yelena had one arm around his neck and the other on his hand which was around her waist holding tightly. The vampire looked back once and spoke. "I think you just picked the wrong person to have a war with Rico."

Then, they were gone. The area was empty except for the two chairs in the corners. Rico ran out onto the patio and looked over to the ground below, but there was no Mr. Black. He growled and slapped both hands on the stone ledge before entering the suite's bedroom again. Lloyd was picking himself up off the floor while Ray lay prone crying into his hands.

"Is he gone?" Lloyd asked.

"Yeah, gone like a puff of smoke in a high wind." Rico stated.

"Well, I can't say that was a lot of fun. Are you all right Ray? Need a doctor or maybe a change of pants?" Lloyd asked the crying man. The only response he got was a shake of Ray's large head as tears streamed down his face.

"You still want the Laurel?" Rico asked Lloyd suddenly.

"What's the stipulation?" Lloyd asked in his business voice.

"You get to run the Laurel, but with our man in the second spot." Rico stated.

"The same one who turned in Eight Ball I would assume? He's a good man, a little skittish, but I'm sure he'll be an asset." Lloyd remarked checking out the second guard with a shove of his foot. Yep, deader than a ten penny coffin nail.

"Ray, go and get my insurance policy from the other bedroom. I left him there making a call when we came in." Rico ordered. The fat man rose slowly from the floor and stumbled out the doors to the main room. When he saw the dead bodies he gave out a third cry of a hairy Christ then the room went quiet.

"Insurance policy?" Lloyd asked while surveying the room. He might only have explain the front door hopefully...oh yeah, and the three dead bodies. He'd have to explain those as well to whoever came to clean up.

"Yeah, someone who knows a little about our Mr. Black there is my ace in the hole, my insurance policy. That jerkoff's going to learn that Rico Hierra doesn't get pushed around, he does the fucking pushing." Rico growled then spit on the ground for emphasis.

"How much do you think he knows about Mr. Black?" Lloyd asked.

A voice spoke from behind him, full of anger and disgust. "I have that mother in my back pocket, I know all about him. I know who you can get so you can hurt his ass!" Kenny stated walking in front of Ray.

"So you're my new partner eh?" Lloyd remarked.

"That's right!" Kenny hissed.

"Well, can you do a better job than Eight Ball? Can I trust you?" Lloyd asked.

"You bet. I'm not going out like Eight Ball did! I'm King of the Hood man!" Kenney stated emphatically.

Rico smiled the kind of smile that reeks of pure unadulterated evil. "Then, partner, you're going help us out with Mr. Black, right?"

"What do you need to know?" Kenny said with the same evil smile.

"All I know is I'm catching the first plane back to New York because I am getting the hell out of here." Ray cried before turning and leaving the room.

People walked back and forth in front of the alley, no one noticed the pair standing in the back by the large green dumpster. Alexander waited patiently for the Chevelle to swing by and pick him up along with his partner, who at the moment wasn't waiting patiently. Yelena paced anxiously in the small space biting her finger nails and he knew exactly why, he just wanted her to say it first. The only problem was she wouldn't and he knew that too. So

Alexander opened the door for Yelena to step through, not charge in like she did.

"Is something wrong pup?"

"My brothers, when do we go to get them?" Yelena said so fast it barely made sense.

Alexander slowly stepped away from the wall he was leaning against. He didn't like the tone in the young lycanthrope's voice. Alexander didn't think she would be stupid enough to attack, but then he wasn't sure what desperation would make Yelena do.

"We will get your brothers back, the process is already underway." Alexander said calmly.

"Het...that is not what we agreed on! I gave you help, I showed you courage, and now I want my brothers rescued from Michaels!" Yelena hissed.

Her body language was telling Alexander so much more than Yelena's voice was at the moment. She had stepped forward but her feet were now shoulder width apart, a classical confrontation stance. The muscles in chin undulated uncontrollable, and her fist closed spasmodically. The change was only seconds away, Yelena was about to become the white wolf, and if that wasn't bad enough Alexander picked up the Chevelle's engine coming by to pick them up. The last thing he needed was Leland and Stephanie to see Yelena in her wolf form, all bristling 400 pounds of it.

"You have to trust me Yelena, I asked you for it before we left this evening and I am asking for it again." Alexander said calmly again trying to soothe the lycanthrope, lull her into calm peace. A shame it didn't work.

"HET!" Yelena yelled suddenly jamming her whole body into a forward thrust as he fist flew toward the vampire.

The punch would have killed a regular man and he would have never seen it coming, like a lightning bolt from the heavens. Her fist was a missile flying toward the oldest vampire's face and with just three inches to go it slammed to a crunching halt, Alexander's palm providing an impenetrable barrier to her attack.

"Calm down, now! I am helping you, but I will not run head first into a slaughter!" The vampire hissed pushing the fist aside like it was nothing more than a piece of paper.

"You lie to me!" Yelena wailed.

"I did no such thing. I said I would help your brothers for the exchange of your trust, which I do not see at the moment!" Alexander countered.

"To hell with you Ancient One, I will save my brothers myself. And then I will come after you!" Yelena spat before bolting past Alexander and into dark toward downtown Atlanta. She was gone before he could answer the threat or try to stop her.

The vampire gave a single thought to try and chase after Yelena, but then the Chevelle showed up by the entrance. He gave one last look at the direction the werewolf ran before moving toward the car. It would be fruitless to chase her and to leave the Chevelle out in the open too long was insane. The greater need had to be leaving the area he thought moving out the alley, round the back of the car, and into the driver's seat. He barely had the door closed before the motorized beast was roaring to life and moving through the crowded streets.

"Hey, where's Yelena?" Stephanie asked from her usual seat in the back.

"She's doing other business for me." Alexander answered covering for the lycanthrope, and mercifully Leland's cell rang ending any chance of digging deeper into the ruse.

The street preacher didn't answer it, just looked at the name and then quickly silenced the ringer. Stephanie leaned toward him asking a question, one that Alexander knew the answer to already. "Who was it?"

"Kenny, I'll call him back once we get back to the Laurel." Leland said putting his cell away.

"What do you know about Kenneth Leland?" Alexander asked directing the conversation, seeing what the street preacher actually knew of the young man. The vampire assumed it was not much, nowhere near enough.

"He's a good kid, came from a broken home where his mother raised him the best she knew how." Leland said answering

Alexander's question about Kenny. The Chevelle sped down the interstate as the vampire kept the speed at a respectable pace. Not to slow, but not fast enough to attract the attention of the state patrol or sheriff.

"Why did Kenneth join a gang?" Alexander asked.

"Same reason we all do, it's the only fatherly love you get. When you're father isn't around to be a role model or show you love a gang takes that place, it's the greatest thing there is in the world until you realize your just being used." Leland remarked.

"Oh, I can see your point." Alexander stated before sitting in silence.

The two rode on before Leland finally asked a question he wanted too, one that Alexander had been expecting for a few minutes. "Why do you want to know so much about Kenny? You suspect he's up to something?"

"No, just wondering about our ally is all. I learned long ago that you have to know a little about everyone before you can trust anyone with your life." Alexander remarked looking out the windshield. And there he was doing it again. Lying to a friend, but it had to be this way. The plan to save Wilma needed everyone to play their part and right now Kenny was playing his. The young man was crucial to everything working and coming together, no one in the car could know he was betraying them at that very moment.

"Yeah, well Kenny's straight man. I've known the boy for a while and I trust him with my life so there's no need to worry all right." Leland stated in a shaky voice. Alexander noted the indecision in Leland's tone and tucked it away in his memory bank. Even the street preacher suspected, which was well enough for now. Kenny had to be the worst spy Alexander had ever known in his long existence and more than likely the worst drug dealer in all of the Laurel Wood projects. Yet, the boy was going to help in his plans to end Dunbar and Hierra.

Kenny was going to be good for something after all.

Chapter Four

"Tell it to me again."

Foster let go of a deep sigh at the Internal Affairs detective's request. How many times did he have to go over the same story, this was like twelfth time in three hours? "You guys must use a lot of recording tape, how come the budget committee doesn't come down on your hand with a hammer like everyone else?"

"We're special." The detective said with a small smile leaning back in his chair.

"Special like when you get a gold star for completing the assignment or special like you have to ride the little yellow bus to school?" Foster asked throwing in a little dig.

"That was a good one, glad it was caught on tape, but it wasn't the best. Now tell me why you were down at the Shangri-La the other night?" The detective asked with a wink.

"I like naked girls, especially the ones with really nice tan lines. There was this one girl last night who had a tan line that looked like a really slinky bikini bottom. Man, she was hot!" Foster smiled with a dreamy faraway look.

"You went there for just the girls?" the detective countered.

"Um, yeah, why do you go? I mean I know with my George Clooney looks it's hard to believe I would have to go to a strip joint at all but I was like what the hell. You know, some days I just don't want to get dressed up to have a girl grind on me."

"And did you speak with or notice Detective Renfroe in the bar when you were there?"

"Listen man, I've worked 55 crime scenes with Renfroe, do you want to know how I know the exact count? Because that asshole has made each and every one so memorable I couldn't forget the exact dates if I tried. When I saw him at the bar I went right to sticking my face in the breast of a rather ravishing girl to keep an extremely low profile." Foster explained stoically.

"And you two never spoke?" The detective asked continuing the questioning on pace.

"Nope, no wait a minute, he did say something." Foster answered shaking his finger at the man across the table at him.

"Yeah, what was that?' The detective asked leaning forward in his chair slowly, his anxiousness starting to show at the chance for a break.

"GET DOWN!" Foster screamed while smiling from ear to ear before laughing.

The IAD detective fell back in his chair with his face beginning to show a whole bunch of anger, the joke was obviously on him and that didn't sit well at all. He stared at Foster for a full minute quietly while in his mind he was using a baton to bash the skinny coroner's head in.

"Ah, I gotcha...I know that look like the back of my hand!" Foster chuckled still smiling.

The detective leapt from his chair and went for the door without as much as a squeak or a whisper. Just as he was going through the portal Foster screamed one last barb from behind. "Hey, when you talk with Renfroe again tell him I got to you too. You can use it to try the whole 'I'm on your side' trick."

The door to the interrogation room almost broke through the jam and came off the hinges from the force the detective used to shut it. Foster chuckled some more then laid his head down on the table for a quick nap. He figured the detective would be back in twenty for another round of stimulating conversation.

As hotels go The Westin wasn't the Windermere by any stretch of the imagination, but it wasn't the local No-Tell Motel either. It had 12 floors of rooms that provided plenty of space to make you feel right at home, even if you were some undead monster. From across the street it looked easy Yelena thought, she just had get inside the hotel and up to the room, which was no problem. There was a stairwell no one traveled and she could pop out at the end of the hall on the floor where her brothers were staying. The floor was deserted of occupants, only one other of the other suites on the floor was occupied so she didn't have to worry about strangers showing up. After she got this far though she wasn't sure what would come next in her plan, it was pretty much 'play-it-by-ear'. And once they escaped Yelena wasn't sure where they would go either. Maybe back to Los Angeles for Svetlana, or north to a small town in the Catskills mountains to hide and regroup, anywhere that Akhenaton was not was the perfect spot for them now. The Grand Lich would probably come for them at some point in time, but at least it would be a fair fight with no one sneaking up on them from behind. She took one last look to make sure the street was as clear as possible, just a few stragglers, before setting off. She crossed the street swiftly rousing no one's attention, went through the lobby without a glance from the night desk, and slipped inside the door to the stairwell before anyone could see. She leapt up each flight stepping once halfway in between before landing softly on the landings above for a step and then leaping the next flight of steps with a gazelle like bound.

She paused once at the 9th floor door, her floor, and sniffed the air. They were here, her brothers and Michaels, but so were the ghouls. The air carried their decaying scent all over the floor and it made the hair on the back of her neck stand on end. She chided herself for getting scared. This was no time for fear when her brothers' lives were in jeopardy. Yelena took a quick breath, said a small prayer in Russian, and moved out from the protection of the stairwell door into the hall. She tip-toed down the carpet not making a sound, past the door to the adjacent suite that was empty she crept while her heart pounded in her chest like a drum. The quiet of the hall was maddening as Yelena listened for any change or pitch of sound that would give her away or signal a trap. After an agonizing few seconds she finally reached the door to the suite, the Promised Land, and that's where she froze.

The sudden feeling of sheer dread came over her, like a cold blanket wrapping over her shoulders. Something was wrong, so very wrong. The metal of the knob was just an inch away and yet she couldn't force her hand to grasp it. Instincts built over long years, like programs on a computer, kicked on in her brain screaming for Yelena to run. The area wasn't safe, she had to leave now! There were her brothers though. She couldn't leave them she yelled back to the voices. The instincts wailed like sirens though, she had to run for her life now or it was over. Everything was over.

Yelena thought she must have looked like a fool there in the hall, her hand hovering just an inch away from the doorknob. Yet she finally gave in to her body, pulled her hand back slowly from the door. She couldn't believe it; she was going to leave her brothers in this prison awaiting execution. No, she wasn't going to do that! Damn her insides and damn her instincts for making her falter. Yelena reached out for the door knob again with forced intent pushing all the sirens and wailing and cursing her mind screamed to stop this to the back of her head. An inch away again her hand stopped short, but this time it was because the knob turned on its own.

The next few seconds slowed down to a crawl, like a movie cinematic effect. She watched as the door swung open inch by inch revealing the inside of the suite behind the silhouette of a man, the room was in a shambles. The furniture was broken and scattered in a field of debris around three statue figures in its center. Some of those slow seconds passed before she recognized her brothers, the three statue figures, standing lifeless like zombies. They were gone her mind screamed, she was too late in coming back from meeting with Alexander. Then the silhouette moved blocking the sight of her brothers and she recognized the ghoul. The black burial suit the loved ones choose for the deceased hung way to loose and its face may have been a man's at one time but after a few years in the ground it was nothing but wrinkled shriveled skin with pieces and patches missing on the cheeks. The eyes were gone as well, long since removed by the mortician or some doctor looking for a transplant, but the sockets weren't hollow. A black liquid pulsed and moved, like a sack of snails, to and fro in semi circles. The ghoul smiled and Yelena saw the teeth, not a set of rotting teeth like you might expect, but a row of gleaming razor sharpened fangs like a shark's and each was tipped with a deadly toxin. A voice sounded from behind it drawing her attention.

"Little Yelena, I was wondering when you would come home." Michaels voice spoke softly with a sharp sinister edge.

The instincts she fought to push away just a second ago, the same ones yelling commands to flee, took over and before Yelena could decide to move she was bolting away from the door in a flash. Her legs churned and her arms pumped hard back and forth drawing power from her small frame in a solid forward burst just as she heard Michaels issue a command that sent a chill down her spine. "Phlegm, fetch!"

That chill running down her spine flooded her body with fear. She could feel him running after her, could sense the ghoul's pursuit. It was a surreal feeling to have the tables turned, to go from the hunter to the hunted in a flash. Yelena didn't think about the feeling though, she only wanted to win the race for the end of the hall and the door to the stairwell. She could fight one ghoul and survive, but if both came for her together than it would be suicide. A ghoul's bite was nothing short of death for her now. Yelena's only chance was to get away now, put some distance between herself and Phlegm, and get help from someone. The door to the empty suite flew by as Yelena's ear picked up the fast approaching ghoul, its feet pounding hard and fast on the floor. The thing was like a heat seeking missile she couldn't shake. She ran straight up to the door to the stairwell stopping just long enough to grasp the handle to open it when she sensed the ghoul's footsteps disappear from behind. Phlegm was airborne now Yelena knew, it was a spear launching from the floor right at her at 100 miles per hour. The handle turned and the door popped free from the jam as she readied for the hit from the beast. She kept moving though, always going forward and never stopping. Yelena lunged through the door just as a poisoned clawed hand slashed down her back tearing the leather of her jacket and some of her shirt in shreds but not cutting into flesh luckily.

The material of the jacket and shirt shredded instantly as Yelena let out a grunt from the blow, but she didn't stop moving to get away. She swung around, grabbed the door, and slammed it across Phlegm's arm with a loud crash and maybe the pop of broken bone. It was doubtful the thing was hurt, ghouls were tough enemies. Yelena didn't wait to see what happened from the slam of the heavy door though. She just spun away and leapt down the stairs. If she was right the counter attack bought her maybe a second or two at the most. Ghouls were truly undead; no feeling in their dead bodies thus there was no pain that would ever stop them short of removing its head or all their limbs.

A quick look back up the stairs told her she was right. The ghoul's arm was perfectly fine as it waited for one second. What was once human only kicked the door forward and walked unusually calm onto the landing pursuing after its prey. The ghoul didn't follow the lycanthrope down the stairs. Yelena didn't care, she kept thinking 2nd floor and the fact all she needed to do was make the second floor to leap to the street. It was the new part of her escape plan, forget trying to gain the lobby because Phlegm was too fast to outrun so the next best choice was the floor above it. And outside meant a better chance for survival, it also meant she could transform. If she could become the white wolf then Phlegm would have to worry about his own survival for a minute.

The ghoul stood on the landing after getting through the door watching Yelena descend each flight of stairs. It knew there was no way to catch the lycanthrope now. The lead was too much to overcome, if he used the stairs, but if it took a more direct approach to the problem. Phlegm looked down the gap between each flight of stairs and the metal rail for a second before with a deft jump it leapt over the rail. Yelena just passed the sixth floor when she saw the black blur fall past her in between the stairs. She knew better then to stop and look over the banister, but Yelena couldn't stop herself from doing just that.

When she looked over and saw down the many flights, suppressing the natural shift of vertigo, her eyes showed her an unbelievable scene. The ghoul was standing at the bottom of the stairwell, the concrete of the floor cracked and broken in a circle all around it forming a weird pattern. Phlegm looked up at her, smiled with those razor sharp teeth, and gave a small cry that sounded sickening. Yelena felt her heart skip a beat as she realized this was a real race now.

At the same time both broke racing toward each other as fast as they could. Phlegm was intent on catching the lycanthrope and bringing her back to Michaels and in one piece wasn't necessary. Yelena gave up on getting to the second floor. The new plan was now to just get as close as possible to the ground and then find a way outside from there. The two passed each flight of stair in unison, Phlegm going past the lobby while Yelena flew by fifth floor. The ghoul was moving faster than the lycanthrope, until Yelena reached down and pulled an extra step from somewhere. She rounded fourth floor just as Phlegm passed the second. So the third floor was it, do or die for both. Neither stopped nor slowed and the ghoul looked to have an edge on cutting the lycanthrope off, but then Yelena pulled out another trick. In an impressive move she leaped the banister with her feet and vaulted the last bit of stairs getting to the landing just ahead of the ghoul.

The door knob practically broke off in Yelena's hand as she ripped the door open. She began to dive through when Phlegm reached her and his hand shot out grabbing onto her right arm. Her skin immediately began to burn from the contact of the claws, the material of her shirt sleeve ripping away. Yelena didn't scream though, she was too strong for that. Instead she stepped back and hit the ghoul with a left elbow to his face with the force of a twenty-five pound sledgehammer. The blow rocked the ghoul, stopping it momentarily, and that's exactly what Yelena was looking for. She broke free from Phlegm's grip and bolted off down the hall in a flash. The ghoul let out its horrid scream again and took chase, the effect of the blow now gone in a flash.

The hall was just a hundred feet long, but it might as well have been a mile to Yelena. The ghoul was gaining on her. It had already erased the gap she gained from the elbow strike. Yelena needed a miracle to get away, and she needed it now. The doors in the hall whizzed by in flashes as the pair ran at breakneck speed to its end, and the large window there. Yelena dug inside and pulled as hard as arms could pull and her legs as fast as they would churn. In the end though she knew she couldn't make it to the window, even with a ten yard lead, but then again maybe she didn't have to. Maybe if she used the ghoul's energy she could still get out of the hotel. The window her mind chanted, she just had to leap through the glass and there was the outside and a chance at living through this. The last of the doors stopped with ten feet to go and Yelena put her faith and life in one last gamble, one last chance. She slowed, on purpose, letting the ghoul gain the last feet needed to entice one more jump to increase her momentum.

And Phlegm took the bait.

The ghoul jumped and landed, while grabbing, the lycanthrope from behind in a bear hug. It didn't sense trouble until it was too late to stop, and even then there was nothing to do but ride out the landing.

Yelena didn't do much because she didn't have to thanks to Phlegm's weight and inertia. She dropped her right shoulder, gave a small twist, and leapt letting momentum do the rest. The pair spun on an invisible axis, turning with Phlegm going through the glass first and the lycanthrope in tow. Yelena shut her eyes as the crashing sound of glass and metal filled the air. For a second everything was semi-stable, and then the weightless feeling of falling took hold. She grabbed the ghoul's hands to keep from getting scratched and to try to steer them down because if they hit with her on bottom then it was really all over, the sidewalk that is she thought while repressing an awkward giggle.

Teddy Roberts didn't mind the night shift, it was quiet and relaxing sort of. He drove the linen truck for Walt's Linen Service, the cleaners for most of the hotels around the city. They washed, dried, and folded everything from table cloths to bed sheets, in any amount the hotel needed. The Westin here did business in the hundreds of pounds a week, which required a forklift to deliver the big loads sometimes. And then there were the special request. The Windermere just down a few streets made him sign a waiver not to steal any linen that their 'special' clientele had used, or to try and sell anything he found in said sheets. Yeah, like he was going take some celebrity's sex stained bed sheet and make a quick buck on EBay. There was no way he was going to do that, how would he even know which sheet to steal. All of them had some sort of a stain and he wasn't the inquiring type to find out what the mark was made of. Teddy was sitting in his truck finishing the log for picking up the daily load at the Westin when he heard the glass break from above. He looked up to the roof wondering what was going on when something close to the weight of a boulder it seemed crashed into the ceiling. The whole truck shifted and rocked from the impact while the overhead sunk a good foot or two in the center. The windshield cracked and the back doors flew open as if a bomb had exploded.

Some kind of training kicked in, from where Teddy wasn't sure, as he rolled out the large door onto the sidewalk in a ball. He gained his feet after waiting for a second or two for a sound from someone or another falling object colliding with his van. When nothing happened Teddy stood up, looked around, and then back to his panel truck with suspicious eyes. The vehicle didn't move but he wasn't going to trust it so Teddy approached it like a man waiting for a snake to leap out. And guess what, one did.

Someone dropped from the crater that was the roof of the panel truck and fell like a stone onto the concrete. Teddy screamed out, noticed the body was a girl, and then ran up to her with a concerned demeanor. Maybe God finally answered his prayer for a little companionship. He knelt and gently took hold the girl's arm, who was attempting to stand up at the moment, while trying to take control of the situation.

"Whoa, wait a minute. You need to lie still after a fall like that. You may have hurt yourself."

The girl though wasn't cooperating and pulled hard against his hand. "We have to run! You have to run away now!"

Hey, was that Russian Teddy thought. Wow, a Russian girl landed on his truck, was this fate or what man! Teddy was too busy figuring out where to go on the first date to listen to Yelena's warning. "Hey it's okay, you're okay now. I'll protect you from whoever's after you!" Teddy offered with a warm smile.

Yelena gained her feet and grabbed two handfuls of Teddy's jacket fully intent on getting her point across with authority. She even lifted Teddy off the ground an inch or two. "RUN AWAY FOOL!"

She just didn't drop Teddy, oh no, she threw him all the way across the sidewalk and into the large hedges that lined the wall of the hotel on loading dock side. Yelena ran form the area on shaky legs, but she made it away and into the dark before anyone could stop her or ask her out on a date.

The hedges were the small spruce type which meant a lot of prickling vegetation. Teddy at the time was busy extricating his foot from a bunch when another body dropped off from the roof of his panel truck. His hope of it being another white haired Russian quickly vanished though as he saw what was standing fifteen feet away. Teddy had buried his grandfather Joe in Scottsboro Alabama last year, a very moving ceremony. And if you were to go dig up old grandpa up you would see something like what Teddy was looking at now, right down to the black dress suit and shoes. The thing turned and locked its empty eye sockets with him, which wasn't the worst part, no way. It was when the thing started to walk toward him with an evil smile and heavy breathing that was definitely worse part. Teddy didn't move, he couldn't, so he just laid there in the bushes scared while death walked at him slow and purposeful. Half the distance, maybe seven feet to go, the thing suddenly stopped looked skyward to somewhere, and then bolted leaving the area in a flash.

Teddy finally took his first breath after two minutes of forced paralysis. There was a policy at work where employees could use the facilities and wash their own laundry for free. Teddy looked down at the crotch his pants and wondered if he could take advantage of that perk tonight.

The alley was dark and she couldn't sense, or smell, the ghoul Phlegm in pursuit anymore. Yelena stopped leaning up against a dumpster to catch her breath, or at least that's what she was trying to convince herself she was doing at the moment. It wasn't working. A wave of guilt so strong it rocked her knees made the lycanthrope fall to the ground weeping. She couldn't keep the sobs in, they exploded from her. The sight of her brothers standing there in the room like zombies crushed her spirit. She had failed them so awfully. The broken furniture scattered among the room suggested they put up a struggle, a fight for their lives, and she wasn't there to help them. No, she had failed her family and now there was nothing left in her world to live for. Her mother was gone, her brothers were zombies, and her lord Ivan and his House had abandoned her. Death was all she wanted, death for failing her family when they needed her most. A bottle gleamed off a stray light from a street lamp, as if pointing itself out to her. Yelena snatched it up, smashed it so she was holding a jagged edge in her hand, and prepared to enter the hereafter with a quick stab to the neck.

Then the image of one person came to her, one person from out of the blue. Clarity, sudden and striking, took hold as the person looked at her with deep eyes. Yelena felt calm serenity fill her soul and she looked at the bottle with disgust. She dropped it and wiped her hand on her ripped mini-skirt. She could help Yelena thought, she was the one person who could help her now. The image of her brothers standing like zombies changed, flowed to an image of all of them alive and walking down some corridor together. And in back, behind them, was the Ancient One again. He could change them back, she understood the image perfectly. Wilma could get her to Alexander and he could return her family to her. Yelena rose from the collapsed position she had ended up in and ran back into the shadows headed for the Laurel as the sun began to rise chasing the dark of night away from the land.

The dawn light from the sun was such a welcomed sight for Foster that he stopped to soak in the rays, stopped right there in the parking lot without a care. After spending twenty-four hours in an interrogation room at the Atlanta Police Headquarters answering a bazillion questions he was ready to go home to Toni.

The thought of her made his tired mind race. She must be worried sick, the image of her pacing frantically in his apartment made him feel guilty. Then he was suddenly angry, royally pissed at the detectives who had kept him in that interrogation room all night. They would pop in every fifteen minutes, ask three or four questions, and then leave just too come back again in fifteen minutes. Their tactic was so simple it was stupid. Anyone with a brain knew exactly what they were doing. The IAD was running over to Renfroe, asking him the same questions, and seeing if the answers jived. And every answer did, which is why they kept them separated all night. They were hoping for one inconsistency, one little slip up. Well, fuck you boys there wasn't one. Now kiss my ass and let me go home to my stripper girlfriend.

Foster was zoned out letting his tired mind and body run on the fuel of his anger. He didn't even flinch or open his eyes when a body brushed by him and spoke in a deep whisper. "You remember where the shop is?"

Without moving he answered Renfroe. "Yeah, but I don't think it's real smart to talk to each other in the parking lot in full view of the IAD detectives who were just busting our balls."

"They expect us to talk, keep our stories running in sync. Hell they've already got officers in stakeout mode following us, so why wait till tonight to talk." Renfroe said.

"What's on for tonight?" Foster asked opening one eye to look at Renfroe.

"We're going over all the stuff we know of our boy and the four Russians so we can arrange a sit down. Meet me at the gas station just north of the shop at 7 and we'll get a bite to eat, until then get some sleep and time with Toni." Renfroe said walking away.

Foster didn't say a word in response. He wasn't supposed to. The folder in his trunk made the choice for him four days ago. IAD asking questions all night made the decision for him. The only thing left was to get it over with and meet Big Bad Leroy Brown in person and maybe exchange notes. Foster walked away and hailed a taxi to take him home to some sleep and Toni's warmth.

Chapter Five

Computations and equations dealing with rocket flight flew through Wilma's brain as she went over her science project for this year. Last year's foray into suspended animation was cool and everything but this year she was going to knock the socks off, as Leland would say, the judges with her rocket project. If her calculations about the booster fuel payload were correct, and she was sure she all the data was good, then she might need to file a flight request with the FAA. Wilma giggled as she imagined some pilot sitting behind the wheel of his plane calmly adjusting a flap or engine speed when a blur suddenly shoot's past his window. She could see the captain let out a small explanative before turning to his co-pilot asking him what the hell just went by the window going straight up. Oh yeah, that would be the rocket with the experimental fuel cell specially created by one Wilma Jackson. Yes, that Wilma Jackson, the scientist at JPL who received the Nobel Prize for Science. There was just one hang up...her mom. How was she going to convince her she wasn't going to blow herself up? She was still busy thinking of just how to do that when the hairs on the back of neck stood up straight up.

A week ago she would have gone into 'Ghetto Defense' mode, keep moving with your head down until you were inside your own house with the doors locked. Yet it was different now, she didn't drop her head or make a bee line for the house. Alexander had passed on to her his strength, not the physical kind, but something better. He had given her strength of heart, of courage and tenacity. She wasn't afraid of the Projects and its evils anymore because in the end Wilma didn't want to live that way one more day. So she stopped being scared, stopped right in the middle of the path to her home, and looked over to a set of bushes by the apartment building to see someone standing there.

"Come on out, I can see you!" Wilma called out confidently.

A second ticked away before someone appeared and it sent a shock through Wilma. She would have never guessed who it was in a million years.

"Hello Wilma." Yelena said with a small smile. She had waited all day, worried and anxious both to see the little girl, to see if Wilma would help or run away in fear. What she received for a response never entered her mind, downright exhilaration.

"Wow, you're the werewolf girl, right?"

"Um, yes I am." Yelena answered in English with her accent glaring. She didn't want to confuse the little girl with Russian, but really, who was the one actually confused at the moment she wondered silently.

"Whoa, you're Russian too, just like my dream! I know some Russian words, but just what I've read in web comics on the school computer. I can say 'Yes' and 'Bathroom' and a few other words."

"Oh, that's very good." Yelena replied with a confused smile. Was the little one really...excited to meet her?

"Hey, are you okay? You look really beat up." Wilma asked with genuine concern.

It felt a little overwhelming for Yelena, to have a human care for her so much. If little Wilma only knew what she had done to other humans she might not be so caring. "I am good little Wilma. I do need your help though, in contacting Alexander."

"Oh yeah, sure, I can help there, but I think you need to rest first. Just stay in the bushes and follow me to my window. It's a sad state of affairs these days but if someone sees a white person around here it could get said person in a lot of trouble." Wilma said walking along the bushes trying to conceal what was happening.

Yelena smiled slightly at the girl, more out of wonder for now, but there was no denying her affection for Wilma was growing. She did as asked sticking close to the building while following Wilma silently. The pair reached the end of the present structure and Yelena stopped while the girl went out midway to the next one. Wilma looked around then gave a small sign, a simple underhanded wave, and with a flash Yelena crossed the empty courtyard. Wilma took another look around and then moved on close to the bushes again. They moved along to the end of this building where Wilma took a left and at the first window she reached over and pushed it open with a small grunt. She turned around again as Yelena went through the open portal with a deft move and after the lycanthrope was in Wilma turned back and closed the window with a plop. She stepped toward the door in a fast walk clearing the ten feet in three steps and Wilma was sure she broke all the known speed records for unlocking all the dead bolts.

The inside of the small living room was lit by what natural light the overcast day provided, which made it a little dark, but not enough to stop Wilma for a second as she ripped off her coat and dropped her book bag by the couch. Stephanie looked out from the kitchen in time to see her daughter run down the hall and into her room like she was on fire. On any other day that wouldn't have drawn even half a look from Stephanie, but after the last few nights her internal alarms started going off. She threw the dish rag she was holding across the kitchen as she started off down the hall after Wilma.

"What's wrong Wilma? What's going on?"

There wasn't an answer from her daughter's room and the alarms going off in Stephanie's head grew louder with each heartbeat. Panic began to claw at her chest but with a shrug she pushed it away. Stephanie called out again with two steps to go till Wilma's bedroom door.

"Wilma Jackson you answer me."

There was nothing in the form of a response and that panic feeling made a surge at Stephanie. She stopped by the door intent on opening it by the knob or simply ripping it free from the jam when someone did the job for her and in the nick of time too. The wood portal swung open slowly, Wilma was standing in the doorway with someone behind her. A second was all it took for Stephanie to recognize Yelena and the fact she was beaten and worn. She looked down to her daughter and the look from Wilma's eyes took every bit of fear and anger from Stephanie's heart and mind.

"She's hurt Mom, her brothers are in trouble, and she needs Alexander really bad."

Stephanie looked up to Yelena and then back to her daughter, a smile slowly working across her face. "Of course we'll help her sweetie, don't worry. Why don't you go and make us some tea while I get Yelena cleaned up, okay?"

"Sure thing," Wilma said with a nod getting ready to run out of the room but just before she did she turned back to Stephanie, "thanks Mom."

"No problem, now get to making the tea." Stephanie said ushering Wilma out with a gentle pat of her shoulder.

"I am sorry for bringing this trouble to your door step Stephanie." Yelena began when Wilma's mother turned to her, but she stopped when she saw the hand come up.

"No need, I'm glad to help. I have some clothes in my room that might fit. Come on." Stephanie said taking the hand she had just held up and reaching over to take Yelena's in hers.

They went into Stephanie's bedroom where Yelena stripped out of her torn top and skirt. Stephanie waited for her to wash off before handing over a pair of jeans and T-shirt to her friend and while the pants were good the shirt was a little big and hung well down past Yelena's waist.

"Sorry for the fit, but it's about the best I can do right now until I do some laundry."

"Oh no, please it will do," Yelena said putting her boots back on and stuffing the pants legs into the high leather material.

Yelena rose from the edge of the bed where she was sitting and looked Stephanie in the eye, willing the woman to look at her. A small tear crossed her face as she spoke. "Thank you Stephanie, I never expected someone to treat me this way."

There was no explanation needed because Stephanie knew what the lycanthrope was trying to say. She could see herself in Yelena, proud and strong, which were never good companions when trying to ask for help. Both of the traits also kept one from seeing the very people around you who would be more than willing to help if you just got off your high horse and accepted it. Yet that's where the problem was, wasn't it, because in the end you didn't want to, couldn't, let go of your pride. You'd rather jump from a plane without a parachute then admit you needed help from someone, and the funny thing, was life knew this about you. It counted on this from your pride and strength because it would always hit when you weren't ready. Life would put some bump in the road in front of you, some obstacle that turned into a mountain, and then you had no choice but to ask for help. At least she did Stephanie thought, asked for help when there was finally nowhere else to go, and some days she wished that her father or Wilma's father had made the same choice when the time had come and not let out for parts unknown to hide out. And now she was glad Yelena had accepted the need to ask even though it left the worst taste in your mouth imaginable.

"No tears now, the last thing we need in here is to start crying out of control and all because I don't have enough ice cream in the freezer to go around." Stephanie said with a laugh.

Yelena laughed at the statement too letting the humor cover her crying. The fact that Stephanie didn't move to hug her or continually tell her that everything was going to be okay kept her at ease. Yelena never liked the attention fawning brought, it was so damn tiring and unnecessary. Wilma suddenly popped her head in and gave the tender moment between the two women her instant judgment, a look of bewilderment.

"Uh, the tea is ready, that's if you two still want some?"

"Yeah, I think we do." Stephanie said with a wink. They all moved out and down the hall to the small kitchen where Wilma had set the table for a service of three, two of the best mugs they owned with two tea bags each and a pot of hot water.

"I need to speak to a Mr. Karl Mueller. I was told to phone this number and someone would pass him a note for me. I have an interested party that would like to sit and come to an arrangement with him and his principal about a certain artifact, a very old scroll that his employer is looking for. If Mr. Mueller's principal completes a task for my client then he will come into possession of the contents of said scroll. Please have Mr. Mueller call me at this number. Yes, you can give him my name. Thank you so very much." Simon said hanging the phone up when he was done and going back to reading a stack of papers on his deck.

He was used to his southern charm disarming both judges in court and beautiful women around Atlanta, but when the phone rang two minutes later he was sure it wasn't his best side that was the reason. Simon picked up the receiver and spoke with his usual quaint colloquialism. "Hello Mr. Mueller, how are you this fine evening?"

The voice on the other end responded in a thick German accent. Simon could almost picture a pair of square metal frame glasses and a patch of black hair cut into a sharp triangle on a very white chin. "How did you find me Mr. Simon?"

"I think you know who I represent Mr. Mueller, a very old client who has some considerable deductive skills. He did not have to put forth a tremendous amount of effort to find you or the one you speak for."

"And this artifact, are you sure it's what you say it is?" Mueller asked quickly.

"Please Mr. Mueller, can we can stop playing games now. You know perfectly well what I have here."

"I need to know if this is, as they say, on the level. If it is not I assure you I will find you and I will hurt you very badly Mr. Simon."

The lawyer in him took over as Simon ignored the threat with ease, like swishing away a fly with a casual wave. "I'm doing very fine this evening Mr. Mueller, thank you for asking, and I can assure you that this is on the level. As a matter of fact I'm looking at the contents of the old scroll right now, a certain piece of parchment from a long time ago which they say was written by the hand of one Jahangir. He was a sorcerer for the Kings of Persia don't you know and some say he actually knew of a spell to bring back the dead. Can you imagine that?"

The phone was silent for a moment but then Mueller finally remarked after a couple of seconds, the last sounding like the hiss of some exotic snake. "Well Mr. Simon, the floor is yours." The hesitation told Simon he had the man's undivided attention.

"My client would like to meet with you at a neutral location and come to an agreement of payment for a special engagement. A job suited particularly well for the one you speak for let's say." Simon said with a smile.

"The Ancient One wants a meeting with me? And this 'old scroll', this would be the payment for completing this 'job'?" Mueller asked carefully, trying unsuccessfully to hide his intention about the scroll.

"Oh dear sir, the terms of payment and the job would be better suited for a face to face discussion Mr. Mueller, but I do know the contents of the scroll will be yours if the job is completed. My employer is requesting you set the time and place and he will be there." Simon said shifting the conversation slyly away from the payment side, but setting the hook with the last bit about the scroll.

Mueller was caught in the net. Simon knew it, had planned it to perfection, so when the man answered after a second the response was already expected. "There is a bar called The Station on the north side of the city, look it up on the Internet. A band called Reality Check is playing there tonight, very good rock-n-roll. I think the Ancient One would enjoy them. I'll be there at 7 PM sharp, table in the back."

The phone went dead with a smile growing on Simon's face. As instructed he called a number and left a message for his client.

"So what's Moscow like?"

The questions came at her fast and furious, but Yelena found herself not minding it one little bit. The excitement in Wilma's eyes was something she had never seen or experienced. The little girl had crept closer and closer over the last minute to the point where if she scooted over another inch she would be in Yelena's lap.

"I haven't been to Russia for a long time Wilma. I'm afraid my memories would not be ones you find interesting." Yelena said with a smile.

"Oh no, I'm all about history. I read a story once about the Czar's, Nicholas I think, and it was so unbelievable! Do you know anything about them? Did you talk with them too, like Alexander talked with William Shakespeare? " Wilma asked so fast her words began to blend one into the next.

"Wilma baby, why don't you let Yelena have a rest, maybe even a little space. She's got a lot on her mind and I'm sure you're not helping with all the questions." Stephanie remarked with a raised eyebrow. A very common sign these days that meant Wilma was treading thin ice.

"Okay, I'll back off." Wilma replied with a dejected look on her face.

Yelena tapped her mug twice with her index finger before deciding to go forward. It was another large step for her, a leap of faith across a giant gorge. "You said you would help me with the Ancient One Wilma?"

"You mean Alexander? I can do that no problem." Wilma said taking a sip from a can of coke she was drinking. Tea really wasn't her thing.

"I have angered him greatly little one. It may not be as easy as you think to have him help me." Yelena said softly, confessing almost to the little girl.

Wilma leaned over, and with the maturity and sincerity of someone twice her age she took Yelena's hand in her smaller one. "We all make mistakes, but nothing that can't be forgiven, because in the end we all need our friends. Alexander understands this better than anyone, believe me. He'll help you and your brothers, I promise."

The statement struck Yelena profoundly, not for the meaning but the sincerity. She couldn't understand how a fourteen year old girl had that kind of compassion, or that kind of a connection with the oldest vampire on the face of the planet. For all that she had been through in her short one hundred years of life Yelena had never met someone like this child and she was quite taken with little Wilma.

"Okay sweetie, I think Yelena needs some rest and you need to do your homework." Stephanie remarked with a cocked eyebrow.

"She can sleep in my room. I'll be real quiet while I work, I promise."

"Girlfriend, you need to slow your roll some. Yelena can sleep in my bed while you concentrate on growing your brain." Stephanie said cocking her other eyebrow.

"All right, I understand." Wilma said with a small frown before getting up from the table. "Can we talk again later? I really want to know about Moscow."

"Da, I would like to tell you of my home." Yelena said with a smile and a small squeeze of Wilma's hand.

Wilma gave the squeeze back, imparting her affection for Yelena in more than words. Then she was away from the table moving down the hall toward her room and her studies while both women watched her departure intently and strangely longing for her company again.

After a second or two of quiet, after Wilma had disappeared into her room, Stephanie spoke softly breaking the silent trance the women were in. "She saved me you know, saved me from going down a bad road with her father."

Yelena looked over to Stephanie with sympathetic eyes, taking in the remark. Little Wilma was more than she seemed, more than anyone could have guessed a human being could be, and before Yelena knew it she was telling Stephanie about the night before. When she came to the end she expected a laugh, even a small snort, because the tale was ludicrous, right? A little girl Yelena barely knew saving her through some flash of a memory in her mind, it was simply inconceivable, you know? Yet Stephanie only smiled. It was the kind of gesture shown by someone who had experienced the same thing, the same feelings and emotions.

"A month after Wilma's father left he called me up, asked me to come to New Orleans and get back together. There was only one catch though he said. I had to leave Wilma behind, cut the ties to her completely. He wasn't the fatherly type he said, wasn't about to raise a child when he was all about having fun and running around."

The werewolf shook her head and whispered. "That is very wrong Stephanie."

"You're telling me, and it took me less time to hang up the phone up than it took to come up with an answer for him. I wondered though for a little while afterwards, what if there was no Wilma. What if she wasn't here? Would I have ended up in New Orleans broke or worse, strung out on some corner selling myself for money? And you know what's even crazier?"

"What?"

Stephanie chuckled and smiled with a sigh, "I spent fourteen years avoiding men like the plague because there wasn't a good one in the bunch and inside a week I came across two that have impressed me like no others. My stone heart started beating again even though I had it tied down and locked away. "

Oh how she knew that too well Yelena thought as her memory of the Ancient One and his compassion as well came up in her mind. She took a sip of her tea and as she did Stephanie asked her one final question.

"If it came down to it, if it were you or Wilma, would you give your life for hers? If it were a split second decision with no time to choose, could you make the ultimate sacrifice?" Stephanie asked, not overly serious as a mother but compassionate like a lifelong friend.

Yelena set her cup down and answered without hesitation, something she didn't think possible two days ago when it came to a human. "Da, for Wilma I would give my life."

"Thank you my sister," was all Stephanie said and it was all that needed to be said. The two turned back to silence drinking their tea before thoughts drifted off to other important things.

Pacing among the remains of the suite's living room furniture Michaels made another trip. Ever since Phlegm had returned empty handed from its pursuit of Yelena he had run scenarios through his mind like some mad accountant at an adding machine, fingers punching buttons for numbers representing plans of ways to go after the Ancient One with only three of the four pups. You had to add it up, calculate the outcome because if the sum didn't come out in your favor then the plan was null and void. Kill only three pups and not all four was bad in any book, all it took was for one to get away and the plan was ruined, just like now. He was rapidly running out of options and plans, coming out null and void every single time. Plan one hundred and ten was quickly on its way to the garbage pile of Michaels brain when his cell rang in his jacket pocket. He jumped from the sudden sound but the surprise turned to anger and for a second he actually thought about tossing the small metallic object out the window. The sensible part of his mind took hold though, screaming it could be a call from his master, which brought him under control with a snap. And when he saw the number was Akhenaton's Michaels sighed with disbelief. He was already in deep enough trouble without getting in any deeper.

He touched a button on the smartphone screen with a flick as Michaels steadied himself. "Sir?" he answered cheerily.

"Were you going to throw me out the window?" Akhenaton asked back quickly, a tinge of suspicion and what might be impatience in his voice.

The wheels in Michaels brain came to a sudden halt from panic, which is why he suddenly started stammering like a fool. "Throw you out Sir? NO! I would never...How could I..."

"Now don't deny it Michaels. You were going to throw me right out that window your standing in front of, weren't you?" The voice hissed slowly.

"Please sir, why would I throw you away? You are everything to me, my reason for being!" Michaels had no clue what he was saying or why he was saying it. He only wanted that tinge of impatience and anger to go away. He was so scared in fact that he didn't catch the words Akhenaton used or that his phone had a weird echo effect going on.

"Michaels, I'm touched. No, I mean it. I really am going to cry over here."

"Sir, I would do any...what do you mean over here sir?" Michaels said finally realizing all the clues. He turned slowly to the doorway of the second room, the one where Ick and Phlegm had emerged, and standing there inside the portal was the Grand Lich himself.

Just the site brought a gasp from Michaels and a cruel smile from the ghouls standing behind him. Akhenaton never left California, never left the security of the mansion, except to take care of personal business. The last time the Grand Lich left the confines of his abode to take care of something, and strangely enough it concerned the Ancient One, a small town in the Alps was complete and utterly wiped off the map. Anytime Akhenaton made a trip it was never good for someone and Michaels did not have to think hard to deduce who that someone was going to be this time.

"Sir, you're here, and not at the mansion. Why are you here sir?" Michaels said trying not to whimper to bad.

"What, I can't take a stroll every now and then?" The Lich said taking a step forward. His wiry frame looked thin, but Michaels knew better. He knew that body was just a vessel, a jar holding unlimited power and destruction. He once watched as Akhenaton stood in a graveyard and with a single spell raised every able dead body in a short moment, before the second hand on your watch could turn twice the Grand Lich had over a hundred Zombies at his bidding.

"Oh no Sir, that's not what I meant at all. It's just that every time you go on a stroll it seems someone gets hurt...very badly." Michaels explained with a small laugh that almost sounded like a cry.

Akhenaton smiled broadly and then threw back his head and laughed with his follower. The move frightened Michaels to the point he winced. He knew it was only seconds away, a searing blast that would burn him to cinders. Yet the Grand Lich just walked over and put his arm around his underling in what might have been a loving gesture, if Akhenaton could have felt love. "I know in the past I have destroyed many a men, women, even children, but it wasn't like they didn't deserve it, right?"

"Oh yes Sir, they all deserved it...in some way or another I 'm sure." Michaels pleaded.

"You're damn right they did, and I take care of my business one time and one time only." Akhenaton stated turning to face his underling with a fatherly gaze. That was the last straw for Michaels. He couldn't take the tension any longer.

"Sir, if you plan on destroying me can you please just do it and stop toying with me like some cat with a fat mouse. I don't think my heart can take it." Michaels said finally breaking down.

"You're heart doesn't beat, it's a proverbial stone, how is it going to stop?" Akhenaton asked with a raised eyebrow.

"I do not know Sir, but I'm sure you can do something like rip the skeleton out of this body or an even crueler fate. I like this skeleton Sir. I've become quite attached to it, and on the inside of my body. Please don't tear out my skeleton." Michaels broke down pleading.

"Whoa little soldier, whoa. I'm not going to rip you're skeleton from your body, at least not while wearing an Armani suit!" Akhenaton remarked with a grin.

"Oh, thank you sir." Michaels responded wearily while wiping his brow.

"No, I think you've done an admiral job in trying to get Alexander to kill those four ungrateful pups." Akhenaton said turning Michaels back to the entrance of the bedroom.

"You really think so sir?" Michaels asked feeling a little better, a little more confident.

"Why yes, listen, you've done everything possible to complete my instructions." Akhenaton explained.

"Yes sir, everything I could think of!"

"You've tried to have him kill those pesky pups, right?"

"My every waking moment has been focused on that purpose since you presented me with task Sir!" Michaels said with a sharp nod of his head.

"And yet that pesky vampire is still walking around and those pups are still breathing, right?" Akhenaton asked feeling the emotion in the room rise.

"Yes sir, that man is infuriating!"

"I know, I know, hell I've known for a century and a half. The vampire is a pain in the ass!" Akhenaton said throwing up his free hand.

"Yes he is sir, yes he is!" Michaels emphatically agreed by raising his right hand.

Akhenaton turned and pointed to the three Epova's standing like stones. "And I know he's protecting Yelena just too rub it in our faces!"

"He is sir?" Michaels asked with a gasp.

"Oh yeah, where else is she going to go? We took care of Ivan's House, drove Victor and Iskra underground with the help of Iskra's own son and kidnapped Svetlana. Alexander is the one and only being she could hope to get help from."

Michaels smiled and nodded as his lord continued. "Well you know what? I say we take care of this tomorrow night! I say we get rid of all of our problems in one move, what do you say to that?" Akhenaton asked.

Michaels shook his whole body with a single gyrating nod. "Yes sir, tomorrow night we finish this! Only, I have been trying to come up with a way to do just that and I cannot think of a way to kill all four of the Epova's now."

"Ah you see my inadequate follower and associate, we've been going at this with the right ideas but the wrong personnel. We need some fresh blood in this thing." Akhenaton responded.

"Fresh blood sir, I'm afraid I don't follow?" Michaels asked not liking the way the conversation was suddenly turning. He was back to thinking he was getting blown up in a rather hideous fashion.

"Yes Michaels, new blood, and by new blood I mean dead necrotic flesh." Akhenaton remarked with a blossoming evil grin.

Before Michaels could ask, before he could think of a word to utter, two behemoths emerged from the bedroom where Akhenaton had come from. They were ghouls like Ick and Phlegm, and yet they were more, so much more. The pair had to turn sideways to pass through the standard sized bedroom door, and duck for that matter. When they walked across the floor Michaels could swear it shook. When they stood side by side in front of him Michaels had to crane his neck to look them in the eyes, which of course were gone. These ghouls were larger than the Epova brothers even, but if that was a good thing the Lesser Lich wasn't sure yet.

"You know what I love more than a fool willing to sell his soul into eternal servitude as my slave for the chance of obtaining some Godlike power he could never hope to control if he did Michaels?" Akhenaton asked.

"No sir, I do not." Michaels answered without taking his eyes off of the ghouls. He missed another obvious remark about himself too.

"Athletes willing to turn their bodies into pharmaceutical cesspools for some silly notion of playing a child's game." The Grand Lich said walking over to the first ghoul.

"They were athlete's sir?" Michaels asked with a deep swallow still in shock.

Akhenaton rubbed the large arm of the first one proudly like a father. "No, they were body builders who pumped themselves full of steroids in a vain attempt to be the best, or some other preposterous athletic goal. They kind of fell short though, died a month apart, and fell right into my grubby little hands."

"Really...a month apart you say?" Michaels remarked with raised eyebrows and a deep swallow.

"Oh yes, big, beautiful, and oh so dead. I made some small improvements over Ick and Phlegm like increasing the bone density, but it was those wondrous drugs in the end that made them spectacular. They're three times as strong as a regular ghoul with half the labor to create and only 8% body fat. I mean they're a work of art. I call them Misery and Woe." Akhenaton stated with blushing pride.

"I can't imagine what you could do with a baseball or football player sir." Michaels remarked with a half-smile shuddering at the actual thought of what the Grand Lich could do with said baseball or football player.

"Oh Michaels, when that happens I'm going to have a hell-of-good time!" Akhenaton replied with an evil laugh.

"So we're going to take the two brutes here and go after the Ancient one?" Michaels asked slowly pointing to the two new ghouls.

"And that's why I keep you around Michaels, because I can't throw anything by you."

"Thank you sir, I think."

"Tomorrow night I want you to take Misery, Woe, and Phlegm and get Alexander to take care of those pesky pups once and for all. You'll have a one in a billion chance of pulling it off probably but I have faith in you Michaels." Akhenaton said with an approving nod of his head.

"Sir, that sounds grand and all, but we still have the issue of getting the Ancient One to kill the pups. He refused at the exotic club to end Dimitri." Michaels stated and then a second later wanting to withdraw the statement.

"In all the watching you and the Epova's have been doing these last few days you're telling me you haven't come across one thing out of the ordinary?" Akhenaton asked quickly moving over to his underling.

Michaels thought for a second, maybe more, before responding. He knew what he wanted to say, just not the way to say it so the Lich wouldn't pull his head off his shoulders. "There seems to be no reason for the Ancient One to be here doing what he is doing. The Epova's couldn't find a reason and I haven't been able to come across one myself. All we know is he's going after drug dealers, like he has some vendetta against them or something."

"Come on now Michaels, you know that vampire's sick reputation for helping those less fortunate, and not quite as dead, than himself. Why would he risk exposure and almost certain destruction just to kill drug dealing scum? Better yet, ask yourself who would he risk exposure for?" Akhenaton wide eyed with a whisper.

It took a second, and only a second, for the gears to click in place. The how and why wasn't important, too much time lost on those unimportant facts. The only thing that mattered was the little black girl and her mother, they were the reason. Alexander was protecting them. Even as the light bulb went on and Michaels looked the Grand Lich in the eyes, Akhenaton was already smiling.

"The little black girl sir," Michaels exclaimed.

"And we have a plan, you get that little girl and I assure you Alexander will kill anything to get her back. You put the pups between that little girl and him and I know the old man will tear the Epova's to pieces." Akhenaton stated with a laugh. After a second Michaels joined in sharing the evil mood of the air with him.

The room echoed with the vile noise until the two regained control. Then Michaels realized something and asked his master for clarification. "Sir, what are you going to be doing?"

"Oh I'm going to go and fetch that package I need while you're taking care of business with that pain in my ass vampire. I'll take Ick here to help me clean up." Akhenaton nodded walking around the room surveying the damage.

"A package sir?"

"Yeah, that nice person who has an exceptional third eye to see the future, she's the package I need. I suddenly came to my senses and realized she's way too important to leave to someone else who has issues with completing my orders to snatch."

The Lesser Lich only smiled ignoring the comment before asking another question. "So we'll be together till we leave tomorrow night sir?"

Akhenaton came to a sudden stop in the room and gasped. "Are you crazy? No, I can only take about an hour with you at the most Michaels. That's why I want you and Misery to go out right now and keep an eye on the package, make sure she hasn't decided to jump on a plane and travel to Hawaii or something."

Michaels took the slip of paper his lord handed over to him noting the address then he watched as the Grand Lich went back to wandering the room looking around earnestly. Akhenaton's underling noticed the way his master was scouring the space and finally gave in to his curiosity. "Um, do you need something sir?"

"Yeah, I don't see a telephone book lying around? I thought the Hotel always put one in every room and suite."

"I thought that as well my lord, but directory might have been misplaced?"

"You know what tops my list for getting upset Michaels?"

"Oh, yes sir, someone calling you 'The Lich King'. I remember sir; never ever call you the 'Lich King'." Michaels grinned proudly as he watched his lord look at him with shock. The name was in reference to a popular online game and once Akhenaton saw how the Lich had been drawn and depicted in the game, and more to the point him, well it didn't sit nicely with the former Pharaoh. He had destroyed more than a few followers who had made the mistake of comparing the way the Lich King looked in the game to the Grand One. Oh really, Akhenaton would say with a sneer, I look like some disgusting rotting corpse living in a dreary old castle. That's what you think of the one who owns your soul? No, the follower would say trying to back away to get out of range, I never meant that sir they would clamor and cry. Then he'd melt them would Akhenaton, right into the rugs those poor dead bastards were standing on without so much as a single regret except one. The Grand Lich really hated losing those rugs, paid quite a bit for each one.

"You just called me that name...twice."

"Did I sir? I'm so sorry, never again." Michaels cringed before starting to walk away and pointing to the door. "I'll just go now sir and keep an eye on this address as you've given me."

He was making a bee line straight for freedom, and Michaels might have made it too if not for the hand coming up to stop him. The appendage belonged to Akhenaton as did the look of frustration in his eyes. "So you're not going to help me find a phone book?"

"Oh yes sir, phone book...just why do you need one so badly sir?" Michaels stammered looking around the floor of the room. He really, really just wanted to get away now after saying that name twice like a fool.

"Because you have to see this trick Misery does with them, rips the damn things in two!" Akhenaton smiled with a glee like a five year old. It was a complete turnaround, a 180 from just a minute ago. Michaels though only smiled half-heartedly and then went to work finding a telephone book for the ghoul to attack relentlessly.

Chapter Six

The night slowly descended on the landscape this Thursday with its usual shadowy path, and with it came the night owls, those girls and boys looking for a goodtime, for a release from the stress of the week by letting go of their inhibitions at bars and clubs all over the city. At one particular bar a band called Reality Check was setting up getting ready to belt out the covers of rock-n-roll songs which would send their fans and crowd into mass gyrating frenzy. One man though sat placidly by himself just out of sight from the dance floor. He absently pushed the square box metal frames of his glasses up on his pointed nose every few seconds while maintaining an 'I'd-rather-be-anywhere-else-than-here' look. Mueller didn't like rock-n-roll, detested the loud noise, and from watching his mannerism for just a second you could have easily guessed that fact. He didn't look at the band which was getting ready to start playing, only at his watch noting that another minute had rolled off the hands. Mueller looked up, then around at the people secretly hating all of them, and finally back to the opposite side of the table. And there stood a man in his fifties with neatly trimmed hair, an expensive business suit with equally expensive tie, and a warm broad smile that screamed lawyer.

"Well Mr. Mueller, you look just the way I pictured you would."

Mueller slowly smiled and pushed his glasses up on his nose again. "And you look every inch the way a lawyer should look Mr. Simon."

"May I?" Simon asked of the empty seat in front of Mueller and before the German could answer he was sitting with that same broad smile.

"I was actually waiting for your client Mr. Simon, you remember, the Ancient One." Mueller remarked with a large bit of sarcasm.

"Oh don't worry Mr. Mueller, my client is having a word with your...why what do you call Mr. Vargas? Is 'benefactor' the proper description of your relationship?" Simon smiled back.

The look on Mueller's face told the lawyer enough, the twist in the meeting arrangement was a total shock, but he wondered which was worse for Mueller. The fact that he didn't see the old bait and switch Alexander had pulled on him or that he knew Mueller's principal would be alone with him. He watched the poor man start to get up and Simon took pity deciding to let Mueller in on the real play here.

"There's nothing to worry about Mr. Mueller, this was all planned in advanced so my client and your benefactor could have a private conversation." Simon stated with sympathy.

Mueller looked to a table across the crowded room and then back to Simon with a glaring suspicious look. "Are you sure that is all the Ancient One wants?"

"I can ensure you a hundred percent that is all my client wants Mr. Mueller, and anyway both men are grown adults...sort of, and they are allowed to have a private conversation are they not?" Simon asked rhetorically.

A minute went by as Mueller cautiously sat back down on his seat while looking over his shoulder back at the bar every other second. Simon waited patiently then enacted the last part of Alexander's plan, the distraction of the guard.

"So Mr. Mueller, I hear you're quite a student of Nietzsche." Simon asked with a grin. The question pulled Mueller in, like a block of steel to a big red magnet. The grin on Simon's face grew an inch or two larger as the lawyer continued on. "I never agreed with Nietzsche's view on human nature quite as much as I did with the philosophy of Descartes. I think it stemmed from the fact I always thought Nietzsche was just too damn full of himself to see the forest for the trees you might say."

"Really Mr. Simon, funny you should mention your dislike of Mr. Nietzsche..." Mr. Mueller smiled finally, being a student of the

German Philosopher the subtle challenge put forth by the lawyer was going to be answered.

Ferdinand Manual Vargas was born originally in 1905 in the city of Madrid, Spain in the slums that surrounded the city. He grew up in the squalors and the failed attempts of King Alfonso's governments to try and run a country. It was no real wonder why he followed his parents into the Socialist Party when he was of age, why he took up the arms of civil disobedience to stop a fool monarch from ruining Spain, and this was not Alfonso he fought. No, by that time he was waging a social war with one Miguel Primo de Rivera, a general who had what historians called a 'mild dictatorship' after taking over from Alfonso. Vargas often wondered what those idiot historians would call Rivera if they had lived through his 'mild' regime, probably anything but 'mild'. It was at the end of the General's run as head of the country when the young Spaniard came across a French man named Adnot, quite the peacock among the rabble of the city. He dressed in fine clothes, spoke quite eloquently, and was the first man who knew of Ferdinand's unusual...'ability'. Even he, Vargas, did not know what he was capable of until the peacock showed him. The French man told Vargas he had come to the city, drawn to these dirty streets by a certain feeling, pulled here from Paris by one lone individual...Ferdinand Manual Vargas.

At first Vargas thought the man was insane, there was nothing special about him that would bring anyone all the way from France to Spain he told Adnot. Then the French man handed over a set of documents from a leather binder, old parchment paper with even older words and symbols and diagrams written and drawn on the collection of documents. As Adnot stared with a small smile, as if he knew already what was going to happen, Vargas looked over the strange words and notes and exhaled slowly. He shouldn't have known what the strange words meant, he was an educated man taught by his parents to read and write, but these phrases and annotations on the paper were nothing he had ever seen before and yet...he knew exactly what each and every one meant. Vargas looked up from the set of papers carefully and whispered...there is an elixir that can prolong a man's life? Yes, Adnot only smiled more while replying, but what should intrigue you more is how you know this. Yes, how do I know what all of this means Ferdinand had whispered with wonder and just a little fear? That my friend is why I was drawn here to you Adnot explained, because only one who can use magic can read the magical writings of a Wizard.

The band got ready to start their set on stage, the guitarist and the lead singer moving into position as the drummer sat behind his drum kit getting ready as well. Vargas sat facing the stage from his seat with the rum and coke on the table where the waitress had set it down. His jet black hair was cut in the usual modern loose layered style and his jeans and sports jacket kept him from looking too out of place from the crowd. Vargas let out a sigh as he thought back on the memories of that night when Adnot had come to take him away, back to Paris to study with the Circle of Ascent, a group of other wizards and magic bearers who looked to the French man as their leader and teacher following him without question.

"I am sorry to hear of Adnot's passing Ferdinand. He was a very interesting man." A proper English voice suddenly said to his right and when Vargas looked over to what used to be an empty seat he unexpectedly saw a pair of dark eyes staring back.

"You must be the Ancient One?" He asked sitting up just a little with a quick look around, his eyes seeking out Mr. Mueller.

"Mr. Mueller is fine Ferdinand, he is sitting with the same man I asked to give you a call and arrange our meeting. By this time they are more than likely discussing who was more accurate in their critical thinking, Mr. Nietzsche or Mr. Descartes." The man replied as the band on stage started up with a cover of an old Allman Brothers song.

Vargas eased back into his seat and eyed the man across the small table, "So you are Alexander?"

The man only nodded and smiled, his lips stretching back just far enough to show a small glimpse of one fang. "I am Ferdinand, and I can assume we may dispense with any further 'confirmations' of who I am."

"Yes we can, but then there is the question of the scroll of Jahangir and its authenticity? I can assume you did not bring it with you Ancient One?" Vargas asked. He had only heard stories about Alexander from Adnot, tales the Spaniard thought at the time were exaggerations but now looked to have more than just a bit of truth. Being this close to the oldest vampire brought back the words of his teacher and fellow wizard. 'Always be wary of any offer Alexander makes, he never enters a bargain that does not benefit him in a secondary secret way.'

The vampire looked to the band tapping his foot to the music as Vargas turned his chair toward him, to face him while they discussed. Alexander smiled inwardly; the wizard had shown his hand too early in asking so directly for the papyrus. He knew the mere mention of the scroll would drive the Spaniard out of his hiding spot in Florida, but to be this straightforward about it so fast gave the vampire an edge in the discussion and it was time to put that edge to the test.

Why won't he look at me? What...was this some sort of a negotiating tactic the Ancient One was using? Vargas exhaled ready to ask one more time about the scroll, he had flown here from St. Augustine on the smallest of chances the offer was real. If this was a hoax-

A single finger tapped the table top drawing the wizard's eyes down to the where the noise had come from. A smartphone sat perfectly in the center of the wood top and on the screen was a picture. Vargas slowly reached out and took the phone in his fingers with a stilled breath as his eyes had subtly deciphered the three words in the image. He stared at the words knowing exactly what each meant even though the phrasing matched no worldly dialect. It was a name, an old name lost to time before the Persian Empire fell but Vargas knew the writing was an exact match to a known Jahangir notation on a parchment he had at his home in Florida. The scroll was true. It had to be Vargas thought. This couldn't be a joke or some fraud, not with this image.

"Give the screen a swipe. There is another image you might find more convincing."

More convincing, Ferdinand wanted to say he didn't need any more evidence this was the true work of the magus Jahangir, but he kept quiet as he swiped the screen. The images changed with a swish and there in the second picture another name appeared in the same handwriting with the same strange word and symbols. If it was hard to breathe before it was damn near impossible now with what he was looking at. Above the music the band was playing, a tune by Bob Seger, Alexander's words floated and barely broke through the near catatonic state of the wizard.

"Akhenaton's name appears several times in the scroll I have been told. It seems the old Pharaoh left some very important paper lying around in the open and a man with a fast hand was able to write down some of the steps one would need to become a Lich of all things."

When the Spaniard looked up the vampire was still paying more attention to the band than he was to the discussion and at any other time that would have set Vargas and his temper ablaze, but the scroll was real and that was all that mattered right now. He had to have it, above anything else he had to have the scroll. "What do you want for the papyrus?"

"The actual scroll is not for sale or any kind of bartering Ferdinand, but the part you wish to see the most can be yours for a song as they say." Alexander answered still watching the band play.

The wizard chewed on his bottom lip just a little then spoke, "I want the whole scroll or we have no agreement."

"Then that is too bad my friend, I am sorry to have wasted your time. Have a nice trip back to your abode in Florida." Alexander promptly stated, calmly never once looking to him.

Oh no, damn it, wait Vargas thought as he began to scramble. "Now wait a moment Ancient One,"

"No, it is obvious you want the entire scroll and that is a shame because I know my man told your man that the 'contents' of the scroll would be yours for the completion of a job, not the whole scroll but just what is written down on it."

"Please Alexander, we can come to an arrangement I am sure," The wizard said quickly with an obvious air of agitation. Damn it he was so close to obtaining one of the greatest magical conjurations ever and he was about to lose it.

"Four static high resolution pictures made from the scroll are all I am willing to barter with wizard, all the magical knowledge you can get from those images will be yours upon the successful completion of a single labor is my offer."

The band slipped into a tune by Buckcherry belting out the mean guitar riffs of 'Crazy Bitch' sending the crowd into its own crazed fueled fervor. Vargas looked down at the images again then back to the vampire who had now turned to face him grinning just a little. He set the phone back on the table and spoke calm. "And what does this job entail?"

"A simple retrieval of a single woman from a compound guarded by five men, a sorcerer like yourself, and a very menacing house cat in the mountains of Colorado," Alexander answered taking the phone back. He noticed the eyes of Vargas watching the images disappear with a cringe of pain.

"If it is so simple Ancient One then why come to me with this offer? And who is this woman, what makes her so valuable?" Ferdinand inquired still looking to where the phone disappeared.

Alexander shook his head, "I cannot leave the city yet and I need her removed from her present situation and here by tomorrow night."

"And she is?"

"The Duchess Svetlana Epova, from the House of Ivan,"

His right eyebrow slowly rose millimeter by millimeter over a couple of seconds as Vargas let the name just roll around in his head. "You want me to rescue a werewolf, when her own kind will not save her?"

"Yes, in exchange for what the scroll of Jahangir will tell you of the necessary steps to become a Lich. Tell me Ferdinand, are you ready to watch what you and Adnot had sought for so long simply walk away?" Alexander asked noting the wizard knew of the House of Ivan and its predicament at this time. When the wizard failed to respond he added just a little more to make sure the man couldn't let go of the deal. "How many dank and dusty old halls have you looked through Vargas for the scroll? Better yet, how many times have you taken the Elixir est adiciet vitam? There is only so long the potion will work to extend your age and you're what now, 109? Even though you look not a day over 40, I'm afraid time is not on your side Ferdinand and here is what you seek, right here at your fingertips."

The last was the final push needed as Vargas nodded and spoke. "I will get the Duchess in exchange for the images, but what if she is dead by the time my men get to her?"

"She will be hurt I am sure but not dead. Her death would bring Akhenaton more trouble than he needs at the moment." The vampire responded knowing from the silence the wizard was turning the offer over and over in his head before speaking. The band finished up their set and began to step down off the stage as the DJ began to take over and spin records.

"Then I agree. I know of some men in Colorado, men who can be trusted to take care of this. They will deliver the Duchess to you tomorrow night as you have asked."

"Good, the images will be delivered by a courier to your abode in Florida ten minutes after Svetlana is back safely here in my sight. Is that acceptable Ferdinand?"

"Yes, that is acceptable."

The waitress walked over and smiled at Vargas speaking in a sweet Southern accent. "You need anything else honey?"

"No thank you, but my frie-"

The seat Alexander had been sitting in was empty now, his presence and the images on the phone gone into the crowd. The waitress looked around in a complete 360 before looking down to Vargas. "Wasn't there a cute fella sitting here a moment ago?"

"Yes...there was."

"Well, I know this is kind of weird and everything, but you wouldn't happen to have his number would you?"

Again Vargas just turned with his one eyebrow rising slowly as he looked to the waitress.

Chapter Seven

"What do you mean they found something weird with the samples?"

Otz had been enjoying his hamburger and fries while sitting in the booth at The Vortex, a bar and grill in downtown Atlanta famous for its food and atmosphere, a very eclectic and sometimes eccentric taste. From the kooky decor to the policy establishing the bar and grill as an 'Official Idiot Free Zone' The Vortex called out to the difference in people courting them to come in, sit down, and enjoy. Renfroe had seen all types in here, from the ultra-swanky to the anarchistic punk to those few who lived about a mile out past the fringe of what society called 'normal'. He once ran into a Transvestite at the bar who looked so much like Natalie Woods it was scary and a little amative back there behind the 'Male' curtains of Renfroe's psyche. If Natalie's real name hadn't been Charles then there's no telling where he might have ended up that night and if truth be told he kind of liked all the attention Natalie's/Charles flirting gave him. Still, the main reason Otz came here was the burgers, those unbelievably 'nasty' combinations and concoctions that once you had one bite you were never going back to eating a flame broiled anything at whatever King. At present he was killing a 'Rebel Outlaw', a half-pound patty covered in pulled pork and topped with a non-healthy chunk of cheddar cheese and bacon and teriyaki sauce. Oh, and don't forget the tater-tots, a grand heap of deep fried tater-tots just finished off the burger. Yes, this was a special place to Renfroe, as was the food, but that was before Foster took a call and told him the lab had found a small abnormality with some results from the crime scene.

"I had the tech call me first with anything he found and not to put anything down on paper till I approved it. He said he found trace DNA around the chest wound of the second male...its Lupine in nature but modified." The assistant coroner whispered after swallowing a half-eaten tater-tot. The large man's reaction to the call was about the same as Foster was having from hearing the information at the moment, a little short of crazy confused.

"Lupine, as in 'Wolf', that kind of lupine you mean?" Renfroe asked with squinted eyes.

Foster nodded while picking up a tot and eating it absently before speaking, "that makes no sense though. The wound was too large for a wolf's maw."

"Nothing is making sense on the here-and-now level of this Foster. It's why I went to see Adria, because this whole thing is swimming in the pond called 'Supernatural'." Renfroe stated just a second before taking a large bite of his burger.

The assistant coroner nodded again then spoke with a very careful sense of trepidation. "And what did your mother say about the guy with the black hair?"

"She said there's more than one," the detective answered giving no outward sign Foster had crossed some line by mentioning Adria as his mother, "a family of four...like a pack."

"Four...as in more than one...as in a pack of wolves," Foster exhaled fighting to keep his tater-tots down.

Renfroe saw the assistant coroner about to pass out and smiled. "Keep it together there Foster. You're doing pretty good so far, just hold in your guts a little longer."

"Yeah," the skinny man smiled for the first time since walking into the bar and grill, "I am doing pretty good huh?"

The detective laughed and shook his head swallowing the monster bite he had chewing on for the past minute. "Don't let that go to your head now, and don't go telling anyone I said it either or I'll beat you down."

"Oh no, of course not, got to keep that level of professionalism between departments and all you know." Foster chuckled just as he began to dig into the plate of what the grill affectionately called the 'Hot Southern Mess'. It was a nice sized fried chicken breast topped with a generous fried egg and bacon and all covered with thick sausage gravy while sitting on a pile of Texas Toast. The Vortex labeled it a sandwich on the menu but Foster just called it good eating...a lot of good eating.

The detective gave a small laugh too then shook his head taking a deep breath, preparing to go where he really didn't want to with the conversation. "What do you know about Werewolves Foster?"

"The Lon Chaney kind or the Twilight version?" He asked back quickly. When the table was silent for a minute he finally looked up from his plate slow, cringing just a little as he saw the stunned look on the detective's face.

"You read the Twilight books?"

"Nooo," Foster whispered swallowing, "I was bored one Saturday night and there was nothing on TV sooooo...it just sort of popped up on my screen. I don't even remember most of it man."

"Yeah, who was the kid who played the werewolf?"

"Taylor Lautner...or some name like that...like I said I can barely remember any of it." Foster coughed with a wave of his hand trying to move the conversation along.

"Uh-huh," Renfroe laughed shaking his head then continuing on. "Well the real thing isn't like either of those I'm starting to think. You said it was a bear that killed that second male and you were pretty damn close with the call Foster. If we run into one of them again just head for the door and don't look back."

"No silver bullet through the heart?" Foster asked pointing to his chest with his fork in a stabbing motion.

Renfroe shook his head, "just a story someone made up and you saw what shooting did to the guy in the club, a whole lot of nothing. I think the wolves are just like our boy, maybe not as tough but damn near."

"Ok, but why is a pack of...werewolves here in town? And how do you know so much about them?"

"Let's just say I've done some reading, and our experiences along with your lab test put a nice glop of icing on the cake. I'm just guessing here, but my thinking is those two from the club have two others running round town and all four are looking for someone."

"Looking for someone?" Foster asked. He was kind of amazed and pleased with himself, being that he had readily accepted the fact there are Werewolves in the world. It was kind of new and different for him, Foster being a scientist and all, like having sex with a beautiful stripper.

"Yeah, those two didn't go to the club to stop Eight Ball's crew or attack Ray. Those two were waiting on someone to show up. Adria said we ended up in the middle of some blood feud and it has to involve this pack of four and our boy." Renfroe explained while wiping his mouth.

"Yeah, I buy that, and it was our boy they were waiting for...the guy in black we saw in the kitchen." Foster added taking another bit of his dinner.

Otz pointed a finger and smiled, "that's what I was thinking too and when he disappeared guess who went with him?"

Foster looked up from his plate and nodded, "your friend Leland."

"You know what Foster. We need to pay a visit to Lee and Stephanie tomorrow night." Otz winked.

"Sure thing, but why wait till tomorrow night?"

"Internal Affairs is still hanging around, just not as tight. If we wait a day then we can move a little easier around town." Renfroe smiled getting ready to take another bit of his delicious burger when he froze. He watched as Foster cut into the mess of food on his plate and shoveled in a big bite before smiling. "How can you eat all of that? It's like a heart attack on a plate; do we even know if they have a defibrillator in the building?"

The coroner swallowed then pointed with his fork at Otz's sandwich while laughing. "And what about that monstrosity in your hands, it's got to be close to the fat and calorie intake a normal human would need over three months. You're getting it all of it in one shot!"

"Yeah, but I'll burn mine off later in the Gym."

"Uh-huh, and I'll burn mine off later with Toni. You know she can do this thing where she bends backwards while-"Foster smiled while bending his head and neck backwards over the seat.

Renfroe just started waving his hands crying out with a laugh trying to stop the coroner from going any farther. "Aw come on man, stop, stop, that's too much information Foster! I have to look at this girl later with a straight face for crying out loud!"

Chapter Eight

They sat on the bench together out under the light of the moon and the few working street lights waiting patiently. Wilma huddled in her large purple jacket holding the cold of the winter night back while next to her Yelena sat in just a large sweater and a t-shirt Stephanie had given her. Obviously she was like Alexander, oblivious to the weather, but where the vampire was dead so he wasn't affected by the cold she was alive so Yelena should feel something, right? Wilma looked over getting ready to ask just that very question to the werewolf when she noticed her friend was a bundle of nerves sitting there waiting for Alexander. Her fingers kept tapping together between her hands which were bouncing in her lap

"Are you all right?" She asked pulling Yelena out of some place her mind had retreated to.

The Russian just smiled and nodded coming back to reality calmly, "Da, I am fine Wilma."

"No you're not. You're nervous about Alexander."

"And how can you tell that?" Yelena smiled for the first time since both had walked out to the bench.

Wilma turned her body to face her and smiled warmly as well, "you're somewhere that's not here for one and second you've been rubbing your hands together like crazy and I don't think it's because you're cold."

"Ah Wilma, you are very perceptive. You would be a very good werewolf." Yelena smiled a little wider.

"Yeah but you have to be born a werewolf and I'm just plain old Wilma Jackson," the little girl said with an exasperated sigh looking away to the shadows. Yelena sighed too remembering how they had spent the afternoon after she woke from her nap. Little Wilma had asked if she wanted to play chess and Yelena had agreed thinking her prowess at the game would surpass the girl easily. She could beat all three of her brothers and her mother with ease so Yelena had decided to play Wilma with a gentle hand, let her take a few pieces before striking. It was a mistake the Russian quickly learned as Wilma backed her into a corner so fast there was no choice but to give up her queen. That's when the girl smiled, held up a book on advanced chess maneuverers that looked like it have been looked through just short of a billion times, and giggled. Oh how could this child think so low of her uniqueness?

"You are special Wilma. Please never think that you are not." Yelena offered trying as hard as she knew to be compassionate. She hadn't been too sympathetic with humans in her past, practically never she remembered, but with Wilma the werewolf felt different. Yelena wasn't sure if she should pat Wilma's shoulder or not, is that what humans do? Is it like she is with her brothers?

"My mom says the same thing all the time. I don't know...I've never felt special. So listen, when Alexander gets here I'll do the talking, okay?" Wilma sighed again looking to her with a weak smile and nod.

She wants to change the subject Yelena thought and with grace she let the conversation stir in another direction. The Russian only nodded and smiled before speaking. "I hope you can change the Ancient One's mind Wilma, but I am not sure even your pleas can after what I have done."

Wilma was about to say there was always a chance to say you're sorry and the sooner the better when a familiar voice suddenly spoke over Yelena's shoulder. "We will just have to hear what our little Wilma offers then, want we Yelena?"

Both the girls jumped a little and yelped as the vampire seemed to appear right out of the ethos next to them. As they gained some composure Alexander only smiled and sat down next to Wilma with Yelena next to her. Somewhere out in the dark the loud screech of a car's tires losing its grip to the pavement wailed through the night. Someone is in a hurry the vampire thought as Wilma looked at him with a stern expression.

"Leland was right, you like doing that too much."

"It is quite addictive, seeing one almost jump out of their skin." Alexander winked with a small chuckle.

Yelena sat quietly smiling at the Ancient One wondering why the vampire was in a light hearted mood, hoping this would help with garnering his help again. He was literally the last hope she knew of for her brothers and mother. There was still no sign of the Great Wolf Ivan anywhere in the world and without him or Victor or Iskra she could expect to receive little help from the other packs scattered across the land. No, she was on her own facing a daunting task of getting her family back from Akhenaton and his undead horde.

"Yeah, I bet it is." Wilma giggled sitting back on the bench getting quiet all of the sudden. Both Alexander and Yelena looked to her then to each other then back trying to figure out what the girl was doing now. The vampire squinted with his eyes looking at Wilma with mock suspicion before turning to the werewolf.

"I think she wants you to start."

"She does?" Yelena asked surprised looking to Wilma too before turning Alexander taking a breath in and starting. "I am sorry Ancient one for acting like I did with you last night. You asked for my trust and I could not give it you. I would ask for another chance, for my brothers and my mother. Please help us, there is no one else?"

The bench was quiet again as the vampire only looked to the werewolf with a cold stare for a very long minute. Yelena took a shaky breath wondering what the Ancient One was thinking on so much and it didn't help that it seemed Wilma had left her alone suddenly to do the job. She began to rub her hands together again nervously when Alexander leaned in and whispered to Wilma. "What do you think I should do?"

"Are you asking me as if I was a 2300-year-old vampire if I would come to the aid of a werewolf who had asked for my help?" Wilma inquired in return turning to look at Yelena with a comical attempt at a raised eyebrow. She just ended up looking like she was having a stroke and Yelena actually had to hold her laughter in.

"Most certainly, if you were a 2300-year-old vampire who had been asked by a werewolf for help would you do so? And remember, said werewolf has family that had tried to kill you." The vampire answered and before Wilma could continue the discussion Yelena held up her hand interjecting a quick point.

"But what if the werewolves had been tricked to attack the vampire and the only werewolf able to escape was very sorry for doing such a terrible act."

"Oh yeah," Wilma said turning to Alexander with a nod, "that is a valid point and it does explain why the werewolf acted so crazy."

"Yes it does, beautiful and intelligent this werewolf is." Alexander sighed with mock frustration while looking at Wilma with a small smile. From the corner of his eye the vampire noticed Yelena was starting to blush just a little from the compliment.

"So, if it were me with all the stated conditions...I'd have to say I would help the werewolf." Wilma smiled with a large nod of her head.

"You would?" Yelena whispered just a touch before Alexander spoke.

"I have to agree with you Wilma. I would, and will, help this werewolf save her family."

With both looking at her Yelena felt a little overwhelmed, all the anxiety up to this point which built to a nauseating crescendo in her stomach disappeared. She fought to hold back a tear and only nodded whispering. "Thank you both."

The bench was quiet one last time as all three remained quiet, then Wilma looked at her watch and gasped. "I have to go. It's our first movie night."

"Movie night?" Alexander asked watching the little girl stand.

"Yeah, Leland is bringing over a DVD player and we're going to watch Star Wars!" Wilma exclaimed happily.

The vampire smiled warmly thinking his friend was beginning to enjoy having a male presence around. It was confirmed a second later when Wilma whispered. "It's kind of nice to have a father even though he's not my real one."

"And there is no one who deserves a father as loyal as Leland then you little one." Alexander nodded making Wilma blush and smile a little wider.

She leaned in and hugged the vampire quickly then turned to Yelena and smiled. "I told you he'd help, and see, you never even needed my assistance."

"Yes you did Wilma," the werewolf smiled just as Wilma hugged her around her neck. Then Wilma turned and ran back to her window and climbed in with only one look back and a wave to her friends on the bench.

A warm smile was on Yelena's face as she watched the little one leave, then she turned back to see Alexander staring at her. His dark eyes blinked once as he spoke. "What happened with you brothers and Michaels?"

"He has taken control of their bodies Ancient One with the ghouls help, all three are no longer my brothers...they are...Akhenaton's now."

He could see the pain in her eyes, the potential loss of her brothers and mother crushing her spirit. Alexander looked out into the dark of the courtyard for a moment then back to see Yelena had also turned her attention back out into the dark with him. He wasn't sure why he did what he did next, maybe it was the same feeling that overtook him the first night he saved Wilma from the pair of thugs that had followed her. Whatever it was he was suddenly standing by her holding out his hand for the werewolf to take. "Come, there is a better place to talk."

She offered no resistance to the overture and simply took his hand and stood to follow. Alexander led her away from the bench and into the dark where he guided her to his parked car back in a safe spot. He opened the passenger door and let her sit before closing the door then moved with a blink and entered the driver's side. The Chevelle started with a deep throaty rumble and the vampire gave it quick pump of the gas just a second prior to putting the transmission in 'Drive'. The car sped out and away from the Laurel with both occupants quiet, neither speaking nor needing to. Alexander drove them to the main strip in Buckhead parking the Chevelle in a small garage away from the throng of people. Yelena climbed out of the seat and then followed the vampire as he led them again through people on the sidewalk to a small dark building tucked away in a corner on a soft turn. The lights were out, it was empty Yelena noted from the sign that offered the establishment for Rent which hung on the front door. The vampire stopped on the sidewalk for a moment then looked right and headed for a wooden fence and a second sign about renting the building. Yelena followed along wondering what the Ancient One was doing and when he looked back at her it wasn't to talk but to check the sidewalk they had just walked down. She looked back and noted no one was around them now, not a soul, and that's when Alexander finally spoke.

"I need to put my arm around your waist, may I?"

The werewolf nodded and then his arm was around her pulling her to him with a snug but not overpowering hug. Yelena gave a small gasp as she felt the ground suddenly fall away beneath her feet and her body gently floated upwards into the night air on invisible wings. The pair ascended in perfect silence to the roof where with a small step Alexander bore them to the large open space that was bare of everything with the exception of a small structure with a door, roof access Yelena surmised. She looked around and there was nothing else except for some crates stacked up by the front façade, a good observation post she thought as the vampire let her go and waved her to the exact spot with his hand. Yelena smiled and followed his lead walking over in quiet and sitting, turning to her right just in time to catch the vampire appearing next to her. It had taken some time to get used to but the 'sudden' appearances weren't so startling anymore Yelena told herself as Alexander looked down on the street below watching the comings and goings of the people below with great interest.

They sat in silence again for a moment with just their knees touching observing the flow of the night just a few feet below them from the dark when Alexander asked a question. "What happened to your father? Why hasn't he tried to help find your mother?"

"Our father is dead Ancient One, killed when he returned to the motherland on a task for our family. It was more than eighty years ago."

"And no one knows what happened to him?"

Yelena gave a small shake of her head while looking down on the street. "Da, all we were told is he is dead. My mother was devastated, so much so I was afraid she would not carry on but she did and she will after I find her. We are Epova and we are strong."

It was the way of the wolf, to survive and live on with an unmatched strength Alexander thought and as he looked to the young one by his side he could see Yelena was very fierce. "Was there no one to help when Svetlana was taken?"

She shook her head as she finally turned back to him and spoke. "There was only Victor, an elder and close friend to my mother, and the other elder Iskra. When he discovered I was going to work with Akhenaton to get our mother back he counseled me viciously against trusting the Lich, that I was being fooled into something deeper and darker. He told me to stay away but..."

"You would do anything to save your mother?"

"Da," Yelena sighed letting the roof slip into silence again. She looked at Alexander and wondered what he was thinking, was he truly going to help her, but then he was asking another question taking her thoughts away from her situation.

"Is Victor involved in your mother's abduction do you think? Is he the next to take over in Ivan's House?"

"He is one of three elders who are under Ivan including our mother. He only has one daughter who came with him when he joined Ivan and his House forty years ago so no, he is not the one to take control if it comes to that. He and mother grew close after we joined with Ivan. I was happy for her because she looked happy. When she was taken Victor disappeared as well which made me suspicious of him at first...but then he would never do anything to hurt our mother."

"And Iskra?"

Yelena shook her head grinning, "No, she is too sweet to do such a thing. I am close with her daughter and my brothers close to her son. She could not take control of Ivan's House either. Only our mother has the numbers to take control, or she did have until she was taken."

"So there are no others allied with Ivan the Great Wolf, but why only three Elders?"

She looked up to the sky taking a deep breath before answering Alexander. "Ivan will take no others into his pack, no other outsiders. He trusts very little and very hard when it comes to others."

The vampire nodded and thought it sounded very much like his outlook only a few days ago then continued asking questions. "What has happened to Ivan? I have tried to sense his presence in the world but he seems to be hidden or covered."

"We do not know where he is. Ivan left one night five years ago on some task only he had knowledge of with one of his sons and told us to follow the orders of our mother, Victor, and the other she-wolf Iskra. No one knew where Ivan went or what he was going to do. We needed him my brothers and I when mother was taken but we were suddenly alone with no Victor and no Iskra to seek help from. We could not request help from the other packs, the ones not allied with Akhenaton without our elders help."

"And Ivan, he is still not under the hand of Akhenaton?"

She nodded quickly answering him, "He would never ally with the Grand Lich. The Great Wolf had no alliance with any Undead before he went missing, which is why Victor was so mad with me. He was right though Ancient One, I made a bigger mess of this and now my brothers are in danger."

"I think you did what any daughter would do if their mother was taken and the only option to getting her back safely was dancing with a snake. To say that you made a bigger mess of a situation that was already a tragedy is wrong Yelena, it's a foolish thought."

Yelena nodded blushing slightly again from the vampire's words as Alexander sat quietly looking out over the street one more time before turning back. "So all of your elders have disappeared?"

"Da, we could find no one to help us...no one but you Ancient One."

"And you don't see that as...strange?"

"It is very strange," Yelena reacted with an exasperated gasp, "yet it made sense when Akhenaton told us our mother had been taken by a group of treacherous Nosferatu. The House of Ivan was under attack so everyone went into hiding."

"Ah," Alexander smiled with a chuckle, "that old terrible name 'Nosferatu', one which I am sure you have called me secretly several times. I use to laugh when I was called the 'Diseased One' by the gypsies."

The werewolf sighed and shook, "something else I must be sorry for, judging you wrong Alexander."

"No Yelena that is something you do not have to feel apologetic for. I was too slow to realize what Akhenaton was up to using you and your brothers."

"He wanted you to kill us so he could use our deaths to force the other packs he cannot control to look favorably at him. He could say you were a killer of innocent wolf pups and that he was the only one that could give all a safe place for those in need of protection." Yelena explained shaking her head with disdain

"Yes, it was a nice idea though it had one flaw." The vampire stated with a small smile.

"And that would be?" She inquired with a small smile of her own.

"I had to kill you and your brothers, which is something I was not going to do."

The werewolf only sighed feeling warmth grow in her heart, "and for that I am very thankful Ancient One."

The pair sat for a few more moments watching nightlife below them pass by without anyone sensing their presence just overhead. Then Alexander rose from the crates standing up and offering his hand to Yelena once again and when she looked at him confused he grinned a little and nodded. "It is time to go and see a movie?"

"A movie?"

"Yes, I have not had the chance to see a movie in a theater yet and Simon was able to persuade a man to let me have the whole place to ourselves. Have you had popcorn?"

The werewolf giggled and nodded with an astonished look, "Da, though I do not like it much."

"Really, how about Goobers, do you like those?" The vampire asked as she stood and looked even more flabbergasted by the question.

"What is a 'Goober'?" Yelena whispered with a shake of her head.

Alexander only shook his head too and whispered like some small child. "I have no idea, but if you try one with me I might chance a taste."

Another giggle went through Yelena, something she rarely ever let happen if she could help it, and then nodded. Then the two left the roof of the building and made their way to a small movie theater located just downtown where Alexander and Yelena spent the rest of the evening. The owner met them at the rear entrance and let the pair into the semi dark building. With the dark hiding most of their features Alexander and Yelena let the man show them to the concessions counter where they tried a 'Goober' and instantly decided a chocolate covered peanut was very good but not what either wanted. Yelena took a small bucket of popcorn and then followed the owner with Alexander at her side to an empty theater. He told them go on down and sit anywhere, he'd get the projector going and then leave them to watch.

The vampire nodded thanking the man then let his companion chose where she wanted to sit in the massive room, complete with stadium seating you know. It reminded Alexander of the

Coliseum in Rome and for a moment the long forgotten memory of the old place came back. He could almost hear the crowd shout and scream for blood again on those long summer nights as Gladiators fought on the sand floor below. He wondered just how close this day and age was to the Romans, how the people of this age screamed for blood just as loud but with different 'sports' as they called the competitions. It really doesn't matter he decided, screaming for blood and death in one age was still desiring blood and death in another.

They sat in the middle and as he sat Yelena put a piece of popcorn in his mouth taking him by surprise for a moment before chewing. He no longer processed food, his internal organs no longer functioning in that way if one thought about it. Still, the popcorn wasn't to awful tasting and with a move so fast the werewolf never detected it he spit the chewed puffed kernel into his hand before dropping it onto the floor. The same move worked just as well with the Goober back at the concession stand.

The movie was based on one of the Tolkien novels, the one called 'The Hobbit' and even though Yelena told him it was the second movie of the series Alexander was lost as to how the movie makers got three pictures out of one book. The movie was amazing he thought with a grin, simply amazing, and the Dragon Smaug was truly a horrible spectacle...it reminded him of Akhenaton in a weird sort of way what with the whole growling 'I am Death' speech at the end. When the movie was done he let Yelena lead them from the room where the owner let them out. The vampire gave him a small nod and a few minutes later the two had found their way back to the Chevelle. He drove Yelena back to the Laurel and escorted her back to Stephanie where the single mother let her in quietly. The werewolf turned and gave one last nod to the vampire as did Stephanie and Alexander only nodded back with a smile to both before making sure the door was secure for the night. Then he crossed the courtyard in a blink and was through the walls of Martha's home without stopping, his ghostly body floating through the material with ease.

It was only when he was in his room, now emptied of all of his things with the exception of a lone book, that he let his mind begin to work again on what was too happen on the morrow. It was Darius again, in a way. He had to let them take Wilma but then he had to be quick enough to retrieve her. He hadn't been fast enough on the plain that day when the men took the Persian King and killed him.

Alexander would not let Wilma suffer the same fate.

Chapter Nine

The day had come and gone...it was finally here...the night of reckoning...

Grammy sat in her old worn out chair slowly running her wrinkled, weathered fingers over a picture of her late husband Jefferson Davis. It had become her nightly ritual of late, the night before this one and the one before that and the one before, to hold him and let her mind float lazily on the gossamer wings of sweet dreams. Tonight though it would all come to a blessed end because Martha 'Grammy' Louis was going home to be with her Jefferson and that brought a sweet smile to her face, oh how it did.

Even though years ago she had lost the ability to look at the photo physically, she could still remember everything about it. More to the point, she could remember everything about Jefferson himself. The way his legs bowed when he walked along side of her all those years ago when they were courting. The smile just before he began that low sounding chuckle, that handsome smile where only the left side of his mouth would move. The smell he carried on those long days he sweated hard from work, the aroma of his manhood would drive her crazy in that secretive womanly way. The night's where she could feel his body lying next to hers, his chest slowly rising and falling in a wondrous rhythm. Jefferson had stolen her heart for all eternity and the day he died, before they wheeled into the operating room to try and save his life, he had promised to wait for her on the other side. He would take her hand when she came home he whispered with one last breath and they could go on a long walk through the clouds of the great kingdom of the Lord.

Outside in the cold of the night the sound of gun fire ripped through the night suddenly.

They had come finally, men allied with the ones who brought the drugs here to the Laurel and men from that 'Prominent' family in New York looking to take over these grounds which were so rich in drug money, waiting for the hands on the clock to just touch fifteen minutes past the Eleventh hour. Alexander watched from the shadows as he always did now and would, gazed and noted where the men were setting up getting ready to fight. At first the men from the ones who ran the drugs here in the Laurel took up a defensive posture forming into small circles at the corners of the buildings waiting for the attackers to show. It might work the vampire thought as he scanned the landscape noting where the attackers were lining up ready to pour in like an army of ants and where the defenders would make their stands. This attempt by the men who ran the Laurel to hold back the coming tide of aggressors would only work if the men defending were willing to die for this land and if some of these defenders who called this hell a home were willing to bleed for it. It didn't matter Alexander told himself, it was all going to burn tonight no matter which side won.

He turned his attention then to the home of Stephanie and Wilma and now the abode of the Yelena the Werewolf. The vampire eyed the front door noting Leland had left thirty minutes ago to attend to some personal business maybe, or it could have been some local gang member requesting a counsel, whatever the reason one of the two Alexander needed out of the home was gone. Then Alexander saw Yelena stealing away the building, from little Wilma's window moving through the shadows of the night like a ghost. Not a single human saw her or detected her as she used her stealth with such an expertise it rendered her invisible to any and all but him tonight. As she disappeared away from the projects Alexander pushed back the guilt trying to claw its way into his soul. Yes, he had arranged a call which would make Yelena leave Stephanie's home, but it was required and necessary. No one could be home to protect Wilma or her mother. No one could chance a rescue just yet. And as he turned back to the front door staring at it four men ran right by him on their way to attack the Laurel. Not a soul noticed or sensed his presence as Alexander exhaled low. The sound of gunfire erupted loudly across the courtyard and somewhere deeper in the buildings of the Laurel.

It would be soon now...he had to quicker than he was when Darius fled he told himself.

He had to be...

The sounds from the war for the turf known as the Laurel raged all around Renfroe and Foster as they waited in Leland's living room. All those years on the police force had taught the detective some, well mostly law abiding, tricks like picking locks on deadbolts and such. A scream let out followed by several shots from a semi-automatic pistol, 9mm it sounded like to Renfroe. Foster drummed his fingers on the arm of the couch he sat on trying to hide the fact that he really didn't want to be here.

"You nervous?" Renfroe asked as more gunshots rang out. He stepped away from the window just in case a bullet went somewhere it wasn't supposed to, closer to the door.

"Gee, does it show? Yeah I'm a little nervous. We just committed a crime in the middle of a riot!" Foster whined.

"Don't worry," Renfroe commented checking his watch as he stood in the entryway, "Lee isn't the kind of man to press charges. And if you haven't noticed we've been committing a crime the moment we decided to not tell anyone about our boy."

"Yeah, will breaking the law isn't as bad as getting shot. I hope Leland isn't the kind of man to shoot first and ask questions later if you know what I mean." Foster said shaking his head.

Renfroe was about to retort when more gunfire erupted and the front door that he had skillfully picked just twenty minutes ago opened. Leland stepped into his apartment quickly and looked up into the broad chest of Renfroe with Foster trying to hide on the couch behind him. "I thought I paid that parking ticket." he stated with a laugh.

"I'm here on personal business Lee." Renfroe remarked coldly.

"Oh, okay. So, what's so important that you had to commit breaking and entering, not that I mind and all?" Lee asked suspiciously.

"Who's the guy dressed in black Lee?" Renfroe asked directly.

"You mean the guy at Ray's the other night?" Leland asked feigning ignorance.

"The thing that saved me from the rather large Russian gent who wanted to tear me limb from limb, that one." Renfroe pointed out.

"That thing...right?" Leland said with a shrug.

"You remember," Foster suddenly piped in, "he was the guy who walked out of the crack house explosion."

"Explosion, you mean that placed exploded?" Leland gasped, almost laughing while making no sense at all. He was trying like the devil to get his story straight.

Renfroe stepped in closer, his body making the statement that this conversation just turned serious. There was no more room for jokes or passing off the question, "The man in the kitchen at the club, who is he Lee?"

Leland stood in silence, his mind fighting with his heart. On one end he didn't want to give away Alexander, the man had become somewhat of a friend to him over the last few nights. However, on the other end, he had to answer Renfroe's question truthfully, the man was his friend and he had to respect that. A second or two passed before Leland sighed heavily and spoke. "He showed up a week ago, just out of the blue. His name is Alexander and I have no idea what he is but I am sure it is not of this world."

"Why is Alexander here?" Renfroe asked.

"He's protecting Stephanie's little girl, Wilma." Leland answered.

"And he killed the two drug dealers and destroyed the crack house?" Renfroe asked quickly.

"Yeah, that was him." Leland answered in a whisper

"Where is he Lee? I need to talk to him ASAP." Renfroe asked.

"I don't know, he said something about making a visit on an old friend. I went out to check on a kid I've been trying to work with. He hasn't checked in with me in a couple of days and I got worried so I stopped by a few places I know he'd hang out at." Leland said shrugging his shoulders.

"Where did you see him last?" Foster asked from the back

"Who, Alexander or my kid?"

Renfroe sighed and cocked his head to the right, "Who do you think?"

"Yeah, right, I don't know for sure and we haven't talked since we found out who the drug supplier for the Laurel is." Leland responded.

"You know who the supplier here is in the Laurel?" Foster asked quickly.

"Lloyd Dunbar," Renfroe answered for the street preacher going back to stand by the couch, "The Narcotics division has known for months."

"What?" Foster and Leland said at the same time.

"Wow that was a neat trick. You two sounded just like the backup singers for American Idol or something." Renfroe chuckled with an uncharacteristic joke.

Leland stormed forward, almost getting in Renfroe's face. "You mean the police know who's bringing that shit in and haven't done a thing about it!"

"Got to have a case to prosecute first preach. Dunbar's got some built in walls between him and the drugs. In addition, he has some heavy protection from the Cartels by way of Rico Hierra. The man's almost untouchable Lee." Renfroe remarked coolly.

"You know the whole damn crew?" Leland screamed.

"Hey," Foster said popping in, "just think of all the trouble you could have saved if you just would have gone to Renfroe here first and asked."

"You know," Leland, said eyeing Foster now instead Renfroe, "If this was a white problem happening in a white neighborhood, all this would have been solved in five minutes."

The street preacher stormed out of the room into his kitchen intent on leaving Renfroe by himself in the living room, only the detective had other ideas though. Renfroe was right behind him as Leland reached in the fridge for a soda. "You think this is a black and white issue! Man, white neighborhoods got it just as bad as the projects. I watch white kids getting arrested every day for the same drug offenses as black kids!"

"Yeah," Leland shot back quickly, 'but you don't see those kids on the six o'clock news every night do you? You don't see a lot of white kids in jail because they can get lawyers to get them probation when black kids get nothing but some worn out public defender who just wants to go home!"

"I don't control the News Lee and I don't control the lawyers. All I know is this drug problem isn't biased. It kills all kids of all colors and we're all responsible if we want to stop it." Renfroe spoke calmly, trying to get Leland to follow suit. It was going to help no one if this all came to blows right about now.

"Yeah, I know man." Leland started to say calming down as well. Then suddenly the world exploded in a hail of gunfire just as Foster dived into the kitchen scrambling for cover. Leland and Renfroe, both veterans of gunfights, instantly dropped to the ground behind the sturdy kitchen cabinets. Renfroe drew his forty-five while glimpsing out of the doorway into the living room. Two men wielding machine guns stood just inside what used to be the front window, another two stood just outside the broken window frame holding identical machine guns.

"Four men with guns," Renfroe whispered to Leland, "sure wish I knew where your friend Alexander was. We could use him right now."

"You and me both man, you and me both." Leland whispered back. Glass crunched under a boot, the men were approaching the kitchen. Off in the distance a barrage of gunfire broke through the night and Leland knew what was going down now. It was an assault, Dunbar and Hierra were taking the neighborhood back by force and somehow they had targeted him. For whatever reason, he knew something was wrong with Stephanie and Wilma. He knew they were in a whole lot of trouble. He had to get to them, yet he was trapped himself. More broken glass crunched as the men were just outside the window stepped in following the other pair.

***

"I'll be seeing you soon Jefferson, you better keep that promise." Grammy whispered clutching the picture to her bosom.

The door to her rundown apartment suddenly flew off the hinges from a vicious kick. Two men charged in and leveled their machine guns on her, their barrels shining in the light thrown from the outside street lamps. Grammy only smiled, still clutching the picture of her Jefferson as the men opened fire with their guns. The apartment lit up with the bright yellow staccato flashes of gunpowder.

Wilma saw the flashes of the gunfire in Grammy's apartment as the large men pushed her headfirst into the Land Rover. Her mother screamed for her from a second car but Wilma wasn't worried. Somehow, someway Alexander would come for them both, he was her angel and he would set everything right.

Someone was going to get hurt real bad for doing this.

Stephanie had fought as hard as she could against the men invading her home scratching and clawing at their bare skin, but it mattered little. They had her hands tied with a plastic manacle after a struggle and then she was being dragged outside screaming for her Wilma and yet the little girl remained so very calm. Little Wilma barely protested as they shoved her headfirst into the SUV. Her mother still yelled and screamed for her as she was pushed into a second SUV in the lead of the one that held her daughter. Then both vehicles were gone, nothing but tail lights in the distance that faded in the dark.

Alexander had watched it all from his vantage point, the whole sickening scene played out for him even as he sensed a large presence, six beings in the dark across the street watching in shock and despair. The vampire knew exactly who it was. He didn't need a magical window or an actual visual sighting of the group to know who it was so he went back to his thoughts no longer worried about them.

Oh how hard was it to watch, to know he could stop the abduction as easily as he had stopped J-Rock that night and yet also understanding this was what had to be. Alexander's plan had worked to a synchronized perfection; Wilma was safe now as the Laurel began to burn. From a small single fire started in one building a conflagration was growing and glowing in the distance as it raced to devour everything it could. She was safe now the vampire told himself, safe and out of harm's way for now. Then he saw the flashes of gunfire from Martha's windows and closed his eyes.

His plan had worked so very, very well...almost too good Alexander thought silently as the rush to the end of it all began.

How in the world did one simple task of getting one vampire to kill four young werewolves become such a monumental task that it would have been easier to solve Global Warming? Michaels stood in the dark with his mouth agape watching the two SUV's drive away with the one person he had been instructed to kidnap. What...was their some kind of demand for the same little black girl? He could only stand there making small whimpering sounds as his brain locked from the sight of his target leaving. How...what...why did this happen? The ghoul Phlegm turned to him and growled some indecipherable words that made Michaels instantly gasp and turned toward.

"We are not informing Lord Akhenaton that we have not retrieved the little girl. Do you want him to burn us alive in a firestorm? Maybe tear our entrails out and dance on them?"

The three Epova brothers stood in a silent watch with stupefied looks, drool oozing from Peter's lips as the large Ghoul Woe added his grumbled retort to the discussion which seemed to have an immediate and thankfully happy reaction from the Lesser Lich. Michaels nodded excitedly and pointed back up into the dark of the shadows. "Yes, yes, back to the car. We have to catch those two SUV's and get the little black girl. Now hurry, hurry, or I swear I will burn all of you to nothing but ash!"

In a mass the group turned and headed back toward where a car had been parked in an abandoned alley. Oh please Michaels begged silently, please let them catch the vehicles and get the girl because if they couldn't...oh the pain would be unimaginable!

"Stephanie!" Leland screamed running through what was left of the front door of the Jackson's apartment. There was no answer and down deep inside the street preacher never really expected one, yet he still ran through the rooms screaming for Stephanie and Wilma both like a mad man. After a minute he returned to the living room where Renfroe and Foster stood watching in silence, the detective's forty-five sidearm smoking eerily in the wash of lights from the outside. Leland never knew how Renfroe got them out of the ambush at his apartment. The man had simply rushed into the room firing the whole clip from his gun. The apartment lit up yellow with the flash of gunpowder and Leland just knew Renfroe was dead, but then detective came around the corner and helped him off the kitchen floor. The four assassins were dead on his living room carpet and Renfroe didn't have a scratch on him except for a small graze on his left hand.

"They're gone, both Stephanie and Wilma!" Leland whispered in shock.

"We'll find them Lee, I give you my word." Renfroe stated looking to Foster.

"Who would take them?" Foster asked nervously.

Before either Leland or Renfroe could answer the assistant coroner a voice screamed from behind them causing all three to spin and look toward the doorway. "They are gone? Where? Who took them?"

"Dunbar," Renfroe answered as he looked at a striking image standing there in the entry way. She was just a little taller than

Foster with hair that was as white as pure driven snow and a pair of eye so blue it was like looking up into a cloudless sky. She was one of them, a werewolf, Renfroe told himself, knew it the second he looked at her. His mother Adria wasn't the only one with certain skills. He heard Foster next to him swallow hard struck just as numb by the beauty as the woman pushed past them to stand next to Leland with a worried look yet her voice was as strong as a piece of steel.

"This Dunbar, is he the same one from the Hotel the other night?"

"Why would he kidnap them?" Foster asked adding his question to the pot. The smell of smoke, already prominent from fires burning the other structures, started to grow and become overwhelming. Foster took a look down the hall and he could see the long dark tendrils of mist reaching out from the old walls of the apartment signaling the conflagration was ready to burn the building to the ground. He turned back to warn the others as more gun fire echoed outside in the projects. This whole place is going to eat itself alive he thought.

The street preacher only nodded to Yelena's question and whispered looking around shocked. "I don't know...I didn't even think he knew we existed."

"I think he knows about you two well enough," Renfroe spoke up reloading his forty-five with a new clip, "and my guess is he wanted to stop Alexander and someone told him that Stephanie and Wilma would do just the job." Renfroe answered.

Leland could only nod in agreement as the identity of the one who had betrayed them began to cross his mind driving his shock deeper. Oh Ken, why the hell would you do it man he wanted to scream when he thought of someone else. What the hell happened to Alexander? He was supposed to be here, to protect them! The man had promised Wilma he was always going to look after her and when it finally came time to produce what happened. Not a damn thing, that's what! Then it hit him, the reason he wasn't here, and it struck at the speed of a bullet. Grammy, where was Grammy? Leland was out the door running before Renfroe or Foster or the woman could pursue him.

They were halfway across the courtyard when an explosion tore through the apartment Stephanie and Wilma lived in. Another minute and all four would have been cooked alive from the blaze.

Lord God does it hurt Grammy thought as she laid prone on the floor of her living room feeling the blood pool under and around her. How long had it been? A minute? Five minutes? She couldn't tell time, it was hard enough just to keep her lungs working and breathing in oxygen so checking the clock had fallen down her list of priorities. For each inhale she could hear a wheeze and it seemed to get louder with each breath. Grammy knew that wasn't good, it couldn't be. A silent footstep suddenly registered in her ears and a small smile crossed her face as she recognized the figure who knelt by her side.

"Hello Mr. Alexander." She whispered trying to take another breath.

"Shh Martha," Alexander said taking her weathered hand in his right while gently rubbing her cheek with his left, "you need to stay still and stay calm."

"I'm dying Mr. Alexander, I know it, and I'm pretty calm about it...saw it coming, you did to I guess..." She replied before a coughing fit made her body spasm uncontrollably.

The vampire held his friend's hand as she groaned from the pain and when she looked calm again he spoke. "Yes, I saw it...you knew I would see it when you helped me see the end of this place."

"I'm going home where I want to be Mr. Alexander...how is...our Wilma?" Grammy asked fighting harder to breath. The wheezing was louder now, so very loud.

"She is safe Martha...the men took her away so she is safe for now." Alexander said still holding her hand.

A second passed by as Grammy fought against the blackness that was pulling at her, taking her to Jefferson. Oh how she wanted so much to see him once again but there was Wilma. She needed to say one last thing to Alexander. Grammy fought against the tide of death, clutching to the vampire's hand as if it was an anchor in a sweeping riptide. Grammy lifted her head off the floor and Alexander instinctively took it in his free hand.

"You saved her from...this place...but you remember your promise to me Mr. Alexander?" Grammy asked fiercely in horse whisper.

"Yes Martha, I remember my promise." Alexander said while gently cupping her heavy head in his hand.

"Then you know...what you have to do...don't you!" Grammy demanded.

"Yes Martha, I know what must be done. Rest now, medical attention is coming." Alexander agreed hoping to calm her down.

"Get her back!" Martha growled shaking as she willed her body to stay in this world just a moment longer, her voice gurgling with the effort. "You can't let anything happen to that angel...some of us have given everything to keep her safe!"

"I'll bring her home Martha I promise you, nothing will stop me." Alexander assured her squeezing Martha's hand gently.

"You know...what you have...to do." Grammy stuttered as her strength finally began to wane. The blackness swept her away from the world, swept away the pain of her body, and for a second she actually felt fear at what was happening. Then there was a comforting feeling, as if someone was whispering in her ear telling her it was okay. It would all be okay from here on. The blackness moved her along while the voice continued to tell her everything would be all right until a small pinhole of bright light suddenly poked through the dark like a lighthouse calling her to follow. Martha moved toward the brightness, swimming along as she had when she was a teenager at the small pond on the farm her father worked. The light grew brighter, and brighter, and then as if she blinked there was Jefferson among a land of clouds. After all the years he had kept his promise and now he was here to take her on the walk he had promised her he would that day so long ago.

Leland stopped at the broken door to Grammy's apartment, the sight inside crushing his soul as if he were hit with a boulder. Alexander was kneeling beside her body slowly and gently placing her arms in the usual pose for a peaceful journey and final rest. The street preacher stumbled in oblivious to the barely hanging door, the broken coffee table, or the bullet holes along the wall behind the destroyed chair. He could only see the dead body of

Grammy, a soul that deserved so much more than to die on the floor of a cockroach infested floor of the Projects. She was the matriarch for so many. She was the mother to so many boys just like him, the ones who grew up without a stable loving energy that nurtured a soul. Renfroe and Foster slowly walked in behind the shell-shocked street preacher as did the woman who moved quietly in. They all stopped at the sight of Alexander and Grammy.

"Oh God, please not her, not Grammy." Leland cried, finally leaning up against a dirty wall to keep from falling to the floor.

The room was silent for a minute, everyone paying their last respects to a beautiful soul as it went heavenward, and then it was over. Alexander stood from his kneeling position and walked over to where Leland was on the verge of cracking from the night's events.

"Are you ready to do what needs to be done?" He asked simply.

"What?" Leland responded like a robot.

"I said are you ready to do what needs to be done?" Alexander asked harshly.

"I don't know-"Leland began but Yelena suddenly cut him with a harsher retort from where she stood.

"Then get ready! They have Wilma and Stephanie!"

The remark scared Leland causing him to jump and break free from the shock of seeing Grammy's body. He turned to the werewolf then back to Alexander and spat. "Where the hell were you? You were supposed to protect them!"

"And I did," Alexander stated with anger. "There were forces here we could not stop, events rolling forward that would have brought about Wilma's death. Even if I would have stopped everything from happening tonight those same forces would have just come for her again and again."

"You know he's right Lee, the minute Dunbar and Hierra decide to get rid of you they'll just keep coming after you till your dead. They'll find you and they'll kill you, Stephanie, and her kid no matter how long it takes. It's what they do to make sure no one stands up to them." Renfroe spoke, adding fuel to the fire burning in the street preacher's heart. Those old days of working the corners started to come back, old feelings of protecting what was yours by any and all means stoked that growing fire as he turned to Alexander. The vampire just eyed him hard and spoke.

"If you want to get Stephanie and Wilma back then it's time to wage war Leland and for that you have to be willing to do anything to succeed."

"I'm willing." Leland snarled in a whisper.

"Are you ready to spill your own blood?" Alexander asked.

"Yes," the street preacher snarled again and this time Yelena joined him.

"Are you ready to face death and not blink?"

"Yes," both responded again.

"Are you ready to kill if need be?" Alexander asked with a snarl.

"Yes," Leland remarked clinching his hand into a fist and pointing a finger with the other at Alexander as the fire in his heart roared and exploded, "I'm ready to do anything for Stephanie and Wilma."

"There will be no one to save you from what you will see and face this night Leland. Only strength, courage, and a steadfast desire will help you against what we face. There can be no turning back from here on Leland. There will be no going back from this moment." Alexander stated.

"I said I'm ready!" Leland demanded. He felt his anger rise in his head and chest, the red beginning to blur his vision. They, whoever that was, had tried to kill him, kidnapped Stephanie and Wilma, and taken the only life in the Laurel that had shined brighter than the others had. Someone was going to pay for this.

"So what's the plan?" Renfroe suddenly asked from behind.

"I plan on unleashing my anger at the men who did this. What are your plans once this is over Detective?" Alexander asked eyeing the large police officer.

"Let's just say my first piece of business is making sure that four Russians catch a plane out of town. From there we'll see how it goes." Renfroe answered putting his service sidearm away.

"See that Yelena," Alexander commented passing the large detective by on his way out the front door," you and your brothers have more help than you expected."

"Wait! She's a werewolf too?" Foster asked abruptly with a whine.

"Da...And it was my brother you shot...both of you." Yelena answered eyeing both Renfroe and Foster just as hard as Alexander had stared at Leland.

"Oh...yeah...well, in our defense, your brother did try to rip me and Renfroe apart." Foster replied with a weak smile.

Yelena's eyebrow went up as the vampire remarked with a sarcastic smile. "And what a shame it would have been if that had happened. Now we have to leave and go rescue our friends."

The men and Yelena left following the vampire as the night air carried the sounds of approaching police and ambulance vehicles. She moved in beside Alexander as he looked to her, the hard line her mouth made as Yelena walked telling the vampire she was more than ready to fight. The fire was extinguished by the firemen before it could reach Martha's apartment reducing it to rubble like the others around it. Grammy's body was finally moved two and a half hours later to the city morgue where it stayed till the morning before being claimed by an associate of one Simon Barnes. Her final resting place was the plot next to her husband under a large oak that faced the morning sunrise in a cemetery in her hometown in Kentucky.

Chapter Ten

"You BASTARD," Stephanie screamed flailing at the arms that held her fast and kept her from strangling the life out of the young man in front of her. A man the size of truck was having a rough time trying to keep her held firm in one spot.

"Yeah, I sold you out bitch!" Kenny yelled back acting tough for the moment. "I smiled when I heard they shot that old ho' Grammy, she's through messing in my business!"

"I'm going to tear your heart out." Stephanie spit.

"Oh, you think you can hurt this OG, well come get you some!" Kenny snarled. "Let this bitch go so I can beat her ass!"

"Tone it down Kenny. We might need her later on." Rico said motioning to the man standing behind Stephanie to keep holding the enraged woman.

"Man I just want to land one punch." Kenney snarled again, faking a quick left at the immobilized Stephanie.

"Listen, I have to make a few phone calls then we move out, got it?" Rico ordered more than asked surveying the room, making sure everyone understood him.

Away from the unfolding fray, Lloyd Dunbar sat behind his large desk watching the exchange intently. He sat there equally divided, part of him wanted to see Kenny beat the woman to a bloody pulp, but the other part wanted to see if she had enough anger to take the young gangster. Lloyd bet if Stephanie could land the right blow, say a nice knee to the groin, then she could stomp all over Kenny here. He was about to get his camera out so as to commemorate the moment in a nice Hi-Res format when he spotted the little girl just to his left, Wilma was her name if remembered right. She was standing perfectly still oblivious to everything around her. The guard didn't even have a hand on her. There was no panic, no fear, and none of the anger that her mother was displaying. Wilma was as calm as the other side of the pillow, as cool as cucumber and any other hooky analogy you could come up with. This immediately intrigued Lloyd, a girl showing the kind of courage most adults couldn't muster aroused his curiosity like nothing else. He rose from behind his desk, walked over, and knelt in front of Wilma so the two could talk eye to eye. Lloyd hated conducting conversations and dealings where he couldn't see the other person's eyes. 'Never do a deal when you can't see the other man's eyes' his father had said once, had to do with trust or something like that.

"You seem very calm sweetheart. You're not scared at all with the bad men here in the room are you?" Lloyd asked.

"No, I'm not scared." Wilma responded calmly.

"Well, you don't worry because nothing is going to happen to you." Lloyd said patting the girl's leg.

"I'm not worried either, but you should be though." Wilma replied back with that strange calmness that was beginning to raise a small bit of concern in Lloyd's mind.

"Oh, really, and why should we be worried honey?"

Neither Lloyd nor Wilma noticed that the room had fallen silent. Kenny, Rico, Stephanie, and the men holding her arms had turned their attention to the two people having a simple conversation. Each and everyone's undivided attention had turned in the room to the pair and rested on the next words spoken by the little girl.

"Because their coming to get me and when they get here they will kill every one of you." Wilma stated flatly, no emotion.

"What?" Lloyd asked with a chuckle.

"Listen sweetie," Rico said pointing a finger at Wilma, "If you're Mr. Black or whoever shows up we're more than ready for him. I got some real nasty men with big guns waiting downstairs just for him."

Kenny laughed first at the remark but soon the rest of the room was joining in. That was everyone except Stephanie and Wilma, and after a second a slow smile began to creep across the little girls face. She went from cute little imp to a mean devil in the time it took for Lloyd to notice it and rein in his laughter. He didn't like that look one bit, not one bit.

"I wasn't talking about Alexander." Wilma responded with a sound that was part elfish giggle and part deranged lunatic.

Suddenly the room was quiet, so silent in fact that you could hear Lloyd's heartbeat pick up in rhythm and speed. Wilma covered her mouth respectfully because of the giggles and Rico felt his blood run cold from the motion, it was as if she were hiding something. The little girl's innocence was gone and replaced by that evil smile that made your breathing short and asthmatic.

"Who's coming honey?" Lloyd asked rising from his kneeling position but never losing eye contact with the little girl.

"The other werewolves and the man without a soul, they followed us here." Wilma whispered before the giggles took her again. It was the only sound in the room and she wasn't done by a long shot as she turned to Kenny lowering her hand and whispering. "But Alexander is coming and when he gets here to save me he's going to do to you Kenny what he did J-Rock. He knows all about you Kenny, everything you've been doing."

The only sound in the room now was the noise Kenny made when he swallowed, a large hollow thump that bounced down his throat right into his stomach. Then Stephanie called out laughing as well, "Not so tough now are you 'King of the Hood'?"

That was it, Rico was sure Wilma was evil and her mother wasn't far behind. He wanted as much distance between himself and that little girl as his town car would provide. He turned quickly to Stephanie and with the speed of a striking snake drove his head into hers. The head butt was crude but effective as the woman went out like a light and would have hit the floor if not for the men holding her up.

"Get the little girl to the hotel now. You know the room number right?" Rico asked the guard on his right as the man left gathered Stephanie in his arms. The man simply nodded at the question as he helped scoop up the unconscious body.

"What are you doing?" Kenny asked with a bit of concern, seems little Wilma had quite effect on the 'King of the Hood'.

Lloyd stepped up and watched the one guard carry an immobile Stephanie down the hall. He mentally noted the fact that Wilma never said a word when her mother was struck or the fact she was being taken away alone when he turned to look at her. The little girl was still just as calm as the other side of the pillow.

"We're dividing up the treasure." Lloyd remarked absently.

"We're what?" Kenny asked with a high-pitched squeal.

"The mother stays here," Rico explained while pointing to Wilma, "and she gets a ride to a safe spot."

"Why are we doing that?" Kenny asked dumbfounded.

"I'm pretty certain Mr. Black would kill for Wilma, but when it comes to the mother I'm not so sure he'd put up much of a fight. If the little girl isn't here then we get the upper hand and we can control him." Lloyd explained in laymen's terms.

The other guard stepped over and took Wilma by the arm leading her toward the door. The girl offered no resistance and followed the man's lead like a leashed dog and yet just as she disappeared from sight, Wilma's voice came calling back, laying out one final warning.

"I hope your life insurance covers mauling by extremely large carnivores!"

The office was quiet for a second before Kenny finally broke the silence with a trembling voice. "You don't think she's speaking for real do you? That dude isn't going to rip me into a bunch of pieces?"

"No way, there's no such thing as 'werewolves' and we got the girl. Mr. Black is going to do what we say because he knows I'll hurt Wilma and won't think twice about doing it." Rico remarked with a shake of his head.

"I don't know about that Rico." Lloyd remarked looking a little white from what Wilma had said as she was taken away. "Do you remember Chico and the way the police found him with his heart torn out?"

The room went silent again and Kenny started to feel the first pangs of regret for getting involved in this war. This may be my final ride he thought fingering the trigger of the gun in his waistband. He was still thinking hard about how he could get out of this if it all hit the fan when the power went out...in the whole house.

"Aw man,"

"You got a backup generator or something?" Rico asked looking around while sounding annoyed. Inside though he was starting to have the same regrets Kenny was, maybe he should keep the girl around just in case?

"Sorry Rico but no," Lloyd sighed biting his bottom lip nervously, "I let the little misses decorate unfortunately. She was more worried about drapes and color panels then the power going out."

"Aw man," Kenny whispered again scared as hell.

"Wow...that'll knock the power out for sure...for the whole neighborhood." Foster commented with a stunned look at the smoldering and crushed substation box that supplied the neighborhood with electricity and power.

"Dunbar owns the whole neighborhood. He built his house on it." Leland responded over his shoulder as he began to walk after Yelena and Alexander.

Alexander wasn't paying much attention to the men who walked at the back though he did smile at the street preacher's response. After arriving and parking the Chevelle a distance away so as not to alert anyone he found the first object he was looking for, the box that provided the electricity for Dunbar's expansive property and house. A fighter loses considerable faith in his cause when he has to fight in the dark the vampire thought, knew from past experiences on the battlefield. He knew there was an army waiting for him at the mansion, how many stayed and fought once they were in the dark with him though, that was the question now.

And as his eyes scanned the shadows the group walked through for any sign of Hierra's men performing a roving patrol of the area Alexander sensed the second thing he was searching for. He knew the others were out there in the depths of the dark waiting for their chance to kidnap Wilma. There was only one place they would be and there by the front gate in the dark were Michaels and Yelena's brothers...and all three of the ghouls. They were here for Wilma as well, still trying to force his hand in killing the werewolves with some idiotic plan. A simple nod to the others confirmed to them what he had stated in the drive here, Yelena's brothers would be out in the night as well around Dunbar's. As he kept his senses sweeping Alexander found Stephanie inside a room in the back of the mansion but Wilma wasn't with her. Rico was taking her somewhere else via car, just as he predicted the boss would. The man was no fool, just full of useless bravado and he knew the only way he would survive the night was to keep Wilma far enough away that the vampire would have no choice but to do as he said. Then out of the dark of the night the group came upon the formidable defenses of the Dunbar Estates, a simple non-threatening eight foot high stucco wall complete with a camera on top, which was out now due to the loss of power. He came to a stop by the wall and then turned to his human friends eyeing each one. They were scared and with good reason. They were entering a world that not a one of them thought was possible a week ago and yet here it was time to go to battle.

"Leland, detective and Mr. Foster, stay together and please retrieve Stephanie. If there is any trouble, try and find a room to barricade in until I can come to help." Alexander explained.

"That wall looks really tall, too tall for me. I guess I'll have to stay out here with the car, you know, in case we have to make a quick get-away." Foster stated with a smile and a quick turn to walk away.

Yelena reached out and touched his arm with a stern look shaking her head with obvious disdain. She turned back and with a quick silent run she practically walked right up the side of the wall reaching the top and sitting down straddling the structure. Then with her own smile the werewolf leaned over and reached down to the man waiting to help him up as the detective went to preparing for the fight he knew was coming.

"What are you going to be doing once we're inside Alexander?" Renfroe asked pulling the slide back on his forty-five to check the chamber, yep, one in the pipe ready to go.

"I think that's a hell of a plan staying here man...that is until one of those werewolves smells you sitting out here and swings by for a look." Leland replied to Foster slapping the man on the shoulder as he walked past. The street preacher followed Yelena's path up the wall taking her hand only to help steady his body before going over and dropping out of sight as Alexander answered Renfroe's question.

"I'm going to make sure Wilma is all right, and then I'm going to end this conflict with Dunbar and Hierra. How do you plan on finding Stephanie?" Alexander answered and asked with one breath.

"You think they can smell me out here?" Foster asked nervously looking to the werewolf with wide eyes.

"Da...You smell of steak." Yelena responded leaning down to take his hand. The assistant coroner just stood there though frozen to the spot with the information he just learned tumbling in his brain. A second was all Foster's mind needed to drum up a picture of a large wolf leaping over the top of the wall with one swift motion and then chasing him, catching him and knocking him down to the ground. Just as the werewolf's jaws drew down for a big bite of Grade A assistant coroner in the image Foster jumped, snapped back to the present, and ran right for Yelena. She barely had time to set herself before the man was crawling on her, over her, and down the other side. The werewolf let out a curse in Russian then disappeared to the other side.

Renfroe sighed and holstered his gun, "I plan on asking nicely once, that's after I make it over this damn wall."

"Oh that's not an issue, mind the landing detective," Otz heard the vampire say with a chipper voice that seemed out of place. He felt a hand grab the back of his jacket just before he was flying, literally up and over the wall with some help from Alexander. The world floated beneath his feet for a brief second before Renfroe was falling back to Mother Earth and just out the corner of his eye he could see the other three just staring at him like he was Haley's Comet or something. The ground came rushing up and if it wasn't for the quick bend of the knees to absorb the shock or the semi-roll on to his back Renfroe might have been hurt. As it were he just lost a good bit of the air in his lungs and decided to lie still for a moment to get it back.

"Well, Otz made it over in one piece...sort of, how is Alexander getting over?" Foster asked just a second before a voice answered that very question from behind his shoulder.

"I just walk through walls,"

The werewolf and Leland could barely contain their chuckles as the assistant coroner gave shrill yelp and danced away from the voice. Alexander only smiled as well as he walked over and offered a hand to the detective who looked up and snarled.

"You threw me over the wall?"

The vampire just nodded once still smiling as Renfroe took his hand. "Yes I did but if you prefer to climb over I can help you get back to the other side quickly to do that."

"Hell no, Renfroe Airlines has officially closed." The detective remarked taking the hand and letting the appendage help him up. Otz noted how cold the flesh was, just like one of the many corpses he had the displeasure of touching since joining Homicide.

The group formed up and began to move in toward the Mansion. All their eyes were peeled and ears listening for any sound of approaching guards. The dark only increased as they began to move into a stand of trees, a small but thick set of woods put in place for an obvious landscape effect. The detective turned to Alexander and whispered. "I guess I don't need to ask how you plan on getting in the house."

The vampire turned to the detective then with a calm expression. "I'm not worried about myself or Yelena getting in. It's you and the others I'm worried about."

"Don't be, I've got the universal key right here." Renfroe said producing a small round object with a metal pin protruding from the top from his coat pocket, a grenade Alexander immediately deduced.

"I see you plan on using stealth." Alexander stated raising eyebrow as he did.

"For the first ten feet or so, then it's all about finding Stephanie." Renfroe smiled taking off his coat. He put the grenade in his pants pocket and drew his handgun.

"Then it is time gentlemen, we split from here to finish this. I will hopefully see the three of you when we are done." Alexander said one last time before he and Yelena disappeared from sight going in another direction.

Renfroe turned to Leland who was holding two nine millimeters and Foster who was holding a small thirty-eight revolver. They looked scared before scaling the wall and both looked just about the same now which was good because there was no time for a pep talk. The detective hoped like hell one of them wouldn't shoot him in the back as they approached the house.

"Okay guys, we're going to move slowly down the tree line in cover formation using the shadows to hide from the lights." Renfroe tried to explain but he noticed the blank stares. Everything just went over the guys' heads.

"Just follow me, and don't SHOOT me Foster." Renfroe exclaimed with a snarl before setting off.

"Why does he always point me out? Why does he do that?" Foster whined.

"I don't know why he does it, just don't shoot me either!" Leland stated with a shake of his head as he followed Renfroe step-for-step.

"Yeah, yeah," Foster spat before trotting to catch up with the other two. Slowly their shapes faded into the dark shadows of the trees heading toward driveway it looked like. A few seconds later another larger shadow followed behind, almost stalking the three men.

The night shift at the front gate was slow, boring, and probably the most important guard duty a man in Rico's organization could draw. You were the first line of defense, the point at which no one got past unless authorized, and the eyes for the boss who might be inside doing business. The gate guard made calls if something suspicious was going down, he sounded the alarm if the police were coming, and kept all gatecrashers away. Eduardo hated the job, it was beneath him, and yet here he was standing in his usual post at the front gate of Lloyd Dunbar's estate along with Luis and Jaime again tonight. Rico always gave him the front gate duty when he came to Lloyd's and Eduardo was beginning to think the boss had it in for him. I mean he never drew the comfortable jobs like driving the town car and tonight would have been nice with the sudden rain and all. He looked up and saw the town car round the house heading toward the front gate, rolling slow and sleek. Now that was a comfortable job.

"Hey Jaime, open the gate. The car's coming out." Eduardo yelled pulling his jacket tighter around him. As the town car rolled to a stop he looked longingly at the warm interior, now that looks like a comfortable job he thought. Wait, he realized, why did the car stop? "Hey Jaime, I said open the damn gate man!"

"Yeah, I heard you man, but the gate's not going to be moving any time soon. Power's out everywhere!" Jaime yelled back from the small guard shack.

Across the two lanes of the secluded street, buried deep in the bushes and trees avoiding the light of the street lamps and detection was Michaels and his group. They watched as the town car was about to roll out of the front gate when the power went out in the shack and the metal gate. The Lesser Lich looked intently at the car as it sat in the drive, his eyes locked onto the top of the head of little colored girl in the back seat as the men ran around trying to figure out how to move the metallic barricade. A small smile crossed his face as he turned to the two large ghouls Misery and Woe just behind him. Michaels gave a small head nod to the pair who nodded back while next to them the Epova brothers did the same. Everyone knew immediately what their leader wanted. The group had come here to kidnap the little girl and thus have Alexander come to them for a final fight, but these men had beaten them to the prize. Now, like a good group of boys, they were driving the prize right back to them with only minimal guard, easy prey for the ghouls and werewolves. Gregor, Peter, and Dimitri slipped forward to stand on the edge of the dark next to the ghouls in the shadows not disturbing a plant or limb from a tree.

"Are you ready to kill for me my followers?" He asked with a low evil hiss. Phlegm growled deep next to him making Michaels smile from ear to ear.

It was time to get the little girl.

"What are you looking at?" Emilio asked his passenger in the backset as she stared out into the dark of the night. Babysitting wasn't the job he joined up to do when he came to work for Rico but it sure beat standing out by the gate in the cold.

Wilma didn't say a thing. She was too busy watching the dark shadows the trees along the roadside created, and even though she couldn't see them she knew the werewolves were out there somewhere watching and waiting. Wilma could sense them out there in the night waiting for a chance to strike. It was Chess, wait for your opponent to show their strategy and then unleash hell on them. She finally turned to Emilio and saw the butt of his gun sticking out just past the edge of his leather jacket.

"How many bullets does your gun hold?" She asked absently.

"Enough" was Emilio's single worded reply.

Wilma looked at the two men upfront and then back to Emilio but choosing not to explain her last inquiry. She had a feeling it would become evident soon enough why she asked as Wilma turned and looked out the passenger window into the dark and began to mentally track the seconds in her head. Then something moved out there in the tree line, just past the magical line dividing light from shadow.

"Not tonight there's not," Wilma responded with a cold whisper. Here they come she thought reaching silently and slowly for the door handle.

That line, that mystical dividing line between what could be seen and trusted and what was hidden and dangerous, abruptly exploded as five large men came running right for the gate sprinting with all their might straight for the metal bars of the barricade. Eduardo and his men began to scream at each other in Spanish warning of the attack. Guns were pulled out in a flash and the bullets began to fly just as the five men slammed into the gate with a loud crunch. The five ignored the rounds and rounds of gunfire that hit them repeatedly, paid no heed to the wounds created by being struck. No, nothing stopped them as the gate bent and screamed before collapsing down onto the hood of the town car jarring the vehicle violently.

Emilio popped out of door on his side just as Eduardo started screaming. He pulled his nine millimeter Beretta and pointed it at the largest of the men. As he pulled the trigger firing the handgun over and over and as flashes of yellow powder burst blurred his vision Emilio noticed one thing readily and easily. Not a round from his gun was hurting the big brute crashing through the gate and as the behemoth descended on him the breach on his nine millimeter popped open with a whack.

Out of Ammo....

A second later the thing brought a hand down on top of his head like a pile driver crushing his neck with ease forcing his head down into his chest with a wet crunch. The last thought of one Emilio Martinez was 'Damn, she was right, not enough bullets'.

The others soon followed Emilio. Jaime was felled by Gregor and Dimitri and their claws as the werewolves attacked him without mercy in their mind controlled existence. Eduardo fought as best as he could as he emptied one clip and was trying to reload a second when Phlegm tackled him to the ground. He was done in a minute screaming in pain as the ghoul tore into him with its long claws ripping away flesh. Woe slammed the body of Luis into the guard shack three times and might have gone for four if not for the fact the wall of the building broke. The ghoul left the man's body lying half-way in and out of the shack's wall.

As soon as the fight was done Michaels ran across the street and skipped over the down gate going right for the passenger door of the car. He had seen Wilma drop down behind the seats ducking for cover when the attack commenced and now he rushed over to claim his prize. Yes it wasn't the best of attempts to get the little girl but in the end Michaels did catch her and that was all the mattered he thought as he flung the door open ready to greet his new prisoner.

Only she wasn't there...the back seat was as empty as Michaels mind right now. The Lesser Lich gasped with his mouth wide open staring the empty seat for a moment before stepping back in utter and mind shattering disbelief.

"Why," he mumbled turning around slowly and looking out at the dark with an exasperated expression. "WHY!" He screamed out in total frustration as Michaels could not comprehend with all of his considerable mental faculties how some fourteen year old girl was eluding him at every possible and conceivable turn! Then, in the middle of his meltdown, the Epova brothers began to whine, low and small noises. Oh he knew what that meant, they had started that same whine back at the hotel when little Yelena had shown. She must be nearby Michaels thought as he turned back to the werewolves.

"You three go find your sister and give her a proper greeting, and by that I mean tear her into tiny little pieces." He ordered quickly going with the idea that popped into his head. He spun then to Phlegm and the ghouls Misery and Woe pointing with his finger as menacingly as he could. "And you three follow me to the house. They still have the little girl's mother so she'll be running there as fast as her legs can go."

The behemoth Misery grunted and grumbled some response that stopped Michaels. "I know the Ancient One is here. That is why you are here, to fight him and protect me!"

The Lich began to walk away when Woe added a few garbled words on Michaels understood. "No one inside the house is to be left alive, but scratch them only if you can. We may still have need of them this night."

Alexander and Yelena stopped as soon as they heard the gunfire and the screaming. The vampire knew Michaels had attacked the gate, and he had a very good idea as to why. He had seen the car or better yet the Lich had seen Wilma in the car. After a quick check with his senses the vampire smiled just a little. He knew the little one had escaped and now the Lesser Lich was in full distress. Oh little Wilma, such a brave and smart girl, always one step ahead in the game. The vampire looked down to Yelena noting she was sniffing the air once then twice before turning to him smiling.

"Wilma is near and so are my brothers."

"Yes, both are," Alexander whispered looking out on the dark, "and your brothers need you more now Yelena. Michaels has sent them out to find you and kill you."

If the news was a surprise to the werewolf she never let it show. Yelena only nodded and whispered, "I will draw them away but please, save Wilma."

Oh how little Wilma has conquered another of us Alexander thought as he spoke, "Nothing will stop me from doing just that Yelena. Now go and remember this, do not transform into your true wolf form. The poison controlling your brothers has almost run its course and Michaels has not had the chance to administer more. All three will soon be free of his control and once they are you must get them to the safety of the car, understand?"

His words had a small hopeful effect on her as Yelena smiled and nodded while whispering, "Da, I will get them to safety Ancient One."

The vampire watched then as the werewolf slipped off silently into the woods to draw her brothers away. He wondered how long it would take for the effect of the ghouls poison to wear off and if she had the strength to fight off three attackers of her brothers' size. Alexander only wondered for a moment as this was Yelena and she was not a weakling when it came to fighting. She would save her brothers and the first part of his promise to her would be fulfilled with the second part already under way. He looked to the house then and knew right where he needed to be once inside, it was all part of the plan.

The branches digging into her side was beginning to itch and being in a scrunched position wasn't at all comfortable for Wilma, but she wasn't about to move. Just six or seven feet away stood three very large half-naked white men, and just past them was the evil man from the other night with the sunglasses. The three large men were Yelena's brothers Wilma knew because all three stood like perfect statues as the evil man threw his fit. He was screaming at the moment, obviously upset because she wasn't where she was supposed to be in the backseat of the car. *You can never shy away from evil girl, never back down to it. Once the demon has you it won't let go no ma'am, it will hold hard to your soul.* Grammy's words came back in her mind granting strength to Wilma, bolstering her will with a courage that flowed through her. *But if you're strong and show no fear then evil can't win you over.* And it won't because I won't let it. It won't because I'm not going to let the evil man hurt my loved ones Wilma thought feeling a growl forming deep in her small chest.

She could see where all the rounds the guards had fired into the three brothers had left their marks, bloody holes and bruises were rampant on their bodies. The brothers stood staring off into the shadows zombie like which bothered Wilma just a little. How was Alexander going to help them if they were mindless? What could he do to save them like this? She was sure the itch in her side from the branches would drive her mad and she would have to scratch it a second when the evil man suddenly started to scream out his orders. He ranted for a moment, what he said Wilma wasn't sure of but she understood the word 'mother' when she heard it and when the brothers bolted off through the dark toward the mansion her heart dropped.

They're going after my mother...they have to be...

The itch didn't matter anymore. It faded from Wilma's mind. Her mother was in danger so there was no time to waste and no chance to panic. Wilma waited just long enough to allow for every sound of feet scraping the ground and deep breathing but her own to be gone before scrambling free of the tree she hid in, scratching like mad at her side where the branch had cut, and then running after the brother werewolves. She knew this was crazy, she had escaped from the evil man and his gang, and now here she was running right back to the house of the men who had kidnapped her earlier. But this was her mother and she was the only family Wilma had, the only one who really wanted her. You never leave your family or friends, ever, which was Wilma Jackson's first golden rule. Her feet pounded into the grass as she settled into a strong running pace hoping to get to the mansion before anything happened to her mother.

Chapter Eleven

The door made a very sweet ding when it opened as someone entered, from a small bell hung by a piece of hemp that was struck with the corner of the swinging portal. The chime of the bell just added to the soft tantric music that played in the store and accentuated the flow of the energy and incense that hung in the air. It was almost closing at the Phoenix New Age shop so it wasn't unusual for Joel to be looking down doing the task of closing out the sales log for the day. He was busy recording the number and type of crystals sold during the shift but he wasn't so occupied that he didn't greet the customer.

"Good evening, we'll be closing soon but please feel welcomed to walk around." Joel said with a pleasant tone while writing in his log. It was just then that a strong smell, a pungent odor, struck his nose and it made his nostrils flex with its strength. The younger brother of Renfroe looked up and felt his heart almost lurch to a stop as he stared into the missing eyes of what he would tell Bear later was a dead man who had just walked into his mother's shop.

But that wasn't the part that struck him full of dread Joel would tell Otz later. It was the man just behind the dead one who had walked in, the man with eyes so evil it froze him to the spot barely able to breath. My blood just turned to ice Joel would whisper and I swear the temperature dropped twenty degrees when he looked to me. My lungs actually burned it hurt so much as he spoke Joel said before stopping.

"We're here for Adria actually. You don't mind if I go in the back and talk to her do you? Thanks so much."

Otz had to kneel and look his younger brother in the eye, who was sitting on the edge of the hospital bed in the Grady ER, asking him what happened, where was their mother?

"He took her Bear, him and that dead man...I know it sounds strange and almost impossible...but I think the man with the evil eyes was dead too...he just didn't look it."

'The necessary lines of communication that every business organization needs to survive are tenuous at best and in times of crisis will inevitably fail'. At least that's what Lloyd's textbook had said about running a worldwide enterprise in his college business class at Yale, and that quote never fit any situation better than his current one. The power was out and it seemed no one at the gate was answering a call on the phone or the walkie-talkie's. The text in the book had gone on to say something about how the forward

thinking company plans for such events that may occur, uses technology to strengthen its reach and blah-blah-blah. It was all lost at the moment to Lloyd as he watched while Rico couldn't raise a soul on the front gate radio or Emilio in the car and that agitated the man's Mexican blood. The Cartel boss sent two more of his men out to see just what the jack-offs were doing at the front gate which left the main house understaffed by two. Something else Lloyd learned at the famous Yale Business School was resource allocation and it seemed like Rico wasn't adhering to the stated rules. You know the one where it states, and I quote, you will leave the main house guarded by a factor of times ten needed when confronted with werewolves and boogeyman who may want to rend the very flesh from your bones.

"Do you think it's wise to send two men outside to check the gate Rico?" Lloyd asked nervously.

"What are you scared of Lloyd? You believe that girl and her bull. Listen, why don't you do me a favor, let me take care of the security stuff all right." Rico said shaking his head with frustration for his business partner who obviously lacked the testicular fortitude to do this kind of work.

"I don't like what's going down here either man." Kenny spoke up while licking his lips nervously. All right, make that both of my partners Rico thought.

"What's the matter with you two? The stuff that little girl said and what happened here with the power are two different things entirely. Now go back to whatever it is you two were doing and stop worrying about the non-essential shit." Rico demanded.

Yet, as much as Rico assured both Lloyd and Kenny, they still felt something was terribly wrong. They looked to each other, Lloyd shrugged his shoulder to say he didn't know what to do, and then they both looked away. Kenny thought hard about an escape route if things got dicey and Lloyd just thought about his college days at Yale.

Renfroe led his band of men down the tree line of the driveway choosing to walk in the grass and the shadows cast by the numerous Douglas Firs and Spruce trees instead of the open concrete. For the most part they were quiet, except for Foster and his continual sloshing in the wet grass. The skinny man had slipped twice and his left sneaker kept squealing as if he was killing a large rat with every step. Renfroe was about to go ahead and shoot the assistant coroner before he got them killed when something made the hairs on his neck stand on end. His right hand shot up in the classic 'Stop' hand signal as his eyes scanned the dark for whatever it was that suddenly caused his internal danger meter to go off the scale.

"What is it?" Foster hissed in a small attempt at whispering. It failed miserably.

"Whatever it is, it knows where we are now!" Leland hissed.

"It knows where we are? We got to get out of here!" Foster remarked while looking around nervously.

"Shhh!" Leland hissed again. He brought the twin nine's up getting ready to blast anything he saw.

Renfroe didn't pay attention to his two cohort's exchange. He was busy trying to locate what was setting off his radar. Suddenly he spun bringing his forty-five up to bear on Foster, the hammer pulling back and locking in place with the pressure of his thumb. Leland instinctively dropped to one knee while falling in line next to Renfroe, both nine's leveled at Foster's small chest. The assistant coroner might have let out a scream but the feeling of a large gun barrel being pressed against his head drove the air from his lungs, like a balloon being punctured with a large needle. A man dressed in slacks and a sports coat stepped out from behind one of the fur trees.

"Drop your guns or I'll splatter your friend's brains all over the fucking front lawn." The man said with a slight accent, maybe Hispanic.

"Go ahead. I won't miss him all that much." Renfroe remarked flatly.

"What?" The man said in utter amazement.

"Renfroe!" Foster yelped.

"Yeah, pull the trigger man. I for one am quite tired of the man's mouth." Leland added with emphasis on the last part.

"Drop Your Damn Guns!" The guard screamed pressing the barrel harder into Foster head.

"Will you two stop screwing around and do what the man SAYS!" Foster wailed while shaking both fist.

"You better do something fast smart guy because I'm going to shoot you in two seconds!" Renfroe screamed back to the guard ignoring Foster.

"Put the Damn guns down NOW!" The guard screamed one last time giving a sharp push to Foster's head for emphasis.

The assistant coroner never knew exactly how close the large claw came to his head or just how much that little shove from the guard mattered. He stumbled forward just as the shadow closest to the guard came to life with a vicious haymaker, the guard's chest becoming impaled on a long set of claws. Something that looked like a cross between blonde wolf and a man appeared out of the dark, the size of a good grizzly bear, and held the guard off the ground while standing on its hind legs which were clothed in a nice but tight pair of pants. For a second no one moved, then the werewolf roared with a sound like a lion, only louder and deeper and everyone took off for the hills. The assistant coroner screamed and lunged toward Renfroe and Leland as the pair opened up with both pair of guns. The night lit up with fiery burst of gunpowder, bullets flew toward the werewolf, but he just used the guard's body as a shield stopping all the rounds from hitting him. From the corner of his right eye Renfroe saw two more werewolves sprinting out of the dark, and then to his left what looked like another guard coming for Leland. It was getting crowded quick...too quick.

"LOOK OUT!" Renfroe screamed firing at the last second. Two rounds from the forty-five struck the blond werewolf dead between its eyes.

"LET'S GET OUT OF HERE!" Leland screamed firing one round from each gun into the werewolf's chest.

The three men immediately broke in a hard run for the front door of the mansion with Foster incredibly in the lead, his lack of muscle and conditioning not hindering him in the least as he fled. Renfroe kept track of the two werewolves running at them from the other side of the estate and with a cringe he watched both take down the other guard ignoring the man's pleas for mercy. The blonde one though, he was coming right for them and the detective knew the race for the security of the mansion was going to be close. He could hear one of the other two werewolves from behind start to chase, its breathing sounding loud but nothing like the giant blonde locomotive barreling down on him and his friends. The front door was thirty feet away but the two werewolves had closed the distance so fast there was no way they were going to make it. Renfroe took a deep breath and then like a practiced ballet dancer he spun on his feet in mid run and fired two rounds from his forty-five at the pursuers on the left, the slide ejecting the spent casings out into the dark on a high arc. He spun back around and pushed his heavy frame toward the doorway faster as Leland fired a few of his rounds at the one blonde werewolf trying to slow it down as well.

Renfroe noted the beasts were all different colors. The two coming from their left were a solid red and a solid black. The one from behind was a solid yellow. Funny isn't it how your mind latches onto the most insignificant things at the worst times. Why in the lord was he noting color schemes right now?

Then they were at the front door. The solid red and solid black werewolves were just a few feet away when Foster skinny body amazingly struck one of the large oak doors hard enough to fling it open. Leland and Renfroe ducked in just as the assistant coroner pushed the door closed. All three werewolves stopping just short in a power slide the detective noted as the portal closed with a slam.

"Christ, I didn't think we'd make it guys!" Foster exclaimed with a gasp. A second later the sound of numerous hammers being cocked back on a great many guns reverberated through the massive foyer. The assistant coroner turned around slowly to see Renfroe and Leland facing eight men, all holding two large caliber guns in each hand at them, and all ready to fire. He instantly noticed the two large grand staircases that led to the upper floors, the small oak table with the ornate vase and blooming orchids in the center of the foyer floor, and the two dark hallways under the stairs that went back farther into the house. Somewhere, back there in the dark, the wolves were coming for them. Foster knew it like he knew the night would give way to the day.

"What'd you do to Eduardo?" One of the guards suddenly asked with a typical head cocked to the left gesture. Foster snapped back to reality looking at the business end of all those guns.

The werewolves slowly became one with the night again. The attack was halted, a command given by something more than speech overriding mental directives. The three obeyed the silent order against their will and moved off as one in direction of the back of the house. They smelled their sister and even though every bit of their will screamed not to do this, not to kill their beloved sister, the Epova brothers ran off to complete the order of their new master now.

"Good evening boys, thought you might want some Amway literature?" Renfroe remarked with a smile and a wave of the hand that wasn't holding his gun.

"Your funny, bet it'll be real hilarious when I shoot you in both your knees!" One guard with a cruel smile remarked with a wink.

Renfroe was about to respond with a good comeback, and it was going to be a good one, when a heavy Spanish accent boomed from above. "Who the hell are these three idiotas and how'd they get past the guards at the front gate?"

"Hey Rico, how's the drug trade treating you these days?" Renfroe answered in a comical non-Renfroe fashion.

Rico looked to the detective and asked a question with a tone that stated he wouldn't ask a third time. "I asked who you are."

"My name's Renfroe, Detective Renfroe of Atlanta Homicide."

"He's a cop!" The guard closest to Renfroe screamed.

"How'd you get passed by my boys at the front gate Detective Renfroe?" Rico asked eyeing the detective closely.

"They're dead, all of them. They were probably ripped to shreds just like the other two we ran into out there." Foster answered cutting in.

"What...what do you mean ripped to pieces?" Lloyd gasped, his presence being registered for the first time.

"They're all dead? Are you saying all the men at the gate are dead?" Rico asked incredulously.

"Well, from all the gunfire we heard earlier I can safely say they won't be coming to dinner tonight that's for sure. By the way, nice place you have here Mr. Dunbar, say you wouldn't happen to have any open windows anywhere would you, maybe an unlocked back door?" Renfroe asked with a nod of his head.

"You Killed Eduardo," the same guard shouted while pointing his gun right at Renfroe's head, "I'm going to blow your head off you culo!"

"Renfroe didn't kill anyone." Leland suddenly yelled taking everyone's attention off of the guard. "Your boys were killed by these things out there that's the size of a bear and as mean as my mother on a bad day."

"Killed by what?" Rico laughed shaking his head.

"The things outside are Werewolves Rico and I don't mean the Michael Landon wearing a cheap costume kind either." Renfroe added as the guard's gun slowly began to lower from its spot on his forehead.

"Damn, I knew it man!" A voice suddenly sounded and Leland looked up to see Kenny for the first time. "What the hell are we gonna do now?"

"Kenny? What are you doing here?" Leland asked in shock though somewhere deep down inside he already knew the answer. He had been betrayed by the boy, given up by a Judas for a hand full of money and power.

"Oh, excuse my manners, this is my new partner. Kenny's taking over the business at the Laurel for us. He's replacing the late Mr. Eight Ball." Rico stated with a smile.

"You little punk piece of shit! You lead them to Wilma and Stephanie didn't you?" Leland screamed and pointed at the boy with a loaded gun.

"No, I told my boss here where to find the man in black and Grammy! Those two bitches were just gravy!" Kenny screamed back.

"Get down here you fucking runt! Get down here so I can stick my foot hip deep in your ass!" Leland yelled pointing both of his nines at the boy now, gone was the street preacher leaving just the gang banger from the corner.

"You want a piece of me? You want a piece of this?" Kenny yelled thumping his chest with his open hand while pointing a large revolver at Leland with the other. "You're nothing but a bitch! I'm gonna run the Laurel when you're gone and it's gonna be OG time baby. I'm gonna have ho's, and bowls of dope, and cars and all the damn money I can spend. It's gonna be just like one of those rap videos, only BIGGER!"

"Hey detective Renfroe, I think Kenny's going to fit right in, don't you?" Rico laughed loudly with a wicked smile. His guards and men started to laugh with him filling the foyer with the echoes of their guffaws and all the while Leland and Kenny were still screaming at each other threatening to break off body parts in orifices that were not meant to have objects inserted unless done by a medical professional. After a few seconds it was more than enough for one person in the room.

"WILL YOU ASSHOLES STOP YELLING AND LAUGHING FOR FIVE SEONDS PLEASE!" Foster yelled loud enough to be heard over the others. Everyone turned to the skinny coroner with a shocked look as he spoke.

"The things outside are Werewolves and they are extremely pissed off tonight so we better figure out how we are going to survive when they come crashing in here to kill us all." Foster said with a sudden rock steady voice.

"If they were coming in here I think they would have just busted through the front door like you did." Rico remarked with that evil smile as he crossed his arms over his chest.

"Not with the way they came to a stop outside. Those beasts could have caught us easily on foot but they let us get inside for a reason." Foster shot back with a shake of his head.

"And what reason would that be?" Lloyd asked suddenly.

"We're like a fish that's been put in a bottle that's just been dropped into a tank holding a great big octopus. The werewolves are going to get in here just as the octopus got into that bottle to get the fish. It's just a matter of time and effort." Foster replied coldly leaving the room quiet for a moment.

"Now I'm sure we're going to need some more guards Rico." Lloyd remarked with a trembling voice though the Cartel boss wasn't totally convinced yet.

"You see the problem here mister is I don't believe a single word your saying and when I don't believe you, well, that's a real problem." Rico snarled ignoring Lloyd's request with ease. Instantly every guard's gun was pointed at Foster just as another voice broke the tension.

"I wouldn't shoot him right now Rico. We got bigger problems to worry about." Renfroe called and everyone noticed the detective wasn't looking at the men with the guns now. He was looking down those two dark halls with a concerned expression.

Gaining entry was easy. One of the many doors on the first floor, one for a patio specifically, was unlocked and perfect for Misery and Woe to access the interior of the house. A balcony on the second floor gave Phlegm the necessary way in with an open window as he climbed the wall with ease. Michaels followed the larger ghouls in then found a hidden set of stairs off the kitchen leading upward to the second floor and while his master's pets stalked in the dark below, slowly and silently, each and all made their way to the foyer. Misery and Woe knew to catch and kill anyone to slow or stupid to flee. The other ones who did get away were to be ushered back to Phlegm so the smaller ghoul could see to turning the escapees into the mindless ones for the master to control.

This was the plan Michaels had, have anyone under his control tend to the other business he had to take care of tonight while he took care of the little girl.

At first no understood what Renfroe was talking about or looking at, but then their ears noticed a sound. It was a clicking, like the sound of a large pair of shoes stepping down heavily onto the hardwood floor of the dark hall. The chill that ran down Foster spine at the sound circulated through the room, evident by each man shaking suddenly from the waist up. The guns of the guards went from Renfroe, Leland, and Foster's heads to the two openings just below them. The clicking sound grew louder with each passing second, louder and closer to the foyer. The lead guard yelled to Rico without looking from the halls and the approaching scraping claws.

"What do we do boss?"

"Just stop whatever's coming at us, "Rico ordered drawing his personal nine-millimeter from under his jacket.

"Somehow, I don't think that's going to be possible." Renfroe added slamming home a full clip into his forty-five. He looked out of the corner of his right eye and felt a bit of relief at the sight of Leland reloading the nine's and Foster pulling the hammer back on his thirty-eight as the coroner spoke up with a voice filled with fear.

"It's not the werewolves,"

"Yeah, how do you know that?" Renfroe asked getting his feet set for the rush of bodies he knew was coming.

The clicking was close now, just out on the edge of the line that separated the light from the dark. Foster pointed his small gun down the hall to the right and answered Renfroe. "That smell, the one just barely out there on the tip of your nose, it's from a dead body."

"A dead body," one of the guards mumbled while another said a prayer in Spanish while crossing his chest in the sign of the cross.

Now the clicking had a companion, the smell of a rotting flesh that stung Renfroe's nose as he realized the werewolves outside didn't have this smell. Then a new deep throaty rumble joined the smell and the clicking, the sound of breathing coming from a very large chest. Only the sounds were coming from both hallways the detective realized. Whatever it was coming to get them was coming in pairs. Renfroe kept his arms loose and his hands just tight enough to hold the grip of his handgun as he whispered a small prayer his mother had taught him. Maybe it would protect him if you believed in all that witchcraft stuff...and fortunately he did.

Chapter Twelve

Wilma's lungs burned like the fires of Hell, which she had been told was very hot by some very reputable people. Being a scientist and all she didn't believe much in the Bible or Organized Religion so she had to take the opinion of certain people that the temperature for the abode for Satan was considerably warm. Just how far had she run she wondered? I mean, the car had only gone up the driveway, but how far down the road was that? It should have been maybe a mile at the most but her legs were screaming as if it was more like ten! Finally though, just when she was about to give up, Wilma saw the top of the mansion peeking over the tree line and a strange excitement took hold sending a burst of energy through her. The small spurt of adrenaline hit her veins like instant gasoline, her legs stopped screaming at her and those fires of Hell subsided in her lungs. When Wilma stopped just inside the shadows of the trees across the front of the mansion, she wasn't sure why. She had every intention of going in. Why else would she run twenty miles back to this stupid place? Wilma's mother needed her help to escape the werewolves and she meant to make sure her mother got away unharmed. Yet, why was she just standing here, outside of the house?

The front door was just a short twenty-five feet away. She could slip in quietly, find her mother, and help her get away from the werewolves. So what was the deal, why was she waiting here and not slipping into the mansion?

Simple, it was because for the life of her Wilma couldn't move an inch toward the front doors for some reason. She commanded each leg muscle to contract and release, to propel her toward the door, but the limbs just wouldn't do what legs were supposed to do. Why couldn't she move? What was this paralysis based on? Suddenly, like a small fly buzzing in her ear, a new idea began to take hold. There was another way in, a better way to gain entry into the mansion. Now she could move because the strange paralysis suddenly left her body, whatever holding her fast to the spot was gone. Wilma trotted toward the back of the house, the smell of chlorine just hanging faintly on the air the farther she went and Wilma knew there was a swimming pool somewhere back here so she needed to be careful not fall in with it being so dark. That's all she needed to do she thought, fall in and have to be rescued from drowning when she was trying to save her mom. Wilma didn't have to worry about the pool though, the small fly that buzzed in her ear pointed out a door just slightly ajar in a small curve of the house. The shadows covered it perfectly and it was nowhere near a source of water. No one would see her slipping inside the house and that would give her the advantage of surprise the buzzing voice told her as she smiled. Wilma ran over and with a gentle touch eased the door open just enough to slip her body through. The small hallway was dark, darker than outside, but the little girl just made sure the door didn't slam shut. She was a veteran of a hundred 'sneak-out-without-her-mother-knowing-to-get-some-air' missions at her apartment and all successful so Wilma knew how to stay quiet when needed. She took a deep breath and started tip-toeing down the hall toward what she assumed was the kitchen. The voice, which had guided her along without a hitch, had mysteriously gone quiet when she walked through the backdoor, yet even in the quiet and dark Wilma had to congratulate herself.

Mission accomplished...time to find mom.

Wake up Stephanie Jackson!

The voice screamed in her head causing Stephanie to sit bolt up in the bed she was occupying. At first she was disoriented, the room didn't look familiar and what the hell had happened to the last few hours. She couldn't remember a single thing for a moment and she had to concentrate past the pain in her head to even remember her name. Then like a tidal wave the memories came back, crashing into her brain and threatening to swamp her for a second. There were the men who came bashing through the front door of her home, the guns being fired as she ducked to get back into her bedroom, and then she remembered Wilma. Stephanie's little girl was running trying to get away just before then the men were grabbing them both and then shoving them into the Land Rover SUV. For a second she couldn't breathe but Stephanie fought back the fear the memories induced while trying to roll out of the bed. The room swam crazily stopping her and that was when she noticed two things rather quickly. One, her hands were locked tight in a nice set of handcuffs in front of her. Two, a man stood just by the door in the shadows watching her every move intently. Stephanie thought she recognized him but the dark confused her just enough to cast doubt.

"Where's Wilma? Where's my daughter?" She asked looking and hoping it was who she thought it was and not one of the men from before.

"She's not safe Stephanie, and at the moment neither are you." Alexander said stepping out of the concealing dark just a step. He didn't want to move to far away from the door in case someone came walking by. Although his senses told him all the occupants with the exception of one was at the front of the house about to meet two very large nightmares he still kept a very cautious demeanor.

Stephanie rose from the bed unsteadily and she might have collapsed if not for Alexander and his quick save. One second she was spinning about to meet the floor in a face ending crash and the next he was holding her tight around the waist with one arm, the other supporting the middle of her back. Stephanie felt warmth suddenly spread through her body from his touch, something she hadn't felt for a very long time until the night Leland confessed his feelings and finally kissed her. The sexual desire inside her came to life and she felt a tinge of fear with it. Was this for Leland or was it for Alexander...or was it something that happened with anyone that came to close to the vampire? She shook her head driving the silly thoughts and the desire away before looking to Alexander.

"Do you have a key for these?" Stephanie asked with a voice that sounded just a little frustrated and not in a bad way.

"I'm sorry but I'm afraid I do not. And if I try to remove them forcefully I might rip off more than just the cuffs." Alexander replied politely while slowly letting go of Stephanie to make sure she was steady.

"Oh, yeah, wouldn't want to go round with a hook for a hand." Stephanie replied while smiling weakly finally before asking again. "Where is Wilma? You said she isn't safe?"

"She's in the mansion again. Rico tried to take her to a safe house but there was a problem." Alexander said walking to the door.

"What kind of a problem?" Stephanie asked quickly after having to chase down the vampire.

"Yelena's brothers and others tried to kidnap her but she eluded them, quite capable our little Wilma is." Alexander responded going back to the door putting a hand to the portal.

"So she's outside somewhere?" Stephanie asked perplexed.

"No, I said she's back in the mansion. Wilma came in through a servant's entrance in the kitchen just a few minutes ago." Alexander said turning away from the door with a slight smile.

"Why did she come back?" Stephanie whined.

"Wilma thought she could help you against the werewolves. She will not let anything happen to her mother." Alexander stated still smiling before turning back to the door again.

"Yelena's brothers are after me now too?" Stephanie asked with her voice sounding as if she was on the brink of a nervous collapse.

"No they are not," Alexander answered quickly trying to layout the confusing field of battle that was Lloyd Dunbar's house, "but Wilma thinks they are. The brothers are actually down by the pool, drawn there by Yelena herself. They are going to attack and kill her, or at least try."

"They're going to kill Yelena, they're sister?" Stephanie whispered totally confused now. Wow, get knocked out for a few minutes and the world goes to pot she thought.

"Yes, because they're being forced to kill her, against their will and all. Yelena will keep them from getting back to the mansion or hurting Wilma."

"And my daughter thought she was going to help me. How the hell did she find an open door to get back in?" Stephanie lamented.

"A voice in her head told her about it." Alexander commented turning back from the door.

"Was that voice yours? Oh please tell me it was."

"No, it was not my voice Stephanie."

"It wasn't? Who's was it?" Stephanie asked trembling suddenly.

"What used to be a man, his name is Michaels. He's the one controlling Yelena's brothers and the one who is now controlling the fight." Alexander answered while trying to soothe Stephanie's fears.

"He's in control now? We have to get out there and help Wilma!" Stephanie exclaimed trying to walk past Alexander, who only stopped her with an upraised hand.

"You can't do that Stephanie." He explained taking her by the shoulders, the flames inside Stephanie rising again at his touch though it wasn't desire this time. "We'll get Wilma out of safely, Michaels wouldn't dare hurt her."

"Oh, you know that for sure!" Stephanie countered. "And how come your so damn positive he won't try to hurt her?"

"It's simple, because he needs Wilma to force me to destroy Yelena and her brothers. He knows that without her he cannot control me and thus his plan is as dead as he is. And he also knows if he harms a single hair on her head I will end him without so much as a passing thought." Alexander answered before turning back to the door. Before shifting his attention back to his senses and where everyone was he made sure of one thing. He looked into her eyes and made sure she knew he spoke the truth, especially if something were to happen to Wilma.

Stephanie didn't reply or say anything else because she didn't feel a need to. The look from Alexander was enough to tell her that he meant every word. He would kill anyone who tried to hurt her daughter. Wilma had two of the best protectors in the known universe, a devoted ancient vampire and a loving mother. She fell in line behind Alexander and waited quietly until he turned back to her and spoke softly.

"In a minute I'm going to open the door Stephanie and I expect you to run through it as fast as your legs can carry you. Down the hall is a right turn, take it, and then cut across to the other side of the mansion. You'll run into Leland and the others there, stay with them no matter what you hear and you might see the light of another day."

Five minutes ago Stephanie would have been going crazy asking all questions about what she just heard. Why did she have to run? What was after them? Yet, she just nodded and began to take deep breaths to ready herself for a quick sprint. She wasn't really nervous and she wasn't seriously scared or concerned about what was going to happen. Stephanie was calm and ready to do what was necessary to stay alive but most of all do what had to be done to get her daughter back. Then the vampire swung the door open with a quick fling and he was gone in a blink as usual. Stephanie didn't stand around wondering what had happened to Alexander for more than a second. She bolted out the open portal into the hall. A second or two later the sound of bullets winging and ricocheting off the walls in the house came from everywhere as she made the right turn at the hall. The screams of so many men echoed in the house just as loud as well.

The boxes of can goods stacked by the wall and the racks of other assorted things and food told her this wasn't the way out. Wilma took a quick survey of the room she had stumbled on. Assorted cans of vegetables, fruits, soups, baking goods, and other sundries lined metal shelves in a neat and very anal manner. She leaned out of the door and looked down the dark hall, thought for a second, and then loaded two or three hefty cans of some vegetable into her coat pockets from one of the shelves on the rack. No way was she going any further inside without being properly armed. The weight felt good in her hands and pockets, a reassurance against the werewolves if needed.

Wilma closed the door to the pantry as slow as possible and the damn thing still squealed like a set of fingernails being dragged down a chalkboard. For a second she gave a good bit of consideration to ducking back inside the small room, one of the werewolves was bound to have heard that. Nevertheless, in the end she just continued slowly down the hall before stepping out in the dark kitchen, nowhere to go but through her mind told her. The kitchen was huge with moonlight gleaming off all the stainless steel accessories and fixtures like twinkling stars in the night sky. Wilma figured it was just as big as her school's cafeteria kitchen when her ears picked up the slightest hint of rumbling and scraping. She froze instantly, her ears trying to pick up the two sounds from the enveloping silence of the dark.

She stood perfectly still listening but there was nothing though, no sound of rumbling or scraping or anything. So Wilma took a few tentative steps toward the archway of a hallway that looked like it might lead to the front of the house, and then her ears heard the rumbling and scraping again. This time she froze and dropped to a knee next to a set of large cabinets of an island probably used for food preparation. Again, silence was the only thing she heard but Wilma knew better, the werewolves were out there in the kitchen somewhere. She leaned up against the cold wood of the cabinet, pulled one of the heavy cans out of her pocket, and readied for the fight.

Time to go to war Wilma thought.

A few seconds passed without any noise and she thought her mind just might be playing tricks on her when the rumbling happened again. This time it was close, so close in fact Wilma could feel hot tingling breath on the back of her exposed neck. Suddenly she heard the scraping again, but the noise was something else now, the scraping actually sounded like words. Wilma came to a horrific conclusion, one that sent a quick shiver down her spine. Drawing up the courage to do the unthinkable Wilma looked up from her kneeling position of safety. There, just a few feet away from her, was the evil man from the night before. He was talking to no one and yet carrying on a full conversation with someone, and it was all in a language she had no clue existed. It wasn't Spanish or French or German, she knew those because her High School offered a class on each. No...The words sounded old...Latin maybe?

Then the house just erupted in sound and noise, gunfire and screaming and things being broken and destroyed. It was a cacophony of destruction and it scared Wilma when it all exploded like some sound bomb. She dropped back down hiding just as the man turned around to take a look at what caused the squeal behind him.

All right, this is no joke, it really is time to go to war Wilma thought swallowing hard.

Chapter Thirteen

Yelena slowed to a walk when she reached the pool, or what some might consider a lagoon because the pool was so large complete with a cabana and an outdoor kitchen and dining area. There was even a small building that must have been a changing room and a shower from what she could tell as she passed it. The area was down a small slope from the house and she had to walk down a small set of steps that passed through and between several well-kept flower beds. Why someone would need a place like this with a house like the one right behind you eluded the Russian, but then she wondered why someone would need a pool the size of the one she was looking at. It was a kidney shaped pool with light blue colored tile and there in the middle were different colored ones on the bottom that spelled out something, what Yelena didn't care. If the pool wasn't quite ostentatious enough already this was definitely the dagger in its bloated heart.

She took a quick sniff of the air and she picked up her brothers' scent quickly, certainly too fast if they were hunting. Oh my precious ones, you don't want to do this as much as I do not, that is why you're not downwind. You're telling me your coming, warning me, but I will not leave you and I will not run. I will help you find yourselves again and then we will avenge our family's betrayal. Yelena closed her eyes and cursed the Grand Lich Akhenaton and his follower Michaels silently for hurting her brothers. She stood there listening to the night and it wasn't long before the sound of heavy footsteps touched her ears. Yelena opened her eyes and there at the other end of the pool by the open air kitchen with a large stone oven and stainless steel grill were her three brothers, emerging from the dark in shambling forced steps. Yelena bit her bottom lip at the sight, holding down the anger it stirred as she watched her brothers fight.

They were in partial transformation, thick coarse hair covering their exposed backs and chests. Their faces were semi-wolf like with the same thick hair covering high cheeks and long teeth but no maw yet. Their arms and legs had stretched slightly and their hands had grown and lengthened into deadly claws. Gregor stepped up grunting with the failed effort of fighting the ghouls poison in their system.

"Run...please!" He spit and growled low.

"No," she whispered back shaking her head, "I will not abandon my family for anything. And I will not kill you even though you seek to kill me."

Somewhere in the house the fight started, the sounds of the beginnings of a raging battle reaching the pool area easily. They stood there staring at each other neither side wanting one instance of what was about to happen, and yet both knew it had to happen. Then the three brothers launched themselves forward running at their sister growling and roaring.

Yelena growled in return charging them thinking one last thought as she did.

Damn you Akhenaton...Damn you...

If you asked who made the first move for the stairs, was it the guards or the three of them, no one could really give you an answer. Renfroe wasn't sure, all he knew there was a deafening roar that broke the silence just before those two huge nightmares came running at them from the dark, and then everyone was bolting up the stairs screaming like first grade schoolchildren running from naptime. A second later the bullets started flying from Rico's goon squad as the stair banister and rail came flying apart in a splinter shower. Leland and Foster fired back blindly and even struck one of the guards in the leg and dropping him like a sack of potatoes as they ran in front of the detective for the second floor. Renfroe just pushed the men up the stairs while covering his face from the flying debris. Then the those monstrosities appeared like ghost, if one could believe something that big would go unnoticed, running right for them ignoring any and all kinds of damage they were taking. The pair broke up, one following each group up the staircase, and as the first behemoth slammed into Rico's men those who had the misfortune of being too slow to get ahead of the others fell, Foster heard the screams for God and his mercy. Nope, don't think the big man or woman upstairs is listening right now fellas the coroner thought just before he told his legs to move a whole hell-of-a-lot faster up the stairs because the other monster was coming for them. Leland actually stole a look over his shoulder and felt his heart, which was damn near about to burst from all this running, freeze because one of the biggest men he had ever seen was just three steps behind him and he didn't look at all nice.

"GO!" Renfroe screamed reaching the top of the staircase then spinning quickly he turned and pointed his gun right into the face of the thing chasing them as the two men kept on moving down the hall. He pulled the trigger firing his weapon point blank, the last possible second before the huge thing was on him, and smiled as the gun kicked in his hand.

The detective wasn't sure if he hurt the thing but he was sure he didn't kill it. The behemoth stopped on the step shaking its head which was all Renfroe really wanted it to do. He followed with a quick step following Leland running as all three bolted down a hall towards the rear of the house now not sure where they were going but knowing anywhere but the foyer was good for the foreseeable future. The men were looking for a door to duck in when Stephanie suddenly appeared from a side hall, both hands locked in handcuffs but still running like a champion sprinter.

<hr/>

"Oh Damn!" Stephanie screamed as a bullet whizzed by just a couple of inches from her head. She was running down the hall like a mad woman when the guards came running up the stairs at her from downstairs and the bullets started flying. The screams that were louder than the guns meant only one thing to her, the situation was sure worse downstairs then it was up here. She ran along the small connecting hall ready to dive out of the way of more bullets when Leland was abruptly there. He instinctively grabbed her under his arm and dragged her down the hall. A skinny guy in front of them hit a large door like a battering ram and the detective from the strip club followed them into a room.

Renfroe pulled his spinning ballet routine one more time firing two rounds from his forty-five. One bullet struck the wall by the big son-of-a-mother who was after them again, but the other struck home causing the large beast to step back and put a hand to the wall for a moment. The detective caught sight of the large thing taking a break before the doors closed and Renfroe finally chanced a look at his new surroundings, a library with no exit save the one they just came in.

"Are you all right baby? Were you hit?" Leland kept asking Stephanie as he cradled her head in his hands.

"I'm good...just get these damn things off me please!" Stephanie exclaimed holding up her hands to show off the bright metal of the handcuffs. Before Leland could turn and ask Renfroe if he had a set of keys to the cuffs a ring of the metal openers hit him square in the chest. He picked them up and freed Stephanie on the second key he tried. She rubbed the feeling back into her hands secretly hoping the red marks would disappear as she looked around. The men all looked okay, no major injuries except for being scared right out of their skins.

"Good job getting us to here Foster." Renfroe remarked to the coroner.

"Yeah, I know I screwed up by running in here but it was the only place I saw open at the time." The assistant coroner answered.

"No Foster, I'm not criticizing you." Renfroe answered. "You ran like the wind and found some cover. Can't fault you for doing what I would have done."

"Thanks," Foster said with a surprised small smile.

"So how do we get out of here?" Renfroe asked aloud.

"We have to get Wilma!" Leland demanded sounding suspiciously like a father.

"I think we need to worry about us right now honcho." Renfroe remarked back. Leland was about to tell the detective that Wilma meant everything to them but Stephanie beat him to the punch.

"We don't have to worry about Wilma."

"Why's that?" Renfroe asked with a raised eyebrow.

"You saw Alexander," Leland answered for the woman he loved.

"He knows where Wilma is and he promised me nothing would happen to her. I think someone in here also knows he'll do anything to keep her alive." Stephanie remarked.

"Huh?" Foster grunted.

"I know it sounds weird but right now Wilma is safer than we are. Alexander will take care of her so let's just get up out of here all right?" Stephanie pointed out.

"I second that emotion!" Leland agreed with a quick nod of his head.

"All right then, here's the plan. I saw Rico and his boys go the other way at the foyer so I'm guessing they have an office or a room they've chosen to hide out in at the front of the house. What do you say we go and pay them a visit?" Renfroe asked with broad smile.

"Pay them a visit?" Leland repeated.

"Are you crazy?" Foster spat from behind.

"Well it sure beats waiting for them to come and get us. I, for one, do not wish to die like a trapped rat." Renfroe said holding forty-five high.

"Man's got a point." Stephanie said with a shrug of her shoulders.

"The man does make a lot of sense." Leland remarked lifting the twin nines.

"Yeah, I know he does. I hate it when he's right." Foster said shaking his head and checking the bullets in his thirty-eight.

Leland tried to pass one of his nine millimeters to Stephanie but she waved him off and shook her head no. "I'll let you handle the gun part of this baby."

"All right people, we ready to move?" Renfroe asked standing by the door. No one said a word, they just looked to each other with eyes that said 'yeah, I don't want to do this, but yeah I'm ready'.

Lloyd and Kenny busted through the doors to the office followed closely by Rico and what was left of his men. The last man in wasn't even through the doors yet before Lloyd and Kenny were closing the entrance. He practically had to dive inside the room or be locked out and there in the hall, just a few feet away the beast known as Woe that had chased and maimed half the guards came to an abrupt stop letting the pursuit come to an end for now. The men inside the room stood in shocked silence as a few seconds ticked away with nothing happening, and then Kenny turned to Rico with a sarcastic smile.

"We got nothing to worry about huh? That little girl is crazy huh? We're crazy for believing her huh?" He spat.

"Listen, I had no damn idea those things existed so you can't blame me for all this shit!" Rico screamed back.

"I don't give a damn about blame Rico. I just want to get the hell out of here in one piece!" Lloyd weighed in with a loud scream.

Before anyone else could say another word a deep growl came out of the dark of the corner of the room. It was pure animal and it was as menacing a sound as anything each man had ever heard. With a slow move every man in the room with a gun raised their weapon and zeroed in on the dark corner where the rumbling came from. One of Rico's men whispered a prayer in Spanish, the same one as before Lloyd thought as he spoke.

"Who's there?"

The growling only grew louder, angrier at the words and Lloyd instantly wished he hadn't said a thing as Rico spat behind him

"What the hell is going here Lloyd?" Rico asked.

"I don't know! Maybe we should have left town like the man in black said to." The business man hissed shaking his head. How the hell was he supposed to know what was going on tonight Dunbar thought? Leaving town was sounding like the choice he should have made when something hit the doors to the office so hard the wood portals shook. It sounded like someone very large hit them with an equally large hammer and every gun that was pointed at the corner shifted and turned back to the doors. Lloyd wondered if the beast outside was intent on getting in and finishing the job it had started in the foyer. He, and the others, totally forgot about the growling from the corner and in the end that was the one thing they should have been worried about more. Phlegm had found his way to the office just as ordered by Michaels and when it was time to strike he attacked the back of the men slashing with his clawed hands drawing blood with cut after cut. Rico never asked for mercy and he didn't scream when Phlegm struck, which is more than Lloyd and Kenny could say. They both yelled and cried as loud as they could when the ghoul came for them in the end.

There was no pause and no hesitation. The brothers three were no longer under the control of their actions and Yelena would not leave them to the mercy of the Lesser Lich Michaels to do awful things. So the fight was on as the brothers intended to do great bodily harm to their sister, only with the first strike Gregor missed with a great awkward swipe of his paw. He's fighting the poison she thought easily ducking the clumsy blow before delivering her own with a swift open palm to her brother's face. The punch knocked the red haired wolf into his brother Dimitri keeping him from attacking but Peter was still more than able to and even fighting against the control of the ghoul's poison he struck hard when given the chance. Yelena turned just time to see her larger brother hit her grabbing two handfuls of her top and then with a heave throw her backwards into and through the side of the cabana with a crash. As soon as Peter finished his throw he reared back his head and screamed with a howl into the night air, a sound of anguish as it was easy to see he was fighting his own body.

Her vision swam and she tasted blood in her mouth but Yelena was too busy getting back up from the wreckage of the cabana and wooden lounge chairs she crashed landed into to think about anything else but keeping her brothers from hurting her and themselves. She staggered out of the cabana front opening holding a large leg piece of a broken lounge chair. There was

Peter finishing his howl and turning back to her while behind him Dimitri was tossing Gregor down turning his attention as well to her.

Fight it my loved ones she thought gripping the wooden club tightly, fight the poison and come back to me.

There was someone back there, behind the island, and Michaels had an idea who it might be as he looked into the dark kitchen. Our dear little girl came back just like she was supposed to, only it was earlier than he hoped for. Phlegm had done his job perfectly along with Woe's help of seizing control of all the men up in the office. The only problem now was there was a very limited time to induce and take control of the men, a small window of opportunity to take over their bodies like he had done with the werewolves. Michaels knew this limited time to complete this part of his plan would be wasted if he began chasing some little girl around the kitchen. His lord would most certainly burn him alive if he messed this chance up. Yet, there was a way to make sure she stayed nearby.

"I guess I'll go see to man who owns this house...and then to your mother little one." The Lesser Lich said politely while smiling cruelly. He didn't wait for a response. He could imagine the look of shock on the little girl's face at his words as he left the kitchen. He went up a hidden stair used by the staff probably so as not to clutter up the foyer with their passing. At the top he followed the hall down to the double door to the large office, the body of Woe filling the expanse of the entryway easily. The large ghoul moved to one side allowing Michaels access and as he entered he saw all the men were standing nicely in three lines and all were acting like perfect little zombies. All ready for me he thought and as he walked in he began to speak those old words Wilma had heard downstairs, phrases in a dialect only but a very few alive could speak in the proper intonation to cause the desired effect. As the Lesser Lich spoke he reached into his jacket pocket and produced a vial of some liquid and to each man he applied one small drop to their lips with his fingertip. The effect was almost immediate as each man, Lloyd and Kenny as well, shook for a moment with small thrashes and throes before calming.

"Ah there, now follow me closely. Will everyone please raise your right hands high above your heads?"

The guards and Rico did exactly what Michaels asked. They couldn't stop from doing it, no matter how hard they strained and told their bodies not to. Suddenly no one in the room could control a single muscle in their bodies. They just stood like statues with raised hands. The Lesser Lich walked up to Rico bypassing several guards who could only watch him out of the corner of their eyes.

"My name is Michaels and I now have control of your body. I need you to go and take care of the three gentlemen who were chased in here. I need you to make sure they are dead and will not be interfering with what happens the rest of the night." Michaels said with a slight smile.

Rico didn't answer back except with a moan. He couldn't talk if he wanted to. He only stared at Michaels with the same blank look he had when the Lich walked in. Then suddenly a rumbling groan sounded behind him and Michaels turned to see Phlegm standing there waiting for the next task to do. "I need you to go to the kitchen and find the little girl. She's hiding there, and do NOT eat her."

The smaller ghoul hissed back before nodding then turning to do as he had been ordered. As it did Michaels turned to Woe and pointed. "Go find Misery and then both of you go and take care of getting the little girl with Phlegm. We need her in our hands before the Ancient One finds her or we all will be in a serious predicament."

Woe did just like his smaller kind, only grumbled and nodded before turning to do as he was told. After the behemoth left the men under Michaels control shuffled out of the room on stiff legs going to do as ordered as they were told, to take care of the three men who were chased into the house. And when the office was empty the Lesser Lich stood in the center thinking and chewing on his thumb nail. He was now plagued with one of the most annoying thoughts anyone being could have, the one where you swear you have checked all the items off your mental list and yet you know you're missing one thing. It just kept buzzing round his head, he had missed something but what Michaels could not think of for his undead life. Yes, he had the little girl captured to all intent and purposes with Phlegm tracking her down. Yes, Misery and Woe would help get the girl and then protect him from the Ancient One. With the girl in their hands Alexander wouldn't risk an injury to her so getting him to finish Yelena and her brothers should be easy enough. So, what was he missing? What could he-

Suddenly it hit him like a lightning bolt from the sky and Michaels gasped from the realization. He cursed his weary brain with a hiss. "The mother, how could I forget about her? Some days I would forget my head if it wasn't attached to my body!"

The Lich walked out of the room and on his second step music abruptly started up with a loud blare that resounded through the foyer and halls from installed speakers. He looked over the banister to the floor of the room below and on the only table in the entryway was a large music box, the kind people carry around to the beach or wherever someone wants to annoy their neighbors with loud 'tunes'. A rough edgy guitar riff began to play, the power chords were followed by a deep drum and a grating voice singing loudly. The man sang about taking a ride, no stop signs or speed limits, and then the band joined in with a loud raucous chorus chanting the main bridge of the song.

I'm on the Highway to Hell...On the Highway to Hell...Highway to Hell...

"Funny Ancient One, but we'll see who is laughing when Phlegm has your little friend in his dirty claws." Michaels hissed at the song and almost instantly, it started over. He turned to Rico with eyes of fire and spit slowly sliding down his chin. "Kill the four in the library, bring their heads to me!"

Chapter
Fourteen

The man had left the room, Wilma was sure of it and the sounds from all the screaming and shooting had died down but yet she was stuck right where she had been hiding behind the island. Fear, stark and strong, held her in a cold grip squeezing her heart and chest. It started when the man turned to look at her but in reality it really began that night she saw him standing outside of Grammy's window. She trembled as the memory came back and it only added to the terror she was feeling. And then, just like before on that night, Grammy's words came back giving her strength.

'If you're strong and show no fear then evil can't win you over'

She took each and every word and put it in her heart letting the power flow through her body loosening the terror's grip. She breathed deep feeling Grammy's will flood her soul and push back the panic. You have no power over me evil man Wilma chanted in her mind sending the icy touch of despair away with each silent assertion of the words. After a minute of stoking her courage she regained enough of her composure to gather her legs under her and slowly stand back up from her hiding spot. To Wilma's relief the man was gone and the evil he oozed with him leaving just the dark of the kitchen and her deep inhales which echoed in it. She looked around wondering where the man had gone and that's when she noticed the can in her pocket and the fact her hand was wrapped around the metal cylinder with an iron clutch.

"Wow...it was almost time to go to war there," she whispered just as the sounds of fighting came from down the hall where the door she came in was. Then the floor started to creak above her, as if something big and heavy was coming back toward the kitchen, and Wilma took a step back away from the squeaking overhead. Each step, creak, was louder than the last and she knew from the number of creaks that there was more than one of whatever it was coming this way. Wilma began to look around for a new place to hide because from the sound of what was heading this way ducking behind the island wasn't going to work this time.

Dimitri hesitated just a moment when he went for Yelena intending to rip her throat out. He was still fighting his body with every ounce of energy his mind could muster and that's what saved him from hurting his precious sister...that and the fact she hit him with the leg of the lounge chair upside his head. The blow was a counter to his off-balanced strike with a claw and it sent him reeling away from her thank the heavens. He went to all fours just as Gregor landed a large backhanded haymaker that propelled Yelena backwards a good six feet before she landed on the stones of the patio that surrounded the pool. She rolled up and was back on her feet just as Peter attacked again trying to punch her but Yelena partially blocked the swing by ducking inside the strike and using her forearm. Then before her brother could react she slammed her fist right into his throat driving him backwards away from her. The punch wasn't meant to kill but stun and it reduced Peter to barely standing as he gagged and gasped for air.

Please, please be gone Yelena begged silently for the ghoul's poison to be done. Her brothers, and herself for the matter, couldn't fight much longer and not cause some type of great bodily harm. Both sides had been pulling punches this whole time but all it took was for one blow to land wrong and she could lose a brother at her own hands or worse, she could be killed by one of them. So Yelena let her guard drop just a bit to make sure Peter wasn't going to die reaching out for him and that was all it took for Gregor to rush her and get his hands around her throat. He squeezed hard closing off her windpipe almost instantly but Yelena still got one last word out before he picked her up off the ground.

"Mother..."

Gregor's face contorted and twisted with pain as he fought his body and growled, "I cannot stop Yelena...I cannot...stop...MYSELF!"

"Save her...please..." She gasped with the last bit of air she was able to take in before her brother began to choke her. Her only thought now was of her mother, of Svetlana as the dark began to narrow her vision. She would have to hurt her brother to get free and that was something Yelena would never do.

The red haired werewolf bellowed with anguish as he watched his beloved sister's eyes start to go dull from lack of oxygen, as his hands continued to squeeze and press on her throat. Then Dimitri was screaming from behind and his hands were grabbing Gregor's wrists and pulling at them to separate his grip. "LET HER GO BROTHER! LET OUR SISTER GO!"

And still Gregor squeezed unable to stop his hands from strangling his sister. Her eyes were so dull now, the life slipping away, and he screamed again as Dimitri tried to stop him by pulling at his wrists with all his strength. She was just seconds away from dying, moments that were utterly agonizing as Gregor couldn't stop what he was doing. Then a pair of fist slammed into his back between the shoulder blades and his hands finally slipped away from her throat. Yelena fell back as Dimitri and Peter grabbed Gregor who screamed and howled fighting the last of the ghoul's poison as it began to fade releasing him from Michael's control. He sat horrified at what he had done and it was only when his precious sister took a deep breath and began to cough that he finally stopped wailing. It was only when she looked to him clutching her bruised neck and smiled did he finally feel back in his own skin.

"Sister," Dimitri cried and slid over to her cradling her as she coughed and breathed deep taking in as much air as she could hold.

"I am fine my brothers...are you all right? Are you free?" she whispered back, her voice barely audible from the damage to her larynx.

Peter only nodded kneeling on the stones feeling worn and exhausted while Gregor shook his head, "If I had killed you."

"But you did not my brother. I am alive, you are free of Michaels and we must flee or the ghouls will come for us once again." Yelena explained pulling her sore and tired body to a standing position with Dimitri's help. She slid over and hugged her brother warmly trying to sooth his pain. She was about to tell her brothers they had to run for the Chevelle and wait for Alexander when the door to the kitchen exploded into a shower of debris that flew all the way down to the pool. The werewolves barely had time to see the smaller of the ghouls, dreadful Phlegm, as it flew across the lawn striking the flower bed high on the wall by the stairs Yelena had come down that led down to the patio.

The body skipped off the dirt and plants before caroming into the center of the pool with a loud splash. Yelena turned from the rippling water and back to the large opening where the door used to be.

"Ancient One,"

Then a small voice touched her mind, his voice. *Find Wilma and keep her safe please!*

The plea moved Yelena in an instant as she rose from the ground and ran for the house while trying to scream at her brothers, "Help Alexander with the ghouls!"

"Where are you going?" Dimitri yelled back pulling Peter to his feet.

She just ran on toward the house hoping her brothers understood why she had no time to yell back. Up ahead, just over the broken back door that Phlegm had smashed through was an open window and just like the wall earlier Yelena never slowed as she approached the house. With three quick steps she ran up the side of the wall and slipped into the window. Her throat burned with every breath and her lungs felt the same but Yelena had to find Wilma. The little one had no idea what she was up against.

If the man from the other night was scary then this new one that silently stalked into the kitchen, obviously looking for her with the way he moved and scanned the dark, this man was about ten times worse. Never mind the smell, which was so putrid she had to cover her nose in a failed effort to keep the strong scent out, it was the way he was dressed and looked. Those are burial clothes Wilma thought from her new hiding spot in the dark corner by the refrigerator down by the other side of the island, and his face...he had no eyes and his skin looked like old parchment complete with small rips in the cheeks. Wilma shook uncontrollably with each crouched step the man took to get closer to her hiding spot but then he slowed near the island and she realized he was looking for her in the old hiding place. She took a long deep breath keeping it as quiet as possible as she watched the man quickly jump around the corner trying to catch her, only she had long given up on that place. The man stood back up and looked confused for a moment, just a quick second, before looking right to her new spot and hissing loudly with a wide smile. Oh God, he's known this whole time where I was Wilma thought with a loud gasp. He was just playing with me she thought on as the man made a quick feint to run at her causing Wilma to jump out of her hiding spot and bolt for the end of the island. It wasn't much but anything between her and this new man was better than nothing Wilma thought as her hand reached into the coat pocket that held the can of corn and squeezed the cylinder again.

This new stalker just stared with a titled head at her as Wilma breathed deep in and out and it wasn't from exertion, it was all from fear. Grammy never said anything about evil looking like this, something without eyes and teeth that looked like a shark's, gazing on her as if she were dinner. Alexander said there were things out there like him but this thing...it wasn't like him at all. The thing growled low as its mouth opened and shut, quivering almost with anticipation.

There is no way this can of soup is going to stop something like this Wilma thought to herself standing there on the other side of the island with the thing staring at her. A small drop of drool fell from its open mouth falling down the front of its black jacket. Oh that was gross Wilma thought as she slowly and with some stealth pulled the can of corn out of her coat pocket trying not to draw attention to the move. There wouldn't be a second chance to try and attack this thing she thought and it wasn't because she only had one can of corn in her hand. No, it was because this thing was quick and she'd only have the one chance to hit it before bolting for any other room in the house than this one. Then the thing did just what she expected and feared at the same time, started forward toward her with three fast steps. Wilma yelped and ran in the same direction he moved countering its approach by running away. Both stopped at the same time on opposite sides of the island staring right at each other across the middle of the granite topped table. Wilma smiled and even giggled a little which sounded so weird at the moment. "I'm the best at ring-around-the-rosie...you want to go for another turn?"

The room between Wilma and the thing was small which should have caused some panic for Wilma but she felt fine for some reason, as if there was nothing to worry about from those shark teeth that gnashed menacingly or eyeless sockets that stared back. Then music suddenly kicked on from somewhere with the heavy power chords of a guitar filling the kitchen along with the strained voice of a singer explaining how he was on the 'Highway to Hell' or something like that. The sudden musical interruption from behind down the hall caused Wilma to turn her head just a little, just enough to catch a quick glance over her shoulder to see what was going on, and that's when Phlegm took advantage of the distraction. With a cat's nimbleness it jumped up onto the island top with both feet closing the distance to Wilma in a flash and the move snapped the little girl's courage clean in half. She yelped again and stepped back raising the arm holding the can of corn ready to lash out with a quick throw of her weapon hoping to injure or maim the thing. The ghoul though just hissed loudly as if daring Wilma to throw the can at it. For a second no one moved, not Wilma or Phlegm, then with a sputter she spoke trying to threaten the thing on the island top.

"Don't come any closer! This can of corn is a lot heavier than it looks!" Wilma was trying to induce at least a smidgen of fear but with her voice quivering like it was the attempt at intimidation was pointless and it was more than obvious it was a failure. The thing just smiled, the skin on its face tearing as it did from being so dry, and hissed louder moving toward her intent on lunging. Wilma was just as ready to let her can of corn fly hoping the tin cylinder would at least blind the thing so she could get a chance to flee when she felt something brush by her in a bolt, a sudden whoosh of air blowing across her face. She watched as the thing on the table top just as suddenly flew backwards away from her landing square in the middle of the large refrigerator with the stainless steel side-by-side doors. Her mouth went slack and her eyes wide as she watched her angel, her Alexander, as he was here to save her once again. He had grabbed the thing right off the island top and, at present, he was slamming its body into and through the refrigerator over and over, its face and head and body going deeper and deeper into the appliance with each slam. The metal doors tried to bend and wrap around the thing but the force Alexander was using to crush it was more than the side-by-side doors could take and both flew into pieces that bounced around the kitchen.

"Run Wilma, flee to safety now!" Alexander screamed with a snarl and little Wilma could almost picture his fangs long and gleaming. "Run away and we will find you!"

The command broke her from the shocked trance and it was just in time as well for a wedge of metal from the obliterated appliance barely missed Wilma's head as it went flying by. She gave a small squeal and turned ready to bolt for what she thought was the front of the house and safety, only someone had blocked the way with a very large man. Wilma froze as the putrid smell from before hit her nose but just about ten times stronger. He's a larger version of the small one, a really large-larger version of the smaller one she thought swallowing hard. Then the mountain moved, the floor shook, and Wilma broke for the stairs while behind her there was a loud crash. Either Alexander had finally mated the refrigerator and the smaller thing with one last thrust of his hands or her friend the vampire had thrown it through the wall to the outside. Whatever one it was Wilma wasn't sticking around to find out as she run up the stairs bounding to the top as fast as her legs could carry her. Below Alexander watched his friend run and a small smile crossed his now transformed face. He had unleashed his full power and it had turned his face into an evil visage as it was down to just him and the mammoth ghouls of Akhenaton's making. The vampire's mouth pulled back exposing the large fangs as he snarled in preparation for the fight.

Wilma reached the top of the stairs almost out of breath. She hadn't done this much running since Mr. Smith's barbaric PE class, seriously, when was she ever going to need to climb a twenty foot rope and ring a bell? She stopped to catch her second wind when something so subtle only Wilma's heightened senses caught it told her that something wasn't right...again. She heard the battle break out below with a loud crash and then to her left gunfire erupted one more time but Wilma refused to look either way. No, the last time she did that she almost got eaten by that thing with the shark's teeth. Wilma just looked ahead as the sounds of fighting echoed in the house and there coming out of the dark shadows was the man from the night before and downstairs, the evil one. She fought the urge to run as the man, still dressed in a black suit and red tie, walked up and stopped and sneered just a few feet away.

"Thank you for coming to me little one. I do detest having to run while wearing my best suit." He quipped, like he was being funny or something. Wilma just stared at him with a cold eye, as hard as any Alexander could give, and when the man took his next step that can of corn she had been holding onto went flying right into this head like a missile. The cylinder struck true with a loud crack sending the man's head back causing him to howl in pain and it was all the distraction Wilma needed or wanted. She turned and ran for the back of the house down a hall pushing her tired legs even more as the can bounced off the man's noggin before hitting the floor.

Michaels stepped back from the blow and grabbed his forehead where the can had hit him, right between the eyes almost. He screamed in anger and shock mostly because his body had stopped feeling anything but horrendous pain a long time ago being dead and all. He looked down to see the can that had hit him then spun howling out to the girl as she ran away. "A can of corn, really? Where did you even get that from?"

***

Misery and Woe...what cheerful names Akhenaton had given these new larger ghouls Alexander thought as he stared at the pair of beasts through his mystical window. Before they died both were men who had pursued perfection of building the body with putting muscle on muscle thus turning themselves into walking giants. And now with the help of the Grand Lich both were as close to that name as one could get, and both were dead as well which meant they felt no pain and would not stop until ordered too or their heads were separated from their large bodies. Somehow the vampire knew Michaels would not halt an attack so that meant he had to put both down by any means he could. Oh this would be a good fight Alexander thought as the two ghouls eyed him side by side for a moment more before rushing at him as one crashing into and through the island in perfect unison. Wood and metal flew in a wild shower of debris along with kitchen implements like spatulas and knives and rolling pins as the behemoths exploded the island into as many pieces as the back door that Phlegm had flown through. Alexander noted the sound of a splash after he had tossed the smaller ghoul away, two points for hitting the pool he thought silently. The vampire met the charge of Misery and Woe, somewhat, by slipping through all the deadly shrapnel letting his body turn ethereal and thus avoiding damage.

As the ghouls hit the wall behind him in a run Alexander became solid again turning to face them. There would be no more ducking or changing from this point on the vampire declared silently. He was on a mission to maim, kill, and destroy these abominations now, for threatening his friends and loved ones Alexander would end both with no remorse. Woe spun to attack him with a loud yell and a lunge but the vampire met the ghoul's charge with a well-placed boot in the behemoth's chest, the kick sending the beast backwards back into the wall and partially through it with the wooden studs and plaster snapping as its large body broke through and the cabinets splintering into kindling as it landed.

The counter though took Alexander off balance just a little because hitting the ghoul was like striking a great boulder. As he took a small step back Misery struck, the ghouls right hand grabbing his shirt as the right fist began slamming into the vampire like a jackhammer, blow after decimating blow. Alexander's head snapped back with each strike, once then twice then three, but as the fourth was coming toward him the vampire reached out with lightning speed catching Misery's hand just as it was halfway from hitting him. All the action stopped for a brief moment as Alexander turned and smiled at Misery showing his large fangs just before his own fist landed square in Misery's chest sending the ghoul skidding back across the floor a good three feet. He held the ghoul's fist in his hand bearing down the pressure on his grip, feeling the bones break under his fingers just as Woe rose from the smashed wall and moved in on him.

And if that wasn't enough, fighting these two walking tanks, Alexander could sense Wilma running down the hall above him. Any second Yelena would hopefully find her and protect her. Then, just as Woe moved in there was more gunfire from upstairs. Leland and the others were having trouble with Michaels and the Lich's newly 'recruited' army. He needed to help them, all of them, and here he was stuck with this pair of walking death and destruction. Woe stepped in swinging ready to land a haymaker blow when the vampire he was intent on leveling ducked and slid out of the way of the punch. Alexander felt the air of the missile that had just missed his head wash across his face, which was how close the large ghoul had come to hitting him, and worse he had to let go of Misery and that one was now coming for him. Both were back to attacking, back to trying to destroy him. The vampire decided quickly the small kitchen was not the best place to fight these two, no, the outside was much better and one at a time. Without thinking or commanding his hand to Alexander grabbed the large cast iron sink from what was left of the cabinets behind him with his right hand and lashed out striking Woe a huge wallop with an overhand strike that sounded just as bad as it looked stalling the large ghoul for a second. Then with a hard straight punch to the face with his left hand, complete with a half twist at the hips to get as much power as possible, Alexander hit Woe hard enough to break its face before it fell back into what had been the only wall left that wasn't damaged by the fight. The plaster popped and broke as the large body hit it then the wood studs that formed the construction of the walls broke as well but held just enough to keep Woe inside the house.

The chance to split up the large pair of ghouls happened quickly then as Misery countered with a swiftness that caught the vampire off guard. The large ghoul hit Alexander with a huge body blow that lifted him a few inches off the floor then followed it with another over the top right cross that rocked the vampire making him take a step back. Misery saw his chance; it was time to end this as it had been ordered.   It pulled back with its left meaning to take the vampire's head off with the looping punch it just threw when Alexander wasn't there anymore, well at least his head wasn't. Then before the large ghoul could do anything else it felt its wrist on the arm throwing the punch suddenly grabbed and Misery knew what was coming was going to be very bad...for it.

Alexander never gave the ghoul a chance to ward off his attack as he latched onto Misery's wrist and spun viciously in a harsh circle performing a textbook jujitsu throw. All the momentum of the ghoul's attack was added to the vampire's strength and his own momentum which equaled enough speed for a large rocket to reach escape velocity for a second or two, the rocket being Misery. The ghoul's balance was gone and it had no control over where its massive body was going, partly propelled by Alexander and mostly its own energy. Misery let something that sounded like a small yelp out as it flew across the kitchen slamming into the ceiling of the hall it was so unceremoniously being thrown down. The vampire watched long enough to see the ghoul disappear then turned to Woe who was trying to get up out of the pile of rubble that was a wall and dishwasher at one time. Alexander growled low then launched himself at the large ghoul hitting it square in the back as it was trying to get up. All at once he shoved the ghoul right out through the wall and into the courtyard beyond in a shower of devastated interior and exterior wall. After he stopped just at the hole in the wall Alexander looked up through the cloud of floating insulation and plaster dust to see Yelena's brothers staring back at him with shock. He was about to ask them why they were still here when a scream from upstairs reminded him of Leland and the others. This plan of his was starting to feel like it may not have been the best choice to have everyone converge on the same spot at the same time the vampire thought taking a quick look around and his eyes settled on a large broken metal table, the perfect tool to address the immediate problem he thought.

The hall was deserted as Renfroe and his group moved slowly toward the foyer making sure to listen for any sound of approaching feet. When the music came alive playing AC/DC they all damn near jumped out of their skins. Renfroe was a big fan of the boys from down under but listening to 'Highway to Hell' right now wasn't helping him any. He looked back for a second to check on Leland, Stephanie, and Foster who were following close behind in a cover formation before turning and moving again. They continued up the hall and then stopped at the sound of approaching feet, two heavy sets moving away and down the stairs in the opposite hall. Renfroe made sure nothing else was coming and then moved them out. They made the corner finally and stopped once again at the turn. The detective moved up slowly and peeked around the expensive molding to check the foyer for guards. Suddenly he spun back just as the expensive wood molding exploded from gunfire.

"GET BACK! RUN BACK TO THE ROOM!" Renfroe screamed while back pedaling into Leland and Stephanie as he brought up his forty-five.

Foster slid across the hall and spotted what Renfroe was taking cover from now. Rico and all eight of his men were coming at them, but there was something wrong with the picture. The way Rico was walking...he looked like a puppet on a set of strings that some drunk man was pulling on, as if he had no control of his body. The other men were the same way and Foster was so hypnotized with curiosity that it never really registered with him the fact they raised their guns or the puffs of smoke as they opened fire. It was only when the hall suddenly blew up with shards of wood and plaster going in every direction from the hail of bullets being fired at him that he realized he was in danger. Foster dropped to his right knee and fired the thirty-eight instinctively at the group hitting one of the guards. Renfroe and

Leland followed his action by firing at the men as well hitting several in the chest and one in the head just above his left eye.

Yet not a guard, Rico, Kenny, or Lloyd dropped from the rounds that struck them. They stepped back, stumbled, and even jumped a bit from each bullet's impact but not a one went to his knees or collapsed from their injuries. Leland even shot Kenny, he even took careful aim to hit the boy in the center of the chest, and Kenny just kept coming at the preacher with the gun leveled and firing. Blood ran from the wounds that Rico's and the others took from all the rounds striking them and still not a one went down from their injuries.

Finally Renfroe, Leland, and Foster backed down the hall retreating from the advancing assault of Rico and his goons. Stephanie ran down the hall ahead of them, ducking from the occasional ricochet while trying to open door after door but they were all locked. She shook each handle hard enough to rip it out of the wood it seemed like but nothing budged. Even the door to the room they were just in was locked now, jammed, or something. It sure as hell wasn't going to open now she decided quickly moving on. Finally, at the very back of the house, a door opened and she turned back to her three companions who were still firing at the mass of men ambling toward them.

"I GOT ONE TO OPEN!" She screamed out to the men.

Renfroe turned to yell at Leland to follow her but before he could say a word the floor just in front of the street preacher and the advancing men exploded upwards. A large metal table, cleverly disguised as a missile, flew past taking three of Rico's men up and out with it but throwing shards of wooden floor everywhere while doing so. Renfroe felt a chunk or two hit him square as he spun to get away from the chaos that was the hall. When he turned back everything had stopped, no one was shooting their guns, not Rico's men or Renfroe or his guys. Everyone just stood quietly staring at the newly formed gaping hole in the floor that went from one wall to the other wall of the hall. Leland looked up from the crater to Rico and the man genuinely seemed confused about what to do. Then Renfroe was grabbing his shoulder and pulling him toward the open door before the assault got under way again. He fell through the portal as Foster slammed the door shut and locked it in one motion. The room looked like a bedroom for guest with an ordinary double bed, a few pieces of furniture, and a window on the back wall.

"Why'd they stop?" Leland gasped looking around from the floor noting slowly someone was missing from the group.

"I don't think they know how to get around the hole." Renfroe remarked helping Leland up off the floor.

"Yeah, where the hell did that table come from?" Leland gasped again still trying to push the haze in his brain away so he could understand why he felt someone was missing.

"My bet's on our vampire friend downstairs." Foster commented reloading his thirty-eight while standing by the door jamb.

"He just bought us some time...wait, where's Stephanie?" Leland asked quickly suddenly realizing who was missing from the group.

Renfroe and Foster began to look around the room quickly just like Leland had done a second before and came to the conclusion they were missing Stephanie just as the street preacher broke for the door in a burst. "I have to get her back!" He screamed actually getting the portal open just as bullets began to fly again striking the wood door frame. Leland slammed it closed out of self-preservation just as Renfroe yelled back.

"She'll be fine. Alexander's out there with her and he'll keep her safe long enough for us to get out of here and get back to her." When Leland looked up and his expression was one that said he wasn't buying into the detective's plan fully so Renfroe stepped up just as the sound of Rico and his men jumping over the hole could be heard.

"Listen, I don't plan on wasting a second of the time Alexander's gained for us. Let's get out of here and then we can come back for Stephanie, cool?" This time Leland only nodded, more from the fact he knew now the hall was a death trap and this room was about to be one. On the somewhat affirmation of his plan from Leland Renfroe looked over to the other body in the room and gave out his orders. "Foster, keep an ear on the door and make sure we don't get walked in on. Lee, let's see how far it is to the ground from that window."

"You think we can make the Chevy from here after we find Stephanie and Wilma?" Leland asked shaking his head as they walked over. He still hadn't bought into Renfroe's plan but it was better than getting shot here in this room.

"All I know Lee is those huge things and Rico, whatever he is now, are inside with us and not outside. Once we touch the ground we'll see about getting back in here and getting Stephanie and Wilma." Renfroe responded while walking to the window as well.

While the other two checked on the window Foster slowly unlocked the door and opened it barely an inch, just enough to look out into the hall. What he saw made his heart sink an inch or two into his quickly shrinking stomach. Rico was in mid jump, he was so off balance it looked like something a first grader would do, but the mob boss had crossed the hole. In addition, most of his men were in the process of following their leader or were already waiting. Foster slammed the door shut just as Rico's gun came back up pointing right at him.

"They're coming for us!" He screamed a second before a bullet pierced the door. Leland grunted and dropped to a single knee pulling up one of his nines while the detective sprang into action.

"No time to make this pretty," Renfroe yelled grabbing a chair with his right hand. He threw it through the glass just as more bullets struck the door splintering it with each successive shot.

No one ever checked to see just how far the ground was from the window. There was no time to and Leland just went with the moment tucking both legs and jumping through the shattered pane. Renfroe looked back to see Foster still standing up against the wall by the door cringing as the bullets crashed through.

"Are you coming along buddy?" Renfroe asked stepping partly out the window.

"Are you going to catch me?" Foster asked back as hands from the other side of the door began to tear at it ripping pieces out of the portal.

"Hardly skinny man," Renfroe laughed with a smile before disappearing from the room by going out the window.

"I am never leaving the lab ever again!" Foster cursed before breaking from the door heading for the window. The bullets picked up in number, as if the goons on the other side knew he was making a break for freedom. The assistant coroner didn't skip a step or stop to gently step through the broken window. No sir, Foster leapt through it like Superman while screaming at the top of his lungs.

What the heck was that crash? The place sounds like its falling apart at the seams, it probably will after all the bullets, fighting, and destruction is done Wilma thought as she ran headlong down one hall. She darted away from the three titans battling it out in the kitchen, as much as she wanted to help Alexander she had to help her mom more. Up ahead she turned right and headed across what she assumed was the back of the house along a dark hallway just barely missing the corner of a partially hidden table sitting against the wall in the dark. Suddenly, Wilma heard approaching footsteps from an opening just up on her right, a hall connecting from somewhere else in the house. That little voice that had told her to hide downstairs when the dead thing came looking for her...that little voice that told her to run the night J-Rock was going to hurt her...well, it didn't advise her to seek refuge this time. It was just quiet, like a church mouse, so Wilma stood in the dark of the hall staring at the opening and waiting.

After jumping in through the window Yelena dropped to one knee listening intently to the silence for any sound that would tell her someone was coming and her senses were strong, so keen Yelena could have heard a pin land on the carpet from the other side of the house. That was if all the other noises of the gunfire and fighting and screaming would die down for just a moment, and strangely enough it did for a minute when she silently cursed for it too. She looked around with a smug smile thinking the Ancient One wasn't the only one with powers, but then the gunfire started up again as well as the fighting downstairs. Yelena stood up, took a sniff of the air and picked up Wilma almost at once. The little one was running toward her now, coming this way fast. The werewolf trotted quietly to the door and cracked it open just enough to scan the hall for anyone and when she sensed it was clear Yelena treaded out into the dark just as quiet as she had crossed the floor back in the room.

With all the clamor and hollering from the fighting Yelena wasn't all that worried about being found sneaking around, I mean everyone was too busy trying to either shoot or beat someone else to death at this stage she thought. The werewolf quietly reached the corner of the hall she was in, Wilma's scent was so strong now and Yelena could hear the little one's heart pounding in her small chest. She peeked around the turn first left then right looking for her little friend and there standing in the middle of the hall was Wilma. Yelena smiled again stepping out just as Wilma sighed and ran to her.

"I knew it wasn't bad." The little girl whispered hugging her friend hard.

The werewolf knelt down and took Wilma in a huge hug careful not to hurt the little one. She gave a small cry of happiness then held her friend back just at arm's length looking her up and down. "Are you all right little one? Please tell me you are fine?"

"I'm fine...are you crying?" Wilma smiled reaching up and wiping away one of Yelena's tears.

"Da," Yelena nodded smiling so wide her face might crack from being so relieved and so happy to see her friend, "I am fine now. I am more than fine to see you are not hurt."

Wilma gave a giggle then reached down and took the werewolf's hand in hers squeezing before the expression on her face changed to concern. "We have to find mom, she's in here still. They took her when they took me."

"Da, I know little one, we will find her I promise." Yelena whispered standing up looking up and then down the hall making sure no one was around. The gunfire, which had stopped momentarily, started up one more time. The large booms though weren't enough to hide the sound of approaching feet and the werewolf sensed someone running at them. She pushed Wilma behind and just as she spread her feet, a growl deep and low began to emanate from her chest as Yelena readied herself to defend Wilma.

Then, with an abruptness that caused both ladies standing there ready to fight to tense and hiss, Stephanie came running around the corner before coming to a skidding stop. Wilma's mother let out a scream of fright at seeing the two so suddenly then her daughter yelled with happy alleviation and ran to her, "MOM!"

Stephanie scooped up her daughter just as quick smiling and crying. "Oh my baby, are you okay? Are you hurt?"

"I'm fine, but why is everyone asking if I'm all right?"

"Because Yelena and I got a little worried when you got kidnapped girlfriend, I am your mother and I do have that right to get scared when it comes to someone harming you!"

The werewolf walked up just as Wilma was about to retort cutting off the somewhat heart-warming moment between mother and daughter. "Please, we need to go and get back to the Ancient One's car."

"Yes we do," Stephanie whispered with a sharp nod while putting Wilma back on the ground.

"Wait, what about Yelena's brothers?" Wilma asked with concern.

Yelena smiled and nodded to the question, "They are fine and free my friend, the Ancient One helped us like you said he would. Now, we need to leave."

"But what about Leland and his friends, we can't leave them either?"

"Listen sweetie, I'm sure Lee and the others already got out and their waiting for us by the car. Now just do what Yelena and I ask and follow us out of here." Stephanie whispered with a mother's intent pushing and nudging her daughter toward the front of the house and freedom. Sometimes she had her doubts about raising such an independent child in one Wilma Lavonia Jackson.

The group started off down the hall taking three steps when a stark cold just dropped on all three, like being thrown into a deep freeze. A dread so thick it smothered the very breath from you covered them causing all three to stop at the same instance, right where their last step fell on the hardwood floor. We're in more trouble now then I was with the guys Stephanie's mind screamed as she swallowed hard just before a voice filled with so much malevolence it made her shiver uncontrollably. Yelena took a quick step in front of her friends as someone stepped out of the dark with a baleful stare at all three.

"I'm afraid the three of you will not be leaving this house just yet."

That growl from before coming from Yelena's chest returned, the low one that signaled to any and all the threat of being torn to shreds was very close to happening if you come any closer. She breathed deep answering the words of the shadow with that throaty snarl. "I will not let you hurt my loved ones anymore...you or Akhenaton."

The shadow moved and Michaels came into full view, a sneer crossing his features as he pointed to the werewolf. "All you had to do my little Yelena was to die at the hands of the Ancient One, but you could not even do that pup. Now I will just have to see to the duty myself."

The werewolf only growled deeper as her body began to transform into the white wolf, as she readied to fight the Lesser Lich. From behind Stephanie took an involuntary step backward meaning to put more distance between her Wilma and whatever this thing was. She sputtered as she whispered out loud, "who...is...that?"

"It's the evil man from Grammy's" Wilma whispered back while tucking in as close as she possibly could to her mother's leg.

Misery finally came to a complete stop just inside the foyer, after bouncing off the ceiling and one wall like a ball, just about a foot short of the only table in the room with the large floral decoration still on its top...still sitting dead in the center. The large ghoul rolled off its back and shook its head grumbling as it did and that's when its eyeless sockets saw the shadows. How Misery could still see without the benefit of an oculus with which to perceive the outside world was only known by the one who created him, but make no mistake the large ghoul could see very well. It looked to the large oak double doors and noticed the pair standing there, a man and a woman. He grunted loudly just as the man stepped forward calling out in a thick accent with a threatening tone.

"Where is our Yelena? Where are her brothers?"

The ghoul only grunted again but this time it added a low growl to its response which drew the female out. Her voice had the same accent and even meaner intent. "If you have hurt our family we will destroy you ghoul..."

Well, with the gauntlet tossed down Misery only grunted deep in his chest while reaching down and grabbing the table with his hand. It accepted the challenge even though the beast knew its orders were to kill the vampire. It tossed the table across the room destroying the piece of furniture and the floral decoration in a flash. Misery roared then and charged the pair, who simply stood where they were. The man and woman didn't stand perfectly still though because as the large ghoul charged the pair began to change into large wolves.

***

The moonlight that streamed down on the courtyard from above glittered off the small particles of dust that drifted on the air from the destroyed outside walls. The Epova brothers, all three, stood watching the large ghoul Woe as it regained its feet. Gregor knew neither he nor his brothers were capable of taking down this behemoth, even with its broken face. They might be able to take the smaller ones called Phlegm and Ick down, but this one ghoul...it was huge. It would have been a great boon if the Ancient One had stayed and helped them, but the vampire disappeared back into the house and Gregor was sure he would not be seeing Alexander again until this was over. The three werewolves began to move slowly breaking apart and encircling the ghoul to try and gain an advantage as they let their bodies transform more into their true wolf forms. A frontal assault was ludicrous Gregor and the others knew instinctively, but if all three came at the thing at once from different sides then the brothers might be strong enough to bring it down. And Woe stood there motionless watching and taking in the trio's moves as all three got into position, as if being surrounded by three werewolves was nothing to worry about. Its broken jaw hung from rotting skin and the left side of its face looked like someone had hit it with a hammer over and over, but that mattered none to the ghoul. It stood still waiting for this new fight to begin and the wait was not long as Dimitri launched himself into an attack a second before his brother Gregor followed. Then both found out why Woe seemed indifferent to them, it was because the beast knew he had little to worry from the pups. It caught Dimitri in one hand before the werewolf reached it latching on to the wolf's throat and clenching down its fingers. As the black haired wolf found himself in yet another predicament where he was being denied air Dimitri could only watch as the ghoul then struck his brother with a massive backhand that staggered Gregor causing him to step back. The ghoul then finished the move by bringing his hand back with a flash sending his fist into Dimitri's face with a loud and painful crunch. The blow at least knocked him free of the ghoul's grasp the dark haired Epova thought, but that was about the only good thing that exchange brought them.

Woe had countered the pair of brothers attacks easily but Peter had waited to just the right moment to attack and when it came he threw his own massive haymaker. The ghoul never saw the punch coming. It was only when the werewolf's fist hit home that Woe finally remembered there was a third wolf still out there and it gave a damn good pop. He turned his head just in time to catch another blow on his right cheek but before the third could land Woe blocked the strike and delivered a head-butt to the blond werewolf. Almost at once Peter's legs went slack and he began to collapse to the ground stunned. Only the ghoul had other plans for him grabbing a handful of the werewolf's head hair and holding him up. Woe balled up his large hand and pulled it back ready to deliver a final killing blow to the young pup when a well-placed and well thrown rock hit him in his head, right about where Alexander had struck him with the sink. The ghoul turned away from Peter to see Dimitri standing a few feet away holding a large stone meant to line the path from the house to the pool. Woe snarled and in his murky mind the foggy thought of him getting ready to throw this lifeless wolf right back at his brother crossed, like the dark haired one had thrown a rock at him, flashed dimly only that was all it was...a single dim thought. As he started to command his arm, the muscles reacting to impulses, something stabbed right through his shoulder and chest. Black ichor flew as well as skin and when the ghoul looked down after a second he saw there was a long shaft of wood sticking out of his dead body.

"Drop my brother!" Gregor screamed from behind holding the long piece of lounge chair with both hands. It was the same one his sister had hit him with earlier and now he held the ghoul with it, or he hoped did.

Its arm wasn't working now. The appendage just hung limp at its side and no matter how much Woe commanded it to move the arm just stayed flaccid. It looked over its shoulder and growled more trying to slide off the wood spear sticking through its body by pulling with its legs but the wolf holding refused to let it slip away. With every step Woe took to try and free itself the lycanthrope just moved as well keeping the shaft stuck right where it was.

"Drop my BROTHER!"

The ghoul took a step forward, which Gregor followed with his own keeping the spear in place. Then Woe stepped to the side and the wolf just followed the step again. It was stuck in a stalemate, or so the werewolves thought. The ghoul knew one way to free its body and with an abrupt turn where it stood it did just that. Woe twisted so fast and so quick Gregor had no chance to follow and he could only watch as the ghoul snapped the make-shift spear with a loud pop. One second the red haired wolf had the ghoul trapped and the next he was face to face with the behemoth holding a useless length of wood. Gregor looked up into the eyeless sockets of the ghoul and watched with a small bit of shock as Woe reached up with its still working arm and pulled the spear from his body and dropped it to the ground.

This is it. The ghoul is going to kill all of us the red haired lycanthrope thought. Yet Woe only stood staring at Dimitri and

Gregor for a minute more without moving before dropping the half conscious Peter to the ground. It snarled one last time as it backed away from the three crossing the patio to where Phlegm had pulled itself from the pool and was kneeling. Woe picked up its smaller kind under its one arm easily and then in long backward strides it left the area. Both Gregor and Dimitri were more than happy to let the beast go and as soon as it was far enough away they stepped over to their bother ensuring he would be safe if this was a trick. It wasn't though and all three lycanthropes watched as the ghouls conceded the fight and the battlefield by slipping away into the night.

"Why did it leave when it could have killed us?" Dimitri asked somewhat bewildered by the quick retreat.

"I do not know brother." Gregor replied looking after Peter while answering, "But I will not forgo this gift. Let us find Yelena and be away from here quickly.

All right, that wasn't a whole lot of fun Foster thought as hands grabbed his shirt and pulled him up next to the house just as the goons from upstairs opened fire with their guns down on them. Tufts of grass flew up from the impact of the bullets and the usual zing sounded as some ricocheted off the dirt. When he jumped out the window Foster lost track of gravity for a second as he fell, flipping through the dark night actually, and then it all came back abruptly with jarring force as he landed flat back on the hard ground. Renfroe and Leland let go of the motionless assistant coroner and returned fire back up the wall at the two men hanging out the window hitting both numerous times, but they still refused to die.

"Get up buddy, they're coming for us!" Renfroe screamed at Foster.

"Just let me get my breath." Foster asked trying to gulp air.

Leland grabbed Foster's arm pulling him up while yelling, "Breathe while you run man...breathe while you run!"

Suddenly a body leapt from a window up ahead, one of Rico's transformed guards fell to the ground with a sick thud landing on his head and shoulder. Renfroe, Leland, and Foster looked on in shock at the body that amazingly started the process of getting to its feet with a jerk. The guard's head hung in an awkward angle on his neck and the ball joint of his shoulder was now almost in the center of his chest. Broken neck and dislocated shoulder the coroner surmised with his pathology acumen before what was left of the man gained his feet, turned, and raised his gun right at him. This is it, I'm going to get shot and die Foster thought. Then fate intervened, another goon had seen fit to jump from the same window and with comedic disaster landed right on his comrade.

The two sprawled across the grass in a mass tangle of legs and arms. Foster almost laughed from the scene, but then Leland was pulling him away down the wall of the house.

"We're up and out of here boys!" Renfroe screamed at his comrades as he ran by. The two men wasted no time in sticking around, they both chased after their companion as more bullets hit around them.

Renfroe caught up to Foster and Leland easily just as more glass could be heard breaking up ahead. A second later, they heard the sound of a body hitting the ground with a meaty thud, just like the two from before. Renfroe turned to Foster, a look of tired anger in his eyes as he put his forty-five in its holster.

"You run right behind me and don't stop no matter what!"

"Where are we going?" Leland asked loading his last two clips in the twin nine millimeters.

"The front door, we go back in and find Stephanie and Wilma before hauling our asses back to the car." Renfroe instructed.

"I'm almost out of bullets." Foster offered up.

Renfroe was about to respond when a slug from a gun struck the wall just above Leland's head exploding wood and stucco all over everyone. The two goons that jumped from the window just seconds before were behind them, but catching up and firing at them. Renfroe spat a curse and ran toward the front of the house and the front doors. "Follow me," he yelled back and both Leland

and Foster did as instructed. More bullets slammed into the wall of the house as they evacuated the area as fast as they could.

The detective, who had grown up under the tutelage of his Wiccan mother and her passive life, let his anger go and fuel him. The emotion sparked a burst of energy, like napalm in his stomach. Once when he was very young Renfroe was given the wooden totem of a bear to channel his energy and growing aggression. Now the strength of the large Grizzly flowed in Renfroe's veins and took over his weary body. A growl escaped from his lips as up ahead he saw two more guards and Rico getting off the ground. Well, that was the other sound of breaking glass he heard. The bad guys were surrounding them. Renfroe never stopped only charged into the group with a roar punching the first guard with a massive blow across the jaw. He struck the second one a great upper cut that took the man off his feet and sent him to the ground.

Rico was last, his gun already up and aimed at Renfroe, but the detective slapped it away letting his anger drive him forward without hesitation or good judgment. The gun fired and the bullet went off into the dark as Renfroe grabbed the mob boss by the head and gave it a savage twist to the right. A loud crack sounded and Rico went limp in Renfroe's hands, whatever force holding him up gone. Foster trotted up and looked at the scene with a shocked expression.

"How'd you do that?" He asked.

"Do what?" Renfroe asked back coming off his fueled rage.

"Kill them! We've shot each of these guys ten times at least and nothing. Now you punch them and they drop like flies!" Foster wailed.

"It's happening to all of them. They just, I don't know, died I guess." Leland rambled.

"Well, in the words of my mother, I'm not looking a gift horse in the mouth right now. Let's get Stephanie and Wilma then get to the car, now!" Renfroe demanded reloading his forty-five.

They ran to the front of the house turning the corner slowly before going back to a trot and when they reached the entry all three were stunned at what they saw. It was one of the large beasts that had attacked them when this whole mess started Renfroe thought. Only now the behemoth was running off toward the dark and what he assumed was the street. The detective watched the large thing disappear into the shadows while Leland and Foster passed him heading in, but then both stopped short going past the entrance. Renfroe walked over to see a man and a woman gaining their feet in what was left of the foyer, torn chunks of walls and broken pieces of staircases scattered everywhere.

"Are they-"Leland began to whisper before Foster cut him off?

The coroner whispered with a raised eyebrow, "werewolves?"

The man helped his female companion to her feet from the floor while eyeing the trio closely, "where are Yelena and her brothers?"

"Yeah, they're werewolves." Renfroe sighed walking past the stunned coroner and street preacher. Great, more people to keep track of. Now that's just what I didn't need right now the detective thought with frustration.

―――――――――――――――――――

"Do you really think you can challenge me Yelena my dear, a Lich with true power?" Michaels hissed eyeing the werewolf up and down harshly.

There was no immediate answer from the lycanthrope. She only breathed deeply letting the growl grow in intensity as the transformation changed her body. Her hands grew in size with the fingertips becoming claws while her jeans stretched from the muscles in her legs which swelled with size and power. Her shoulders thickened as did her neck and Yelena's face shifted as she took on the lupine look. She stopped short of becoming the full white wolf, kept her body from becoming the full lycanthrope because she didn't want to scare Wilma. And the weird part, if Yelena had known, was Wilma thought the lycanthrope looked especially cool. Deep down the little girl wanted to see her friend in her full form.

"You are no Lich Michaels. Akhenaton did not transform you completely. He still holds you short of being anything but a ghoul on a leash. You are nothing to me." Yelena snarled finally snapping her teeth at the end warning the small man to stay back.

The Lesser Lich though sneered and in the moonlight his eyes turned to a full black as he did. "I am his right hand and my lord calls for your destruction pup!"

Yelena roared at Michaels last causing the walls to shake and the Lich replied, only not with words. His hand came up and out with the fingers outstretched in a fan before slowly closing, squeezing the air itself. The howl of the werewolf suddenly morphed and transformed into a wail of pain, a shriek of agony as Yelena felt her heart cramp and stop. Michaels, he was somehow doing this. He was trying to kill her by stopping heart, crushing the muscle from afar like a grape. The werewolf reached out and put a hand to the wall to steady herself as the pain in her heart exploded. And there was the Lesser Lich smiling as he squeezed his fingers together, grinning as he killed her. "I am his right hand...I took your blood with a small scratch Yelena and now you will feel my power."

Then from behind her Yelena heard a high pitched yelp, a loud plea from a voice that touched her spirit. "STOP, STOP HURTING HER!"

Wilma...oh little one...run please Yelena thought as Michaels just grinned on and squeezed even harder causing her heart to erupt with more pain. The werewolf yelped again as Wilma cried out from behind for the Lich to stop, only Michaels was far from letting this enjoyment end. "Know this Yelena, I will kill the mother and the child once I have killed you and know this as well...I will enjoy every moment as I do."

Stephanie had been watching all this unfold frozen to the spot in the hall with fear, rooted to the floor in terror. She had watched as the man threatened them, as Yelena had changed before being attacked secretly, and now she stood perfectly still watching the man kill her friend. She knew Yelena was close to death and here she was doing nothing...then the man said he would kill Wilma once he was done with her and her friend. Well, that was a mistake because there is nothing stronger in the universe than a mother protecting her young, that indomitable will and strength that a woman feels and shows for her child when that young one is threatened with death. Down in her stomach Stephanie felt that will and strength flare to life with a bright flash and before she could think of doing it she pushed Wilma back from her and she ran at Michaels crossing the space between them in three long strides before the Lesser Lich could react. She didn't try to grab him or push him or even slap him. No, Stephanie held nothing back but her fist which when it reached the farthest point it could on her swing she brought forward with all the strength she had. Her fist hit Michaels face like a hammer and it was more than evident he had grossly underestimated the mother's intent and her power because Stephanie stunned him long enough to land another blow.

"You're Not Going To Touch My Daughter! You're Not Going To Touch Her!" Stephanie screamed loudly as the Lich stepped back and turned toward her.

Michaels forgot about Yelena and the hold he had on her. He had to or else this woman would beat him to nothing but a blood stain. She landed one more fist to his head and then the Lesser Lich fought back blocking the next thrown punch before lashing out with a vicious slap to the woman's face. As she fell back a step leaving just a small opening Michaels instantly moved to go after her and finish this without hesitation, but then something hit him hard stopping him cold in mid-step. The Lich looked down to see a large hand, or paw, in the middle of his chest with the long claws embedded deeply into his body.

Yelena, he had momentarily forgotten about her. He looked up from his chest to see her standing now, strong and ready, glaring at him as a deep growl rumbled from her chest. "Do you know how much this suit costs, and you just ruined it?"

"I will not let you hurt them...ever!" Yelena spat pressing her now oversized claws deeper into the Lich, squeezing him more with the knife like ends. She hadn't expected much of an answer from Michaels though it still surprised the lycanthrope a little when he reached up and grabbed her by the throat with his hand. It wasn't as much a desperation move as it was frustration from the fact she had now stalemated him, nowhere to go and no way to get there.

Wilma stepped over to look at her mom, check on Stephanie, as she watched the pair now locked in a deadly dance stare at each other. She knew whatever hold the man held over Yelena was gone now but if it was due to the werewolf spearing him with her claws Wilma wasn't sure and she didn't feel like asking. She took another step toward her mother when she suddenly stepped into something, a body that wasn't there just a second before. Wilma actually bounced off it for a moment before she looked up to see her angel staring down at her smiling just a little. "It will be fine now Wilma, take my hand and trust me."

She looked up at Alexander with a puzzled expression, what did that mean Wilma was thinking when that feeling of dread from before turned into a one ton weight that sat right on her chest.

He had sensed his arrival the moment he stepped foot in the house.

Oh Akhenaton had tried to hide his presence, but it was impossible to do so once he was this close Alexander thought. It was the same for him when it came to the Grand Lich, the ancient vampire unable to cloud his being once the proximity of Akhenaton was this close. What was the Grand Lich doing here the Ancient One asked himself silently as he felt the air around him gently ripple with spitefulness from the arrival of his enemy? Alexander turned to look out at the Epova's readying themselves to battle the large ghoul and he knew Victor and Iskra had arrived somehow, someway, and were now fighting the one called Misery in the front of the house. He knew both could use his help against the massive ghouls but he couldn't because of Akhenaton and what he might do now that he was here. So why are you here old friend the vampire asked himself again looking up to the second floor of the house, as if he could see the Grand Lich through all the plaster and wood and dead space in the walls, right to the small room he was in now.

Leland and Renfroe lost Stephanie, but that's nothing to worry about Alexander thought as he sensed Yelena about to converge and meet with Wilma in the hall. He turned his head at the sound of someone man-sized being tossed into something immovable up front, Victor and Iskra were having a rather hard time fighting the large ghoul while upstairs the controlled men had jumped over the hole he made with the table and were now pursuing the others and Yelena had found Wilma and Stephanie had found them, which would have been good thing at any other time except Michaels had found all three of cutting the group's escape. Outside the brothers were trying to fend off the one called Misery when Alexander felt Akhenaton begin to move and the Grand Lich was walking toward Yelena and Michaels...and Wilma. The vampire heard the loud retorts of gunfire outside now and he knew the men had chased Renfroe and the others out the windows of the bedrooms upstairs.

I can't help them...I have to save Wilma...this was all for her and I have to help her the voice in his mind chanted as Alexander felt his body begin to float and ascend while becoming incorporeal. Up through the floor he floated, up to the second floor in a room that was empty when he stopped. Alexander's feet barely touched the rug on the hardwood floor before he was gone in a flash quickly finding Wilma and the others in the hall. He watched as Yelena stopped Michaels from hurting her friends, her human friends, and it made the vampire smile just a little seeing how the werewolf had fallen into the role of protector as well...that was till he saw Akhenaton arrive standing back in the shadows. Alexander walked quietly up to stand next to Wilma just as the little girl felt the foulness of the Grand Lich, the evil pressing down on her small soul and squeezing. He reassured her and held his friend's small hand just as Stephanie felt the same heinous and oppressive force that was Akhenaton clench her like an iron claw causing her to shiver uncontrollably even more. Alexander guided Wilma over to her mother slowly putting his free hand on Stephanie's shoulder letting his power push back the invisible wall of terror that Akhenaton used to such a perfect effect and as he did the former Pharaoh stepped out from the shadows locking eyes with him.

The Grand Lich, The Creator of Undead Armies and Vile Monsters had arrived and was about to hold court. "Tell the bitch to let Michaels go, now."

"Do not refer to Yelena as a 'bitch' Akhenaton, if you want her to release that silly lap dog of yours than just ask Michaels to let go of her, and you might as well call off your ghouls. The night is not yours." Alexander replied coldly. Lines deep and drawn long ago in the sand were quickly reappearing out of the foggy past as the two foes faced off. The Grand Lich let a small chuckle out as he grinned evilly.

"Sure thing old man, I just thought we were past all the niceties and all. Let the pup go Michaels."

"Are you sure sir? I can kill her for you easily." Michaels hissed just before the cloth of his suit, tie, and shirt ripped more as Yelena squeezed her hand dragging her claws through his dead body slowly.

"I will tear you apart before you could blink." She snarled low.

The hall was quiet for a moment before Akhenaton sighed and shook his head. "Please don't tell me this is going to take all night because I need to get back home and see too a few things."

"Let him go Yelena please. I need you to take Stephanie and Wilma out of the house and back to the car." Alexander stated never letting his eyes leave the former Pharaoh.

It was still a long minute before she complied, but then with a quick pull Yelena removed her hand and claws from Michaels chest standing still as he held her throat. "Let her go Michaels, time to call it quits on this one." Akhenaton ordered and his man followed the command releasing the werewolf.

Both combatants stepped away from each other slowly, backing away while eyeing the other with a mean stare. "This is not over little Yelena, take that as a vow."

"Do not let me find you straying too far from your master's protective reach ghoul." She replied reaching the vampire's side. Almost at once she felt a small hand take hers and squeeze along with a small voice pleading.

"We need to leave Yelena, please, let's just leave like Alexander says to."

The lycanthrope looked down to see Wilma with a look of fear on her face. Yelena felt the sudden ache from guilt as she saw just how scared her friend had become. I came up here to keep her safe and look what I've done the werewolf thought, well no more. Her body shifted back to human slowly as she spoke.

"Da," she said nodding to Wilma and smiling before looking up to Alexander, "I will take them to the car Ancient One and wait for you with my brothers."

The vampire smiled warmly in response and that ache of guilt in her stomach turned to butterflies for some reason making the lycanthrope blush a little. "Thank you my friend,"

Yelena gave a small nod in return not wanting to meet his eyes, not wanting the Ancient One to see what she was feeling suddenly now. No, she just took Wilma and guided her and Stephanie back out of the hall and down a turn where for some strange reason she knew another staircase leading downstairs would be. It's him Yelena told herself silently, Alexander, showing her the way to safety...keeping a watchful eye on her and his friends. The trio made it quickly and quietly through the mansion working their way to the front without issue and without the feeling of foreboding death that Akhenaton gave off. It was there just before the foyer that they found the group of loved ones looking for them, Leland instantly moving to take Wilma and Stephanie in his arms while whispering over and over how he was so worried for them. The little girl actually giggled as her mother kissed her man's cheek whispering how happy she was to be with him. Yelena took in the sight for only a second because it was all she was allowed as a familiar voice called to her and when she looked up her mouth turned into a smile. Iskra stepped up hugging her quickly asking in Russian if she was all right, was she injured. Then Victor was next to her saying they had to leave before Yelena could answer so the group made their way out of the house, but not before she took one look back wondering just what the two oldest of any undead anywhere were doing now. Either one couldn't hurt the other so what were the Grand Lich and the Ancient One going to do...talk?

Michaels slinked away after whispering a word to his master. Alexander watched it closely and with some glee he had to admit. The Lesser Lich cast one last look over his shoulder to eye the Ancient One before moving off into the dark. Akhenaton turned back to him smiling at first before his face changed to a look of disdain as he looked the vampire up and down. "What are you wearing?"

"What do you mean, what's wrong with the way I dress?" The vampire asked looking down his body then up back to the Lich.

"You're the oldest vampire in existence, the fabled 'Ancient One'...you look like you're ready to smoke a bowl of your favorite bud while giggling your way through the extended cut of 'Wayne's World'."

"I thought I fit in very well with what the humans wear these days." Alexander replied with a raised eyebrow considering every word he said. The talk was pleasant for now but it would soon change, it always did.

"That's the problem, you do, but would it kill you to wear a nice suit and tie. You know, maybe dress like a 2300 year old vampire is supposed to dress."

Alexander shook his head still grinning, "I grew so tired of wearing handmade suits and shirts. I like looking...like this. It's truly kind of fun."

"Yeah, oh well...welcome back. How do you like the 21st Century?"

"It has been," Alexander replied with a pause while watching his enemy, "interesting to observe as I pass through. It was a bit...overwhelming at first I would have to admit."

The Grand Lich just nodded emphatically with the obvious truth and laughed, "Oh I know, I know. Of all the ages I have passed through, all the eras and civilizations and societies, this one right here takes the cake. I mean, the other day I typed the word 'squat' into Google and the shit that popped up made even me cringe."

What exactly was going on here Alexander asked himself suddenly stymied by this 'new' Akhenaton? Where was the arrogant megalomaniac bent on destroying me the vampire continued on as he spoke? "How is California and Hollywood? Is it really the land of dreamers as they say?"

The Grand Lich just shrugged his shoulders. "Eh, it's a cesspool most days but the cemeteries are very nice. You get to meet some very interesting dead people when you raise them from the grave out there. I like to just sit on a bench and watch them shamble around. By the way, nice play with rescuing Svetlana last night...totally did not see that one coming."

"I had to keep my promise Akhenaton, and it was not hard to find her."

"Yeah, I wasn't really trying to hide her and guess what? Your still being all heroic and shit...it's why I went ahead and called Victor and Iskra to let them know where to find you, get the whole gang together. You know, Vargas won't get anywhere with what you gave him. Do you know how many steps there are to transforming ones' self into a Lich?"

"Seven I believe, not counting the necessary components and such?"

Akhenaton's lips squeezed a little tighter giving away the fact the vampire's response was right and a little too close for comfort. Alexander grinned a little wider and continued on feeling it was time to get this meeting going in the right direction. "Why did you send the Epova's after me knowing the four could never hurt me much less end my existence? What game are you playing at now?"

"Let's just say I got a little bored while you were away and needed to have some fun buddy." The Lich replied staring back and grinning now. "I missed you old man, thought you might enjoy the taste of Yelena's blood. I'm thinking it might be pretty sweet, she's a real looker."

The vampire's brow furrowed as the Lich's last made very little to no sense when it came to their 'relationship' if you could call it that. "We are not and have never been friends. We have been trying to destroy each other for almost 2000 years Akhenaton. We razed a small village to the ground the last time we met face to face and fought."

"Hey yeah, that old Austrian village in the Alps, I remember now. The one that had the gentleman who painted those small pictures that goes in lockets. I don't remember the name of the place though."

Alexander shook his head, "The name of the place is lost to time Akhenaton, same as the village itself the moment we showed up on its doorstep."

"We did make a mess of that town didn't we? You still have that locket the little man made for you?"

"His name was Stefan and yes I still have the locket he made me." Alexander answered with cautious words. He was still trying to figure out just what Akhenaton was doing here, what all of 'this' was about, and with him dodging questions it was just a little frustrating.

The Grand Lich smiled and leaned in whispering, "Is that why you saved that little colored girl, because you feel guilty about what happened to dear old Roxanna and your boy? That's who Stefan painted for you right?"

"Be careful where you step Lich, be very careful." Alexander whispered coldly letting his gaze and intent warn the undead master to stay back from certain topics.

"Really, that's all it took to upset you...it was less than five minutes. Oh well, guess we're always going to hate each other like a couple of Real Housewives from Orange County, but really I didn't think this little get together would end on a happy note." Akhenaton sneered.

The vampire shook his head and growled growing weary of this dance. "Just answer my question, why did you want me to kill the Epova's?"

Akhenaton sighed again but this time there was no attempt to rile the vampire. No, this was the old evil Pharaoh coming through, the snake who was nothing but pure malevolence and who had every intention of picking a fight and it showed as the Lich snarled. "You woke up at the wrong time old man and on top of that you showed up in the wrong fucking place."

Well, if he wasn't confused before then Alexander was totally lost now. He looked at the Lich with a raised eyebrow deciding not to reply and Akhenaton took the silence as a signal to keep talking. "While you were away from the world getting your beauty sleep we've been turned into a joke, a punch line with a great ending that just never gets old."

"We've become a what?" Alexander asked cocking his head to the side.

The Grand Lich stepped forward getting close to the vampire still snarling. "We're no longer the scary myths we used to be old man. We're no longer the nightmares who frighten and haunt the living. No, we've been...accepted into society if you can believe it. We've become...popular to those cows out there in the living world, some even running around dressing like us on Halloween. The humans use to whisper our names and make the sign of the cross for protection for fear of being cursed and now they walk around screaming out our names like we're the best of friends. Do you know they've made movies about Zombies and Vampires, hell there's a hit TV show right now and a talk show afterwards about being undead and people love it? We have become nothing but adorable and 'awesomely spectacular bro' across the whole world. "

"And that's a bad thing as you see it?"

"It's fucking disrespectful is what it is." Akhenaton snapped with his hand coming up and finger pointing to the sky. "Have you seen what they've turned us, you and me, into?"

Alexander stared into the eyes of the Grand Lich and he could see the crazy just swimming there, like it was doing laps in the black of his pupils. "We have become celebrated I will admit, but-"

"But what," Akhenaton spit cutting the vampire off, "it's okay with you that all the hard work and effort and time we put into being feared and reviled for all those centuries has been for nothing? Have you looked us up on the Internet, our likenesses are on T-Shirts someone can buy for $9.95!"

"Really, I'll have to check on that. I need to replace some of my t-shirts." Alexander smiled. He couldn't help but grin. He had forgotten just how crazy the former Pharaoh was.

The Grand Lich though shook his head and whispered. "They put me in some computer game, did you know that? Millions of computer nerds can kill me over and over and over for a monthly fee if they want. Is that fear I ask you? Is that the respect I should receive after all the people I have killed? And you, well just throw on some body glitter while letting a big fan blow though that long hair of yours and there won't be a pair of dry panties from here to Manhattan. You've become nothing more than a body-oil drenched heartthrob for every screaming teenage girl, hopeless romantic and lonely housewife to swoon over. People actually think you're a sweet guy who just needs a little TLC and you'll be all better. Your just misunderstood is all, just give the old vampire a hug and he'll be your boyfriend."

Alexander barely held his snicker in at the last, dry panties, now that was a new one. "We cannot hold back change or time Akhenaton. Both will take us where both will and maybe it is a little strange having people admire us but it's not the end of everything."

"Are you sure of that? You know me vampire, am I the kind to just let a slight like this go by without dealing out some form of retribution?"

No, no he was not the kind to let any form of a perceived disrespect slide. The Pharaoh would kill anyone who stood up to him or against him personally and it was this realization that made the final piece of the puzzle pop into place for Alexander. He knew now why the Lich had sent the Epova's and Michaels after him. "You used them as a diversion, the Epova's. You had something else planned this whole time and you didn't want me to find out?"

Akhenaton smiled a little wider, the smug grin one gets when an opponent discovers what you're really up to just a little too late to save one's position. "You actually had me scared there for a moment. Here I am about to obtain the most important piece I need for my evil plan to get revenge to work and you suddenly come awake and show up in the same city I'm about to go and visit. I tell you, I thought karma was spitting in my eye yet again till I thought 'what is the best way to keep you busy' and it hit me. Putting a puzzle like the Epova's and all their problems in front of you was the perfect preoccupation, just the thing to let me slip in and get the one I was looking for before you caught on. See, I knew you'd have to play the hero and try to save those silly pups."

"What plan...what are you going to do?" Alexander asked with a low whisper.

Akhenaton just chuckled with that menacing laugh and shook his head. "You think I'm going to tell you what I have planned? That only happens in the comics and James Bond movies old man. I will tell you this though. I'm going to have a lot of fun doing what I'm about to do."

"You cannot kill innocent people Akhenaton?"

The former Pharaoh just chuckled and stepped close again whispering coldly. "I can do anything I damn well please. I am a God and I am about to unleash judgment day. Let's see them film their TV and talk show after I reduce this world to an undead Hell complete with me as the Head Lich in charge. Let's see them play their computer games and buy their t-shirts after I turn this world upside fucking down on top of their silly little heads."

"You know I will not let you hurt anyone I care for...I will not let you endanger anyone I hold dear." Alexander stated with the tone of someone making a solemn vow. He was slowly starting to realize just how far Akhenaton and his plan were in front of him at the moment. How do you stop a train that's already gathered so much momentum it can't be stopped? The Pharaoh must have gleaned what the vampire was thinking because he stepped back letting the smile fade from his face.

"I know you are and have always been a thorn in my side, to expect that to change for the better is just crazy. I don't expect you to join my side or my cause either old man, not once since your awakening have I thought you'd do such a thing."

"And you would be right in assuming such Akhenaton."

Akhenaton carried on right through the vampire's last, acknowledging and dismissing the words with a single motion. "So count this as our last 'cordial' meeting vampire, after this night if we meet in person again I will not hesitate to create an endless dead army to send after you. No old man, you do what you have to but take some advice and listen well to it. Take those you care for and find some small spot out there among your humans to go and hide and prepare. I'm coming to destroy this world and I'm bringing all my zombies and ghouls with me to do the job."

There were no other words between the two, what else was there to say? Alexander stood quietly glaring back the Grand Lich as Akhenaton gave back the evil eye to the vampire. There would be no fighting or clash of fist. It was pointless as the Lich couldn't hurt Alexander and destroying the body of Akhenaton would only force him to inhabit one of the many other vessels he had prepared back in Los Angeles for just such an occurrence. The two only stared at each other before the Lich stepped back into the shadows smiling once again, a smug grin that told Alexander he had missed the mark this time, but the vampire knew there would be another night facing the Grand Lich.

There is always another night when you're immortal.

"How long has it been?" Foster asked standing next to the Chevelle.

"Two minutes from the last time you asked." Renfroe responded from by the side of the vampire's car.

Stephanie and Leland stood outside with Wilma watching the large group of lycanthropes as they huddled together talking in their native language. The minutes had ticked by agonizingly slow as they had made it back through the house but when Yelena saw her brothers and the other two werewolves she gave a small gasp and ran to them. The walk back to the car had been uneventful though because suddenly Rico's goons didn't move or do anything except lay where they fell. Now there was just waiting while watching the werewolves confer and that was a killer for Renfroe and the others. The detective knew the quiet was short lived. All the shooting and fighting had to catch someone's attention even with the size of this place so it wouldn't be long before the police would be showing up. And even though Rico and his men were dead now, technically, that didn't mean they all couldn't just pop up and start attacking again. Then, approaching slowly, two headlights cut through the darkness heading toward them. Renfroe and Foster pulled out their weapons while Leland stepped just in front of Stephanie and Wilma. A large black Suburban pulled up and stopped in front of the the two groups before the heavily tinted passenger side window began to lower on its loud motor.

"If it's Rico I swear I'm going to shoot that car full of holes." Renfroe whispered just as a familiar face came into view sitting behind the driver's wheel.

"No need to shoot detective." Alexander remarked putting the large SUV into park before getting out. He walked around the front of the car and was quickly greeted by Wilma who was smiling brightly.

"Where did you get the gas guzzler?"

The vampire smiled and nodded back, "I found it in the garage with the keys in it. I think someone was about to try and make an escape when we showed up."

"It was probably Rico, but since he's not going to be using it..." Renfroe grinned putting his weapon away just as the assistant coroner spoke.

"Why let all that gas go to waste I say."

"I was thinking the very same thing. Victor you and the werewolves can take the Suburban and follow me." The vampire pointed out.

Victor only shook his head to idea stepping out past Yelena before she could stop him. "Where is Svetlana? The voice on the phone said you took her."

"No Victor, the Ancient One did not take mother. It was the Grand Lich Akhenaton, he took her." Yelena quickly countered moving up to his side touching his arm gently. When the elder looked to his young pack member she only nodded before he turned to look at her brothers. All three nodded as well then Victor turned back to the vampire as the other Elder Iskra spoke.

"Then where is our Svetlana?"

"Patience my friends, follow me and I promise your questions will be answered." Alexander stated. He waited quietly and calmly letting the werewolves come to the realization the only choice was the one he was offering. And if there wasn't enough incentive with finding their mother and elder then what the coroner said next pushed them along.

"Well, we better get going soon. I think I hear sirens coming this way." Foster stated looking over his shoulder.

The elders of the lycanthrope looked to each other before Victor agreed to the vampire's request this time with a single nod. The werewolves slowly slipped inside the large SUV while Alexander and the others packed into the Chevelle. Soon the car was moving off into the night with the SUV following closely. Three speeding police units blew by them on their way to the mansion, not a one slowed down to look at the two cars exiting the area. The Chevelle and the Suburban rolled out of the neighborhood and onto the highway ten minutes later speeding toward downtown Atlanta.

 Chapter Fifteen

Don Reynolds got out of his car after popping the trunk via the handle under the dash and surveyed the landscape, there had to be about hundred cop cars on the estate's grass and driveway. He pulled a blue windbreaker from the trunk with the letters 'GBI' printed on the back in big yellow font and proceeded down the driveway to the large house that was bathed in the flood lights put out by the police. CSI personnel, police officers, and detectives ran inside and outside of the house while a couple of groups collected evidence in various spots all around the grounds outside. A deputy stopped him until Reynolds produced the necessary ID to get past the crime scene tape. When he entered the main foyer the devastation of the scene hit the GBI Agent like a big bag of bricks.

There were bullet holes in everything, a body that looked mangled being photographed on the stairs to the second floor, and blood just about everywhere. He stopped to take the site in and almost got run over by a detective doing a power walk going to the back of the house.

"Hey buddy, where is Jones?" Reynolds asked the fast moving police detective.

"And just who are you?" The detective asked acting perturbed at being stopped to answer a question.

Reynolds leaned forward and twisted his shoulder enough to display the large yellow letters on the back of his windbreaker. "The letters not big enough for you pal?" Reynolds shot back.

"Oh, yeah, Lieutenant Jones is this way. Just follow me and watch your step all right special agent." The man said turning to walk away.

Reynolds had to walk fast to catch up, but kept his eyes open just to take in the whole crime scene. The hall was brightly lit with floodlights. Up ahead he saw the entrance to the kitchen, and the huge hole in the wall and ceiling where something large had been thrown down the length of the passage. The special agent from the GBI had seen all kinds of crime scenes but this one shocked him to the bone, it was unbelievable. He stopped by the hole in the ceiling, which was cordon off by a ring of tape for a safety precaution, and looked right up into the twinkling stars of the night sky. To his left was yet another hole in the wall, the floodlights from the outside blinding him momentarily.

"What the hell did this?" Reynolds asked dumbfounded pointing at the hole in the ceiling.

"A metal table we found lying outside just beyond the pool." A voice called from the mass of people in what was a kitchen at one time. The GBI agent looked over to see his old friend from the local Police force walking up.

"Are you kidding me Bob, a metal table?" Reynolds asked shaking his head. "Did an explosion throw it that far?"

"Do you see any evidence of an explosion Don?" Robert Jones, Lieutenant with the Atlanta Police, replied with a wave of his hands.

"Then how did a table go up through there?" Reynolds asked.

"Someone threw it or at least that's what forensics says is their best guess right now." Jones answered with a sarcastic smile.

"You didn't call me down here for this did you? Please tell me you are not going to get me involved in...this?" Reynolds asked holding up both hands in a mock gesture of giving up.

"Nope, follow me and I'll show you why we called you." Jones said walking back to the front of the house.

Reynolds stood for a second looking at the hole wondering how someone could throw something like a metal table through two floors, a roof, and still clear a pool in the backyard. The problem was there wasn't anyone capable of doing it and he knew it. Yet, forensics said someone threw a table through two floors and a roof so there had to be somebody out there in the world walking around that could do it, right? The thought died quickly as Reynolds turned and trotted to catch up with Jones who was already heading up the stairs to the second floor, thank God he chose the stairs that didn't have the body lying on it. The GBI agent pulled a pair of rubber gloves from a pocket and pulled the sticky material on with the usual snap as he surveyed more of the damage. Bullet holes lined the wall, lots of them, which meant someone had one hell of a firefight. The mangled body was now covered in the standard white sheet as a forensic tech checked for prints along the banister by it. The two made their way to an office that was unscathed and looked rather homey in Reynolds opinion.

"Hey boys, give me and the agent some time alone." Jones ordered the group of personnel in the room. They filed out and the door closed to the office as the last one left.

"All right, what I say right now doesn't go any farther than this room got it?" Jones turned to Reynolds saying.

"Wait a minute Bob; I'm not going to involve myself in some kind of a cover up either." Reynolds pointed out. "If there's something going on here between you and your local boys then I'm out of here like Casper, understand?"

"It's nothing like that Don." Jones said walking over to the desk and handing over a ledger. "We found this in Dunbar's bedroom, a safe in the floor under the bed."

Reynolds took the book and read the page that Jones had opened already in the ledger and after just a few lines his eyes shot back up to the police Lieutenant. The man had literally found the pot of gold at the end of the rainbow, at least when it came to police work and drug dealers.

"This is unbelievable. You've got documented evidence of every drug trade that's gone down with one of the largest Cartel's. You have bank accounts, amounts and shipping dates, and it list Rico Herrera by name. You've got the whole damn operation Jones." Reynolds pointed out with a shocked look.

"What I 'got' is Rico Herrera's body outside under a white sheet. He's thirty bullet holes heavier, a broken leg from jumping out a window, and a broken neck." Jones shot back walking around the desk to stand by the GBI agent. "I have eight members of his crew shot up, four have huge unexplained claw marks, and not one shred of physical evidence to tell me how it all fucking happened Don."

"Rico's dead?" Reynolds asked in shock.

"As dead as dead can get," Jones said shaking his head.

"Wait, wait one second," Reynolds stammered waving one hand while setting the ledger back down on the desk. What the Lieutenant had said just a moment before was finally sinking in to his stunned brain. "Rico was shot to death and his neck was broken?"

"I never said anything about being shot to death." Jones offered.

"What do you mean?" Reynolds asked after taking a moment where he was truly trying to keep up with what his colleague was saying.

"The spot where his body is, there's not a splatter of blood. The forensic boys tell me he wasn't shot there and from the wounds he sustained he shouldn't have made it more than a few feet." Jones explained while one finger tapped the top of the desk. "And the broken leg, it's the same type of fracture a man would sustain falling from a second story window."

"Fall from a window?" Reynolds whispered in even deeper confusion.

"Exactly how I feel Don, nothing is adding up here and I got a lot of press waiting for a briefing down the road." Jones clamored.

"Why would someone shoot Rico and break his neck?" Reynolds asked rhetorically.

"How did Rico fall out of the God Damn window and break his leg if he was already shot and dead somewhere else in the house?" Jones spat.

"This is all preliminary right? The CSI need more time to go over what they collect and turn in their findings?" Reynolds asked.

"Yeah, you think we could stall?" Jones asked.

"On the weird stuff with the bodies, definitely. What about the rest of his crew, what happened to them?" Reynolds asked. He knew the drug lord rarely went anywhere without his small army of men, his crew.

"The same as Rico, all of them have at least twenty gunshot wounds to their bodies. And guess what?" Jones asked.

"They were shot somewhere else too?" Reynolds said with a quick guess.

"The man wins a cigar!" Jones whistled.

"I'm going to make a call to my supervisor, get some more people out here, and get a handle on the press. We need to make sure no one leaks a damn word about any of this." Reynolds ordered producing a cell phone from his pants pocket. Somewhere outside a dog howled but he paid it no attention, his mind was going so fast he barely remembered the phone number for his boss.

Chapter
Sixteen

The Chevelle came to a rumbling stop in the parking lot of what had been a small local grocery store at one time but was now nothing more than an oversized run down shack for the homeless to sleep in. Alexander shut off the engine then sat back in his seat watching the Suburban to drive up and come to a stop behind his car. As he did Wilma, sitting from the back on her mother's lap, couldn't help but notice the glow off in the distance. She knew where she was at the moment, the old store was one of the many places you avoided when traveling the hood. It was nothing but bad, a haven for the darker element here in the projects. Leland had once asked the city council to demolish this place, put an end to the blight the street preacher had stated, and yet the money it would take to do such a job spoke louder than Leland ever could and the request died silently and rather quickly. You can't expect the city to pay to clean itself up Wilma thought as she did some quick map correlations in her head and came to a sudden and startling realization.

"Mom...I think the Laurel's on fire."

Her mother looked at the glow then turned to Leland quickly with a look of concern but before she could say a word he responded. "Yeah, they burned it sweetie...all of it...right after they took you and your mother."

"Who burned it down Lee?" Stephanie asked quickly, the anxiety one would expect to hear in a person's voice when learning their home had just burned down absent. Maybe she was tired Lee thought or maybe she was secretly happy that place had finally met its fate. Either way, it didn't bother Leland as he only looked at the lady he loved while Renfroe answered her question.

"Does it really matter who committed the final act? The Laurel needed to be burned, the ground cleansed and made ready for new life to grow."

So true Alexander thought quietly as he looked to the detective, rebirth can only begin once the soil has been made ready to grow new life. From the back he heard Wilma sigh sadly then speak. "I guess I lost all my journals and books and stuff."

"We'll replace all of it Wilma, I promise." Leland said quickly with a reassuring touch to her shoulder.

"Yep, we're going to replace all of it...somehow." Stephanie stated with her man though not with the same conviction the street preacher had. She was already thinking of replacing furniture, dishes, and every other basic necessity one would need to live.

"Sure, I know you will. Hey, someone's coming." Wilma pointed out solemnly before getting excited while looking through the back window to see headlights approaching.

"Who is it?" Foster asked quickly just as Alexander opened his door.

"The men I have been waiting for." The vampire remarked stepping out into the cold night.

As he exited Stephanie pointed vigorously at the passenger door making the same shooing sound everyone makes when telling people to hurry while trying not to attract attention. Renfroe had barely climbed out of the Chevelle before Leland almost fell out from being pushed by the love of his life. He turned to ask Stephanie to calm down but never got the chance to say a word because Wilma hit him in the legs and bounced off running around the front of the car eager to see the new arrivals. As a large van slowly crept up the werewolves poured out of the Suburban, Victor led the pack to stand close to where Alexander stood waiting, "what is happening Ancient One?"

The vampire turned to the elder lycanthrope then to Yelena with a grin and spoke warmly as the van parked a good distance away from the group. "I am fulfilling my end of the bargain. Are all werewolves so impatient now? You know, I do not remember Ivan being this eager ever in his life."

The lycanthropes all looked at each other confused shrugging their shoulders and Alexander had to chuckle at the sight. From the passenger side of the van a man stepped out dressed in military garb, a vest bursting with ammunition and other things jingling from a hundred separate pouches as he walked. A large assault rifle hung perfectly in the center of his chest from a set of straps, the scope and forward grip making the weapon look even more menacing in his hands. The man stopped halfway between the cars and called out. "Who here is Alexander?"

He crossed the distance between himself and the man in a blink stopping right in front of him. "I'm Alexander. You're with Vargas I assume?"

The man jumped a little from being startled then looked back to the van, as if checking to make sure his backup was watching. The vampire only waited patiently, those men in the van wouldn't be the slightest of help if he decided to attack the leader here. The man turned back after a second and Alexander noticed the leader's finger was resting on the trigger of that very large and very scary rifle.

"Yeah, we're with Vargas." The leader stated coldly while looking over the vampire's shoulder to keep an eye on the large group. His training was good the vampire noted, and while he was admiring the way the leader handled himself that mystical window opened and the man's past played out for him. The leader, feeling somewhat satisfied with his safety, turned back to Alexander speaking in that stoic vernacular men with military bearing use. "We have your package. Orders are not to turn it over to you till Vargas has what you offered."

Alexander nodded then pointed toward the van, "How is she?"

"She's weak, looks like she hasn't been fed since being taken and was probably given some drug to keep her docile. What they gave her I don't know and Vargas told us not to address it."

He only nodded again as Alexander pulled his phone from his jeans pocket. As he dialed a combination of numbers he had memorized Yelena looked at the van and took a sniff. She gasped immediately before shifting to stare at Alexander with eyes filled with hope. "Is it Mother, did you rescue her?"

"Is it our Svetlana?" Iskra asked quickly with the same look of hope.

Alexander returned the look and spoke a single word to whoever it was on the other end who answered the call. "Go,"

He hung up and put his phone back into his pocket still calmly keeping eye contact with the werewolves who only became more restless with the wait. Iskra exhaled with exasperation while Yelena bit her bottom lip with anticipation and Victor was close to screaming something at the vampire when the loud ringer of a second phone cut him off. Everyone watched as the leader pulled a large satellite phone from one of the many pouches on his vest. He opened the long antennae then pressed the button to accept the connection using loudspeaker on the unit. "What's the verdict?"

A lone voice on the other end spoke, a distinguished Spanish accent. "We are good, let them take the package."

With a simple single nod the leader gave the order to his men inside the van. The door slid open and three men dressed in the same military attire and weapons stepped out leaving a pile of blankets in the middle of the doorway as the only thing in the van. Even the driver got out and stood on his side with his weapon up and at the ready. No one with Alexander moved because they were all afraid to, if they did then this all might come to an end. Then the pile in the van moved, slow at first as if stirring from a nap, and a form sat up and looked out at the group. From under a tangle of long brown hair a pair of tired green eyes looked out before a shiver ran through her body, which was marked with beautiful tattoos up both arms. Alexander had worried for a moment that Vargas might try and pass off a double, but as soon as the werewolves saw their elder they all gasped. They knew she was in the van before the door had even opened the vampire realized, Svetlana's scent carrying on the night breeze just enough to tell her family she was safe and home now. Yelena gave a small cry and ran to her mother just a step ahead of the rest of her pack. The three men quickly stepped back letting the werewolves gather around their loved one.

Wilma walked up and took Alexander's hand in hers while smiling with pure joy and whispering. "That is so cool...you're the greatest Alexander."

He only continued to smile as he watched the wolves gently touch and hug their elder. Svetlana cried just a bit as Victor took her in his arms whispering something sweetly in their native tongue in her ear. Alexander's Russian was a little rusty but he knew the words for 'My love' and it took very little to assume the relationship between the pair was more than what Yelena had told him, and speaking of the young one she looked over to him with tears in her eyes as well. Alexander only quietly returned the warm expression till the leader of the men held the phone out.

"Vargas wants to speak with you."

The phone was cold as Alexander took it while the werewolves with Victor holding Svetlana in his arms walked over and Leland with the others looked to him, all waiting to hear what he said. "Yes Vargas,"

"Are we satisfied?"

"We are satisfied Vargas, are you?"

The phone was silent for a second before the wizard came back. "We are very satisfied Ancient One. The photos are being scrutinized as we speak."

"Remember Vargas, what you have is only a part of what you seek. Be very careful with what you have and where you look for the rest." Alexander replied. He could see a look of curiosity on Yelena's face as Vargas responded.

"We will be careful Ancient One. In the future if you wish to do business again please do not hesitate to contact me through our mutual men."

"Thank you Vargas." Alexander said signaling the conversation could end now.

"My pleasure Ancient One, have a pleasant evening." The voice said before ending the connection. Alexander watched as the leader of Vargas's men put the phone back in its pouch while the werewolves stared at him, all putting together finally just how their elder and mother was rescued.

"We're done here. If we don't see each other again have a nice life." The leader said while giving a hand motion that told his group to get back into the van. He started to walk away when Alexander stopped him by calling out.

"Your father would be proud of what you've done here."

The leader looked back with a confused expression, just what the vampire had been prepared to see as it was the usual reaction when he told someone what the mystic window showed him. Alexander shook his head carrying on, "You're named after your father, Gabriel Sanchez, and his father before him. On certain long nights when you cannot sleep it's because you wonder relentlessly if what you do now, if being a hired mercenary is what your father would consider 'honorable'. Well Gabriel, tonight you did a very honorable thing."

Yelena stared at Alexander stunned just a little as she watched. The leader of the men who had rescued her mother was obviously shaken by the revelation as he stood there in quiet disarray not moving till one of his men called out asking if he was coming. The leader turned and walked away then as the van came to life but just before he climbed into the passenger side he took one long look back at Alexander. He's thinking just what is this man who I've never met before and how does he know my name Yelena thought with a little pride for the Ancient One. He's very suspicious and skeptical with most everything but yet he'll accept what was just said because even though it sounds crazy it feels right deep down. She watched the van pull away, the leader eyeing Alexander all the way till the vehicle was gone, as the pride grew in her heart. Victor easily cradled Svetlana who looked weak but more than capable of living through the night.

"You knew where our Svetlana was being held?" He asked quietly, respectfully.

The vampire's eyebrow rose slightly, "Once Yelena asked me to grant her mother sanctuary I began to look for her, sense her presence in the world. I stumbled on her you might say, captured and held by some of Akhenaton's followers."

"You can 'sense' someone and find them...anywhere in the world...the Entire world?" Leland asked with eyes wide and full of surprise.

"its okay baby, just remember he's really old." Stephanie winked with a chuckle hugging the street preacher. The wolves laughed as well, all except for Svetlana who reached out offering a hand to the vampire. Alexander took it and felt the weakened state of the elder werewolf but he also felt the strength that flowed in her. Given time to heal and recuperate Svetlana would be a force again soon enough.

"Thank you for helping my family." She whispered as Victor added to her words when she finished.

"The House of Ivan owes you much tonight Ancient One. Whatever you ask of any of us we will give you."

"Thank you Victor, but what you need now is to find a safe place to hide and let your pack heal." Alexander remarked letting Svetlana take her hand back. The elder only nodded and for a moment the group was quiet, no one speaking or talking till the smallest among them said what they all knew was coming.

"Yelena and her family are leaving, aren't they Alexander?" Wilma said with a voice that bubbled over with sadness.

The vampire only nodded as Yelena answered her friend, "Da little one, we must go now and heal."

"And that means you're going to leave too, doesn't it?" Wilma whispered looking up to Alexander and as the words touched the wind Stephanie sighed sadly from behind the pair. She had known that Alex wouldn't stay here with them forever, not even a full week. Oh she knew he had other things he had to attend too, a vampire almost certainly had other things that needed looking after. The only thing Stephanie feared would be how her little one would take losing her friend, her Angel. At the moment Wilma looked strong enough to handle the departure but that could change so fast.

The vampire looked down into his friend's eyes and with an intended slowness he knelt to look at her directly, as a dear friend and not a child. "Yes Wilma, I am leaving tonight. I have to start living as you once told me to do not so long ago, to not be afraid of this world."

Everyone watched, waited with a held breath hoping the little girl wouldn't fall to tears, and they were all a little surprised when she didn't. She was too strong to let everyone see her fall apart, too smart to let her emotions cloud the situation. Wilma only smiled and wiped the single drop on her cheek away as she spoke.

"I kind of knew you'd have to leave, being a vampire and all. Can you make me one promise though, like when you promised to help Yelena?"

"Yes my lady, what is it you wish of me?" Alexander asked bowing his head again just like the other night. It was very dashing Yelena thought as Wilma smiled at the act sending a blessed sigh of relief through the others.

"Can I write you, so you won't forget me?" The little one asked with a small whisper, a plea that brought Alexander's face up to hers again with a gentle smile.

"I could never forget you my Wilma. You are the one who had kept me from slipping away again to sleep this lowly life away. You have shown me such strength and courage that I now wish to find my place in this world like you will one day. No Wilma, I will never ever forget you because as much as you call me your angel in truth you are mine."

Oh those words, those precious words Yelena thought shaking her head while holding back her own tears as she watched Wilma hug her Alexander around his neck as hard as her little arms could do while whispering in his ear with pure warmth. "I love you my Alexander, my angel'."

Leland reached up and quickly wiped a tear away hoping no one saw him only to spot Renfroe staring at him with a crooked grin. Yeah, even the tough ones have a soft spot the detective's glance said as he looked back to the vampire who whispered back to his friend.

"And I love you Wilma Jackson, my angel."

There's not a dry eye in the house Renfroe thought grinning at the sight just as Foster spoke up. "I hate to break this up, but we better start thinking how we end this thing tonight and what we tell people tomorrow."

"Yeah, I'm pretty sure IAD will have a few questions for me and Foster. What's the plan with you Lee? You have some place to stay?"

The street preacher started to say he had a brother who had a couch that Stephanie and Wilma could share for a few nights till better accommodations were available, but the vampire only stood up and offered a better option. "A suite has been booked for all three of you at the Windermere, for the next week. I hope it will suffice."

As Stephanie and Leland's jaw dropped open along with Yelena's little Wilma only giggled and looked up to Alexander. "Isn't that the hotel where all the famous people stay?"

"Yes it is and strangely enough they had an incident down there just a couple of nights ago. You wouldn't have been hanging around there that night huh Lee?" Renfroe asked still grinning.

The street preacher only coughed as Stephanie shook her head. "No we haven't...I mean we may have driven by...just a quick step inside to see the lobby."

Alexander finally laughed as there was no holding back his mirth at watching the pair. Then he felt the small hand he was holding squeeze and he looked down again to Wilma. "Where are you going from here?"

"I do not know little one, anywhere my feet take me I guess till I reach the coast." The vampire answered.

"Wait, what about the Chevelle? You're not taking the car?" The street preacher asked quickly.

There was a small jingle sound and then the keys to the muscle car were flying straight to the point where Leland caught the ring with a quick hand. He looked at the keys in his hand then back to Alexander who only winked. "I couldn't think of a better man to take her than you Leland."

He was struck numb and flat dumb by the move. Leland had never owned a car like the Chevelle though he had dreamed of it for so long. The smile began slow, creeping almost, as what he was holding in his hand began to register in his brain. The Chevelle...it was his...and that smile turned into a small laugh as he turned and kissed Stephanie before speaking. "Thanks man...thank you!"

The vampire only chuckled as Victor turned to him. "We are going now Ancient One. We will never be able to repay you for what you have done for us."

"I never expected a payment for my help Victor, only your friendship."

"And that you have, forever my Ancient One." Yelena whispered sweetly.

The tone couldn't be missed. The undercurrent of emotion the werewolf seemed to let flow from her to the vampire. Alexander sighed and replied never letting his eyes leave Yelena's though what he said was for Victor more than the young lycanthrope. "There is a phone in the glove compartment. I had Simon put the phone numbers of people you can trust in the contacts, people who can help you to hide and protect you. Also, in case of an emergency, I have arranged for a bank account to be opened you may use if you need money."

Svetlana gasped at the news while Victor and the brothers only looked on in shock. Not a one of the werewolves could have foreseen the help the vampire would give them, it had never been dreamed of. Lycanthropes accepted aid only from their kind and only when there was no other acceptable choice. Now, one of the lowly Nosferatu who they called unclean was helping them, which was nothing short of life, by giving them unquestioned aid. Well, there was one who had seen this side of the vampire and at the moment Yelena felt her heart skip just a small bit.

"All right Wilma...we have to go as well baby." Stephanie suddenly said with the sound of her voice low and tinged with sadness.

"I know mom, I just need a minute more." Wilma whispered before abruptly breaking from Alexander's side and running to Yelena who knelt and hugged the little girl warmly. "I'm going to write you too so don't get mad if there are a lot of questions about Moscow."

"And I will answer everyone my friend with happiness." Yelena replied kissing Wilma's cheek before standing back up. Wilma ran back hugging Alexander one last time, his hand gently rubbing her back. Then she quickly ran to her mom's side as Leland reached over and shook the vampire's hand one last time as well.

"We'll keep you in our thoughts Alex, be safe wherever you go."

"Yes Alex, be safe and we will keep you in our hearts as well." Stephanie added as she hugged her daughter. Then the three left with Renfroe and Foster following, the group heading for the Chevelle.

He just smiled and nodded one last time before watching all leave for their cars. Alexander watched Leland and his crew get into the Chevelle while the lycanthropes filed into the Suburban.

Yelena was the last of her pack to enter and just like little Wilma a moment before she suddenly trotted away from the SUV and over to the vampire. Without hesitating once she rose on her toes and kissed him long and sweetly, slightly pulling on Alexander's bottom lip as she let go. "My Ancient One, mine," Yelena whispered tenderly but with a loving assertiveness before turning and running back to the Suburban.

The vampire watched her climb in and the taillights come to life. He watched both cars pull out of the parking lot heading for the start of new lives, the beginning of a new day. Alexander looked skyward noting the moon and its beautiful glow. "Alone once more," he whispered noting the weary tone that was there when he arrived in the city was gone now.

The breeze blew across the open space of the lot as he pulled out the locket from his pocket. It popped open as if some force wanted it to be and there they were staring at him, beautiful eyes and warm smiles of his family past. The vampire let out a small sigh and then whispered low. "I take it I'll never really be alone as long as I have you three and my locket. Well, where shall we go?"

There was no answer but the wind yet if one listened just right, with the proper intention, then one might have heard a small word there gliding along on the breeze. Alexander shook his head closing the locket. He heard the word and knew exactly where they wanted to go. He put the pendant around his neck then pulled a small black box from his back pocket. His MP3 player kicked on with a slide of the bar on the screen from his thumb. The Allman Brothers came through the ear buds he put in, the harmony of 'Midnight Rider' drawing out a nice sigh. Alexander looked to the moon one last time, thought of Yelena and Wilma and then Grammy.

"It's time to start living again," he whispered before disappearing from the lot without a sound.

Epilogue One

"Is the any word on Alexander or where he might be wandering around?" Akhenaton asked from behind his large desk in his study at the Mansion he owned. At the moment the Pharaoh was looking into a baseball sized piece of amethyst crystal, perfectly round and polished. Why no one knew and the three sitting on the other side of his desk would never chance the fates in asking him either.

"No Lord Akhenaton, there has been no sign of him." Michaels answered stretching. He wasn't quite use to the new stitching that was done for his body. Being dead and all there was no real need to heal a cut or gash, no need to worry about blood loss. You did have to repair said cuts though or risk the skin ripping more. That was usually done with any choice of a sturdy thread and needle, just like sewing up a new jacket. All of Yelena's claw marks had been closed but it took some getting used to the hemp used to sew him up.

"And what about Svetlana and her pack?" The Grand Lich asked next.

All the way to the left the heavy set man on the end of the three spoke up, his leather jacket creaking with a pop as he shifted his large body. His name was Ross Young, a very sought after custom motorcycle builder with a popular shop downtown and for now till the end of time a Lesser Lich in servitude just like Michaels. Ross Young though really wasn't Ross Young. He was really Dave Duketz from Cleveland, Ohio who Akhenaton had found in 1974 sitting in his basement drinking a cold beer surrounded by a very large amount of child pornography. Three months later Dave became Ross and in doing so was one of only a handful who had survived the transformation ritual to being a Lich. He did so well that Akhenaton had marked Dave very high on his list of those to keep an eye on. It wasn't because he liked Dave, it was quite the opposite. You always keep the ones who can easily take your place close and under a very watchful and thorough gaze the Pharaoh had learned over these long years.

"There has been no news of her or the other werewolves. The map's been clean ever since you returned." Ross answered looking at the Grand Lich while chewing on his thick Fu-Manchu moustache. The room was silent as Akhenaton continued to look into the purple sphere.

"Do you think the pack is still with the Ancient One my lord?" Michaels asked quickly almost panicky.

In the middle of the three sat a very sweet looking lady, her blond hair cut short and spiky fitting the way she dressed. The blue blouse, white slip on shoes, and baggy jeans sat well on her tall frame while enforcing her 'look' of being just another soccer mom. She bit her bottom lip and then spoke with a clean southern accent. "The Ancient One is most likely out sight-seeing. He and the wolves' have parted ways I'm sure being that Lycanthropes and Vampires don't like each other very much."

For the first time since the trio had entered and taken a seat in the large study the Grand Lich broke from gazing into the amethyst and looked over to the only female Lesser Lich with a smile of surprise, "very astute Lily, very good. I want you to go and give yourself a gold star on the board when you leave the room."

The woman only smiled happily back, very 'mommy' like. Now there was true dichotomy in that look, true 'ninja' like skills the Grand Lich thought. Lilith Featherston came from a very pious Southern Family. Her father was a preacher sermonizing and calling out the gospel from the pulpit every Sunday and Wednesday, right up to the moment he died on the church steps from a massive coronary. Lily, as Akhenaton called her, though was a cruel sadist on the inside. She was a calculating monster with a mean streak and she was so good at breaking down men and women during torture she had her own little room downstairs everyone called the 'Pit' and everyone steered very clear of it except for the Pharaoh. Oh the screams that came from that room on those special nights when Lily was working, oh the sweet pleas of someone crying out. It made the Grand Lich so proud he had transformed her he just beamed when he thought of it.

"So we have nothing to worry about from either then?" Michaels smiled.

"I wouldn't think so." Akhenaton said turning his attention back to the sphere in his hand before speaking again. "What do you hear about the other wolf packs Ross?"

"It's like you said, the minute the news got out you had kidnapped Svetlana the other wolves either moved to join you or went underground to get away."

"And what's the number like, how many joined against how many went and hid?"

"More joined than ran, but there are still enough wolves out there that they can make a problem." Ross answered shifting in his seat again.

The Grand Lich shook his head while gently putting the sphere down on the desk. "A few pathetic wolves won't stop the train from rolling down the tracks Ross, but I would like to know about Magda. What are she and the 'Sisters' doing?"

"Alexander's brood haven't changed their movements or tried to run my lord. They act as if nothing has changed; as if they have no clue the Ancient One is awake." Michaels stated.

The chair Akhenaton sat in creaked as he leaned back in it smiling still. "They know, Magda and Kazahiro might not have been sitting around just waiting for their daddy to come home but they know that old man is back. Keep an eye on them, if anything changes let me know."

"Agreed," all three said and the Grand Lich was suddenly reminded there was a fourth missing from their weekly meeting. He sighed and cocked his head just a little.

"Is the body ready for Hilga?"

"Yes it is. All it needs is your final touch sir." Michaels answered with a sigh of exasperation.

"Is it the right size this time?" Ross asked quickly.

"Yes, it is the size that she requested." Michaels answered sighing again.

"It better be. You know Hilga likes her curves and if you give her one of those stick thin supermodel bodies again she will have a fit." Lily added with a sharp nod.

"She'll probably blow herself up again to get rid of it." Ross snorted shaking his head.

That's what Akhenaton liked about being a Lich. You never died, just shifted bodies from one to another like changing suits when the time was needed. The only drawback was that for the Lesser Lich's the bodies had to be dead all ready, a certain limitation he didn't have to worry about. It was good to be the king to quote a movie phrase. Hilga's essence, her very soul, was housed now in a rather large Emerald secured in a very secret location and here in a day or two he would perform a ceremony to let her take control of this new body. Hilga was a very well built German lady who had an insatiable need to know things, any and all things it seemed. It was this curiosity that led her to him, to being transformed, and into a very nasty explosion in a warehouse in town where she kept her lab. Her old body had been burnt to a crisp, well the parts they could find anyway.

"I spent all night in the body room downstairs and reaching out to our contacts to find the one she wanted. It took me sometime but I have a very voluptuous body prepared for her." Michaels spat shaking his head. He didn't really like Hilga, she liked to whine too much in his opinion.

"Is everything set for Owens and the potion? Did he get the notes from Hilga, the ones that didn't burn up?" Akhenaton asked taking on a fatherly tone suddenly.

"Yes, but we're still making the preparations." Ross responded.

"Why is that?" The Pharaoh asked quickly.

"We have all the steps to make the potion my lord. It's just most of the components to create it were lost in Hilga's lab accident and finding replacements takes time." Michaels replied.

"I don't like delays people. Just tell me when the potion's ready to cook again so we can fire proof the lab. The priestess I found in Atlanta, is she ready at least?" Akhenaton said looking at the three with an intense stare.

"She's refusing to help out, stalling, but I'm sure Lilith can persuade her if needed." Ross replied shifting in his seat one last time.

The Grand Lich looked to his Lesser Lich and the soccer mom only grinned back. "I'm quite sure I can get her to change her mind if asked the right way."

The door to the 2X2 storage space sat closed just two feet away, yet Renfroe couldn't bring himself to open it. This part of his younger life was just that, the past, locked away because he shut it out. Then Alexander came into the picture two weeks ago and now he was facing that door he closed years ago. Would the supplies still be good? Would the components still work? He knew the answer was yes because he'd packed everything so meticulously, the way his mother taught him.

The thought of Adria scattered everything he had been working on for the last twenty four hours threatening to send his plan into the mental trash bin. His mother meant the world to Otz and even though he acted cold like she didn't Adria was always in his heart. Now someone had dared to cross the line and take her, hurt her. Renfroe stopped his brain right there, wrestled it back under control, and got it back on track. He had a plan damn it, just follow it!

Yes, it would all work just as it always had for him. The only question is will your heart let it work, will your mind let the intention and energy flow. Renfroe suddenly stepped forward grasping the Master lock with a burst, inserting the key and giving it a vicious twist. His hands were sweating as the door opened to the dark and musty space.

No turning back.

There, lying on the floor was a single black duffle black. He starred at it for a minute then reached out quick and grabbed the handles, as if the bag was a large snake that might bite him if he didn't strike fast and first. Renfroe popped the trunk to his 68 Camaro Super Sport and tossed the bag in the back with a single throw. The car was something else he had put away thinking he would never need it. From his coat pocket he produced a single piece of paper given to him by Alexander's lawyer. Simon wasn't a tough person to find and he gave up the address to a group in

L.A. just like Alexander. A family of vampires the lawyer called 'The Sisters', that's where Alexander was going probably.

After getting in the former detective looked to the passenger seat where his brother sat quietly with a determined cold expression. "Are you sure you want to do this?" He asked already knowing the answer. Renfroe just wanted one last confirmation before he put the car in motion.

No turning back.

"They took mother. If you think I'm going to sit here while you go after her your crazy. Now let's get going." Joel stated never turning his head toward his brother.

Answer accepted Renfroe noted mentally while nodding silently. The car kicked over with a loud roar, the engine rumbling with race cams and oversized pistons. Renfroe went over the plan again in his head. A straight run to Los Angeles, get Alexander's help in getting his mother back, and then use that black duffle bag to make sure whoever took her paid for messing with his family. The muscle car laid down a sizable black mark as Renfroe lit up both tires leaving the parking lot of the storage lot.

The sun was setting and it looked utterly amazing Yelena thought, standing there on the porch outside the large log cabin in the Smoky Mountains where they were hiding. The pack had fled Atlanta in a rush but only went as far Tennessee and the mountains. A number in the phone the Ancient One had left for them was familiar to Iskra and after a quick call the refuge they had need of was obtained. Svetlana grew stronger each day, the drug used to make her docile gone and with food in her belly the elder was making long happy strides to returning to being normal again. She had even assumed some small resemblance of control of the pack giving orders to the others to fulfill. It was the day after they had arrived though that she learned just how her mother had been betrayed and taken so easily. Iskra's son Vadim had turned on them, his family and his house, choosing to join with the Grand Lich. He had lured Svetlana with a lie that Yelena her only daughter had been hurt to a secret spot and then shot her with a poisoned dart rendering her unconscious. Yelena learned that Victor and Iskra had been lured away in the other direction by a separate call from someone saying Ivan was alive and in hiding needing their assistance. That was why no one could find the pair. They were up in Canada looking into the lead. It wasn't till someone left them a written message in the hotel they were staying in, a letter under the door, did they come to learn of Svetlana's fate and the others.

Did you have something to do with that my Alexander? Did you bring them back here or was a third person involved in this somehow? The questions just bounced around in Yelena's head for a moment before slowly and subtly shifting to another. She smiled as her mind and reflections rolled uncontrollably to him and the werewolf didn't mind when it happened, not at all. She wondered where he could be now, her Ancient One. Was he seeing this new world each little piece at a time? Wherever he was Yelena found herself wanting to be there at his side, close enough to touch and take in his scent.

"You're thinking of him again," a voice called out from the door of the cabin.

"Da," Yelena answered without looking back. She knew it was Alla, Victor's daughter, who had come to check on the quiet one of the pack. The six-foot-tall form of the she-wolf approached slowly, edging up as the breeze blew her long dark auburn locks around. Alla was the same age as Yelena and the two were as close to sisters as a pair without a blood relation could be. "I find myself thinking of him more and more every day."

Alla crossed her arms across her chest looking out at the sunset. "Your mother knows you're in love with Alexander and I am very sure your bothers do too. Victor and Iskra know as well so there is very little reason to try and hide now."

"I think everyone knows sister. I have not been very good at hiding it, nor have I wanted too. I miss him greatly Alla."

"I know sister and one day soon you will see him again. And that will leave you with one last problem." Alla said turning to look at her friend and pack member.

"What is that?"

The tall werewolf leaned in and whispered warmly. "How do you plan on telling Ivan when he comes back that you have fallen in love with an unclean Nosferatu?"

Yelena just chuckled at the question before looking back at the sunset. She knew her sister was only joking, making a jest, but the unspoken intent was there. When Ivan returned she would have to explain what happened in Atlanta? He would expect an accounting of her heart and why she felt the way she did for the Ancient One but that was not Ivan's concern. Where she lay and with who was no one's business but her own. So as the sun fell slowly below the horizon her thoughts went back to him. Where could he be tonight she thought silently.

Where could he be?

Epilogue Two

The setting sun dropped across the highway making it look as if the cars in front of Alexander were driving into the burning ball as he made his way to New Orleans. He spent the day in a hotel along the highway just outside of Memphis reading and ducking the little pain that sun light still caused him. The windows on the refurbished 55 Belair were covered with dark tinting, not as dark as the custom black paint job on his new car or the sunglasses he wore, but enough to protect him if need be and yes technically he was almost immune to the sun now but old habits die-hard. He still felt the need to seek cover at the approaching sunrise twilight but just an hour before sunset Alexander decided to get moving again ignoring the pain it would cause. The Belair rumbled and sped along with no particular destination in mind, the driver just following the road to where ever it took him as he drove with his arm resting easy on the open window. There was so much to see now, so much to experience and he wanted to take it all in.

As Johnny Cash sang out from the high end stereo telling everyone to get rhythm just like the little shoe shine boy on the corner a car slipped up beside him, a long station wagon complete with a family inside and several large luggage cases tied down on top. The vampire turned to look at the wagon as it slowed to keep pace with his car and there in the windows were two small faces of the kids in the back and in front the face of a bored wife sitting next to a husband who kept trying look past her at the gorgeous ride next to theirs. The vampire grinned as the young boy and little girl made funny faces at him while he stared back. The sight of the pair caused Alexander to begin to think about Wilma and the story Simon told him before he left the hotel.

Yesterday her mother Stephanie opened the front door to the suite at the hotel they occupied to find Simon waiting politely with a brown leather satchel under his right arm. He had arrived promptly to the hour to pick all three up, Leland and Wilma and Stephanie. The lawyer was his usual engaging gentlemen using his charm to keep them occupied with a story as he drove to a secret spot. When the Mercedes pulled into the small gated community in Alpharetta Stephanie asked why they were in such a nice neighborhood, all the houses lining the street looking so grand and so expensive. Simon just laughed as he pulled his sedan into a drive way and up to the closed garage doors before climbing out after shutting off the engine. The lawyer began to explain how there was a nice Private School just down the street, one of those charter types that specialized in Science and Math. Little Wilma would love it, if she could get use to wearing the school uniform every day. There was a Whole Foods Market maybe a mile in the other direction to buy groceries. Leland asked Simon again why they were here at this house, the tone in his voice a mix of hopeful and fearful. The lawyer simply produced a small key and handed it to Wilma letting the little girl do what she already had guessed she was supposed to do with it.

The key opened the door easily even though Wilma's hand shook from being nervous. They stepped through slowly to the expansive fully furnished five-bedroom house as Simon told them the two acres of land would give Wilma enough room to run around. Leland barely heard anything the lawyer was saying being totally lost in the shock of the moment and all, but he heard every word when Simon said Wilma would also be safe from any 'issues' when it came to the Laurel Projects and all that had happened there. Stephanie turned to him and whispered low trying not to kill this dream with the sharp stab if reality. We can't afford to live here Simon; it's not possible she stated trying not to cry. No ma'am, the affable lawyer smiled warmly, the owner of the house is looking for a nice family to look after the place, care-take you might say. There are no house payments to be made and actually there's a stipend paid to the ones who stay on. So we can stay here Wilma smiled and Simon just nodded before reaching into his satchel and pulling out a carefully wrapped package. Mr. Alexander wanted you to have this Wilma the lawyer said handing the package to her and the little one knew instantly it was a book.

Wilma pulled the wrapping back slowly as the leather bound book within was slowly revealed inch by inch. Her eyes went as wide as half-dollars the second the letters 'The Plays of William Shakespeare' registered in her mind and a small tear rolled down her beautiful brown cheek. The pages inside were aged she could tell as each slid tenderly between her small fingers and a magic old and unseen wrapped itself around her small heart making her feel so warm. The book was hand crafted and printed in a different era with artistry and love and a caring for the written word. Wilma clutched it to her bosom and silently thanked him for everything, for being her friend and angel.

She was safe now...no names on any papers for anyone to trace. No one could find Wilma or Stephanie or Leland. The house was paid for in full with the funds from a private company owned by a trio of the many aliases the vampire had used over the years. His vast fortune was stretched over so many accounts and businesses it would take an accountant several months to try and track down the identity of any name that appeared on a document and when she or he did find a name it would lead to nowhere with any search.

Alexander slipped back to the here and now seeing the kids in the back of the station wagon were still making faces while the husband was trying to explain to his bored wife what a great car that rebuilt Belair was. The vampire grinned a little more at the kids then and just for fun he let his mouth open wide exposing the large fangs hissing. All at once, at the sudden change in appearance in the man, both the boy and girl slowly slid back into their seats quietly while staring straight ahead, neither wanted to even chance seeing the boogeyman riding alongside again. He reached up and lowered his sunglasses with his free hand a bit as he looked to the wife who he watched sigh and turn to see this gorgeous ride her husband wouldn't shut up about. As she did the vampire locked eyes with her and suddenly the wife's head hit the window and began to fog with her heavy breathing. She began to claw at the glass just a little, like she wanted to jump cars and trade places, but then the wagon turned left taking the on-ramp to another highway. Alexander watched the wagon disappear before putting his glasses back in place and turning back to the drive.

He looked over to the passenger seat for a moment and smiled because there sat Wilma's book that she gave him, her treasured copy of Shakespeare given to the one who saved her as a most precious gift. He touched it lovingly then felt a sudden urge rise in his chest. Magda and the Sisters, maybe it was time to go and see them. No rush though, he could take his time getting to LA.

The Belair rolled on down the highway as night set in and the cars headlights came on. The MP3 player sent the next song to the stereo and the speakers belted out CCR's 'The Midnight Special' as the vampire got on to living just as a dear friend suggested.

The End

About the Author...

R.Kane lives in the Southern US with his family where he was born. He enjoys the occasional fishing trip for bass and throwing the ball with his Golden Retriever.

Please visit the website for updates -

http://www.rkanepublications.com